the Chess man enigma

M.S.KOLL

MEMOIRS

Cirencester

Published by Memoirs

MEMOIRS
PUBLISHING

25 Market Place, Cirencester, Gloucestershire, GL7 2NX
info@memoirsbooks.co.uk www.memoirspublishing.com

First published in England, July 2012

Book jacket design Ray Lipscombe

ISBN 978-1-909020-69-6

Printed in England

For

Mr Russell Millner
Mr Ajay Nigam
Dr Cheryl Rees

CHAPTER 1

On the first floor of a small terraced house, three people sat at one end of a large pine table. Each had two files in front of them. In about fifteen minutes, they were expecting two visitors. The time was a quarter to eleven, the day Tuesday, the 13th of November, location, a quiet street somewhere in Cardiff, Wales.

As usual, D.I. Jones was early. He had been instructed not to use his own transport, so he'd taken the train from his home in Taffs Well to Queen Street. On exiting, he headed towards an address in the Cathay's Park area, arriving at the house over ten minutes early. He liked punctuality so to kill some time he sat on a bench in the small communal gardens across the street from his destination. There were two other occupants in the park, a man and woman. They were sitting together talking. There was a slight drizzle and unlike D.I. Jones, they had no umbrella, but it didn't seem to bother them.

After five minutes, D.I. Jones rose and crossed the road. As he crossed, he noticed a small black Fiat parked two doors down. A young man of about twenty-five sat in the driver's seat reading a broadsheet. From his appearance he looked like he would be hard-pushed to read a comic, thought Jones. Pressing the buzzer, someone asked him his name. He gave it and the door clicked open. He had been instructed by the voice to go up the stairs and knock on the second door to the right. On entering what seemed to be a large open kitchen-cum-dining room, he was requested to take a seat in one of two vacant chairs at the bottom of a large table.

On the other end sat a woman, flanked either side by men all casually dressed. D.I. Jones recognised one of the men as Chief Constable Clarke.

The woman spoke first: "Good Morning, Detective Inspector Jones."

"Good Morning Ma'am," Jones replied in his highly accented Welsh brogue.

"Please bear with us a few moments; we are expecting one other person. Would you like some coffee?" D.I. Jones declined.

Detective Inspector Mikhail Karetzi had also taken the train to Queen's from his apartment in the Bay. He was running late and although he did not wear a hat or carry an umbrella, he did not rush.

At exactly eleven, he reached the top of the terraced street. For a few seconds he stopped outside a small café, which was empty apart from a chauffeur in uniform drinking a cup of tea. Opposite stood a large official looking car. Karetzi walked down the street towards the address he'd been given, about a hundred yards. It was still drizzling; he was still strolling. Karetzi entered the room ten minutes late and made his way to the one remaining chair and sat down.

"You're late, we said eleven and that's what we meant D.I. Karetzi," said Chief Constable Clarke.

Before Karetzi could say anything, the Chief made the introductions. "Mrs Andrews, Welsh Assembly and Mr B, National Security Services, and you both know who I am."

Karetzi smiled and the Chief caught it. "Something amusing you, detective?"

"Not really Sir, but I guess it's just a little quirky."

"What is?" demanded the Chief.

"Being interviewed, if that's what we're here for, by Messrs. A, B and C, and one wonders if the guy downstairs is part of the alphabet, maybe Mr Door-opener!"

The Chief scowled. Karetzi squirmed. Jones sat more upright in his chair and turned to Karetzi. He offered his hand: "D.I. Evan Jones."

"Mikhail Karetzi, call me Mike, it's easier," answered Karetzi, shaking Jones' hand.

The Chief went on again. "You are not being interviewed; you have already been selected by me and others to form a new partnership for the sole purpose of carrying out one, just one, murder investigation. Actually, I lie; the investigation is not about one murder, but eight, and rising. A serial killer whom we have code-named The Chessperson. You have all heard the rumours, some true, some not. Everyone has a theory in the Forces throughout Wales but no one has a clue about the killer's identity. The most puzzling aspect to all this is, what is the motive and why does the killer leave a beheaded chess piece as a calling card? Is it symbolic in any way?"

"Let's not forget that there are 32 pieces on a chessboard. Unless we get a result soon…" The Chief's voice faded, his throat dry. He whispered, "We could be only a quarter of the way through this madness."

Emma Andrews, a lady of about fifty, smart, well dressed and Chief Advisor to the First Minister, could not keep her eyes off Karetzi. She glanced at the file for about the tenth time. Six foot and a half-inch, black eyes, impossible, she took another quick glance. Karetzi turned and held her gaze until she lowered her eyes back to the file. She felt like a silly little schoolgirl.

Yes, his eyes were black and seemed to sparkle. Full head of unruly jet-black hair, 14 odd stone, and broad shouldered, aged 35, very fit, still playing football regularly, hobbies football, and fifties/sixties American music. The small scar under his left eye, shaped like a teardrop, did nothing to detract from his good looks. He looked like a film star, and dressed like one too. Armani jeans, black moccasins, beautiful grey cotton shirt and a soft, navy blue leather jacket made up his wardrobe.

No jewellery except what looked like the ugliest, biggest steel watch she had ever seen. Very strange considering the rest of his attire.

Whilst Emma was salivating over D.I. Karetzi, Mr B was appraising the other average height, age 54, grey/brown hair, slightly overweight. Looked like his old Maths teacher, spit and polished black shoes, leather elbow patches on a Harris Tweed jacket, white shirt, plain brown tie with a large Windsor knot. The thin end of the tie was longer than the wide end and was tucked into his trousers. He wore purple thick socks and brown corduroy trousers with turn-ups. Where the hell did this man buy his clothes? Mr B hoped that he was a better detective than he was at clothes shopping. Maybe his wife bought his gear.

These two were like chalk and cheese. Mr B had a good gut feeling. The opposites that the detectives obviously were would complement each other: one would think, the other would act.

The Chief Constable was now in full swing. He told them everything he knew about The Chessperson. He told them that they were not sure with any degree of accuracy as to the gender of the killer. No idea of height, hair, colouring, weight, and age – only that ninety five per cent the killer was white, nationality unknown.

The victims ranged in age between 20 and 70, all male, all in different geographical areas of Wales. They had nothing in common: some were rich, one unemployed. Why, what was the motive? No connections; no apparent motive.

Silence ensued only to be broken by the theme of the Lone Ranger – the ringing tone of a cell phone. Everyone looked at Karetzi. D.I. Jones shamefacedly switched off his phone.

The Chief frowned. Emma smiled. Mr B Spoke. "This gentlemen, is a poison chalice. You are being asked to solve crimes where the combined forces of Wales, Merseyside, Manchester, Bristol, Chester and Scotland Yard have, with all their manpower and expertise, failed. They did not get past the starting post and I doubt if you will either.

"I hope I'm wrong. It's nothing personal but where do you start with an invisible, motiveless murderer? Why do we have no real leads after nearly five months and eight victims?"

"Why Chief, do we have two officers of the same rank and only Inspectors at that? Why isn't there someone higher? Who will be the leader? Will the other listen? From the files one seems the maverick type, the other looks like a professor and dresses like one. D.I. Jones is older. D.I. Karetzi dresses like he's going to a party," said Mr B.

"It's just unrealistic to expect these two detectives to crack this case. Have you any comments Emma?"

"I have, Brian."

Mr B sat back. All he had said was true but he had wanted to see what reactions he would get and deep down he knew that these were as good detectives as anywhere in the Force. He wished that his men were as good. Yes, he had a very good feeling. He would report back to London to the top man that he was confident that with these two the tide would change. But he still wanted to see their reactions. It was important to find out if they could gel and fight for each other, if they would work together, not as friends but as detectives.

Before speaking Emma sipped some water. "It is my belief, and of course I have no expertise in these matters, but my women's intuition tells me that D.I. Karetzi and Jones will do the job. For some reason I think we have the makings of a superb partnership. I think that they should now tell us what they think. It's been two hours and they haven't said a word."

The Chief stood. "Well detectives, your turn. Anything that you wish to comment on? Anything you don't understand, go ahead talk."

Jones stood up. "Firstly I would like to say that I can work with anyone and it will be a pleasure to work with my new, younger partner. Maybe I can teach him how to dress properly." Everyone laughed. "Of course, we all have knowledge of these murders."

"I propose that we will rename the case 'THE CHESSMAN', because I can categorically state that it's a man. Do you agree Mike?" Mike nodded. "In one stroke we have therefore cut our list of potential suspects in half. We've only been on the case a few minutes and we're progressing. I also think, no I know that no case, not one premeditated murder case is without its motive. That to me is the key and yes, it is unrealistic, as Mr Brian says that we can be expected to break this case, and I know that he is expecting some kind of indignant reactions from us but I am afraid I personally will disappoint him.

"Mike you want to say something?"

"I agree with what Evan says. I think we are different, but why should one of us be the leader, and one the follower, or the dissenter? We will do our best together. From what I see we could be a good partnership. I'll give you an example. If in our investigations we come across a closed door that we need to enter, Evan will keep knocking forever if need be until he is let in. I will knock a couple of times and if I'm not let in, I'll break it down. Either way between us we will gain entry. That's what this case needs, someone thinking, someone acting and both of us solving."

"That's exactly what I wanted to hear," said Mr Brian. "Do you have any other observations in particular about the meeting here, not a police station? Why were you asked not to come in your own cars etc. etc?"

Mike turned to Evan, and gestured for Evan to speak. "Okay, Mr B, this I can assume is a safe house, probably used by Internal National Security for whatever. It wouldn't remain so if the neighbours noticed a Police Chief full of braid and silver buttons arrive in a large chauffeur-driven car, hence the Chief is in casual wear."

"There's security downstairs, the voice on the buzzer is different from either yours or the Chief's. The said security is probably listening to me speak right now, ready to move in case of some problems up here. There's a couple in the park opposite, sitting in the rain without an umbrella, pretending to be lovers. They are sitting on a bench facing this building. Five yards away there's another bench, under a tree facing into the park. That's where lovers would sit, somewhere more secluded and protected from the rain. Obviously police."

"Two doors down there's a young chap, in a black Fiat, not an official car, probably waiting for you Mr B, one of your boys? Next time he has to do a similar job tell him to read the popular tabloids, not broadsheets – he sticks out like a sore thumb."

At this point Karetzi intervened. "I noticed the Fiat and the official car for Mrs Andrews parked outside the café a hundred yards away at the top of this street. The chauffer is inside drinking tea and is strategically placed to have a full view up and down this street. I would hazard a guess and say that the Chief Constable has parked his car in the next street or so. And last but not least we were requested not to come in our own vehicles, so that in case of an emergency it would be difficult for entry or exit if there were parked cars outside the front door."

D.I. Jones stood. "I would like the tapes destroyed, Mr B."

"What tapes are those?" asked the Chief.

"The ones being recorded downstairs by Mr B's man or men."

"Is that correct Brian, didn't we agree, no notes and no taping?"

"Yes, Chief, they would have been destroyed later-on tonight after we run them through once more."

"Just our standard procedure," added Mr B.

"Well it's not my standard procedure, Brian. I made it clear that there would be no recordings or notes and you agreed. Isn't it so Emma?"

"That's what we all agreed," replied Mrs Andrews.

Mr B spoke out aloud to no one in the room. "Bring them up, Jack."

A wiry little man of about forty entered the room carrying three tapes which he put on the table in front of Mr B. As he was about to leave D.I. Karetzi restrained him. "We will also need the tape recorder and the other tapes." Jack looked at Mr B who nodded. He departed but was back within two minutes, recorder and tape in hand.

"How the hell did you know there was another tape, Detective?" queried the Chief.

"Simple case of mathematics. It's twenty past two. We've been here over three hours and each tape is sixty minutes long," said Karetzi.

The Chief plugged in the tape recorder and at random slotted in one of the tapes and his voice boomed out: "…any degree of accuracy as to the gender of…". Jones reached over and ejected the tape. "Sorry Chief, I think we must ascertain that these are the only tapes, so we should hear the beginning of Tape 1 and the end of Tape 4."

This was done and they were satisfied. Jones took all four into the adjoining kitchen and destroyed them by setting them alight.

Emma rose and took a long black coat from the hook on the door. The Chief helped her into it. Emma wished everyone good luck, carefully averting her eyes from D.I. Karetzi's. God, if I were only twenty odd years younger, she thought. She handed D.I. Jones a card. "If the Assembly can be of any help, just call."

"I think you've a new friend there," Mike said to Evan.

"No, I think you have Mike," said Evan. Inwardly Mr B was on the same track. No hope in hell for poor old Emma with this Karetzi chap.

Next to leave was Mr Brian. No one in the room knew his surname or for that matter his Christian one. One thing for certain, it wasn't Brian. He also handed D.I. Jones a card. No name or address, just a telephone number. "This number will get you past any red tape, quicken things up, smooth your paths, make things happen. Just ring anytime, 24-7,"

Yes, thought Jones, this bloke was like Cod Liver Oil, good for you, but tasted like shit, and his new partner (he'd heard the rumours), unconventional, dicey methods, crazy, but well-liked and respected by all.

His thoughts were interrupted by the Chief asking them if they would like a coffee. Both D.I.s replied in the affirmative. Black for Karetzi; milk, two sugars for Jones. It wasn't everyday a Chief

Constable made coffee for his men: actually, this was a first, and a last.

The coffee was ready: three mugs all different sizes and type. They were placed on the table together with a small soup bowl. "You may smoke, this is not an office, that's downstairs," the Chief said. Karetzi shook out a filter-less cigarette from a crumpled pack and lit it with a gold and silver lighter. Jones lit up his small clay pipe with a throw-away lighter. The tobacco smelt sweet. It was a cherry-based product.

When everyone was comfortable the Chief opened up his briefcase. He handed them new warrant cards. They read 'Special Detective Inspector'. He handed them a mobile phone each and corporate credit cards. "There are unlimited funds at your disposal. I don't need to say, don't abuse them, no personal stuff on the cards, police business only."

You still said it Chief, thought Karetzi. And that was the beginning of the S.C.S serious cases squad.

"Your salaries will be paid in the normal way and before anyone asks, no, there is no pay rise." The chief carried on: "You will be joined tomorrow by Gilberts. Amber will live here and coordinate everything. We've seconded her from Bristol. She's the tops, the best."

"I assume you're talking computers?" asked Jones.

"And more, Evan, much more and she's a local lass to boot."

"Sounds good to me," Karetzi said.

It would to you, Jones thought. He wasn't so sure about Karetzi and women, together, hours on end in a small house. He could see complications; somewhere in the back of his mind he'd heard about his new partner's passion for the ladies. He made a decision. Jones would make sure that his new partner and his daughter, Jasmine, would never meet.

"Amber has every police and witness statement, every piece of known paperwork, including local newspaper clippings and reports, photos, everything that we have as a Force on this Chessperson, I mean Chessman. She also has a list of telephone numbers of various people or establishments including judges who will help cut through any red tape. This as they say in the U S of A is our Wales Public Enemy No. 1."

"It's a tall order, eight victims, not one lead, no motive. This man is an invisible. Where does one start? He's a needle in a haystack, in a field somewhere in Wales."

"Any questions?"

"Just one," said Karetzi.

"And what's that?"

"Who the hell is that Mr Brian?"

"Ah, Mr Brian, the Whitehall enigma. All I can tell you is that he is in National Internal Security and has the ear of the most important people in Britain. Does that answer your question, Mike?"

"Yes Sir," replied Mike, no clearer as to who Mr Brian was or where he came into this case. Nevertheless, he was obviously useful.

"Who do we report to?" asked Jones.

"Amber has all the information. I will now bow out of the case and leave it up to your goodselves. Oops, I nearly forgot, you can pick up an unmarked car from this address – ask for Sandy." He pushed over a piece of paper with an address on it. About ten minutes' walk from where they were currently sitting. "I envisage there will be a lot of travel and overnight stays in places. Any of you have a problem with that?" There was no answer.

Chief Constable Clarke had finished. He looked at his watch – just gone three. He felt drained and despondent. These two detectives against the Invisible Chessman. He couldn't quote any odds of success, the numbers were incalculable. He shivered, and his legs felt like rubber. He had difficulty standing up to shake hands with the detectives, who were ready to leave. The Chief passed over two front door keys and the alarm code.

Prior to leaving, the detectives visited the bathroom separately. They descended the stairs and Karetzi tried the door of the office.

It was locked. He tried his new key – it wouldn't fit, so he tried it on the front door that worked.

Once outside, in the fresh air, there was an uncomfortable silence between the newly formed partnership. Neither was sure about the other.

It had stopped raining. No need for Jones to unfurl his umbrella. For that he was grateful. It was too small to share. "The garage is that way across the park and to the right," Karetzi said. They crossed the road into the park which was empty apart from the couple on the bench. They were soaked and cold. Jones waved. They didn't wave back. The distance to the garage was short but both knew that the road to their goal would be long, strenuous and would in all likelihood end in failure. The detectives were gripped in a state of despair. Both were thinking the worst, obviously someone, somewhere wanted scapegoats and it seemed they had been selected Special Detectives; Special Patsies would be nearer the truth. They found the garage.

CHAPTER 2

Over 50 miles to the West of the garage that Karetzi and Jones were about to enter, Peter James, sitting on a big easy chair in front of the television in his front room, opened another can of Ginger Beer. He was watching Countdown and was feeling very content.

He raised his glass and proposed a toast. To the future, and the riches that would be theirs. Riches for all, for Bob, for Andy, David, Michael, Amy, Boris, Trudy, Steve and last but not least, Uncle Pauli and Carl.

He laughed, no one laughed, no one raised a glass, no one else was in the room. Not physically, just in his mind. He was not mad, he was the Chessman. The future was his.

Within a week Brian from Barry would be joining them, another chess piece would meet his maker, and he sure as hell was not talking about any games manufacturers. He was talking about THE MAN in Heaven, GOD.

So far, he had used five pawns, two castles and a knight. The pawns were easy, not too much preparation, but the others needed timing, legwork and organisation.

The police were stupid. They had not one meaningful clue. Lots of clues such as footprints, hairs, scars, rings, even a video of him, all useless information, disinformation. So the profilers would profile. Motive: without that there is no basis, nowhere to start. The cops had bagfuls of identity, all completely different. The idiots had not one clue, not a half of one.

Peter worked from home – an end of terrace in Swansea. He

was a coin dealer, mail order and on-line. He sold to collectors everywhere. The study and collecting of coins is called numismatics and is derived from the Greek word for coin which is nomisma. Peter didn't specialise but preferred dealing with British, American and Canadian coinage.

Business ticked over, he made good money, was well off, not rich yet, but well off. He had inherited good money from his parents and he'd invested well, owning two homes, the one in Swansea and, under a different name, a small flat in Cardiff. He had no mortgages and a bit of money in various banks, all again under aliases. Soon he would be rich, guaranteed.

At half six, just after the local news, Peter, the thirty-year-old, brown haired, causal jeans and open neck shirt type, went into his bedroom and changed. Five minutes later 'Uncle Paul' emerged. A sixty-five year old, grey haired, small whitish moustache, wearing a dark blue, double breasted woollen suit over a white shirt, a blue tie, black leather shoes and socks made up the person known to Jim and Pat, his neighbours, as Paul. He opened the front door, closed it, stepped over a low brick, dividing wall and rang the doorbell. Jim answered. He was ready. It was Karaoke night at the local, The Red Parrot, and Jim always sang, hopefully Peter's favourite.

They made small talk as they ambled the half mile to the pub. Jim was sixty-nine and didn't like rushing. "How's your Peter these days? Don't see him around much recently."

"You know Jim, Peter's always on the computer, doing business, or surfing, browsing, whatever they call it."

Jim nodded. The internet, computers, mobile phones, they had all passed him by as they obviously had to his friend Paul. Jim was wrong there. Jim was wrong about a lot of things but he had a great voice and Paul was looking forward to one song in particular.

Paul made a mental note to come as Peter and talk to Jim sometime during the next couple of hours, otherwise he'd have to find an excuse and go and see Jim and his wife Pat in the morning as Peter. Luckily any excuse would do. Their neighbours had no children, no visitors except a nurse, for Pat, who suffered from acute arthritis. Pat didn't get out much. Jim did all the shopping but Peter/Paul helped out now and then.

Two years they had been neighbours and the stupid idiots next door had no idea that Uncle Paul and his nephew Peter were one and the same. Actually, maybe they were the perfect neighbours, Peter thought, under the circumstances.

Paul and Jim ordered and after greeting a few acquaintances, took up a vacant table. They were fortunate; over seventy people were jammed inside, many standing at the bar which had the best view of the small stage.

A dumpy freckled woman with huge hair and even bigger breasts was murdering 'Summertime'. My God, thought Peter, never mind 'Summertime' in Swansea, it was like bloody 'Wintertime' in Siberia! She was booed off-stage, rightly so. Next up was a young lad of about twenty-one or two who did a good Elvis with 'Are you lonesome tonight?'.

The crowd wanted more from the Elvis boy but he refused, probably because his girlfriend was waiting by the door, impatient to go somewhere with a bit more life. The average age in the Parrot was fifty plus.

Elvis was followed by a Sinatra devotee, singing 'My Way', not bad thought Jim, who stood up ready and eager. He walked slowly to the stage.

The room was noisy. With a few drinks inside them, the Tuesday regulars had warmed up, their tongues looser.

"Oh, Oh, Oh, Yes, I'm The Great Pretender" – Jim was better than good. The noise lessened quite a few degrees. Quite a few joined in singing along with Jim but not Peter; he was waiting for his favourite part. It soon came around and Peter joined the others singing, "Oh, Oh, Oh, Yes, I'm the Great Pretender, adrift in a world of my own, I seem to be what I'm not you see…"

By now everyone was singing, but still the voice of the person on stage came over loudest and sweetest. The applause was deafening. Jim sang another two Platter's classics and then returned to his table. "Brilliant Jim, just brilliant. I love that first one. I just love it, love it, love it," said Peter.

"I'll get some more beers in Jim," said Peter, rising and moving towards the bar. "You need a nice cold one – lager as before?"

"Thanks," replied Jim.

Fatty big breasts had got a hold of the microphone again. This time she was murdering another classic. It was so bad Peter couldn't fathom out what the song was meant to be. She finally killed off the song and was about to kill another one when the manager and a bouncer helped her out into the street. She was still singing; anyway, that's what she thought she was doing. Everyone who had ever heard her knew that was an untruth.

Whilst waiting for the beers, Peter knew he had to be ultra-careful with Jim. A while ago he was about to look smart and tell Jim that when he heard the song first by Queen, he knew it would be a great classic.

That would have been a big mistake. The song was fifty years old and Paul at sixty- five would surely have known that. It was a massive hit. Peter paid for the drinks and took them back to his table and sat down.

He took a sip and then, without warning, suddenly jumped up. "Damn, I think I've left one of the gas plates on the hob burning. I won't be long Jim, better safe than sorry."

Peter left and ran the whole distance back to his house without breaking sweat. Once inside, it took him a few minutes only to change once again into Peter.

On re-entering the pub, he looked around. Jim saw him and waved him over. Peter walked over. "Uncle Pauli having a pee, is he Jim?"

"No son, he had to pop back home. He won't be long. You just missed him."

"I wish he'd keep his mobile on, I can never get him when I want to."

"I'll get you a drink in. What'll it be sonny?"

"Thanks Jim, but I'm in a rush. I've got someone waiting for me in town and I have a feeling I won't be back home tonight," said Peter smirking.

"A hot date Pete, can't remember the last time. Oh, never mind, get moving son and make sure you have a good time. You're only young once and that once has passed me and your Uncle Paul back a long time ago."

Peter left, ran again to the house, and changed. He walked back. He was feeling the strain and was tired. He was also pissed off. He wondered if he could spare a pawn for Jim. No, no pawns but an accident, a fatal one might just be in order. Could he find the time? Was it too close to home – bring unwanted attention? He'd think about it. There must be a way.

"Well Paul, was the hob on?"

"No, Jim, a waste of time. I'm too old for going back and forth. Who needs the hassle? Mind you, my memory is bad Jim."

"Talking of memory Paul, I nearly forgot to tell you – Peter's just been in looking for you, said he tried calling you on your phone."

Jim recounted the conversation he'd had with Peter. Paul already knew of course, but he sat patiently listening.

Paul took out his mobile. "Peter's right Jim, it's switched off. I hate the thing but I guess I should keep it on."

"Did I tell you Jim, Peter's going on a business trip, seven, eight places, North Wales, Chester, Liverpool, Manchester and other places? It's all set up. He'll be away for weeks."

"Never was sure, something to do with money, that's Peter's lark isn't it?"

"Yes Jim, it's coins actually, old coins he buys at auctions and from private collectors and resells over the internet and through respected dealers, all over the place. He does well with it or so it seems. He never complains."

They finished their drinks and left. It took them ten minutes to get home. Within an hour Peter was asleep. He never had any problems getting to sleep. He had a clear conscience. As usual he dreamt of riches. What he would buy: a yacht, Ferrari, holiday home in Barbados. His list was endless as was his imagination.

Pat was still awake when Jim got home. "Had a nice time Jim? Did a little singing like the old days?"

"Yes love, one day we will get down there together when the weather changes for the better. Make a foursome with Paul and Peter, what do you say my love?"

"I look forward to it Jim, but tell me something."

"What Pat?"

"Our neighbours there, what can I say? Strange, no: different."

"In which way Pat?"

"I don't know Jim, it's just a feeling. I can't put my finger on it."

Jim got into bed. Even after forty-seven years of marriage they still slept in the same bed. Jim couldn't get to sleep. He was restless. Pat was usually uncannily right. The neighbours were nice decent folks. He could call them friends but something next door wasn't kosher.

He tossed and turned all night. The morning wouldn't come fast enough. He just lay there hoping it was later than it really was. The bedside alarm clock proved that there were still sixty seconds in a minute and sixty minutes in the hour. Hope just didn't come into it. Time was time.

CHAPTER 3

The detectives stood outside the garage, a brick and concrete affair. Ugly was too kind a word for it. Two large double garage doors and a small regular door all painted navy blue front the ground floor. The one and only floor above had four small windows, each one covered with steel bars; they were also painted blue. It was a garage without a name, a secret car hideaway.

Jones tried the small door. It creaked and opened into a room about fifteen foot square. There was a metal desk, a couple of storage units, two chairs and a filing cabinet; metal again. There were two brick walls, one with pictures of racing cars plastered all over it. The other had two large notice boards full with pieces of paper held by magnetic round discs. The other two walls were half-bricked from the floor with glass up to the ceiling affording a good view to most of the garage that they overlooked. One had a door for entry into said garage.

A youngish, curly haired man in blue overalls greeted them. When he spoke, one could see that he was missing one front tooth.

"Are you Sandy?" asked Jones.

"No, I'm Robbie – Sandy's checking over a vehicle. Can I be of help?"

"Yes, you can Robbie. Please tell Sandy that Special Detective Inspectors Karetzi and Jones have come to pick up a car."

Through the glass windows the detectives could see Mercs, BMWs, Jags, a small van and a Ford, bonnet open. Peeking into the bonnet was a small, stocky man of about forty. He had straw-coloured hair.

"I guess that is Sandy," said Jones.

"Must be," answered Karetzi.

Within a minute straw hair together with curly hair entered their office; straw hair confirmed that he was Sandy. "I was expecting you," he said, offering his hand. It was black with oil and dirt. The Detectives didn't shake hands with Sandy who seemed offended by the snub. Tough luck.

"Let's see some identification please," said Sandy. Warrant cards were produced and inspected carefully by Sandy who then asked for further proof of their identities.

"Further proof?" said Jones. "Why do you need that?"

"Well, these look too new to me. It's like they were made last night and no car goes out of here until I'm completely satisfied as to the identity of the recipient. I'm in charge here." Curly nodded.

"So, no proper identity, no car. Comprende my friends? No transport. We can call a taxi and he will give you a discount." Sandy and Curly laughed.

"We seem to have got off to a bad start Sandy," Karetzi said, ignoring the 'No Smoking' sign and lighting up his fourth of the day. He allowed himself max five or six daily. A pack would last him four days on average.

"Put it out Detective. This is a no smoking area. It's against the law to smoke in the workplace."

Karetzi inhaled and blew the smoke straight into straw hair's face. He inhaled again before speaking. "Sandy, my new partner Special Detective Inspector Jones seems to me to be a very patient man who could chew the fat with you forever over a nice cup of tea. Unfortunately, I'm the opposite and behind my back people call me 'Crazy Karetzi'. Me smoking in here will be the least of your problems, comprende my friend?"

More smoke streamed into Sandy's face. Karetzi then stubbed out his butt on a sheet of papers resting on the desk.

"Your car's over there," said Sandy. "The one with the open bonnet. That's the one I have assigned to your goodselves."

Straw hair and Curly took great delight at seeing the two crestfallen faces before them. Having ascertained that his partner's cigarette butt would not burn the garage down, Jones politely asked why they couldn't have one of the other cars. The answer was logical. They were assigned to high-ranking officers but Jones was still unhappy. "This was fun," thought Sandy. "I bet they wished they shook my hand now."

"I'm going to have a look. Evan, you just start the paperwork with the boy here." As he opened the door to go into the garage, he heard Sandy say, "It's in top condition detective. I personally checked it over before your arrival."

As Karetzi neared the car, he reached into his comb compartment on the inside of his leather jacket, squatting down next to the passenger side front wheel, completely out of sight. He stabbed the tyre three times, puncturing it. He remained squatted until the tyre was flat. He folded the knife and returned it to his comb pocket. He strolled back to the office.

"Well?" asked Jones.

"It's a piece of shit on three wheels, Evan. What is known in the trade as a shitmobile."

"Three wheels?" queried Sandy.

"Yes mate. One's got a puncture and there's a pool of oil under the engine."

"No way!" shouted Sandy, "Absolutely no way."

"Come and see for yourself," said Karetzi.

Everyone made a move for the door. Sandy first, then Karetzi, who turned, blocking his partner's and Curly's exit.

"I'll sort out the car with Sandy. If you could finish the paperwork with Curly, Evan, it will save time." It made sense to Evan. He was no mechanic and he was certain he was more efficient than his partner with paperwork, so he agreed. Jones grabbed Curly by the arm and manoeuvred him to one of the steel chairs next to the desk. Evan remained standing. He couldn't see

Sandy but could see his partner from the waist up. Curly couldn't see anything except Jones' back.

Even before kneeling down Sandy could see that the tyre was flat. Obviously, the lunatic detective had tampered with it. It was fine half an hour or less ago. He would report this wilful damage of police property to the Chief Constable himself.

"Do you see the oil puddle, Sandy?"

"No, I don't detective," Sandy replied, going through the motions. He stretched palms flat to the floor, head down, under the car. "There's nothing there, just like I thought."

Suddenly and without warning Karetzi planted the heel of his left foot over the mechanic's right hand. The pain was excruciating. Sandy whimpered but did not cry out loud.

"Let me give you some facts, you cocky little grease monkey," Karetzi whispered. "Fact one, I weigh over two hundred pounds and if I shift my weight even slightly, I will break every bone in your hand. Fact two, there is not much call for one-handed mechanics. Fact three, I will drive one of the other cars out of here within half an hour with your blessing. Now Sandy, you seem a bright sort of a chap, being in charge here and all that, you must know a fact or two." Karetzi shifted his weight.

"Don't, please don't."

Karetzi relaxed his foot a little. "I'm still waiting for a fact that will make my day, as they say in America."

"The red BMW in the corner, next to the van is now available," signed Sandy, tears of pain streaking down his face onto the dirty concrete floor.

"If you turn you head and look up Sandy, you will see that I am holding a knife with a five-inch blade. Do you see it?"

"Yes."

"Good, I don't want any change of heart regarding the red Beamer. Remember a no-handed mechanic is even worse off than a one-handed one. I mean with one hand you can still pick your nose and scratch your arse."

Do we fully understand each other, Mr Sandy Campbell?"

"Yes, yes," replied Sandy.

Karetzi lifted his foot and helped the mechanic get back onto his feet. They walked to the office. Sandy tried to clench his fist, but could not. It was very bruised.

"You guys were a long time," Curly said. "Any other problems with the car?"

"Plenty, it's un-driveable, so we're taking that red Beamer instead," responded Mike to Curly's question. Curley looked at Sandy, bemused and lost. What was going on? Sandy nodded.

Jones was also lost. He noticed Sandy's hand and he could see that the mechanic had been crying. What was going on? What the hell happened out there? The paperwork was changed accordingly. Curly signed it off. Sandy couldn't. One pair of the big blue garage doors were opened and with Special Detective Inspector Karetzi at the wheel, the beautiful red BMW 330, two-door Club, Sport Coupe, rolled out into the Capital's streets.

"I think, Evan, that went off quite well, wouldn't you say? I mean, this is a beaut of a car. Let's see if we have the blue light and siren?" Evan found the light. "Stick it up on the roof Evan. Let's see what this babe will do," said Mike putting on the siren and pushing his foot down hard on the accelerator.

When they touched a hundred and twenty on the motorway, Mike was satisfied and so was Evan not to be stopped by traffic police. They could hardly say that they were running-in a new car. First day at work with his new partner and Evan was bricking it, his knuckles white, his heart beating so fast it was doing more revs than the car. This man driving was not only crazy but bloody dangerous.

"Can you tell me, Mike, what exactly made Sandy change his mind about the car? He was adamant before you showed him the tyre. It must have been the oil leak. That's what it was I guess."

"Actually Evan, I mistook some old dried oil as a leak. There wasn't one."

"Then why the change of mind? It only takes a few minutes to change a tyre in a garage with all the necessary equipment to hand."

"I agree with you there, Evan. I suppose when I accidentally stepped on his right hand and didn't realise it, he must have thought I was trying to break his hand and panicked into giving us a better one."

Evan said nothing. What could he say? He felt very uneasy knowing that he would have to work with Mike every day. The Detective was a maverick. More worryingly for Evan was the fact, not rumour, that his new partner carried a large knife.

"If it's okay by you Evan, we'll drive down to my apartment in the Bay and we can have a chat and get to know each other better. Then we can have a bite to eat at a local bistro I frequent before going back to the house and having a proper look round."

"That's fine with me but no point in going back to the house. The office part is locked."

"Don't worry about that Evan, I'm sure that we'll find a way in. I'm confident that a small locked door won't stop us."

"My God," thought Evan, "he's going to break and enter!"

It's as if Mike read his mind. "After all, Evan, my friend, it's not illegal to find a way into your own office."

Evan had to concede that his partner had a good point. "That Brian chappie, he seemed to be in charge and I think that's who we will be reporting to, but who the hell is he and why is he involved?" said Evan. "I mean he's some kind of high ranking spook. Why is the government so interested in our Chessman?" Evan added as an afterthought, "It doesn't make any sense."

"I can tell you this Evan, it's all very strange – keeping it out of the newspapers, the connections of the severed chess head pieces, running such a massive case with low-ranked officers out of a terraced house in Cardiff. If ever there was a job for Scotland Yard, this surely must be high on their list of priorities, yet here we are, Evan, just you, me and a woman called Amber."

"I get this feeling Mike that this Mr Brian has opened the door of desperation for us two and we've no choice but to go through."

"Let's hope they're revolving Evan and we can come out on the right side." Evan smiled.

"By the way, Evan, I bet you a quid to a penny that the spooks have got copies of those tapes."

"Of course they have Mike, they're probably listening to them right now and later they will have them voice and speech analysed to determine what kind of characters we are."

Approaching London on the M4, George the Fiat driver asked Brian what he thought of the two detectives. All three had rerun the tapes, picking out what the Boss thought relevant. Jack in the front passenger seat worked the tape machine, slow, fast forward, slow, repeat, fast forward and so on and on until they had heard the parts they wanted. Hopefully, the experts would dig out anything of use later in the lab.

"Those boys are good, better than good, they will progress on the case. One is patient and fastidious, the other sharp and cunning," Brian said.

"But Boss, they can't be that clever. They have no idea we copied the tapes," Jack proudly pointed out.

"I very much doubt that we fooled them Jack, they probably guessed that we were running two tapes simultaneously, but what could they prove and what could they do about it, and more to the point, do they care, do I? Answer that Jack."

"Any information we extract about their characters is useless and they know that as well as I."

Evan liked the apartment. The furniture was a bit sparse and modern for his taste but he liked the third-floor flat overlooking the Bay. It had a big lounge and balcony. The views were great.

Two good-sized bedrooms, both with double beds: one made up, the other not. In the corner of the unmade bedroom there was a bathroom and just outside there was a pile of women's lingerie.

Evan thought, what kind of woman forgot her bra and knickers? She must have been in one hell of a rush to get out. The kitchen was a good size and well equipped and there was another bathroom. The flat seemed twice the size of Evan's.

How could his partner afford it? What with his expensive clothes, he probably has a Porsche parked in the undercroft garages. It was very disturbing. He had that uneasy feeling again. There was a lot he needed to find out about this new partner. He hated prying into anyone's personal life, but he needed answers, otherwise he would find it difficult, if not impossible, to work with his partner, Special Detective Inspector Mikhail Karetzi.

Mike let Evan wander around appraising everything before putting on the telephone voice recorder.

Three messages: his mother asking about his well-being, Mandy asking about her left underwear and Tanya asking him if he was on to go out that night as she'd just flown in and would be in the City for a few days stop-over before her next flight. Obviously an air stewardess, reasoned Evan. He thought of his daughter Jasmine, not that she was an air stewardess, she worked in a large department store in the City as a beauty consultant in the large cosmetics department but he thought of her nevertheless.

One thing he knew, one thing he could guarantee, that his daughter wouldn't be another girl, leaving messages on Mike's phone. He'd see to it that they never met.

Mike asked Evan if he wanted a soft drink. He explained that he never used milk or sugar and therefore had none in the apartment. Evan settled for a diet Coke.

Evan rang his wife, Edna, told her he would be back very late. Told her about his new case, new title, new partner. Edna was fine with everything but she had reservations about her husband being partnered with a Pole. One of the new wave of immigrants flooding the country. Did he speak good English? Was he savvy with our ways, our traditions? She would find out. She'd invite him to dinner tomorrow. She would use her mother's good fine dining Japanese dinner service. We must show these Poles that we have standards to uphold.

She rang Evan and asked him to invite the Pole, his new partner, for dinner tomorrow. She also wanted to know if he was a Christian and whether or not he had a good grasp of the English language.

"Yes, Edna, I think he's a Christian. He speaks perfect English and he's not Polish but of Russian descent. I think he was actually born in Wales and yes, again, I will invite him to dinner. Eight prompt." Russian, thought Edna. She'd never met one before. I suppose he drank Vodka. She'd get some in.

By the time Evan had got off his phone, Mike was ready. A new shirt, black pair of slacks and a new comfortable pair of moccasin shoes. He sat down opposite Evan on a small leather easy chair, a black coffee in his hand. "Let me tell you about myself Evan," Mike said lighting up his fifth cigarette of the day. "Please feel free to smoke." Evan took out his tobacco pouch and pipe. This was going to be very interesting, he mused as he stuffed the tobacco into his small clay pipe.

"I'm thirty-five years old, nearly thirty-six. I was born in Cardiff. Mother Welsh, father Russian. My father passed away when I was twelve, my mother is alive and well and lives in a small bungalow in Penarth.

"I play football for a small local team. It keeps me fit. I follow City at Ninian Park and see as many home games as possible. I love music, most of all fifties, sixties stuff. I love boxing, especially when Joe Calzaghe fights. I believe in God, but don't attend any church. I'm not married but enjoy the company of women. I like a drink, sometimes two.

"Some people call me crazy and I don't think it's a term of endearment but it does rhyme nicely with my surname. I'm a fair bloke but if the need arises for the good, I will bend or even break the rules and still sleep easy at night.

"That, Evan, in a nutshell, is me. I like to think I'm a good cop. I am a little unconventional but I produce results."

You can say that again, thought Evan, his mind going back just an hour or so to the garage.

Down in the garage, Sandy and Robbie just sat there. What was he to do? How was he going to tell Chief Superintendent Freddie Fowler that his assigned car wasn't assigned to him anymore? Fowler was foul, a nasty, red-faced bully but the Russian named cop was completely crazy. At one stage Sandy actually feared for his life.

He did the right thing, it was the only thing he could have done. He hoped and prayed that the car would run perfectly. Another session with the crazy cop would send him over the edge. He looked at his hand. Robbie looked at it too, but was wise enough to keep his mouth shut.

Sandy was a great mechanic, one of the best, but when it came to brains, well, it wasn't fair, was it? Like Baldric in Black Adder, he had an idea. He picked up the phone, cradled it between his shoulder and cheek, then dialled with his left hand.

"I would like to speak to Chief Superintendent Fowler, please."

"Who may I ask is calling?" asked a woman police sergeant.

"It's Sandy from the garage. It's regarding the Chief Super's car."

"Just wait a minute and I'll put you through."

"Thanks."

"Hello, is that Chief Superintendent Fowler?"

"Of course it bloody well is, you asked for me, didn't you?"

"Um, Yes Sir, that's right."

"Well, what do you want?"

"It's a bit difficult to explain Sir, but your car is no longer available."

"No longer available, what's happened to it, stolen, crashed, what?"

"It's just left the garage on an emergency reassignment, top priority I'm afraid. Nothing I could do about it. We will of course source a similar car as soon as we can Sir. Hopefully within the next week or two." More like a bloody month or three, thought Robbie, who was listening to the conversation.

"Are you fucking people stupid, incompetent or both? I've been waiting over six months for that car and the day before I'm finally going to get it, you let someone else fucking have it! Who the hell has got it? Tell me, before I come down there myself and bang your bloody heads together. I want that car, and I'm not waiting for another six months and personally I don't care if you've assigned it to Prince Charles, it's my car. Now names, addresses of the fucking thieves."

"I have two names, Sir, a Special Detective Inspector Karetzi and a Special Detective Inspector Jones. I also have an address and phone number, landlines and mobiles."

"You gave my car to two lousy, miserable D.I.s and they have priority over me, a Chief Superintendent?" and with that he slammed the phone down on Sandy. The Chief was seething. He was enraged. It took him a full two minutes to calm down enough to start dialling. He had no luck with the landline or the mobiles, but first thing in the morning he would pay the car thieves a visit.

"How do you think it went Sandy?" Robbie asked.

"Fine, just wait till that foul mouthed bastard Fowler tries to get anywhere with that crazy Karetzi bloke. My money's on the Russian!"

Both laughed. Time for a nice cup of tea.

CHAPTER 4

"You hungry, Evan?" Mike asked.

"I am. It's been a long day. Been up since seven this morning. Crikey, that's over twelve hours."

"Good, so am I. Do you like Italian?"

"I like everything," replied Evan.

"Well, just follow me to food heaven," said Mike. "I know a great place just down the road." Mike led, Evan followed.

Angelo the owner greeted them at the door. "Good Evening, Mikhail. You are joining us for a pleasant Italian meal?"

"No, I've come because I hate the food here Angelo and because it's over-priced and dirty here and mostly I keep coming to hear someone actually pronounce my name correctly, apart from my mother."

A wide grin spread across the dapper little Italian's face. He hugged Mike. "Welcome. I will get you a table near the window." Angelo showed them to a table. On each table there were flowers, freesias in fact. Angelo took them. Where Angelo obtained freesias from at this time of year beat Mike.

Within seconds a waiter brought a carafe of iced water, some fresh bread and a bottle of Pino Grigio with two glasses.

"No flowers," said Mike.

"The boss, he say, no woman, no flowers. Wine is on the house." The waiter left, only to return with two menus.

"Angelo always sits me next to the window, why beats me. I mean you can't see out because of these blinds and even if you could, it's as bloody dark as a blackboard out there." Evan didn't answer. The place was nearly full. It must be good, he thought. Angelo didn't do 'Happy Hours' or 'Early Birds'.

They ordered Veal a la Lemone for both. A green salad for Mike and chips for Evan. A selection of vegetables came with the meal. Mike poured the wine. "You drive the car tonight Evan. You need to get used to it. I'll walk home from the office. It's not that far." Evan sipped his wine. This was lovely but one glass was all he could have.

Both the S.D.I.s ate slowly, savouring the delicious taste of the veal. "I guess you'd like to know a bit about me", said Evan. "If you wish, Evan." "Not much to say but I'll try to be as brief as possible.

"I'm 54, married, one grown up daughter. My parents are alive and live in Pontypridd, as does my only brother Bryn. Like my father before him, Bryn teaches English in the local comprehensive. He's four years older than me and retires at the end of next year.

"I follow cricket as much as I can. Glamorgan in particular. It's been a bad two or three years for the County but I love the game and will always support them, through thick or thin. I follow the Blues at Rugby. I understand that there is some talk of them ground-sharing with City in the new stadium."

"So I hear, Evan."

"I like all music, especially Welsh choirs, and am partial to the old style country and western. Hank Williams, George Jones etc. My wife and I attend Chapel regularly. In general we live a simple life. A small caravan in Rhyl does us for holidays.

"Good," said Mike, "I like those artists too. Something we have in common."

"Twenty-seven years I've been in the Force. I don't cut corners and don't distort facts to support anyone's stupid theories for personal gain. I think I'm a good cop. Maybe, slow and pedantic but I get there, Mike. It's like I'm the tortoise to your hare. In three years I will hope to retire and watch more cricket. My wife, Edna, loves it as much as I do. Funnily enough we met at a cricket match in Abergavenny over thirty-three years ago. It seems like yesterday. I wish it was." Evan was finished as was his dinner.

"Evan, I think we'll get on fine as partners but one thing I need to ask you."

"Yes?" said Evan, fearing the worst.

"Can you please explain to me the rules of cricket?"

Evan smiled. He was warming to his new partner.

"By the way Mike, Edna my better half, has invited you for dinner tomorrow. Can you make it or do you have something prearranged?"

"That will be nice. Thank you and thank your wife. What time?"

"Eight, Mike."

"Eight it is then, Evan."

"Coffee Evan, or a sweet, or both?"

"Just a regular white coffee's fine. Difficult enough already getting into some of my clothes. I should really get on a diet sometime soon."

Mike ordered a double espresso and a regular. He also ordered a large brandy. "I assume you don't want one?" asked Mike. "As you are driving."

Evan nodded. He noticed that his glass of wine was half full. Mike's was empty, as was the bottle. He wasn't worried. The rumours said his partner was a little crazy but no one had ever mentioned that his new partner had a drink problem.

With the coffee and brandy finished, Mike called for the bill. Angelo brought it himself.

"You enjoy the meal?"

"As always Angelo. It was lovely."

"Very good," added Evan.

"That is why they come to Angelo's. Best food in the City.

Always full except on Mondays."

"That's because you don't open on Mondays, you rascal," said Mike, fishing in his jacket for his new credit card. "Add twenty per cent for the staff Angelo and thanks for the wine. Give my best to Donna. Tell her...."

"Tell me what Mr Detective?" Donna, the chef and Angelo's wife, had just appeared at the table. A petite fresh-looking lovely of Angelo's age, forty.

"I was going to say, Donna, tell her I love her, but you know that, don't you?"

"Your friend, he no like the wine?"

"I love it, but I'm still on duty and driving," Evan replied to Donna.

Mike formerly introduced Evan to Angelo and Donna. Donna gave Mike a big hug and a kiss before returning to the kitchen. "You keep your big Ruski hands off my little doll, Mikhail," said Angelo laughing.

"Difficult Angelo, but I know you need her in the kitchen and I need to come and have a good meal as often as possible."

"Mike, that's as fine a meal as I've had in a long while, but do you think twenty per cent excessive, and should you have used the corporate credit card for personal use? You remember what the Chief Constable said when he gave us the cards."

"Yes, Evan, I can remember. The Chief said there were unlimited funds for police business. Right Evan?" corrected Mike.

"Well, we're on duty. We had not eaten all day, so as we are on a case and hungry, it's police business. As for the tip being excessive, I have to disagree. The bill was £45.50 with a ten per cent tip; we'll call it a round £50, a twenty per cent tip adds say another fiver. Do you agree Evan?"

"That's correct, Mike."

"So, Evan, we gave five pounds extra tip and saved ourselves nearly £18 on the wine. So we are thirteen pounds up and a lot of goodwill for any future visits. Do I rest my case, Evan?"

"The way you put it Mike seems fair." But fair to whom, thought Evan privately. Mike had a strange way with him. He bent the rules but who got hurt?

"One last point to ponder, Sherlock," said Mike addressing his partner.

Evan waited. What now? He thought.

"What do we do about overtime? When do we charge? Who gets the bill? I think it's only right, Evan, not to worry about today. Let's forget the long hours and hassle of today but this looks like it's going to be a long and hard journey."

"Jesus Christ Mike, one minute you're charging the Force for meals, the next you're waiving our, I repeat, our money for overtime. You're an enigma Mike."

"No, Evan, I'm just a fair man; in a different way to you. Perhaps everything evens out in life. Sometimes I take the short cuts, sometimes I go the long way round it, but I always end up at the destination I want."

What the hell was he talking about? Had the wine and brandy affected him? He was rambling on and on. Time to change the subject. They were near the BMW now. Mike handed Evan the keys. "What do you drive Mike?"

"I'll show you Evan. It's just over there in the undercroft." Mike lit up – his seventh of the day.

Mike led Evan to the corner. A two-door Mercedes Benz 280 SL Auto stood there.

"Is that it?" Evan asked.

"It sure is, 83 vintage, less than 50K on the clock, power steering, electric windows, ABS, music systems, the lot."

"A fine car, Mike; tell me, what would you call the colour?"

"It's described as Pewter over Silver. Thank God I've never had a bump. I don't think anyone will be able to match the paint. If it ever does need a touch-up I will take it to Sandy and his mate, the one missing front tooth wonder!"

"I doubt whether they could do a good job. It would need a specialist," Evan countered.

"I know, Evan, just joking!"

"How long have you owned it?"

"Nine years Evan."

"I'm impressed. Must be worth a bit."

"Don't know, to me the value is immaterial. I love beautiful cars nearly as much as I love beautiful women."

Evan got that uneasy gut feeling again. It worried him. Mike had expensive tastes, good designer clothes, not his choice of gear but nevertheless expensive, a classic Merc, large flat on the Bay, eats out a lot. Where did he find the money?

Mike could read his partner's thoughts. Evan was thinking about his finances. He was adding two and two together and getting twenty-two. When the time came he'd put him straight or buy him a calculator.

"I'm looking forward to meeting Amber, Evan."

"I bet you are," mused Evan. Anything in a skirt. Mind you he was single but that didn't mean you have to be promiscuous. His mind leapt to his beautiful Jasmine, then back to Karetzi. They would never meet.

Back in the real world, Evan spoke. "I don't think Amber will be there until tomorrow, Mike."

He received no answer. They got into the car and Evan drove towards the City. Maybe Evan was back in the present, but Mike was back in the past as they drove slowly up through Bute Street. How the street had changed since his childhood. Gone were the multicultural cafes, the ship chandlers, even the old North Star pub.

Only the Greek Orthodox Church remained. He went a couple of times with his father, who of course was Orthodox. It seemed to a child, a huge ornamental building with murals depicting Saints everywhere. Huge lights hanging from a very high ceiling and candles everywhere; big ones, thin, small, fat candles were everywhere. He wondered, was it still the same? He tried to remember exactly how long ago it had been since he last went. Probably twenty-eight years. Aghios Nicolaos. Yes, the Aghios meant Saint and St Nicolaos is the Patron Saint of the sea and seafarers.

The car slowed. Evan had to park over fifty yards away. All the other spaces nearer were taken by the other residents of the street. The BMW was by far the best car. Evan wondered. Did anyone care? Strangely enough he found to his surprise that he did. He was proud to drive such a vehicle. For that he had to thank his partner but how had he done it, how had he got the people there to change their minds? He would never really know.

"We're here, Mike," Evan said.

"Go ahead Evan, give me a couple of moments. I just need a bit of time."

Evan passed over the keys. "Okay Mike, see you inside." He could sense that his partner was somewhere else and needed his own space. He let him be. Everyone needed a few moments to himself and Mike was no different, Evan guessed.

Mike was physically sitting in the car but mentally he was still in the Greek Church. He could smell the incense and he could see the candles flickering like little lights on a Christmas Tree. Eventually he stirred, undid his seatbelt and was about to open the door when he saw the big black man carrying a large dark bag, slowly creeping up on Evan, who was engrossed and struggling to open the door.

Silently Karetzi opened the car door and stepped onto the pavement. In one quick movement he removed his knife, opened it and put the lock on. He moved fast when he saw the mugger reach into his bag and produce a gun. Karetzi's heart raced and he was about to throw it, when he realised that the mugger didn't have a gun, but a banana.

With the office door still unopened and a gun resting on the small of his back, Evan froze. The assailant obviously had the upper hand. Evan expected to hear the assailant's voice, but the next voice he heard was his partner's who had his knife at the mugger's throat.

"Mister, you won't kill anyone with a banana, unless of course they slip on the skin and crack their head open, but this here knife will slice through your throat in a second. Drop the bloody banana and the bag, then turn around very slowly. It's been a while since I cut anyone's throat."

The bag and banana were dropped. The would-be mugger turned. Mike had taken a step back just in case. Staring at him was a woman, not a man, about sixty years old, sporting a short style haircut and wearing a black trouser suit. She was black, probably Anglo-African. Evan turned and walked around facing her.

"What stunt are you trying to pull here, Madam?" asked Evan, his heartbeat still not normal.

"I thought you were trying to break into my house. I live here."

"Are you Amber Gilberts by any chance?" Mike asked.

"Yes I am."

"Nice to meet you Amber. I'm S.D.I. Mike Karetzi and the guy you tried to shoot with a banana is S.D.I. Evan Jones."

They all shook hands.

"May I ask what the 'S' stands for? Is it Superintendent?"

"It's not Superintendent or shit, it stands for 'Special'. Our speciality is apprehending dangerous criminals wielding bananas and you're the first we've nabbed," said Mike.

"I see you have a good sense of humour Mike, but Evan looks a bit pale. I'm sorry I scared you Evan."

Before Evan could reply, Mike said, "Lucky you are wearing brown trousers, partner."

Amber giggled. Evan didn't.

"I'm afraid, Mike, that your first arrest wouldn't get to court."

"Why's that Amber?"

"If you only have a licence to nab banana-wielding criminals, I was holding a plantain, a relative to the banana, but not one."

"You're one smart and may I say, beautiful lady," commented Mike.

"And you Mike are a very bad liar, but thanks anyway."

"Shall we go in? I've seen a couple of curtains twitching. Our neighbours are getting nosey," said Evan, picking up the bag and plantain.

Amber opened the door. "No need to worry about the alarm. It will never be on. I hate the damn things."

The detectives followed Amber upstairs. She was taller than Evan and weighed at least thirty pounds more. She never wore makeup or jewellery. Born in Cardiff to a Jamaican father and Welsh mother, she attended university, graduating with a First in Sciences.

"This is the lounge, which you know, and here is the kitchen," Amber said, plonking down her big shopping bag on the black granite worktop. On the hob was a pan, lid off and Amber started the gas underneath. "My supper," she explained. "I love food, especially Caribbean. I wasn't expecting you, otherwise I would invite you to share but I'm afraid there's not much."

"We've eaten, thank you," said Evan who, looking at the stew in the pot, reckoned it was enough to feed a large family and still have enough for their dog.

"One day I'll cook us up a nice meal with some decent Red Stripe lager. The only beer I drink. I have some decent rum and a bottle of good whisky if you're interested."

"Thanks again Amber, but it's been a long day," said Mike.

"Fine. I'll show you the rest of the house. The bathroom I guess you have already visited. The toilet seat was still up and the bath towel wasn't replaced tidily when I came in this evening." She looked at them both.

"Best write a letter to Chief Constable Clarke then, Amber. He was the last to use it, telling him not to be so bloody careless."

"Okay, okay, my mistake, sorry about that, but remember, I live here and I like it tidy," said Amber.

"Point taken," replied Evan.

Amber's smile was dazzling. They were going to get on fine, the three of them. She had had her reservations about working in a small office with two officers both unknown to her, but they seemed harmless enough.

The older one was kind. The stroppy one was the one to watch. She could understand women falling at his feet but she was no fool. Old enough to be his mother, she had no chance. Not that she was interested. Married, divorced, married, divorced, married, separated, that was enough for one lifetime. With hindsight, it was mainly her fault nothing ever worked out in her love life. She was and still was married to her work.

Thankfully no children; just her work which she loved and, according to all, she was very good at it. She intended to help these detectives nail this Chessperson. No-one had told her that the case was now labelled 'Chessman'.

"This, gentlemen, is my room and a no-go area for you. Is that understood?"

The S.D.I.s understood. Evan noticed that it had a lock. The only room upstairs with one. The bathroom did have a bolt on the inside.

"And this is your room, if you ever need it." She pushed open the door to reveal a small dark room, comprised of a single bed and bedside table, a wardrobe, a sink with a mirror above it. A single bulb hanging in the centre of the room was the only source of light except for a small glazed window. There were no curtains, carpets or lock. A prisoner would turn his nose down at this, thought S.D.I. Jones.

"If we catch this Chessman, I'm going to put him in this room as a punishment."

"You mean, when we catch him Mike," Evan said.

"Yes, 'when', thanks for the correction."

"That just leaves downstairs. The nerve-centre." Evan glanced at his watch – nearly eleven. He'd better ring home again. He fished out his mobile. It was the new corporate one. He was about to replace it with his own personal one when he changed his mind. He spoke to his wife and replaced the mobile back into a pocket. He heard Mike say, "Well done Evan. I see you're getting the hang of this expenses business." Evan blushed but he was still on duty. Why not save some money?

Once downstairs, Amber unlocked the door. "By now I guess you know that your front door key won't work in this door." Mike mumbled something. Amber gave them a key each.

The room was massive, about forty by twenty feet of which ten foot was an extension. This was carried on upstairs adding over four hundred square feet to the original house. To the rear there were double-glazed doors, which led out to a small, enclosed, paved back yard. The large room itself looked like the bridge of the Starship Enterprise. To say it was impressive was an understatement. Evan could understand why Amber was seduced by technology.

Out of place with the rest of the surroundings were three old-fashioned steel desks and two swivel chairs. Both desks were piled high with boxes and files. "I insisted on having the most up-to-date technical appliances available. These cost a fortune, but they will pay their way eventually," said Amber.

"Will an early start tomorrow be okay for both of you? Say eight a.m.? We need to go through the boxes over there," she said sweeping her hand over in the direction of the desks. She didn't wait for confirmation. She just added a 'goodnight' and they let themselves out. There was a nice spicy aroma wafting from the kitchen. Evan felt a twinge of hunger. He wondered what Amber was cooking. It looked good.

Evan dropped Mike off and then drove on to his apartment in Taffs Well. Edna greeted him with a kiss. She was in her dressing gown. "Get changed Evan, you must be dead beat. I'll make you a nice cup of cocoa and then you can tell me all." Evan did and told Edna everything.

Mike had thought of taking a taxi to the pub where Vicky worked. She finished at midnight. He knew that Vicky liked him and he liked her but what about Tanya and Amanda? Life was complicated enough and things looked like they were going to get busier with this new job. He undressed and went straight to bed.

D.I. Jones let himself into the house, he knocked twice and entered the office. Amber was sorting out files. Without rising she greeted Evan. "Coffee's in the pot. Help yourself. I drink lots all day long. It keeps the brain stimulated." Evan poured some coffee, added two cubes of sugar and some milk and sat in the remaining chair. He played with his clay pipe. Amber noticed. "If you wish to smoke you can either go outside into the yard or upstairs to the lounge."

It was cold outside and Evan couldn't be bothered with the stairs, so he passed. Above the door a cheap plastic clock about one foot in diameter hung. The second hand ticked very loudly. About 400 ticks later, the door opened and Mike walked in. He was five minutes late. He said 'Good Morning' but didn't apologise for being late.

Mike poured a black coffee for himself and reached into this jacket pocket for his cigarettes. Even with her back turned, Amber spoke. "Smoking outside or upstairs." She'd heard the rustle of the cigarette pack.

"No problem Amber," said Mike, sitting on the edge of one of the now cleared desks.

"All the files are now in chronological order. I've been at it since six," Amber carried on. The first victim was in Bala. The second Abergele, third Dinas Powys, fourth Machynilleth, then Abergavenny, followed by Bridgend, Tenby and the last in St Dogmaels, a small village near Cardigan, known affectionately by the locals as St Dogs.

"At first I thought there was a message in the names. So it seemed until I go to Bridgend. Look what I mean – by taking the capital letter of each location, we can read BADMABT. Now if Bridgend had been Newport or Neath we'd have got BADMAN.

"I then ran these letters through the computer but the computer couldn't come up with any sensible anagrams. I tried connecting up the places, no recognisable figure emerges. The distance as the crow flies is about three hundred and ninety miles; six hundred and twenty four kilometres. No joy there. I have exhausted all avenues concerning places, names, dates, mileage, locations including weather patterns. Everything and we end up with nothing.

"The only constant at all is the fact that all these crimes were from Friday night to Sunday night suggesting that our Chessman has a nine-to-five job.

"Before we progress any more I am going to tape all our conversations so we don't need to take millions of notes, but can in an instant recall any part or parts that we made later on. That way we don't miss anything which could be important." She switched on the machine and the taping started.

"As you are well aware, nothing connects the victims. Not age, status, not workplace, location, only the gender. They are all male. Next, to look at is method. No connection again. The victims were knifed, shot, poisoned, strangled and so on.

"Motive," Amber proceeded. "Motive – without that we have nowhere to start." She towered over the detectives. Mike was seated leaning back in his chair. Evan was now on the edge of the desk, sitting rather uncomfortably, unable to relax.

The doorbell rang. Everyone glanced towards the plastic clock as if it would give them a clue as to who the caller was but it could only tell time and that was precisely nine a.m.

Amber moved to the office door and pressed a button. "May I help you?"

A woman's voice replied. "This is Sergeant Williams. I have with me Chief Superintendent Fowler who wishes to talk to Detective Inspector Jones and Karetzi on a very urgent matter."

"I'll buzz you in. First door on the right."

"Thank you."

Amber looked at Mike then Evan. It was obvious they didn't recognise the name and when the Super and Sergeant walked in, they didn't recognise the faces.

The Super had his hand out. "Which one of you has my keys? I assume you're Jones. Do you have my keys?" His hand still outstretched.

"Yes, I am Special Detective Inspector Evan Jones and no, I am sure I don't have any of your keys."

The Super stepped forward. "No, look here you fucking thief! I want my car keys back now. I'll deal with the paperwork."

"Excuse me, Chief Superintendent, could you refrain from swearing? There are ladies present."

"And who the fuck are you, the cleaner or the fucking cook?" he asked Amber.

"Now Chief, take it easy," said Jones. "Apologise to Amber and then we will discuss your problem."

"I don't do apologies to cleaners or pathetic snivelling little car thieves."

Amber was on the verge of tears as was Sergeant Williams who had tried to fade into a corner.

"Don't bloody hide Williams. We might have to make a few arrests."

"Please Chief, you must calm down. You're a big man and your blood pressure will go through the roof," said Jones. "You see Williams, the detective thief is also a doctor. That will be handy to know."

"Just pass over the keys, Jones, and we'll be on our way. No hard feelings and I might throw in an apology to the cleaner if you hurry," he said, poking Jones in the chest.

"You're just not making yourself clear, Superintendent Fowler."

"It's Chief Superintendent."

"Yes Sir," Jones added. "Please clarify why do you think we have your car keys?"

"Are you the most stupid detectives in Wales, Jones, or are you just pretending to fucking work me up? Yesterday you went to Sandy's garage and picked up my BMW, for which I have been waiting six months."

"Is that so? Well, we did go to Sandy's garage and we did take a BMW which was assigned to us. All the paperwork was in order."

"That was my car and I intend having it. Is that fucking crystal clear to both of you?" the Super said, looking at Karetzi who was still sitting and observing the situation with a wry smile creased across his face. "And you," he said pointing at Karetzi. "You stand up when a superior officer enters a room."

"Superior in rank, but not in brains or manners," countered Karetzi.

"What the fuck did you say?" The Super was now shouting.

"It's what I'm about to say that you should worry about Sir."

"Oh, now we are trying to threaten a superior officer are we, you bloody foreigner? I'll have you both busted down to bloody traffic before the day's out. You can count on it, can't they Williams?"

"I was about to advise you Chief that …" Sergeant Williams suddenly spoke, her words barely audible. "I need to use the toilet."

"Upstairs, first door on the left," Karetzi said. She exited. She wanted to be sick and she was, but at least she had escaped.

"As I was about to say Super, this whole conversation is being taped. You're on Amber's camera. Don't switch it off Chief Superintendent. Leave it." And with that Karetzi switched off the tape.

Evan, Amber and the Super were dumbfounded. What was going on? "You shouldn't have switched off the tape you fat, stupid lump of lard! No one will know how you slipped and damaged yourself."

"Are you fucking crazy man?"

"Yes, Chief, I am. Everyone in the Force knows that. As do a lot of other unfortunates. You will first apologise to Miss Gilberts, our lab technician and friend and colleague. You will do it now while you still have all your teeth and your nose is in one piece.

"If Miss Gilberts accepts your apology, then you will apologise to my partner and if that's okay we will wait for your Sergeant's return and you can apologise to her.

"Me, I don't need any apologies. I just hope you don't. Then I will beat the crap out of you, superior or not." Mike poked the Chief Super twice in the chest and then knocked his braided cap off. The bully had become the bullied.

Amber spoke through her tears. "It's okay Mike. No damage done."

"I'm sure the Super's happy with that."

Head bowed in acute embarrassment and total defeat, the Super nodded, avoiding everyone's eyes. Sergeant Williams returned looking like a ghost.

The Super spoke. "I am very sorry about the events of today. I completely over-reacted. I was rude and I whole-heartedly and unreservedly apologise to everyone in this room, especially the ladies."

"Now see, Super, not so difficult to be civil. Amber, please order the Super a taxi. Sergeant Williams can drive their car back later after we have a little chat."

The Super left in his taxi. Amber put on a fresh pot of coffee and produced an ashtray from somewhere. "This is now a smoking office," she proclaimed.

Mike lit up a non-filter, Evan his pipe and Sergeant Jane Williams a menthol cigarette. No one spoke until they had finished smoking. Evan stood and shook hands with Mike, then, completely out of character, hugged him. The bond between them was complete. Amber kissed Mike on both cheeks, tears raining down from her eyes onto Mike's shirt.

Sergeant Jane thanked Mike. Even though she hadn't been present she could see the reactions of the other two. "May I have a piece of paper and a pencil or pen?" she asked Evan. Evan handed her his biro and a piece of paper. She started writing.

44

THIS WHOLE ROOM IS BEING TAPPED. ALL CONVERSATIONS ARE BEING RECORDED. "Let's get some fresh air," Amber said, pointing to the yard at the back. They all trooped out into the cold.

"How do you know Sergeant?"

"I can tell. My husband does a lot of this type of work; surveillance work, wire-tapping, camera work, etc., for the police as outside contractor. I've picked up a lot from John, that's my husband.

"Somewhere within a range of, say eighty or so yards you will find a van, a decorator's, butcher's, something nondescript. If I'm right it's very near and it will relay the information back to somewhere else for analysis."

Evan looked at the Sergeant. She was blonde, petite and plain, and married; she would be okay. Not Mike's type, he guessed. Evan made an executive decision. "Jane, may I call you that?"

"Sure," answered Jane.

"Well Jane, we are shorthanded here and we have a massive case to pursue. It would involve both myself and Mike with a lot of travelling, leaving Amber all alone. Anyway, do you want to join us?"

"I'd love to, if you could swing it."

"I'm sure we can. I'll ring C.C. Clarke. Mike will ring his friend Mrs Emma Andrews and Amber will arrange for a few more chairs. Go home, don't worry about Fowler and ring this number, in two, no make it three hours."

When Sergeant Jane left, Evan said to the other two, "I hope I haven't jumped the gun here. If you are not happy with Jane we can always say that we couldn't get the transfer."

"No, I think it's a great idea," said Mike.

"So do I," Amber said.

Do you think we can get her husband to do a little overtime on the quiet?"

"For what?" asked Evan.

"To bloody well sweep this house for bugs as a start," Mike said. "We can't sit out here in the bloody cold every time we want to talk."

Phone calls were duly made. Wheels set in motion.

"Fancy a walk around the block Evan?"

"Yep, let's see if we can find ourselves a suspicious van."

"And if we do?" Evan said.

"I'll puncture a few tyres, remove a light bulb or two from the car lights and we'll call in the local cop shop to remove an abandoned vehicle," answered Mike.

Evan had to admit to himself that it wasn't exactly legal but tapping wasn't either. Mike walked a fine line when it came to legalities and it looked like he was just behind him. After nearly two hours of looking, two hundred yards radius of the house they came up with nothing. "It could be Jane is wrong Mike. Who the hell would want to bug us? Who knows we exist except for, except for Brian, who for unknown reasons has already taped our conversations once?"

"Do you know Evan, that is the point. Why is he tapping into our case? Again, what motive does he have? Is there a hidden agenda? Are we being used, set up, but whom, why, what's going on?"

"Well," Amber, "maybe Jane got carried away and wanted to look smart."

"I don't think so, Mike, but give me ten minutes and then I think we will have some useful info which might be of help."

Evan started opening the phones. Mike looked under the desks, under the carpet, everywhere. Either there were no bugs or maybe the detectives were not good enough to find them.

"I'm ravenous," Amber stated. "It's already gone eleven." Evan was too. He'd only had a boiled egg and a piece of toast for breakfast. Mike had nothing but a black coffee but wasn't particularly hungry. He could easily last out until dinner.

Amber's breakfast was slightly different to Evan's and Mike's. Two fried eggs, two sausages, black pudding, four rashers of bacon, beans, tomatoes and two pieces of toast. Three cups of strong tea and a large orange juice had just about kept her going but she didn't want to fade away. Food was her vice. It gave her energy. How else would she do such a demanding job?

Within fifteen minutes Amber had made four different types of sandwiches all in lovely soft barm cakes. A total of eight. Evan ate two, Mike one and the remaining five Amber disposed of. A big pan of curry was bubbling away on the stove. Amber's dinner or maybe just a snack until dinner, Mike thought.

On finishing, they moved downstairs. Amber printed off something from one of the computers and handed it to Evan who was smoking his clay pipe. "How does this help Amber?" he asked, passing the list of names and addresses over to Mike.

"So we know who lives in this street. Mr and Mrs Richards and two small children, the Patterson's with three kids, Mr Smith and Miss Lavers and so on and on." Mike stopped reading and looked up to Amber.

"A fine bunch of detectives I've been lumbered with. Do some detection boys. Work out what that list is telling you." They looked again. Just names and addresses, nothing sinister.

"I give up Amber," said Evan.

"Me too," said Mike.

"Come outside and I'll explain," said Amber. Once outside she said, "All the houses in this street are occupied except next door."

"So?" asked Evan.

"Why is smoke coming out of the ventilator? The heating must be on. Somebody is in there. Someone who doesn't open the curtains, put out a bin – today is bin collection day. We've got someone who wants to keep a low profile. Either some squatters or an undercover surveillance team. That's possibly why we couldn't find a van", concluded Amber.

"You put us to shame, Amber. I guess it's time the gasman knocked on next door for a meter reading," said Mike. "Although

I doubt if anyone will answer. Squatters won't, nor will undercover boys, but I'll give it a try." Mike left and within five minutes returned. "As I thought," he said. "No answer but something has to be done about the yobs mucking around in the park opposite. They're likely to break someone's windows."

"What yobs?" asked Evan.

"The ones who ran away after the accident to next door's front window."

"Jesus Christ," Mike said. "No, Evan, just yobs."

"Don't they have double glazing like us?" asked Amber.

"No Amber, they don't need it. It's unoccupied, probably up for sale."

"Look Mike, this isn't right. I can't be party to it."

"That's fine Evan, let's get the desks and put them out here where we can freeze to death whilst our friends in there are breaking nearly every privacy law existing. Oh, and while we're out here freezing, I wonder if the Chessman will take pity on us and refrain from killing anyone until the summer."

"Which window Mike?" asked Amber.

"One above the door to the left as you look at it from across the road."

"Damn it Mike. I've got a good arm; without you we would have been in big trouble this morning," said Evan, moving towards the front door.

Mike followed, as did Amber. As they stepped out onto the pavement, the phone began to ring. Amber re-entered to take the call. Evan found a piece of stone, balanced it in his hand, took aim and threw. True to his word he did have a good arm. The window shattered.

A head popped out from behind the curtain, then a second, her cheek bleeding. "Yobs down there!" shouted Mike. "Call the police before they get away. I'll get you a doctor. You look bad."

"It's okay," answered the man. "Thanks, but we'll deal with it."

"Too well dressed for squatters," Evan said as they walked back to their own house. Amber greeted them with the good news that Jane Williams would be joining them on Monday. When the phone rang again it was Sergeant Jane. "Get her phone number Amber and tell her we will ring her back in five minutes but give her the good news first," Evan said.

"All out," Mike said and out they went. It had now started raining. "What you thinking Evan?"

"I'm thinking Mike that phones will be bugged."

"But we didn't find anything, Evan."

"Aye, but we're hardly experts, are we? Anyway, the way I see it is the phones are not clean. I'm going up the road to where the café is. I'll ring Jane from the phone box outside there. I'll ask her to get her husband down here pronto with all his gear. Then I'll go into town and purchase two new phones, pay as you go mobiles and put them on my new credit card."

"Evan, you're picking up too many bad tricks from your partner," Amber said laughing in that delightful way she had. "I bet you they even know what I eat," said Amber.

"I don't think they are that good Amber," said Mike.
"I'm hungry. I get hungry if I talk about food. Can I get anyone anything?"

Both detectives declined. Amber went upstairs to get something to eat. Evan went to phone. Mike stayed down in the office. He closed his eyes and tried to concentrate.

CHAPTER 5

Josh Armfield picked up the phone and dialled. "Hello, this is Josh. Can I speak?"

"Of course you can. Is it an emergency?"

"I guess so, Mr Brian. We've been rumbled."

"How Josh? Are you sure?" Josh told him. "Pack everything up and leave. Make sure that they see you and Debra leaving."

Mr Brian closed the phone and immediately dialled out again. "We need a meeting asap. When is convenient?"

"Six, Room 13," replied his superior, the Director of National Security.

Mike opened his eyes. Fifteen minutes had passed. Amber had polished off nearly a packet of crisp breads, topped with butter and cream. She left a couple. She wasn't greedy, but on the other hand you just can't leave two, can you? She just ate them plain—no butter, no cream.

"Let's go outside Amber. No, not the back. Onto the pavement." Once outside Mike pointed to a blue Cortina. "Has that car moved, Amber, since you've been here? All the others have. I'm sure I saw that car there yesterday morning Amber."

"No, that car hasn't moved to my recollection. All the others have at one time or another," Amber replied.

"Good", said Mike. "Why don't you go back inside and put on a fresh pot of coffee. I've got work to do out here."

"You think it's the spook's car from next door, don't you Mike?"

"Ninety per cent, Amber. We will get in some pretty hot water if it's the missing ten per cent. Best you go in now, Amber."

Mike walked the fifty or so yards to the car which was parked on the side of the communal gardens. He leant on some rails which bordered the gardens. He lit up, four today, not good and then he noticed the camera hanging from the tree. My God, they're filming us too. Within a few minutes he found another, hidden in another tree directly opposite the house.

He took a walk through the gardens. Nothing unusual apart from the unlocked garden shed. He opened the door and stepped in. It reeked of cigarettes. He could smell stale coffee. There were breadcrumbs on the floor. Someone, probably two, had recently been in here and stayed a while. In one of the empty flower pots he found about fifty cigarette butts. He emptied them onto a shelf; three different brands.

He returned to the Cortina. The cameras were focused on the house. He knelt and took out his knife and punctured both tyres on the passenger side. They would have a spare but not two. He smiled. He was the king of tyre slashers. Numero Uno.

"Someone won't be travelling anywhere in a hurry, Amber. I just hope it's our next door neighbour's and not some poor old salesman who needs his car to work. Keep an eye out, Amber. I'm guessing they'll be pulled out for the time being and other arrangements made. They will have reported back to base and told whoever that they had been compromised."

"You phoned, Evan?"

"Yeah, Mike. Jane will speak to her husband John and he will just turn up as soon as he closes his shop. He sells various electronic ware. I see you got us new phones Evan."

"I did, Mike. But they're useless. I was followed Mike. I clocked him from the phone box first. They will know I phoned Jane but obviously they can't know what we talked about. They wouldn't have had time to tap her phone."

"But why are the new phones useless?" Amber asked.

"Because my follower went into the shop after I left and they would have got our new numbers. I tell you Mike, this is a big operation. I am at a loss to understand what is going on. Why are they interested in us? What's going on? Who are they? What do they want?"

"What do we have that is of any use to them? Again, who is 'them'? Can you enlighten us in any way Amber?"

"No I can't but I suggest as follows: Mike goes down to one of those nasty, dicey pubs. I'm sure there's a few in Cardiff, and sells the phones to two different people for a fiver and when I go shopping I will buy another two mobiles from one of those supermarkets."

They all heard the front door of the neighbours' house slam, not once, not twice, but three times. "They want us to know they're leaving Mike. They're not going far Evan, not in their car anyway. If that blue Cortina is theirs. It had a slight accident."

"Another tyre problem, Mike?"

"No, Evan, two tyres."

All three of them stepped out. Two men and a woman were crossing the street, each loaded with two suitcases. They headed towards the Cortina. They opened the boot and squeezed two cases in. They opened the rear door and put the remaining cases on the back seat. One of the three was obviously not riding in the car.

Before crossing Mike heaved a big sigh of relief. He'd called it right.

"How's your cheek love," Evan asked. She didn't answer.

"Oh, by the way, do you need any help with the tyre?" Mike asked, pointing. "It looks like you got a flat."

"Shit, get the spare out George." The man called George opened up the boot and took out the two cases and then the spare tyre and tools.

"These cars only carry one spare, George?" asked Mike. No answer.

"You lot aren't the talkative types are you?" said Evan.

"I think they're the listening type Evan," said Mike.

Three of them laughed. Three didn't.

It took George nearly ten minutes to change the flat. He reloaded the boot. "Thanks George."

"No problem Josh."

"But you are wrong there Josh. There is a problem. See, you have another flat. You unlucky sods; two flats in one day."

"You fucking bastards. You did this, didn't you?"

"My, my, Josh you are fast, but please could you cut down on the swearing. There's a lady present and it's not you," said Mike, looking at Debra.

"When you get your car fixed, make sure you come back with a ladder, otherwise you won't be able to reach those cameras up there in the trees. Oh, I nearly forgot, clean up the crap in the garden shed. I think it will be appreciated by the gardener."

In room 13, the Director, Professor Benson, Mr Brian and Jock Whittaker, technology expert and Chief Advisor to the Director on those matters, waited for the coffee to be served before anyone said a word. When she had finished, the secretary left closing the heavy door behind her.

"Are you telling me, Brian, that we spent over a hundred grand on the most up-to-date bloody surveillance stuff, rented cars, houses, paid overtime as if we were the CIA, and we get fucked by two country Welsh yokels who you said, in your words, were 'past it and crazy'."

"Mr Director, I said that. That was why we picked them, after viewing their files. However, at the initial meeting with the two detectives, I realised that they were quite smart and observant. This I reported to you on my return."

"You did Brian, you did, but it seems that they are getting smarter by the day. If this keeps up they will be sitting here instead of us." No one laughed. The Director turned to Jock. "I thought you said the taps were undetectable, the best."

"I sent two Grade A men, Mr Director, they don't come any

better. I can't understand it. They must have just struck lucky."

"Run me through what's happened from this morning until now Brian."

Brian reported everything from the time each entered the house. The conversation prior to the Fowler incident. The following of Evan. Everything. "So they stopped talking inside. Just after this Superintendent left?"

"So it seems Mr Director."

"Okay, this Gilberts woman. She's their expert. Correct?"

"Yes sir. Computers, photography, lab work, but not surveillance."

"Anything else about her that's relevant?"

"No, Sir, except that she likes cooking and eating."

"I said relevant, Brian."

"Sorry Sir."

The phone in the middle of the conference table in Room 13 rang. The Director picked it up and handed it to Brian without saying a word. Brian listened for a few minutes and then cradled the receiver. "More problems Brian?"

"Yes, Mr Director."

"Let's have them Brian," and Brian did.

"This is unbelievable," Jock muttered. "I've never seen anything like this since I began in the department. These are two very smart cookies."

The Director took a sip of his coffee. "Do me a favour Jock."

"Yes Sir."

"Check under the table, will you?"

"For what Sir?"

"For bugs Jock. It wouldn't surprise me to find that our two intrepid detectives are now bugging us." The Director laughed. After a few seconds so did the others.

"Where do we go from here?" asked Jock. "We still have got the bugs in place unless they rip the place apart; they won't locate them. That I guarantee. Maybe the phone bugs but not the others and don't forget we have their new mobile phone numbers. We're not out of it yet."

"Of course we're out of it, Jock. I think DI Jones tagged our man, following him. Those phones will get dumped. Worse still, sold cheaply to have us in a real muddle. I'll bet you Jock that within a day they find someone to do a sweep and locate your little roués. They know three of our operatives, maybe more. They know me and will have worked out that I'm involved and all this has happened in less than a day."

"Our little lambs have turned into Lions. I have a sneaking regard for these yokels, Mr Director."

For the first time the Professor spoke. "I can see that these detectives are on the ball, but let's face it they talk about anagrams, diagrams, mileage, weather; all pointless. Whereas we know who is behind all these crimes and we know the motive. I say, let's just tell them what we know and that we're using them as bait and get on with it. I'm seventy, this is my last big case before I retire. Just tell them, I think they'll be relieved to know what's going on." The Director nodded. Jock was happy, he could still use his equipment and no-one need ever know that he had failed. "You don't seem happy Brian. Do you disagree with what our esteemed Head of Finances and Business department is saying?"

"I'm afraid so Mr Director."

"Pray, please tell us why, Brian. I am interested to hear your theories."

"I've no theories but find it unbelievable that one of the hundred biggest corporations in the world, namely Nakamura Heavy Industries, would hire a hit man to go round killing people in Wales in order for NHI to monopolise the air and sea instrument business. It does not make sense to me."

"It doesn't stand up, Mr Director, not even one per cent, but John has always come up trumps when big business and finances have been involved."

"My team have a mountain of documentation, accounts, press clippings, inside financial information. We know Nakamura's businesses and finances better than they do. Everything points to an aggressive manoeuvre in the industry of instruments and if the Japs get it right they could make billions."

"Professor, take Doctor Elwin and go with Brian down to Cardiff. Talk to these detectives, put them in the picture. Although I am far from convinced that NHI has anything whatsoever to do with the Chessman but we have blown our cover. Look, how do I account for it?"

CHAPTER 6

"Shall we get on with it?" Amber said. "It's nearly four and we've not got off first base." The phone rang. Amber picked it up. "Fine, ten o'clock, Monday morning. That was Mr Brian's secretary. He's scheduled a meeting here for Monday. He will be coming down with a Professor John Benson and a Doctor Terry Elwin."

"The plot thickens. Now we will be bored into submission by a Doctor and a Professor," said Evan.

"Submission of what?" asked Mike.

"Submission of something or other. They're hardly coming down to try out Amber's cooking are they?" replied Evan.

"I don't know. They could do worse." Amber liked that. Just as they were about to start, the doorbell rang. Amber answered it. "It's John Williams. You are expecting me." Amber buzzed him through. If he had a bit more hair and a dress on he would be his wife Jane's double.

"Pleased to meet you all. I'd like to thank you for what you did to that arse Fowler this morning and again for getting my wife this job. If I can ever do anything for you guys just call. It's free. On the house."

Having said his piece John unzipped his big blue holdall, took out his gear and began working. He systematically swept the whole house from top to bottom. He even opened the windows and checked outside, the radiators, the clock. He lifted the carpets, checked the kitchen drawers, utensils. It took him until six before he replaced his gear. Eight in all: three in here, one in the hall, one

57

on the landing, two in the lounge and one in the kitchen. "They are the most sophisticated bugs I have ever seen. May I keep them? I want to dissect them and find out all about them. It's my business."

"Go ahead John. Are you sure you got them all?"

"One hundred and one per cent." He said his goodbyes and left.

"Another day has flown by," Amber said. "It's gone six and I'm hungry. We will reconvene in the morning. Eight, which will be our usual time. By that I mean mine and Evan's usual time, Mike. I suggest you put your watch back ten minutes Mike. That way you'll be on time."

"I already have Amber. That's why I'm only ten minutes late."

"You are incorrigible Mike." They all laughed.

Outside Evan got into the Beamer, then opened the door and shouted to Mike, "Remember Mike, 8 p.m., number 7. Don't forget." Mike raised his hand in acknowledgement as he kept on walking towards his apartment.

After a few minutes he came across a small flower shop. It had closed but he could see two women inside tidying up. He rapped on the glass window. Both women turned. He gestured, making a 'please open' sign by pretending that he had a key in his hand and was flicking his wrist left and right.

"Let's see what he wants Mum. He looks rather dishy."

"Too old for you, darling. He could be your dad," replied the mother.

"Bet you wish he was Mum." For that she received a playful clip across the back of the head. They opened the door.

"Can we help you sir?" asked the mother.

"I hope so, I know you're shut but I desperately need flowers, a nice bouquet."

"What type?" asked the younger. "Red roses? No, you tell me."

"It's for an older lady."

"My age?" asked the mother.

"Oh, no, this lady is probably about fifty, twenty years older than you Mam."

"Mum's forty. I'm twenty-one."

"That's incredible. It's true then that flowers keep you looking young," Mike replied, not having a clue what he was talking about. Neither did Mum but who cared. She only looked about thirty according to this lovely hunk in front of her. The daughter wasn't impressed. Not at all, but he was fanciable; very much so.

Five minutes later and Mike walked out with forty quid's worth of mixed flowers. The Champagne he had yet to find but there was a decent off-licence just down the road. He hit it for a bottle of the best one in store; another thirty-five pounds. Thank God for the new corporate credit card. Next door he bought a new pack of smokes and a Chronicle.

After he had shaved, showered and dressed, he sat down and starting with the back page he read his paper. He stopped reading as soon as he read that City were talking about giving up their two best players. With City it only meant one thing: they would be sold in the next transfer window. What the hell did they do with all this money from transfers? Over twenty million in transfers over the last few years and still over £20 million in debt. He threw the paper down in disgust. He rang his mother. She was fine. He liked to ring her at least twice a week and he visited as much as he could.

The trip to Taffs Well was uneventful. Joining the A470 he crossed over the M4 junction 32. He bore to the left, joining the A4054. Just before the railway station and half a mile later he reached his destination: a large five-year-old block of flats overlooking the River Taff.

He found a parking space in the visitors' section. It suddenly occurred to him that he had no card to go with the beautiful flowers he had bought. Grabbing the flowers from the passenger seat he opened his car door and proceeded to what looked like the main entrance to the block of flats. For a change he was five minutes early he thought, stopping to check the time on his watch.

There he stood rooted as if his shoes were glued to the tarmac.

A beautiful statuesque strawberry blonde had just come out of the building and stood under the lights above the doorway rummaging through a large leather bag. The door remained open.

Mike was guilty, very guilty of optical indulgence. He couldn't get enough. At last his brain connected with his legs and like a zombie, started walking, drawn to this vision of beauty. He stopped two feet from her. She had amazing cornflower blue eyes and Mike was mesmerised.

He handed her the flowers he held in his hand. "These are for you." Strawberry was taken aback, lost for words but she clutched the flowers with both hands staring wide-eyed into Mike's dark eyes. A tingling sensation ran all the way up her back. Her eyes were fixed on Mike's.

"Thank you but I cannot."

"Of course you can. These flowers are addressed to you. See, on the greeting card. It says: 'To the most beautiful girl in Wales'." Before she could speak, he took two steps and pushing the partly ajar door fully open, he entered and in a daze walked to the four elevators he saw in front of him. For the first time in nearly twenty years, he started whistling the tune 'The most beautiful girl in the world'. Charlie Rich, he thought as he whistled waiting for the elevator.

Trance-like, he walked into the chrome and mirrored cabin and pressed the second-floor button. He started ascending. It was the elevator door opening that jolted him. He stopped whistling. He didn't get out but pressed the ground floor button. He looked into the mirror and mouthed, meet Mr Stupid. There was nobody to contradict him. On the ground floor, he waited impatiently for the door to open. Once open he rushed through the lobby to the front door and out into the car park in front of the building. The door slammed shut behind him.

He was too late. He had no name, no phone number, no car type, no number plate. What a klutz he was, but hope was eternal. He was after all a detective and he would have to start detecting.

He was smitten for the first time since his first love at the tender age of twelve.

Mary – hadn't given her a thought. He wondered what she looked like now. Probably fat; married with kids.

He stood cursing himself for being so slow. The girl, woman in every sense of the word. was like a dream, an angel. He had to find her. He didn't care if she was married, had children, the mother from hell, nothing would deter him. He had to find her. His mind raced. She either lived there in the apartment; no, he'd discounted that. People who looked like her didn't live here. Eighteen apartments. That left seventeen after excluding Evan. He'd made a start, a very small one.

He walked back towards the entrance, then turned after remembering the Champers in the car. No flowers. They had gone to a good cause. A beautiful strawberry blonde. Anyway Evan and Edna would prefer a nice bottle of Champagne. Of course they would have liked both but then beggars can't be choosers. He looked at his watch. He was only fifteen minutes late, not so bad. Actually he was twenty-five minutes late. He'd forgotten that he had put his watch back ten minutes.

She pulled over about half a mile down the road. Her legs were trembling, her hands shaking and her heart beating. She had never felt like this, ever.

She took the flowers from next to her and smelt them. The fragrance would always remind her of him. A tall, dark stranger, lean, handsome in a dangerous way; brilliant eyes. She would love to run her fingers through his curly jet black hair. She looked for the card, didn't expect to find one and wasn't disappointed.

Since her divorce two years ago she had not looked at a man. Three years with Taylor, her ex, had put her off men. For the first year of her marriage things were fine, then when he broke his leg and couldn't play rugby any more he had become morose, started drinking too much; used his fists too freely and too often on her.

She stopped caring. Actually, the whole marriage had been a mistake. She realised it now. She didn't, not until half an hour ago, ever want another close relationship.

From friends she'd heard that Taylor had stopped drinking, had got a good job as a fitness trainer in one of the top health centres in Cardiff. At six foot four he was an imposing figure and when he was sober he could talk the talk. He had tried to contact her on many occasions. She had changed her address, phone, everything.

She started her car, a red Mini convertible. She loved the car but at five foot ten in her stocking feet, she sometimes felt a little crammed in the car but tonight, it seemed different; the car seemed bigger, better, faster, and she sped off into the night, her heart filled with excitement and joy. She must find the stranger. 'The flower man.' That's what she would call him.

When DI Jones got home, the first thing he did was to remove the picture of Jasmine from the lounge. He replaced it with a green painting of a heavily wooded forest which not only matched the carpet but luckily was on top of the pile under the spare bed. Fortunately, the new picture was larger and no one would be able to tell that it had replaced his daughter's portrait.

He lied to Edna. This he did very rarely but it was for the best. His guest was, from the little he had seen and heard, a serial womaniser. Jasmine had been hurt more than enough in the past and it was best that Mike never met her. He was a dangerous person. Even Evan had started breaking the law, after less than two days with his new partner.

He told Edna that the string had snapped. The string that held the portrait up and that he would repair it tomorrow. Edna was mystified. It was fine until her husband had got home. But she let it pass. Evan had his reasons for whatever he did and he would explain when he was ready.

Evan changed and relaxed until at seven-thirty his daughter appeared. She had come round to drop off her dad's tobacco which she had bought that very day. A little surprise for him.

She stayed half an hour. Evan was shitting himself. First, he had to explain why her portrait had been replaced. The broken string crap. Then he had to somehow manoeuvre his daughter out before eight. Edna kept on asking her to stay for dinner and meet her father's new partner.

She declined. She hated police talk and avoided meeting any of her dad's colleagues who as a whole talked rubbish and bored her. Anyway she was catching a film with a girlfriend who she had already let down twice.

Jasmine left at five past eight. A relieved DI Jones thanked God for that and thanked Mike for always being reliably late. Edna wondered what was going on. She asked Evan if he was all right. She was worried about him. He was acting very strange, very unlike the predictable husband she knew and loved.

"I hope your new partner hasn't lost his way?" asked Edna. "He's nearly half an hour late. I mean I suppose as a foreigner, the language difficulties and other things, I mean they drive on the other side of the road don't they?"

"Look Edna, he'll turn up and for the tenth time, he was born in Cardiff and grew up there. His English is good, as good as anyone's. He's just your regular guy." Another bloody lie, thought Evan. Mike was anything but regular. At that moment the buzzer went. Evan answered. It was Mike. Evan let him in and waited with the door open for his arrival.

"Sorry I'm late, Evan. Had a few problems to sort out."

"No problem Mike. Come in and meet my good wife Edna."

"Pleased to make your acquaintance."

"It is Mike, is that right?" Mike nodded. "I'm Edna. You are most welcome. Thank you for the Champagne."

"Make yourself comfortable. Would you like a drink? A Vodka perhaps?" asked Edna.

"I think Mike would like a Whisky love. Isn't that so Mike? I have a good Laphroaig."

"Ah, one of my favourites. I love that heavy peaty taste."

"Do you know Evan, that it's Prince Charles' favourite Malt and that during prohibition in the USA, doctors were allowed to prescribe it for its Islay medicinal character."

"My God, Mike, you know your stuff but tell me how exactly do you pronounce it?"

"Easy Evan, LA-FROY-HA."

There were two sofas: both two-seaters. They were covered with blue velvet as was the easy chair. Mike sat down on one of the sofas. Evan, after preparing Mike's whisky and his ale, sat opposite on the other sofa. He placed the neat Whisky and his ale on dainty coasters on a dark mahogany coffee table which separated the sofas. There were two ashtrays on the coffee table. Both men lit up.

"Are you sure you don't want any water or soda with that Mike?"

"No thanks Evan, a Malt should always be drunk neat. Blended, well then I add some water."

Mike took a good mouthful. He felt the liquid warming his insides. He relaxed and thought of the blonde. She must have thought I was mad, handing her flowers. A perfect stranger. His body tensed and he knew that no amount of favourite malt would cover his pure unadulterated stupidity in not even asking her for her name. Could he redeem the situation? He had to try and he'd start right now.

Edna had been busying herself in the kitchen preparing her meal. Welsh lamb with Rosemary and garlic, roast potatoes, green French beans with fresh mint sauce, bread and butter putting with custard. She let the men talk and get work talk out of the way. Evan was right, this man Mike looked foreign. A very handsome kind of foreign but acted as one of them. He was much younger than Evan, probably had different ideas and hobbies but she could see that they seemed comfortable in each other's presence.

The detective starting detecting. The hunt was on for the strawberry blonde. "Lovely place you have here Evan. Been here long?"

"Since they were built Mike, nearly five years ago."

"Good neighbours, Evan? I suppose you know everyone after five years? It must be like a small insular community."

"Not really Mike, our immediate neighbours we know well and a few others by sight. These days people keep themselves to themselves."

"Mostly people of your age group I suppose?"

"Yes, definitely older couples. I think that there are very few children in the block."

Edna came in with what looked like a gin and tonic and sat down next to her husband. "About fifteen minutes, is that okay?"

"That's fine darling," replied Evan.

For the first time since he had walked in, Mike was able to get a good look at Edna. Taller than Evan, same age but looked younger, good figure, very pleasant face, dyed auburn hair cut short, must have been a looker once, still attractive. Evan had done well for himself. It was obvious to Mike that they were still in love.

"Another whisky?"

"No thank you Edna. I'll wait till we eat."

"What about you Evan?"

"I'm fine too darling."

Over dinner which was delicious, as was the wine, a perfectly chilled, delicate Chablis, they made small talk about work mainly. Edna laughed when her husband recounted the Fowler incident and was nearly in hysterics when Mike told her about Evan's stone throwing.

Evan was surprised that Edna found all the law-breaking so amusing. She was very law-abiding, held Christian values very highly, yet here she was encouraging wilful acts of damage and God knows what. "Sometimes dear husband, the end justifies the means. Think about it. Will you use just normal methods to catch this killer with the chess pieces, or whatever he does? I bet you, he's thrown away the decent way to kill rule book, Evan. I have a feeling, a good feeling Evan, that your attitude will change as time goes on. I like you Mike and I think that you and my husband, although obviously very different, will get on like a house on fire."

"My God Edna, you're not expecting me to be an arsonist too!"

"No Evan, but you know exactly what I'm saying. After all, after thirty-three years of blissful marriage, I have never interfered or asked questions about your work and now all I'm saying is, you've three, possibly four years left. Make your mark. Start by catching this killer. Get him in any way you can and, if it means bending the rules: then dear, break them."

Evan was speechless. What a woman. What a wife. She knew that he could get into big trouble but was backing him to the hilt. His partner had, in the space of one hour or so, altered his wife's attitude to life; their life.

The question was, could he change? Did he want to change? He'd been happy plodding along doing things slowly in a correct way and getting good results. A tortoise was in the long run better than a hare. He looked over at Mike. Was he a harmless hare or a bloody tiger masquerading as a hare? The latter was probably true. His partner seemed a good man and a good cop but he was dangerous, extremely so.

CHAPTER 7

Mike had to say something. He wasn't so sure what. "Edna, the meal was fantastic, thank you. I would like to say that I will not allow your husband to do anything stupid, any really daft things. I will do, I'm known for that. It's probably in my Russian blood."

"Rubbish Mike, you might be a little crazy but you're not daft and whatever goes on, good or bad we'll be in it together. I think I already owe you that. Edna is right. I may not like it, but it if we're to catch our madman, we're going to have to bend some rules. All I hope is that if we end up in jail, we're there after we have apprehended the ratfink."

"The ratfink, Evan? I'm not familiar with this term."

"Well Mike, I don't think you will find it in a dictionary. It means a nasty, undesirable type of person."

"I see," said Mike. "This is exceptionally fine china Edna. Is it Japanese?"

"Yes, Mike, and it's very old, handed down from my grandmother." Mike had scored another point with Edna.

"Coffee Mike?"

"Black please, Edna."

The men sat back on the sofas, the same positions as before dinner. Both lit up their respective poisons whilst waiting for the coffee. This, together with brandy, which Evan had purchased on the way home, was set on the table.

"Can I help you clear up?" asked Mike.

"Thanks but I'll do it later Mike. Right now I want to know all about my husband's mysterious partner. How come you were born here in Wales? How did your father come to be here?" Edna was interested. It wasn't every day you met a Russian or a Welsh Russian.

"It's a long story. I don't want to bore you Edna and I don't want to overstay my welcome. It's been a great evening and I don't want to ruin it."

"You won't Mike," Evan said. "To be entirely honest I'm interested too, please tell."

"Okay, but I have warned you," Mike replied. "Where do I start?"

"At your father's birthplace would be a good point," Evan said.

"Right, my father Demetri Karetzi was born in Archangel, a large port in the White Sea, Northern Russia. A very, very cold place from what I know. The year was 1926. He was an only child to a schoolteacher and farmhand. At nineteen my father was robbed of his parents, my grandparents, when a freak railway accident proved fatal to both.

"My father was training as a marine engineer and by 1964 had reached the rank of Second Engineer in the Russian Merchant Navy. In that capacity, he had joined a ship carrying pit props to Cardiff. Outside Cardiff, the vessel's main engine malfunctioned. Luckily tugs were already alongside and with their help the ship made it to the discharging berth. The ship was scheduled to stay about ten, twelve days. The problem was that the big diesel engine was of Russian construction and didn't carry the correct spares and of course they could not buy the replacement parts in the UK. They had no choice but to make the necessary repairs on the berth.

"They arranged with a local dry dock company to make the parts in their workshop about a mile away. The plans and diagrams were of course in Russian and the dry-dock needed someone to translate and oversee the work. Apart from the Captain, my father was the only person who spoke reasonable English. He'd been taught by his mother who taught English at the local college. As he also

knew the engineering side it was logical that he would be the one
to help the dry-dock manufacture the parts.

"Together with the ship's Commissar, these people were officials
of the Soviet Communist Party, placed on ships and responsible for
the political education and wellbeing of the crews. In effect spies
who were feared and hated by all. Anyway, together they would
go ashore, one to do the work, my father, the other to make sure
he didn't pick up any bad western habits or try to abscond. The
Commissar spoke no English but that was irrelevant – he was
completely in charge.

"They were picked up daily at eight a.m. by the dry-dock and
returned a few minutes past six p.m. Lunch, provided by the
shipyard, was between one and one forty, tea breaks at ten and four,
each for twenty minutes.

"The shipyard employed over one hundred people. There were
two or three in the area at the time. I think none are still going.
Times and of course ships have changed radically as has Cardiff
which is no longer a port as such.

"Returning to the story, my father and the Commissar ate daily
at the yard's small canteen which was run by a lady and her
daughter. They did the cooking, the serving over the counter and
the cleaning. They were subcontracted by the Yard. The
Commissar drank beer every lunch but would only allow my father
water from the tap. When my father needed the toilet, the
'Politico' would accompany him and stand outside the toilet. He
would check the food, any drawings or such made by Father for the
yard, even though he was clueless in these matters. Suffice it to
be, the Commissar was scared by his own shadow. They were dark
days in Russian history. Everyone was scared of everyone. There
was no trust. It's difficult to understand now, but that's the way it
was then.

"The Commissar would smoke English filter cigarettes offered
from time to time by shipyard staff but my father wasn't allowed to

accept these simple acts of friendship. He had to smoke horrible Russian-made cigarettes that had hollow cardboard tubes instead of filters.

"All the staff liked and respected my father and detested the Commissar. On, I think, the seventh working day, Sunday overtime was out as the Russians didn't believe in it. Two days before the ship's departure and on the eve of the completion of the manufacture of the parts, my father was made aware by the chief fabricator in the yard, a Mr Elwyn Williams, that he was to be ready for a big surprise the next day. To cut a long story short, my father prepared himself for all eventualities. At lunch as usual, my father drank water and the Commissar his free glass of beer.

"Within minutes of supping this beer, the Commissar fell fast asleep, his head resting on the table. Within half a minute the staff had redressed my father, in the shipyard's overalls, given him ten pounds in change and had someone drive him to a small B&B in Bute Street. The establishment was run by a Somali who until a year before had worked in the shipyard as a welder. In a small battered leather bag, with which they provided him, my father put in all his worldly possessions. These included five antique religious icons and this knife." Mike produced a thin, lock knife with a five-inch blade, and an ivory handle which for some reason had three drilled holes. He handed the knife to Evan.

"He had smuggled the icons out that day. He had intended making a break for it, little realising that he was going to get all the help he needed from his sympathisers and new friends at the yard. He was wearing this." Mike pointed at his watch which was still going strong, ugly but still going strong.

"That night he had a visitor. Two actually. The engineering foreman Elwyn Williams and his daughter Alice, one of the dinner ladies, and my father's future wife, my mother. The police half-heartedly looked for my father. The Russians didn't make a big noise about it. It was bad for morale. The Captain told the crew that my father had an accident and was hospitalised. On return to Russia the Commissar would probably have been tried, found guilty of something and at best jailed.

"Through the shipyard contacts my father worked throughout South Wales doing small engineering jobs and repairing boilers, both domestic and industrial. He made good money and was very happy. Everyone he came into contact with liked him and eventually he obtained residency documents.

"I was born in Cardiff; my father had sold two of the icons for very big money, bought a house in Grangetown and a small truck. I was named after my grandfather.

"One night, just before my twelfth birthday, my father was mugged by persons unknown. He died from his wounds, ten minutes after being mugged. Now it's just my mother and me. My grandfather, Mr Elwyn Williams, died a few years ago at a ripe old age. My grandmother had passed away before my father married and that, folks, is my story. I told you it was boring."

Edna had tears running down her face. Evan had opened Mike's knife and was examining it closely. Half an inch wide, it had been sharpened both sides above the clasp, about three inches down, a very lethal weapon in the wrong hands. Lethal in anybody's hands.

"That was a beautiful story, Mike," Edna said. "Would you like another brandy or something else to drink?"

"No, I've already had far too much. Could you call a taxi for me?" Edna did. Evan handed back Mike's knife which he returned to the slot intended for combs on the inside of his jacket. "Could you bring my car down tomorrow Evan?" Mike asked, passing him the keys.

When the taxi arrived Mike again thanked the Jones for their hospitality. They had enjoyed his company. They said their goodnights and Mike gave the taxi driver his address and was on his way back home. On entering his apartment he realised he'd forgotten to leave his cleaner money. Mrs Alibi was good. Every

Wednesday she'd clean, change the bed, launder and wash his clothes, tidy up the fridge. She was a diamond. He trusted her. She had her own key and the front door code. He would have to remember to pay her double next week.

CHAPTER 8

At eight prompt both the detectives had arrived in the office. Both had slept well. Amber was already at work and the coffee was bubbling away and for a change it was a nice bright morning. Thursday, second day on the case. It seemed like two weeks, not two days. "Let's get started. Let's do some detecting shall we boys?" They didn't get a chance to begin. The door buzzer went. "What now?" said Evan. "Probably the new chairs. They promised me that it would be their first call and the factory's only just outside Cardiff."

It wasn't the chairs. It was Jane, Sergeant Williams. "What you doing here Jane?" Evan asked.

"I've come to start work," Jane answered. "I'm not required anymore at the station so I came down to help. It's all in order. The Chief Super has agreed. I guess he didn't want me around."

"That's about the only thing that idiot has got right then," added Mike.

"I understand John did a good job down here yesterday."

"Top man, Jane," said Evan.

Mike rose from this chair. "Use this chair Jane. We're a bit short on our seating arrangements but we expect to rectify that soon. Have a coffee and relax. You're not a Sergeant here. You're Jane, part of the team. Would you like something to eat Jane? I've some nice biscuits and a sponge cake, oh and a few cream cakes." Jane declined.

"I could do with one of those cakes, Amber."

"In the fridge upstairs Evan."

As he left, Evan said, "How about you Mike?" Mike also declined but Amber asked Evan to bring her one.

Amber ate hers standing up, Evan sitting on the other chair, the one left. They finished their cakes and were about to begin. The buzzer again. This time it was the chairs. "Right, we have four chairs for four people and three desks.. Now that's sorted, let's see if we can sort out the Chessman. Shall I go through from the beginning what we know for Jane's sake?"

"Go ahead, Amber," said Jones. "I think what I will do is start with a summary of the first murder in Bala. On completion we will look at the photos, read the statements, police and witness ones, and anything else that we think is relevant to that particular murder.

"So, Bala, Gwynedd, Sunday 15th June, Father's Day. Time about 14.30 hours, victim 34 years old, white male, named John Harris.

"John and his girlfriend Judy were enjoying a stroll at Bala Lake, Llyn Tegid. Having walked about a mile Judy needed the toilet and leaving John sitting there on the bank, walked to the north of the lake where there are facilities. On returning about twenty minutes later, she found John floating head down in the lake. She called some other walkers for help and they dragged him out. He was dead. There was no sign of a struggle and there were no witnesses. The police, local boys, found a mark on the back of his head but the pathologist thought that the blow would only have stunned John, not killed him, so the killer must have dragged John in having stunned him and then held him under the water until he was dead. The police at Bala found a severed chess pawns' heads in the victim's trouser pocket. Remember it was the first and the chess pieces had no significance to anyone.

"The victim lived with his parents in Bala and worked as a cashier for a small seven/eleven outlet locally. He was well liked, financially sound. The local boys could not find a motive. His watch, money and credit card were all there. How did the murderer get away so fast? A bicycle or scooter? All outlets were checked for rentals, nothing came of their enquiries.

"On a lighter note, one stupid rag blames the murder on Teggy. That is Nessie, The Loch Ness Monster's equivalent in Bala.

"Here are the police statements, photos, etc. I can find nothing. Nothing stands out."

They all checked and looked carefully. Amber was right. Nothing.

"Abergele, Conwy, Saturday June 28th, time about 09.30 a.m. 52-year-old, white male, named Jason Roberts became victim number two. As the previous victim, decent, no known enemies, widower, worked as a technical analyst for BAe. Stabbed through the heart with what is consistent with a small serrated kitchen knife.

"A witness, Mrs Audrey Smith, saw a tall man wearing dark jeans and a dark cotton jacket running away from the scene, a bus stop, towards the town centre.

"She tried to help the victim but it was too late. She called the local police station and they were there within a few minutes. A severed pawn head was lying next to the body. No connection as yet with the Bala murder.

"Police made enquiries in the town centre for the tall man and got no results. It seems our Chessman disappeared into thin air. This man was carrying a plastic shopping bag and he probably had another jacket in it.

"These are the photos, police and witness statements. Again, nothing that helps or stands out. Again, no motive.

"Saturday, 13th July, time between 11.40 and Noon. Mr George Williams, 47-year-old white male, partner in a large firm of solicitors, married with two children aged 12 and 14. Place: Lettons Way, just a few yards from Dinas Powys Castle.

"Mr George Williams lived nearby in a half million pound detached house. He left home at 11.30 with his golf bags, walking the half mile or so to the Golf Club. He played most Saturdays with the same three people, always booked their round for 12 o'clock.

"Beaten to death with a golf club, one of his own, appropriately a number three iron. Third victim, number three iron, get it? The club was missing from the bag and the police at the scene on interviewing his playing partners ascertained that he always carried a number three iron. The body was found at five past twelve by another golfer who had just finished and was on his way to his car. Next to the body on a damp piece of ground, a size 11 footprint was found, new and very clear. The local CID here in Cardiff think it was left by the murderer. A chess castle's top half was found next to the body. A painstaking search was made for the golf club. Even sending divers to a nearby disused quarry but no sign of the golf club. No witnesses. No suspicious cars. Again nothing, but the Chessman must have had transport of some sort. A house to house proved a dead end.

"Here again are the photos and we do have the footprint cast. Do we have any comments here, anyone?"

"Yes," said Evan, "a few. Firstly, I don't think this was a random killing and secondly I think that the shoeprint business is a red herring. I'm not sure why, but why leave such an obvious clue? He's too smart for that."

"Nevertheless," said Mike, "I agree with both points, but let's check out the shoe. It might help."

"Okay," said Amber. "After we have gone through them all, we'll have a good look at the print to see if it helps us any."

"Victim number four, Machynileth, Powys, Sunday 2nd August. Joseph Hanson, fifty- three year old, unemployed, white male, poisoned whilst drinking in the Green Bear Inn, Maengwyn Street, opposite Parliament House."

"Did you say Parliament House?" asked Jane.

"Yes, it's a building which houses and charts the rise and fall of

Owen Glyndwr, self-proclaimed Prince of all Wales in the 15th Century," replied Amber. "If I'm not mistaken, this small town of about two and a half thousand people was shortlisted in the 1950s as the Welsh Capital."

"Of course Cardiff eventually won through," Evan offered as a footnote to Machynileth history.

"That's correct Evan, however get on with it."

"Our victim Mr Hanson was seen talking and drinking with a stout, red-haired man of about sixty. He had a very large mole on his nose and was wearing a dark suit and tie. The time of death 14.10 hours. Autopsy showed he was poisoned – arsenical solution. In this case the trioxide used in weedkillers, rat poison, etc. We have the pathologist report marked MAL 3097/DW/08.

"Now of course we must ask ourselves how did the Chessman get a normal, sane person to drink that vile tasting stuff? It seems that since losing his job, Mr Hanson worked as a manager in a small specialised clothing manufacturer. Mainly military stuff, uniforms, etc. He had started drinking heavily day and night and was seldom seen sober. Anyway, according to the barman at the Green Bear, the stranger, the red-headed man, continuously bought Mr Hanson drinks, rum and coke, gin, whisky, brandy, a right mixture. I think he would have drunk diesel oil without any problem.

"The Chessman left about five minutes before our Mr Hanson's death by what was assumed at the time to be a heart attack. Everyone assumed it to be a heart attack and by the time the coroner had made his findings, two days later, it was pointless looking for our red-headed friend, the Chessman, who had placed a severed pawns' heads in Mr Hanson's top jacket pocket.

"This by the by is the first time a connection was made by our boys – that a man leaving severed chess piece heads was a serial killer. Enquiries were belatedly made in regards to the red-headed man who was obviously their prime suspect. Machynileth is a small place, isolated with basic rail connections.

"How did the Chessman come? Did he stay the night or the previous night? How did he get there – car, bus, what means of transport? Again no-one seems to have seen Mr Red Hair with the big mole after he left the pub; incredible." Amber had finished, exhausted and hungry. "We're half way through and it's nearly half eleven. Let's break for a bite to eat."

Mike offered to go and get everyone some pizza and Coke. Evan had brought the car and it was outside. Mike returned twenty minutes later laden with boxes and cold cans of soft drinks. Everyone ate heartily, especially Amber who probably ate as much as the others put together. No-one spoke during the meal. Evan was deep in thought. Now at least he knew why Mike had money. It eased his mind a lot.

"Number five victim is our Mr David Donovan. The date: Saturday 23rd August. Place: Abergavenny, Monmouthshire. This we will leave to the end as we have it all on videotape," said Amber.

"So we have an identification?" asked Jane.

"Yes and No," answered Amber. "On to number six, Bridgend. Date: 7th September, a Saturday. Time between 10.05 and 10.15. The victim, Sir Edward Pettiford, white, male, aged 72, frail and wheelchair bound, strangled in his own home. A massive creaking mansion just on the outskirts of town. Main witness, Mr Alan Starling, butler to Sir Edward, aged 76 and this is what the butler saw, in his own words:

" 'At about four o'clock, the doorbell rang. I answered the door and was confronted with a man in overalls who said he was an electrical engineer who had come to repair some fault. I explained to the man that we had no fault and to the best of my knowledge had not reported a problem. He explained that the fault was showing up at his station and could result in a blackout. He showed me some kind of identification card and I could see the letters SWALEC on his blue overalls. This I assumed to be the South Wales Electric Company. I asked him to put out his cigarette and enter. This he did, kindly picking up the remainder of his stubbed cigarette and putting it in his pocket. He was wearing leather gloves. Mind you, it was a very cold day. He held a large bluish-type bag. He was wearing what the youth of today call "white training shoes". The man had black hair, a cloth, four-piece green tartan cap, about average build and five nine, five ten in height. Aged about 40 years old. Strangely enough he smelt of black boot polish but his shoes were light coloured. Apart from Sir Edward who was watching a sport's programme on the library's television and myself, nobody else was in.

" 'Saturday is the cook's day off. The maid was ill and the daily cleaner is usually finished by noon. I directed the engineer to the main fuse box and left him to it. About ten minutes later, maybe fifteen at most, he comes into the kitchen and tells me that the fault is rectified. It was a very small problem. I thanked him and showed him out. He had no van in the courtyard. I didn't think anything of it at the time. I called into the library to see if Sir Edward wished for anything and found him to be dead. I called the doctor who arrived within ten minutes. He noticed the neck marks and called the police. The police came and I told them all that I am telling you.'

"The 'you' being CID. The doctor first sees the severed chess knight's head in Sir Edward's lap. Even though the response by our boys is fast, no clues were to be found and obviously no Chessman.

"Let's fast-forward to Tenby in Pembrokeshire. On the 28th of September, a Sunday. A beautiful warm and sunny day. Mr Alan Carver, divorced, white male, aged 48 together with another twenty-two colleagues were on a works' day out. They had travelled from Newbridge where they all worked at a small technical research centre. In Tenby they had all broken into small groups. However, Mr Carver had drifted off alone and, having purchased some fish and chips from a nearby establishment, was leaning against a wall overlooking the harbour eating.

"The witnesses, two fourteen-year-old boys, say that they saw or thought they saw an old lady push Mr Carver over the wall to his death. The lads were sitting about twenty-five yards away on a bench eating ice-cream and they had noticed the old lady talking to Mr Carver.

"They had noticed her because it was very warm and most people were walking around with their jackets off. It was about twenty past one and most people were in town or on the beach having lunch. As I was saying, the lads couldn't miss her. She was wearing a dark greenish tweed coat and to quote the lads verbatim, 'The old lady had on thick, tight things on her legs; she had white hair, no hat.' They think she was wearing glasses and both agreed that she was wearing dark woollen gloves.

"For some reason the boys could not recall the old lady having a bag. A third witness, a Mr Chow, did not come forward until the lads had pointed him out to the police. His command of English is limited and he was extremely uncooperative.

"He works in a local restaurant. A crowd had quickly formed and in the confusion the old lady had vanished. The local boys searched the town and surrounds. A young lady had seen the old woman enter the toilets in the town centre and another couple had seen her walking up the main drag, possible just before entering the toilets.

"An obvious assumption here is that the woman, or the Chessman, changed identity in the toilets. Somewhere on his person he must have been carrying a bag. The area was thoroughly searched but no tweed coat. Our Mr Carver had a pawn head in his jacket pocket which was still lying on the wall.

"The lads say the old woman was very old, say seventy, frail and no taller than them, about 5 foot 4 inches. Mr Carver was five seven and about ten stone. This obviously was a random opportunist kill by the Chessman. There are the documents, the photos and the weather report. One last thing: it's not much help but his immediate boss at the tech centre says that in the last month or so they had had a spate of petty pilfering. Do you think it worth looking into, boys?"

"No, Amber, an absolute waste of time. Nothing to do with the case. Let the local Newbridge lads sort it out," said Evan. Mike agreed.

"Our last victim, just over two weeks ago, was a Mr Bryn Evans. The date: Friday 31st October. Halloween night. Location: a caravan site in St Dogmaels, Cardiganshire. The time: midnight.

"Mr Evans, a twenty-nine year old white male, was returning to his caravan from a nearby hotel where he had been drinking heavily. He'd recently parted from his partner who had returned to their main home in Taunton.

"He was accosted by someone wearing a black cloak and a devil's mask. A struggle ensued and Mr Evans fell, bleeding. He was stabbed repeatedly (you're not going to believe this but here we go) with a small gardening fork. The occupants of nearby caravans on hearing the commotion came out to see what was going on. By that time the perpetrator had vanished just like a puff of smoke. There were no actual witnesses. The description of the assailant came from Mr Evans, who died before the police and ambulance arrived. Next to his body lay the severed head of a pawn. A search was made; you can guess the result for yourselves. Before we see the video does anyone have anything to say?"

Evan spoke: "This man has opened the doors of disappearance. He's a ghost."

"Let's hope they are revolving, Evan, then we can catch him when he comes around again." Nobody laughed. It was not a laughing matter. Even Mike who made the quip knew it wasn't funny.

"Here are the photos, not of any help but they do show how isolated this caravan site is. Here's a map: one road in, one out."

"A boat perhaps?" said Jane.

"I don't think so, Jane. "On the beach opposite people were having some kind of beach party. They were contacted and say they never noticed any boat out in the river.

"And now for the film show where all will be revealed. An identification on camera at last, but then see for yourselves." Everyone lit up, except for Amber who was munching into some Bounty bars of chocolate. She pushed the start button and the forty-eight inch screen came to light in black and white. They watched the full two hours and fifteen minutes of tape and after ascertaining that the blonde was the first and only customer they replayed the vital minutes in slow motion over and over again, a total of twenty-one times.

"So what do you see Evan?" asked Mike.

"Same as you. A tall, long-haired blonde, wearing black trousers or jeans, shoes, long black raincoat with dark scarf, walks into the pawn shop at precisely nine minutes past nine in the morning. Mr Donovan, the proprietor, is standing behind a grilled counter but makes the mistake of coming to the side where there is no grill. He says something to the customer."

Amber butted in: "He says 'good morning, how can I help you?' The local boys in Abergevenny brought in a lip reader."

"Thanks Amber," said Evan who continued. "From what we can see there are two cameras, both static. One facing the counter, the other one, the entrance door. Unfortunately only one is working. The one facing the counter. The blonde is carrying a large plastic bag, the top of which is just visible from this bag. She produces a gun – looks like a Luger with silencer already attached.

"She takes two steps and fires rapidly; a distance of about four feet. The first hits Mr Donavan in the shoulder. The second misses and the third goes right through the heart. She replaces the gun, turns, opens the door and walks out into the street. It all happened in less than two minutes.

"Prior to leaving, she throws something over the counter towards the prostrate body of Mr Donavan who, because of the counter, we cannot see. This is what I see," Evan concluded.

"You are right Evan, the gun is a Luger," agreed Mike. "The

something he threw was a severed rook's head, or castle if you prefer. I notice Amber that we do not have one facial shot of the so-called blondie, as she stoops after the murder on the way out and we only get a picture of the top of her head. I'd guess the Luger is at least seventy-odd years old, probably a war souvenir picked up by our conquering army of dead Germans. God, there must be thousands and thousands around but it looked in good condition. Someone must have looked after it."

"Impossible to trace," said Evan. "Without the actual gun and again our blondie was wearing leather gloves, so no prints of hers on the doorknob. This again was pre-meditated. I think we can all agree on that." All concurred. "Amber, is it possible to work out how tall blondie is?"

"Not really," Amber said. "The problem there is we must allow for hair because it's a wig and we don't know what footwear she was wearing: high-heels, flatties, boots. We could get a rough figure but what's the use?"

"Look," said Mike, "let's start with the video and just note any points that we can find, then do the rest one by one."

"Okay," said Evan. "I'll go first.

"Where did she get the gun? I mean he. Are any of the clothes he wore branded? I mean, exclusive? Can they be traced to a shop? Why is he such a lousy shot? It took him three shots, one actually missed from four feet. Edna would have done better and she's never even touched a gun. Have they checked any street cameras? What type of bag is she holding and let's look at all the pawn shops' recent videos. He must have done a recce. Why leave a castle head in this case? Those are the questions. Now can anybody provide any answers?"

Mike stood and paced up and down the room. "Firstly, as we've said before Evan, all these disguises tell us something. That he is not anything like any one of those. He's pretending to be.

"Do you have a summary of the profiler's reports?"

"You mean the Behavioural Investigating Analysts?" said Amber.

"Yes, them, and what have they come up with?"

"Male, aged between thirty and fifty, white collar worker, banker, solicitor, salesman, nine to five, Monday to Friday, five ten to six two, average build, own transport, blah, blah, blah, absolutely no use. Oh, this part I like best, probably that he lives in a rural part of Wales and that he or someone close to him has been cheated in some kind of deal, a complex type of deal, something like a game of chess and the white pieces represent those that cheat. The motive simple: revenge."

"Where do they come up with such crap?" said Mike. "No excuses for using that word instead of 'shit'. Both have the same meaning.

"At the moment I see two things: our chessman is more than likely to be left-handed, hence the bad shooting. He was using his right hand and it seems that the three victims which were left back row pieces were rich or well off; the pawns were given to the others – just ordinary Joes."

"It makes good sense to me," said Evan. "Look at the marks on Sir Edward's neck. Obviously strangled with electrical wire from behind. It would be impossible to strangle him any other way."

"What about the marks Evan"? asked Jane.

"They are deeper cuts on the left-hand side of his face," Amber answered. "The sign of a strong arm prevailing over the weaker. The stabbings with a knife in Abergele; look at the photos again. One wound to the left as seen from the front. Then the heart. The same with the Halloween victim; six large wounds: five to the left of the body and only one to the right." Amber finished by apologising to Evan for interrupting him.

"No probs, Amber. I think we've nailed his left-handedness. I am interested in the plastic bags that seem to be cropping up here and there. Why not a briefcase or small lightweight suitcase? Do we know anything about them?

"Did the witness, Mrs Anne Smith in Abergele, notice what make of plastic bag the man running away held?"

"It's Audrey, not Anne, Evan," Amber said. "I'll contact her and see if she can help out with this bag business, and I'll also contact the couple in Tenby who saw the Chessman as an old lady walking through town. See if they noticed if she was carrying a plastic bag.

"That leaves the plastic bag on the video. Let's re-run and see if we can get a better look at the plastic bag."

They did re-run it, froze it, enlarged it and came to a conclusion. The bag had dark handles, either black or navy blue and the same colour for the top three inches before at least two inches of a lighter colour. They could see no more. As a clue, it was about as useful as tits on a boar's arse.

Jane's keen eye had caught a white mark on the scarf. During the previous re-runs it had been overlooked as a trick of light in the shop. It was enlarged and a clothes tag emerged. Slowly and painfully Amber, in between bits of a large chocolate bar, had unearthed its secret and revealed a brand name: MU-ST. Nobody recognised the brand. Amber would look into it.

"We still have the footprint cast to look at before we pack up for the day," Evan said. "Personally I think it's a waste of time. Another red herring but let's go through the motions." Each one in turn looked at the cast and the photos. Each one passed until again Jane asked Amber for a magnifying glass. Amber obliged.

"See here," said Jane, pointing to a spot on the soles just before the heel. She ran a finger up and down. "There is a brand here. I think it says IV, the Roman numerals for the number four. Actually, I'm wrong. Look at this: it's IVI, not IV." And so it was. "These are very expensive shoes. Look at the stitching, the patterns on the heels and if I had to guess they are very old. I mean thirty, even forty years old.

"If I had to hazard a guess, I would say that these were custom made and worn only on special occasions."

Amber thought about it and agreed. "Tomorrow, Jane, you look into the shoes as you seem to know more about these things. I'll look into the scarf and the plastic bags."

"I think we can now see light at the end of the tunnel," said Evan.

"Let's hope it's not a fucking freight train hurtling down on us with its headlight on," said Mike. "Do you know something?" he said to everyone in the room. "I think I have stumbled on the motive."

Everyone looked at Mike. No one spoke awaiting Mike to go on.

"It's easy: the Chessman wipes everyone off the board, thirty-two perfect murders, writes a book about the murders under a pseudonym, makes a fortune and retires to the Bahamas. He wiles away the time playing chess and drinking rum with the locals."

"That's not funny Mike," said Evan. Amber and Jane suppressed a giggle.

"It was gone six. Mike drove Evan home in his car then returned. He was meeting Amanda for a meal and other things. Jane went home to her husband John and Amber had a nice meal: Jerk-style chicken, rice, bread, washed down with Red Stripe Lager.

CHAPTER 9

Friday morning. Peter the Chessman had just finished his breakfast, toast with butter and marmalade, coffee with cream. His first job was to drive his car to his lock-up about five hundred yards down the road, then he would walk back, change into Uncle Paulie and bring Uncle's car out of the garage at the back to the front. The whole business was getting out of hand. Running three cars was not only time-consuming but expensive. The cost of the lock-up, his Mini, Carl's 2-litre BMW, and Uncle Paulie's Rover, Car Tax, MOTs, forged documents. It all added up.

As Carl, the toy salesman, he lived in the Cardiff flat. Carl was five years younger than Peter, blonde, trendy and loud, like all good salesmen should be. He knew all his neighbours in Cardiff. They all had accepted that as a salesman he was on the road continuously. He kept various cheap toys in the BMW, his samples.

Now and then he would give his neighbour, a single mother with a small boy of six, a small toy or two. The mother, Susan, he would bring flowers, cheap champagne and chocolate. She was most appreciative.

He rarely had to change bed sheets in his own flat. At most he was there, once a week. He enjoyed being the toy man.

Now as Uncle Paul he had finished all the necessary car manoeuvres. He'd bought Pat from next door some flowers and knocked on the door. As usual Jim answered. "Morning Paul."

"Morning Jim."

"I've got some flowers for Pat."

"Come in and have a cuppa. Pat's made a lovely carrot cake." Paul entered, gave over the flowers which Pat put in a vase and sat down.

"And how are you today Pat?"

"Getting by, but this weather is bad for my arthritis. I can just about get around," replied Pat, offering Paul a cup of tea and a slice of cake.

"Will Peter be joining us?" asked Jim.

"No, Jim, he left for his business trip. I told you on Tuesday about it, remember? He'll be gone at least two weeks, probably three."

"I didn't see him leave," said Jim. "Did you Pat?"

"Strange he should leave on a Friday. You wouldn't think there's much business over the weekend."

"I think there's a big auction early tomorrow in Liverpool or somewhere round there. I guess Peter wanted to prepare himself," replied Paul.

These two old farts were very nosey and had nothing better to do than sit in the lounge looking out the window. They were beginning to get on Paul's wick. He would have to do something but at least he had created for himself a three-week period of grace.

He finished his tea and cake and returned to his home next door. He was still thinking about his neighbours. Maybe he should smack them both over the head with Pat's bloody concrete hard cake. He smiled. Agatha Christie never came out with such a good title for one of her books. 'Death by Carrot Cake.' Brilliant, he thought.

Paul was now ready. He needed to get down to Barry once more and have one last good look at the location before Sunday. Every day for the last three days he had followed Priestly's Volvo down to the Knap in Barry. It was a round trip of about 120 miles but it was worth the hassle. He knew everything he needed to about his next victim. But he would check it out once more. A bishop piece was ready. He was ready. Poor old Priestly wasn't. Today he would have no choice but to take the Rover. He had to return by six as he had prearranged a tennis game in the indoor courts with his doubles partner Jack.

More complications. Jack knew him as thirty-five year old Peter. He was also in the coin racket but more into Greek and Roman antique stuff. They would tip each other off about various collectors and collections. Sometimes joined together to purchase. Other times pretending to bid against each other. He chucked his racquets and gear in the boot of the Rover and headed East on the M4 motorway.

Heading in the opposite direction were Special Detective Inspectors Karetzi and Jones. S.D.I. Jones was driving. They had arranged to meet Mr Alan Starling, ex-butler to Sir Edward, at the mansion in Tenby and then were to go on and meet Mr Chow and the two young boys in Tenby when they had finished school.

They had not as yet been able to get hold of the elusive Chinese gentleman.

"Are you okay Mike?" asked Evan. His partner, he had noticed, was not his usual chirpy self.

"I'm fine thanks Evan."

But Mike wasn't. His date with Amanda had been a disaster. All his fault. He kept comparing Amanda with the strawberry blonde. It was no contest – strawberry won hands down.

For the first time in his life Mike reckoned that a bird in the hand is not worth anything. He wanted what he couldn't get. Not yet, anyway. He'd find the strawberry. He only wished he had a name. Little did he realise that sitting next to him was the man who could give him that name and much more information about his strawberry blonde if he was so inclined. Evan of course wouldn't be; no way.

They reached Sir Edward's mansion, parked in the large driveway and rang the bell. The butler answered the door. He was still in uniform. The Detectives showed him their credentials and were let in. The butler led them to the library room and offered them a seat. They sat rather uncomfortably for the butler was still standing. "May I get you detectives some refreshments?" The detectives declined.

The butler still stood. Evan stood and addressed him. "You are Mr Starling?"

"That is correct Sir. I assume that you must be wondering why I'm still here working with Sir Edward now gone?"

"I am, Mr Starling," replied Evan.

"I have been asked by the Trustee Estate to remain in my present capacity until things are sorted out. They say it will probably be about six months. It's very complicated so I understand. It's just me and the cook. The maid has gone and the gardener is not here today."

"I see," said Evan. "Could you sit down while we have a chat?"

"I would prefer to stand Sir. At my age it's difficult to get up after sitting and in all honesty I'm used to standing. Always on call as you might say."

Mike stood up. "Just a few small questions, Mr Starling. Did you see any vehicle on the day of Sir Edward's murder? By vehicle I mean bicycle, motorbike, van, car, etc."

"No Sir, nothing in the driveway."

"And the gardener? Maybe he noticed something?"

"I'm afraid not Sir, he was away in London that day delivering documents and things to Sir Edward's banker."

"I didn't think banks opened on Saturdays, Mr Starling."

"I understand that Mr Jackson, the chauffer-cum-gardener, delivered these documents to a private house in Hampstead to one of the directors of the bank."

"Do you know what was in these parcels or what the documents referred to?" Mike asked and thought he knew the answer. He was surprised when the butler told him that he knew.

"They contained plans and details of a new factory. Sir Edward wished to build a site near Cowbridge. I helped him get the documents packaged. A job that was usually done by Sir Edward's personal secretary who dealt with all these matters. However, she was in Bristol visiting her Aunt and Sir Edward wanted an early answer to the financing aspect of the deal."

"Okay Mr Starling, you mentioned something about 'training shoes'. Is that correct?"

"Yes Sir."

"Do you mean 'trainers'?"

"No Sir. I mean something like people use to run in or play games with."

"Rugby, football?"

"No Sir, softer, very strange footwear for this time of the year."

"You say in your statement that these shoes were light coloured. Is that so? Describe the colour please."

"The best description I can give is that they were the colour of sand."

"And this height you give is five nine or ten?"

"Yes Sir."

Evan paused and went back to the shoes. "Did they have heels?"

"They do indeed, about half an inch at most."

"Did they have laces or other means of fastening?"

"Laces, Sir."

"Thank you," said Evan.

"Mr Starling," asked Mike, "may I ask you to guess roughly what my height is including my shoes?"

"No problem Sir, my guess would be six foot, maybe six one."

"Thank you, Mr Starling."

The butler didn't ask if he was correct and Mike didn't confirm it.

"One last question. You say you smelt black shoe polish."

"I did Sir. My guess is that he rubbed it into his sideburns, an old army trick. It is supposed to make you look younger if you don't show grey hairs."

"Anything else Mr Starling?" Evan asked.

"Yes Sir, it occurred to me that he was younger than he looked. Maybe five, eight years and he was lean and fit, I could tell. The work overalls were too big for him."

"You have been very helpful Mr Starling. We thank you for your time. You are very observant. May I trouble you just once more – can you describe the bag?" asked Evan.

"Yes, it was a long leather bag, greenish blue in colour, about a foot in width with a zip. No brand name that I could see but it had a white logo of some sort. Unfortunately, I didn't really take much notice of it. Sorry Sir."

"That's more than good enough. Again, thank you."

"We'll see ourselves out," said Evan. The butler couldn't help himself and showed them to the door.

"What do you make of him, Mike?"

"He's not gone gaga, Evan. He's all there. Very observant and accurate. I think we're looking for a man, average build, five ten in his shoes, aged between twenty-five and forty at most."

"Spot on; the bag, the shoes."

"That I'm not sure about, Evan. It's a job for Jane or Amber. Shall we give them a ring on our new phones, Mike?"

"Might as well. You drive, I'll call. See if there has been any news."

There was. Mrs Smith confirmed that the man running away was carrying a plastic bag. Unfortunately she didn't recognise the brand or shop but would know it if she saw it again close up.

As for the scarf, they had identified it as coming from one of two shops. The MU-ST collection, ladies wear; both had closed down over eight years ago. The first in Cardiff had lasted three months more than the one in Swansea.

With regard to the shoes, nothing. "Well, Evan, that's something. Tell me why are we so interested in the plastic bags."

"In all honesty, Mike, I don't really know, but we just don't seem to have anything else to follow up."

"What about the docs the butler and Sir Edward sent down to

London, Evan. Nothing sinister there, but let's stop in one of those big sports shops and pick up a couple of catalogues, see if the butler can match shoes or bags with the so-called electrician's gear."

"Okay, Evan, go into Swansea. There's bound to be one in the town centre. It's on our way."

They found a big store near where they had parked. They collected every single leaflet, brochure, etc., that they could lay their hands on. Nearby was one of those new coffee places.

They ordered and started looking through the catalogues, marking various shoes and leather bags with a pen. They arrived in Tenby at precisely three p.m. They had arranged to talk to the lads at quarter past at one of the boys' homes. They lived next door to each other.

Both sets of parents were there. The boys ran through their story once more. They could add nothing to the original statement that they had made. They couldn't remember any plastic bag but at the time they were in shock. Neither though could rule out the plastic bag one hundred per cent. "That just leaves the inscrutable Mr Chow," said Evan. "Has Amber tracked down his address, otherwise we will have to wait until the restaurant opens?" They rang Amber who couldn't trace his address yet but gave them the name and address of the restaurant.

It was your typical old-fashioned Chinese eatery. Heavy red curtains, red dragons made of wood everywhere, red tablecloths and carpet, red doors and a red sign above the red entrance door with the restaurant's name: 'The White Crab'. It was closed, so the sign said, but there was movement inside. An old Chinese man dressed in some sort of uniform, red of course, was putting flower vases on each table. Every vase had a red carnation.

Evan tapped on the window to catch the man's eye. When he did, he beckoned him over. The man shuffled to the door and opened it. Mike showed the old man his warrant badge and explained that they needed to speak to Mr Chow.

The old man spoke good English. He was the owner and told the detectives that Mr Chow was a chef and he gave them his address which was just a few minutes away. They found the house, a large house, developed into six small, one-bedroom flatlets. Mike rang the appropriate doorbell and, after a few minutes, a small balding Chinese man of about forty-five opened the door.

Thankfully Mr Chow's flat was on the ground floor and the door was open otherwise Evan doubted if they would have got in without a warrant. Mr Chow was ironing. The TV was on: horse racing. A paper opened at the racing pages was on a small table. Various horses had been ringed with a blue biro.

"Any winners, Mr Chow?" No answer. "Do you speak English?" No answer. Mr Chow just sat there shaking his head. After twenty frustrating minutes Evan decided that without a translator it was pointless and decided to go back to the restaurant and bring back the owner.

In reality Evan needed the break. The smell of weed was overpowering in that small enclosed space. All the windows were shut. "You okay with our Chinese friend for ten minutes or so Mike, while I go and get the owner to interpret? Someone must stay in case he does a runner."

"Yeah, take your time partner. I'll watch the Gee Gee's on TV."

Evan left. Mike shut the door after him and locked it. Mr Chow didn't move but Mike did towards the iron. It was still on and red hot. Mike unplugged it and suddenly in one swift movement had Mr Chow in a head-lock with his left arm; in his right he held the iron.

"Now Mr Chow, you're going to have to learn English in quick time. I will ask some simple questions. For everyone that I don't get an answer to, I'm going to rest this iron on your bald head. I hope for your sake you can understand me, so here is the first question. You answer me quick, chop, chop." Mike lowered the iron to within a half inch of Chow's head. Chow started shaking. He could feel the heat.

"Do you live here? Don't nod, you will burn yourself, Mr Chow. Speak; your mouth is nowhere near the iron."

"Yes."

"Good start, Mr Chow. Did you see the murder on the 28th September?"

"Yes."

"Good, Mr Chow, very good so far. Did the old lady pick him up and topple the man over the edge?"

"Yes."

"Did you notice if the old lady was carrying anything?"

"Yes."

"What was she carrying?"

"A bag."

"What type of bag, Mr Chow? Remember, Mr Chow, my hand is getting tired. Do you understand what that means? Do you?"

"Yes, sir a plastic supermarket bag."

"Do you know what supermarket?"

"Yes, sir, it is KostKing." I have some in draw."

"Good, Mr Chow. One final question. Where did the old lady go after the incident?"

"She walk to town centre. I see she cross road and walk fast, you understand sir?"

"Excellent Mr Chow, you see how easy it is to learn a new language," said Mike releasing him and replacing the iron on the board. "Now let's have one of these bags." From one of the drawers Mr Chow produced a KostKing bag, navy blue, three inch top and handles, the rest pink with a navy blue, five-inch diameter crown on both sides.

They were parading the winner at the last race on the screen. Mike glanced at the newspaper. Mr Chow had picked a winner. "It's your lucky day Mr Chow. You learn a new language and get a winner all in ten minutes."

Mike folded the bag into a size that he could fit into his pocket, unlocked the door and turned facing Mr Chow, who was still shaking. "Some words of advice from your friendly laundryman. Wash the clothes before you iron them and more important, stop smoking whatever shit you're doing. I really don't want to come back and search this place."

With that Mike left. He opened the front door into the street and stepped out. He could see Evan walking towards him, alone. He lit up his third of the day, inhaled deeply and started walking.

"He wouldn't come, Mike, said he was too busy. Nothing I could do to make him."

"No need for him Evan. Once our Chinese friend realised how important his health was, we managed to iron out our language difficulties and got on rather well."

"What health problems, Mike?"

"Something to do with his head, Evan. You know the Chinese herbal remedy, acupuncture."

"I guess that stuff he was smoking didn't help much either, Mike."

Mike produced the KostKing bag. "This is what the Chessman was carrying."

"Never heard of them, Mike."

"Nor me, Evan, but it could easily be the same as the one on the video." Mike rang the office. Jane answered. Mike explained about the bag. Jane said they would review the video, check with Mrs Smith, with the new description and check out where KostKing had stores.

"What now Evan?"

"Back to the butler or to the office direct."

"Butler again. Maybe we will get some tea and scones. I'm hungry, Mike."

"Right Evan, I'll drive. We will get there faster."

Mike drove fast, blue light flashing, siren going. Evan hung on for dear life. He shouldn't have mentioned being hungry. At this rate he doubted if he'd have a stomach left, never mind filling it with scones and cake.

The butler opened the door, offered them tea. Both accepted. There were no scones or cakes. Probably for the best. Evan's stomach was still queasy. The butler looked through everything the detectives had. He pointed out two pairs of shoes which he said were similar but not exactly the same. The bag again; something similar but not exact. He did however pick up on the logo. A small green crocodile. The Lacoste brand. They thanked the Butler and with Evan driving slower than Mike without the blue light and siren. After about six miles on, heading East, Evan, doing just over seventy in the outside lane, shouted out: "God, I just thought I saw my grey Rover heading down the opposite way."

It was a Rover. It was grey but it wasn't Evan's. It was the Chessman going home to play tennis after his afternoon in Barry. For a split second the detectives were only feet away from the Chessman. It would be a while before they got that close again.

The Chessman had had a good day. He was a little tired but he looked forward to his game of tennis with his friend Jack.

On entering the office, the S.D.I.s were greeted by Amber who had made a huge coconut cake which she and Jane were now enjoying with a cup of tea. Mike was happy to do without the cake. Evan had two slices of cake. He would have had a third but decided against it. He would be having dinner soon.

"We have news," said Amber, her mouth full of cake. "Can we see the bag first?" Mike handed it over. "Yep, just as we thought. Mrs Audrey Smith is ninety-nine per cent certain that he was carrying a KostKing bag. After we described it to her, she remembered the pink vividly and the top rim and thinks that ninety-nine per cent it's the same bag as in the video. These bags are not particularly strong so I would assume it's not the same one in each incident. I don't think they are meant to last – cheap to produce. Used once; at the most, twice," concluded Amber.

Jane carried on for Amber who had already put another chunk of cake into her mouth. "So it's logical to assume that the Chessman or someone in the family shops at this supermarket which logically must be local to them.

"They have stores in Haverfordwest, Pembroke, Milford Haven, Carmarthen, Tenby, Llanelli, Neath, Port Talbot, Ammanford, Gorselnon and three in Swansea. They are also opening up another three or four within the next year. They are smaller sized supermarkets, something like Aldi or Lidl. They seem to use more local fresh products: meats, fruit, veg and other things produced in West Wales. Prices are actually cheaper than the bigger supermarkets. Obviously they have less overhead costs."

"Thanks Jane. What about the shoes?"

"Nothing still. I don't think we will ever be able to progress on that front," answered Jane.

Evan told the girls about their talk with the butler, the conclusion being that the Chessman might be a tennis player. All indications pointed to him playing some kind of game, like tennis. Mike himself was a keen tennis player. It could be bowls, but like Mike said, he thought the Chessman too young for bowls and bowls usually had a squarer, more solid type of bag. They were quite heavy. No, it had to be tennis. The length and size of the bag were the discerning points. Just right for a few racquets, balls, gear, etc., and according to Evan, it was not really a cricket bag – not being long enough, didn't sound right.

Amber expressed her surprise that without a translator Mike and Evan had obtained so much information from Mr Chow. Evan was too and wondered if 'The White Crab' would have its full complement of staff tonight. For some unfortunate reason he didn't think so. Evan was right, they were a man short that night and it was a very busy night. Mr Chow had phoned in saying that he had a bad headache – apt, really.

It was time to call it a day. Evan drove Jane home then went to his home. Mike walked to his, stopping on the way to pick up a 'Cardiff Chronicle'. He read as he walked. Back page first. Man City had made a big offer for another one of Cardiff's young players.

He read it twice, three times. The transfer of another young player didn't make sense, but something else did. He turned on his heels and headed back to the office.

Amber was just about to eat. "Hello Mike, come to keep me company? Didn't feel like eating alone. There's enough food for two." Actually, the leg of pork would have fed the local police force.

"Thanks Amber, just a quick one. Have you got a piece of paper, a pen or pencil?"

Amber got them. "Look here Amber, IVI – that's what's on the shoe."

"The I after the V being twice as thick as the I before the V, right Mike?"

"Well, now look: 'M'. Just by elongating the lines it changed to 'M'. The top part just faded with wear."

"It could easily be Mike, easily be. I'll look into it after I eat and get back some of my energy."

Mike left again. The 'M' in Man City had clicked something in his mind. It was useful to read the back pages first. They were a mine of information.

Jane and John had fish and chips at home, as did Edna and Evan. Mike grilled a pork chop which he had with a tomato and onion salad, olive oil and lemon dressing. Amber polished off her roast pork, roast potatoes and veg. In no household was any alcohol drunk. A very strange occurrence for all of them.

The Chessman did, though, at his local Indian restaurant. He had three pints of Kingfisher lager, his favourite beer. At home he only drank ginger beer but with the hot King Prawn Vindaloo and the other spicy food he needed the cold lager to counteract the burning in his mouth and throat. He looked forward to Sunday. All being well and Mr Priestly would be another statistic in this great game of chess which would net him a fortune one day soon.

When Mike got home he just sat trying to concentrate on a crossword in his evening paper. His mind though was elsewhere. It was on the strawberry blonde, but where do you start looking. Impossible, no time. Tanya the air hostess had left a message on the phone. She was a beautiful looking girl but my Christ could she talk! Tanya was the second air hostess he'd dated and Marilyn, the other was also a big talker. He didn't bother to ring back. He just wasn't in the mood. He'd have an early night.

He was in bed by eleven. Very early for Mike. He slept like a baby who'd just been fed. At seven a.m. the alarm brought him out of a deep sleep. He reached out for the strawberry blonde but all he got was a handful of thin air.

It took Mike a while to realise that he'd been dreaming but now he knew and with one quick slap he sent the alarm clock spinning into a corner.

That's for waking me up when I was having such great dreams, he said to the clock. If the clock was a speaking type it would have told Mike to grow up or something to that effect.

Mike got up. A black coffee, piece of toast with marmalade and a cigarette constituted breakfast for him. It was Saturday and he was ready.

CHAPTER 10

The chessman was reading his morning paper. He'd been reminiscing intermittently throughout the night. He'd thought of his parents, Gillian his mother who was scared of his father Jonathan. Not that he beat her or anything like that. She thought she was intellectually inferior. His father thought the same and did what he wanted without any opposition from his mother.

She got used to being treated like a slave; cooking, cleaning, ironing and helping out in the large men and women's fashion shop they owned in town. She had no friends to speak of; a sad and lonely woman. His father on the other hand socialised a lot.

Every day from the age of eleven his father would pick him up from school, letting his mother close the shop at five thirty. He would then play chess with his son Peter. This went on every day except Sunday. Six days a week, sometimes two games a day for five years. A total of two thousand, five hundred games. Peter never won, not that he cared – he actually tried his best to make losing faster and dreamt up ways of making stupid moves to annoy his father.

He could hear his schoolmates playing games outside, in the street, football, cricket using the green garage door opposite their house as the goal or in summer they drew wickets on the garage with chalk.

Later when he reached fourteen the boys would hang out with the girls, having a sly fag, a sly kiss or grope. It was all happening outside when he was playing chess inside. His mother would come home at six, cook supper and then supervise him while he did his homework before bed.

Rarely was he allowed to watch the television because his father wouldn't leave until nine. Where he went, no-one knew. No one ever asked. His father would be back about midnight but he was never drunk.

Peter was sixteen when he realised that his father had other women. He was lucky to get to a good school when they moved that same year to a bigger house in a new area. His father had now given up on the chess games but for Peter it was still bad. New school, new area, no friends. He hated his father with a vengeance.

It was the chess that had ruined his life but now ironically chess would make him a millionaire. At seventeen Peter could have gone on to university but wanted out of the system and joined a large jewellers. He learnt a lot about all kinds of jewellery but he was fascinated with the odd coins that the jewellers used.

He took various courses on art and jewellery, antiques, coins. He studied hard doing these courses. After the death of his mother when Peter was twenty, his father started drinking heavily and started forgetting things. The shop was run by good staff. His father rarely there, spending most days in the pub. He let himself go. Suddenly there were no women. He was dirty in appearance and the way he spoke.

One Sunday out of boredom Peter had rummaged through his father's desk and found a will. It was signed by both his late mother and his father. The manager from his father's shop had witnessed it. Peter was being left everything. That is unless his father pissed it all away.

The very next day, his father met with an accident. He fell down the stairs whilst drunk, breaking his neck. A push from behind helped propel him like a rocket downwards. There was no remorse. Peter waited over an hour before calling an ambulance. He undid the shoelaces from his father's right shoe. It was to be the Chessman's first victim.

It took over three months to clear up all the details. There were a few distant relatives and that was that. The funeral, the selling of the business and then the house, the tax elements to everything.

Peter moved to the house he now occupied, then under a new name with the help of some iffy documentation he had acquired. He bought the flat in Cardiff. He created his Uncle Paul just eight months ago and at the same time he rented the big lock up. He had not thrown away his parents' clothes. It must have been a premonition that they would come in useful one day.

Today Uncle Paulie would do the weekly shop. It was only a mile to the local supermarket KostKing. Their fresh produce was excellent. He also needed to stock up on ginger beer – a celebration would be in order tomorrow. He popped next door as Paul to enquire of any shopping they might require him to get.

S.D.I. Jones and Sergeant Williams both arrived at ten to nine. S.D.I. Karetzi arrived twenty minutes later. Greetings were exchanged. Evan was tieless. A first for him at work and instead of his normal white shirt, he was wearing a grey one which matched his grey flannel trousers.

Mike wore designer jeans, dark slip-on shoes, a pale blue open-neck shirt and a dark blazer with gold buttons. If it wasn't for the heavy rain and sleet outside, Evan would have sworn that his partner was geared up for a picnic.

Amber was just sitting in front of two monitors. She seemed to be working them both.

"What's Amber doing, Jane?" asked Mike.

"Contacting shoe people."

"Who are shoe people, Jane?"

"Everyone involved with shoes, manufacturers, cobblers, shoe shops, mail order companies and so on. She's working on the new logo that you think the shoe had. The 'M' with a thin and thick vertical, Mike."

"We all agree here that it's a possibility," said Evan.

"Can you take over now Jane?" Amber asked. "I need to crunch some figures with our sleuths here. This is why we have Detectives. These are not necessarily facts but for our purpose they are near enough. The Chessman is a white male, about five ten, average build, light to medium dark hair, age about twenty-five to say forty-five and living in a triangle which starts, say, Porthcawl, cuts up to and includes Newcastle Emlyn one way and from Porthcawl to Milford Haven the other way.

"The population for this area is roughly six hundred thousand but this reduces to half that amount because he is a male. We agree that the probability of his being left-handed is overwhelming. Only ten per cent of the population is, so we're down to thirty thousand and that reduces further to about ten thousand when we take into account his age group.

"We have ten thousand suspects at best. If we're wrong with any of our assumptions we could still have half a million suspects. We have to be positive. In just three days we have achieved a lot. Somehow we must narrow the field down – but how?" concluded Amber.

Evan took out his clay pipe, packed it and lit up. Mike played with his knife, sharpening a seven-inch pencil to three, then two inches. Mike grabbed another and cut it into two. It was as easy as slicing through butter. He started sharpening one of the halves. He felt inadequate and deflated. In reality, they had achieved nothing. "We need to know why he strikes over the weekends. What does he do for a living? What are his hobbies and last but not least, what is his motive? That's the key," said Mike.

"I don't think he plays any tournament Chess. It's the same people nearly every tournament. They all check out. The tennis angle might help."

"But how? We can't round up all left-handed tennis players in West Wales and we're again not sure that the tennis shoes, bag, etc., are not red herrings."

"But let's not discount it. What about his work? Is he self-employed? More than likely. At least two, maybe three of the murders were planned. That takes time and preparation and a bit of money, petrol, disguises, train fares, loss of work. He is reasonably well off but still we are left with the big 'Q' – Motive?" Mike stabbed his chair with such fury that the knife quivered for nearly ten seconds.

"That's police property," Amber said quietly.

"Sorry Amber, I thought for one minute there that it was the Chessman." Mike removed the knife, took off the safety, folded it, and returned it to his inside jacket pocket.

"Got it!" Jane exclaimed. "We've got it. A Mr Joey Martins says that that was his family's trademark up until twelve or so years ago when he, this Joey chap, took over his old man's cobblers in Swansea."

"Get him on the phone Jane, ask him if he actually made shoes. If they did do they keep records." They got Mr Martins on the line. Yes, Jane reported, in the sixties and early seventies they made custom-made shoes – his father and uncle. In nineteen seventy-three they stopped. Not enough customers but carried on repairing shoes with their mark on the sole right up until ninety-one.

They did keep records but along the way they were not required anymore and they were disposed of. "One thing for sure," Mr Joey Martins added, "shoes with the Martins' 'M' must be at least seventeen years old." Those made by his father or uncle would be at least thirty-five years old, and still going strong? No way! He would say this was a repair job.

"One last thing Mr Martins," Jane asked. "Can we have the address of your establishment?" Jane wrote it down. "Thank you, Mr Martins."

Jane put on her coat. "I'm going to get a large-scale map of Swansea. I think we will need it."

"Take this card Jane," said Mike. "Here's the card number." Jane departed.

"Sergeant's okay Mike?" said Evan.

"Sure is Evan, who else would go out in this weather, without an umbrella?"

"You would Mike," retorted his partner. "I should have lent her mine."

On her return Jane, soaked to the skin, had purchased the large street map. The scale, four inches to the mile. It was one of those that folded two ways, down and across like a concertina. Fully open it nearly covered the whole desk. Jane hung up her coat over one of the radiators and then took off her shoes, again placing them on another radiator.

She retired barefoot to the bathroom where she dried her hair and repaired her make-up. On returning downstairs to the office, she found the other three huddled around the map. Amber had three markers in her huge hands, each a different colour.

With the green marker she put two crosses on the map. "Those represent the supermarkets, KostKings." With the blue she marked the site of the now defunct MU-ST clothes shop and Martins the Cobblers. With the red she marked off all the other major superstores in the area, a total of six major players within a radius of three and a half miles from the city centre.

Evan picked up one of the two-inch pencils that Mike had sharpened. He pointed to a spot and said, "If you live here you would shop at this supermarket, here, at that supermarket, here, at this one."

"He must live in this area," Evan concluded, drawing a pencilled ring around an area North of the A4118 to about a mile South of the M4. No one argued; there was a total murmur of agreement. A section of about one square mile was now the focus of attention.

"It's perfect for a person on the move. Near a main railway station and the main road network in Wales. The sea's not too far either. Now all we need is a bloody house number and street name and…" Mike had not finished the sentence. They had stretched all the material they had at hand to breaking point; a lot of assumptions, guesswork, coincidences had led them to this point but hand on heart they could be completely wrong. The Chessman could still be based anywhere from Anglesey to Wrexham to Chepstow to even twenty yards down from their office.

However, the others were more optimistic. It all made sense. It all added up. The Chessman lived in the area ringed.

"That's as far as we can go today," Amber said. "It's Saturday. Jane and I are going shopping together. Can one of you men give us poor females a ride into the town centre?"

"No problem," said Evan. "I don't think Mike's little car will accommodate both of you comfortably."

"Are you saying I'm overweight, Evan?"

"Maybe a little, Amber, only a little."

Mike turned to Jane. "First thing I would buy would be an umbrella, Jane. Put it down to expenses – I would. Oh, and have lunch on the force too. You're still officially on duty."

"Actually Mike, I'm not. Not until Monday, remember."

"Well, let Amber pay on expenses. You have a card, don't you Amber?"

"Of course I do."

"Well then, lunch solved, not bad hey, Evan?"

Evan couldn't fathom out if Mike was joking or not. He decided that he wasn't.

"See you all Monday," said Mike. "Have a good weekend."

Evan dropped the girls off, then headed home to pick up his wife Edna. They were also going shopping and would drop into the cosmetics department at his daughter's place of work and have a chat.

Mike headed for home. He needed to pick up the Belgian chocolates he had in the fridge. They were his mother's favourites. You couldn't miss his mother's small bungalow in Penarth. It was painted purple. Alice, his mother, had lived there for thirteen years and every three years had the exterior of the house painted, always a shade of purple.

The door was open. Mike had repeatedly warned his mother about leaving the door open but she took no heed. A very trusting person, his mother. He pushed it open and walked straight in through a small lobby and into the lounge.

Mike heard the shriek before he actually saw his mother who was rushing over to him, arms outstretched. "It's my little boy, my little Mikhailee!" She gave Mike a big hug and lots of kisses. It was the same every time he saw her, even if he had only visited two hours previously. He was embarrassed. Another three elderly ladies were in the room drinking tea and eating fruit cake. He felt like one – the fruit cake part.

"How are you mother?" Mike asked, handing over the chocolates.

"I'm fine son. Are you okay?"

"Of course I am mother, right as rain."

"Would you tell your little mother if you weren't, Mikhail? I do worry you know. You're not in the safest type of job. Why couldn't you be an engineer like your father?"

"You know why mother. Anyway I see you've got company. Why don't you give them a chocolate or two? The fruit cake looks dry to me."

Alice laughed. Her boy knew how to change the subject.

Alice was sure that Mikhail was still looking for his father's muggers, even after all these years. She was right. That was the main reason Mike had joined the force. Mike spent an hour with his mother and her three friends. Between them they finished the whole box of chocolates and the fruit cake which was not dry. Alice's cakes were always good and never dry.

Mike drove back to the Bay. One of the reasons he had bought in that area was that it was very close to his mother. His only living relative that he knew about.

He poured himself a whisky and prepared himself a small steak sandwich with lashings of mustard. English, not that bloody French stuff which was only fit for hotdogs.

He ate his sandwich, drank his whisky and switched on his TV. He liked following the scores on a Saturday. That's when he wasn't watching City play. They were playing away to Plymouth; a long trip and he had neither the time nor inclination for such a journey. He had a lot on his mind. His father's muggers, no murderers, the Chessman, the strawberry blonde, even his footballing days were coming to an end.

Playing for the Casuals had been fun and fulfilling but lately he had begun to miss training sessions and his bones ached for hours after every match. He wondered if he could see out the season the way things were going. He might not be left with the choice. It was a conundrum. Want to play and not get picked, don't want to play, get picked to play, don't play and you miss the buzz, the rush, adrenalin, play and you probably let everyone down and ache all over to boot.

No, he was being too hard on himself. He was still an integral part of the team. Together with his lawyer friend Toby they formed the defensive stability the team needed. He had known Toby from school, some twenty-six years ago and they had remained friends all that time.

Both Mike and Toby once could have played in a much higher grade of the game. Not the highest maybe but a much higher level. Both had chosen different arms of the law. The similarity ended there. Toby was now married, with two small children, a dog, a cat and probably a goldfish. Mike wasn't sure about the goldfish. At least he was fit for tomorrow's cup game. He lit up, and watched the scores. City had lost.

CHAPTER 11

Sunday, the 16th November, and all was well at the Jones' residence in Taffs Well. They had attended Chapel and now were reading the Sunday Papers. For Evan 'The Times' and Edna, 'The Mail'. For lunch Edna was making roast beef, Yorkshire puddings, roast potatoes, peas and carrots. A nice white was cooling in the fridge. They would eat about one, one thirty and then Evan would relax in front of the TV and watch the rugger. It was going to be a very good day.

Amber was also cooking. She had invited Sergeant Jane and her husband to dinner. She was also cooking a joint of beef. It was at least three times the size of the Jones's. Amber was worried. Would it be enough? No wine, but a few crates of Red Stripe lager would complement the roast. Actually according to Amber, Red Stripe would complement any food and it tasted just as good without food. Yes, definitely, Amber was on her third!

For Special Detective Investigator Mikhail Karetzi the day had also started well. A brisk walk to the local newsagents for cigarettes, then down to his local coffee bar where he could read all the papers over an espresso or two, whilst talking to Emma, a waitress, whom he had fancied for a long time. Unfortunately, until today Emma had given him no encouragement. Mike left a good tip and returned to his apartment and prepared his football gear.

They were playing at Llantrisant about half an hour away; kick off 3 p.m. He would leave about two o'clock. Mike was always early for a match which was strange as he was always late for everything else he did.

Bill Priestly, a small bespectacled man of fifty-one had driven his Volvo from his home in nearby Wenvoe down to the knap in Barry. He had done so every day for the last two weeks roughly at the same time. It was cold and drizzly but inside the car it was perfect; warm and secure.

Since the divorce, six years ago, he had thrown himself into building up his small innovative instrument manufacturing factory and built it up. Large freehold premises, sixty odd staff and fully trained. Financially strong, he was in a very good position, but how much further could he take it and did he want to?

The offer from Nakimoto Heavy Industries was very fair. The workforce would be kept intact, apart from the other three directors who would be well compensated. As for himself, he would clear well over three million pounds. He could do everything he ever wanted. The problem here was that he didn't know what exactly he wanted. He could return to his roots in North London, take a cruise or two.

Tomorrow was deadline day. He had to make a decision by midday tomorrow. High Noon.

He reversed the car into a parking place overlooking the pebbly beach and facing the sea. It must be one of the most beautiful spots anywhere, he thought. The tide was in and there were only two other cars. The nearest was parked over forty yards away to his left.

He fiddled around with the radio until he located the station that he wanted. A huge container ship was coming down the River Severn, heading for the Atlantic. It could even be one of NHI's. Now that would be some omen, if it was.

The live commentary was coming from White Hart Lane. Spurs, his team, were playing a local derby against their, and his, hated rivals, Arsenal.

The ref obliged and blew. The drizzle persisted like a weeping boil. Just when you think the puss is out, it starts again, little by little. Bill didn't want to put his windscreen wipers on. They made too much noise and he wanted to listen to the game.

Out of the corner of his eye he could see a hooded figure, knapsack on his back, walking slowly in his direction. He was reading or trying to read something that looked like a map. Bill dismissed the person out of his mind. Probably some day-tripper who'd lost his bearings.

Goal, just three minutes on the clock and Spurs had scored. At that very moment Bill made his decision. He would sell. From now on he would watch his beloved Hotspurs, live. Yes, live. He settled down to follow the game, a weight off his mind.

In the mud and rain at Llantrisant, there had been another goal. The Casuals were one down and Mike Karetzi was gutted because he was at fault. He had been suckered into a challenge on the big opposing centre forward, a mistimed challenge which had resulted in a penalty.

Mike and Toby were having a torrid time against the No. 9; he was all elbows and small cynical fouls on the blind side of the ref, who was the opposition's secret weapon, their twelfth man. The second goal came fifteen minutes later. The No. 9 had dived like a Kingfisher after fish. No one was anywhere near him. Another penalty 2-0. Mike tried to keep calm. He'd already been booked but when the big No. 9 left his leg trailing causing a bad injury to his friend Toby, Mike began to see red. The whole situation was getting out of hand and the ref was doing nothing. It was time to redress the balance and give the centre forward a dose of his own medicine and that Doctor Karetzi decided he would personally dispense.

The Chessman stopped about thirty feet from the Volvo. He sat on the sea wall separating beach from tarmac and spread out a map, his back to the car. Mr Priestly was alone in the car. He had been on all of the occasions that Peter had followed him. Everything was going to plan. The Volvo was hidden from the many flats overlooking the beach by a grass bank. The nearest car was fifty yards away and for some absurd reason the Volvo's windscreen wipers were not on. He hoped that Mr Priestly hadn't dozed off unless he'd left the car unlocked.

Brian, the name he had selected for the Barry operation, carefully selected one of the millions of pebbles on the beach. It had to be the right size and weight. Small enough to hold, big enough to kill.

He put the pebble into the large left pocket of his hooded nylon anorak and half folded his map. His leather gloves served two purposes. One was to keep his hands warm, the other to protect his fingers from leaving any prints.

Brian, looking less than his real years, slowly sauntered towards the Volvo, map in hand, pebble in pocket. Bill Priestly saw that the person with the map was now nearly upon him. He wanted to get rid of the intruder as fast as possible, so that he could listen to the game in peace.

Activating one of the levers on his dashboard he electronically lowered his side window. "Are you lost?" Bill asked.

"I'm not sure," said the stranger. "I'm looking for Porthkerry Park. It's around here somewhere." Barry looked at his map as if puzzled.

"Who's playing?" Brian asked as if interested. He didn't care a hoot but it seemed the right thing to say as he waited for the right moment to strike.

"Spurs and Arsenal, and we, I mean Spurs are winning. Porthkerry Park is over that way," said Bill, poking his head out of the window and pointing. That was a big mistake. Brian smashed the pebble with such force that Bill's head split like a watermelon in a press. One blow was enough Bill was gone. As Brian pushed Bill's head back through the window Arsenal scored and drew level. He threw the severed bishop's chess piece head and tossed it through the open window onto the victim's lap, together with the blooded stone. Priestley's spectacles fell off.

Brian, The Chessman, took one more glance, turned and walked away in the direction of Porthkerry Park. He'd only taken a few steps when he heard a roar. Arsenal had scored again.

It was turning out to be a bad day for Spurs' supporters, especially for Bill Priestly. Brian took off his knapsack, opened it and removed a damp cloth with which he cleaned the spots of blood from his nylon anorak. He replaced the damp cloth together with his gloves and map into the knapsack. He kept on walking and passed in front of another car in which a young couple were necking.

It was an old Mini and the windows were all steamed up as were the young couple who paid him no attention. They had better things to do. Brian smiled.

As he neared the end of the beach, he came to a small pitch and putt golf course. He took the small concrete path for thirty yards and then cut to the right, a steep set of over a hundred steps in a heavily wooded area.

Halfway up he ducked behind some thick bushes and Barry emerged as Uncle Paul and within twenty minutes he was back to the car which was parked outside a ruin they called Barry Castle.

Mr Priestly's body was discovered by a man walking his dog. The Chessman was nearing the motorway by then.

In Flat No. 17, Evan was watching the rugby when the phone rang. Edna was in the kitchen, still loading the dishwasher. It had been a great meal and Evan felt a little bloated and slightly tipsy. The wine had gone down very well but he rose and walked over to the phone. It was probably Jasmine, his daughter It wasn't, it was Amber. She sounded agitated, very unlike her. "Evan?"

"Yes, Amber, anything wrong? You sound distant."

"I've just received a call from Barry Police Station. The Chessman has just claimed another victim, down on the Knap. Do you know where that is?"

"I do," replied Evan. "Have you contacted Mike?"

"I can't Evan. He's playing football in Llantrisant and his phone is off."

"Okay, Amber, leave it to me. I'll contact you later."

"What's happening Evan? Why are you putting on your shoes and jacket?" Evan explained to his wife. "You're over the limit, Evan. You can't drive."

"I'll call a taxi."

"It will take too long love. I'll just rinse out my mouth with that mouthwash and be off. Time is of the essence. I need to pick up Mike and get down to Barry." And with that he left.

Even as he was driving Evan felt uneasy. All week he had been breaking some law or other and now to top it all he was driving whilst under the influence of drink. What next, drugs?

Halfway through the second half, the Casuals still 2-0 down, Karetzi seized his opportunity. The big lumbering oaf of a man masquerading as a centre forward bore down on Mike, ball at his feet and that was the last thing he remembered for over an hour. The two broken ribs would stay with him for a long time, as would the missing teeth.

Mike saw red and the ref showed Mike red. Mike's team mates applauded him off, as did a few of the opposition but in an ironic way. As he trundled off Mike saw Evan, who had just that minute arrived. He picked up his pace and met Evan on the touchline.

"Let's go Mike, you're driving, no time to explain."

The forty or so spectators, mostly home fans booed as Mike walked towards the tin shed which they used as dressing rooms.

"Come on Mike."

"All right Evan, let me at least put on a pair of trousers."

Mike took off his boots and shorts. He put on his jeans and shoes, threw everything else into his kit bag. On the way out he put on his watch, small gold cross and with leather jacket in one hand and kit bag in the other they walked towards Mike's car.

"Where you going Mike?"

"To my car, Evan. Leave the BMW here. We can pick it up later. Where we headed?"

"Barry, Mike."

Mike gunned the car and they sped off towards Barry. It was half past four, just over an hour since the victim had been found.

Evan explained. Karetzi lit a cigarette. He ached all over. He needed to rub some oil into his calf. He also needed a shower and to change his football shirt which was covered in mud and blood. He laughed out loud. Mike had just remembered that he was still wearing his football socks and shin-guards.

It had been a long time since Mike had been to Barry. His father took him to Barry Island when he was six or seven. He remembered that big beautiful sandy beach on the island but couldn't quite place where the Knap was.

Mike followed the signs, past the huge Dow Corning Chemical Plant on the left and onto the Ffordd y Mileniwm. To the right, the impressive Dock Offices with the statue of David Davies who built Barry docks over a hundred years ago, dominated the front of the building.

To the left of Barry Docks, two ships were in: one discharging timber, the other loading scrap metal. Hundreds of new apartments on what had been the Docks' storage area. It was now named 'The Waterfront'.

Mike crossed the Gladstone Bridge and turned left into Broad Street which he followed, leaving Barry Station on the left. A few minutes later they had arrived at the edge of a harp-shaped man-made lake. To the side were a few shops, cafes and restaurants.

More apartments overlooked the sea and they were on the promenade of the Pebble Beach which ran from Cold Knap Point past Bullnose Cliff and onto Porthkerry Bay. Mike parked as near to the cordoned off crime scene as was possible.

A Chief Inspector, a DI, four constables, a SOCO team, a photographer who had obviously just finished, a young couple, an old man and his dog were at the scene.

"Understand that you are the Specials running this case?" said the Chief Inspector who introduced himself as Tony Brand. Mike nodded. "This is D.I. Haggarty. That is Mr Evans who found the body and the couple over there think they saw the killer. Medical bloke's just left, murder weapon's a pebble, still in the car; time of death about 15.30 give or take five minutes," added Chief Inspection Brand.

"I'll be off now. D.I. Haggarty will be on hand to help you," and with that he left.

"In a rush were we?" asked D.I. Haggarty, looking at Mike from top to bottom. "Where do you wish to begin?"

"Let's start with the radio, shall we?" said Mike.

"Okay," replied Haggarty. "What about it?"

"Was it on when the body was found?"

"Yes, it was."

"Which station?"

"BBC Five Live."

"Good, could you please switch it off," said Mike. D.I. Haggarty did.

"Next, do we have an ID on the victim?"

"We do, a Mr Bill Priestly, address in Wenvoe. Next of kin has been notified. Still trying to locate his ex-wife who lives somewhere in South East Kent I think."

"Where's the chess piece?"

"Still on his lap, Sir."

"A pawn's head I suppose?"

"No, it's actually a bishop's head," replied Haggarty.

"What else do we know about the victim?"

"This is his card," Haggarty said, passing it over to Evan.

"It's Tom, isn't it?"

"Yep."

"I'm Mike and this is Evan. Look Tom, please don't be fooled by my appearance. I may be wearing a football shirt but I can assure you that I can read." Mike took the card out of Evan's hand.

Tom reddened. "Sorry, I didn't mean to offend you Mike."

Mike read the card. B J PRIESTLY, Managing Director, Priestly Instruments and Electronics, telephone number, fax and address followed.

"Ever heard of PIE, Evan?"

"No, Mike."

"You Tom?"

"Yes, the company is situated just outside Barry, near the airport. It's been news in the local papers recently. I think it's being sold or has received a large offer from some Japanese firm. I've got a copy of this week's paper in my car if you want it."

"Thanks Tom," said Mike.

Tom turned and walked to his car. Evan looked at Mike. "Let's assume this guy is rich. So, the Chessman leaves a back row chess piece. A bishop because of the name Priestly. Obviously not random, premeditated, but how did he know that this Priestly guy would be here, at this time and in such a spot, well hidden from all those apartments?"

"I can't answer the last part, Evan, and I agree with all your other points. Here comes Tom with the paper. Let's talk to the witnesses before we all catch pneumonia. I'll take the old man, you the couple, but first I suggest we get a good look at the victim and inside the car."

The detectives walked to the car. The victim was sitting in the driver's seat, head to the side. The blood had coagulated. It was everywhere. His plain grey tie was now a red polka dot and grey tie. The window was fully down.

Twenty minutes later the three D.I.s sat together in one of the Parade's coffee servicing shops. Mike had used the shop's facility to change his shirt, wash and generally tidy himself up. After two coffees Evan was feeling as right as the rain beating down on the large shop's front window. He read and re-read the article that Tom had marked in his newspaper. From what he could gather poor old Priestly had everything to live for. Mike returned and sat down, his legs aching. He stood again, opened the door and lit up.

"Is he okay?" Tom asked Evan.

"He's fine Tom."

"Isn't he the cop they call Crazy? I've heard about him. He's a hero to some of the boys and girls. Yes, most of the girls."

"One and the same, Tom, but he does have method in his madness," said Evan laughing. Tom joined in. He liked these people. They were open and honest, not like sour-faced Brand.

Mike finished his fag, threw the butt into a pool of water which had formed near the pavement, watching it disintegrate.

A car, music blaring, passed at speed and splashed water all over his shirt and trousers. He was just too tired to react in time. He sighed, shook his trouser legs one at a time and re-entered the café. "Not my day Evan. First I get sent off, first time in my life, then the bloody Chessman business and now I get soaked just after changing shirts."

"It could be worse," said Evan.

"Could it?" answered Mike. It did; the establishment's espresso machine had broken down, so Mike was forced to drink instant.

"What did the young couple have to say Evan?"

"Well Mike, not much really. They were sitting in the car about 50 yards from the victim. Their car was steamed up. They were canoodling. They thought a man in a hooded anorak, carrying a knapsack passed by them walking towards the park in the opposite direction of the lake. That's it, Mike. They gave Tom a description of his clothes but they saw nothing."

"And you, how did you get on with the old man?"

"Not much there either, I'm afraid. Mr Rodgers was walking his sheepdog Alfie along the prom. The dog sniffed something and ran up to Mr Priestly's car, barking. Mr Rodgers who lives nearby tried calling his dog to come back but Alfie just stood there barking. Eventually Mr Rodgers went over to see why the dog was barking and discovered the body. From his cell phone he contacted the local boys, Tom here."

Tom nodded. "We got the call at five past four. We were on the scene within five minutes."

"Look Tom, there's blood everywhere in the car. On the victim's clothes, outside the car. The murderer must have blood all over him. Surely someone must have noticed him walking to wherever he had stashed his car," said Evan.

"We're doing a house to house; nothing so far. Remember," Tom looked at his notes, "this man was wearing what the couple describe as a dark nylon anorak. Even with a handkerchief or tissue he could clean up a nylon jacket."

"True Tom."

"Did this couple notice his shoes, what type of shoes?" Mike asked.

"No, no mention of footwear, Mike."

"Someone must have noticed him before he struck. He didn't parachute in, did he?"

"We're asking, Evan, but we're not getting. It's as if this guy is invisible, a phantom. He appears, kills and disappears."

"Tom, have you checked train stations, bus stations, taxis? Hooded knapsack carriers would stand out."

"Being checked out as we speak. Don't hold your breath though," added Tom. He'd read some of the Chessman files.

Tom didn't want to say it, but the two detectives sitting at his table might be good but they were no match for this Chessman bloke.

Evan paid the bill. "Thanks, Tom, keep us informed. Send us statements, photos, etc., to the address I gave you. Oh, and please send us the pebble and medical report." Mike added.

"Will do," said Tom, walking out into the rain and towards his car. They want the pebble, he thought. Well, they do call him Crazy Karetzi. The pebble, one of millions, and they wanted the bloody pebble.

As Mike drove back towards Llantrisant to pick up the BMW, Evan summarised the murder scene as he thought it played out. Mike concentrated on driving. It was still raining and was very dark but Mike listened to what his partner was saying.

"The Chessman pretends to be a rambler, twitcher, holiday maker, anyway an 'out of towner'. He's probably holding a local map or something. He approaches Mr Priestly's car on the pretext of asking directions. Priestly opens his window to see what the stranger wants. For some reason he puts his head outside the window. We know that from the blood on the outside of the car. Yes, he puts his head outside the window either to look carefully at a map or to direct the stranger. The Chessman already has the pebble in his pocket. He's probably wearing gloves. Bang, one hard downward movement and Priestley's dead.

"The Chessman shoves the victim's head back through the open window, tosses the Bishop's head and the pebble into the car and walks away. The nearest car is fifty yards away. The young couple are otherwise engrossed in whatever. Their windows misted up and any noise that Priestly might have made is drowned out by the radio."

"Ten out of ten, Evan, but to earn a star you must come up with a motive."

"Do you know, Mike, that I would love to come up with a motive just as much as I would love to know why no-one seems to notice him before and after he strikes."

As they arrived at the car park, just off the football ground, Evan asked, "How will the pebble help us, Mike?"

"It won't as such Evan. I just want to hold it, feel it, get some idea of how big his hands are."

"I see," said Evan, but he didn't really.

Mike let Evan out and waited for him to drive off before leaving himself. Evan drove carefully. He still wasn't sure if he would pass a breathalyser test. He made it back to Taffs Well without being put to the test.

The Chessman was back home too. After burning the anorak, cleaning his shoes and washing his shirt and trousers, he relaxed, opened a beer, ginger beer, and caught the news. He was the star again but only he knew it. The invisible star. He toasted himself and of course, Brian Barry.

CHAPTER 12

A new day, a new week. The four of them sat around the three desks in the office. Three of them were smoking, one eating. They discussed yesterday's events. It had been the first that the team had been directly involved with from the start.

The main topic of discussion was not who, but why. Why, why, why?

They did agree that the Chessman's richer victims were premeditated. The others random killings. Why? You can't blackmail the dead. The dead can't pay up.

They talked and talked, killing time before the meeting.

A mile away, Mr Brian, Professor John Benson, Doctor Terry Elwin, together with Chief Constable Clarke sat around the breakfast table. All the other hotel guests were finished and gone about their daily work. Mr Brian phoned the Director; the fifth time that morning.

That Nakamura was involved somehow now seemed indisputable to all except Mr Brian, even after yesterday's connection. "So, Chief, you'll have to attend the meeting. Don't you agree?" said the Professor. "This has gone on far too long. We need to set the wheels in motion and set the trap." The Chief reluctantly agreed.

At precisely ten they entered the office. The Doctor could smell the smoke. He saw the ashtrays. He was about to comment when D.I. Karetzi held out his hand. "Welcome to our house Doctor Elwin." Mike put a huge emphasis on the word house.

The Doctor was disarmed. How did he know I was the Doctor and not the Professor and is he trying to tell me that in one's own house, one can smoke? They said these people were smart but were they smart or lucky? Probably both.

After the introductions, the men went upstairs. The women, Jane and Amber, were not invited. "I guess we're not a safe house anymore Mr Brian," said Evan.

"Why do you say that S.D.I. Jones?" replied Mr B. Evan just glanced at the Chief in full uniform. "I get you, in a way you're right. All will be explained," said Mr Brian.

"Doctor Elwin, our eminent criminologist will lay the foundations of the case as we know it," the doctor began. He had a loud voice and obviously liked hearing himself. "I will not bore you with statistics but there are four types of male serial killers.

"We have what we call 'the visionary'. These are usually psychotic, i.e. Mentally deranged. They suffer from hallucinations. They kill randomly and spontaneously, are disorganised and typically concentrate in one area.

"The second type is the 'Power Killer'. All that motivates this killer is the desire to have control or the power of life and death over the victim.

"Next is 'the Missionary', a man with a mission to rid the world of particular groups. These groups usually include one of the following: gays, prostitutes, drug dealers, users and religious groups. Those he deems undesirable. He is usually organised and plans his murders.

"Last, but not least, are the hedonistic serial killers. Lust, sex and violence walk hand in hand with these killers. Part of this group is the thrill. Killers who keep their victim alive as long as possible in order to relish their suffering. Sadism and mutilations can be linked to all of the hedonistic group. You will obviously have noticed that a certain type of serial killer is missing from the last group. That of the contract or comfort killer. Those who kill for material or financial gain.

"Our Mr Chessman is without doubt a contract killer. Paid to kill. I will pass you over to the Professor."

"Thank you Terry. That was well summarised. We have the motive but only the Chessman's financial gain, but who is the paymaster and what's his motive? Again as you will see it's money and power.

"You probably have not been able to make the connections between the victims because it's not really obvious to people not familiar with the intricate world of high finance. What goes on behind the closed doors of large corporations. How they think. How they work. How they get an edge on their rivals. What sums of money are involved. Who pulls the strings and so on.

"As head of the Business and Financial department, of the Special National Security Office, my work usually centres around fraud, industrial espionage, money laundering, off-shore banking, dicey financial dealings, takeovers. I could go on but you are all wondering, that is, the two detectives here are wondering, what the hell this has got to do with the Chessman. Well, let me tell you, it has everything to do with the Chessman, but first let me go back to the connections.

"Including yesterday, we have nine known victims of the Chessman of which six, yes six, or two out of every three, are connected. The connection is the aerospace industry. Before you interrupt me, let me tell you that the other three, the unconnected three, are red herrings. A very clever ploy to throw us off the real reasons for these murders."

Like a schoolboy Evan raised his hand. "Yes, detective? Would you like to say something?"

"I would Professor. Why were we being bugged? Where does that come into it?"

"There are reasons which we will come to at the end.

"Jason Roberts, Abergele, Technical Analyst BAe. George Williams, Dinas Powys, Solicitor. We will come back to him in a minute. Joseph Hanson, Machynileth. I hope I have pronounced that correctly. It's pretty hard for an Englishman. Anyway you know where I mean. Unemployed, but previously about six months or so had been Manager of specialised military clothing company manufacturers.

"Sir Edward Pettiford, biggest shareholder in PM Electronics, Manufacturers of Radar, Echo sounders and other air and marine equipment.

"Alan Carver, Tenby, Technical Researcher mainly for the military, Newbridge Engineering Ltd. Bill Priestly, Barry, Managing Director and Founder of Priestly's Instruments and Electronics, makers of all fine aircraft equipment. It is common knowledge that he was sitting on a massive offer from Nakamura Heavy Industrial. The solicitors, Messrs Williams, Wright and Reynolds were acting for NHI. George Williams, our Dinas Powys victim, was one of the senior partners.

"Those are the facts. What you don't know is that apart from making a substantial offer for Priestly's company they have also last week made a bid to buy out Newbridge Engineering and fifteen months ago they had a go for Pettifords, an unsuccessful one, but from what we understand they have not given up.

"No doubt about it, with Sir Edward gone and without Mr Priestly at the helm of PIE both these companies are vulnerable to a takeover."

Again, Jones raised a hand. "How do NHI profit by owning or controlling these companies?"

"In a nutshell, by owning these companies and amalgamating them with the companies they have in the UK and France, they will virtually control the European market in Marine and Aircraft specialised instrument and sonic equipment manufacturing industry," said the Professor. "I can give you figures and estimations of potential profits. We're talking about hundreds of millions of dollars if they get it right."

A rapping on the door curtailed any further conversation. Jane entered with about six A4 size typed papers which she handed to DI Karetzi who was nearest to her. "Best we could do in the time. Hope it helps," she said as she left.

Everyone looked at DI Karetzi who spoke. "Now Mr Brian, what about the bugging business? Can we have our explanation?"

"It's best that I answer," said the Professor. "It's been three weeks since we discovered the connection. We had been monitoring NHI for other matters which do not concern you and found a pattern which we subsequently followed down this very winding path.

"For obvious reasons we couldn't just walk into their European head office, which is incidentally in London, and confront them with our findings, so we looked for another means. If Mohamed won't go to the mountain, blah, blah, blah.

"Through various channels at our disposal we were about to leak certain information to NHI; part of that info was that a Special Force had been formed in Cardiff specifically to look into the various aspects of Nakamura's trade and finances in the UK. It would also mention that certain documentation of a highly classified nature was being stored there and that they concerned NHI target companies in Wales."

"And I guess we're the Special Force and we just wait for something to happen. Like what?"

"That we don't know D.I. Jones, but we were prepared for the worst. We had twenty- four hour surveillance; seven operatives within a minute of this building."

"So now you can see that you have set us back somewhat and we badly need to restore our systems as they were."

"I would like to point out that your Chief Constable was not aware of the real reasons for the set up here until a few hours ago."

Chief Constable Clarke rose: "As I said in the hotel, I agree with the idea, but it should be left to my men to decide whether or not they wish to remain as bait. Why not use your own people, Mr Brian?"

"I'll tell you Chief, I'm getting my orders from a high authority. I have made it clear that I'm not convinced by a long way that NHI has hired out a contract killer we call the Chessman. It doesn't make any sense."

Mike lit up, as did Evan. The Doctor, Terry Elwin sniffed the air and waved his hand in front of his face up and down. "Would you like me to open a window Doctor? You seem uncomfortable."

"Yes, I would. It is a very bad habit you both have and as a doctor I would advise you both to give up the filthy habit."

Mike moved to the window and opened it. "I think Doctor Elwin, you are correct on the smoking front. Actually, I know you are right but on this NHI business I'm afraid you and the Prof here are to my mind way out. I think I speak for my partner also. Japanese Instruments, high finance, absolute nonsense. In less than one week we have narrowed down a good identity of the Chessman. His build, height, the fact that he is left-handed, that he lives in Swansea to the north of the city and that it's our guess, more than a guess, that he is working for himself. He is not a contract killer."

"And his motive, Detective, is what?" said the Professor. Mike didn't answer, he couldn't. "I thought so," said the Professor.

Evan then spoke. "All you have are a few coincidences, nothing more."

"Look Detective, five of the best men in this line of work have worked for nearly a month to make the connections: experts, London-based, top men. Myself and Terry have led this team. We were ninety-nine point nine per cent certain before yesterday. Now we're one hundred and one per cent certain that NHI are behind all these murders. Would you agree detectives that a contract killer may live in Swansea, may be left-handed, may fit your height and build, etc.?"

Evan and Mike conceded that the Professor was right. After all, Evan thought, there is no law that states serial killers cannot live in Swansea or anywhere else but the laws state that if caught serial killers are jailed for life.

What a bloody load of nonsense, Evan concluded. Mike would have agreed.

It looked to the Chief Constable that the Prof and Doc were getting through. Would the Detectives agree to hang on in as bait? He was soon to find out.

"May I tell you gentlemen why you have wasted four weeks and so much manpower and come up with a load of rubbish?" said Mike.

"And a whole amount of money," added Evan. "We could have done a door-to-door in our Swansea area with the money you've pissed away."

The doctor's eyes flashed anger and frustration. Were these peasants so completely detached from reality or were they just plain stupid? He cleared his throat. "Detectives, have you understood what the Professor and I are saying? What the experts are saying? What is obvious to all but you two?"

The professor looked at Evan. "Surely D.I. Jones, you at your age of life can grasp the finer details of our case. It's simple enough. I'd like to take you through the connections again, but is it really necessary?"

"No, it isn't," piped up Mike.

"Thank God for that," muttered the good doctor. "At last our friends see sense."

"That we do," countered Mike. "But do you? There lies the problem. People like you and the Prof," said Mike, looking directly at the Doctor, "usually find what you look for and usually hear what you're listening for but in this case you've found out the wrong things and heard the wrong things and two wrongs don't make a right."

Oh, Christ, thought Evan, here we go again. What was Mike on about?

Up until now Mr B had been a casual spectator. His had to be the calm voice of reason. He had to bring this meeting to some sensible conclusion. But how? Common-sense had to prevail.

"Look John, Terry, let the detectives try and prove our theories are wrong. You've both said your piece. The Chief is as open-minded, as am I. Let's see what the detectives say, shall we?" The Chief nodded his approval.

The Professor needed a rest from arguing his point. "Let them speak Terry. It should be interesting to hear counter-arguments even if they are wrong. We have a duty to listen."

Terry defiantly crossed his arms but sat down ready to hear another load of mumbo jumbo. He could hardly follow what the young trendy one was on about. He hoped the older one, Jones, would do the talking. He didn't get his wish.

Karetzi stood up and just to annoy the doctor, lit up. He actually didn't feel like one at the moment but it was worth it, just to see the doctor's face.

"My father, a decent, hardworking man with principles, was born in Russia. In his native country they have a saying which I think, with all due respect to the learned Professor and the good Doctor, applies to them and their team of experts.

"The saying covers your theories perfectly. It is 'There's none so blind as those who don't want to see'. In other words you only see what suits you and discard what does not. Let's take the solicitor, George Williams. You state as a fact that Mr Williams was acting on behalf of these NHI people. His firm was, that is correct but Mr Williams was not representing his firm." Mike shuffled through the papers that Sergeant Jane handed him. One of the partner's, Mr Rodney Wright, together with his assistant Janet Briggs actually handled the account.

"Take Priestly of Priestly Instruments. Three co-directors who, between them, have twenty-five per cent of the shares, all say that the offer from NHI was too good to turn down and that they were sure that Mr Priestly would have sold. He'd indicated as much to them. The deadline for signing was noon today.

"Yes, NHI were turned down by Sir Edward Pettiford a while back but only because they, the Japanese, would not allow Sir Edward to remain as Chairman for three years and it seems that Newbridge Engineering has accepted NHI's offer in principle."

Mike consulted his notes again. "Then we have the Abergele victim, Jason Roberts, a widower. This man was emigrating to Brisbane, Australia, in mid-January to be with his sister.

"As for Joe Hanson in Machynileth, he was sacked for being continuously drunk at work where they made military uniforms; big deal. Hardly something of importance to one of the world's largest corporations turning over billions of dollars yearly.

"In the UK alone NHI own, let's see, eighteen companies. In France, seven. Mexico, Brazil, USA, Canada, South Africa. Do I need to go on?

"They have the muscle to buy virtually any company they want. According to all the financial statements we have accessed they are going from strength to strength. Half a billion is like loose change to them.

"To say that someone in an organisation as large and powerful as theirs would hire a hit man is just ridiculous. It's ludicrous. I say go back to London, stop wasting the taxpayer's money and leave the detective work to the detectives. Eventually we will get the Chessman and I'll bet you he won't be wearing a kimono."

The professor was stunned into silence. In his briefcase he had over two hundred pages of proof that NHI were behind the murders and other wrongdoings. He slowly opened his case, took out the documents and slowly placed them on the table.

"This is the proof that NHI is using shady tactics and doing dodgy deals. Most of them could be classified as illegal or at best borderline in legal terms. Take a look Detective, see for yourself."

"We don't need to, Prof," said Evans. "What you have there are the mechanics of how big business is done at that level. Those who don't break all the rules fall by the wayside. It's dog eat dog when you're in the top league."

"May I ask one more question?" said Evan. No-one answered. "Are you a Doctor of Medicine, Doctor Elwin?"

"No," was the brusque reply. Mr Brian smiled inwardly. He liked the old Prof and the Doc was okay but as he knew all along, they'd fucked right up. He knew it was nonsense as did probably the Director but there was that one per cent chance. Where the hell did these boys get their information? Another knock on the door. It was Amber with a tray of sandwiches. Jane with a tray of cakes and cold drinks. "I thought you might be having a break by now. I hope that's okay."

After laying down the trays, she beckoned Mike and Evan into the kitchen. "There are three big sports clubs in the Swansea vicinity, two have indoor tennis courts. They also have bowls, squash, snooker tables, golf courses, swimming pools, bars, restaurants and about eight thousand members in one and six and a half in the other."

"Any chance of getting…?"

"No way Mike, Data Protection Act."

"What about one of our so-called friendly Judges?"

"Again, no way. Way too big a warrant. To search a house or building we can swing it, but a powerful sporting organisation, no."

"Thanks, Amber, and thanks again for the notes. They saved the day," said Evan.

Mr B came into the kitchen. "Anything I can do? I have a feeling that you've killed the NHI business stone dead."

"I hope so; a waste of time as you rightly said. What happens now Mr B?"

"I'm not sure Evan."

"Will they close us down?"

"I doubt it, Evan."

"The Chief and I agree that you should carry on. There's a serial murderer out there."

After finishing the sandwiches Evan lit his pipe. Mike just sat thinking. How was he going to trace that Chalky White fellow? Was he still living in Cardiff or had he returned to London?

What was the pub called where all the petty conmen and thieves gathered together with the fences and other low-life? He'd remember. It would come to him. He had a job for Chalky, who owed him big time.

The sandwiches were finished and Evan cleared the remains away into the kitchen. The good doctor however was not finished. He returned his attention to the matter in hand. He did not want to lose face. He scanned his notes. These two detectives had some valid points but they had one flaw in their ideas. Back to motive. They readily admitted that they had found no motive, whereas the Prof and he did. It had been shot down by the detectives but it was the best thing that was on the table. It was the only one.

"Motive, gentlemen. We have a motive: greed, financial gain, power. We must not dismiss NHI. I will concede that maybe the Corporation's top men are not involved, but the guys running things over here would be in a position to do something off their own backs. Is that correct John? I mean, have they a lot to gain personally: promotion, better salary, better standing in their own social placing."

"Possibly Terry but who and where did they get the money to pay for a contract killer?"

"Slush funds John. We know how these people work. Untraceable, ready-to-hand money."

Evan didn't want to completely demoralise the team from London but the farce would not continue.

"Look, why don't you in London follow that angle? I think you'll be wasting good time and I'm sure that you have bigger and more important cases to crack. We will just plod on down here and see if we can get a result. Is that correct Chief?"

"Yes, Evan, I will now be your reporting station. If necessary, I will pass on any information to London. We're set up now. We have the team and we're making progress," added the Chief.

Mr B agreed. "I will confer with the Director soonest and make sure that your team is left to carry on as they are. We will see ourselves out. Again, Detectives, you know how to contact me if I can help you in any way."

After the three from London had departed, the Chief sat back in his chair. "What do you boys need?"

"We need some luck Chief," Mike said. "We need a break and the Prof is right, we need to have a motive or catch the bastard red-handed."

"Do you think we will hear anything more from London Chief?"

"I think Brian is an ally. He could be very useful to both yourselves and me. I will stay in touch and keep him informed."

"Give me regular updates. Amber can contact me. By the way, what do you think of her?"

"She's the best," said Evan.

"Better than that," said Mike.

"And the new girl, Sergeant Williams?"

"Coming along fine Chief; a good asset. Her husband helped out too. He debugged this place Chief," said Evan.

"One thing more Chief: we need some membership lists from a couple of sports clubs. Can you help?"

"Sorry boys, no go. I doubt if even Brian could get them to give you access to personal data of their members."

The Chief left. Amber and Jane entered. Evan told them what had happened. What was said, by whom, when, the conclusion and next time, if Amber could make more egg and cress sandwiches, as the non-medical doctor had eaten most of them.

"What now then?" Amber asked. "We've exhausted all our leads except possibly these sports centres. Let's go down Mike."

"And do what?" replied Mike.

"See if we can find any left-handed bowlers or tennis players?"

"Well, we should have a look round, take a few pictures, talk to the receptionist, manager, see if we can learn anything."

"Right mate, you drive. Evan and Amber and Jane, please do me a favour. Try and locate a Charles Frederick White, better known as Chalky White. White male, born East End London, age about thirty, cat burglar. Did a spell in nick. Will be on file. Ask around. All these types of low-life drink somewhere and pass around information."

Mike and Evan left. Within an hour they had reached the first of their destinations. Both started taking pictures on their mobiles and Evan was also carrying a small camera which he used for the long range shots.

In London all was not well. The Director had received the accounts to date. Nearly two hundred and fifty thousand pounds had been thrown at this Nakamura business and was still rising.

The head of accounts had joined the Professor, Doctor and Mr B and the Director. Two jugs of water were already on the table and five glasses. Agnes, the accountant, guessed that the Director was already trying to stem the flow of money going out. No coffee, tea, soft drinks; a saving of at least ten pounds calculated.

"What a bloody farce, Brian! What a fucking farce. Sorry, John, but I am lost for words. Do you know how much money we've poured down the drain, because I do."

Agnes kept her mouth shut as she would do throughout the meeting. After all, she didn't authorise the spending on all that technical stuff. She was the accountant but someone else was going to have to pay for this disaster.

"I still believe, Mr Director, that we have something. My gut feeling tells me that Nakamura is still involved," said Doctor Elwin." "And so does the Professor. We have the documentation."

The Director was in a very angry mood. He felt like telling the Doctor to eat his bloody documentation, then maybe he'd have a different gut feeling. He managed to refrain. "Brian, what can I say? Mr Director and I were unconvinced before our trip to Wales and nothing has changed."

"I hear you Brian."

"Tell me, John, how could these boys destroy four weeks' work in less than four minutes? Did they have information we didn't? If so, why and where did they obtain it from?"

"They interpreted the information in a different way to us and in all truth they came up with more up-to-date info, all of which helped them break our theory." The Professor lent forward and spoke quietly. "Even when we were in the meeting, they were talking to people."

"Who was talking to whom?"

"The detectives in front of you," Brian interjected. "I think that John means that the two women downstairs were contacting people."

"You mean this Gilberts woman and this Sergeant Jane?"

"Yes Sir," said Brian.

"And who did they contact and why was that important Brian?"

"They found out that the solicitor Williams did not personally handle NHI work, one of his partner's did."

"So why eliminate him?"

"Plus the fact that Mr Priestly according to his partners was ninety-nine per cent agreeable to the sale. The deadline for such sale being less than a day away."

"Why kill Priestly then?"

"The guy in Abergele was emigrating to Australia in a month. Everyone in the firm knew that, as would NHI if they had wanted to. Mr Hanson, an unemployed alcoholic – what kind of threat is he? Sir Edward…"

"That's enough Brian. How come we didn't have these facts John?"

The Professor hesitated. He had to be very careful with this answer. "We look at the big picture, Mr Director, the financial angles, the…"

"Fine, I've heard enough. The Detectives did their detecting.

We read reports and financial brochures." The Doctor fidgeted in this seat. The Professor squirmed in his. The Director sat and looked around the room.

"Any suggestions from anyone? Can we rescue our position? Account for the money? I'm open to anything that makes sense."

Brian again spoke first. "We here in London, that is the Professor and his team, carry on probing NHI financial dealings. Eventually, I am sure that they can be nailed for some misdemeanour or other. That will be a result for us. As for Cardiff, they requested our help. We provided equipment and expert help i.e. The Prof and Doctor. I became the contact between Cardiff and us, thus my involvement. I honestly believe that eventually the Welsh boys will get this Chessman and we can say that it was a dual effort."

"All that's left is to change these," Brian pointed to the accounts, "to reflect our involvement and expenditure in such a way that it looks to everyone that it's money well spent. In the meantime, we put the word around that we are helping to finance the operation in Cardiff. That part at least is true.

"Who can complain about finances when we are trying to catch a mad dangerous serial killer? It's with our help that the Police in Wales have so far managed to progress. Also, I suggest we send Jock and another specialist in that department to Cardiff for the day. They can check the equipment and help in any way they can. It will look like we are completely involved in the operation down there."

"Thank you Brian. Give them a call; tell the Chief, what's his name?"

"Clarke, Sir."

"…that they will have our total cooperation and help in any way necessary. Do it tonight. Oh, and write him a letter, ask if the equipment is fine. If our people, namely the Prof and Doctor Elwin helped with the Chessman case, mention that our top tech bloke is to visit them. You know the drill. As of this minute NHI is a

London thing. Nothing to do with the help we are giving the locals down in Cardiff.

"That's it for tonight. Agnes, please remain. We need to do some massaging to the accounts. I hope you have some ideas, Agnes, otherwise I could always call up the yokels from Cardiff. I'm bloody sure they would sort them out." Joking apart, the Director thought they probably could. If he had time he'd like to meet these detectives. So far they'd run rings around his people. Not many people did. Not since he was made Director eleven years previous.

CHAPTER 13

Vincent taylor, Jasmine's ex, lost his job on Thursday. He had broken someone's jaw at the gym where he worked. The jaw belonged to the Manager.

For two days Vinny sat in his rented flat staring into space. He really didn't know what to do next. Over those two days he finished the carrot juice, the prune juice, he ran out of vitamins and he ran out of self-control.

A few hundred yards away, the off-licence was just closing when Vinny walked in. He bought himself a cheap bottle of whisky and went back to his flat. He put it on his mantelpiece and until his resolve broke it lay unopened. The time was five a.m., Saturday morning.

He had his first alcoholic drink in over six months. He needed just the one. One wouldn't do any harm; after all, he was six foot four and weighed seventeen stone. One drink wouldn't even register on any type of scale. At seventeen minutes past eight, he'd finished the lot.

He felt fine and in complete control, but he needed just one more. The local garage down the road sold cans of beer. They would be open.

Vinny never made it, he fell asleep drunk and didn't wake up for four hours. When he saw the time he realised that the local would be open, so after splashing some cold water over his face he headed for the nearest watering hole. He didn't bother changing. That would be criminal, a waste of drinking time. Vincent had to make up for the previous six months No-one could begrudge him a few drinks. By six he was gone again and fast asleep at home. He slept for nearly eighteen hours. When he eventually surfaced he realised that he'd run out of money and needed more. He searched through his pockets. He was lucky; no money but the address of Jasmine. Of course she didn't know that he had her address. A month or so ago he had spotted her outside a department store. He followed her to her new home.

His intentions had been honourable. All he wanted was for her to see that he was sober, a new man. At the last moment he had chickened out. He couldn't face the possible rejection.

But now it was different. He didn't want to get back together. He just wanted twenty, thirty quid for a few days. Nothing else. She'd understand. He staggered to the toilet, rinsed out his mouth, combed his hair, tidied himself up as best he could in his state.

On the way out he grabbed a handful of peanuts from the top of the sideboard. Food would settle his stomach and soak up the booze. The fifteen-minute walk to his ex's apartment took nearly forty minutes as he swayed from side to side, stumbling and falling at least three times. Pedestrians gave him a wide berth. He was a big man, not fat, just big. One could see that he was, in his sober times, a very fit young man. That he was. He was a fitness instructor, one of the best, or was, before that idiot of a Manager had overstepped the mark.

He stopped outside the small block for over five minutes. Vinny knew she lived on the first floor but without a key couldn't get entry into the building. His chance came when some old dear arrived carrying two heavy shopping bags. She fumbled with the keys whilst trying to hold onto her shopping. Eventually she got the door to open. She had her back to the door to keep it open whilst she manoeuvred her shopping through the half open front door. Vincent pushed the door open further, giving the old bag enough room to move in with her shopping. He got no thanks but was in. Thankfully, the lady lived on the ground floor. She waited for Vinny to take the stairs before she opened her own front door.

Vinny took the steps two at a time. It was easier for him than going step by step. There were fourteen steps and Vinny made it without mishap. He licked his fingers and slicked down his blond hair. He was ready. He'd ask for sixty and hope to get forty.

Evan and Mike took their photos, the brochures, layouts, timetable of events, talked to whoever was there. Mike noticed the security, CCTVs, he noted everything that would help Chalky. It was time consuming. "What we need, Mike, is an inside man at the places."

"Why Evan?"

"We need to contact the local CID here. See if anyone is a member and then if one of ours is, what then?"

"It will help Mike."

"I don't see how, Evan."

"Nor do I at this moment, Mike, but it will help I'm sure."

Mike wasn't sure but what he was sure about was that Chalky could help. All they needed was some expensive equipment to help Chalky. One good thing, they had unlimited money on the credit cards. They also had Jane's husband. That left Chalky, but would he play ball? Chalky owed him big time.

He rang the bell. No answer. He rang again. Still nothing. Maybe he was at the wrong door. Then he noticed the spy hole in the door. It took him a while to realise that Jasmine could see that it was him and wasn't opening her door.

He rapped on the door, not too loudly. He didn't want to scare her. All he wanted was some money. He didn't want to go in, he just needed the money until his last week's pay came in. Oh, how he regretted buying that car a few weeks ago. Six thou was a lot of money and cash at that. He'd gone to the limit on his overdraft and his credit cards; he'd drawn everything.

Jasmine was confused. What was Taylor, as she liked to call him, doing outside her flat? How did he find the flat? What did he want? Vincent kept on ringing and tapping on the door.

"What do you want Taylor? I'm not going to let you in. Go away. I don't want to see you."

"You don't have to see me, Jas. I just need some cash. It's important. I need it badly."

"You sound drunk."

"I've got a very bad cold. Look, Jas, just slip me forty quid through the letterbox and I'm off. I'll pay you back next week."

"Are you sure you haven't been drinking?"

"Of course I bloody am. Haven't had a drink for nearly a year, Jas. I just have a lousy cold. I'm short of money. Thirty will do."

Jasmine hesitated. She had heard that Taylor had stopped drinking but what worried her was that he was so desperate. "Hang on a minute, I'll go and get some money." She got a twenty and pushed it through. "That's all I have at this moment Taylor. Now please go away. I don't want the money back or you."

Vinny pocketed the money and stood there looking at the door. Was that all he was worth, a measly twenty? "I need more. I told you I need more, you fucking bitch!"

"Go away, Vincent. I know you've been drinking. If you don't go I'll call the police. Do you hear me Vincent?"

"Will you call big bad daddy, Jas? Fat lot of use he is. Just a fat old fart."

"Right, I'm calling the police," Jasmine said, turning away from the door and heading for her bedroom where she kept the phone.

The second time that Vinny threw his weight against the door, the lock gave in. The small chain went the same way. Vinny was in. Jasmine needed to get out.

Just after ten p.m. Mike and Evan, both exhausted, called it a day. The recon finished, they climbed into the car and headed for the town centre. Both were hungry. They settled on grabbing a bite to eat at a small Indian restaurant.

They ordered chicken for both, one Masala for Evan, the other a Vindaloo. Some Pilau rice, a Keema Nan and two bottles of Kingfisher lager, completed the order.

A few minutes later Evan received a call from Amber. He passed the phone over to Mike. Amber had found Chalky's watering hole. The Cutty Sark, just outside the city centre in Canton.

"Let's switch these bloody phones off," said Evan. "At least whilst we eat." They switched both mobiles off and started eating. If the phones had still been on Evan would have received a call from a very upset wife, who when answering her door, found a hysterical daughter standing there, clothes dishevelled, makeup running in streaks and blood seeping from her mouth and nose.

A mother's first instinct is to hold and cuddle their children, protect them in every which way. Edna was no exception.

In between the sobbing and hysterics, Edna managed to extract the full story from Jasmine. Once Jasmine had mentioned the name Taylor and the word drink, she knew the score.

"Where's Dad, Mum?"

"Gone to Swansea for something. Can't get him on his mobile. It's not like Evan."

"What about calling his partner, Mum?"

"Tried, that's switched off too."

With ice on the black eye, warm face flannels covering the mouth, cotton wool in both nostrils, ointment, then plaster on the cheek, the broken fingernails, bruised leg, it was a miracle that Jasmine had driven from Cardiff to her parents without having an accident.

"Shall we call the police Mum? He might come here. I'm scared. I think he was going to kill me."

"We must get hold of your father. He wouldn't like it if we called his colleagues."

"Look, we'll have a drink and then we will get a taxi to the hospital, unless I can find your father."

"I will be fine, Mum. I don't want to go to hospital."

"Vincent's very heavy-handed darling. He might have caused you internal damage. I insist that we go. I will leave your father a note. Where the hell is he? I can't understand why his phone's off, or his partners."

At eleven Edna could still not get through. She'd only had one drink and that she hadn't finished. She left a note and drove Jasmine to the hospital.

As they left the restaurant Evan switched on his phone and found two texts and five voicemail messages from Edna. She urgently needed to speak to him. He rang home, no answer. He rang Edna's mobile, no answer. Probably went to bed. But why all the urgent messages? Something was up.

"Anything wrong Evan?"

"Can't get hold of Edna, landline or mobile."

"She's probably gone to bed Evan."

"Don't think so Mike. She's left half a dozen messages saying she wanted to speak to me urgently."

Evan drove as fast as he could. He dropped off Mike and pointing the car in the direction of home, he sped to Taffs Well.

He read the note. 'Have gone to the hospital with Jasmine. Everything looks okay, Love Edna.' What the hell is this? Why go to the hospital if everything is okay? What's going on? He didn't waste time trying to phone the hospital.

He got into the car and drove like a maniac back to Cardiff. Why hadn't Edna taken her mobile? Was she in such a rush? Was she ill and contacted Jasmine? Which car did they take? Damn it. He hadn't noticed but they had been drinking. He had noticed the two glasses on the coffee table. Did he also see a blooded towel on the small sofa or maybe he was just paranoid and imagining things.

He was shown a chair next to an empty bed. She'd been crying. "Where Jasmine?" was all he could say, the panic slurring his words.

"Thank God you're here, Evan. I've been trying to contact you all night."

"What's happened? Where's Jasmine?"

"She's having x-rays, Evan."

"Why?"

"That bastard Taylor beat her up badly. He was drunk." She told him the rest; everything she knew.

A few minutes later Jasmine was wheeled into the room. Evan gave her a big hug and held her until the nurse intervened. "She needs rest. We're keeping her in for tonight, just for observation. The doctor says he doesn't think there's anything broken or any internal bleeding but it's best we keep her here for the time being. You must leave now. I'm sorry, but those are the rules."

Evan and Edna managed to stay another half an hour before they were pushed out. Evan drove the BMW home. Edna followed in Jasmine's car. They didn't sleep until tiredness closed their eyes. Both slept on the sofas.

Both were awake at six. Jasmine had had a good night and wanted to get out. To go home, not her home. That wasn't her home anymore. She wanted to be with her mother and of course her father.

Vincent sat on a small leather sofa in Jasmine's flat. How the hell did she manage to escape? He looked around. Not too much damage. He righted a chair, straightened a picture, picked up a few broken ornaments and put them in a bin. He found a half bottle of Vodka and a full bottle of wine and Jasmine's handbag. He emptied the contents on the coffee table. Another thirty-five pounds in notes and lots of change. He left the credit cards.

On the way out he wedged the door shut as best he could, in his drunken way. He doubted whether Jas would call the police. As for his ex-father-in-law, he wouldn't want to lose face at the station.

He was home and dry; bottles in a plastic bag which he had found in the kitchen and nearly sixty pounds better off. He left, stumbling and tripping all over the place. The Vodka never made it to the part where he lay down and slept. The wine didn't either.

He drank the Vodka and broke the wine bottle when he fell for the umpteenth time.

Evan took an empty suitcase and, together with Edna, headed for the hospital, only to be greeted with the news that although Jasmine felt fine, the doctor felt otherwise and wanted her to remain another day.

The doctor was worried about her physical state. She was traumatised and he was afraid that mentally the worst was yet to come.

It took a while to convince Jas. Tears flowed freely from all except the doctor. He'd seen all this many times.

Edna remained with Jas. Evan left. He bought a new lock and went to Jasmine's flat. He sat on the chair and cried out of sheer frustration. Evan changed the lock, filled up the suitcase with clothes, cosmetics, shoes, whatever he could find and departed.

He rang his brother Bryn and tried unsuccessfully to contact his old friend and Jas's Godfather, D.I. Mick Maloney. Mick was on holiday. He would have to confront that bastard himself.

He rang Amber; told her that he would be late in. Mike was late. On arrival he asked Amber if she knew why Evan hadn't appeared. Amber told him that he telephoned and would be late.

"So what do we do today?" Jane asked.

"Let's look into this sport's business," Amber said. "We can't get the membership lists. We're trying to see if any of our colleagues belong to any of the clubs. We're not even sure that the Chessman belongs to them or if indeed he plays any games. Shoes, bags, could be another of his red herrings."

"I would have to agree, Amber, but apart from murdering innocent people over the weekends, he must have some other hobby. Why shouldn't he relax and play bowls or whatever? What do you say, Mike?"

"I say there must be more angles on this than a fifty-pence piece. Leave the lists to me. I think I might have a way."

"What do you mean Mike, more angles than a fifty-pence piece?"

"We're trying to get things in the normal legal way but there are other ways, other angles – do you follow me, girls?" No one did.

At eleven Mike said he had to go. No sign of Evan. The Cutty Sark was a pub straight out of Dickens. It was dowdy, badly lit, smelt of mould and inhabited by undesirables. To be fair they were at home there.

It was also their office, shopping centre, bank and most of all their information centre. Information on everything and anything illegal. Here all the conmen, safe men, forgers, fraudsters, burglars bought and sold their wares, whether it be jewellery, funny money, silver, booze, tobacco, everything.

The kingpins were the fences but strangely enough no one dealt or pushed drugs. No strong arm stuff, no violence. This was a very specialised club. The members had mostly avoided getting caught. They had helped each other with information which one just couldn't buy anywhere else.

As Mike walked in all conversations stopped. About fifteen or so sat in various corners of the establishment, all male; no surprise really, the business was male orientated.

Mike walked up to the bar, and still no one spoke. The bartender looked at him, placed his hands on the bar top and asked Mike sarcastically if he was looking for directions. Someone sniggered, someone else laughed. Mike said nothing. This wasn't going to be easy. The barman smirked. "The police station is just down the road friend, but you know that don't you?" Still Mike said nothing.

"Well, are you going to say something or do we have to guess? You know, like on one of those game shows on TV?"

Mike turned on his heel, walked out and looked above the door. After a few seconds he returned. The barman squinted his eyes as if in deep thought but said nothing.

"I see that you have a licence to sell alcohol to the public. In which case, I'll have one. Triple rum and black and one orange juice with ice."

The barman was too stunned to move, but eventually he did. Still no-one spoke until Mike pointed to a sign. "I've heard of the 'No Smoking Policy' but I've never come across a 'No Talking' one."

"You a cop?"

"Yes," answered Mike. "Special Detective Inspector Mikhail Karetzi at your service. I'm looking for one Charles White, better known as Chalky. Here's my card. Get him to ring me on the mobile."

Mike took a sip of the orange juice. The barman took the card. Mike passed over a twenty and picked up a beer mat, placing it over the run and coke. "That's for Chalky."

"Look Inspector, I don't know this Charlie bloke. Doesn't drink here but if he ever does come in I'll give him the card and of course the drink." The barman smiled.

"Okay; look Bonzo, at the moment you have a permit to sell booze. Fuck with me and you won't even get a permit to own a dog by the time I'm finished with you."

Mike walked out. Everyone started talking. One or two had heard of Mike. Heard he was crazy. Now they had first-hand knowledge that he was.

Within twenty seconds of Mike walking out, the barman had Chalky on the blower.

Mike would give him half an hour. He took a stroll around the area. Chalky would immediately have to get down to the Cutty to explain to everyone that he did not know this bloke, Karetzi. If he didn't nip it in the bud, Karetzi knew that he would be ostracised by his peers, a leper, and Chalky wouldn't work again.

Charles White was a born and bred East Londoner, a cockney. The apples and pears type. He was twenty-nine and average in every way except for his hair which was white as chalk. White as his name. He was well educated and had a great voice. He was once the lead singer of an up and coming band, the EELS, East End Londoners. They were on the verge of making it big, when tragedy struck. Two of the five band members were involved in a car accident; both died, one was Charlie's younger brother, his only sibling.

That was ten years ago. Charlie had changed. A year after the fatal car crash Charlie fell in with a bad lot. He realised that he had magic fingers that would unlock anything, doors, locks, safes. He was a natural. This combined with the head for heights and his great balance made him one of the top men in his new profession, that of a burglar.

Charlie was fearless; he taught himself how to bypass alarms. He had everything but still got nabbed. He served six months as a guest in one of her Majesty's hotels.

He could have avoided doing a carpet, slang for a six month spell in prison, but after a successful caper he and his partner had carried out, his friend slipped and fell breaking a leg and Charlie had turned back to help him when he could have easily got away. He vowed that day that he would, as from that moment, always work solo and he had, quite happily.

After prison he moved around ending up in Cardiff doing odd jobs, mainly bar work. He heard about the Cutty Sark and slowly he was trusted and accepted by the other animals of that particular zoo.

Everyone recognised greatness when they saw it and when it came to cat burglars Chalky was the best. He was the man. Two years ago he had his big break. He was approached by one of the specialist fences who dealt mainly with art, any form of art.

The fence cornered Chalky, whom he knew well. He passed Chalky a photograph. "That painting is worth over a quarter of a million; to someone it's worth one hundred thou; to you it's worth fifty."

"Is it in a bank, a gallery, strong room?"

"No, it's hanging up on a wall in an apartment down on the Bay. I doubt very much if the people know its worth. They have not taken any extra precautions against its being stolen. I have a feeling that it's not even insured."

Chalky knew that the fence was not telling him the truth. He guessed the painting to be worth more. How much more he couldn't tell but this was a life changing opportunity if he could get the right money. On the face of it, it was a very simple heist.

"One hundred, not one penny less."

"Come on Charlie, you trust me. I need to make something. Fifty grand is a lot of bread Chalky."

"I know it is, but a hundred is double. Lots of bread."

"Look Charles, I'll take a smaller cut and give you sixty. That's it. Take it or leave it. It's up to you. They," he said, making an arc with his hand as he pointed all round the pub, "would do if for half."

As soon as the fence had called him by his given name Chalky knew he would get his hundred grand.

"You know that only two people apart from me can do this job – that's why you're sitting here buying me a drink. Little Alfie is ill and Birdie Smith is otherwise detained, I think for another six or so months. It's a hundred, not one penny less."

"No can do Chalky. Maybe you're right but I must get my commissions. Let's call it a two/one split. You get the two; that's over sixty-six and a half grand. Not bad for a few hours' work."

The fence smiled, and from his pocket produced a brown envelope. He knew this was his ace in the hole. They couldn't resist cash up front when they saw it. He laid it down in front of Chalky. "10K, in there. Go on, open it. Count it. It's yours, upfront money, the balance of fifty-six off when I get the painting."

Chalky opened it and flicked through the fifty pound notes. "You're fifty short, Jimmy." The fence laughed. Why not, it never failed. Cash was king. He stopped laughing when Chalky pushed it back to him. It's a look Jimmy couldn't understand. "I want one hundred."

Chalky got up. Maybe Jimmy was telling him the truth after all but it's the buts that get to you. "Goodbye Jimmy, thanks for the drink," and Chalky headed for the toilets. He needed a leak. He'd probably just pissed away a life-changing moment and all he wanted was a leak.

After relieving himself, whilst washing his hands, he decided that he would settle for seventy thou but changed his mind when he found Jimmy standing outside the toilets waiting for him.

"Let's sit down, Charlie. One hundred it is. Take your ten now. Keep the picture. I've written the address on the back."

They shook hands, both were very happy especially Jimmy Jones the fence. His profit was now two hundred and he didn't have to lift a finger.

Chalky would need a month at the most. That was acceptable to Jimmy. Two hundred grand was worth the wait. Jack knew that Chalky had to do his homework. That's what the top professionals do. Charlie left singing the 1960s number-one hit 'Good Timin' by Jimmy Jones, the American singer.

For three weeks he watched the penthouse apartment. He established without any doubt the movements of the occupants. Two middle-aged Italians or Greeks. Weekdays they would stay in, but on Saturday the shorter one would go out alone. The tall, bald headed one would go out on Sundays. Saturday man would take a waiting cab at about seven p.m. and he'd return in the early hours of the morning in another cab absolutely plastered.

Sunday man would take his big Merc out from the garages underneath the apartment blocks at about ten a.m. and return two hours later with the weekly shopping.

Their laundry was picked up on a Tuesday and returned on the Wednesday. They had no visitors as far as Chalky could ascertain.

Wednesday night was the only time they both went out together. At about nine p.m. Sunday man would get the car and park outside the main doors. A few minutes later Saturday man would exit the building carrying a large leather bag which he would put in the boot.

He would then climb into the front passenger seat and Sunday man would drive off. Invariably they would return at about one in the morning.

Together they would park the car and together they would take one of the lifts to their penthouse apartment.

On the fourth Wednesday, Chalky dressed in a suit and tie and carrying a small briefcase parked his car a couple of hundred yards away. It was nine p.m. He walked slowly towards the building. He saw the men leave in their car. He had at least three hours.

It took him less than twenty seconds to open the main doors. He rode the lift to the penthouse and was confronted with two doors. He heard noises emanating from one so he started working on the other. Chubb lock first, Yale lock second.

He nearly messed up with the alarm but with seconds to go had managed to bypass the system.

He was in. It was dark in the hall but he could see some light in both what looked like a lounge and what was obviously the kitchen.

He switched on his torch and moved stealthily into the lounge. The lounge was bigger than his whole apartment and every wall was covered with pictures.

It took him only seconds to locate the one he wanted. He couldn't mistake it. Two feet by one and a half. The picture, an oil painting depicting a Victorian picnic scene. Two adults and three small children were sitting on a grass bank next to a river. Before them lay their picnic. Hams, cheeses, bread, cakes, beer, lemonade and various other culinary delights.

Chalky had never ever had a picnic and the scene made him quite envious but a hundred thou would make up for that.

He did a recon; any jewellery, small objets d'art, money, silver that would be a bonus. He systematically went through the lounge, the kitchen and two bedrooms. He found nothing of real interest. The third room was locked. It looked like another bedroom.

Again, it took less than half a minute to open. He pushed open the door and entered, torch on.

His eyes nearly popped out of his head. There must have been at least a hundred bags of flour, stacked on two shelves above a large modern safe. Six digital entry code, two keys, foreign make. He doubted if he could crack it in two hours, if at all. He'd never encountered such a sophisticated safe in his career.

Now Chalky was streetwise, although anti-drugs, he knew coke when he came across it but just to make sure he removed his glove and tested the goods with the top of his index finger.

This was bad, not good. Chalky was beginning to panic. Suddenly he didn't want the money. You don't mess around with these types. Life was cheap to them and Chalky valued his at more than ninety grand, much, much more.

He began to sweat. He'd come for the picture, the rest was not his business. He exited the room and relocked it. He went back to the lounge. From his pocket he took out the small sharp pen knife. It was now or never.

He would cut the painting out from the frame. His hand shook as he placed the small sharp blade in the top right-hand corner.

He had reached the life defining moment in more ways than he cared to think about. He'd been in the flat nearly three hours engrossed in his work.

He lowered the knife. Could they trace anything back to him? Jimmy, the ultimate buyer, he wasn't sure. These people had power, money and connections. If they knew the value of the painting and it was worth a hell of a lot more than what Jimmy had told him, then he could be asking for trouble.

He looked at the other oils on the walls. They all looked expensive to Chalky. He guessed that these people knew their art. If they weren't insured, he shuddered. They would hunt him down.

For the right type of money someone would grass. After all, how many people in Cardiff could pull off this job? Not many, if any. He folded his knife, picked up his briefcase and left, closing and locking the doors behind him.

Taking the lift down, he glanced in the mirror. He was sweating like a pig. He felt relieved. He had never until today aborted a heist. He had a feeling that he had just saved his own life. He pressed the large white button that released the lock of the front door and stepped out into the crisp night air.

Chalky took two steps and stumbled. He fell awkwardly. His briefcase burst open spilling its contents at the feet of the two strangers, a man and a woman.

That man was D.I. Karetzi returning from a local Italian restaurant with his girlfriend Mimi. He lived on the third floor of the apartments that Chalky had just left.

A torch, various keys, picks, small empty pouches, a magnifying glass, small camera and mobile were strewn everywhere. Karetzi was slightly tipsy but could see the tools of a cat burglar.

From his jacket pocket he produced his warrant card. Chalky froze. He could make a run for it. This bloke was half cut. He'd have a chance but the bloody mobile had all his particulars and the cop had it in his hand.

"Empty your pockets and put the contents on the floor." Chalky did. "What's your name and address?" Mike asked him, picking up a piece of paper that Chalky had deposited on the floor. Chalky told him.

"Why are you carrying all that? I assume you're not a locksmith doing an emergency job this time of night."

Charlie told Mike the truth. At least this Charles White had not lied to him about his name and address. The piece of paper Mike had picked up was a gas bill that Charlie had forgotten to pay and it corroborated what Chalky had told him.

So he might get Charles White for breaking and entering but was it worth the hassle, the paperwork? After all he hadn't got him for stealing or possession. Mike felt in a good mood. "Look Charles, put everything back in the case, close it, hand it to me and go."

Charles did, except for his car keys. "Can I keep these? I need to get back home."

"Okay, now get lost before I change my mind." Charles left. Mimi had already gone up to the apartment. Mike lit a fag, picked up the case and entered his apartment block.

Mimi was in bed waiting for Mike who joined her after dumping the briefcase in the lounge and getting undressed. Mike and Mimi carried on celebrating in the only way they could.

Mike came out of the building at nine a.m. as usual. He was running late. Chalky was there waiting. "You again, Mr White."

"Me again. I need my briefcase and contents, Detective."

"Sorry, Mr White, not until I've studied them carefully. Who knows what goodies they hold."

Charlie was desperate. He felt like a puppet on a string and this cop was just about to cut the string. He had important telephone numbers on his mobile, in code yes, but in time they could break it.

When that time came Chalky would be Public Enemy Number One to all his acquaintances and contacts in the underworld. There would be no place to hide, anywhere in the U.K.

"If I was to give you information that would result in the biggest drug bust ever known in Cardiff or Wales for that matter what would you do about my personal gear?"

"I would think, Charles, that you'd lie through your back teeth. Sell your grandmother and sister to anyone in exchange for that mobile – it's got to be the mobile, am I correct?"

"I don't have a grandmother or sister, neither do I have a father or brother, Detective; only a mother and she's ill. As for lying, I didn't yesterday, why would I today? You're a cop. This is your big break and probably my life. If we can come to some logical conclusion here."

Mike had already guessed what the mobile contained. For some reason he liked this guy. He would listen. This Londoner was different and he had balls. Mike pointed towards his car. "Let's talk, Charlie."

Mike drove to the cafe bar he frequented and they ordered two coffees. The waitress he fancied wasn't on duty so Mike had no distractions.

"Here Detective, is trust me time. You hand me the briefcase first and I will hand you an address. Briefcase with all my stuff; I mean all."

"Charlie, I can run you in right now. Get the info if it exists and keep the briefcase with its secrets which I have no doubt will be of great interest to us down at the station."

"That is true to a point Detective. You already have the briefcase but you don't have my information and I guarantee you that you never will if I don't get my stuff. To you I might just be nothing, a petty crook but if you asked around you will find that I'm honest, reliable and never bullshit."

"Get in the car Charlie."

"Where are we going?" asked Charlie.

Mike didn't answer. Charlie resigned himself to more interrogation downtown. He tried to prepare himself mentally and physically for the coming ordeal but to his surprise the detective with the Russian sounding name drove back to the apartments on the Bay.

"Okay Charlie boy, stay here, don't move and don't try to steal my car. Got it?"

"I've got it. I wouldn't try to steal your car Detective. It would be as easy as opening an envelope."

Mike laughed. He was really warming to Charlie.

Five minutes later Mike returned, briefcase in hand. "Check it Charlie." Charlie did. "Everything there?"

"It is."

"Well, you have your briefcase, Charlie, and even if you do give the info promised and it works out, you will still owe me big time."

Charlie weighed up the options. "I agree."

"If of course the info is rubbish, you have big problems Charlie."

"I understand. Can you drive me to my car? I'll give you the whole nine yards as we drive. It's just down there about half a mile." Charlie noticed that the detective had locked all the doors. Mike noticed that Charlie had noticed. He smiled. He was being paranoid. This was getting ridiculous.

"There's over a hundred kilos of Coke, a safe full of money and oil paintings worth millions in an apartment not too far from where you live, Detective.

"The safe full of money part is a guess, Detective. If it's not then it's got something more valuable than money in it. I've never come across a safe like that in a private residence before. I doubt if anyone else has either.

"The day it all happens is a Wednesday. That's the day to strike. Actually Thursday morning at about one a.m. There are two occupants, both male, both about forty-five, fifty. They look foreign. I think Italian or Greek. Every Tuesday their laundry is picked up by TALC, The Ace Laundry Company. You won't find them in the telephone directory or anywhere else. They don't exist. I've checked.

"They return the laundry on the Wednesday in the afternoon, only they return twice as much as they take. At nine on the same day, at night of course, the two men leave the apartment together; one is always holding a large brown leather case and returns at about one a.m. again with the leather case. They drive a big blue Merc." Charlie gave Mike the number plate. "That is the one and only time they are out of the apartment together."

"And where is this Aladdin's Cave, Charlie?" asked Mike, just as Charlie told him to stop.

"Oh, didn't I mention it?" said Charlie, picking up his case and opening the car door. "It's the Penthouse flat in your block of apartments. I think the number is 21." Charlie slammed the door shut and opened the door to his Fiesta.

"Christ," Mike thought. "Christ."

A week later and Detective Inspector Karetzi was the toast of the local Force. Twenty- three arrests, over two-hundred kilos of Coke, three million pounds in various currency and gold coins, four million pounds worth of oil paintings and all from just one anonymous phone call to Mike. For the record Saturday and Sunday men were both Maltese, not Italian or Greek.

Mike checked out Charles White. Just a three-month stretch, elusive and good. They had him down for at least five major jobs in the six years, probably more. Chalky, as he was known, was a non-violent, old fashioned, cat burglar; a little Raffles clone.

The Cutty Sark was as he had left it. It still stank. It was still dowdy and the low-lifes were still sitting in the same positions with the one exception. Chalky was at the bar.

"That's yours Charlie," Mike said pointing to the rum.

Chalky turned. "Shit," he thought.

"I've got you down for three jobs I hope you've got alibis for, Chalky." Mike read out three dates from his phone bill. "That, Chalky, is the last booze you're going to have for a very long time."

"I've no bloody idea what you're talking about."

"But you will Chalky, you will. Come over here and let's talk about your alibis, shall we?

"I'll have another orange juice, barman. Put it on my slate."

"You don't have any credit here," replied the barman.

"The twenty knicker you pocketed half an hour ago says I do. Oh, and don't forget the difficulties in obtaining a dog permit, my friend. Bring the orange over to my table over there. That's a good man."

At that moment Charlie made a clumsy attempt at making a break for it but was tripped by Mike who then picked him up by the collar and marched him to a table. Chalky protested and got a slap on the head. Chalky sat down. Then Mike sat. The barman brought their drinks over.

Mike winked at Chalky. "Bit half-hearted try at escaping eh Chalky."

"But the slap wasn't half hearted, was it Detective?"

"I made it look good as did you Chalky. We both know the score. You can't be known to associate with the other side, can you Chalky?"

With that Mike slapped Chalky hard on the cheek which reddened with pain and embarrassment. Chalky went to rise. Mike restrained him. "Sit, shut up and listen Chalky. Cast your mind back two years. You owe me and I'm here to collect.

"Don't bother with any, I don't do that type of thing anymore. I'm going straight or whatever is going through your mind Chalky. Do this and we're even."

"You know, Detective, that I won't do anything illegal. Yes, I owe you but I'm damned if you are going to set me up and pin a whole lot of other things on me for your own personal gain. What is it you want, a promotion?"

"What is my nickname Chalky? You do know it; you're the type who would have checked."

"I know."

"Well, you also know that you're going to pay me back, don't you? You won't like the consequence if you don't Chalky. I won't either. I hate hurting what I know to be a good honest, decent and reliable person. Have you heard those words before, Chalky?

"Think about it. You don't have any options here. I want repayment and you want me off your back. In one hour meet me at my apartment. I'll be outside. Don't be late. Now tell me to fuck off in a loud voice. Finish your drink and leave."

Chalky did. It was the best part of his day so far.

Mike sat and finished his drink before pretending to slink out unnoticed. "Good old Chalky," said one customer. "Sure told that pig where to get off," said another. Everyone agreed Chalky had seen off that crazy Karetzi cop. Drinks were ordered, people smiled. Chalky was one of their own.

Before getting back to the hospital, Evan phoned through to the office, told Amber that he wouldn't be in that day and probably not the next. He gave her Vincent's name and last place of work and asked her to locate his address and call him on his mobile.

"Jasmine looks worse today, Edna. Anything changed?"

"She's in shock Evan, reliving the mauling she took."

"Is that what the doctor says Edna?"

"Yes, Evan."

"When can she come home?"

"I think she will be here for a few more days Evan. We all have to be very patient for Jasmine's sake."

"What about Taylor Evan? Are you going to speak to your colleagues? He's a menace to society. He might kill someone unless he's locked up."

"I'll deal with it Edna. He's not getting away with beating my daughter to within an inch of her life."

"But what can you do Evan?"

"I can do lots. Just leave it to me."

"Before we go back in Evan I want to know what you intend doing?" Evan was about to answer when Amber called him on his mobile with Vincent's address.

"Who's that Evan?" Edna asked.

"Nothing, just police work love."

"Look, let's get back in and see Jasmine."

Edna knew better. She knew something was afoot. Evan was lying, probably about Taylor. He was going to do something stupid, but what?

At nine they had to leave. On getting home Evan told his wife that he needed some papers from the garage. Edna made a mushroom omelette. Evan returned empty handed. "Couldn't you find them darling?"

"I'll have to sort out that garage one day so we can find things."

They ate in silence, both in their own thoughts. "Are you frightened?" Edna asked.

"Of what my love?"

"Of Taylor of course. Do you think he'll attack our girl again?"

"Don't worry about anything Edna. It will be sorted out."

"What are you going to do Evan?"

"I'm going to confront him. Have a word, warn him."

"You know he won't listen Evan, and if he's had a drink or two he'll kill you, Evan. You're too old, too small and unfit. I will not allow you to go anywhere near him. I mean it."

"I said I'm only going to have a word with him Edna. No violence. I must do something. Jasmine's our daughter. That's the least a father can do."

"I don't want to be visiting two people in hospital. We must talk to the locals. You must know some of the boys at the local police station."

"It's my daughter, my responsibility. As soon as Jasmine comes home, I will go and talk with him in as nice way a way as I possibly can. You know me, Edna."

"Yes I do Evan, that's why I'm afraid. I know you and I know Taylor."

That same Tuesday evening, Jim, the Chessman's next door neighbour, phoned to cry off from their usual Karaoke night out at the local. Pat his wife was suffering badly from her arthritis and he was staying in to be with her.

The Chessman was glad. He'd done a very good deal that morning but it was a long and hard tranche of negotiations. It always was with the Yanks.

He opened a can of ginger beer and pulled out his new book, one he had recently purchased. It was a book on handwriting, titled 'All you need to know about handwriting'. Three hundred pages long. Things were coming to a head, once he had mastered at least half a dozen different styles.

The Chessman began reading and practising the various forms of writing that he would require in the near future.

Mike met Chalky as planned. They took the lift up to Mike's apartment and Mike served coffee. Mike lit up. Chalky didn't. He had never even tried one. They eyeballed each other for over two minutes.

"Why are you Captain Cooking me, Detective?"

"Chalky, I suppose to you, being a Londoner, this rhyming slang shit means something. To me it means nix so please don't act the wise guy. I've a lot on my plate at the moment."

"What is it you want Detective?"

"I want you to break into a sports club Chalky."

"An office?"

"Yes, and I want you to photograph all their membership details."

"Where is it?"

"Llanelli."

"When?"

"Tomorrow night."

"How many owls?"

"Owls?"

"Guards, security."

"One I guess."

"Are these in a safe, Detective?"

"I've no idea. I wouldn't think so. Just in desks I would presume."

"You know that I'm a lone star, don't you?"

"Chalky please stop talking like a 'B' movie actor. I can't follow you."

"I work alone, Detective. Lone star, do you see? Will I need a Jacob?"

"Chalky, I don't know any Jacobs and I thought you said you work alone, a lone star!"

"A Jacob is a ladder, Detective, as in Jacob's Ladder."

"Chalky, if you say one more fucking word that I don't

understand I'm going to bounce your skinny arse all around this room. Now, here are some pictures and plans of these offices. The 'X' marks the room where the membership files are kept. Tomorrow I will get you a specialised camera which can handle the volume of work that I anticipate. There are over eight thousand names on those lists. So we will meet here tomorrow. I will get the camera Chalky, then, as I said, we're squared up."

They shook hands. Charlie left. Before Charlie left he told the DI that he didn't need a camera. He had all the equipment necessary.

Chalky didn't switch off the tape recorder until he had climbed into the car and switched on the radio. He switched off both the radio and the tape recorder after approximately one minute.

Now he had Karetzi by the balls. He would not be going to Llanelli. Karetzi now owed him. Pity, because he was getting to like the man.

From his window, Mike watched Chalky walk to his car. He noted that Chalky remained in the car a few minutes before starting it up. Mike laughed out loud. These guys always think they know everything.

He'd give Chalky a ring in an hour or so. The so-called plans of the building in Llanelli were of course worthless.

Mike left for the office. On arrival he was greeted by Amber. Jane had to go home. "No news on Evan?"

"No Mike, he won't be coming in at all today or probably tomorrow."

"What's wrong with him? Is he unwell?"

"He sounded a bit down when he rang but didn't say he wasn't well."

"Where was he phoning from, Amber?"

"No idea. I think he was on his mobile."

"Not at home then. Probably shopping. He could do with some up-to-date gear Amber. I think I'll go and have a haircut and then it's time for a good night out. See you tomorrow Amber." Mike walked to the door.

"Oh Mike."

"Yes, Amber?"

"I forgot Evan asked me to trace an address."

"So?"

"It might have something to do with him not coming today, Mike."

"Let's see. Doesn't ring any bells for me, Amber. Must be private."

"Guess so," replied Amber, not really believing that. Nor did Mike but everyone had their secrets or things they didn't want other people to know about.

"You try starva me Mike. Three times you no comma to see Andreas."

"Andreas, you weigh over two-fifty pounds. I'm sure you're eating fine. You won't starve."

"You lika shave, razor cut, special Andreas cut, hair massage? No lika old days Mike, now no smoke in here, soon no drinking coffee in my shop. I know you lika Greek coffee, eh Mike, very strong, one sugar."

Andreas the Greek was a great barber but he talked too much. Mike accepted a coffee. "I love Turkish coffee, Andreas. It's the best," teased Mike. Within a minute Andreas had gone to the small back room and come back holding a dark green packet of coffee.

"You see here, you read Mike." Andreas prodded a podgy finger at the writing at the bottom of the packet.

"I see it Andreas."

"You read Mike."

"Made in Greece."

"Is betta than Turkish, made in my country Mike."

"Yes, Andreas. You cut my hair as normal, okay, like every other time, no different."

163

Mike took a sip of coffee. My God, he thought, you could stand a bloody spoon in this and it was so sweet Mike felt he was drinking pure unadulterated warmed up honey but without the sugar it tasted like gasoline.

Mike closed his eyes, his ears too. If only he could find a way of closing Andreas' mouth, all would be hunky dory.

Fortunately two more customers entered the establishment. They were in for a hard time. They weren't wearing ear plugs.

On leaving Andreas's Mike had time to go and buy some Belgian chocolates. He'd go to see his mother. She'd be pleased to see him. He wanted her to see that he'd had a haircut. She was always saying that a bit longer and he would look like a girl. Something reminded him of the strawberry blonde. He was yearning for someone he didn't know, couldn't find. He realised he had his limitations. One obvious one was that his detection powers needed some brushing up.

Six thirty, a cold, wet and miserable Wednesday morning outside. Even colder in the garage. Edna looked around carefully. What did Evan want in here? Nothing had been disturbed as far as Edna could see. Whatever it was Evan was after he either couldn't find it or he did and put it somewhere else.

The only other place, of course the BMW, the firm's car, the firm being the police. Edna went back up, found the keys and returned to the car. She looked in the boot, nothing unusual. The glove compartment – again just the normal things one would find there.

She was about to close the door when she saw the object. Evan's old truncheon peeping from under the driver's seat, just the strap visible. Edna didn't say anything. Evan was still asleep. She replaced the keys. Evan wouldn't know that Edna knew about the truncheon.

They left for the hospital at eight. Evan was obviously worried. He didn't have breakfast. Unheard of! Edna was driving Evan's Rover.

For a change Mike's mother was alone watching television. She was pleased to see her son. Mike stayed a few hours, then left directly for home. He needed to make a phone call.

He never made the call. Ten minutes after arriving at his apartment and just as he was about to ring, Chalky called.

"Hi, is that Detective Karetzi?"

"It is Chalky."

"I think I'll give tomorrow a miss, Detective."

"You might think that Chalky, but I know otherwise."

"I took out some insurance Detective, listen." Chalky played back the tape from yesterday's meeting and Mike listened till the end.

"Very interesting Chalky. Have you checked out this Llanelli office address?"

"No, but who cares? It's called something. That's it, entrapment. That won't go down well in court, would it, let's be honest Detective. I think that you and I are quits. If anything you owe me big time."

"Tomorrow here, ten o'clock, Charles Frederick White. Don't be late Chalky because I will have to contact certain mutual friends and have a word with them."

"What mutual friends, Detective?"

"Hum, let me see my list. Let's start at 'A' – We got Abrahams, Abel. No Bs or Cs, but Ds; we have Darlow Jack, Downs Peter, Dawson, Roger, then on to E. 'E for Eknardt, Eddy.

"Shall I carry on Chalky? It's quite a long list, about thirty, thirty-five names. Strangely enough I recognise a few of them. I haven't bothered to break the code Chalky but I know a woman who would do it within an hour, then I suppose we'd know a lot more."

"Detective, I thought we had an agreement two years ago? My info for the briefcase."

"We did. I gave you your briefcase intact but maybe I forgot to mention that I extracted the names from your mobile first."

"Ten o'clock it is then, Detective." Chalky laid the phone back into its cradle softly. He was absolutely drained. This detective kept on bettering him.

Mike lit up. Chalky had insurance but his insurance company had just gone bust. He had Chalky trapped tighter than a dirty penny under Gordon Brown's size ten shoe.

Mike got dressed. The only company he wanted tonight was unavailable. Actually he hadn't even found her yet. What he needed was a quiet drink, alone, not Angelo's. He was treated like family there. Some place walking distance away where he wasn't known. It took Mike fifteen minutes to find that place. A small hotel that actually served Macallans.

It was gone midnight when Mike returned home. A steak sandwich, some fries and nearly half a bottle of whisky had done the trick.

He made a large black espresso and drank half of it. The other half he spilt. He tried to read his paper and gave up. He eyes wouldn't focus on the words.

At one thirty he undressed to his boxers and climbed into bed. He dreamt beautiful lovely dreams.

At seven his alarm went off. He put the clock back half an hour. He did the same a half hour later. At eight he got up. The clock said seven o'clock in the morning. The best dream was the one you can remember. Mike had a head like a drum. It just kept on banging and banging but he could remember his dream. He took a couple of Anadin.

As he made his coffee the dream wouldn't go away. A tune was in his mind. It transferred to his mouth. He parted his lips and the words came despite his pounding head.

In dreams, I dream of you,
In dreams you're mine, all of the time,
In dreams, dreams of you.

Mike didn't know if he had the right words, couldn't remember who sang it. Was it Roy Orbison, Conway Twitty? It didn't matter.

They summed up his night, his mood, maybe his future. Charlie would have known it was Orbison, 1963.

He wished he could go back to bed, sleep and have more dreams. He was afraid. What if the dreams stopped? You can't force good dreams into your sleep. It's something that happens naturally, just like nightmares. Nightmares he'd had plenty; always the same. He could see and hear the muggers who killed his father quite clearly but he couldn't touch them. He'd got close, reached out, but could never lay a finger on them and worse; they kept changing their faces.

Chalky was there at ten prompt. In his hand he had a tape. Without a word he passed it to Mike. Mike tossed it into a waste basket. "I promise you, Detective, that is the only one. I have not got a copy. I've come to pay my debt."

Chalky took off his jacket, his shirt, trousers, everything until he was down to his 'Y' fronts. Mike looked at him. "What are you doing?"

"I'm proving myself to you, Detective. No more tapes."

"Get dressed Chalky. People might get the wrong idea. I've a reputation to uphold. Only beautiful women get undressed in my presence.

"Sit down Chalky. Let's go through the plan. It's simple but all good plans are. Chalky, there's a hell of a lot at stake here. I can't say any more.

"You must believe and trust me like I'm going to trust you from now on Chalky."

"Give me the plans Detective. Let me look at them. I need a bit of time. I can't just hope for the best. I must be prepared."

Mike's phone rang. "Yes, who is it? I can't hear you. Speak up. Who is there? Speak up for Christ's sake man!"

"It's me Mike."

Mike recognised the voice but couldn't place it. A woman, not young, not his mother, not Amber or Jane.

"I'm at a disadvantage madam. You seem to know my name but I don't know yours."

"It's me. Edna. You know, your partner, Evan's wife."

"Of course, sorry, but could you speak up a little? Is something wrong?"

"Mike, I hope I haven't disturbed you but I'm desperate and I need to talk to you." From her voice Mike could hear pain.

"Go ahead Edna," said Mike, in the nicest way he could muster.

Edna told Mike about Vincent, what had happened, then told him about Evan and the truncheon. She was scared, scared for herself but more so for Evan.

"Where are you Edna?"

"I'm outside the hospital in the car park."

"And Evan?"

"With Jasmine."

"What do you want me to do Edna?"

"Can you talk some sense into Evan before he gets himself killed? Taylor is a lunatic, especially when he's had a few drinks."

"Leave it to me Edna, I'll look into it and have a word with Evan. I'll come on some pretext tomorrow morning early and I'm sure we will find a solution."

Mike sat down. His head didn't throb any more. It was as if the conversation with Edna had sobered him up.

Ignoring Chalky, he picked up the phone and dialled the office. Jane answered. "Hi Jane, Mike. Is Amber about?"

Jane handed the phone to Amber. "It's Mike for you." Amber took the phone.

After getting Vincent Taylor's address he sat back down. Chalky knew that something had changed. He didn't say anything. He just waited. He could see that the detective was unhappy. He felt sorry for him, why he didn't know. He just did.

Mike reached into his pocket and produced a folded piece of paper. He handed it over to Chalky. "That's the only one, no copies, Charlie."

Chalky unfolded the paper. It was the list of his associates, fellow criminals, bent lawyers, fences etc.

"You won't need those diagrams Charlie. I've changed my mind but there is one small thing you can do for me tonight."

"No problem detective." That phone call had changed everything.

"Of course Charlie, with that list in your hands, you don't have to do anything that you don't want to.

"Before I tell you what the small favour is, let me tell you a story. Then you can make up your mind. Is that fine with you?"

Chalky nodded. As far as he was concerned, apart from killing someone he would do anything for this man. The man had shown his respect but more importantly he had trusted him.

He looked at the piece of paper with the names, reached over and took the detective's gold and silver lighter. He burnt the paper and placed it on a large ashtray. He watched as it burned into ashes.

Mike watched too. That was it. He had no leverage left now.

"That's it Chalky. No more tricks as far as I'm concerned."

"Detective, I still want to hear the story."

"Five years or so ago, a young woman married a quite well known rugby player with the blessing of the parents. Her father was a very keen rugby fan and pushed his daughter towards the union. Unlucky for her this sportsman is not what he pretends to be. He's actually a nasty, violent monster both on the field and at home.

"At first his violence comes out only when he's playing and rarely at home unless he's been drinking. After he stops playing, due to a broken leg, he starts drinking heavily. He starts beating up on her, Chalky, until the girl can't take any more and cites for a divorce after running away.

"After the divorce, this man allegedly stops drinking, gets a good job as a fitness instructor and for nine months the girl hears nothing from him.

"That is until a few days ago, when in a drunken fit this animal appears at her new apartment demanding money for drink.

"It all goes wrong, he beats the girl within an inch of her life and would have killed her if she hadn't managed to escape.

"Now let me give you a physical description of our monster. He's young, six four, fit and extremely strong and extremely violent when drunk.

"The father of the girl is the exact opposite. He's fifty-four, five eight, overweight and unfit.

"As a father, a father who in his mind pushed his daughter into the marriage, wants to atone for his mistake or what he thinks is a mistake. He wants to confront his ex son-in-law. He regards it as his duty. This man is my new partner, an honest, decent cop.

"The phone call I just received was from his wife, begging me to talk to him. She is afraid for her husband. The oaf as she calls him would kill him as easily as squashing a tomato.

"You heard me promise that I would go and see him tomorrow morning."

"But you're not going to, are you?" said Chalky. "Is that address you just obtained the animal's?"

"Yes, it is Charlie."

"And can I assume that you will be paying him a visit today?"

"That's the idea, Charlie."

"Are you sure that's a wise idea Detective? I think this bloke can do you a lot of damage by the sounds of it. Permanent damage if you get my drift."

"I get your drift Charlie. That's why I need an element of surprise to even up the odds a little. That's why I need you. The small favour I was talking about."

"I don't follow you, Detective. Look at me; I abhor violence. I wasn't built for any of that rough stuff."

"No Charlie. I wouldn't put you in any danger. All I need is for you to get me into his flat. I can hardly ring on his doorbell, can I? You get me in, and then walk away and get on with your life. I have nothing on you Charlie. You open the doors and walk. You can forget me."

"I'll do it. Like I said, I still owe you and I know you trust me", Chalky said, pointing at the ashes. "But from what you told me, my advice would be forget going in alone, forget getting involved personally. I can arrange some goons to talk to him. They give him a good lamming, nothing will ever come back to you or your partner. I will deal with the money side of it."

"Charlie, thanks, but I can't do that. Just get me in and walk away."

"Okay Detective, give me the address. I'll do a recce and go and pick up my tools. I'll be back at say two o'clock."

Mike handed Chalky the address. Mike went to the office. Evan was there sitting down with the girls, drinking coffee and smoking his little clay pipe.

"Hi Evan, are you okay?"

"Fine Mike, a bit tired. My daughter had an accident and is in hospital. Edna's with her now."

"Serious Evan?"

"She's okay, Mike, coming out tomorrow hopefully."

"What happened to her Evan?"

"Had a very nasty fall. No broken bones but I think she's still in shock."

"Nothing happening here Evan. Everything under control. We're still looking into the sport's angle otherwise it's all quiet on the Western Front."

"Take a few days off Evan," Amber said. "We can handle everything and wish her the best from all of us here."

"Thanks everyone," Evan said, pushing open the door and exiting.

"He looks awful," Jane commentated.

"It's like he's carrying the whole world on his shoulders," added Amber.

Mike didn't comment. He had a coffee and the one remaining chocolate biscuit. Evan seemed in a stupor, he thought. Maybe

Charlie was right. Why was he getting involved? He should just stop Evan doing something but Evan would have pride. He very much doubted if he could talk Evan out of confronting this Taylor chap.

Maybe it was his Russian blood, rushing to his heart and not his brain, or maybe it was the helping of a damsel in distress just like one of King Arthur's knights. Mike said goodbye and left for his chariot, a Merc. A modern version maybe.

He drove home and awaited Charlie. Charlie didn't appear until gone four. He wasn't happy. He'd seen Taylor, a giant of a bloke, tall, wide and lean. He told Mike.

"Are you going in tonight Detective?" Mike nodded. "Would you still go in even if I don't help you?" Mike nodded again. "Thought so," said Chalky. "One thing Detective: when I saw him he was coming back from the offi. He looked loaded and he has obviously not finished yet. He had a bagful of lunatic soup."

"The offi I guess is an off-licence. The soup?"

"That's right. The lunatic soup is your cheap booze, rough wine and cider, you know what I mean. Drink enough of that crap and you end up in an asylum. You go mad."

"Tell me Charlie, where do you pick up this way of talking?"

"In the knowledge factory. I'm sorry, I mean in prison, Detective."

Mike gave up. Charlie was a one-off. Mike fried some bacon, cut a few tomatoes and made some sandwiches which they ate, washing them down with a couple of bottles of diet Coke.

Chalky noticed the small carriage clock on the mantelpiece. He was fascinated by the thin red second hand. It was the colour of blood. It never stopped moving. Chalky followed it for over a minute.

He remembered sitting with his late father and watching this old film, 'High Noon'. The tension built up and up. The clock ticked away; good would conquer evil in the end, just after midday.

This reminded him of that film, but he had an ugly feeling in his stomach. Would the outcome be the same? He felt a pang of sadness; he didn't think it would. The blood-coloured second hand went on and on happily. Chalky wished he could do the same.

"Have you got the necessary tools Charlie?"

"Yes boss I have."

"Will we have a problem getting in?"

"No, it's just a gingerbread door." Mike looked at Chalky. "That, Detective, means it will be easy. Sorry, I keep thinking you're one of the boys down at the Sark."

"I'm going to change Charlie, clean my teeth, the inside of my mouth is like a bird cage. Make yourself at home." Mike left.

Chalky sat there. From Charles Frederick White, to Chalky White, to Chalky, now Charlie, not Charles. This D.I. Karetzi, he liked him.

If the boys at the Sark could see him now. He didn't want to think about it. He could still walk but this man lived up to his nickname. He was crazy! But there was empathy between them and Chalky's mind spun back, a different time, a time that was way in the past.

All he could see was pain. The pain in John's eyes and legs. The pain of seeing his friend. Chalky come back for him, knowing that they would be caught.

Did the DI feel that way? Did he think, I've got to do it whatsoever? Did he realise that he couldn't win? Does he care? Is he stupid, crazy, both? The 'Charge of the Light Brigade' came into Chalky's mind.

In the shower Mike wondered if Chalky would still be there when he came out. He was glad he gave him the list. Damn it, he'd made his reputation on the back of Chalky's info two years ago. In a way he hoped Chalky wouldn't be still sitting in a chair outside in his lounge.

Mike came back in the lounge. He felt better, the throbbing in his head gone. He was dressed carefully. Trainers had replaced the moccasins, a short sleeved shirt, the long sleeved one, loose fitting jeans with an elastic belt and no jewellery except his watch. No mobile, credit cards, money, comb or his penknife.

"Time to go Charlie. You ready?"

"I'm ready. Are you sure you are?" replied Charlie, putting on a pair of gloves and dark blue bobble hat.

Chalky pointed to the knife. "Don't you think you should take that boss?"

"No, Charlie, I go with a knife, he grabs a bigger one from the kitchen, you understand, things escalate out of all control.

"Follow me in your car," Mike told Chalky. "You will park about five hundred yards away – remember you're not involved. I will park outside. I am involved."

On the way out Mike grabbed a half packet of his cigarettes.

Twenty minutes it took. After parking Chalky walked the five hundred odd yards to where Mike had parked. He opened the passenger door and got in.

Mike was smoking, the hand holding the cigarette shaking ever so slightly but more than noticeably.

A last cigarette for a condemned man, thought Chalky. He looked at the detective. He could see his eyes, black as tar, just staring through the windscreen. Chalky guessed that he was preparing himself for battle.

Mike recognised the symptoms of fear, dry mouth, sweaty palms and accelerated pulse. He could taste the metallic flavour of adrenalin flowing through his body.

He could use it, but didn't want the adrenalin to take over and create panic. Mike kept his breathing as steady and balanced as he could. He tried to focus. He needed to.

Mike crushed out what remained of his cigarette, glanced at Charlie and opened his car door. Charlie did the same. Mike locked the car and, crouching down, placed his keys on the inside of the front wheel, completely out of sight.

With two steps, they crossed the pavement. There was no gate and with another two steps they reached the front door.

They paused for a few seconds, then Chalky did his job and they were into the building.

Taylor's flat was on the first floor. There were two on each floor, a total of four. There was no lift so both took the stairs, making as little noise as possible.

They shouldn't have bothered. The noise emanating from the target flat was enough to wake the dead.

A gangster film of some sort was playing at full volume on the TV. There seemed to be a lot of shooting. Mike put his right index finger to his lip and with his other index finger on his left hand he pointed to the lock.

If there was a dead bolt on the other side Mike would be in trouble. There was, but it hadn't been locked. Mike's luck was holding. Or that's what he thought.

The door opened. Mike tapped Chalky on the shoulder and pointed to the stairs. Chalky whispered "Good Luck" and crept back down the stairs, very slowly.

Once outside, Chalky started running as fast as he could towards his car. To get back home Chalky had to pass the apartment again. He only lived a further mile down the road. He wondered what was going on in that flat. Best he forgot the whole bloody business, he thought, but he couldn't. It was just gone eight p.m. and Maggie his partner was still at work. Maggie was a nurse and on the late shift. She wouldn't be home until gone midnight.

Mike just stood there in the small lobby. To the right there was a door obviously leading into the lounge from where the TV was playing.

He waited a few minutes. He had to be sure that Vincent was not in the kitchen or the bathroom. He remained still. He also had to make sure that Vincent was alone. If there were two of them he would get out as fast as possible. That's why he left the door slightly ajar. The same applied if Vincent had female company.

Another minute or so passed. Mike's breathing was faster than he'd liked. There was no turning back now.

He pushed the cheap wooden door open and adjusted himself to the semi-darkness. The only light was from the TV which was showing a black and white film.

His heart pounding like a piston engine, his legs like jelly, he tried to take in the room as fast as his brain could collate the information.

CHAPTER 14

The room was square shaped, about fifteen foot each way. At the back an archway led to a small kitchen, to the right a TV. Opposite the TV was a two-seat sofa, in front of which was a small wooden coffee table. In the middle of the room was an easy chair.

On the opposite wall there was a bookcase full of magazines with a few ornaments on the top shelf. The carpet was a faded red. It was dirty and there were bottles, all empty, everywhere. A half full bottle of cider was on the table as was a large dirty tumbler.

It was hot in there. The double radiator on the wall next to the bookcase was red hot but Mike felt cold. He was shivering.

He knew immediately that he had made a big mistake as soon as he had seen the occupant of the sofa. A huge, ape like man, shirt undone to his navel, revealing a toned, well-muscled body. The ape man had discarded his shoes.

He was obviously drunk. It took him a while to register that he had an uninvited and unwelcome guest in his front room. So, Mike thought, this is the animal and woman beater.

"Who the fuck are you? What you doing in my house?" Vincent shouted.

"I'm a friend, Mr Vincent. I come to give you a piece of advice."

Vincent raised himself unsteadily from the sofa, knocking the half full bottle of cider off the table. "You're not my fucking friend and I don't need any advice. Get the hell out of here before I tear you apart, you stupid bastard!"

Without warning Vincent charged, head down. The easy chair

took the brunt. Again Vincent charged. Mike stepped aside but in doing so lost his balance, the wall stopping him from falling.

Vincent turned and threw a massive haymaker which just grazed Mike's chin. If Vincent's punch had connected Mike would have been the first man on planet Mars.

A punch to the ribs sent Mike crashing to the floor. Vincent followed up with a kick to Mike's unprotected stomach. If Vincent had been wearing shoes it would have been all over.

Mike crawled towards the bookcase and another kick from Vincent caught him in the nose. A fountain of blood followed. Two more kicks followed; one opened up the old wound under Mike's eye, the other catching Mike's left hand.

Karetzi was desperate. Vincent stamped on Mike's ribs. The pain was unbearable. Vincent attempted another stamp to Mike's ribs but this time lost his footing and crashed into the bookcase which instantly became firewood, such was the load landing on it.

Both rose simultaneously, very slowly, one because he was drunk, the other because of the pain in his side.

Vincent threw a right just catching Mike on the shoulder. He followed with a left again to Mike's ribs.

Vincent smelt blood. He charged again, this time tripping and landing on the coffee table. The coffee table went the way of the bookcase.

Vincent took his time getting on his feet again. Mike couldn't take advantage of the situation.

Mike tried to gather some strength. He tried to forget the pain. He was near complete exhaustion. Mike now knew he was going to get hammered. He thought of his mother, his father. Was this the end?

Mike could only watch as the animal staggered to his feet, stood unsteadily, then advanced on Mike who he felt was rooted to the spot.

A short left jab split Mike's lower lip. Vincent prepared himself to throw a right but telegraphed it and Mike blocked it with his left.

Mike's elbow caught Vincent in the throat, forcing his head down.

The head butt did it. Vincent sank to his knees; a kick in the groin had the right effect. Vincent started screaming but still he started to get up. Mike was weak and again conceded his advantage. Nothing could keep this animal down, thought Mike, pain racking his body, blood flowing from both his nose and mouth.

He took a pace back, wary of being rushed again but Vincent was back on his feet. He lumbered towards him. Mike pretended to move to his left. The animal, brain slowed by the booze, and pain in his groin, moved to his right to counteract his opponent's position.

Summoning every last ounce of strength in his body, Mike planted his left foot firmly on the floor and, using his right foot like a scythe, kicked Vincent in the knee.

Vincent's leg gave and he collapsed in a heap. Mike moved swiftly and decisively aimed another kick into Vincent's groin. But Vincent wasn't finished. From where he lay he had grabbed hold of one of the bottles which he threw catching Mike on the head, breaking the skin.

Now both were on the floor. Vincent couldn't move. He was in agony – the bottle had been his last act of defiance.

Mike's left eye had closed, his other covered in blood which was pouring from his forehead. Mike could just about see Vincent. He felt the ground for a bottle, finding instead one of the broken coffee table legs.

He picked it up with his right hand, his left now swollen and numb. He had no feeling in that hand.

He crawled the five feet to where Vincent was lying and, raising his right arm, brought down the mahogany coffee table leg, not once but twice with all the force he could muster, down onto Vincent's right knee, smashing the bone to smithereens.

He brought his arm up again and again brought it down as hard as he could, this time breaking every bone in Vincent's right hand.

Vincent was screaming hysterically like a banshee. In between screams he was cursing Mike to high heaven. No-one could hear him. The couple next door were away on holiday, the flat directly below was empty, being decorated ready for renting out, and the old man living next to that one was tone deaf and usually in bed by nine.

Mike felt nauseous. He wanted to throw up but didn't even have the energy to do that. His head was spinning like one of those big wheels you find at the fairground. His ribs were on fire. Blood was everywhere, every bone ached. He knew he had to get out.

He crawled to the front door which fortunately he'd left slightly ajar. With great difficulty he opened it further and tried to stand using the doorknob as a prop.

The film on the TV had finished, the good guy had won.

He tumbled out through the door, his legs giving up on him once more. He was saved from falling head first down the steps by the banister. He tried to stand only to kiss carpet once again. He descended the stairs backwards like a baby would do.

At the bottom of the stairs Mike used the newel post, dado rail and letter box to stand long enough to open the door.

His first step into the front garden was his last for quite a while. He fainted, falling onto a holly bush and cutting his arms badly.

As he came round, a hand grabbed him. He couldn't understand it. It wasn't his hand. He couldn't see. My Christ, it was Vincent, the fucking man was indestructible!

It took nearly fifteen minutes for Chalky to get Karetzi into the Mercedes. He'd seen where Karetzi had put the keys and now that he had him in the passenger seat he had to work out how to drive the car which was an automatic.

It didn't take Chalky long to fathom it out. He drove Mike to his home which was only five minutes away and fortunately was on the ground floor.

Karetzi seemed to be comatose. Chalky thought about taking

him to hospital but he didn't need the questions. The detective wouldn't want them either.

It was nearly midnight and his partner Maggie would be back in less than twenty minutes. As a nurse she'd know what to do.

Chalky boiled some water and cleaned up DI Karetzi's wounds, stemming the flow of blood. From the medicine cabinet he produced a bottle of Iodine and with cotton wool he dabbed the mixture over the wounds.

On the eye he put a handkerchief full of ice. The detective was talking nonsense between groans. Chalky wasn't sure what damage the detective had sustained but it was obvious that he'd taken one hell of a beating.

Chalky had put the detective on his bed. The white duvet would have to be changed, it was covered in blood. Chalky heard the key in the door. Maggie was home, thank God.

Maggie immediately sized up the situation. This wasn't the time to ask too many questions but one she had to ask. "Who is he, Charlie?"

"A policeman. Someone I owe. We can't call for a doctor or go to hospital unless it becomes a life or death situation."

"He's in a bad state, Charlie. Take his shirt and trousers off, shoes too, obviously."

Chalky did.

At around three in the morning D.I. Karetzi came round. His right hand was bandaged, as was the top of his head. It felt like he had an iron belt around his chest, more bandages. He was having difficulty breathing through his nose and even his mouth.

More worrying was that he could only see out of one eye. With his one good eye, he could see a nurse at the bottom of the bed. "Take these tablets," she said to him. She helped him take them as he could only use one hand. "They will help with the pain," the nurse Maggie explained.

"I suppose a smoke is out of the question?" said Mike.

"No, you can smoke, but it will probably make you sick," Maggie replied, handing Mike one of her own and lighting it for him. "I'll get you an ashtray."

My God, thought Mike, what kind of hospital allows smoking in the wards or anywhere else for that matter, unless of course he was dying and they were turning a blind eye.

Just four puffs later and Mike dropped the cigarette, closed his one eye and drifted off to sleep.

Chalky had taken a cab to where he had parked then drove to Taylor's flat. The door was still wide open to the flat. Chalky crept upstairs. He could hear the deathly cries coming from inside. He went in and saw Vincent.

Christ, he was in a very bad way, much worse than the detective! Chalky knew that this bloke wouldn't see the night out unless he received medical help.

He left the flat and got into his car. After a few hundred yards, he stopped at a public phone box and dialled 999. He gave them Vincent's address. They asked who the caller was. He hung up the phone and drove home.

Within an hour the emergency services arrived and whisked Vincent Taylor to the hospital – perversely, the same hospital that Jasmine was in. He refused to answer any questions.

It was nearly seven a.m. when Mike came round. The effect of the painkillers had worn off and the pain in his chest was excruciating. Where the hell was he? He cast his mind back and remembered the altercation with that Taylor, an animal in all but name. He remembered smashing his knee, breaking his hand, coming down the stairs backwards and lifting himself up to the front door. From then on, nothing.

He heard a voice. "Are you okay, Detective?" He tried to sit up and couldn't. It was a voice he recognised.

He tried to speak but his mouth felt sore, his nose blocked up.

"It's me, Boss, Charlie, Charlie White. Do you remember me?"

Mike did and didn't. His brain was fuzzy. "Where am I?" asked Mike.

"You're a guest at the Casa Charlie Hotel," Chalky answered, trying to make light of the seriousness of the situation. "Are you feeling any better? Do you want anything?" said Chalky. There was no answer. Mike had dosed off again.

When Mike did come round a few hours later, Chalky was still sitting on a chair at the bottom of the bed, half asleep. He was tired too. His partner Maggie, the nurse, was in the small bedroom also sleeping but had left various pills for Mike to take to ease the pain.

The room was hazy. It was like a carpet of mist had covered everything in Mike's sight. From his one good eye he managed to focus on Chalky who was now standing next to him.

Mike mumbled Charlie's name. At least he recognises me, thought Charlie.

"Don't speak Boss." Chalky helped Mike sit up. "Take these pills. Later I'll go and get something stronger."

Mike dutifully swallowed the pain killers.

"Where did you find the nurse Charlie?"

"She lives here, Mike, Maggie is my partner."

As if by magic, Maggie appeared at the door, now out of uniform and wearing slacks and a pullover.

Not the best looking broad that Mike had come across, but then neither was Florence Nightingale, but she was a good nurse.

"Are you Maggie?" asked Mike.

"Yes, that's me. You realise you should be in hospital, don't you?" said Maggie.

"I can't go. Thanks for fixing me up. I'm sorry that I have caused you so much trouble. I'll be out of your way as soon as possible."

"I'm sorry Detective, you are not fit to go anywhere for at least a day," said Maggie. "You can't even stand, never mind walk. You need somebody around to help you."

The pain was unbearable. Over the counter products weren't strong enough. "What's the prognosis Maggie? Will I live or not?" Mike said, tongue in cheek.

Maggie laughed. This guy was some tough hombre.

"I'll list your ailments. You have a two-inch gash on the top of your head, a broken nose, a black eye, a wound under your other eye, looks like an old wound that's re-opened. Your lower lip is split, you're heavily bruised around the face and one arm and that's the good news. You have probably cracked a few ribs, your left hand is probably broken and you could have internal bleeding."

"I shouldn't have had that haircut then, no protection on top," Mike said.

Chalky laughed. "I don't think you will be playing any football for a while Boss."

"No problem there Charlie. I'm banned for six games."

"Another fight Boss?"

"Something like that, Charlie."

"Do you have any alcohol here, and I'm dying for a fag, Charlie?"

"I've Greek firewater," said Chalky.

"What's that Charlie?"

"It's cheap cooking brandy. Maggie uses it when making things in the kitchen."

"If it's okay in food, it's okay to drink Charlie. Do you know where my car is?"

"Just outside, I brought you here in it Boss."

"Could you get my cigarettes for me?" Mike winced as he spoke. The pain was taking his breath away.

Charlie returned, cigarettes, ashtray, brandy already poured in a glass, about four fingers high.

Mike took a massive gulp. The heat of the liquid ran through his body like a steam train. Mike lit one of his cigarettes. He smoked three, one after the other and then finished off the brandy.

Chalky and Maggie just sat there saying nothing, giving the detective room. Chalky made a call, took down an address and handed it to his girlfriend.

"How do you do it Chalky?"

"Contacts, Maggie, contacts. I can just about get anything."

"Will he want money?"

"No, I'll square up with him later." Maggie left.

When she returned an hour later, she had a litre of liquid morphine, more cigarettes, Mike's brand and a bottle of whisky. The best she could get.

"Tell me Charlie, does Maggie know what line of work you're in?"

"I guess so Boss, but she pretends not to and turns a blind eye. Although lately, I've been trying to go straight. I've got some consulting work for two insurance companies, but it's part time."

"The poacher turned gamekeeper."

"Not quite Boss. Like I said Boss, I am trying, but one has to live and you need money for that."

"So Charlie, tell me, what happened? I remember coming down the stairs backwards, then what?"

"You opened the door somehow, took a step and collapsed as if you'd had a blackout. I got you to your car which was just a few yards away and drove you to my flat and you are currently in my bed."

"Sorry Charlie. Why did you come back? I thought I told you to go and forget everything. Why did you return?"

"That one's easy boss, it was the song from that film 'High Noon'."

"What are you talking about, Charlie? Didn't we agree no more slang, riddles? This 'High Noon' I suppose means 'something soon', Eh Charlie? I think I'm getting the hang of it," said Mike.

"No Boss, 'High Noon', the film with that Gary Cooper chap, a bloody old film. Anyway like I said, I tried for hours to remember the theme tune. I can recall all British hits from 1953 to 1977 but this one was 1952 and sung by Frankie Laine."

"You've lost me again Charlie."

"Sorry Boss, after letting you in I ran to my car and came back here for an hour. I couldn't get that theme song out of my head, when in a flash the first line came to me."

"And what was that Charlie?"

"It sounds a little stupid detective. I won't sing it. It's a little twee."

"For Christ's sake Charlie, what is the first line, just spit it out."

"Okay Boss, if that's what you want – it's 'Please don't forsake me oh my darling'."

"And that's what made you return?"

"Yep, it was the word 'forsake'. It grated on my mind," said Charlie. "I was outside for over two hours. I was going to give you ten minutes or so, then I was going to go up and find out what was happening. I would have called the police if you had problems."

"Charlie I think Taylor is in a very bad way. I mean a hell of a lot worse than me. I hope I haven't killed him."

"He's in hospital boss. I rang the emergency services. I've checked he's in Intensive Care – that was four, five hours ago. I saw him. You really hammered him, boss."

"Where did you phone from Charlie, your mobile?"

"No, I phoned from a call box."

"Well done Charlie," said Mike.

"Could you ask Maggie to come in please, Charlie?" asked Mike, taking a massive slug of the liquid morphine.

Chalky and his girlfriend Maggie stood at the bottom of the bed.

"Tonight, or to be correct, this morning, you Charlie saved my life, twice; the second time being when you arranged for Taylor to get to a hospital. I could have been on a murder charge if you hadn't, Charlie, and you too Maggie, I owe you both."

"You owe it to yourself Detective to and get some x-rays and proper medical attention," said Maggie. "You might have internal bleeding," she added.

Mike held out his good right hand. "My mother calls me Mikhaili, my colleagues call me D.I. Karetzi, my enemies 'Crazy' – but to you and Maggie, Charlie, as friends, you can call me Mike."

Chalky was absolutely speechless. He couldn't find anything to say. He just shook Mike's hand as did Maggie.

Chalky turned away and walked through into the hall, tears welling up in his eyes.

"You've embarrassed him," said Maggie. "Deep down he's a very decent and sensitive man."

"I know," said Mike. "I needed to tell him how much I've appreciated his help, in more ways than I can ever say. I needed to, before I..." and with that Mike fell asleep, the morphine doing the job.

After picking up Jasmine and taking her home, Evan left for the office. Both the women in his life were safe and sound and now Evan had decided that he was ready for Taylor.

Tonight, he would confront him. It would all be over, one way or the other. He arrived over an hour late.

Amber was preoccupied but she had noticed that Evan seemed his usual self. Spit and polished shoes, tidy and clean-shaven. Now where in the hell was Mike?

"No sign of Mike yet?" Evan asked Jane. "He's even later than his usual lateness, if that makes sense," said Evan. Probably involved with some woman, thought Evan.

Everyone was looking for Mike, the office, an ex-girlfriend, current girlfriend, Edna, his mother and Angelo; someone had broken his restaurant window.

By two in the afternoon Amber had tried the mobile, landline and had despatched Evan to Mike's flat. No car, no Mike. A bloody mystery, thought Evan.

His wife Edna could not understand why Mike hadn't appeared at the flat as planned to talk to Evan. Where was he? She was sure that Evan was about to do something. Call it women's intuition.

It was nearly three o'clock when Mike woke. He still felt drowsy. He felt that he needed to phone the office. The problem was, tell them what? That he wasn't feeling too good? No good. They'd be around to his apartment. If he said he had had an accident, the same, someone would be round.

He was in a conundrum. It was a riddle without an answer. Not a decent answer anyway.

Maggie came back in with a large cup of tomato soup. "I hope you can get this down you. Leave it a minute, it's too hot at the mo."

"Thanks," said Mike. "My lip's very sore."

"It should be Mike, you've split it, but the good news is I don't think your nose is actually broken and I see that you're opening your eye a bit now."

"I suppose that it's just bruised," said Mike.

"Yep, you've got a real beauty there but it's only a black eye, no real damage. It's still weeping blood from the gash on your head. It needs stitching.

"How's the pain in your side?" asked Maggie.

"Bad, Maggie, but it's subsiding. It's better than it was a few hours ago. Where's Charlie?"

"Fast asleep," said Maggie.

Sip by sip Mike drank the soup. It was good, warming and very tasty. It was homemade and had basil and cream in it. When he finished, Mike took another slug of morphine and when Maggie had left the room, he got out of bed.

He stood there on the spot for a few minutes, his good hand holding onto the bedstead. He didn't attempt to walk. For now it was enough that he could stand.

He got back into the bed and within minutes was asleep, unlike Vincent Taylor who was wide awake, out of Intensive Care, operations complete.

"So, Mr Taylor," said the detective standing at his bedside. "What we have here is a burglary gone wrong. Two intruders broke into your apartment with the intention to steal. Is that correct so far? You confront them, a fight ensues, they nearly kill you, they run – taking what?"

"I've told you Detective Inspector Simpson, they took my money and jewellery, over two thousand pounds, rings, gold bracelet, gold chain and some other items."

"From the drawer in your bedroom? Is that correct, Mr Taylor?"

"Yes, Inspector, how many times do I have to go over this?"

"And the descriptions, Mr Taylor?"

"Both about five eleven, well built, blonde, twenty-four/five year old, both wearing gloves. I would recognise them if I saw them again."

"Thank you Mr Taylor. We'll be in touch when you're out of here." The inspector left. What a load of crap, he thought to himself. He didn't believe a word of what Taylor had told him. He confined everything he'd heard in the last hour to his mental dustbin.

Tomorrow he would go around to the flat and have a good look around. D.I. Simpson would have to make a bloody report tomorrow after he'd seen Taylor's apartment.

It was his youngster's birthday and he promised that he would take all the family out to their favourite restaurant.

Vincent looked at his raised leg, his broken hand in plaster, as was the leg. He knew he would never work again as a fitness instructor or anything, period.

He reckoned he was lucky to be alive and he wanted to stay that way. Whoever his assailant was, and he wouldn't ever want to know who it was, was crazy, absolutely mad. He had nearly killed him. He would never contact his ex again.

If he ever saw her in the street, he would cross the road, that is assuming he could still walk.

But every cloud has a silver lining – he was still heavily insured. He wouldn't ever have to work again.

"Still no sign of Mike," Amber said. "You'd think he'd ring in."

"Maybe he's had an accident," Jane said.

"No, I've checked all the hospitals."

"Maybe we should get into his apartment. Could he be there, unconscious in a coma, whatever?" said Jane.

"I'll go down there again," Evan said. "Speak to a few people before I head off home. Someone must know him." Evan said goodnight and was gone. A quick drive down to the flat in the

Bay. He stood outside the door speaking to everyone who came in and out of the building.

A neighbour had seen Mike drive off in his car yesterday at about six, half six. He said he was talking to someone, a young chap, shortish with white hair. Evan checked the undercroft for Mike's car – it wasn't there.

Evan left. It was very dark now. He felt for his truncheon. It was still where he had left it. The torch was in his pocket. He parked about fifty yards from the address and waited.

About fifteen minutes later he saw an old man walking very slowly towards the house. Evan got out of the car and moved as fast as he could, truncheon up his sleeve, towards the door. The door had been opened by now. Evan went in with him.

"Don't worry my friend. I'm with the police. Just checking on Mr Taylor upstairs."

The old man was obviously deaf or very hard of hearing. Evan needed to shout but was afraid of warning Taylor so he showed the old man his credentials. At least the old man's eyesight was fine.

Evan slowly climbed the stairs as quietly as possible, retracing the exact route taken by Mike and Chalky twenty-four hours previously.

At the top he fingered the truncheon. Deep down he didn't want to talk to Vincent. He wanted to beat the shit out of him. The first blow would be decisive. If it didn't fell the arsehole, then Evan knew that he would be the one ending up in hospital; if he was lucky.

He was about to ring the doorbell when he realised that the door was slightly ajar. The lights were on and he could hear a television.

The bastard was probably pissed out of his mind. He rang the doorbell, once, twice, three, five, ten times. There was no movement. With his left hand he pushed open the door; in his raised right he held the truncheon.

He walked straight through the door to what was obviously a lounge which was open. He stepped through.

He viewed the scene, the broken furniture, the blood. This was bad. He wondered what had gone on in there. On the way out he cleaned off his palm print from the door, before closing it behind him.

Edna was waiting for him, no dinner cooking. She was so relieved to see her husband that she just burst into tears. Evan stood looking at this wife completely bemused.

"What's wrong Edna? Where's Jasmine? Something wrong? What's happened?"

"Jasmine's asleep, Evan. I was very worried about you. I thought you might do something stupid."

"Like what?" said Evan.

"I thought you might go and see Taylor. I was afraid for you."

"I did love. I went to his flat." Evan told his wife the rest.

"Oh my God, Evan! What have I done, what have I done?" cried Edna. "I contacted your partner Mike and told him what had happened. He was meant to come here earlier today and talk to you. Now I can't get him on the phone."

Evan's heart sank. "Mike didn't turn up today in the office and we've tried to contact him with no luck. I've even been down to his apartment. He was last seen over a day ago."

Evan got Amber on the line. "Amber, Evan here. Did Mike ask you for any address lately?"

"Yes, Evan, the one I got for you, a Mr Vincent Taylor and a few days ago he wanted me to trace a certain Charles Frederick White, also known as Chalky White."

"This White bloke, do you have an address?"

"No, just where he drinks, a place called the Cutty Sark, a place of ill repute, Evan."

"Do you think we could get an address for White, Amber?"

"I'll try. I have an old address. I'll work from there and call you back."

Mike had whisky, a ciggie and a walk around the room and to the bathroom, in that order.

A bath was run and Mike had a good soak in the warm water. Maggie re-bandaged his chest and ribs but Mike had to wear the same clothes which, although they had been washed and ironed, still had bloodstains on them and the shirt was ripped.

"I'd lend you one of mine, Detective, but you're twice the size," said Chalky.

"It's Mike, Charlie."

"I'm making an omelette, Mike. Could you eat that?"

"I think I could manage that; then I think I need to get back to my own apartment but obviously can't drive myself."

"Don't worry Mike, I will drive you in your car. Maggie will follow in mine but first let's eat."

They ate and Mike, with Chalky's help, got to his car. Mike had a plastic bag in his hand. In the bag he had the whisky, cigarettes and the morphine. Maggie followed in Chalky's car.

Two minutes after they had left Evan appeared at Chalky's door. He rang the bell, tried the knocker. No-one was at home and no sign of Mike's car.

He turned his car around and headed for the Bay. Where the hell had Mike and this Chalky White bloke got to?

As he neared the Bay, his mobile rang. It was Amber. "No sign of Mike, Evan, but on a hunch, when I rang around the hospitals I also enquired about Vincent Taylor and I found him."

"Where Amber?" She told him. "He's just come out of Intensive Care. He's in a very bad way. A.D.I. Simpson interviewed him about a burglary that went wrong at his flat."

Mike, Chalky and Maggie had just opened the door to Mike's apartment when Evan arrived outside the building. He saw the Mercedes parked in his partner's space and he knew that everything was fine.

Someone was coming out of the building and Evan got in. He took the lift and was ringing on Mike's door. A woman opened the door. Not what Evan would have thought was Mike's type at all.

"Is Mike in?"

"Yes, who may I say is asking?" the woman said.

"Evan, Evan his partner." She stood aside and Evan entered.

Chalky spoke first. "I'm Charles, Mike is just changing. He'll be out in a second or two. This is my partner Maggie." Evan shook his hand, then Maggie's

Mike entered the room. He was wearing a dressing gown, no pyjamas or slippers. Evan could hardly keep the shock off his face. His partner was shuffling towards him. He looked as if he'd been run over by a bus.

Mike was also shocked, seeing Evan there. He just about made it to the sofa.

"Can I get you a drink Evan?"

"Um, yes, Mike."

"Whisky do?" asked Mike.

"That's fine, thanks Mike."

"Could you do the honours Charlie? I assume you've been introduced."

Charlie poured out the drinks. "I'm off, Mike. Maggie's got to get ready for work. You know where to find me if you want anything."

"Thanks for everything Charlie, and you Maggie. I'll contact you in a few days."

With that they took their leave.

CHAPTER 15

"So Mike, I see you're still alive."

"Yes Evan, but please tell me what day it is?"

"Wednesday Mike."

"Shit, Mrs Alibi will be here shortly. Can you reach into my jacket Evan and see if I've got sixty quid for her. She's my cleaner by the way."

Just as Evan found the money, the doorbell rang. "That must be her Evan. Give her the dosh please and tell her she's not required today."

Evan did so. Mrs Alibi was more than happy.

"She okay with that Evan?" Mike asked when Evan returned.

"Bloody right she was, sixty pounds!" said Evan. "I'd do it for that."

"That's two weeks and she also includes the laundry and ironing in that."

"I see," said Evan.

"Sit down Evan and have some of my medicine. It will calm you down."

"Take morphine, Mike? No way," replied Evan.

"Don't be stupid Evan. I didn't mean that. I meant the bloody whisky, best medicine a man can have." And with that Mike attempted without success to stand.

Evan rushed over. "I'll get whatever you need Mike."

"What I need is the toilet!"

Evan helped him get there. Mike shut the door and started vomiting over and over again.

It was unbelievable that someone could vomit so much, thought Evan. If it were an Olympic sport Mike would run away with the gold medal.

Eventually the toilet door opened and as ashen-faced Mike re-entered, stumbling his way to the easy chair via a wall, the floor and the back of the sofa; he was breathing heavily. Evan handed him two glasses, one with morphine, the other with whisky.

Mike gulped down the alcohol first, then took the other glass from Evan, dropping the empty glass on the floor. He then took a large mouthful of the liquid drug before finishing it off with another mouthful.

"Should you be mixing those together Mike? It's dangerous."

He received no answer from his partner.

"Did you hear what I just said Mike?"

"I did Evan. You're the one that gave them to me."

This time there was no reply from Evan. He felt embarrassed. Deep down he felt guilty and just didn't know what to say next. He pretended to study the bottle of whisky.

"I always thought that whisky was spelt with an 'e'" said Evan, wanting to make conversation.

"In the States and Ireland it is, but the proper stuff, Scotch, is spelt without one. Did you know that it was Welsh descendants who founded the American whiskey industry in Bardstown, Kentucky in about 1730. Eighty years later more Welsh immigrants founded Jack Daniels bourbon and a little after that Southern Comfort.

Evan didn't and couldn't care less anyway but again he pretended to be interested.

"Mike, do you realise that Taylor will come looking for you and next time he will come prepared?"

"I doubt it Evan. What with one good leg and one good hand. No Evan, he won't be looking for seconds when he leaves hospital."

"I owe you. No, my family owes you and are in debt forever, Mike,, but pray, please tell me, why did you get involved? This was personal. I would have dealt with it. You don't even know my daughter and for that matter you hardly know me."

"Oh but that's where you're wrong, Evan. I know you. I know that you're fifty-four, unfit, overweight and not thinking straight in this case. That guy Taylor would have killed you. You are a decent upstanding man with Christian beliefs. Taylor is the devil. No contest, Evan."

"You still haven't answered me Mike – why?"

"Because, I on the other hand I am fit, youngish and fight dirty and, more importantly, I never let a lady down. I might not live up to all their expectations but I never let a lady down. When your good wife Edna rang I did what I thought was best for both of you. I just picked up the gauntlet and acted."

Evan listened carefully.

"You don't owe me, okay? It's over, but we both owe Chalky a lot. I owe him my life. Twice, once for saving me and once for saving Taylor, otherwise I would be up for murder now."

"How did he save Taylor, Mike?"

"He contacted the hospital, Evan."

"I see. I've been to the apartment, Mike. Your fingerprints will be all over it and if Taylor talks then both our careers will go up in a puff of smoke and worse."

"Don't worry about Taylor, Evan. He will not talk. That's a guarantee."

"I've got to go, Mike. Will be back in two or three hours. Anything you want, anything I can get you?"

"No Evan, just remember the code for the door downstairs and take my keys. They're over on that shelf." Evan did and headed for the hospital.

He found Taylor and walked in. Fortunately no-one else was there. No doctors, nurses, friends if he had any, no one.

Taylor's eyes darted from left to right and back again at least three times in quick succession. He was scared shitless.

Evan looked at him. He looked like one of those Egyptian mummies, bandages and casts covering most of his body.

"Do you know who I am, Taylor?" Taylor nodded. "Do you have any problems with my daughter or any of my family, Taylor?" Taylor shook his head from side to side. "Speak up you little bastard."

"No, I have no problems with anyone or ever will have, so help me God."

"Don't bring God into this, you bloody heathen, and don't lie or I swear the next time... Well, you can guess about next time. You've got plenty of time available."

"As from yesterday Mr Jones, I mean Inspector Detective Jones, I don't know you, your daughter, just please leave me alone, please."

"Have the police been here?" Evan asked. It was standard procedure for a hospital to report to the police in cases where a patient in Taylor's condition had been admitted.

"Yes, detective Simpson, his card is on my table."

"And?" asked Evan.

"I told him it was a burglary that had gone wrong."

"Good, keep it that way and we won't have to meet again. I suggest that when you leave you find somewhere new to live, like say the Shetland Islands."

On getting outside, Evan, hands shaking, lit up his pipe. Taylor had taken the hiding of his life. This episode of Evan's life was coming to an end. One more thing to finalise. He rang his wife, his brother and gave them his instructions. He met them outside Taylor's flat.

They had buckets, cleaning up detergents, cloths, scourers and a mop. It took two hours for them to complete the work and leave the flat clinically clean.

All of them wondered where Taylor's neighbours were. It was like a cemetery. Were they all dead? Each went their separate way. Evan via a fish and chip establishment where he bought some soft drinks and fish and chips for two.

They ate. Mike got through about half and managed to keep it down.

Evan recounted his steps since leaving Mike. He told him about seeing Vincent and then about the cleaning job.

He helped Mike get the bandage off his left hand. The swelling had gone down a little and was now itching.

Mike lit up. He tried opening and closing his hand. He could see and feel a little movement. A big smile crossed his face.

"You seem happier Mike," said Evan.

"Just thought of something nice Evan."

"What's that?"

"I was wondering if Taylor plays tennis."

"I've no idea Mike. Why do you ask?"

"When I left him Evan, his testicles were as large as tennis balls."

Evan laughed. "I guess we won't see any little Taylors coming into this world for a while, eh Mike?"

Mike laughed and took a slug of whisky. He still couldn't hold it in his left hand but his right was fine.

Evan got up. "Before I go Mike, I need to say something."

"Go ahead Evan. Your secrets are safe with me."

"It's not a secret. It's just that I want you to know how much I appreciate what you have done for my family. I'm humbled and honoured to be your friend and partner. How can I ever repay you?" Evan carried on now crying softly like a baby.

Mike opened his mouth so speak but vomited instead. The fish and chips had decided not to remain where they should.

Evan cleaned up and made Mike a cup of black tea with some lemon in it. He waited whilst his partner recomposed himself. For a few minutes no one spoke. Evan got up again ready to leave.

"You don't owe me anything," Mike said. "I'm crazy. I did what I had to do and I would do the same tomorrow if the need arises. Go home Evan. Edna's waiting. Just remember, Chalky might be a petty thief but I count him as a friend and both of us owe him."

By the time Evan got home, Mike was fast asleep, dosed up on whisky and morphine.

Jasmine looked much better and the three of them talked for over an hour.

When Jasmine retired to her room she knelt down and said a prayer of thanks. It was the first time in over twenty years that she had prayed in private.

Mike slept reasonably well considering and when he got up it was nearly nine o'clock. Without too much of a problem he got to the kitchen and fixed himself a coffee.

Within minutes Evan arrived. Five minutes later Chalky and Maggie, who changed Mike's dressing and applied various balms and ointments to his damaged parts, left.

Even thanked Chalky at least half a dozen times.

Chalky wasn't used to getting praise from the police and felt quite embarrassed.

Within the hour Mike dozed off and his three companions took the opportunity to leave. Evan returned in less than forty minutes. He'd been shopping and had bought all the ingredients for a hearty breakfast including some sugar as he knew that Mike never kept any in the apartment.

Half an hour later Mike woke up. "How you feeling?" asked Evan.

"Aching and old. Nearly as old as you, partner."

"Ah," said Evan, "That old!"

Mike laughed.

"I've been out, got us some breakfast and some strawberries."

"Strawberries?" queried Mike.

"Yep, you were talking about them in your sleep Mike, just before I left."

"I hope you used the card Evan."

"Of course I did Mike," Evan said, as he left for the kitchen.

I must be getting better, thought Mike. Why else would I be thinking about the strawberry blonde.

Evan made breakfast. The works. They ate in silence savouring the food especially the strawberries, washed, pared and dusted with sugar.

After cleaning up Evan left and Mike started making his phone calls. The food remained in his stomach.

First his mother, who he told that he had the flu and wouldn't be going to see for a while. His mother, being a mother, said no problem, she'd go around to his flat with a flask of chicken soup. It took a while but Mike managed to talk her out of it. He then phoned a few friends, mainly female, and last but not least Angelo at his restaurant. Mike again managed to put off someone from coming around with food.

On leaving Mike's, Evan headed directly for his office. He found Amber and Jane talking about ways and means of getting the membership lists of the two clubs in Swansea.

They asked how Mike was doing. Evan told them. Amber had made a lasagne and had kept a piece in reserve for Mike. Evan said he'd drop it off later.

They sat and talked about food, Mike and the Chessman.

Mike slept on and off. During the time he was awake he drank whisky and morphine when absolutely necessary for the pain which even the alcohol couldn't tame.

All he wore were his boxer shorts, the ones with little pink elephants on. He got himself to the veranda and opened the door before stepping out into the cold icy wind. It was sleeting but Mike was oblivious to the weather.

He looked up into the sky. It was dark and grey which perfectly matched his mood. He looked out onto the water and could see the little white horses forming everywhere.

He welcomed the peace. His mind regressed to his childhood, to his father.

He'd joined the police to somehow avenge his father. He'd failed but wasn't giving up. One day he would go to Russia to his father's birthplace and tomorrow or very soon he would go to the cemetery where his father was interned. He'd take his mother, although she did go at least twice weekly and liked to be alone when she went.

Some sleet hit him in the face. It was then he realised for the first time that it was very cold. He reckoned that Russia was colder.

He went back in, closed the door and picked up the whisky which he knocked back in one. It was then he noticed that he was holding the glass in his left hand. He carefully put down the empty glass and tried to make a fist. He just about succeeded.

In the kitchen he found a huge catering box of Clingfilm, something his mother had probably supplied years ago. With great difficulty he opened it and extracted the contents. As best he could he wrapped the film around his chest and waist. He felt like Mr Blobby.

He had a nice long hot shower, the bandages remaining ninety per cent dry. He shaved and cleaned his teeth.

At ten to six Evan arrived, in one hand an umbrella, in the other the 'Chronicle' and a plastic bag with the lasagne in.

Mike wondered why Evan needed an umbrella for the ten yards or so from the car parking space to the foyer door. He couldn't come up with logical answer when really it was simple. Evan didn't want to get wet.

"I've got some food from Amber and a 'Cardiff Chronicle'. Turn to page fourteen, bottom right-hand corner."

"Not another Chessman killing surely?"

"No, just turn to page fourteen."

"I need to wash my hands Mike. Can I use the toilet?"

"Use the en suite Evan. I think there is something wrong with the other."

Mike turned to the page and scanned it. It wasn't easy reading with one eye only.

Jasmine was feeling much better and more relaxed. She was staring out of the window which overlooked the car park.

She was trying hard to concentrate but she just couldn't remember the car from which the stranger with the flowers had alighted from. Hopefully, he would come back again. She would know the car. She needed to find him and this time she wouldn't let him go.

After washing his hands, Evan could not resist opening the cabinet above the sink. It was full of aftershave and eau de colognes, most still unopened.

He read the labels. Prestige, Atkinsons, Hidalgo, Phileas, Jordache Man, Grey Flannel, Aqua del Elba, Royall Lyme and a lot more. Evan was pushed to actually know most of them. He himself liked good old fashioned Imperial Leather aftershave, always did, and always would. He closed the cabinet door.

"Do you wash in aftershave Mike? You've enough stuff in there to open up a perfumery or whatever you call them French places."

"Aye, I've got quite a range Evan, but only use two, the Grey Flannel in the evening, over twenty years now and the Royall Lyme during the day. I buy the Grey Flannel and my mother buys me the other every birthday. My father used to wear it. Try some Evan."

"I'm fine Mike, and the others?"

"What others?"

"The other scents, gifts from various female admirers I suppose?" said Evan.

"Something like that Evan. Just presents. If you like the look of them take some, try them out, they won't kill you Evan. I'm sure Edna would appreciate them."

"I doubt it Mike. She's used to what I wear and I'm sure she likes it – always gets me some for Christmas."

"So," Mike said, "the great Melvyn King will be signing his new book on Saturday at Horton's Bookshop. One of my heroes. Never saw him play in the flesh but lots of old games on the TV. Over three hundred goals for Cardiff and Wales. Incredible and unsurpassable."

"Fantastic record, Mike, but did you know he played cricket for both Glamorgan and the MCC? At just nineteen he was one of the world's leading all-rounders. That means, Mike, that he could both bat and bowl to a high standard."

"How come he switched sports Evan?"

"Training accident. Broke three fingers in his right hand. Both his batting and bowling suffered. Fortunately there was nothing wrong with his feet or head so at the age of twenty-two he gave soccer a go and the rest is history."

"He's never been knighted Evan."

"Of course he hasn't, he's Welsh. He can't act or sing, so no gong. Same goes for Gareth Edwards, John Charles, etc. The list of Welsh super world class sportsmen is endless and the knighthoods for these world stars is a fat zero.

"Anyway do you think you will be able to come on Saturday with me and see Mel? Get a book signed?" said Evan.

"I'll make it even if I have to crawl there. He was one of my heroes and I don't have too many of them, Evan."

The Chessman was also going to meet the great Mel King but not to shake his hand but to do him a big favour. He would immortalise him. Tomorrow he would do a recce. See how the land lay. He had a street map and a plan but he'd still check out the area.

From his old chess box he picked up the White King and with a Stanley knife he severed off the King's head. He wiped the head clean of prints with a cloth and deposited it inside a small plastic pouch.

He checked his clothes for Saturday. The trousers needed a little ironing and the black leather shoes a bit more shine. He got down to it immediately. He liked to be organised.

He then started reading his book on handwriting again and again, underlining a word here, a word there, a sentence or whole paragraphs in some cases. He made notes in the book's margins and then read and re-read all the underlined words and all his notes. When he felt he had mastered and understood what he needed he began to draft a letter.

It was difficult to incorporate all twenty-six letters of the alphabet in his letter but somehow, after over forty attempts, he had a rough draft. Not perfect but he was tired and hungry.

He opened another can of ginger beer. Two thick slices of white bread toasted, two ounces of coarsely grated Cheddar cheese and another two of Caerphilly cheese mixed in a pan with a little dry mustard, a knob of butter, a splash of Worcestershire sauce and half a glass of Brains Best Bitter and hey presto – Welsh Rarebit. He added salt and pepper and when the mixture became creamy enough he poured it over the toast and put them under the hot grill until they were bubbling and golden. When he became rich he would still eat this at least once a week.

He opened another can of ginger beer and sat down to eat and read the rest of his newspaper. Halfway through his meal his eye caught a small article about a Japanese conglomerate called Nakamara Heavy Industries. He read the article twice. It seemed that this massive international company was or seemed to be using underhanded ways of muscling into various technical-based companies in and around Wales.

Various opponents of rival firms had met with untimely deaths. A list of these firms was printed. Peter recognised a lot of them. He read on – a dedicated office had been set up in Cardiff by the police or Government. It was a little ambiguous to ascertain what N.H.Is involvement exactly was.

NHI was quoted as saying that they had absolutely no idea of what was going on and were calling in their London lawyers, presumably to sue the paper or someone.

This was interesting. Peter finished his rarebit and walked to the mirror. He was about to convene a meeting.

"Thank you for attending at such short notice, my friends and colleagues. Our quest is nearing its end but we still have a few minor problems to overcome.

"Just leave it up to me. I think that we will have to use another pawn. We will know who and when after Chester has completed his assignment in Cardiff on Saturday.

"Thank you for your time and goodnight." With that he turned, sat back down and turned on the television.

Peter knew this wasn't normal behaviour but he felt good about it. It was just play acting like on television or film. No harm done, he thought, forgetting the nine dead people. Someone else had committed those murders and the latest member Chester Cardiff would be responsible for the next two.

Friday was just like any other day in November, heavy rain with a few thunderstorms thrown in for good measure. Evan arrived at the office five minutes early. Jane was right on time. They took coffee and sat down in their normal positions.

Amber handed them both a copy of yesterday's 'Chronicle'. She'd highlighted the NHI article. They lit up and read in silence, the only noise coming from Amber who was demolishing a packet of chocolate biscuits.

"This is ridiculous," said Evan. "I can just imagine the Chessman reading this and laughing his bloody socks off."

"I agree Evan, everyone is on the lookout for nasty little Japs whilst our killer goes about his business."

"Any luck with finding out a way of getting those lists Amber?" Jane asked.

Amber shook her head because her mouth was filled with chocolate biscuits.

"Let's go through all the documents we have again. Maybe we missed something," said Evan.

"Okay," said the girls in unison.

Three hours later they all agreed that they could find nothing new.

"Look," said Evan, "I don't think we will progress properly until we have the motive. We need the motive. I just can't understand it."

By twelve thirty the Chessman had driven to Cardiff, made his recce and was now in a public phone box. He dialled and spoke to the woman who answered the call.

"I have important information about these NHI murders and wish to speak to someone."

"I'm sorry sir, could you repeat that?"

"I can. I'm talking about the casualties at Nakamura Heavy Industries' casualties, not the people you see at your local hospital but about the murders. Do you understand?"

"Yes, sir. May I have your name?"

"Look lady, either put me through to whoever is in charge now or I'll put down the phone."

After a brief pause the voice of a man came on the line. "Can I help you?" asked the voice. "I'm Chief Superintendent Heslop."

"Are you dealing with the NHI case?"

"No sir, but I can pass on any relevant information."

"Goodbye Chief." The Chessman put the phone down and took a walk.

Twenty minutes passed before he phoned the Chief again from another phone box.

"Hello Chief, it's me again. Last chance. I need a name and number."

"Ring back in five and I'll have something for you," said the Chief, simultaneously routing through his files to find the number of the so-called Special Investigative cowboys who were supposedly working the Chessman, now NHI case or cases.

After getting a phone number out of Chief Heslop, he again walked to another phone box and called.

As soon as the anonymous caller had finished, Heslop rang the number himself and warned DI Jones to be on standby to receive a call. It might be a crank but on the other hand, who knows?

Jones waited and was rewarded after ten minutes.

"S.D.I. Jones here, who may I be talking to?"

"You may be talking to the man who can tell you about these NHI murders," said the Chessman. "What would you say, Detective, if I tell you I know how the killings are connected with a certain board game?"

"I would say that you have lost me completely. I have no idea what you're talking about and unless you are more specific I'm going to terminate this conversation," replied Evan.

"Then in that case Detective, terminate this call and we will both lose."

"And why is that?" asked Evan.

"Because put in simple terms, you need to catch a serial killer and I need the reward money."

"What reward money? What serial killer?" said Evan, but the line went dead and Evan's last words were spoken into thin air.

Both Amber and Sergeant Jane Williams who had been listening in were at a loss to explain the call.

"He knows a lot, Evan," said Jane.

"Very interesting Jane. I think Nakamura would willingly pay up and then make the government pay in one way or another. They couldn't lose, after all, we know and they know that they have nothing to do with the murders," said Amber.

"How old do you think our caller is, Amber?" asked Evan.

"Difficult Evan, he was disguising his voice, changing depth and pitch continuously. He seemed to know a lot about the Chessman but then quite a few people have a little information on these murders," said Amber.

Jane was about to speak when the phone rang again. Evan picked it up. He preferred it that way, even though it was still on loudspeaker.

It was the same person. "I understand the reward is for a quarter of a mill. Can you confirm that, S.D.I. Jones?" the Chessman asked.

"For the right info I think that would be in order," said Evan.

"Then can we meet outside Cardiff Central in ten minutes?" asked the voice.

"Make it twenty, and how will I recognise you?" asked Evan.

"I will be wearing a red hat, and you, Detective?"

"A blue Glamorgan Cricket Club umbrella," said Evan.

"Come alone Jones," said the voice before the line went dead.

"Right Jane, got a brolly?"

"Yes, Evan."

"Good, grab it and follow me. Keep about fifty, sixty yards behind me. If I make the meet carry on past me and wait."

"And if you don't?" said Jane.

"If I don't then I will turn and head back, same route. Wait and then check to see if I'm being followed. If I am, call me on my mobile. You have the number."

"I do."

"Okay, let's go. Remember what I said. It's important that he is trapped in the middle if I don't make the meet and he follows me."

Peter the Chessman adjusted his cheap blue plastic raincoat and gave his grey cloth cap a good shake. With his old-fashioned glasses and greyish moustache he looked a lot like the late Fred Dibnah.

Stationing himself behind the steel barrier in the corner of the bus station where Central Square and Saunders Road met, he had the perfect position. If only he knew from which direction they would approach. He was certain this Jones chappie wouldn't come alone.

He saw the stupid cricket umbrella. It was probably used in the summer for shade in the sun. Now that was a laugh. Summer and sun in Wales! Nevertheless, it was doing a job in the drizzle.

The Chessman got a better view of the policeman when he passed only yards by him and now he waited for the backup man. The cop stopped just outside the front of the station.

Two lads of eighteen went into the station, a woman with a suitcase; three people were loitering outside the station, two with cases, another with a briefcase. All were smoking.

A blue over-coated lady passed holding a small purple coloured brolly. She headed straight into the station.

In the next five minutes six more possibles passed. Maybe the cop had come alone. He scanned the area again. Nothing suspicious.

He moved to the next place of shelter and suddenly noticed that the cop had gone. No sign of him.

Evan had given up. What was this bloke's game? He went into the station and looked carefully at his watch, tapping it and shaking his head at the same time. He then walked out and headed back to the office.

Sergeant Williams had got the message, waited a few minutes and also left.

The Chessman saw Evan walk out of the station and walk slowly back the way he'd arrived. He waited a few minutes and was rewarded. The woman with the blue overcoat and purple umbrella came out of the station and headed in the same direction as the cop. So no train luv. Twenty minutes in the station. He was sure she was the backup.

For a so-called sixty-five year old, the Chessman moved very fast through the bus station, across Wood Street and turned left into St Mary's Street. Bluecoat lady was about eighty yards ahead.

He followed.

From his left pocket he extracted a plastic bag and, from his right, a small umbrella. Still in full stride he put cap, glasses and moustache into the bag whilst at the same time he unbuttoned his coat and, stopping for just a second, he also placed it into the bag. He unfurled his umbrella and kept following.

All was well until the small park when the blue coated lady disappeared. No police station in sight, so they must have entered one of the houses opposite. Very strange.

It was now gone two. Peter circumnavigated the park and found himself a phone box. He called the cop's number. A woman answered. An older voice with a slight Jamaican twang, obviously not the one he had followed from the station.

In his best Jamaican accent the Chessman asked if he could speak to Detective Jones, and Amber, without another word, just passed the phone over to Evan.

"Jones here."

The fake Caribbean voice spoke. "I'm sorry Detective but I was compromised. It was impossible to make it to the station but I still want the reward and will get in contact again soon. Bye for now."

"Were you followed Jane?" Evan asked.

"Absolutely no way, Evan. No one at the station who would fit the bill. Lots of people with small kids, young couples, station staff. I don't think he came and outside just a few, mainly with suitcases having a quick ciggie before travelling."

"Lousy accent," said Amber.

"Somehow I think he knows it was but what I cannot understand is why all this subterfuge when he knows that we must meet for him to claim any reward," said Evan.

"Will he phone again?" asked Jane to no one in particular.

"If he's genuine then he will. If we can entice him with a reward," Amber answered.

"How will he know that the reward is there, guaranteed without any comebacks?" asked Jane.

"First job is to find out who NHI's lawyers are and request a meeting with them here in Cardiff. We tell them that we have a possible good lead which could exonerate their clients but they need to put up a very large reward," said Amber.

"If they don't agree then we might have a bigger problem than we already have. Maybe the London boys are on the right track and we, well, we are really in the shit," Evan said.

"Time for tea." Amber said. "I'm sure we could all use a cuppa and a slice or two of my Victoria cake."

It sounded fine to Evan.

The Chessman ordered a slab of Dundee cake and a pot of tea. He was pleased with how his day had panned out so far. The voices he'd used for the calls were perfect. No one still had any real clue as to his real voice or age and now all he had to do was kill an hour or so before returning to the park and waiting until they left the house. There were at least three of them. The two he'd seen and a Jamaican woman.

Amber turned on her swivel chair and faced the other two. "Wilhelm, Western and Wright."

"Who might they be then?" asked Jane. "NHI's London lawyers?"

"Ah, the three Ws, great cricketers from your party of the world Amber."

"The big hitters from London," giggled Amber. "The Law Society's equivalent to Walcott, Weekes and Worrell."

"I think they will smash poor old Prof and friends for six," said Evan who could hardly contain himself from laughing with Amber.

Poor old Jane, having no interest or idea of the game of cricket didn't have a clue of what they were on about and frankly didn't care.

"This is how we will leave it," said Evan. "If our man of many voices contacts us and we are satisfied he has the information which will help nail the Chessman, then we will talk to the three Ws. Until then we do nothing."

"I'm off to see Mike, then home. Can I give you a lift Jane?" asked Evan.

"Thanks Evan but now that it's stopped raining I'll walk," said Jane.

The Chessman clocked Evan coming out of a house and crossing the road to a BMW. He made a mental note of the registration number. It might come in handy.

He moved closer to the house from which the detective had

211

emerged. He knew he couldn't follow the car on foot so he just waited for someone else to leave. He hoped it would be soon. Not only was it cold, but it had begun raining again.

At last he saw movement. The front door of the unimposing terraced house opened and the woman with the blue overcoat exited. She crossed the road into the park.

The Chessman watched her carefully. He noted the path she took until she was out of sight. He followed her route, turned and went back, then turned and did the route again.

Now satisfied, the Chessman walked to where he had parked his car. It was time to go home. Tomorrow was a big day. On the way home, the Chessman had lots of time to think. He thought mainly about Mel King and wondered if Mr King would get a good night's sleep, not that it mattered much, as from tomorrow Mr King would make up for any shortage of sleep tonight. He would be dead.

When Mike heard the doorbell ring, he glanced at his watch. It was running fast. It said ten past six, yet the six o'clock news hadn't even started.

He pushed himself up and wandered slowly, half-cut and half-drugged to open the door. It was Evan.

"Hi Mike, you look better."

"Thanks Evan. Generally I do. One more good night's sleep and I'll be fine for tomorrow's book signing. By the way, do you have the time?"

"Yes, Mike, just gone half five. Get yourself a coffee or cold drink, Evan."

"No, I'm okay Mike, just popped in to check out if you're still alive. And to bring you up to date" – which Evan did.

"Sounds strange to me Evan. I'd give a pound to a penny that it's the Chessman."

"Yes, it's crossed our minds too," said Evan. "On the other hand it could be Nakamura's people. I'd personally give you a tenner to a penny on that," added Evan.

Mike thought about it for a second or two before replying. "You know Evan, your tenner would be safe. I completely agree with you and if we're right about this, then we're wrong about our theories on the Chessman."

"I know Mike, I know, if the guy doesn't contact us, we're back further than when we first began on this case. I just can't contemplate such a scenario. We'd be finished Mike. Back to God knows where."

Mike glanced again at his watch. Still nothing. He tapped it hard on the table – still no movement. It was broken, probably during the fight with Taylor. Mike took it off. He was very upset.

"Something wrong Mike?"

"Yeah, my father's watch is bust."

"Let's have a look, Mike." Mike passed it over. "An Exacta, East German, Mike. I think it might be a bit hard to find spare parts for this. It also needs a new face. It's scratched badly. It looks like a nine," said Evan.

"I think it's a six, because when I got the watch it read six minutes past six and the winder was pulled out to lock the time."

"Was your father wearing the watch when he was attacked?"

"Yes, but he was attacked at about five o'clock and also the watch was not on his wrist but in his pocket."

"So you think your father was leaving some kind of message. A clue to who the mugger or muggers were?"

"I guess so Evan. I've thought about it countless times and just can't make any sense of it. The way I see it, my father was attacked by at least one assailant. He is stabbed and robbed. For some unknown reason they panic and run away. All they take is money. They leave the watch because, being foreign, it is traceable and not worth much anyway.

"They also leave his wedding ring, purely I think because they could not get if off his finger easily. My mother now has that. She says she will give it to me when I marry.

"So as I see it, my father then knows he is dying, after being beaten so badly, that he somehow has enough savvy to try and leave a clue. So he takes off his watch, scratches the six on the face with whatever he finds to hand, say a very sharp stone or nail, and then sets his watch to six minutes past six. He pockets it so that the police know it's an important piece of evidence and a clue to his attackers."

"Okay, Mike, let's say three sixes, not a phone number; couldn't be a car registration or a house number – can't say anything comes to mind which would help."

"Evan, I've had twenty years and more to decipher the code, clue, whatever. I've gone through my father's books, record collection, everything that I could that was my father's but to no avail.

"I've tried line six, page six, sixth word, page sixty-six, sixth line, sixth record in sixth album alphabetically, then sixth song, sixth verse. I could write a book on what permutations I've used."

"Have you given up, Mike?"

"No, Evan, and I never will."

Evan let the matter rest. His partner was visibly tiring and getting quite despondent so he changed the subject.

"Will you be okay for tomorrow, Mike? I'll pick you up at about nine?"

"Nine is fine Evan. See you then."

They said their goodnights and Evan left.

Within ten minutes of Evan leaving Mike, who no longer needed the morphine as such and was fed up drinking whisky, which he'd polished off and had no choice, decided he would try and get to Angelo's and some solid Italian food. It took him a while but he made it in one piece. Everyone was happy to see him and made a fuss over him. Mike didn't mind in the slightest. The free meal and drink helped restore Mike to something like his old self.

Before getting into his car outside Mike's, Evan phoned home and told Edna he would pick up a Chinese takeaway for dinner for all of them.

Over the meal the discussion turned to Evan's partner.

When Evan told them about the watch, it was unanimously decided that they would buy Mike a new watch as a small token of their appreciation for what he had done for them regarding the Taylor incident. Jasmine could get a thirty per cent discount in the jewellery department of the store where she worked. She was about to start working again on Monday and had decided to stay with her parents until the New Year.

After dinner they sat and watched television. They were all content and happy. Suddenly Edna started shouting. "I've got it! I've got it, Evan!"

"Got what darling?"

"I've solved the puzzle. Well nearly," replied Edna excitedly.

"The puzzle?" queried Evan.

"The three sixes. It's the devil's number, the number that represents hell or the devil!" cried out Edna, now on a roll.

"So you think the devil attacked Mike's father, do you love?"

"Don't be silly Evan, you know I don't mean that, but that's the clue, Evan. I'm sure of it."

"Dad."

"Yes Jas?"

"I think mum's right. It could be something written on their T-Shirts, like on football and rugby shirts. That type of thing."

"Two things, Jas: it was mid-winter so forget the T-shirts, and even if they were stupid enough to walk around half naked in the cold, I cannot think of any sporting organisation which would carry that many players in their squad."

"No, Dad. We're talking here of street gangs, motorbike gangs, that type of thing."

"I think you're onto something girls," Evan said, rising and moving to the phone which he picked up, dialled and waited for Amber to pick up.

Amber with a mouthful of fried ribs, picked up and listened.

"Okay Evan, all gangs in the South Wales area from 1960 to 1975."

Working with Mike and Evan was always interesting she thought, and this was no exception. She started work. This should be easy. Easy as eating another rib which she bit into.

By midnight everyone was asleep, the Jones family, Mike, Jane, Peter the Chessman, Melvyn King, everyone with the exception of Amber who was still on the computer.

CHAPTER 16

Saturday 22nd November, 08.15 hours. Mike was awake. He could see out of both eyes, his hand was fine, ribs a bit sore but all in all he felt good. Well, maybe he couldn't do a marathon but a bit of hand shaking, no problem.

He was expecting Evan at about nine so he made a large espresso and checked himself over before drinking it. Comb, knife, cigarettes, lighter, credit cards; something was missing – no watch.

Evan left in plenty of time but the car was behaving strangely. Every time he stopped for a light, the car stalled and he was nearly fifteen minutes late.

Mike was waiting patiently and when Evan arrived late Mike knew there was something amiss.

Evan explained the problem and Mike rightly said to get it to Sandy's and they could walk around to Horton's from there while it was being repaired. It was obviously something simple.

Evan agreed and they set off. When Sandy saw them, he dropped his newly made coffee onto his lap. His right hand began to twitch and he went pale. He looked at Curly. "We have a problem mate."

Curly looked up. He could see that the boss was sweating and stupidly asked for Sandy to verify that they had a problem.

"Do you see Father Christmas, Curly, or do you see Detective Dread?"

"Dread Sandy?"

"Just button it Curly. I'll have to see to this as usual."

"Hi boys," Mike said. "Do you remember us? BMW, problem stalling at lights." Evan handed Sandy the keys.

"Can I get you detectives a coffee while we look over her?" Curly asked.

"Thanks," Evan said, "one black, no sugar, one white with two."

Evan looked at Mike smiling. "I think you've scared Sandy, so much he's pissed himself." Evan pointed to Sandy's crotch which had the dark stains of the spilt coffee.

The coffee came and both mechanics left to look over the car.

Mike lit up again blowing smoke rings at the 'No Smoking' sign.

After a few minutes, when Mike had stubbed out his cigarette on the floor, he took out his knife and started sharpening a biro which was lying on the desk.

"That's not a pencil," Evan advised Mike.

"I'm just bored Evan. You see that Ferrari sign over there?"

"I do."

"Do you see the fifth letter, the 'a'?"

"Of course I can Mike."

While Evan was still uttering the words the knife flew like a jet straight into the centre of the letter 'a'.

"Incredible," said Evan.

"Not really, just five years or so of daily practice, throwing it at an old apple tree we had in the garden," said Mike. "In the beginning I could only hit the tree once in ten and make it stick. You see, the knife wasn't correctly balanced, so I drilled these holes, first one, then two and got it right with the third. Now I can hit any target, nine times out of ten, but every so often it bounces back." Subconsciously Mike touched the teardrop scar under his left eye. "I stopped practising when I think I killed off the old apple tree," Mike said laughing.

Sandy returned just then with the news that it would take an hour or so to repair the car. He had smelt the smoke and noticed the knife in the wall. He was worried.

Without even bothering to ask what the problem was Mike thanked them and, after retrieving his knife from the wall, they left telling the mechanics that they'd come back at about twelve, if that was all right with them.

It was, and the detectives departed. Sandy and Curly both breathed a sigh of relief. The job would only take a half hour but Sandy wanted to make sure that the car didn't have any other problems. He remembered the knife. How could he forget it? His hand started twitching. No, he'd never forget the knife.

Sandy noticed the cigarette butt on the floor. He gave it a nudge with his foot and it went under the desk. He then opened the door to let out any remains of the smoke. Exhaust fumes, oil and grease smells he was used to. But cigarettes – no way, unless the smoker was that crazy detective. For him he would make an exception. In reality, he had no choice and he knew it.

Evan walked slowly. Even at the best of times he walked slowly, but today he walked even slower. He knew his partner was still hurting. Every fifty yards or so, they stopped for Mike to rest and they eventually arrived at Horton's at just past half ten.

There was a queue of over a hundred people and it was getting longer by the minute.

They headed towards the entrance and flashed their warrant cards. Mike mumbled something about pickpockets and they settled in the queue with about twenty people ahead of them. Evan estimated that at a minute per person for each signing they would be there for at least twenty minutes. He wondered if Mike could last that long but decided not to say anything. His partner would have worked it out himself and if he was okay with that, then fine.

Everyone in the queue was so excited. They would come face-to-face with a living legend and shake his hand.

Unfortunately, for most in that queue they would never shake Mel King's hand. In less than half an hour the word living would not apply to the legend Melvyn King who was happily signing autographs and writing messages inside Horton's bookshop.

The Chessman had been there for nearly two and a half hours. Luckily, for him and the people who were queuing the rain had held off. It was cold but no rain.

He had seen Mel King dropped off by a friend or relative and enter the bookshop where a table with a pile of books on top was ready. Mr King had seated himself and taken a sip of coffee from a plastic cup. He seemed in very good spirits.

That was about to change drastically. Born in Cardiff, died in Cardiff. Mr M. King would soon be Mr M. King R.I.P in Cardiff.

The Chessman, or now Chester the Chauffeur, caught his own reflection in one of the nearby shop windows. High black boots with extra heel insoles, he looked at least four inches taller and the padded shoulders of his oversized grey-double breasted uniform made him look broader.

Steel grey hair, white shirt, plain dark blue tie with a small white letter 'K' embroidered on it, well, not quite embroidered but carefully painted on with some typing correction fluid. In his hand he held a plastic CostKing bag which contained his leather gloves and chauffer's cap.

At five to eleven he crossed the road, pausing in a small doorway to put on his cap and gloves. He folded the plastic bag into a neat small square and put it into one of the inside pockets of his jacket.

He buttoned up his jacket and marched purposefully towards Horton's which was about sixty yards away.

The Chessman took the longest steps his legs would allow; after all, he would soon be a TV star – CCTV cameras abounded in this area. He touched the fake scar on his cheek and felt his grey moustache. Green contact lenses would also help in his bid to be recognisable to all and sundry.

Again, he crossed the road and entered Cara's Coffee and Donut Café. It was modern and tastefully done up. About thirty people were enjoying the cafe's fare – about half the capacity.

Two roving security cameras were in use; one picked him up as soon as he entered.

He could see four staff. One couldn't miss them, they were outfitted in a hideous vivid pink and white striped tracksuit and all four were wearing pink baseball type caps back to front. In blue lettering C.C. was emblazoned on both the upper clothing and cap. Not one of them was over the age of eighteen.

If Peter, alias, the Chessman, alias Chester in this case, could change anything, he would have spared King and killed the designer of the bloody uniforms.

"Good morning," the Chessman said, when he reached the counter. "Mr Melvyn King would like another coffee and some doughnuts." Whilst speaking he fingered his tie; the two youngsters dressed like pink clowns followed the movement of the fingers and noted the small white 'K', just as the Chessman had expected.

"You the chauffeur to the actual real Mel King?" asked one.

"I am son."

From nowhere a small, fat woman of about forty appeared. She was decked out completely in black, obviously the owner Cara, the Chessman correctly reasoned.

"I'm Cara. I own this place and I assume you are Mr King's chauffeur?"

"Dead on," replied the Chessman. The word 'dead' set his heart racing just a little. It was a good feeling. "Mr King would like another coffee and some doughnuts."

"Okay, same as before, a regular Americano with one sugar and what type of doughnut?" asked Cara.

"I think he's heard about your special," replied the Chessman.

"Everyone has; my own special recipe," Cara said pushing out her ample bosoms and standing as tall as she could which made her nearly five foot with the four-inch heels.

"That sounds perfect. Mr King is so looking forward to the special doughnuts, Mrs Cara, and please can you make it two coffees? I could do with one. It's been a long day already and could I have mine first?"

"No problem and it's just Cara, not Mrs. I'm not married," she said, looking into the emerald green eyes.

Funnily enough that last statement didn't surprise the Chessman.

He waited a mo for the coffee and when it was ready he made to pay with a twenty-pound note. Cara waved away the money. "It's on the house, please make sure Mr King knows."

"That is very kind of you." I'm sure that Mr King will appreciate your gesture and the free publicity you will get from it, thought the Chessman as he picked up his coffee.

As he walked towards a table, partly hidden by a large pillar but unoccupied, he said to himself, "Lose ten or so stone and maybe you can prefix your name with a Mrs."

After seating himself the Chessman, alias Chester, lifted the lid off the coffee container, raised it to his mouth and pretended to drink. He rested the carton next to the pillar out of sight to most of the customers and staff.

From the side pocket of his jacket he removed a small phial of liquid which he delicately poured into the coffee with his left hand, his right hand positioned in such a way as to obscure his movements with his left from prying eyes.

A moment later a small plastic tray, bearing a coffee and three doughnuts, was put beside him on the table. He guessed that one of the doughnuts was for him or else maybe Cara must have assumed that Mr King's appetite was as big as hers and he could deal with all three.

He waited a moment, then stood up, his back to the two customers who could see the tray and he quickly swapped coffees. He piled the doughnuts one on top of the other like pineapple rings in a tin. He finished by dropping the severed chess piece in the doughnut ring pile.

The Chessman, or Chester as he called himself that day, was pleased that he had had the foresight to order the special doughnuts and not different types. Mr King might have preferred the one on the bottom of the pile and everything would have been ruined. It was so easy to make stupid mistakes but then he wasn't a cop.

Leaving his coffee on the table, after taking off the lid, he walked up to the counter, tray in hand. Addressing the pimply youth whom he had first encountered on entering, he spoke.

"Look here Jon…" The name was on a badge pinned to his so-called uniform. "I've no chance of getting past that crowd outside Hortons. They probably will think I'm queue jumping and I've got this uniform on as some kind of disguise but you, in your outfit, will have no problem getting in and you will be able to meet the great man himself, face to face. He might even shake your hand."

Jon glanced at Cara, who was hovering nearby who nodded her approval. She knew publicity when she saw it.

There's no such thing as bad publicity, the Chessman thought, but if tomorrow's heading reads MEL KING POISONED BY CARA'S COFFEE, then maybe there was such a thing as bad publicity.

The Chessman returned to his seat and watched Jon crossing the road holding the tray as if it was a delicate baby. Jon had no problem getting through the crowd both outside and inside. Detective Karetzi and Jones were in seventh and eighth position in the queue respectively.

As Jon approached the desk, the crowd stood aside giving him more room in which to manoeuvre. Mel King looked up slightly bemused.

"Complimentary coffee and doughnuts from Cara's Coffee Shop Sir," Jon said, setting down the tray.

"Thank you, thank you very much. It's very much appreciated. It's thirsty work book signing." Mel King stood up and shook Jon's hand, then immediately sat back down and took the lid off the coffee carton.

Before attending his next customer Mel took a bite out of the top doughnut. After signing a book, he took another bite and a sip of coffee. It tasted a little bitter but it was still good. Another signature and another couple of sips. One more and a few sips and a bite of the doughnut.

By the time the detectives were third and fourth in line, Mel was dead. A heart attack, according to a doctor who happened to be just behind Evan, and who brushed past everyone to administer some help when Mr King started having a seizure, but it was too late.

The word soon got around, people crying, screaming, the whole spectrum of human emotions when someone near to your heart dies.

Mike flashed his badge at the store's Manager. "Get everyone out now – come on, move it!" With the help of his staff and a doorman, who happened to be an off-duty policeman, they managed in five manic minutes to get everyone out, apart from the detectives, doctor, staff and policeman.

"Listen up now," said Mike, "first thing is to cover the shop window with whatever. It's like a goldfish bowl in here; next, don't touch anything and you," he said pointing to the off-duty policeman, "phone your local boys and get them in with an ambulance a.s.a.p. and everyone don't touch anything."

Everyone outside and inside the bookstore was in a state of shock. The word had spread like wildfire and there were now at least four hundred people milling around outside.

Evan had been crying but now had managed to pull himself together again. Mike would have cried too, if he had the time to let everything sink in.

"Are you sure, doc, this is a heart attack?" asked Evan.

"Ninety-nine per cent," was the reply. The staff covered the windows and everyone just stood there not knowing what to do next. Mike felt he needed a cigarette, not in the bookstore as he might contaminate the scene so he asked about the back, if there was space outside. There was and Mike had his fag.

When Mike was on his second, Evan joined him. "What a rum do eh Mike? I can't believe it. The guy was ultra-fit, even at his age."

"Sod's law, Evan," replied Mike. "Maybe the bloody doughnut killed him," he said, sarcastically.

"Everything's possible," Evan said, "but what a sad way to go."

"I don't know Evan, he's in the limelight again. I bet you the reporters are outside. Someone should give them a statement of some sort."

"Let the locals do it. We will leave as soon as they get here."

The Chessman sat and drank his coffee. He didn't have a care in the world. He just sat and waited for Jon, or Pimples, as he now called him, to return.

"Any problems Jon?"

"No," John replied excitedly. "I shook his hand. Dad won't believe it – he's dad's hero."

Was, thought the Chessman, was his hero. It was time to leave. Closing the carton of coffee, he walked out of Cara's, coffee in one hand, cap in the other.

Turning left he started strolling towards the Castle. After fifty or so steps he knew that his mission had been accomplished. He could hear the crowd behind him. He didn't turn around. "Welcome to the club Chester, my friend, a job well done," he said to himself.

A little further on and he ducked into a small alley. He poured the remaining coffee down a drain and then placed the empty carton in the plastic bag which he had put in his jacket pocket. His cap, moustache, scar and grey wig followed as did his tie. The contact lenses followed the coffee down the drain.

He ran a comb through his blond hair, undid his jacket and the top two buttons of his shirt. At a brisk pace he walked the mile to his car where he opened the boot and threw in the plastic bag and his jacket which he replaced with a dark blue blazer.

The Chessman also took out another two bags, one containing toys and one with wine. These together with some flowers he put on the front passenger seat.

Before he drove off, he switched on the radio. He wanted to hear the breaking news. He drove carefully to his flat in town. When he heard that Mel King had died from a suspected heart attack, he was satisfied. Chester had joined the family but some credit had to go to Pimples as it was he who had applied the coup de grace. He arrived at his flat, put the flowers in the sink, half full of water, the wine in the fridge and then he changed into jeans and T-shirt.

After giving the locals a statement, Mike and Evan left, then glumly walked towards the garage, battling against the crowd who had ghoulishly arrived from everywhere. It seemed like a football crowd on the way to a match. Both were fighting back the tears. Mike had forgotten the pain in his ribs; the pain he felt had transferred to his heart.

They picked up the car, Mike surprisingly shaking both Sandy's and Curly's hand whilst thanking them profusely.

"Christ, that was strange. What's got into him? He was nearly human, Curly."

"Who is nearly human Sandy?"

"The fucking crazy Russian Detective, you bloody idiot."

"Right Sandy," said Curly as Sandy walked away in disgust.

The car seemed fine, not that the detectives would have noticed. They were in another world, a very sad place.

Evan parked and they entered. Amber had heard the news and was really upset. Half an apple pie and custard had remained un-eaten on her desk; the custard had congealed. Amber was obviously extremely upset.

Mike rang his mother telling her he would be round later and Evan phoned Edna to tell her the news. She already knew. Everyone in Wales and probably the world knew by now.

Chief Inspector Janet Ridley asked the pathologist George Massey, who was a big fan of the late Melvyn King, to confirm that it was a heart attack so they could move on. She had a bit of shopping to do and didn't want to hang around. She really didn't know anything about Mr King. She hated all forms of sport, especially cricket.

Massey agreed that it looked like a heart attack. There were no pills in Mr King's pocket or briefcase. He would check with Mr King's family doctor as soon as he could.

He made some notes and with the pencil he was using, pushed the half-eaten doughnut aside and was about to do the same with the second when the doctor noticed a foreign object at the bottom of the pile.

"So what do we have here then?" he said out loud. "That's strange, it looks like a chess piece." He poked it out with his pencil. "It is half a King. The head only, how weird is that."

The Chief turned smartly and moved closer, bending down and eyeballing the object with great intensity.

"Oh shit," she exclaimed. She was not prone to swearing.

"Get those detectives who were here before. It's going to be their case. We now have a murder enquiry. Nobody is to leave this building. I want statements from all, the CCTV camera footage inside and on the streets. I need the coffee and doughnuts analysed and Tony, get across the road to this Cara place and keep everyone inside. No one is to leave the café. Stay with them and if they have CCTV get the tapes and hold them until further notice."

Evan had just lit up his pipe when the phone call came. "Mike, they want us back at Horton's immediately."

"Why?" asked Mike.

"I don't know, the guy on the phone said his boss C.I. Ridley just told him to get us back there urgently, like yesterday. It seems there has been some kind of development."

"No point in taking the car Mike. Won't get anywhere near the bloody place."

They were in such a rush to get back that Mike forgot the pain in his side and Evan his umbrella.

When they got there, a crowd of about forty were still milling around, half of them reporters, waiting for news.

A ten-foot area had been cordoned off and three PCs stood nonchalantly on the inside of the cordon.

Evan showed his card to one and with that the reporters started asking Evan and Mike for answers to a thousand different questions.

"No comment at the moment boys. We're just here to help as witnesses, no more. We will keep you advised," said Mike. Like hell he would. Someone unlocked the door and they entered.

The Chief walked over. "We've found a severed chess piece head. I understand this is your domain. I've had photographs taken," and she told them what else she had got done or organised.

In sympathy with the dreadful news coming from inside Horton's, outside the sky had darkened and it was beginning to rain.

Flower tributes had already begun to arrive. The nearest florist was having its best day ever. The flowers just kept on mounting up. It just showed how much Melvyn King was loved and respected in his native Wales.

Chief Inspector looked at the flowers. She could not understand why a man who had either kicked or hit various types of balls could have so much hero worship. She had no time for such people and their stupid games. Thank God she could pass on this particular case.

"Look," she said. "I'm sorry but I have other pending problems I'm afraid. The music has stopped and you two have been left holding the parcel."

From her bag the Chief produced some dark glasses. They were the size of shire horses. What was more than irritating to Mike was the fact that she was chewing gum, making a noise like a horse nibbling carrots.

On the way out she turned and just said, "Good Luck, I'll leave my lads here until whenever."

Evan said thank you. Mike wanted to say so something else, two words only but managed to keep his mouth shut. Evan was again surprised. He could see that the Chief was getting up Mike's nose.

Mike turned to the ambulance boys. He pointed at Mel King. "Take him and be careful, cover the body properly, no photos, okay?

"Now Evan, let's clear the room. Firstly you, doctor, I'm not sure of your name."

"Smith."

"Well, thanks for hanging around Dr Smith. Have you given a statement?" asked Mike.

"I have, to Sergeant Cooper over there."

"Thank you, you may go home now."

Mike turned his attention to Doctor Massey. "Sorry to keep you, doc, I'm D.I. Karetzi and my partner is D.I. Jones. Have you anything to add to what we already know?"

"I'm afraid not. He was obviously poisoned which might or might not have brought on a heart attack. Within a day or two we will have the results from the lab when we have analysed the coffee and doughnuts, but you have seen these chess pieces before I can assume, detective?"

"Yes doc, it's not really a secret in the force. We have a serial killer on the loose. This is the tenth. Always leaves his calling card."

"All I can say is he took one hell of a chance today. Hundreds of witnesses including the Police," said the doc.

"He's good, doc, very good at what he does and the problem we've got is there's no motive and no connections between the victims," said Mike.

The doc had nothing else to say so Mike bade him goodnight.

Evan came up to where Mike was standing. In his hand, he had a bunch of papers; witness statements. Seven staff, the Manager and the off-duty policeman – moonlighting.

"Anything there of interest Evan?"

"Not really."

"I suggest we let the staff go apart from the Manager and we keep the off-duty boyo, name of Wilson, and the Sergeant Cooper."

"I agree Evan. What about the three outside? They are actually drawing the crowd here. The quicker we release them the better and we also have one across the road in a place called Cara's, and all the staff and customers. From what I know, about forty people. They will be chomping at the bit now."

Mike and Evan walked over to where Sergeant Cooper was. "Sergeant, I'm D.I. ...", but before Mike finished what was going to be the introductions, the Sergeant butted in, "Yes, I know", in such a way that it bothered Mike.

"Is there a problem?"

"Not exactly Sir, but I was off duty half an hour ago and wanted to make the kick off at Ninian Park."

"Well matey, I wanted to play tiddlywinks with my grandmother but we all have to make sacrifices in a murder case.

"Now that we've sorted that out I would like you to go across the road and help the PC already over there in Cara's to take everyone's statements, if that's okay with you Sergeant Cooper."

Cooper trudged off, not happy at all.

"Bit harsh with him Mike," said Evan. He never got a reply as Mike had moved on to the off-duty PC.

"Now PC Wilson, have you anything to say?"

"No Sir, I was at the door as you know. People came in, bought their book, had it signed and walked out again."

"Except for one person," said Evan.

"That's correct – a lad in a pink suit. You must have noticed him; came in with a coffee and some doughnuts, then came back out again empty handed."

"Okay, son, have you made a statement? If the answer is yes, go home or wherever, go and see Cardiff play. There is at least one seat available."

"Maybe we should call Jane for some extra help?" said Mike.

"She's on her way. I've already spoken to her. That's her at the door. I'll go and let her in," said Evan.

Jane joined them. Now they were four – the three police persons and the store's Manager.

"Let's get started," said Evan. "Firstly, do you have the tapes or whatever for the last five hours or so?"

The manager pointed to the tapes, one of which was already in the machine, ready to be viewed.

"That's an in-house tape Mr Denzil said."

"The Manager, David Denzil?"

"Yes, it starts at eight when I came in and started it up."

"Let's see then."

Nothing of interest until the camera panned Mike and Evan just inside the door, then ten minutes later the coffee and doughnut incident, then the spasms and shaking of the head by Mel before passing away. It ran on for a while until Chief Ridley and the rest appeared.

"Shall I put on the next one?" asked the manager.

"No David, that's fine," said Evan, "but we need to ask you a few questions. How did Mr King arrive and from where, if you know?"

"By private car. He was coming from the Angel Hotel."

"Apart from a briefcase, was he carrying anything else?"

"No, sir."

"Who supplied him with his first coffee?"

"I did. I asked him if he wanted anything and he said an ordinary coffee with one, so I went across the road to Cara's and got one."

"Where is the empty container now David?"

"In the bin at the back."

"Could you please retrieve it for us and don't spill any coffee that still might be in it."

David was off and returned in thirty seconds, coffee carton in hand. There was still about a centimetre or so left at the bottom.

"So what do we know? That the poison was not administered here. We've seen the tape and we know that the first was brought in by Denzil, the manager," said Jane.

"Therefore by elementary deduction, it must have been added either in Cara's or on the way, but it's highly unlikely that the boy or Cara herself did it. It doesn't make sense," said Evan.

"Have we got hold of the CCTVs in the street?" asked Mike.

"Not yet. It's coming from Central. Get the last three days' worth. This was organised murder. The Chessman must have looked over the area in advance and Jane, please get Amber to get all Mr King's personal data such as address, children, doctor's name, etc."

"Okay Mike, I'll get right on to them."

Evan went through Mel's personal effects. Just the usual: money, comb, keys, credit cards but no ID or pills of any sort. The briefcase fared no better: just papers, pens and a few magazines on football.

"No mobile, eh Evan?"

"No Mike."

Mike turned to Evan. "Mel was murdered right in front of us and we haven't got a clue regarding motive."

"Let's cross over to Cara's," said Mike. "And as for you Denzil, thanks for the cooperation. When we have gone, lock up and go home."

The people in Cara's were very agitated. Evan raised his hands and said, "Calm down folks. We need just another few minutes of your time and you are free to go about your business."

They quickly scanned the statements, the problem being that apart from the staff, not one of the customers had been in the café at the time of the incident. Nevertheless, they went through the motions of speaking to all twenty-six customers.

Mike advised them that they could go as could the PC, which left them with just the sergeant, Cara and five staff.

"Right," said Evan, "I will speak to Cara, Mike, to this Jon boy and Jane – see what the rest have to say."

"And what about me?" said Cooper, the sergeant. Mike looked at him, it was now half three. "You can go; if you rush you will make the second half."

Sergeant Cooper rushed and did indeed make the whole of the second half.

"So let's compare our notes," said Evan, after he had finished with Cara. "What do we have description-wise?"

"So we all agree, male, 6'2", in chauffeur uniform, broad shoulders, grey hair and moustache, blue tie, white shirt, green eyes, leather gloves, black shoes and a white 'K' embroidered on the tie," said Jane. "That surely can be tracked down. It's very unusual."

"You're right Jane, get Amber to run it down. We might strike lucky."

"So," Evan carried on, "this guy comes in pretending to be Mr King's chauffeur, orders on behalf of Mr King, poisons something, probably the coffee, and dupes the young lad into taking it to Mr King. Have I got it right, Mike?"

"Sounds about right Evan. Let's have a look at the tapes now."

The tapes confirmed everything that they already knew. "So he had his own coffee which he took out with him. We need to find out where he dumped the empty," said Mike.

Jane volunteered to take a quick look at the bins within a couple of hundred yards radius of the premises. Within five minutes, she returned. "No way, everyone has about thirty, forty Cara coffee cartons. The bins haven't been emptied for a week."

"I think if we could find the transport the Chessman used, assuming he didn't come by bus or train, we would crack the case. Let's see the CCTVs from around the area Mike."

"Amber's already on to it. They should be at the office by now," said Jane.

"Good, nothing more for us here. Let's go," said Mike. They left Cara to reopen.

The half-eaten apple pie and custard was still on Amber's desk, Evan noticed. He was moved to speak.

"Look Amber, we will get him, I promise you. He's made mistakes, especially with this one."

"I'm not so sure Evan. I've been through all the street CCTV tapes; our Chessman came out of Cara's, turned left and a few yards further down turned into an alleyway and disappeared. No sign of him on any camera. It looks like he changed appearance in that little lane and, poof."

"Any luck with Mr King's address, next of kin?" asked Mike.

"All in hand. He now lives in Taunton, married, one son, who owns a couple of sports shops in the West Country, name of Michael, who is currently abroad in Germany on business. I understand that he has been contacted by his mother and is on his way back from Germany. They have our phone number."

"So what next then?" asked Jane.

"Check this out if you can," Mike said, handing the coffee carton to Jane.

"How am I supposed to do that Mike?" asked Jane.

"Take a few sips and if you are still alive in ten minutes we will know it's not poisoned." Everyone laughed and Amber just picked it up and said, "I'll deal with it and by the way Evan, I have some names for you regarding your call yesterday."

"What's that about Evan?"

"I'll tell you later when we come back."

"Why, where are we going?"

"The Angel Hotel. Have a quick look at Mel's belongings. They still must be there. He was doing a morning interview for some programme in Cardiff."

"How the hell did you know that Evan?"

"Easy, Denzil told me."

"A mine of information, our Denzil."

"Yes Mike, but he's not our Chessman, is he? He's far too stupid and nice."

"Okay girls, we will be back within the hour." And they were true to their word.

On the way Evan drove. It wasn't that far. "What I can't understand, Mike, is why didn't he just walk the short distance from the hotel to Horton's?"

"I guess," said Mike, "that the only two explanations are that he, like me, has problems walking, or probably being a very humble man, he didn't want to be mobbed in the streets by well-wishers."

"Or reason number three, Mike. The Chessman threatened him in some way and he felt safer in the car and while we're at it, who was the driver?"

"Good point Evan. The driver part. The rest, I doubt it. The Chessman does not warn his victims. It's just not in his make-up. It's more than a game to him. If only we had a motive."

The detectives methodically went through Mr King's personal possessions. All he had was a small overnight leather bag containing a change of clothing and toiletries.

"Did you expect to find anything Mike?"

"No Evan, did you?"

"No, let's go downstairs, ask a few stupid questions, receive a few stupid answers and we can go."

They asked their questions, got their answers, but before they left Mike left a card. "When the guy who picked him up this morning appears to pick up his belongings, get his phone number and address and ring me there, on the line."

"Did you notice Mike," Evan said on the way back, "that Amber is off her food?"

"I did, and she's not the only one. I don't think I will ever eat another doughnut in my life," Mike replied.

They got back. It was now dead on six o'clock.

"Anything new girls?" asked Mike. "Cause I'm absolutely beat and could do with getting back to my flat. My ribs are on fire, so is my head. Can you drop me off, Evan?"

"Sure Mike. What about you Jane, you need a lift?"

"I'm okay Evan. Meeting up with John at seven in town. The

walk will do me good. I do not want to be early and sit in a restaurant by myself, so I'll leave in about half an hour, but thanks Evan."

"You cooking something nice tonight?" asked Evan, looking at Amber.

"No Evan, I'm just not in the mood and to be honest I'm not hungry. It's a strange feeling."

"Maybe a good night's sleep will help. That's if I can get to sleep," said Amber.

"Well, goodnight everyone. Shall we convene tomorrow at ten?"

Amber nodded, as did Jane and with that Mike and Evan left.

The Chessman meantime was lying down resting, his alarm on for half four, just in case he dozed off. His girlfriend and her son from the next flat were visiting a relative in Swindon or somewhere and wouldn't be back until the next day which suited the Chessman just fine as he or rather his colleague Chester had one more duty to perform.

Next to the alarm clock he had two, two pound coins and a severed pawn head. The serrated kitchen knife he had already put in his jacket pocket.

By quarter past six, the Chessman had found a spot in the park far enough from the house but near enough to witness the comings and goings to and from the house. He saw the two male detectives leave together so there were four residents in total. He hoped that the woman he'd followed was still in the house and had not left early. He also hoped that she didn't have a car with her or that she would be picked up by a husband or friend. There were a lot of 'ifs', if he was to pull this one off tonight.

He was rewarded at quarter to seven. The door opened and the woman he'd followed came out. There was only one 'if' left – would she take the same route?

On the path he laid the two coins, heads up. That side caught the light better. Then he positioned himself behind the large bushes and waited. Thankfully no one seemed to use the park much especially after dark. It was probably too dangerous and it was soon to become notorious.

Sergeant Jane Williams ambled up the path. It had stopped raining and she had lit up a cigarette. She was in no particular hurry. She wanted to arrive after her husband who hopefully would have ordered some good wine or champagne for her birthday.

Spotting the money she stooped down to pick them up. An early birthday present, she thought as her fingers clasped the money.

The first blow to the back of her head sent her spinning to the floor. In a daze as she tried to rise, still on all fours, she was dealt a second heavier blow.

Grabbing her by her blonde hair the Chessman jerked her head back and in one quick movement slit her throat. He then dragged her behind the bushes and placed the severed pawn in her hand which he clenched. After wiping the knife clean on her clothes, he looked around and headed for his car, first picking up the coins and pocketing them. Four pounds was four pounds. Life was cheap, he mused.

All had gone well and to plan. It was deathly quiet in the area.

By eight, he was back in his small apartment. He had a long hot bath and celebrated Chester's double assault in Cardiff with a few ginger beers and a cheese omelette. He did not feel particularly tired but knew he would sleep well that night.

John had arrived at the restaurant a few minutes early. After making sure he got a good table, he ordered a bottle of Champagne and a beer to keep him going until Jane's arrival. He opened the little black jewellery box and fingered the gold bracelet with the heart, his birthday present to his wife.

At quarter past, John called Jane on her mobile. It rang and rang. By half past John was frantic. Why hadn't she called, why couldn't he get her on her mobile? Something was amiss here. He contacted her office and when Amber told him that she had left nearly fifty minutes ago, he was beside himself with worry, as was Amber who took it upon herself to ring the local police and hospitals with no result.

John rushed down to the office and they studied the street map until they had decided which was her probable route.

John set off to follow the route and Amber contacted Mike and Evan. Fortunately, neither had had too much to drink. Evan abandoned his chicken curry and drove down. Mike his Macallan Malt. Mike took a taxi.

John in the meantime had cut through the part following the quicker route from office to restaurant. He passed within six feet of his dead wife. Once outside the park he again rang Jane's mobile. No change. Again, he left a message. By this time, he knew things were bad.

It was Drumbeat the Alsatian who found Jane. He was being exercised as he was most nights by his owner Derek.

Derek had never seen a dead body before, not one with a slashed throat. After bringing up his dinner, he managed to compose himself enough to phone the police. It was ten minutes past eight.

Mike, Evan and Amber sat behind one of the desks deciding who would do what when they heard the police sirens. They all went to the front door and out. Two police cars, five police, of which three were in uniform.

Even before asking, all three somehow knew that it had something to do with Jane.

They ran to where everyone was assembled and Evan flashed his warrant card to one of the plain clothes men.

"A woman?" asked Evan.

"Yes, throat slashed."

"Where?" asked Evan.

"Just over there behind that bush. Man with Alsatian found her, chap named Derek Hadfield, local, walking his dog, still in shock, poor bugger," said Detective Inspector Downing, who introduced himself.

One of the policemen had a torch on Jane's face.

"Why the clenched fist, any idea?" asked Evan.

"I think she's got something in her hand," added Mike, moving closer and bending down to open the hand.

"Best not touch anything," said Downing to Mike.

"She's one of us, a Sergeant Jane Williams, works out of our office," said Mike, opening her fist with great difficulty. "Shit, shit, shit!" Mike showed the pawn minus head to Evan.

Amber was sick.

"Do we have a contact number for Mr Hadfield and his address?" asked Mike. "If so, tell him to go home. We will contact him at a later date. Have we contacted forensics, especially a photographer?"

"All in hand," said the policemen. "Let's cordon off the area and see if we can find John."

At that very moment John entered the park and was running towards them.

Evan tried to waylay him but couldn't. John went crazy. Two of the policemen had to restrain him from touching the body.

"So what do you want us to do?" asked D.I. Downing. "I've been advised by my Super that this case has absolute priority and that you guys will handle it and we are to remain until further notice."

"Thanks," said Evan. "As you are well aware, this is his second strike today. We must catch him."

"Are you making inroads?"

"We are slowly."

"Can one of you lads drop John off to his house? He shouldn't be hanging around here. He's in no fit state," said Evan.

"Sure, but he doesn't want to go."

"He's going," said Mike. "I will have a word with him but either way he is going."

Mike explained to John that he was hindering the investigation and that it didn't help him or them and time was of the essence for any clues not to be missed.

John didn't really understand what Mike was on about. How could he when Mike himself wasn't perfectly sure of what he was on about? However, he did agree to go and was escorted to one of the police cars and driven away.

"Let's try and re-enact the scene. You, Amber, are Jane. Go and walk up to me," said Mike.

"Can't do it Mike. Can't do it." She was crying like a baby.

"Right," said Mike, you" – pointing to a young policeman. "You will be the victim. Go back twenty yards and walk slowly to me."

"Yards. How many metres is that, Sir?"

"Twenty metres. Go back twenty metres and come to me slowly."

The young PC did as he was asked. When he was a metre away Mike stopped him.

"What is it Mike?" asked Evan.

"There's fresh blood here," Mike said, pointing it out on the floor. " I don't think she was standing upright when attacked, Evan. She stopped around where our man is now standing."

"She dropped something and stooped to pick it up," said Evan.

"No, Evan, I think the Chessman was hiding behind the big bush. He wouldn't know she would stop at this exact spot."

"Then he must have put something on the floor which she went to pick up," said Evan.

"Yep, that's it." Mike put a pound coin on the floor. "Evan, you get behind the bush ready to attack. When he goes to pick up the coin, give him a pretend rabbit chop on the back of the neck."

Now, the policeman stooped to pick up the coin and Evan charged out, but was a microsec too late.

"I think, Mike, he put a few coins or whatever, to give him that extra second, then it would be more than possible. He then killed

Jane when she was stunned by a blow or two and dragged Jane behind the bush. You can tell where the drag marks are on the grass."

SOCA arrived and started their investigations.

Mike lit up and walked slowly towards a nearby bench. He sat down. Evan joined him. "I feel guilty Mike."

"Why Evan?"

"It was my idea for Jane to join the team."

"No Evan, she was very happy working with us." He was about to say something more when the pathologist walked over to where they were seated.

"Hi, I'm Walter. I understand that you have already worked out the time of death and how. All I can add which might be of use is that the victim has a bruise on the back of her neck consistent with a Karate style chop downwards, maybe two.

"I'm not a hundred per cent at this moment but I would say the murder weapon is a common standard kitchen knife, five or six inch blade. She didn't put up a fight so I guess she was taken completely by surprise. We are combing the immediate area for clues but somehow I think we will come up empty handed but then I understand you know who the killer is from the chess piece.

"I will, though, add that this was a clean kill. It was planned perfectly. You are dealing with a very dangerous man who is possibly schizophrenic."

Evan began to cry.

Walter, embarrassed, walked away. Mike put his arm around Evan's shoulders. He couldn't find any words to say to his friend and colleague and anyway he was ready to cry himself.

Back in the office Amber, full of anger and frustration, had put some music on. Prince Buster singing Reggae. She played this same one over and over again. It fitted her mood perfectly as did the bottle of rum she had opened and was drinking like it was lemonade. She had lost a friend and someone was going to pay, she thought, staring at the phone.

Rummaging through her desk she found the card she was looking for. The receptionist told her that Mr B was unavailable and would Amber like to leave a message? Yes, Amber would.

Amber calmly gave her name and telephone number before launching into a massive tirade blaming what had happened on Mr B, the Prof, doctor and all the other arseholes that associated with them.

The message was loud and clear. Mr B was played the tape by the receptionist over the phone. Mr B spoke to the Director requesting permission to travel to Cardiff which he obtained.

Before packing Mr B called D.I. Jones on his mobile who, together with Mike, was still sitting on the park bench.

Evan took the call but was far too distressed to be coherent, so Mike took the phone off him and agreed a meet at ten the next morning.

Mr B had thought it best not to contact Ms Gilberts. Hopefully, she'd cool down by tomorrow. He had to laugh though, he'd never been called a pigmy with a banana stuck up his rear end before. Better than the old fart professor with a dictionary up his. Ms Gilberts' words. As for the good old doctor and the receptionist, they fared even worse.

Mind you, he thought, Amber had every right to be angry. The people in Cardiff needed help, two murders on their doorstep.

Mr B packed and left in his car. He would find a hotel in Cardiff easily enough. He needed to get hold of the local papers and, in the morning, all the nationals. It was a two and a half hour drive and that's exactly what it took him.

Mike advised Amber about the meeting at ten. Amber told him about her phone call which had probably precipitated the early meeting with Mr B.

Both Mike and Evan took cabs home. Evan wasn't fit to drive. Mentally he was wasted.

When Evan got back he was distraught. He told the girls what had happened and immediately after that retired to bed.

Mike made himself a cup of tea with a slice of lemon then again checked the football scores on Ceefax. Cardiff City 0 Preston North End 4. He already knew the score but was hoping against hope that someone had made a mistake but the score still remained the same and Mike switched off the television in disgust.

By ten the next morning both Amber and Evan were on their second cup of coffee. Amber still not wanting to eat, had laced hers with rum.

Evan had his Sunday best on. Dark grey suit, light grey shirt, brown leather shoes and as a sign of respect, a black tie.

The front pages of most of the Sundays led with the death of Mel King with a suspected heart attack. The back pages also had stories of the legend. Somewhere in every paper, the murder of Jane was reported.

"How much longer do you think we can keep a lid on the Chessman?" asked Evan. "Someone somewhere will break the story and we will have a real problem trying to explain things."

Mike had driven; a few twinges here and there, but had driven up. He was to be ten minutes late as was Mr B. Prior to leaving Mike had scanned the papers and was relieved that none had connected the two murders. Mr B also read and reread all the papers, forgetting the time and that was why he was late.

They arrived simultaneously, both Mr B and Mike. Somewhat sheepishly, Amber asked Mr B if he wanted a coffee.

"Thank you Amber, that would be nice and by the way I'm five foot ten."

Mike and Evan looked at each other perplexed as to why Mr B would tell Amber how tall he was.

"Before we start. This Mr B business is ridiculous. My name is Brian."

"You are correct there Brian, but it isn't as ridiculous as that bloody article you leaked to the papers concerning the Japanese company," Mike said.

"Come on, be fair, you know I was completely at odds with this hired hit-man stuff," Brian said. "Utter nonsense, but in my business you go with the flow, otherwise you don't go anywhere."

"And what business is that exactly?" asked Evan.

"National Security, Evan."

"Do you know Brian, up to the present time all you have managed in the way of help is to provide us with a paper boat and set us adrift in a sea of shit," Mike added.

"You have a strange turn of phrase Detective Karetzi, but think what you will, I am here to help," said Brian.

"Like you have with the membership lists," said Evan.

There was no comment forthcoming from Brian.

"Do you know where you are sitting Brian?"

"What do you mean Evan?"

"You're sitting where Jane used to sit. You notice I'm using the past tense, Brian. Will that help to concentrate your mind?"

"My mind's concentrated. You must realise that I'm here to help but I'm answerable to others and I can't do much about certain policies that are employed by the firm."

"Forget all the bickering between us," Amber said. "No one is sadder than me, but it won't help catch the bastard if we waste all our time scoring points off each other."

"Motive," Mike said. "We have no motive, except possibly for Jane's. That is either a warning to us or he's trying to promote this Jap-hired hit-man crap which your 'firm' in London will buy. Is that why you're down here so fast, Brian?"

"Do you have any theories Brian? I mean logical ones, not the pie in the sky type?" asked Mike.

No answer.

"I guessed not but we have and in this I think we might all agree. The well-to-do victims get back row pieces, kings knights, castles; the others pawns. We think money has something to do with it. We have a key but no bloody door," said Mike. "We need help with those crummy membership lists Brian. Soonest," Mike added.

"Look, if I could help I would," said Brian. "But not with these lists."

"Okay Brian, for such an organisation not to be able to provide a few lists doesn't make sense. Please take off your jacket and shirt, Brian."

"Why?" asked Brian.

"You know why."

"You think I'm wired, don't you?"

"Take off your shoes too, Brian."

"Christ, this is pathetic but I will do as you want." And he did.

"Thank you Brian. Now please open your briefcase and empty the contents on the desk."

Again, Brian complied.

Mike sifted through the various documents, taking apart a biro and a nasal nose spray container. He then checked the shoes for false bottoms.

Evan did the same with the briefcase.

"Satisfied?" said Brian, red faced and angry. "Was this really necessary?"

"It's a matter of trust, Brian. Now that we have resolved the trust part we can talk freely," said Mike as he helped put Brian's belongings back into his briefcase.

With his shirt back on, a humbled Brian needed to regain some self-esteem and control of the position he had not expected himself to be in.

"Off the record, I personally will help you get this Chessman legally or illegally, but if something goes wrong and it concerns the latter option, then I walk, no qualms."

"Now we need a tiny favour from you. A legal one, nearly," Mike said.

"Fire away," said Brian, fidgeting with his biro.

"We need twenty grand in cash. We need it tomorrow."

Not only did he take Brian by surprise but Evan and Amber too. Brian noticed that.

Mike carried on. "There is an element of the underworld here in Cardiff who have important information for sale and we badly need certain information which will be costly. In these cases, there are no receipts, contracts, agreements, nothing, just an exchange of cash for information. Needless to say, we don't have that type of cash. It's all about trust but could lead to us apprehending our man sooner rather than later.

"It makes sense Brian, you know it does," Mike carried on. "What is twenty grand to your boys, a weekend in Rome, a night or two in Paris, a day in Monte Carlo?"

Neither Evan nor Amber said a word.

"I don't know who you think we are Mike. Twenty thou is one year in Essex, fifteen months at a stretch. You're crazy."

Mike was just warming up. "People out there in the streets don't realise what they know until money changes hands. The Chessman lives somewhere, has neighbours, friends, colleagues. He shops, drives a car, goes to the pub, plays bowls or something. He is not invisible. He does exist and we need to find him quick because we all know what is likely to happen if we don't. A chess board has thirty-two pieces." By now, Mike was exhausted.

"I need to make some calls," said Brian. "I'm going back to the hotel. It might be a while as it's Sunday; not an easy day to raise certain people."

"Where are you staying?" asked Amber.

"The Adam," replied Brian.

"Good choice," piped up Evan

As he was leaving, Mike shouted to Brian, "The money must be clean, no new notes, not marked. You know the drill Brian, and small denominations, tens and twenties, no fifties."

Brian did indeed but he could guarantee that they wouldn't get any money. He wasn't even sure he would mention it to the

Director. These people! Well, the one who did all the talking was living in cloud cuckoo land.

"Mike, what the hell was this all about? Getting the guy to undress, looking for mikes or recording equipment?" asked Evan.

"It was bloody embarrassing," added Amber.

"I knew he wasn't carrying but I had to find a way of looking into his briefcase. We need to know who we're dealing with exactly."

"And what did you find out, Mike?" asked Amber.

"I got one, the briefcase combination – well nearly, and I've got his real name."

"His real name?" asked Amber. "And what is it?"

"It's bollocks," said Mike, smiling.

"What's bollocks, Mike?" Evan asked.

"His name is pronounced Bollocks but spelt Bollok, singular."

"You're having us on, Mike."

"No I'm not. It's Brian T. Bollok, without the 'c'."

"So he and the misses are collectively known as the Bolloks, assuming he could find anyone to marry him with that name."

They all laughed. It was the first time in over a day.

"Let's go back a bit Mike," said Evan. "Why did or do we need the briefcase combination?"

"Because, Evan, there were envelopes containing documents which I'm sure will help us identify who our potential paymasters are plus other relevant information which we will be able to use some time."

"Mike," Evan said, "we have a snowflake's chance in hell of them handing over any money. Surely you realise that and no one will buy into this information for sale."

"I agree," said Amber. "There's no way. You also mentioned the combination number Mike."

"Yes, I think it's 070568. That was the number on the case after it was opened and I guess it could be his birthday. The 7th of May 1968."

"Bravo," said Amber. "All we need is to find his room number and if he comes back here after his calls, and leaves his briefcase then we find someone to creep in and look through the gear."

"Easy, peasy, illegal, impossible and very dangerous," said Evan, looking at his watch. Chapel would be over. Edna home. He'd give her a ring and tell her not to expect him for lunch or, the ways things were unfolding, dinner.

Mike was about to look at this watch before remembering that it was broken and not on his wrist.

"Tell me, Amber, do you think there is anyone who can repair a sixty-year-old East German stroke Russian watch?"

"I doubt it Mike. I'll ask around though."

"Thanks Amber."

Evan looked at Mike. Tomorrow when Jasmine went back to work she would find a watch for Mike. After all, he must have broken it fighting Taylor and a new watch was the least they could do for Mike.

Mike excused himself and walked out of the room where he rang Chalky. "Is that you Charlie?"

"Yes Mike. How are you feeling?"

"Thanks to you and your lady, I'm fine. I need another favour, Charlie. I know I owe you but this is important." Mike then told him what he needed. "So go and wait nearby Charlie, and wait for my call."

"Going now Mike. Just collect a few tools and my camera and I'm off."

"Thanks Charlie."

Amber was back playing Prince Buster. "I feel the spirit – Yeah. Well down inside of me. Glory Alleluia, so I sing Glory, Glory Alleluia." She seemed to be lost to the world.

"Reggae Mike."

"What's that Evan?"

"I know that Evan, but…" Mike spread his arms out in a 'What's going on there?' type of gesture.

By the time she played it for the sixth time running, Mike crossed over to where Amber was sitting.

"I'm sorry Mike. I can't help myself. Do you want me to play something else? I got Mickey Finn, Zoot Sims, Derrick Morgan, Jimmy Cliff."

"No Amber, we need you with us. Our two brains don't match up to half of yours. We need to be together on this otherwise God knows. Isn't that so, Evan?" Mike said imploring Evan to help him out.

"You've never said truer words Mike. We need to avenge Jane's death and Mel's too. We really need you to be strong, Amber."

"I don't know if I can. I've never felt so useless. Two murders within a mile of us; one just across the road and what can we do? Nothing. It's so demoralising." Amber started crying.

"Listen Amber," Evan said in a low, kindly voice. "Maybe we should book you into a hotel or maybe you should have a break somewhere else far from all of this mayhem."

That seemed to do the trick. The music was turned off and Amber stood up.

"I'm not going anywhere. Like that bloke on Mastermind says, 'I've started, so I'll finish', and I will tell you something else. Jane told me that the happiest days of her career were here working with us. When she first came she was slightly worried as I was, that you boys, especially you Mike, were cutting corners, not doing things by the book, but only the other day she told me and I agreed with her, that we should throw away the rule book and get this bastard before, well before he got any more victims. Enough is enough, we must do anything we can to get him, legal or not."

"Well, well, well," said Evan, "the gloves are off, no rule book. I can see my pension going the same way."

"I'm glad you've come to the proper conclusion," Mike said, "because Chalky is awaiting a room number and when he has that he will wait for Brian to leave and do what he does best."

"And how are we going to get his room number Mike?" Evan

asked. "We can hardly ring up and ask for Mr B or Mr Bollok without a 'c'. He's probably registered under a false name."

"True," Mike said. "Have we got his mobile?"

"No," answered Amber, "and by the way, no one checked his mobile for any listening devices and you call yourselves detectives!"

"I told you Amber, our two brains don't make up half of yours," said Mike. "Can you think of any way we can get his bloody room number?"

"Just ask him," said Amber.

"When?" said Mike and Evan together.

"When he comes here of course," Amber replied.

"And why would we want his room number?" said Mike.

"So that we can send him some important document which we are expecting which might exonerate NHI," said Evan.

"Good, that sounds okay to me," said Amber.

"And me," Mike added.

"Right then," said Amber, "that's sorted. Now we have this to look into." She handed both the detectives a sheet of paper, each with four names typed on them.

Mike was puzzled. He read the names out loud. "The Devil's Advocates, The Reaper, Painted Angels and The Demonics."

"I think your father was mugged by one of these gangs Mike. That was the message he left on the watch; the three sixes. The Devil's number. Edna and Jasmine, God bless them, worked it out and Amber tracked down these gangs that were prevalent in the seventies and eighties."

Mike sat down, his heart pounding. Could it be after all these years, he'd got a break, a glimmer of hope? A picture of his father flashed through his eyes; his hand automatically went firstly to his wrist, then to the cool ivory handle of his knife. He felt hope. There was a God after all.

He murmured his thanks before asking Evan, "So one of these gangs wore 666 on their jackets?"

"That's my guess," replied Evan. "Amber is still trying to find out which if any did have that number somewhere on their attire."

"Is anyone hungry, apart from me?" asked Evan. "I can go out and get us all something to eat."

Amber shook her head. Evan looked at Mike, then said, "I'll leave it for a while. Maybe you'll change your mind later Amber."

Brian laid down his briefcase and made sure it was locked, before putting it away in one of the cupboards.

He hit nine on the hotel phone and got himself an outside line. He dialled three different numbers before tracking down a very pissed-off Director.

Brian explained the situation and the need for the twenty thousand pounds.

The Director explained his situation and why he wasn't going to give anything.

For over fifteen minutes they discussed the matter. The Director won by putting the phone down on Brian.

Brian phoned the professor who was at home. He listened to Brian and agreed in principal that some money should be given. He didn't care how much. He was retiring in about a month and he honestly believed that if the chaps in Cardiff could flush out the killer, it would only help prove that NHI was behind it, otherwise why kill that Sergeant Williams?

"Look Brian, I'll do my best with the Director, but my gut feeling is he won't listen to me either."

"Look Professor, these people are crazy. I've had a hard time stopping them breaking the Chessman story and their theories to the press so please take a prescription of some sort from your friend the Doc for your gut and get on the blower. Any story right now and we will lose Nakamara."

"We don't have long. I'm on my mobile. Do you have my number?"

"I do Brian."

Brian sat back, exhausted. He had lied. It wasn't the first time, it wasn't the second and it certainly wouldn't be the last.

The call came just as Brian was resigning himself to failure and was stealing himself for another meeting with the detectives.

When Brian entered, without briefcase, Mike knew that they had got some kind of result.

Ten thousand, that's all. It would be coming down tomorrow with one of the Agency men. It had to be signed for and all the money would have to be accounted for.

"That's only half," said Amber.

"There's no more and we must know where and to whom it goes. I'm sorry, I did try, believe me, I really did."

"By the way Brian," Evan said, "we have some very important information coming tonight. What's your room number so that we can get it to you?"

"Information on what?"

"NHI, Brian, very important. We assume your people will need to see it anon."

"Room 19."

Mike excused himself and contacted Chalky.

Chalky had never been to the Adam Hotel but within ten minutes he was inside Room 19. Drawer by drawer he checked everything. One drawer was half an inch open and that's the way Chalky left it when he closed it again.

The briefcase was in a cupboard. He noticed its exact position before lifting it onto the bed. He noted the numbers that were on the lock in its closed position and then opened it with the numbers that had been supplied by Mike.

Every single document was scrutinised. He made various notes before closing the case and resetting the original numbers. He replaced the briefcase in the cupboard. In that same cupboard he found a suit hanging up. He rifled through all the pockets. He left leaving the light on because that was the way he had found it.

On the way out he checked around the bar, the restaurant, nearly full. The roast beef looked good.

The staff seemed pushed to the limit. He needed to get the receptionist away from her desk. He wanted to get to the computer and see if Room 19 had made any phone calls.

He studied the keys hanging up on the hooks behind the receptionist's desk. On the first floor numbers 11, 12 and 19 were missing. Were the guests occupying 11 and 12 out or were they eating or, worse scenario, were they in their rooms? He had to find out. He stopped outside 12 and listened; he could hear voices and when he listened outside 11 he could hear both the television and a man's voice.

He headed back towards the stairs when the sound of a door closing alerted him to the fact that someone was exiting on that floor. A couple were now waiting for the lift so Chalky took the stairs and waited. The couple didn't hand in their key but walked straight out into the street.

He waited a few minutes and then crept back upstairs. In number 11, the TV was still on but all was quiet in number 12 so he let himself in and called reception on the internal phone.

"Reception, can I help you?"

"Could you please come up to Room 12. My wife has a problem. It's rather delicate and she wishes to talk to you."

"I cannot leave the desk Sir, but I will send someone up."

"No, my wife insists that she can only talk to you. Please come. It won't take more than a minute or so."

"Okay Sir, but only for a minute."

"Thank you very much," Chalky said and after closing the line, he ran the tap in the bath and then lifted the phone off the hook and left, taking the stairs two at a time, making it just in time to see the doors of the lift closing behind the receptionist.

A quick glance around, the coast was clear. Chalky darted behind the desk and entered Room 19 onto the computer. When the bill to date came onto the screen he got a printout and hastily stuffed it into his pocket. He then cleared the screen and just walked out into the street.

Davina, the receptionist, was at a loss. She repeatedly knocked on the door but there was no answer, nothing, and she could hear the sound of running water. She did have a pass key but felt it prudent to call the manager. They entered together.

The manger turned off the tap, replaced the phone and sat on the bed. The windows were locked and everything seemed in order. It was a complete mystery and became even more so when that evening he spoke to the occupants who assured him that they had not phoned reception or left the bath tap on and he had no reason to disbelieve them.

Mike's phone rang. It was Charlie. "Yes mum, I will come down and let you in. Yes mum, I don't normally work on a Sunday.

"I've got to take a few minutes off. My mother has just turned up and I need to let her in. Whilst I'm gone maybe Brian can help us with those lists, Amber."

"Good idea Mike," replied Evan.

Brian was handed the list. "Is this connected to the Chessman case, Amber?"

"In a way it is Brian," replied Amber.

"And what exactly do you want to know?" Brian asked, "Because in all honesty I doubt if we can help. We don't keep files on this type of low-life."

"Did you use the word honesty and your people in London in the same sentence, Brian?" Amber carried on.

Brian blushed.

"We need to know everything about these people, names, addresses, ages, anything and everything. You may not keep files on them but you do have access to the people who might," said Amber.

"Tell me the connection between this lot and your case," Brian said, tapping the list with his forefinger.

"Without the information we can't," said Evan. "But be assured there is."

"That's not good enough. I can't justify the time or cost. Damn it, how can we be expected to find information relating to some minor petty thugs from thirty odd years ago? I'm sorry to use a cricketing term. I've already batted on your behalf once today. I went out on a limb to secure you some money, albeit with strings attached.

"To do so I had to lie to my superiors; a very dangerous thing to do but nevertheless, that's what I did. I wasn't born yesterday and I know that you're not telling me everything." Brian laid the list on the desk.

There was no comeback from either Amber, or Evan, who was deep in thought wondering what Mike was up to. He knew it wasn't Mike's mother who called.

"Hello son," Chalky said grinning.

"Hello mother. My, my you look different today."

Both laughed.

"Any problems, Charlie?"

"None Mike, I could have done the whole floor and no one would have known."

"So what do we have then?" asked Mike.

"We have the full name, Brian Terrence Bollok, who works out of this address in London. His boss is nameless but calls himself simply the Director."

There was a photo of him posing in front of a quite large detached house with a woman and two children, both girls, one aged about four, the other say, six years of age. "The photo is three years old and was processed in Ealing so we can assume that that is where the house is.

"Five phone calls were made from the hotel room, two to landlines, three to mobiles. Here are the numbers. I would suggest one of the landlines was his boss, this guy they call the Director, the one he called first. The other might be his home.

"There's a relatively new two-piece suit hanging in the wardrobe, bespoke, Saville Row, name of Allen and Smart.

"There were lots of documents, some kind of contract with the MOD and others, but I couldn't understand them. Oh, he had a letter of acceptance from St Juniper's accepting his daughter Lucy as a pupil to join her elder sister Mary in September just gone." Charlie checked his notes. "It ended with regards to Brian's wife, Abigail.

"There were half a dozen cards with only a mobile phone number on. I borrowed one. Here it is," said Charlie, passing it over.

"Thanks," Mike said, "that's his number. Anything more?"

"Yes, we have a receipt from Harvey's Wine Merchants in Acton. This is their address and telephone number, and that's it, Mike."

"That's good Charlie, very good. Just one more thing, is this Acton place anywhere near Ealing?"

"Yes Mike, as a matter of fact I think it's just a mile or so up the road from Ealing."

"Good Charlie, as from now you are on the staff, unofficially of course, but you're one of us."

"So I am unofficially, but officially as far as we are concerned a Rozzer, but do these unofficial people get any dosh, Mike?"

"Yes they do, Charlie," Mike said. "We will open a special fund for new employees who are not on the books."

"Do the others in the office know about my new position, Mike?" Charlie questioned.

"Not yet."

"I see," said Charlie.

"Don't worry Charlie. It will be sorted out before your next job, and thanks, Charlie. It looks like I'm always in your debt."

"Give me a call when you need me, Mike" – and with that

Chalky walked away towards his car, about a hundred yards away.

The pain in his side was just about gone but that pain in the arse Brian was still hopefully in the office. He was. They were all having a cup of coffee. Evan was sucking on an empty pipe.

"Mother all right Mike?" asked Amber.

"Fine" said Mike. "A little pale, more white actually, but she soon warmed up in the apartment. Still thinks I'm a child. To her I suppose I am." Amber laughed and belatedly so did Evan. He now knew that Mike had just seen Chalky, hence the word 'white'. It was a clue for them.

"Enough of my mother's health. What have we agreed here with our friend Brian?"

"Not good," said Evan. "To start with, no go on the gangs. Too much work for the boys in London."

"And the money?" asked Mike.

"Ten thou to be signed for and accountable, i.e. receipts for everything including ten pence if you go to a station toilet," said Evan.

"Money is tight at the moment," said Brian. "Or so I'm led to believe."

Mike sat back in his chair. He needed to think things through. He needed a little time so he took out his cigarettes and took his time extracting a cigarette and lighting up. He exhaled deeply and blew smoke up towards the ceiling. He thought his actions were the sign of a man in control. He knew otherwise.

The big wall clock's second hand did two full circles and an old Elvis song came into Mike's thoughts. He had to say something. It was, 'It's Now or Never.'

"Can I make a suggestion, Brian?"

"You can, but it won't change anything," was the coarse reply from Brian.

All eyes turned to Mike but Mike's eyes were on Brian. He needed to strike a blow and see whether or not it landed or just passed into thin air.

"Why doesn't the Director come down here himself and see the situation at first hand, Terry?"

Brian showed surprise on his face but he recovered quickly. "Unfortunately Mike, the Director is far too busy to spare the time." There was after all no point in denying the existence of his boss. It wasn't a big deal and as for them knowing his middle name, so what.

Mike was taken aback. He had not scored a hit. Brian had bettered him.

"Okay Brian, why don't we come up to London. Up the M4 through Ealing and we're there. No time at all," said Mike.

"It's ten thousand, Mike, and every penny accountable. The money should be here in the morning and remember, veiled threats won't help your cause one iota. You're stabbing in the dark, Detective."

"So give us some light Brian, a torch, not a fucking match," Mike said. "Maybe that would help our cause out. Between you and us, there's a murdering madman on the loose."

"I've done my best. I'm sorry I couldn't do more but that's the way it goes. See you tomorrow." Brian walked towards the door. No one got up. They heard the door slam. Brian wasn't a happy bunny.

As he drove back to the hotel, he realised that he had made a mistake coming down. It was interesting that they had mentioned his middle name and Ealing. Not that it mattered but it was slightly unnerving. What other information did they possess and of what use was it to them?

"Here are five numbers, Amber. We need names and addresses to go with them. What are the chances?"

"These what Chalky got from Brian's hotel room?" asked Evan.

"Yes," said Mike, telling them all that he had got from Charlie.

"Charlie will also be joining us part-time on and off for very special consignments, if that's all right with everyone?"

"Look Mike, are you sure that's wise? I mean, I know we will do nearly anything to get the Chessman, but hiring a known criminal, that's going a bit too far for my taste, Mike," said Evan. "And I feel very uncomfortable, the line must be drawn somewhere."

"Amber, what about you?" asked Mike.

"I can't believe what I'm about to say."

"Say what you will," said Mike.

"If this Charlie White chap can help get Jane's and the other poor souls' killer, then to hell with what is right. Let him help us and if we get the Chessman I will personally pin a medal on him."

"Look Evan," Mike said, "what if only I deal and communicate with Charlie? Then if things go wrong I get it in the neck and no one else is involved."

"You damn well know I couldn't let you do that Mike. I'm not happy with it but we are a team and your instincts have come up trumps more than once and not forgetting the Taylor incident."

"And Charlie was instrumental with getting us all out of a big fix," said Amber. "You both owe him and we all owe Jane, don't we?"

Head bowed, Evan turned to Mike. "I'm sorry Mike, of course you're right. We can use Charlie. He can get into places and do things which we can't. A perfect example has been today."

"We are now a team of four: three on the inside and one on the outside," said Mike. "Now that's sorted, what next?"

"Call the three mobile numbers but not from here or our mobiles," said Amber.

"We need another mobile or two," said Mike. "I'll pick some up first thing tomorrow. I'll use some Polish addresses. It will go on my card. It's becoming quite indispensable."

"I told you so Evan, remember?"

"I do Mike," and again they all laughed.

The light was still on. The briefcase in the correct position with the dials set on the numbers that he had carefully used. His coat and more importantly the hangers were as left. The room seemingly undisturbed, but Brian knew better. Someone had been in his room, someone good, not your ordinary, everyday chap. It was very perturbing.

He made discreet enquiries with the management, receptionist and other staff – nothing. With shaking hands he opened the mini bar and grabbed a small bottle of cognac which he emptied down his throat; a second went the same way. From his mobile, he phoned home. All was well. For some unknown reason that was a great relief.

He packed, paid and called a taxi. He found a new hotel. The car he left at The Adams. He would pick it up the next day. It was better that way.

It was ten in the morning when Roy, one of the securities accounts people, contacted Brian. Roy told Brian that his ETA was 11.48 hrs and Brian gave him the address before heading off to the Adams to pick up his car.

Mike arrived in the office just after ten. First thing that morning he had visited his mother. Then he had gone to a local supermarket where he had used an AMP cash machine to draw money on his corporate card before purchasing two mobile phones, giving them a Polish address and speaking in broken English.

Evan had dropped off his daughter at her place of work and was now sitting opposite Amber who was finishing off her third bacon butty. Her appetite was back with a vengeance.

Brian arrived at 11.45 and Roy at 12 o'clock. There were four forms, all in triplicate: one copy of accounts, one for the detectives and one for somebody else. The detectives and Amber signed all of them, with Roy countersigning and Brian witnessing as Mr B.

Everyone was happy. The money was clean and all there.

"Remember," said Roy, "we need proper accounts, proper documentation. Kindly keep me informed and up to date with expenditure. We must balance the books."

"Don't worry about paperwork Roy, because we won't," said Mike.

Roy looked at Brian who just shrugged his shoulders.

"Were they joking Roy?" asked Brian on the trip back to London in Brian's car.

"No Roy, they were deadly serious."

"I don't think I should have handed over the money. I have a bad feeling about how these people are going to spend our money and I'm not sure about their honesty, Mr B."

"Stop worrying Roy, you're just the messenger, you delivered, got their signatures and that's that."

"You're right Mr B, why should I be sweating. It wasn't my money."

CHAPTER 17

When Charlie arrived about half an hour after Roy and Brian's departure, he was introduced to Amber. He already knew Evan. Chalky had a car registration number which he handed to Mike who, on handing it to Amber, told her it was Brian's.

"I'll check it out, so let's get down to work, shall we?"

"Okay," Mike said, straddling a chair directly opposite Charlie. "Two sports clubs in the Swansea area. We need copies of their membership lists. These lists run into thousands. You need to get in and out PDQ. Start as soon as possible. It will give us time to sort out the corn from the wheat."

"You mean chaff from the wheat," said Chalky.

"If you say so Charlie."

"Can I ask why?"

"Yes," Mike said, "one of the members is our Mr Chessman who has murdered in cold blood at least eleven people including Mel King and our own Jane who worked with us.

"Do you like to be called Chalky or Charlie?" Evan asked.

"As friends, please call me Charlie."

"Okay, let's get this straight. You just want the membership lists?" said Charlie.

"Correct. Nothing else. I mean nothing Charlie," Mike said, handing him a sealed envelope.

"What's this?" said Charlie, knowing full well that it contained money.

"A monkey for now, another monkey when we have the lists."

"Anything to sign?"

"Nowt," said Amber and Mike in unison.

"A monkey for some monkey business," added Evan, who thought he'd made a good joke, not that he was sure how much exactly a monkey was.

Apart from Charlie no one found Evan's joke hilarious.

"I will do it tomorrow night. Well, one anyway 'cause tonight I've got to see my 'old and bitter'," said Charlie.

"You going out for a drink?" said Mike, having worked it out.

"No Mike, I'm going with the wife to see the mother-in-law."

"Right, got you," said Mike, not having a clue how one got from old and bitter to mother-in-law and it having nothing to do with drink.

After Charlie had left, Evan came clean and asked how much money a monkey was.

"Five hundred Evan."

"Thanks Mike. I get mixed up with all this slang."

"Are we sure Charlie's up for this, Mike, because we really are crossing the line now?"

"Don't worry Evan," Mike said. "I think we crossed the line a while ago. It's too late to change direction. It's full steam ahead."

"Well, let's hope we're not on the Titanic," said Evan.

Again everyone laughed. It broke the ice and for a minute or so, they forgot what they had just endorsed.

Mike took out two new cell phones, as the Yanks liked to call them. They had both been activated. From his pocket he pulled out the wine merchant's receipt and dialled.

"Good afternoon, Brian Bollok. Is that Harvey's?"

"Good morning Sir, Basil Harvey speaking. How may I be of service Mr Bollok?"

"I don't know if you remember me, Basil. I bought a dozen bottles of your excellent Special Cuvee Brut in September I think."

"Of course I remember Sir." He didn't but all customers were important to him.

"Well, I would like another dozen of the same. Do you still have it in stock?"

"Of course we do Sir," Basil answered.

"Could you deliver as I'm away. By the way Basil, to which of my residences did you send it last time?"

"Just a moment Sir," Basil said, extracting an address from one of his ledgers and reading it out to Mike.

"Good, that's fine. Abigail will sign for it."

"This afternoon be okay, Sir?"

"That's fine Basil. Thank you very much. I'll pay you when I return at the end of the week and please give my wife a ring prior to delivery to make sure she's in. Do you have my telephone number?"

"Yes Sir, is it…" and Basil read out a number.

"That's the one, thanks again Basil."

"Thank you Sir. We are always at your service here at Harvey's".

"Fantastic Mike, both address and telephone number, but of what use are they?"

"At the moment of no use but it lets Brian know that we know more than we actually do about the London people, and anyway Brian deserves an early Christmas present for all that sterling work he has been doing, Amber."

"But it's hardly a present if he's paying for it himself Mike," Evan grinned.

"That's true, Evan."

The phone rang. It was an irate Chief Constable. He was on his way down and no one was to leave before he got there.

No 'good afternoons', 'hello' or greetings of any kind were forthcoming from the Chief Constable. He was really uptight.

"Do you know why I'm here?" bellowed the Chief Constable.

"It's about Saturday's incidents," said Evan meekly.

"Of course, it's about this whole damn business. The Chessman, Jane Williams, the others, but it's also about something that has been recently brought to my attention."

The room was as quiet as a funeral parlour.

"You ride rough shod over witnesses, garage mechanics, even policemen with higher ranking and God knows what else, but obtaining money by deception takes the biscuit. Did you think I didn't know about these things and now you top it off by obtaining money from our London friends. Who do you think you are? There are channels for raising finance and in this case they all go through me." The Chief hardly paused for breath. "You're acting like a bunch of cowboys in the Wild West. This is Cardiff, not Dodge City."

"Is this about the ten thousand Sir?"

"Of course it is Evans."

D.I. Evan Jones didn't correct him. This wasn't the time.

"I ask you, Evans, as you seem the most likely of the two to give me a straight answer. What in the world made you ask for funds through London?"

"It's Jones Sir, not Evans, and in answer to your question, it was offered, Sir."

"What do you mean offered, Jones?"

"Mr B specifically came down to Cardiff to help us. He asked us how he could help, extra manpower, equipment, etc., etc."

"And, Jones, did he mention money? No, I thought not!" said the Chief Constable when Evan failed to respond. "Is this money set aside for more equipment, Jones?"

"Not exactly, Sir."

"Then what for?"

"It's for information Sir," said Mike.

"Information! What the hell do you mean by that, detective?"

"To buy information and save time and in the long run, money," said Amber, trying her best to help out. "And where, can I ask, do you buy this information, the library, W H Smiths, the University, where?"

"From informants, Sir?"

"Oh my Christ. Are you people crazy? Those type of people

will sell their grandmothers for a fiver, and you lot…" the Chief started laughing uncontrollably. "You will give the money back."

"Too late Chief," said Mike. "We have already disposed of most of it and we are not inclined to give the remainder back. We have a signed contract and we need to complete what we started."

"What? In a matter of hours you have put forward some deranged plan on which you have spent the money, without any receipts? I would really love to hear more," said the Chief sarcastically.

"The money is out and we're awaiting the information it buys," said Mike. "Of course," he continued, "there are no receipts, but I'm sure the adoring fans of Mel King, John, Sergeant Jane Williams' husband and the other victims' closest friends and family will worry about how the ten thousand was spent and if we had all the correct paperwork when we catch the Chessman."

"It's about doing our job in the best and fastest way," Amber said.

"And at this very moment we take any route that brings us a step nearer to our goal," added Evan.

"Very touching, but I am in between a rock and a hard place. Do you know that London has given us a month's notice on this place and the equipment we are using?

"Some things are out of my hands. I don't want to disband the group and move you to other stations. I know you're making progress but you have upset some powerful people," the Chief Constable said.

"These people who keep creeping out of the woodwork," Evan said. "These faceless grey people with strange names and non-existing lines of work should not be allowed to hinder our pursuit of the Chessman."

"Amen to that," said Amber.

"What about you, Detective?" the Chief asked Mike. "What's your position on this?"

"That's easy Chief. Deep down you want us to finish the job and that's what we will do, conventionally or otherwise. The money is of no consequence to the suits in London. It's a piddling amount which they spend on lunch every day between them."

"Let me get this straight. Because in your opinion it's a trivial amount of money, you think that you can squander it unaccountably, willy-nilly, is that so Detective?"

"We've advised them where it's gone or going. If they need accounts, tell them to contact their local Tax Office. Better still, tell them not to buy any more paper clips for a week. That way they can recoup the money," Mike said.

"Don't be flippant or a wise ass with me, Karetzi, and don't try my patience. It's already at breaking point."

"Chief, I don't think my partner was trying to be clever, but he is right," Evan said. "I can't see what the problem is. They offered us help, we accepted it in the form of cash; end of story."

For the first time since entering the office, the Chief sat down, his brain in turmoil. "The problem is twofold. You should not have sourced the money from London and you cannot or will not provide any accounts for that money.

"Will we get him? By him I mean the bloody Chessman," the Chief asked.

"It's only a matter of time," said Amber. "We have the best motive in the world for doing so. He murdered our friend Jane and we want to avenge her."

"I need to make some phone calls," said the Chief.

"You can use this line Sir. It's clean. We will leave you alone," Amber said, handing him a memo pad and biro.

They all trooped out and went upstairs for a cup of tea and biscuits.

The Director, Brian and Agnes Beswick, the head of accounts, were in conference discussing business entirely unconnected with the things in Cardiff when the call was put through.

"Who?" asked the Director. "Ah yes, put him through. It's the Chief Constable from down in Wales Brian, you speak to him. He asked for you."

Brian spoke for a few minutes.

"Well?" asked the Director.

"He said he would try and resolve the financial problem and was requesting in a roundabout way a few more months."

"A few months?"

"Yes, I think he was talking about the lease of the house in Cardiff, Sir. But there is no lease or rent, nothing. We are footing the cost in its entirety. Isn't that so, Agnes?"

"Yes Mr Director."

"Also, Mr Director, he said that we owe his men the chance to nail their suspect and that they were very close to doing so."

"Rubbish, he's been conned by his own men. They are no nearer to a result than they were when they started. What were you telling me about motorbike gangs? Then we get something about bowls players in Swansea!

"By the end of this year they're history. Get a letter out to them for the Chief Constable's eyes only; confidential and make sure that they are in no doubt about what they take. All the equipment is to be intact. Now, enough time wasted on our Welsh friends. Let's get down to some proper stuff."

"The money. What shall we do about the money, Sir? It looks extremely likely that we will have a hard time getting receipts of any sort from them according to Roy who went down with the money."

"It's that chap Kanasta. He's the problem. He is the conductor orchestrating this whole sorry mess."

"Karetzi Sir. I guess you are thinking about the card game?" said Brian.

"Thank you, Brian, that piece of information helps us a lot. Agnes, lose the ten grand. Let's draw a line underneath it and if we get it back then bully for us."

Agnes nodded. It was easy to do. She'd done it hundreds of times and for hundreds of thousands.

Using the internal phone the Chief asked the three to come down.

"I've spoken to Mr B and in essence I'm waiting for them to come back but I do not think that my call will alter their minds. Focus on our immediate problem and please let's make it our one and only problem."

"Well, thanks Sir. We will try and keep in touch with any news," said Amber.

"Don't try. I expect updates every day," said the Chief, "and I want to know where the money is going. Are we all clear on that?"

"We are sir," said Amber.

"And you two?"

"Yes Sir, both of us are," Evan said.

"Well, goodbye for now."

"And with you too," said Evan, as the Chief left the room.

" 'And with you too Evan' – what's that about? It doesn't make sense," Mike queried.

"Goodbye – it's just a contraction of God be with you, Mike."

"Fine my friend, today you learnt about monkeys and me about farewells."

"We have a new telephone number boys. All we do is hit recall and bang, we speak to people in London," Amber said.

"Well, what you waiting for?" said Mike.

"Here we go. Get ready to talk, Mike."

"Why me, Amber?"

"Because Mike, I'm a woman with a Jamaican accent and Evan…"

"Fine, let's get on with it," said Mike.

"Tangent Import and Export Services," said a young plum voiced woman.

"Hi, can I speak to Roy Bentley in accounts, please?"

"I'm sorry Sir, we do not have a Mr Bentley on our books."

"Then, sorry to disturb you. I must have dialled incorrectly."

"Look Mike, when I rang the other night the number on the card Brian left, I got the Alaskan Fur Trading Coop and my message obviously got through to Mr B.

"When I tried to check out the name for an address, nothing – it was non-existent; however, I feel that I'll have better luck with Tangent." She was correct. They had an address and two numbers.

"Are we a team or are we a team?" shouted Evan gleefully.

"The best," added Mike, planting a big kiss on Amber's cheek.

"We have another number to ring boys. You can just make it out on the memo pad. The Chief's hard handed and if you hold it up to the light, you can see another number. I would say a mobile. Let's ring it, shall we? You this time, Evan."

"No way, let Mike do it again. He's good at it. He has the magic touch or rather the magic voice."

"What a load of bollocks, without the 'c' of course." Smiles only this time.

Mike dialled on one of the new mobiles. "Hello, is that Janet?"

"No, you have the wrong number."

Mike cut the connection. "Funny that," he said, "I think I recognised the voice but I can't place it. Do we have the Chief's home number, Amber?"

"We do Mike. I'll get it for you." Mike rang. "Hello, is that Mrs Clarke?"

"It is," replied the Chief Constable's wife. "What do you want?"

"Well, we are doing a survey on the merits…" Mike didn't finish because Mrs Clarke told him that she didn't have time for any surveys and put the phone down on him. "So he didn't phone his wife and it wasn't his office."

"Never mind," said Evan.

"Hang on a tic," said Mike. "Have we still got that Welsh Assembly woman Carol what's-her-name? Something rings a bell. I think it's her. No, I'm sure it's her."

"Here it is, Emma Andrews. Bingo, same number!" said Amber.

"Interesting eh," said Evan. "I think she is carrying on with our esteemed Chief Constable."

"If 'carrying on' means having an affair, I think it's possible, but not probable. It could have been just an innocent call about his predicament here. He's not the type for any hanky panky," said Mike.

"But she is," said Evan. "Remember that first day. I am sure she was eyeing you up, Mike."

"Another job for Charlie, our intrepid little hero."

"To do what, Mike?"

"To follow the Chief of course. See what he gets up to," said Mike.

"And so he's doing naughties with Miss Welsh Assembly – how or why does it interest or help us catch the Chessman?" said Amber.

"I don't have all the answers Amber, but if he is being naughty then we will take the appropriate action," said Mike.

"And what might that be when it's at home, Mike?" Evan said. "Are we not getting a little bit too preoccupied with things that really don't concern us?"

"It's just a piece of the jigsaw. Maybe it will be useful, maybe it won't."

"But let's keep our mind on the Chessman, shall we? Don't forget our time here is also running down," said Amber.

At least all three agreed with that.

The meeting was just about over when Brian's mobile went. He'd forgotten to switch it off before the meeting started. The Director was not impressed.

Brian checked out the caller. It was Abigail. It had to be important otherwise she wouldn't have rung.

"Yes, darling, something wrong?"

"I have a delivery at the doorstep from the local wine merchants.

Two cases of that Champagne we didn't like the last time."

"What made them send it, Abi?"

"He said you phoned and ordered and that it was to come to this address, not our other."

"What other, Abi?"

"Our other home, Brian."

"But we don't have another home love."

"I know we don't Brian. Do you think I'm stupid?"

"Tell them that we're sorry. There's been some misunderstanding and I will see him in a few days' time."

"Okay darling, bye for now."

"Bye."

"The colour has drained from your face. Have you got a problem Brian?"

"I'm not sure, Sir."

By now Agnes had left the room and they were alone.

Brian was just about to tell all to his superior when Agnes knocked and re-entered the room.

"Forgotten something Agnes?"

"No Director, I just thought that I ought to tell you I have just been informed by reception that someone phoned asking for Roy Bentley."

"And who is Roy Bentley, Agnes?"

"He's one of my accounts staff."

"So?"

"Well Sir, all calls as per standing orders number 359C. All private calls are to be made or taken on personal mobile phones at specified times of the day."

"Get on with it woman," said the Director.

"The call was taken on our classified line Tangent, not Alaskan."

"This Roy Bentley. Is he the one who came down to Cardiff?" asked Brian.

"The same," answered Agnes.

"Okay Agnes, noted; please leave us alone. Now to your problem, Brian." Brian told him.

"This has got something to do with those Welsh retards, hasn't it?"

"More than likely, Mr Director," said Brian sheepishly.

"I can't understand them. Are they stupid? What are they trying to prove, Brian?"

"I think they are sending us some kind of message."

"A message Brian? Explain."

"They are pissed off. They are on some kind of mission or so they think and now they think we are hindering them. First we tell them that they must leave our safe house, then it's this money business; they wanted more, no accounts, nothing."

"Okay Brian, don't the idiots realise that all they are achieving is hastening their own demise – so what kind of message is that?"

"May I speak frankly and openly Sir?" The Director nodded.

"We are a covert agency who employ over two hundred people to protect our country blah, blah, blah, but they are telling us that we are not that secret to them and that because they know how to contact us, then we have no real power over them. Take the problem with the money. How can we retrieve the money if the contracts can never see the light of day because we are a covert organisation in the main?"

"Bullshit Brian. Maybe it's time someone explained their position to them and told them to stop rocking the boat before it sinks. They are behaving like little children who have just had their sweets confiscated. Do they realise that one or all of them could meet with fatal accidents? Tell them to shut the fuck up before they get into my bad books. Who the fuck do they think they are messing with, a kindergarten teacher?"

The Director by now was purple with rage and Brian was worried. The boss was talking some pretty heavy things.

The Director picked up the phone. "Get me Professor Benson, Doc Elwin, Jimmy Johnstone and Agnes Beswick now and organise some coffee and sandwiches."

Agnes arrived, first followed by the Prof and Doc. Now they all sat waiting. "Where the hell is Johnstone and the coffee and stuff?"

When Agnes heard the name Johnstone her feet started tapping, slowly at first, then faster. It always was the case when she got nervous, which she was now.

Jimmy Johnstone was synonymous with all that was bad in the Agency. He and the others who worked with him arranged 'happenings', as he called them, and these so-called happenings were all bad.

Stories abounded in the Agency about the fires, car crashes, heart attacks, suicides even. Fatalities all attributed to JJ. He, though, thoroughly enjoyed his work.

"I don't think I'm really needed here," Agnes said. "I've a lot of work on, Mr Director."

"Just sit down," the Director said. Agnes did as ordered.

Eventually Jimmy arrived, at five foot five, slight with a nice open, kind face; he did not look in any way threatening. He looked more like a choir boy.

In the seven years Agnes had been in the Agency, she had only met Jimmy once. That for her was more than enough. Jimmy looked at Agnes and smiled. He had a beautiful smile, nice white straight teeth. Jimmy never let on that they were false. He lost his real teeth in a fight somewhere in the past in his native Glasgow.

One of Jimmy's teeth was gold; one was slightly crooked. It made the rest look more authentic.

The Director looked at Jimmy who didn't speak or shake anyone's hand. He just stood there smiling.

"Glad you could join us Jimmy." The wee man just stood there waiting. The Director went on. "As from this minute, Jimmy, you and the rest of your men are on standby. Do not leave the building until I speak to you again."

Jimmy did a mock salute, turned and walked out. He was happy. Something big was coming his way in the form of what he liked to call work.

"We are here to discuss what measures we will take against the dangerous and crazy bunch of detectives who had stolen from the Agency and were now threatening certain members with ..." He wasn't sure what! He went on and on, never giving anyone a chance to speak.

Unfortunately for Agnes, when she was nervous she also needed to use the toilet and seeing Jimmy had made her very nervous so she had to say something.

"Excuse me, Mr Director, but I must leave the room for a moment."

"Listen to what I have to say first and then go and do whatever you have to," said the Director. It was more like a command than a request.

Agnes stayed, her legs now crossed so tightly even George Clooney wouldn't have been able to pry them open.

The Director kept talking. By now, it was obvious he was planning something pretty nasty for the poor hapless souls in Cardiff and his messenger would be Jimmy Johnstone.

Eventually the Director called the meeting to a close. Five minutes too late for Agnes – she had wet herself.

In Cardiff they sat around the finished pizzas; a new bottle of wine was opened and all was well with the world.

With everyone out of the room apart from Brian and the Director, it was Brian who spoke first. "Mr Director, why don't we just give them a call and explain to them that they could be in serious trouble unless they repay the money, or account for it accordingly.

"They will be out of our hair by the end of the year and if by any miracle they apprehend this Chessman or whoever then we can claim some bonus points in giving them help.

"We do not want this small problem to escalate by letting Jimmy loose. He's not a full shilling either."

"What you say makes sense, Brian, but my blood boils when I think of the arrogance of the bastards, plus the fact that they are trying to make it personal. I mean, that wine business; this Bentley business. I will talk to them but I'm still inclined to get JJ down there to crack some heads. Get everyone back in, including Agnes. She must have changed her underwear by now," said the Director smirking. Brian didn't find it funny but smiled anyway.

When everyone was back in with the exception of Jimmy, the Director advised them that he was about to call the people in Cardiff and wanted witnesses to the conversation. Brian put the line on loudspeaker. He dialled and Amber answered.

Amber put on her line's loudspeaker and asked Mr B to go ahead. This was a turn up for the books, Evan thought.

"Firstly, let me advise you that the Director is here in the room with other interested parties. Do you understand?"

"We do," said Amber.

"Right, the Director wishes me to convey the following to your good selves. He only wishes two things: one, that the money you have borrowed is accounted for in the correct manner and, two, that when you move out at the end of next month no equipment is removed."

Mike tried to light up, but the cigarette was having none of it. His hand was trembling too much.

"Does anyone wish to say anything down there?" asked Brian.

Amber answered. "Brian, we get the message. It's a pity that you want us out; fair enough it's your property and I know the Force isn't reimbursing you for any lost rent or lease. Of course we won't take any of the equipment. It's not ours and, to be perfectly frank, I can probably do the same work with a laptop and a few phones.

Even our police force can afford that. Unfortunately the money is a different kettle of fish."

"The Director wishes to know why," said Brian.

"Because Brian, most of the money has gone to buy information which we need urgently since you leaked that ridiculous NHI story to the papers."

"It's Professor Benson on the line. It is not ridiculous. You people have absolutely no idea about this matter. Isn't that so, Doc?"

Before the good doctor could confirm it, the Director cut in.

"Do you people agree to the simple terms I have laid down or do I need to do something that will impress on you that you are dealing with things way out of your league?"

"If that is you, Mr Director, please understand we do not disagree with anything you say. It's just that we do not have the money but are more than willing to call it a loan and pay it from our wages over an agreed period. What more do you want?"

"And who am I talking to now?" asked the Director.

"It's Special Detective Inspector Jones, Sir." Mike tried lighting up again. This time the lighter wouldn't spark.

"Listen up, Detective Jones, there are no deals. I'm sorry about your colleague Sergeant Jane, but you can hardly blame us for your inefficiencies. I would suggest you concentrate on your work, getting this Chessman bloke.

"I am also well aware, Detective Jones, that you have been prying into certain personal details of my staff. That is another no-go area and for that alone you people must be taught a lesson."

"Is that a threat Sir?" asked Evan.

"Detective listen, you all listen very carefully. Are you listening down there in Wales?"

No one spoke.

"I hope you're listening because you're piloting a paper aeroplane and I'm going to piss down on you from a great height."

"We are trying to compromise here," said Evan. "All we want

is the killer of our friend and the others. We are all on the same side. We cannot understand why you are taking this high-handed attitude and threatening us for no reason."

"There are reasons Detective, and I'm fed up with giving you them. I have nothing further to say to you."

The phone call had finished.

"What's wrong with these people?" said Doc Elwin. "Don't they realise what a powerful organisation this is? We could make them disappear and no one would bat an eyelid.

"Hand me the file, Brian, or better still, read it out loud for us all to hear. I want everyone to understand what scum we're dealing with and they call themselves policemen. What are the criminals like down in Cardiff if these are the police?"

"Shall I begin, Sir?"

The Director nodded.

"Chief Constable."

"Forget him, Brian."

"Ms Amber Gilberts, age 60, black, Jamaican father, welsh mother, big girl, very heavy set. Expert at nearly everything, especially with computers. First with Honours Cambridge."

"Is she the one who found the bugs?" asked the Director.

"No Sir, that was probably John, husband of Sergeant Jane Williams, the one…"

"I know who she is or was. Get on to the next one."

"Detective Inspector Evan Jones, age 54, Welsh through and through, 5'8", slow, pedantic, married to Edna, lives in Taffs Well."

"Strange that," the Director blurted out.

"What's strange?"

"Their Christian names. Only one letter different, both four letters, get it, only the 'V' in Evan and the 'D' in Edna."

"Taffs Well."

"Shouldn't that be Taff Wells?" said the Doctor.

"Who cares Doc, get on with it, Brian."

"One daughter, Jasmine."

"Um, has a nice ring to it," said Agnes. "Jasmine Jones."

"Yes it does, Agnes," said Brian.

"For Christ's sake Brian."

"Sorry Boss, one brother Bryn, older; parents both alive and living in Pontypridd. Christian, attends Chapel regularly."

"Enough of PC Plod, get on to the other one."

"Detective Inspector Mikhail Karetzi, born Cardiff, Russian father, Welsh mother, age 35, six foot plus, fit, still playing football, currently serving a ban for violent conduct on the field, sharp, cunning, bit of a playboy, drinks whisky, smokes non-filter American cigarettes, carries a knife with five-inch blade on his person, not married, mother alive, lives in Penarth, no other family. DI Karetzi lives alone in an apartment in Cardiff Bay, dresses smart, Christian, probably orthodox but has never attended any church. His musical tastes run from…"

"I think we get the picture Brian."

"There's more on DI Karetzi Sir, and I think you should read it."

"No, Brian, you read it."

"Okay, here we go. The following are all mainly attributable to D.I. Karetzi but none will actually file a complaint as such. It's all off the record.

"Chief Superintendent Fowler, they or, to be exact, Karetzi, stole his assigned car and then manhandled the Super. A garage mechanic was stepped on, threatened with a knife but won't say a word on the record. A Chinese man, witness to the Tenby murder threatened with a hot iron."

"A hot iron, Brian."

"Yes Sir, the type used for ironing clothes. Then we have the case of Vincent Taylor, ex-husband of Jones' daughter, beaten to a pulp by Karetzi, nearly killed the man; note that this Taylor guy is only 30, a fitness instructor, 6 foot 4 inches, not a push-over.

"Our surveillance people have a few stories too – slashed tyres, smashed windows and more. There are rumours too about…"

"Why hasn't anyone made a complaint, for God's sake? A Superintendent Detective Inspector, a man beaten to within an inch of his life and yet this guy is walking around large as life. It doesn't make sense," concluded the Director.

"And yet, Mr Director, he didn't say a word in anger today when we were on the phone. What made him keep his mouth shut?" Agnes pointed out.

From his notes the Director read out a list of names "Alice, Edna, Jasmine, Amber, Evan's Mother, Edna's Mother. Take away the women and what have we left, Brian?"

"Left for what, Mr Director?"

"For Jimmy."

"I don't quite understand Sir," said Agnes.

"Nor I," added Professor Benson.

The Director ignored them and carried on. "The Chief Constable, not really. He isn't the problem and that leaves just two, Evans, I mean D.I. Jones and the other, D.I. Karetzi. Eeny, meeny, miney, mo, catch a bastard by the toe, never, ever let him go. And the winner is… Karetzi. First prize, an evening with Mr Jimmy Johnstone and friends.

"We will teach Mr Karetzi a lesson in humility and at the same time show them just how powerful and far reaching our Agency is."

"With all due respect Mr Director, is this the right course to take? As far as I can see the Detectives are only doing their job, a little zealously yes, but then they do have a serial killer down there," Agnes said.

"Agnes, understand where you're coming from but you really do not understand this side of the Agency and I do not expect you to, but as Director I must sometimes make painful decisions for the good of the agency and in the long run the Nation's well-being."

"What do you have in mind exactly Sir?"

"A simple message: Jimmy goes down and has a quiet word or

two with the detective. He will then realise the error of his ways and all and sundry can go about their work happily," answered the Director.

"On your way out, Brian, could you get Jimmy back in?"

The meeting had ended.

"Well," said Amber, "I don't think that went too bad."

"Not too good either," commented Evan.

"It's unlike you, Mike – not have anything to say?"

"I'm not happy, Evan. I just don't feel my normal self. These people are after our blood. I can't understand why they are pushing us. I mean, we even offered to pay them back the money. They are looking for a fight and by speaking I would have given them a good reason. I can't hold my tongue."

"You restrained yourself very well Mike," Amber said.

Back in London, the Director and Jimmy had a chat. "Just slap the bastard around a bit Jimmy. Don't tell him why or who is behind this thing. A few broken bones, a few smashed teeth. You know the drill. I needn't spell it out."

Jimmy turned to go when the Director spoke again.

"Tomorrow Jimmy; I need you to go Paris before the weekend, so make sure it's all done and dusted by tomorrow."

Jimmy smiled. A shiver ran through the Director's body. He was a little afraid of the Scotsman but at least he was on their side – he hoped.

Before leaving the offices at Tangent, Jimmy paid a visit to the Accounts Department. Only piss pants Agnes was there with another person. The others had obviously gone home.

He headed directly for Agnes. Thank God Pauline was still there. What in Hell did he want? Twice in a day.

"I need travelling money, say three hundred pounds."

"When do you need it?" asked Agnes.

"Now."

"Are you planning on going somewhere tonight? The safe is locked at six."

"Well, unlock it and give me three hundred pounds. I don't want to come back in the morning."

He was now standing over her menacingly. Pauline moved towards her boss in an act of support. Jimmy spun his heels and just looked at Pauline who at six foot towered over him.

"And you," he said, pointing at her, "what can you do for me?"

"I think we have that amount in the petty cash box, Agnes. Shall I get the money?"

"Yes please Pauline."

"Just sign here please, Mr Johnstone." Jimmy did. Usually he sent one of his errand boys to deal with the money side but today he thought he'd come up and have a look around himself.

As he was signing, his mobile phone went off. Jimmy answered it. "You and Tony, we leave at five thirty. Be there at about eight, got it?" snarled Jimmy and with that he walked out stuffing his pockets with the money.

No 'goodbyes', no 'thank yous' – that wasn't his style.

"Who the hell was that?" said Pauline.

"That's the infamous Jimmy Johnstone Pauline."

"Is he the one that goes around and…"

"Yes he is, Pauline. Let's go Pauline."

They switched off the lights and left. Pauline headed for the Tube, Agnes for a public telephone box.

"We've done absolutely fuck all today," said Mike.

"I agree. This London business has taken up all our time, and for what?" said Evan.

"For ten thou which we're going to have to repay out of our pockets," said Mike.

"But we still have, or will have, nine thousand left after Charlie's money."

"What we could do, Mike, Evan," said Amber, "is use our credit cards and draw out three fifty pounds each to cover the money. That way we don't actually lose anything. It's just expenses."

"Yes, we will do it tomorrow," said Evan. "I'm wacked out. Shall we call it a day then?"

They all agreed.

The phone rang. Amber picked it up. She listened for about a minute and replaced it. She was visibly shaken.

"Something wrong, Amber?" Evan asked.

Amber was finding it difficult to speak.

"Anonymous call, woman, trying to disguise her voice. Anyway, message simple. Someone called Jimmy Johnstone, together with at least two others, will be paying you, Mike, a visit tomorrow early morning. According to our caller, this Johnstone chap is a very, very nasty piece of work."

Amber was working the phone again. "London phone box. Can get the actual position. Will take time."

"Forget it Amber," said Evan.

"We know who this Johnstone guy works for, don't we?" said Evan.

"We do," said Mike.

"I think, Mike, you should use our spare room here tonight and that we call the locals in the morning," said Amber.

"To do what Amber?"

"To stop them doing something to you Mike – something bad."

"I agree with Amber, Mike. This has escalated into something which we can't deal with alone. Maybe we should advise the Chief Constable."

"Evan, we can't do that. Let's work it out, shall we? Three people are sent down, one will sit in the car, two will come up. They won't break in. Pointless; one will knock on the door, probably trying to deliver a non-existent parcel or flowers, etc. The other will wait outside hiding until the first has gained entry."

"Then Mike, assuming that's the way it pans out, then what?"

"I don't know, Evan. What I do know is that for some unfathomable reason we were tipped off by someone close to the top of the Agency; most wouldn't have an idea about this Johnstone bloke coming down, would they Evan?"

"No Mike, but I say, just call in the locals. I know a few of the lads down there as you probably do, Mike."

"And what will they do? We need to split them up, Evan. I have a plan," said Mike.

"So did Baldric in Black Adder," Amber said.

"Very funny Amber, but my plan is simple. I need the following: a pair of handcuffs, a baseball bat which I will supply, and good camera. The last I guess is your department, Amber."

"I have one, a Polaroid Instant."

"You, Evan, need just to hunt down their car and on the signal from me, report a suspicious person or persons to your D.I. mate. Oh, and if you could lend me a pair of handcuffs, I'd be obliged."

Evan passed them over. They were on his person. You never knew when they would be needed.

"If you can be there at mine Evan, say seven sharp, we can prepare accordingly."

"I just don't like it, Mike," said Amber. "Too many things can go wrong."

"They can, Mike. I'm sure it would be better all round if we let the locals get them."

"Arrest them on what grounds, Evan?" Mike said. "And then of course they will know we were prepared for them and, the big question, they will come again and we won't be ready for them."

On the way out Mike stopped Evan. "One last thing, Evan. I need a Taser stun gun. I didn't want Amber to know. I need it tonight ready for tomorrow."

Evan looked at Mike carefully. "You've got to be careful with those things, partner. They can do a lot of damage in the wrong hands."

"Look partner, Johnstone might be armed. Who knows with these types and would probably have some special permit if he is."

"He is?" asked Evan.

"Armed," said Mike.

"My ex-partner, back in the good old days, Big Mike Maloney, D.I., Irish, big, big man, tough as teak and godfather to my daughter. He will have access to one, no problem."

At seven precisely the door rang. Mike glanced at the clock. It had to be Evan and it was together with somebody who looked as if he'd gone the full distance with Mike Tyson.

"Hi Evan, punctual as ever."

"Morning Mike. This is Mick Maloney, he insisted on coming once I told him about the Taylor business.

Mick offered his hand. It was the size of a bear's. Mike took it. "Do you know what you're letting yourself into, Mick?"

"No and I don't want to. If Evan says it's okay then it is. Me and him go back a long way and he's saved my skin a few times over the years."

"As you have mine, Mick," said Evan.

"I can't get you to change your mind, Mick. This could end up disastrously. These guys are working for MI5 or 6 or 7, or anyway, they are not pansies and more than likely one or all of them could be armed."

"So Evan told me," Mick said, completely unconcerned or worried.

"I'm Irish. I've got a thick skull but I'm not thick. As I see it we are expecting three; one remains in the car, standard procedure, and two come up, correct so far?"

"I think that's the way I would play it," said Mike.

"As I see it there is no way for me to hide in the hallway outside your flat, so I will have to go up that last flight of stairs and wait," said Mick. "Okay with that?"

"I'm with you Mick," said Mike.

"The first baddie you let in and zap him. Fine, he's out for a while but baddie number two barges in and nails you, Mike, and I won't have time to stop him 'cause I'm a stupid lumbering Paddy who can't get down in time, unless…"

"Unless Mick, I slam the door shut behind the first. You are warned by the slamming of the door, giving you time to come down before the guy outside figures out what to do next, and Bingo. I leave it up to you. I'll handcuff the first bastard and tie his legs up with this here piece of rope I have standing by in my pocket. I will then grab the bat and cut the second down to size if he's still struggling with you."

"And me?" said Evan.

"Like we talked about yesterday, two things: you locate their vehicle, then warn us when one of them enters the building before ringing the locals about a suspicious man in a car who seems to be dealing."

"That seems easy enough Mike but we could still face a problem that we haven't allowed for," said Evan.

"Tell us Ev," said Mick

"What can we do if all three come up or if there's four of them and three come up?" said Evan.

There was silence from Mike and Mick. "Coffee anyone?" said Mike.

They all moved to a small table where the coffee had been prepared. Milk and sugar were in a jug and bowl for those who needed them. Evan had milk and two, Mick, milk and three.

"They wouldn't send down three people to deal with one unaware target," said Mike.

"But if they do?" said Evan.

"Then you warn me on the mobile and we call in the troops," said Mike.

"They will walk away," said Mick, "if that happens. We can't hold them if they do nothing. All we are doing is preventing you from getting a thorough beating today. I emphasise the word 'today' Mike, because they will be back some time in the future and someone in their organisation will be in big trouble," said Mick.

"Who?" said Evan.

"The person who tipped you off, that's who," said Mick. "Do you know who it is?"

"No," said Evan, "just that it was a woman."

"How many time we gonna drive past this fucking place Boss?"

"Until I say otherwise, Gaz?"

"Yes, Jimmy, sorry."

"You will be, Gaz, if you don't stop talking. This will do, stop over there. You get a good view of the front door and that balcony. Keep your eyes on the balcony, dumbo. When I come out onto that balcony, I will signal you to get ready to leave. Got it Gary?"

"Yes Boss, what about the Rosko?"

"The Rosko – you are the fucking pits! The gun will remain in its place. There's one bloody little policeman probably still fast asleep unless he's got a bird up there, then he might be doing some early morning exercises," said Jimmy.

"Why would he want to do that, Boss, if he's got a bird with him?" said Gaz.

"Oh for fuck's sake Gazza."

"Shut up the pair of you, before I get angry and take it out on you two instead of that arsehole up there," Jimmy said.

"If there's a woman, a few hard slaps, Tony. I don't want any hysterics. Got it?"

"Got it."

"And then lock her up in the toilet or something."

"Okay Boss."

"Let's go, remember what I said Gary. Watch for my signal."

"Have you got the chocolates, Tony?"

"I have Boss, but forty quid for a box of foreign chocolates! Why couldn't we just get some flowers, a fiver's worth?"

"Look dickhead," Jimmy said, stopping in the middle of the street. "Belgian chocolates are the best in the world, not Swiss, not

American, not English, Belgian. Flowers to a man, a bit silly, eh? He's hardly going to open the door for some pansies or Chrysanths is he?

"The chocs are on my expense account. I will be reimbursed and I'll have them with my girlfriend tonight. A man with no teeth can't eat chocolates, can he Tony?

"It's ten to. I said we would be in by eight, didn't I Tony? Now listen up, when the next person comes out we go in. We take the lift up if there's room in the lift. You remain out of sight in the lift. As soon as I get in, I'll take him out and either leave the door open or re-open it for you. Then it's bang, crash, wallop, balcony signal, down again, car waiting, chocs in hand and back to the big smoke. Aye, I'm quite looking forward to meeting our PC Plod," said Jimmy, licking his lips in anticipation.

When the young chap came out, Jimmy wished him a Good Morning whilst keeping the front door open for Tony to enter.

"Plenty of room in this position to hide, Tony. From now on it's all go. Let's go out and enjoy."

When the call came, Mick went up the stairs and Mike got ready, towel over his right hand which held the Taser.

Evan had spotted them, the second time they drove past the apartment block. Thankfully, there were only three and as Mike had reckoned, one was left in the car. Evan made a note of the registration number and then the call to Mike as soon as they had gained access to the building. Two guys: one short and wiry, the other big and slightly overweight. Who Mr Johnstone was he couldn't say but if he had to bet, it would be on the small man. It was the way he walked. He walked with authority if that made sense – he swaggered. Evan likened him to one of those American Wild West gunslingers. Let's just hope he's not packing, thought Evan.

Mike heard the doorbell, counted to ten slowly, then with his left hand, opened the door.

"Yes?"

"I have a box of Belgian chocolates for a Detective Inspector Karetzi. I hope I've pronounced it right," said Jimmy.

"I'm not expecting anything," said Karetzi. "Could you please just put them on that small table over there while I dry my hands."

"No problem Sir," said Jimmy, thinking what a bloody plonker and they sent me all this way just to deal with this arsehole.

Mike slammed the door shut with his foot. It was so loud that probably Evan outside in the street would have heard it. Tony hiding in the lift certainly did as did Mick at the top of the stairs.

Jimmy jumped, dropping the chocolates. He turned only to be zapped hitting the floor like a sack of coal.

Mike stood over him. "You know, Jimmy, I had a lot of respect for you when you were playing football for Celtic and Scotland, but now you're dealing with people in a different league."

Mike got Jimmy's hands behind his back and handcuffed him, then with the piece of cord he tied Jimmy's legs together before rapping the cord around a radiator and tying it tight.

All hell was breaking loose outside his front door. Luckily, his only neighbour on the floor, a young yuppie type, had left a few minutes earlier.

On opening the door Mick came flying in, blood streaming from a broken nose, followed closely by another big bloke, if anything bigger than Mick. The baseball bat behind the knees brought him down and a kick from Mick in the balls kept him down. Mick was breathing heavily. He could hardly talk. Mike handcuffed him and between them they dragged him into the kitchen where Mike, after kicking him once more, took off one of the cuffs and locked it onto the over range door.

"I've no cotton wool. Take some tissues Mick and here, drink this. Sorry it's not Jameson's but it will help. Christ Mike, I'd drink whisky from Uganda right now. He's one hell of a strong bugger."

"Thanks Mick, you did great today. Let's not forget the guy's half your age."

"True Mike, true, but I should have taken him."

"You did Mick. Go and sit down; try and stem the bleeding."

From out of nowhere, a mobile rang. It was emanating from Jimmy's pocket. Mike extracted it. "Yeh?"

"It's me Boss. I've been moved by the locals. I didn't put up any fight 'cause of the, the, you know what I mean Boss, didn't know what to say."

Evan came running in, truncheon in one hand, umbrella in the other. Both Mike and Mick burst out laughing.

"You can put the umbrella away Evan, everything is under control," Mick spluttered, still laughing.

Poor old Gary on the other end of the phone couldn't make out what the hell was going on up there. His brain just couldn't get round it.

"Are you still there Boss? I think I've got a crossed line."

"Boss is still here boyo. Trussed up like a turkey about to be roasted," said Mike.

"No Mike," said Mick, "it's the other one over there nearest for roasting."

"True," said Mike, "did you hear that matey? If you want your friends to join you, I suggest you go and park somewhere quiet and ring again in an hour. I've not had my fill of fun yet today and I might just come looking for you. Stay put, no calls to anyone expect to me, understood?"

"I don't know, Mr… I just don't know."

Mike closed the line.

"Insubordinate little fellow. Jimmy, you need to make sure he follows orders and the orders of the day are: one, give us some information – namely, who authorised this stupid attempt to intimidate me and, two, why?" Mike said.

Mick stood up. "Time for me to go. If you need me again Evan you know where I am. I'll come up and see you soon. Both you, and of course Edna, and my little girl. Tell her, her godfather sends his love."

CHAPTER SEVENTEEN

Mike butted in. "Nice to have you on our team Mick. Good luck to you and if you're ever around this part of town, just come up. I'll get some Jameson's in for you.

"Great bloke, Evan, pity about the nose."

"What now then Mike?"

"Ring Amber. She's probably fretting and if she worries too much she'll empty the fridge and store cupboards of everything."

After ringing Amber Evan took nine photos of the two: six of Jimmy and three of the other one with Amber's Polaroid Instant.

Mike took out his knife, felt it for sharpness. It was as he expected, razor sharp. He laid it on the table, then changed his mind, picked it up and cut the pink ribbon holding the lid and bottom part of the box of chocolates. He read the contents list carefully, before choosing a marzipan one. He bit into it. "These are nice Evan. Have some." Evan did. He had to agree they were fantastic. They had quite a few each.

"You've got good taste Jimmy. Did you know Evan, our mate Jimbo here, played a good game of football in his other life? That is before he became slow and stupid."

"I didn't know that Mike," Evan said in all seriousness. "I've got an ordinary camera in the car. It would be good if we took a few more pics. We might need copies."

"Fine Evan, sounds like a good idea to me." Evan left, taking both his truncheon and the umbrella.

"Are you going to say something Jimmy? 'I love you' would do for starters."

"Fuck off, you fucking Russian twat," said Jimmy, spitting in Mike's face and then turning his back to him just in case Mike punched him or even spat back.

With one quick movement, Mike stabbed Jimmy hard in the left buttock. Jimmy squealed like a pig. He turned and spat again at Mike.

Mike slapped Jimmy hard twice, once on each cheek, then

seeing an irresistible opportunity to cause the Scotsman more embarrassment, he stabbed him on the right buttock. Little pools of blood had formed on the floor beneath Jimmy.

"You're messing the floor Jimmy. I've got a good mind to send your lot my cleaning bill."

"What's going on in there?" Tony shouted.

"I've given your Boss another two arseholes to go with the one he was born with."

"I'll kill you," hissed Jimmy. "You're dead meat. If it's the last thing I do, I'll rip your throat out."

Evan returned. He saw the blood and asked Mike what happened. Mike told Evan and Evan wasn't too happy and told Mike so.

"Take lots of photos, Evan, and call for Amber who can develop them and make some copies."

When the cab arrived, Mike wanted Evan to take them down to him but Evan insisted that Mike did it. He didn't know what Mike would do when he was out of the apartment again.

With that finished and the time just gone eleven, it was Mike's turn to wonder what they would do next.

After a coffee and a smoke, they decided to phone Mr B. This was getting tricky. Jimmy's wounds needed to be seen to. That's when Mike decided to call Charlie and ask him if Maggie, his live-in partner, was available and could help.

She was. She would be round with Charlie in about fifteen minutes with the necessary gauzes, plasters and painkillers necessary. All Mike had to do was take off Jimmy's trousers and underwear. No problem, thought Mike undoing the cord around Jimmy's ankles.

The internal buzzed. It meant someone was downstairs waiting to be invited into Mike's apartment block. Evan answered it. Amber was outside. Evan buzzed her in.

One quick glance told her all. Her first instinct was to help the poor little chap in the foyer. He was bleeding. By the time she walked into the kitchen she wanted to throw up.

She turned and gave both Mike and Even her fiercest look. Evan said he was sorry. Mike just sat there and was the first to speak.

"What you sorry for partner? You wanted them to beat me to a pulp?"

"Of course not Mike, but I do feel a little bad about all this," Evan said, spreading his hands horizontally.

"Did we need to do this?" asked Amber, tears coming to her eyes.

"Just patch up the wee footballer," said Mike and as an afterthought added, "and think of Jane."

Amber turned on Mike. "Jane has nothing to do with this, Detective Inspector Karetzi and you damn well know it! I'm ashamed of you, and you!" – looking at Evan who blushed profusely and turned away.

"One fucking normal person in this zoo?" Jimmy interrupted.

Mike got up and viciously kicked him in the balls. Jimmy whimpered, clutching his private parts; the pain ran right through him.

"Christ Mike, did you need to do that?" Amber said.

"No, I guess not, but one gets a lot of satisfaction doing so."

"You disgust me," Amber said.

Evan just looked on. Things were getting out of hand and he didn't want to be party to it.

Mike aimed another kick to the same place, then another, even harder. Jimmy fainted.

"I'm going," said Amber. "This is not what I expect from my co-workers." She moved towards the door.

Evan grabbed her. "Listen Amber, I don't like violence and to both of us it is anathema, if that's the right word. Anyway, you do your job, I do mine and he," pointing at Mike, "does his, or as far as he's concerned, he does."

"Not for me, Evan. I abhor violence. It's not the way decent people act. I'm off and in all honesty I'm not sure what the future holds."

Jimmy had come round again. He saw Amber heading for the door, the one detective trying to stop her.

"What about me, you big fat slug? You're here to tend my wounds?"

"Go on then, fix him up, Amber," Mike said.

"Come on bitch, or should I call you Florence?"

"Florence?" said Evan.

"Yes, Nightingale."

"Come on slut, down on your fucking knees, help me, and when you've finished you can give me a blow job."

"Shut up arsehole," said Evan.

Mike lit up, sucked in and blew out rings of smoke everywhere.

"My, my, you're wee in stature and even smaller down there," said Amber. "If you say one more word, the iodine will overspill and I promise you that you will be very sorry."

"Do your worst, bitch."

Amber did, with great effort. After she'd finished she rose and slapped Jimmy so hard that his upper false teeth popped out. Jimmy looked down dejectedly. For the first time in memory he felt vulnerable.

Evan for some reason felt sorry for him. Amber didn't.

"Have we anything to eat in here Mike?" Amber said.

"Not really Amber. Actually, nothing as such unless of course you want a liquid lunch."

"I'll phone for something," Evan said. "Sandwiches do, pizza maybe?"

"Anything," Amber said, "just make it fast and don't forget something for Jimmy, something with a straw," Amber added.

Evan left. He wanted to pick exactly what he wanted to eat.

Mike got up and crossed over to where Jimmy was cowering. Jimmy feared the worse. Amber didn't care anymore. No one had ever called her a slut; fat, yes, and she was. Black, no problem, she was, but slut? No way.

"Open your mouth Jimmy. I said open your mouth." Jimmy did, there was no fight left in him. Mike stooped, picked up the upper false teeth and placed them in Jimmy's mouth, turned and walked back to his seat.

Amber looked at Mike, astonishment all over her face. Mike shrugged and said, "It's demeaning, not having your full set."

What a strange man, thought Amber, but in her estimation Mike had risen quite a few pegs, as he had in Jimmy's.

When Evan returned with various sandwiches, Mike asked Jimmy what he preferred. Jimmy said 'anything', so Mike gave him egg and cress. The same for Tony and Cokes for both. Mike now unlocked the handcuffs and tied Jimmy's one hand to a radiator, so that he could eat.

They all ate in silence. They all knew they had a problem. What to do with their captives.

When Jimmy's phone rang, Mike passed it to Jimmy who looked at Mike for what to say.

"Just tell him to go back home and not say a word to anyone," Mike told him. Jimmy did and handed back the phone to Mike.

"Where do we go from here Jimmy?" Mike asked.

"I don't know mate. I haven't understood exactly why I was sent here and it looks like I fucked up. First time in my life. You were expecting me, otherwise I think things would have turned out differently. You held all the aces."

"I did and still do, Jimmy. Let me try to explain once you have apologised to Amber, who did solely come to help you with those wounds."

"Missus, I was out of order and I'm sorry. Thanks for tending my wounds."

"Apology accepted," said Amber.

"So let's hear this story, Michael."

"It's Mike, and better if Amber tells you everything."

Amber started right from the first meeting with Mr B. Mike shut the kitchen door; there was no reason for the other guy to hear.

It took ten minutes. Jimmy didn't butt in or ask any questions.

He just nodded occasionally and when Amber finished he said, "I see."

"You have a dilemma Mike. Let us loose or keep us here or turn us into the local boys in which case we will be released within hours and there will be lots of questions asked of you. Can you answer them?"

"That sums up our problem Jimmy," said Evan. "So we have a right old conundrum here," added Mike.

"I'm not sure that's the word to use in this context," said Amber.

"Well, I know what I mean and I'm sure everyone else does," said Mike.

"Can you at least tell me who tipped you off about me coming down? It was only to have a quiet word in your ear, Detective, warn you off digging into the organisation too deeply and now we have a snitch in the Agency."

Evan's phone rang. It was Charlie. They had been held up with a flat tyre. Evan told him that everything was under control and not to bother coming.

"I can only tell you that he rang yesterday. We've got him on tape. It's not a voice any of us recognise, although I think he was trying to disguise it by speaking through a hanky or scarf."

"I'm sorry about your friend Jane," said Jimmy, "and I understand how badly you want to catch this Chessman, but keeping us here does not help you, now does it?"

"It might," said Evan. "It just might, if Jimmy spoke to the big man in London."

"To say what?" asked Amber.

"To tell him that we are of little or no threat, or rather to persuade him that we can co-exist. They do whatever they do leaving us in peace to catch our man."

"You're wasting your time. The Agency is, well, how can I put it? 'Inflexible', that's the word," said Jimmy.

"Okay," Mike said. "There's only one way to find out. Maybe we will get through if we use Jimmy's mobile."

"It will make no difference. Can I make a suggestion before you phone?" said Jimmy.

"Why not?" said Amber. "You speak up Jimmy."

"Fine. If you ring, within an hour they will be breaking down the front door. You can't use the photos and implicate us in any way and even if you could, how would they help you? The photos wouldn't see the light of day and if by some miracle they did surface you and others would be contravening the Official Secrets Act and then prison."

"Your suggestion Jimmy; all I hear is doom and gloom," said Evan.

"Let us go and I will tell them that we've had a good chat; everything is great down here in Wales," said Jimmy with all the sincerity he could muster.

Mike looked at Evan. Evan nodded. After cutting the rope binding his legs, Mike used the key to uncuff Jimmy and then helped him get to his feet.

The punch to his stomach took Mike by complete surprise. Not as much as the kick rendered by Amber to Jimmy's backside, hitting the stab wound on the right buttock. Both were now on their knees. Mike winded and Jimmy screeching in agony. Evan stood over Jimmy ready to cause him more anguish. Tony inside was shouting obscenities. He didn't see anything but he could hear Jimmy's screams. It was like a Tarantino film.

Still kneeling, Mike slowly got his breath back and looked at Jimmy who was writhing in great agony. He was about to ask why, but was pre-empted by Jimmy who now held out his hand. Mike took it and they shook hands.

"Sorry Mike, I had to do it. It's the way I am. I had to get in one good blow. I couldn't walk away without throwing a punch. It's all about pride." He then turned and with all the dignity he could muster he faced Amber and bowed.

"Never mind Jimmy Johnstone's footballing skills, look at

Amber's – what a kick!"

"A bloody bull's-eye," said Mike.

Everyone laughed, Jimmy louder than most. "You lot having a party in there?" shouted Tony.

"Shut up Tony!" Jimmy shouted.

"I think it's time our friend Tony was released, Mike," Evan said, picking up on the name as if knowing it would be of some use.

"Would you please explain to him that everything is hunky dory. He's a big brute and I don't want my apartment wrecked. I'm expecting female company tonight."

Amber rolled her eyes. Evan blushed.

"Anything else to eat Mike?" Amber asked.

"You know there isn't, Amber."

"Can I phone the driver to pick us up?" Jimmy asked.

"Yes, go ahead."

"Is that you Gary?" asked Jimmy. "Where are you?"

"Not quite sure Boss," answered Gary.

"Well, find out and then find out where the nearest chippy is and get me six large fish and chips and mushy peas, sausages and an assortment of cold drinks; oh, and a few faggots while you're at it. Have you got all that Gazza?"

"I have sir, but where am I going to find the faggots in the middle of the day?"

"At the fucking chippy, you stupid fucking moron, where else would they be?"

"Sorry Boss, I thought you were on about gays," said Gary.

"Gays, Gary, give me a break, gays! You... never mind, get on with it!"

"Yes Boss, immediately."

"And Gary, lots of salt and vinegar, okay?"

"What's all that about then Jimmy?" asked Mike.

"Dinner before I leave, I'm starving," said Jimmy.

"So am I," said Amber.

"And me," chirped Evan.

"But we've just had sandwiches," said Mike.

"That was just the starters," said Amber.

Jimmy was back on the phone to Gary. "Don't forget to get a receipt, Gazza."

Jimmy turned to the others who were now all sitting and just said, "Expense Account."

Mike smiled and said to Jimmy, "Sit down Jimmy, the war is over, let's give peace a chance."

"Lennon," said Jimmy. "Can't sit at the mo." Amber smiled.

Again, Tony shouted, "What about me? Don't forget me. I need a piss!"

"Marble, Jimmy."

"Good," said Jimmy, shouting to Tony to keep his mouth shut.

"Marble Mike?" Amber queried.

"Yes Amber, the kitchen floor is marble, so it's piss proof if Tony soils himself."

"That is disgusting and unhygienic Mike," Amber said.

"Not if Tony can control himself it aint," replied Mike.

"While we await our food provider Jimmy, maybe you can help us with a small problem," said Evan.

"Maybe," said Jimmy.

"Do you know anything about motorbike or other gangs based here in Cardiff in or around the nineteen eighties?"

"Not off hand, but we do keep some old files in the basement. Why?"

"Because one of these gangs killed my father and I want to stamp on the damn cockroaches that did it. It's personal."

"Ask Mr B Mike, he could easily get access," said Jimmy.

"Have, and it's no go even though we told him it was connected to our Chessman murders. He says they don't have anything on file."

"Give me the list if you have one and I will get any information on file, in exchange for the photographs. Is that a deal?"

"It's a deal," said Evan, not giving Mike a chance to speak.

"Do you speak for everyone detective?"

"He does," said Amber. Mike nodded.

From her bag, Amber produced a pen and some paper. She wrote down the names and passed them to Jimmy.

Jimmy pocketed the piece of paper without looking at it.

"There might be more than what's on the list," said Evan.

"Don't worry, whatever is there you will get. I also know some other people who will probably have the information."

"What about the tape?"

"What tape," asked Evan.

"The anonymous caller with the tip-off about me. I want it," said Jimmy.

"No way Jimmy. What with voice recognition equipment and God knows what else, you will track him down and we can't have that, can we?" Mike said.

"Can I hear it for myself then?" said Jimmy.

"No, Jimmy, I think it should be destroyed. We don't want an unexpected burglary," said Mike.

"Pity, but I understand," said Jimmy.

When Gary rang again, he was situated outside in the street opposite Mike's apartment.

"Okay, Jimmy, I'm going to unleash the beast next door. Do you want to come in and help?" said Mike.

Together they walked in. Mike handed Jimmy the key.

"About time," Tony said.

No tell-tale puddles on the floor, Mike thought, looking carefully everywhere around the big guy.

"Things have changed," said Tony. "Everyone seems luvvy-duvvy with each other."

"Don't say another word Tony or I'll slap you from here to hell and then back again. Now Tony, go downstairs, have a pee in the bushes and pick up four fish and chips and sausages and other things and bring them up."

Tony was mad with rage. Jimmy kept himself in between Tony and Mike, who held the Taser behind his back.

"Don't think about it Tony 'cause I will teach you a lesson you will never forget. Things have changed here and I need you to be in control of yourself. Now go. I'm hungry."

"Don't you want a faggot Mike?" Amber asked.

"I'm not too sure what they are," said Mike.

"It's just seasoned chopped meat which has been fried," said Amber.

"What type of meat?"

"All types, liver, beef," said Amber.

Mike took one. They weren't bad.

It was three o'clock when Jimmy left. He'd been in Mike's apartment six hours.

"No news from Jimmy yet?" asked the Director to Brian.

"Nothing Mr Director, but we all know that Jimmy's not much for communicating."

Amber cleared up, Mike and Evan lit up. "What do you think Jimmy will tell them?"

"He will cover his arse best he can, Evan."

"You didn't tell me about the chocolates Mike," Amber said, her mouth full of the product.

"Sorry Amber, a present from Jimmy. Take them with you. I don't eat much chocolate, only the ones with marzipan."

"Thanks Mike, I'll take out the ones with marzipan for you and put them in the fridge."

Before leaving, Jimmy had borrowed a small cushion. He needed it badly. He had eaten standing up.

Mike finished his fag and started pacing up and down the room.

"Why are you pacing, Mike? What's wrong?" asked Evan.

"We need to call London, Evan. This has got to finish Evan, otherwise we will never get anywhere near the Chessman. We will spend our life looking over our shoulders."

"Right then, here we go. It's show time," Mike said. Evan shuddered.

"Tangent," said the voice, a new receptionist not long on the job. "How may I help you?"

"I would like to speak to Mr Bollok, without the 'c'".

"And you are Sir?"

"I am Special Detective Inspector Mikhail Karetzi, spelt KARETZI.

For a few good seconds there was silence before the receptionist spoke again.

"What may I tell him it's about sir?"

"Cardiff."

"Did you say Cardiff, as in Wales?"

"That's correct miss, Cardiff, the Capital of Wales."

"Could you please expand on that sir?"

"Yes of course, Cardiff became the Capital in 1955. The population is about three hundred and ninety thousand. It's situated about twenty-five miles west of the bridge that crosses the River Severn, which is the longest river in the UK. There are two bridges: one motorway, the M4 which runs just outside Cardiff, one way to Swansea, the other way taking you into London and did you know that you pay to enter Wales when you use the bridge but it's free going out?" Mike didn't pause from breath. "You must have heard about the Millennium Stadium with its retractable roof where we beat all-comers at rugby; then we have a new stadium being built for the Bluebirds and..."

"Thank you sir, could I ask you to ring back in five. Mr B is on the phone at present."

"No problem Miss, give them the tape and I will ring back."

"You should join the Welsh Tourist Board Mike," Evan said laughing.

Mike glanced at his wrist, no watch. He smoked one and then rang back. The girl at reception put him through to Brian who was sitting next to the Director who was extremely surprised. He had tried unsuccessfully to raise Jimmy since Karetzi's first call.

"Yes Detective, how can I be of help?" said Brian.

"Leave us alone please. I've had a word with Jimmy and his mates and we all agreed to let well alone, no more, no less."

Forty minutes it took; the ten thousand would have to be shown to have been used; the offices would be rented to the local police force as from January the first if they could come to some agreement with the Chief Constable and/or the Assembly; ditto the equipment.

They would also help, if they could, with the list Amber had given them. The ones Jimmy was also going to look into.

It was now five in the afternoon and Amber asked if Mike was sure he liked the marzipan chocs. She had systematically polished off the others, one by one and in some cases two by two.

Mike said that he could live without them. Amber obviously couldn't and raided the fridge.

"What a fantastic day's work," Evan said. Everyone agreed but knew that they'd moved no further to catching the Chessman.

"I wonder what the Chessman is up to right now?" said Evan.

At eight p.m. the three were now just sitting in the office.

"We must do something. We can't allow ourselves the luxury of just sitting here and waiting for the worst."

"But what can we do?" said Mike.

"It was an inspired trick of yours, I must say," said Evan.

"I don't understand Evan," said Mike, completely mystified.

"Saying we have a tape of the anonymous tipster. I especially like the red herring you threw in making the caller a 'he' and not a 'she'."

"Yes, if I say so myself; Jimmy can tell them that the mole in their organisation is a man and he is sure of that because we have a tape, which we will not release to them for obvious reasons."

"We could give them the tape," said Amber. Mike and Evan stared at Amber in shock. "Did you actually tape the call, Amber?" said Mike.

"No I didn't, but it doesn't stop us fabricating one. Very simple really, all we need is a man speaking through a handkerchief from a local phone box reading out from a sheet of paper," Amber replied.

Evan thought it was a reasonable idea but they should not waste the time and energy and just tell Jimmy that they had destroyed the tape.

Mike concurred it was the last they would speak of the matter.

In London, they were talking about the same subject – the Director, Brian and Jimmy who was standing up.

They concluded that they would never get hold of the tape and that the mole would have to be flushed out another way.

When Jimmy had left the room, the Director turned to Brian. "I never in my lifetime though that anyone would get the better of Jimmy, Brian."

"Me too, but the Ruski had the drop on Jimmy, poor guy. Rumour has it that our boyo down there in Wales gave Jimmy a new arsehole or two," said Brian.

"So I hear. Pity, because Jimmy was supposed to go to Paris this weekend. Guess I'll have to find someone else."

The Director stood as did Brian. "Ah, well, tomorrow is another day," sighed the Director. "I hope it's better than today."

"Amen to that," added Brian as he walked out of the door.

CHAPTER 18

That evening Mike cried off from dinner with Cheryl, a hairdresser from Roath. Instead he paid his mother a visit and together they went to the cemetery which, although closed to the public, was open for Mike and a twenty-pound note.

Evan was shown the watch that he, together with his wife and daughter, had chosen for his partner. It was an Omega, chunky just like Mike's broken one and made of gold and silver which perfectly matched Mike's lighter. All that was left was the inscription and, after nearly two hours, they settled on just the word "Thanks" above the stamp on the reverse of the watch and underneath the stamp of the astronomical observatory with the eight stars and below the date of the fight with Taylor in Roman numerals to match the watch's face numbers.

All of the Sunday following Chester's double murder on Saturday, the Chessman had stayed in his girlfriend's bed only surfacing to eat. Murder was tiring and that Sunday night, it was time to leave Cardiff and head off back to Swansea. He had gone through all the papers with a fine toothcomb looking to see if anyone had picked up on any mistakes that he might have made. They were still not mentioning the chess element or that Mr King had been poisoned. He knew that that would change soon enough.

During the past month, Peter the Chessman had dealt with his finances. Together with his savings he would have over three hundred thousand pounds. Both his house and flat he mortgaged to the hilt, the cars heavily financed. Orders were coming in for

Christmas; a good time to sell coins. Whatever remained at the end of the month would go into auction at the beginning of December. He expected to clear another thirty odd thousand from the coins in total.

All the bank accounts had been set up. He had two new passports in different names, one British and one Canadian. He would just walk away when the time came. He had no emotional attachment to the house, flat, cars, or for that matter anything. He wanted a new life. He'd taken lives to make a new and better life for himself. It was that simple.

Tuesday morning, ten o'clock precisely, the Chessman was in his bank, a small independent. There weren't many left anymore. The bank took a four per cent commission and within the hour had remitted the balance of three hundred and eighty-six thousand pounds to a Panamanian company account in a Luxembourg bank. This was converted to American dollars at the current rate and for a further four per cent they sent the new balance to a Liberian company account in a Brazilian Bank within an hour of receiving the money.

Another four per cent ensured that his money winged its way to another account in the Cayman Isles inside one hour. A citizen of Canada, André Dubois would be the final name on this financial tap dance.

From the Cayman Isles, it was a two-hour flight to Montego Bay in Jamaica, the money's final resting place. Mr Dubois would take it in cash.

Yes, he lost about fifteen per cent of the money but because of the time zones involved, the money sent from Cardiff would be in the Caymans the same day and in his account.

The banks involved had been warned to expect more, very large amounts of money to be forthcoming from the same source within the month and to earn their exorbitant service fees they were to act immediately without further instructions.

The Chessman looked forward to retiring as such. Murder was such a toilsome business. It took it out of you. It was very tiring.

A nice mansion with a bit of sandy beach, a tennis court, a little land with various exotic fruit trees, a servant or two, and sun all the year round. And women of course; plenty of them.

He had selected six of the richest people in Wales and the Bristol area. Their wealth ranged from twenty million to forty-five million. Their ages from thirty one to forty two. All were male, married with young children. Their wealth totaled just shy of 200 million and all he wanted was a measly ten per cent. He expected to make about five or six million. That was enough because being a realist he calculated that he would get a greedy one or two who wouldn't part with a penny; one would have to be removed as a lesson to the other five.

To the Chessman, it was crystal clear. Enjoying the rest of your lives with ninety per cent of a lot of money was much better than being dead with a hundred per cent of a lot of money.

The Chessman started on the letter again. This was getting tedious he thought but then so were many things and you didn't get a good pay day out of them.

Wednesday morning and by five past all were present and having their coffee. Amber was also nibbling on a toasted cheese and tomato; it had been over an hour since breakfast.

The call came five minutes later. It was Brian. He was about to send a fax if they would stand by.

The fax stuttered through; first on the list was The Reapers; they didn't start a gang until after the death of Mike's father.

The Painted Angels: into prostitution and booze in the Newport area; now disbanded.

The Satans, pure motorbike gangs, mainly hanging out around scruffy cafés. Generally, completely harmless except for various instances of noise pollution and speeding. Gang ageing, but still running.

The Devil's Advocates, disbanded late seventies and last on the fax The Demonics, harmless bunch of lads, all holding down normal daytime jobs such as welders, decorators, painters, petty theft, a few boozed up fights at football matches, nothing big. Now disbanded.

Names were supplied where appropriate, those with records.

"What a bunch of nobodies," Mike said.

"I think we are on the wrong track. Look at this lot."

"The Reapers seem a bit nasty, but based in Newport. I reckon we can discount them," said Evan.

"You can discount them all," said Mike.

"At least we tried and give Brian his due he got what we wanted and now we find out that it's not what we needed."

Mike sat down, dejectedly. He'd start from scratch again but he hadn't reckoned on Jimmy.

The phone rang. Evan picked it up. "It's Taj."

"Who's Taj?" asked Amber.

"Three Arseholes, Jimmy."

"You mean Jimmy Johnstone?" said Amber.

"Of course I do," replied Evan.

"Well, what does he want?"

"He has information on the gangs," Evan said.

"We have that already," answered Mike.

"He knows that Brian sent us a fax but he has additional material which he has gleaned from his own sources. Generally it's about gang members, names, addresses; that is old addresses and various other tidbits. He's asking if he can have the photos including the Polaroids and of course any copies as agreed."

"Ask him where he wants us to send them," said Mike. "We keep our word but tell him not to bother sending the information which is of no use to us but thanks anyway," said Mike.

Evan took down a PO Box address from Jimmy or Taj as he liked to call him and handed it to Amber who would arrange the collecting and mailing of the photos.

Within a minute, the fax machine started up again. Jimmy had sent the fax as proof that he had collected the information Cardiff wanted.

Again, it was names; some with home addresses, some with work addresses.

"Interesting, The Satans had a burning cross on their black leather jackets and here we are Mike, we've struck gold. I can't believe our luck. Look here, The Demonics had a treble six tattooed on their wrists."

Mike jumped up and ran over to where Evan was standing reading the fax. "Holy Mackerel, we've cracked it Evan! Good old Jimbo. I can't believe it, what a break!"

"Let's open a file Amber. How many names. Do we have addresses? Let's get it all down on one sheet of paper."

Mike grabbed a piece of foolscap and a pen. He wrote quickly. When he had finished he read aloud:

"The Demonics, gang consisting of between ten and fourteen members. Ages of them now forty-four to forty-eight/nine. Tattoo on wrist. Five names, two home addresses when twenty years plus old, one work address, eight years old and one prison address, current. These five members had all been inside for various misdemeanors. All this from Jimmy. Two different names, no addresses on Brian's fax, so seven gang members to try and track down. Well, they knew where to find one – in prison."

They didn't hear Charlie coming in. He had no key but then Charlie didn't need one. The alarm was off, not that it would have hindered him.

Mike looked up when he sensed that someone had entered. He was surprised to see Charlie standing there grinning from ear to ear.

"Hi Charlie. Was the door open?"

"Hello everyone. No, I used my own. Didn't want to disturb you."

"Maybe we should change the lock," Amber said.

"Won't make any difference to me or anyone worth his salt," said Charlie.

"Never mind that," said Mike. "We've been trying to get hold of you."

"I was working," said Charlie.

"What type of work?" asked Evan.

"I've been doing a little finangling," said Charlie.

"Now you've completely flummoxed me," said Amber. Is that something to do with fishing?"

Charlie laughed. "Finangling: behaving badly, like stealing documents from a sport's club. I have a list of 231 names with their addresses and contact numbers. Here, take them Amber."

"How the hell did you get them without a camera, Charlie?" said Mike, eyeing about a dozen sheets of paper.

"Easy. I bypassed their Mickey Mouse alarm system, picked the office door and cabinet locks and then using their photocopying machine I copied the relevant numbers."

"Relevant numbers?" queried Evan.

"Yes, I eliminated women, the partly disabled, those under twenty-five and over fifty and all those belonging to only the snooker and table tennis group who are just anoraks."

"Christ Charlie, that doesn't make sense," said Mike.

"It does to me Mike. Believe. It's not one of those groups," said Charlie.

"Just because they play ping pong doesn't exclude them from being the Chessman," Mike said.

"It's not one of them. I promise you. I know Mike, trust me," said Charlie.

"What about the other sports company down in Swansea," Amber asked.

"I have it on good authority that we will have the full list by tomorrow," said Charlie.

"What do you mean Charlie, by good authority?"

"A friend of a friend has a cousin who works for the company who insures the club and therefore has access to their membership list. It will cost another five. Too many people with their noses in the trough," said Charlie.

"And this friend of yours, he's Kosher? No comebacks if there's a problem?" said Mike.

"No, he's an old mucker of mine. Met him when I was in her Majesty's Hotel," said Charlie.

It took Evan a few minutes to work out that mucker was not a mispronunciation of a profanity, it just meant mate.

"Another day, a little more pay," Amber said.

"For me," Charlie said.

Amber handed Charlie a photograph. Charlie studied the photo. Mike tapped out a cigarette and lit up. Evan began loading his pipe. Mike sucked on the smoke and then blew it out; a strand of tobacco had settled on his lower lip and he spat it out. It landed on the photo which Charlie had laid aside, a dark brown spot between the Chief Constable's eyes.

"Good shot Mike. You've given the Chief Constable a third eye," said Charlie.

"He will need it if he's to detect you following him," said Evan.

"How did you know he's Chief Constable Clarke, Charlie?" asked Mike.

"I know he's a Chief Constable from his uniform and his name I know 'cause you just told me."

Everyone laughed.

"Look everyone, I've got to be frank," Charlie started saying before Mike butt in with "Well I'll be Jesse."

The three of them looked at Mike for an explanation of some sort.

"Frank and Jesse James, American Wild West bank and railroad robbers," said Mike.

"Where the hell do you come up with these things Mike?" asked Evan.

"As I was about to say," said Charlie, "I have never followed anyone. It won't be easy. I mean, doesn't his rank allow him a chauffeur or something?"

"Yes, but we are betting on him not using an official car, Charlie. We think he is playing away from home," said Evan.

"Tell me more. I need some info. What am I looking for? Is he walking on the wrong side of the street?"

"What?"

"No he's not gay, Charlie. We think, and of course we could be way out, that the Chief Constable is seeing this lady," Evan said, showing him a picture of Emma Andrews in a Welsh Assembly brochure.

"They are both married. Here's their addresses and places of work," said Amber, handing Charlie a sheet of paper.

"I can do my best," said Charlie, "but I can't promise you will get a result." He added jokingly, "Is there anything else I can do in between jobs?"

"Yes there is," said Mike. "I need a personal favour."

"If I can, Mike," said Charlie.

"Thanks Charlie. When you next go down the Cutty ask some of the old timers that frequent the place if they can help me trace any of the following who belonged to a gang in the seventies, eighties. They have a tattoo on their wrists. The sign of the beast '666'."

"Let's have the list then, Mike," said Charlie. Mike passed him the list.

"I will tell you something for nothing," Charlie said.

"Aye, what's that?" asked Evan.

"If you add up all the numbers of a roulette wheel, you arrive at a total of 666."

"Now I know why it's a devil of a game to win," said Mike.

"Anything regarding the funeral arrangements for Jane?" asked Evan to nobody in particular.

"Nothing Evan, big one on Sunday for Mel, but heard nothing about Jane's," Amber said.

Charlie left at two. Amber went upstairs to the kitchen to grab a bite. Evan followed her. Mike sat and put all the numbers through his calculator. Charlie was right. 666 was correct; another piece of useless information.

"Alone in his own world he closed his eyes and saw the image that he always saw, the beautiful strawberry blonde; another problem he couldn't solve.

Over forty minutes he sat there alone, thinking and all the things that he thought about were all the things that he couldn't face; that in reality they were no nearer to catching the Chessman, or his father's killers or even finding the woman he wanted. He began feeling depressed. He needed a drink or two.

"Are you asleep Mike?"

Mike opened his eyes. It was Charlie.

"I thought you'd gone, Charlie."

"I did but I got a call that the list was ready and they wanted the money, so I collected the list and gave them the five that you had given me."

Charlie put the list on the table. "I'm afraid that there are over 400 names on this list; all the males. They could only separate from the women members, Mike."

"That's fine Charlie." Mike got up and from the internal rang the kitchen. Amber answered, her mouth full of food.

From what Mike could gather they were just finishing and would be down shortly.

"Grab a pen Charlie and a sheet from that list. Knock off any one over the age of 55 and under 25 and anyone who is disabled."

Charlie started on one sheet, Mike on the other. By the time the others arrived nearly fifteen minutes later, the list had been reduced to 189.

Mike opened his bottom drawer, withdrew five hundred pounds and handed it to Charlie.

"We've got a total of 420 potentials. I'll run their addresses through the computer and eliminate those not in our little triangle."

It took two hours plus before Amber gave everyone a printout. One hundred and six names left.

"Bloody Hell," Evan said, "how are we going to go about this, interviewing one hundred and six people? We can ask for help. We need a dozen or so detectives – each takes eight or nine addresses."

"You will need a cover story," said Charlie.

"You can't knock on people's doors and not knock on their neighbours because they're not on your list. And what do you say? Do you say we're looking for a left-handed serial killer. Do you have a chess set with some white pieces missing, one size 11 shoe, a hooded anorak, wigs, chauffeur's garb, leather gloves, grey overcoat, women's…?"

"Okay Charlie," said Mike, "I think we get the gist and we wouldn't even get the manpower. No way. We can't, hand on heart, say that the Chessman is one of these 106."

"Firstly, we whittle down the numbers," said Amber. "And then we see what we will do next."

"And how are we going to do that?" asked Evan.

"Local newspapers, such as say, the 'Barry and District', the 'Port Talbot Tribune' series. All the murders happened during the weekends, agreed? So anyone of our 106 playing football, cricket, tennis, bowls, whatever, cannot be in two places at the same time, can they? And local papers report all the names and places in the minor local leagues. It's a big job but if necessary, I will stay up all night," concluded Amber.

"I therefore suggest that we go home and tomorrow we will see how we have fared and what numbers we have left."

Everyone said their goodnights and went their separate ways, each driving.

Mike needed petrol so he headed for his normal garage which was slightly out of his way but he trusted them with repairs and naturally used them for petrol.

As Mike pulled into the garage, a woman was attempting to inflate an absolutely flat tyre on her Mercedes sports car. It was a beautiful new car as was the female to whom it belonged. To start with he could only see her perfectly rounded pert bottom. That was enough for Mike to become Sir Galahad and ride to the rescue.

She was about his age, very, very nice looking brunette, and no rings. The tyre was punctured so Mike put the spare on, at the same time extracting a dinner date for half eight that same evening. It was more than part her idea. She insisted on treating Mike as a 'thank you' for changing the tyre. Her name was Barbara. Mike's spirits lifted. They arranged to meet at Angelo's.

Mike rang Angelo to tell him to set a good table aside. Either way if she didn't turn up then he'd still have a good meal and a good drink. He needed both.

Jasmine arrived just after her father. The watch had been inscribed. Everyone was very pleased with the result.

Amber worked steadily. In a way it was quite therapeutic. She was not tired and this kept her mind busy. She eventually finished; only forty-two names remained. The boys would be pleased. The time was four a.m.

For a moment, Charlie was fooled and nearly missed the Chief. For some stupid reason he expected the Chief to be in a suit and tie, not as the clubs say, smart/casual. The Chief carried his uniform in one of those nylon suit carriers which he had deposited into the boot of his car.

Charlie followed the Chief for over two miles before the Chief parked into an all-night garage and started walking.

Charlie did the same, camera in hand. They walked a good three hundred yards before the Chief stopped at a small restaurant. He looked around and then entered. Charlie waited. It was very cold but at least it was dry.

The Olive Branch was Greek. Charlie recognized the flag that was hanging from a pole outside. He didn't know too much about Greek food. He assumed that the Chief did.

Now was the Chief eating alone, with colleagues, his wife or this Emma Andrews? The cold was getting to Charlie and he could wait no longer. He entered the restaurant not knowing what his next move would be and not particularly caring. At least the place was warm.

At one end of the restaurant stood a small bar with two stools. He slowly walked towards it keeping his eyes peeled for the Chief and took one of the stools.

He ordered a bottle of Greek lager and when he was asked if he required a table he replied in the affirmative but didn't wish to sit until he had finished his beer.

After his eyes had adjusted to the dark of the tavern, he scanned the room. He could not see the Chief but in the corner a woman sat alone at a table laid for two. He tried to match her face with the one in the brochure. It was possible but not a certainty. The woman wore a wedding ring. He concluded that the Chief was visiting the men's room and a few seconds later the Chief passed Charlie and headed for the table with the lone woman at it.

The Chief sat, smiled and over the table they tentatively held hands for a second or so. Bless them, thought Charlie, suppressing an urge to laugh out loud.

On finishing his drink Charlie was shown to a table and handed a menu. The menu was a little alien to him but he eventually settled on the Fried Salt Cod with a side dish of chips. The Greeks called it Bakaliaros. Fair enough but fish and chips is fish and chips in whatever language. He ordered another lager. It was actually quite good. He wondered how he could get in a couple of shots with the camera. Fortunately, he still had plenty of time because the Chief and friend were only just on their starters.

When the meal arrived he was glad he had ordered the chips as the fish was accompanied with Mash potato, just two mouthfuls, and a salad with everything but the kitchen sink in it.

The fish was burnt, no batter and full of salt. The chips were cold but Charlie did not complain as he didn't want to draw attention to himself.

Charlie tried another mouthful. It felt like the chef, if he could call a person who dips fish in salt instead of flour before frying, was intent on poisoning him. He gave up on the salt fish and tried a mouthful of the mash. Grabbing his napkin he spat it out. It was like eating pure crushed garlic. My God, a teaspoon of this stuff would see off Dracula from a hundred paces.

"Is everything okay, Sir?" asked the waiter who had witnessed Charlie's struggle.

"I think I probably asked for the wrong dish. Have you got a burger?"

"We do Keftedes, Sir; meatballs you would call them Sir."

"Great, bring them on and another lager," Charlie said, preparing himself for the worst. Nothing in this place was what it seemed. He was more than pleasantly surprised; the meatballs were just out of this world, fantastic. Why hadn't he ordered them to start with?

The two central tables had remained unoccupied and after clearing them the waiters carted them away. A high stool was brought in from somewhere and placed in one of the corners of what now was going to be used as a stage-cum-dance area.

In front of the stool one of the waiters placed a microphone. A massive black mustachioed, small, thick-set man made his way to the stool, carrying what looked like a large mandolin which Charlie at least recognised the instrument to be a bouzouki.

After adjusting the mike and fine tuning his instrument, the moustache started playing. Charlie recognized 'Zorba the Greek' as one of the tunes.

By the third tune, ten people were on the makeshift dance floor. They weren't exactly dancing, more like prancing, thought Charlie. The waiters were smashing white plates, half a dozen at a time on the dance floor and customers were buying plates and joining in the plate smashing.

The Chief and the lady he was entertaining were neither

prancing nor plate smashing. They seemed content holding hands and grabbing a quick kiss now and then.

Some of the customers started taking photos which gave Charlie his chance to catch the Chief and friend in very friendly positions. Charlie felt sorry for the Chief in a way. He hoped that it was the Chief's wife, but somehow he doubted it.

A couple of miles away, down on the Bay, Mike had resigned himself to dining alone. It was a lady's prerogative to be late but thirty-five minutes? It was going to be a no-show.

Mike was on his third glass of Pinot and they were large. The table was laid, flowers – the works.

Angelo tried his utmost to lift Mike's spirits but wasn't making any headway.

"Maybe your friend lost way or maybe have accident," Angelo said kindly.

"Or maybe she's not coming Angelo," Mike said, sipping his wine and wondering if he should order. He was getting hungry. It had been another long day.

The door opened. Angelo turned and let out a wolf whistle. "You very lucky man I think Mike."

Mike could see nothing as Angelo was obscuring his vision, so Mike stood up just in time to see Barbara flounce through the door and head towards him.

She was wearing a stunning black trouser suit, high heels and her hair long. The whole restaurant stopped talking and looked, the men lusting, the women envying.

"I'm ever so sorry Mike. I had a last minute emergency."

Mike kissed her on both cheeks and then waited until she had made herself comfortable.

"Absolutely no problem," Mike said. "I was late myself," he lied. This was looking like a great night and Mike was up for it. He had missed a woman's company; all work and no play. Now he was about to make up for it.

"Would you like a drink Barbara? Some wine perhaps, what's your preference?"

"Thank you, I'll have a sparkling water with ice and lemon please," said Barbara.

"Some Champagne to go with it?" asked Mike.

"Actually Mike, I don't drink alcohol. I can't advise my patients not to drink on the one hand and then partake of the stuff myself. It would be hypocritical of me," said Barbara.

"Did you say patients?" asked Mike.

"Yes, I'm a doctor, work at the Heath."

Well, let's not worry about that Mike thought, I'll make up for you but it did make things a little awkward.

On the other side of the coin Barbara had a great body, was stunningly beautiful and wore some real nice perfume which excited Mike's nostrils.

Unfortunately things got worse. The good doctor Barbara was a vegetarian and to cap it, was also on a diet. How the fuck could vegetarians go on diets? It didn't make sense to Mike.

She picked at her food whilst Mike polished off a massive veal chop, fried in oil, butter and herbs; the spaghetti with just plain tomato sauce and lots of parmesan cheese also went down a treat as did the bottle of Pinot Grigio which Angelo had suggested as enhancing the meal.

It had been a long time since Barbara had fancied anyone. Now thirty-six and looking ten years younger, she knew she could get absolutely anyone but hadn't come across anybody she liked enough. This guy could be the exception. She wanted this man with the sparkling black eyes, unruly black hair. She was fascinated by the teardrop scar. He was tall and he looked fit even though he ate copious amounts of food, drank excessively and probably smoked. Nevertheless she could live with that for this man.

"Tell me about you," Barbara said.

"Welsh born, Russian father, mid-thirties. I'm a police

detective, like good food, drink and I smoke non-filter American cigarettes. I play a little football to keep fit, though at the moment I'm serving a ban. I work long and strange hours but in general I'm happy with life. That's about it," Mike said.

"Is there anything else that you like to do? Any hobbies, going to the cinema or something?" Barbara asked teasingly.

"Yes, I like beautiful women."

"And would you say I fit into the category Mike?"

"Very much so," answered Mike honestly.

"And you have no one at the moment Mike? I find that very surprising."

"No Barbara, I'm all alone. Like I said, my work hours are unpredictable. I could say the same for you. No man on the go, Barbara?" said Mike.

"Like you, I never seem to have time. Being a doctor is hard work although I do enjoy what I'm doing immensely."

With the meal almost over, Barbara knew that this man was hers for the taking and she wasn't going to miss out. The guy was like putty in her hands. She was really getting excited. For the time being forget about the drinking and the smoking and he didn't act as if he was taking drugs. She could tell; it was part of her job.

She wondered how she would let him get her into bed. It was so obvious he wanted her. All the signs were there. She wished he would move things along a little faster. Any opening line would do, however corny. He would have to do something about his breath. She abhorred the smell of tobacco and drink.

Relaxing wasn't coming easy for her. She was in a rush. It had been a long time and she was very impatient, so when Mike ordered a large brandy out of the blue, it took Barbara by complete surprise. He had also ordered a coffee and asked Barbara if she wanted anything. She declined.

Okay, she thought, he was obviously nervous as to how he got to the next stage of bed. Men were like that around her, but one thing for sure, wherever they ended up she would do the driving.

At that point a nasty thought entered her mind. Could the guy perform after all that drink? He seemed completely in control of all his facilities but when he went into the fresh air, what then?

"So where do you live Mike?"

"Just down the road. I walked from my apartment to the restaurant. It took me about ten minutes. And you Barbara?"

"Llandaff, and, thanks to you for changing the tyre – I drove down."

At last she thought, we are now getting somewhere. He's making his move, arranging where they would go on after they had finished here; and about time too.

"I must say, the food is good and the atmosphere tops," said Barbara.

"I'm glad you liked it," Mike said, wondering on what basis she had come to that conclusion when she had hardly eaten any of her meal, and that being vegetarian.

When Mike had spotted Barbara at the garage, he had mentally given her a mark of eight out of ten. When she had walked into the restaurant this went up to nine; now it was six and decreasing. Barbara was beautiful but they had nothing in common, even where music was concerned. She liked classical, he liked anything but. She didn't drink, eat; a little stoic for Mike. Beautiful and classy, yes, fun, hardly.

"Do you drink like this on a regular basis Mike? I suppose it's the job, chasing criminals all day and night. I suppose it would be futile for me to advise you, as a doctor of course, to cut down a little. It's very bad for your health-wise, as is the smoking."

It was now five out of ten. If Mike wanted someone to preach to him he would attend a church.

"No, I can honestly say it is not on a regular basis; sometimes I drink more and other times much more," said Mike laughing.

Barbara assumed Mike was joking but wasn't sure. She gave him the benefit of the doubt. She really wanted this man with the fabulous film star smile and rugged good looks. Strange that he didn't have someone in tow, or maybe he did.

She realized that she had made a little mistake lecturing him on his smoking and drinking habits. This type of man didn't take kindly to being patronized.

The night was dragging on and Barbara decided to hasten things by calling for the bill. She did say it was her treat after all.

"It has already been settled," said Mike.

"How, I've not seen anyone bring over the bill?"

"It went on my account. I'll settle with Angelo some other time," said Mike.

"But it was my treat," said Barbara, slightly miffed.

"When I have dinner with a beautiful lady, Barbara, I pay. It might seem a trifle old fashioned, but for me that's the only way. I hope I haven't offended you."

"No Mike, not at all. I just didn't expect to find any, dare I say it, gentlemen, in this day and age. Thank you."

The perfect man, Barbara thought. A man of principals to go along with all his other plus pointes, but he was rather slow. She knew he was gagging for it and yet he was prolonging his agony needlessly.

She caught her reflection in one of the many mirrors decorating the restaurant. She looked good, amazingly good. All the men's eyes were on her. Mike was a very lucky man to have crossed her path.

Mind you, there were also a lot of women's eyes on her man. He really did measure up. She was very happy. Her body tingled with anticipation of what dessert might bring.

Mike rose, slowly. "Are you ready Barbara? Do you need to use the ladies before we leave?"

"No, I'm ready Mike."

Guilio, one of Angelo's waiters, pulled the chair out, giving Barbara room to swing out her long legs accentuated by the four-inch heels. She took her time. She was the centre of attraction and wanted to milk it.

Mike slipped Guilio a twenty-pound note. He knew that Guilio would share it with the other waiters. They were all cousins.

Angelo was already at the door which he held firmly open, first for Barbara to pass and then Mike, who he wished a good night. It had a double meaning; even Barbara caught on.

Mike had lit up even before the door had closed behind him. Barbara caught the smell of tobacco as Mike exhaled gratifyingly. He wouldn't be smoking in her car, absolutely not and for the first time that evening she got something right.

By the time they had walked to her car Mike had had his nicotine fix and he dropped his cigarette into a small puddle. Barbara noticed. At least he knows he's not smoking in my car, she thought, opening the doors automatically from her key ring.

She turned to face Mike who was behind her. Surely he didn't think he was going to drive after the amount of drink he'd downed. That happened to be the furthest thing from Mike's mind. "Barbara, thank you for a very interesting evening. I hope it's not too late for you. I suppose you have a busy day ahead of you like I have. In truth I could have done with another brandy," and with that Mike gave her a peck on the cheek before somehow getting the car door open.

As she sat down her mind was racing. Was this man for real? Was he just going to walk away and leave her? This was a first. She slipped out of her stilettos and without bothering to put on her flats, she gunned the engine in her bare feet and sped off into the night.

Mike was about to wish her a good night and tell her to drive carefully. She had travelled over a hundred yards before Mike moved.

Barbara drove until she couldn't see the restaurant before stopping. She was shattered both physically and emotionally. She burst into tears. It was then that she realized she hadn't put on her seat belt; another first. It was a night of firsts for Barbara. A night she'd never forget.

What a pain in the arse, Mike thought as he walked back to the restaurant, another cigarette in hand.

"What a happen Mikhail, lady no like you? She no like food, the vino but maybe she lika jiggy jiggy, eh Mikhail?"

"Yes Angelo, maybe she like jiggy jiggy and so do I, but not with her, do you see Angelo?"

"No I not see, she very beautiful Mikhail."

"She is Angelo but if I did jiggy jiggy with Madame, I would be afraid."

"Afraid?" questioned Angelo, calling for a large brandy for his friend.

"Yes Angelo, afraid of finding out that my penis was the wrong shape or that my balls weren't the right size medically speaking. She's a doctor, Angelo."

"Aha," said Angelo, handing Mike the brandy. "I see," when of course he didn't. Only Mike knew what he was talking about.

"Any women here who are not too fussy Angelo, waitresses, kitchen staff, customers?"

"Nobody my friend, only my wife Donna in the kitchen," Angelo said, rising to the bait.

"Get her out here then Angelo. She can't be that fussy if she's married to you."

Angelo laughed. His wife Donna was a real Italian beauty and Mikhail was like family to both of them. He guessed that his friend had turned the woman down. She was up for it. He wondered if his friend was okay in himself after his illness or whatever it was that had stopped him coming.

Charlie took the photos and when he paid his bill, he asked the waiter why the mashed potato was full of garlic.

The answer was simple. It wasn't mash potato but garlic with potato called Skorthalia, an accompaniment that is served with Fried Salt Cod, like mint sauce is to lamb or apple sauce with pork. Charlie nodded. Vinegar was the more logical as with fish and chips.

Charlie left before the Chief. If the woman was not the Chief's wife he would not be in the least surprised. Holding hands and kissing in public at their age. Infidelity was not only for the young but rife with the more mature whose relationship had gone stale. Yes, he was quite the philosopher was Charlie.

He drove home and then took a taxi to the Cutty. He took over three hundred pounds. He'd already given Mike's list to the barman but even amongst your own you paid for information. Information was King and he also needed to buy some for a personal job.

On entering he ordered a rum and black. He looked around and was given the nod by a small bespectacled man with wild ginger hair. The required info was ready.

He crossed to where the ginger haired man was sitting, leaving his drink on the bar top. From his pocket Ginger took out a plain brown envelope and placed it on the table. Charlie picked it up and put it in his jacket pocket. Then Ginger raised two fingers in a 'V' shape. Charlie counted out two hundred pounds underneath the table, folded the wad and slipped them to Ginger underneath the table. Ginger pocketed the money without counting it. Not a word had been exchanged. There was honour amongst thieves.

On returning to the bar for his drink, the barman whispered the words 'Little Dick'. Charlie passed over two twenties and a two pound coin for the drink and then turned his back to the bar.

As usual Little Dick sat alone doing a crossword. No one was quite sure where Richard got his nickname, maybe it had something to do with the size of Richard's apparatus, or maybe his height since he was only five foot one. Charlie decided not to dwell any further on that particular subject and moved over to where Little Dick was sitting, taking a seat opposite him.

"Hi Rich, understand you might have something for me."

"I do Chalky, I do. You're looking for stuff on the Demonic gang, yes?"

"Yes," said Charlie. "What exactly do you have?"

"I have a recent address to a name on your list. I have a name not on your list and I have a work place for two on the list plus I can throw in some background on the whole gang. How's that for starters?"

"How much Rich?"

"Say two fifty," said Little Dick.

"Two hundred, half now, half tomorrow Rich," said Charlie, taking out what remained of the money he had brought.

Little Dick agreed and Charlie handed over the money making sure that Little Dick could see that he had only one twenty in total.

"Throw in a pint of Brains, Chalky, while I go and have a pee."

Charlie ordered with a form of semaphore without the flags. First he caught Todd the barman's eye then pointed to Richard's nearly empty glass before pointing to his own nearly filled one. He then held up his last twenty pound note which indicated that he would pay with that and he needed Todd to bring change.

Before either Richard or the drinks came Charlie picked up the crossword that Rich was engrossed in. It was from one of the Red top dailies and was four days old. It was half complete and done in three different coloured biros and a pencil. Richard was no Einstein but when it came to getting information about past events he was the best. God knows how he did it.

The drinks arrived before Richard, who had obviously had a fag in the loo. He stank of stale tobacco. He rolled his own and they had a particularly distinct smell to them.

Little Dick thanked Charlie for the drink and then began rummaging through his pockets for his notes.

Having found his notes, Richard, or Little Dick, as he was generally known but not to his boat race, began:

"Around 1978 four school friends aged seventeen and eighteen and no longer attending school, formed a gang. They were all at the time unemployed. The gang's main activities were pick pocketing, shoplifting, breaking into electricity meters and the like.

"Within a year, the gang had grown and they had a leader, not one of the original four. They called him The Whistler, not his real name but his nickname, because he was always whistling. This Whistler character closed the membership when they numbered twelve in membership.

"They called themselves the Demonics and they all without exception had the number 666 tattooed on their wrists.

"By the end of 1980 they were into intimidation, burglary, knocking over small shops and newsagents. Most carried knives, knuckledusters, bits of pipe, etc. They were fearless and were ruled with an iron fist by this Whistler bloke, who was a couple of years older and was the brains behind their escapades. They were into violence and got away with some good money which it was rumoured was stashed away. Again, rumour had it that they were planning on knocking over a local bank, but still needed a little more easy cash to buy one of the bank's employees and various pieces of equipment.

"Anyway, in September of that year, 1980, two were arrested attempting to rob a Post Office and another died in the middle of 'doing a newsagent' – he slipped and cut his head open on a steel corner unit with sharp edges. This happened on the same day.

"The Whistler within an hour of the arrests disappeared, taking all the money with him. The two were given two years apiece and within days, the gang disbanded. Look, here's your list, Charlie:

Jeff Entwistle	
Gareth Jones	Prison, current
Ifan Reece	
Tom Rider	
Tim Spillane	H. Address – 20 years old
George Surridge	W. Address – 18 years old
Toby West	H. Address – 20 years old

"Now to that list I have the recent address for West and another name, Barry Davies. Plus, we have a recent works address for Reece and Rider and of course the gang leader nicknamed the Whistler.

"It's thirsty work this, Chalky," said Rich.

Charlie stuck his hand up in the air and made a circular motion to Todd, who brought over another round and took another fiver for his efforts from Charlie.

"That's better," said Little Dick taking a long sip from his beer. "Now, where were we? Ah, yes. Entwistle was the guy who had the fatal accident, so cross him off the list. Surridge and Jones were the two jailed."

"And this Gareth Jones in for another spell, Rich, do we know what for?"

"Fraud, cheating old ladies out of money, forging docs."

"Okay, Rich, carry on."

"Well, about five or six years ago, Surridge was killed outside a pub in Carmarthen, a hit and run. He was blind drunk. Police never caught the driver. One emigrated to Australia, no name, at the same time as The Whistler's disappearance.

"That's it Chalky. To conclude, you now have eight names of which two are deceased plus a nickname of the gang leader and you know that he emigrated to Australia. Your best bet is to speak to Jones, he's not going anywhere for a while. Maybe he can provide the missing names."

Chalky got up, shook hands with Little Dick and was about to walk away when he remembered. "By the way Rich, three down is Baron."

"Thanks Chalky, I'm getting there albeit a little slowly, but that will help me quite a bit."

Charlie walked away. He waved to Todd and spoke to a few acquaintances on the way out. When Charlie let himself in at midnight, the first thing he did was make himself a coffee. He took a couple of Anadin and then sat at his small table.

Taking out the brown envelope he'd got from Ginger, he opened it and studied the diagram carefully. It was a piece of cake. Old alarm system, prehistoric safe, quiet area. Yes, he would do it tonight. Thankfully, Maggie was on nights and he could slip away without any questions being asked.

In the Evans' household that night it had been decided that tomorrow, Jasmine during her lunch break would come with the watch and personally give it to Mike. Edna also felt that she should be present as she was the one who had got Evan's partner into it.

Evan had no choice but to seem happy with the arrangement but deep down he harboured some uncomfortable feelings. He really didn't want his daughter to meet his partner; it would be a recipe for disaster and tears. His daughter had been hurt enough in the past. But, and a big 'but' at that, Mike had taken a savage hiding for Jas and they owed him more than just a paltry thanks and watch.

"So, just after one, I'll see both of you in the office," said Evan.

It was nearly five when Charlie returned from his shopping trip in Chepstow. All had gone well as he had expected. He emptied the contents of the cloth bag, also borrowed from the jewellers, on the table.

Diamond, emerald and ruby rings, one of which looked to be about three carats. Gold chains, bracelets, necklaces and other bits and bobs. Charlie was no expert but he reckoned on about sixty grand total for which he would get at best a third in cash.

He figured the big diamond ring. He really fancied it but Rule No 2 stopped him. Never hold on to any of the merchandise. Rule No 1 he'd already dealt with: never get caught. He packed the gear away and hid them under the floorboards. He'd see Mike with the information he had bought from Little Dick.

By ten to nine, Evan was hanging up his raincoat. His umbrella had taken most of the bad weather; it was chucking it down. He opened, shut and shook it a few times before plonking it into the stand.

Amber had just made some bacon butties and asked Evan if he would like some. Evan said "Yes" even though he'd had his breakfast less than an hour ago. Evan made himself a coffee. They chatted about the weather, not work. Amber didn't want to repeat herself, so she would wait for Mike who turned up fifteen minutes later, soaked to the bone.

"Swim up, did you?" laughed Evan.

"Yes, I did actually, but I forgot to change into my bathing suit," Mike said.

"Get your gear off Mike," Amber ordered.

"Trousers and all?" asked Mike mischievously.

"You can use my dressing gown, I'm sure it will fit you," said Amber.

"I think so, Amber, probably fit both me and Evan," said Mike, now down to his strawberry printed boxer shorts.

"Don't you have a vest on, Mike, in this weather?"

"No, rarely; they irritate me, so I tend to avoid them," said Mike.

The blue velvet dressing gown was as big as a tent for four. Mike nearly lost himself.

From his jacket pocket, he produced a crumpled damp packet of cigarettes. There were three left. He took them out and laid them on one of the radiators. He tried his lighter but obviously that was damp too so he just left it on his desk. He hoped that by the time the cigarettes dried, his trousers would be ready to wear. He felt very uncomfortable. Maybe Evan did have a point; an umbrella was handy sometimes.

Evan handed Mike a coffee; the butties had gone by now.

"Boys, I have some good news for you. We are down to forty-two suspects. Now it's up to you to get down and interview them somehow.

"That presents problems. How do we go about it?" said Evan.

"There is no way without seeing them," said Mike, "absolutely no way."

The door buzzer went. It was Charlie.

"Can't understand why he didn't just walk in as usual," said Evan.

"Because I put the bolt on," said Mike. "I'll go and let him in."

"Better if I do," said Evan. "You're not dressed for the outside world."

When Evan opened the door, Charlie just stood there holding a small umbrella.

"Christ man, I nearly drowned out there. I should have brought a canoe."

"We have coracles here in Wales," said Evan, letting Charlie in. "Before you ask, Charlie, coracles are small round boats used like canoes." Evan added.

As Charlie entered the main room, he heard Mike telling him not to laugh. Charlie didn't for precisely two seconds.

Mike rescued his twice-toasted cigarettes from the top of the radiator and lit up, his lighter now in working order. Charlie helped himself to some coffee; he'd only managed five hours sleep and needed the caffeine to keep alert.

"So, Charlie, you look pleased with yourself," Amber said.

"I am," said Charlie.

"Well, let's have it?" said Mike impatiently.

"Okay. I've got these photos of the Chief and another person. I developed them this morning and it cost."

"What you need is a digital camera, so that way we can put them straight through the computer," said Amber.

"Forget the fucking cost Charlie; you know we'll see you right."

"Yeah, sorry. I keep thinking I'm bartering with the Cutty boys."

"So, let's see them," said Amber.

" 'Let's' flip side of 'Seranta' – Susan Vaughan '1960," said Charlie. No one acknowledged his bit of music nostalgia.

"My, my, you naughty people," Evan said when he saw the pictures.

"Is it this Andrews woman?" asked Charlie.

"It is. Did you follow them anywhere, Charlie?" Evan asked.

"No, I left before them," said Charlie. "I have a bloody headache from the plate-smashing and I was worried about the fish I ate."

Mike let it pass. "Okay, give the negatives to Amber. We will need copies and that was a bloody good job by the way."

"Good result," said Amber, to which Evan agreed wholeheartedly.

Charlie flushed with pride and took a sip before speaking again.

"I've got more. Yes, I've got info regarding the Demonics," and he laid out the list as he now knew it.

It was now ten to eleven. Another hour and twenty minutes and Edna and Jas would be coming round with the watch for Mike.

Mike studied the list then said to Amber, "This is the way I think it should be done. Evan tries to find West from this recent address and has a word. I, together with Charlie, if you've got your car here?..."

"I have wheels a hundred yards up the road, Mike."

"Good, then we, or to be precise I, will speak to Messrs Reece and Radley at work. Amber, if you can arrange an interview with this Jones for tomorrow, I'll go with Evan and we will have a chat."

"Well, we are making inroads into both problems, Mike," said Evan, "but we really have got to find a solution to the forty-two men in Swansea.

"It could take months to speak to them individually. I mean, some will be at work, away at work, holidays. It's a massive job and we can't really entrust it to the local force, can we?" said Evan.

"You need to do the reverse con," said Charlie.

"What the hell is a 'reverse con', Charlie?"

"Well, I've just made it up to be truthful. What I mean is, instead of conning somebody, you let him con you," said Charlie.

"Charlie, even by your double speak, this is complete mumbo jumbo."

"Explain, Charlie, in a way we 'thickos' can understand," said Mike.

"Okay, but this reverse con needs money; quite a lot of money in fact."

"We're still with you Charlie," Amber said. "I'm dying to hear your ideas."

"Well, we send all these forty-two people a letter telling them that the number allocated to them in October's correspondence has won them a brand new Sony television or something. This, with a few year's guarantee. All they have to do is come on a certain day between the times of whatever, bringing with them proof of identity to pick up their free prize. When they come at the allotted time and date, you make them sign a form, a receipt or something and have a word with them about your other products. That way you can gauge whether or not they're your man and of course if he's left-handed."

"I think I'm following you," said Amber "but I cannot understand why you say it's a reverse con."

With that, Evan butted in: "Because they have not received any previous notification or correspondence from us, i.e. the company offering the prize; they think that we have made a mistake. By turning up and collecting their free gift, they are in effect conning us, but we know otherwise if all falls into place. Is that right, Charlie?"

"That's about it. All you have to do is locate a decent electronics retailer, come to an arrangement with him, say give him ten, twenty per cent over the wholesale price for say forty whatevers and in effect, he makes money. His shop is heavily advertised and we hopefully get our man.

"Remember three things: the pickup point must be in Swansea so that the punter doesn't have far to travel, the prize is worth having and it must be after six so that our man does not have to take time off from work. Oh, and the product must have a few year's guarantee; we do not want them to think we might be giving away knock-offs," said Charlie.

"Can you arrange something, Amber? Ring the retailer and before you do so can I have my clothes? Charlie and I are going visiting."

Evan looked at the clock: it was half past eleven.

"How long do you think you will be out, Mike?"

"About an hour, hour and a half tops, Evan. Why do you ask?"

"No particular reason Mike. Just wondering if I should try and catch this Toby West as we have an address and be back to compare notes with you."

"Good thinking Evan," Mike said, putting on his trousers which were still a little damp but wearable, as was his shirt.

It was still throwing it down but they had reached Charlie's car without getting wet thanks mainly to Charlie's umbrella.

Mike got Charlie to stop at his favourite newsagent where he bought another pack of cigarettes. They then headed for the small industrial estate north of the city.

They arrived at the small industrial estate and parked on a grass verge next to a high wire fence. There were three businesses working out of the estate: a garage doing bodywork repairs, a storage centre, which looked shut, and Eastern's Steel Fabrication Ltd.

"Right Charlie, I'll go in and have a word; you can stay put or have a walk around."

"What, in the rain? I think I'll stay inside with the heater on full blast," said Charlie.

Mike walked quickly the twenty yards or so from the car to the small office in the building. Two men were seated on plastic chairs behind a square wooden table. One wore a cheap black suit, the other dirty blue overalls. Across the top right-hand pocket of the overalls, the word 'orema' was visible. Mike assumed, correctly, that the one in the overalls was the foreman. The suit didn't look up from whatever he was doing but the foreman spoke without seemingly opening his mouth.

"Yeah?"

"I would like to speak to the manager."

"I'm the foreman, what do you want?"

"I'd like to speak to a Mr Ifan Reece and a Mr Tom Radley," said Mike.

"Why?"

"Police business," said Mike, flashing his card.

"Not in my time, mate," said the foreman.

"Okay," Mike said, "when is their time?"

"Twelve to half twelve," the foreman replied.

"So in five minutes. I'll wait here if you don't mind," Mike said.

"Do what you like," said the foreman; the suit still hadn't said a word.

Lunchtime came a few minutes later, a siren ushering in the break. Four men trotted out, each carrying a plastic bag or box containing their meal.

There was a shelter nearby and they all sat out of the rain on two small plastic benches.

Mike left the office and strolled over, lighting up as he went along. It was still drizzling.

"Any of you Ifan Reece or Tom Radley?" asked Mike, not getting a verbal answer but a pointed thumb towards the building from a youth in a hard hat. "Thanks," Mike said, not meaning it.

There was a gap in the large steel double doors of the workshop and Mike stepped through. The place was full of assorted size mild steel boxes. Down at the far end two men were eating some sandwiches and drinking what looked like tea, which had been poured from a flask. Mike walked up to the men: "Sorry to bother you in your lunch break. I'm Detective Inspector Karetzi and I'm making some enquiries about some old cases with which, assuming you are Mr Reece and Mr Rider, you may be able to help."

"I'm Rider and this is Reece. Why do you think that we can help?"

"Well Mr Rider, I understand that both of you belonged to an organisation called the Demonics. Isn't that so?"

It was Reece's turn to speak "That, Mister, was a long, long time ago and we've nothing to say."

"It's 'Detective', Mr Reece."

The double act played it straight. It was Rider's turn to speak.

"We're busy now, Detective."

"I can see that you're eating. I only want a few questions answered – it won't take a moment."

Get lost sonny, we don't have to answer any questions from you," said Reece.

"Now Gentlemen, that's not a nice way to talk to a policeman," said Mike. "It can lead you into problems you never knew you had."

"Man, if you don't leave us in peace to have our lunch, I'm going to...." Rider never finished his sentence, because at that precise moment the man in the suit came towards them.

"What's the problem, Tom?" said the suit.

"He's asking questions about us," said Rider.

"He's a fucking cop," added Reece.

"Okay. I'll handle this. Go outside and finish your lunch, you've only got ten minutes left," said the suit.

"I'm Bill Eastern, owner of the company. What precisely do you want?"

"I need to speak to them about a gang they belonged to in the late seventies/eighties. We're tying up some loose ends before we move the old files to storage."

"Well, Detective um?"

"It's Karetzi, spelt with a 'k' and a 'z'."

"I don't know how we can help you Detective," said Eastern.

"We, plural... are you an ex-member Sir?"

"I am. It was a long time ago. We were just kids really, playing at being tough guys," said Eastern.

"You did pretty well all told, that is until the Whistler took off with your ill-gotten gains."

"There was no real money. Andy was the brains, the driving force. He kept us all in line," said Eastern.

"This Andy, does he have a second name?" asked Mike.

"Yeah, Williams," answered Eastern.

"Where is this Williams guy now?" asked Mike.

"No idea. They say that he went to Scotland. I don't know, I've not been in touch with anyone outside Ifan and Tom, other than Timmy who I last heard from about five, no six years ago. Lives, or lived in Darwin. He was very ill, the 'Big C'. That was the last I heard from him and Jonsey, serving time for conning some old dears out of their savings, always was a charmer."

"Timmy who?"

"Croft."

"Anyone else? Names; how we can track them down?"

"No Detective. No names. It's a long time ago and as you can see, I've moved on. A good honest business built on hard work," said Eastern.

The siren went off again. It was twelve-thirty and the workforce started filing in.

"One last thing, Mr Eastern."

"Yes?"

"Can I see this famous tattoo of yours?"

"Why?" asked Eastern.

"Just curiosity, Mr Eastern."

"Will you go then, Detective, and let us get on with our work?"

"You have my word Sir, one quick peep and I'm history," said Mike.

Eastern stretched out his left hand so that his watch was visible and with his right hand unbuckled the leather strap of his watch. Although it had faded, it was still visible to Mike. Each number was about three quarters of an inch in height and the total span was about one and a quarter inches, easily hidden by a watch.

"Thanks Mr Eastern. Did all the members have the exact same tattoo?" Mike asked.

"Yep; the Whistler used the same tattooist for everyone; it was like he was branding us. We belonged to him. Pathetic really, but there you go. As I said, we were easily impressed. He must have been three or four years older; it made a big difference." And with that, Eastern turned without shaking hands and walked back to his office.

Mike stood there for a few moments. He looked around. He could see Reece, who was busy welding; Rider was nowhere to be found.

Once outside, he found Rider, who was sweeping away the puddles that had formed outside the big steel doors. Eastern was standing at the office window looking out, probably waiting for Mike to go. Mike tapped hard on the driver's window. Charlie had locked the doors and had nodded off. He was dead beat and didn't stir so Mike rapped the window even harder with his knuckles. This time he got Charlie's attention.

Once inside the car, Mike just sat staring at the road sweeper, Mr Ifan Reece. Mike was thinking; Charlie let him be. For over five minutes, they just sat there like two tailor's dummies, oblivious to the world. Then Charlie, getting worried, spoke: "Are you all right Mike?"

"The campanologists are having a field day in my head and I don't know who's actually pulling the ropes. I just can't put my finger on it. Something is not right, Charlie."

Poor old Charlie was lost; whoever or whatever these campanologists were, they were really getting to his friend. Something must have happened inside the building.

"Take me to the cemetery please, Charlie."

"Which one Mike?" Mike gave him the address.

Things were getting weirder by the minute, thought Charlie, but held his tongue. No point in asking Mike, he was sure he wouldn't get a sensible answer.

On arrival at the cemetery, Mike asked Charlie to wait; he'd be a while if that was okay with Charlie. Charlie said it was. Mike switched off his mobile; he did not want to be disturbed.

After half an hour, Charlie got fidgety and a little worried for his friend, so he ventured into the cemetery. It took him ten minutes to locate Mike, who he could see was sitting on the side of a grave, smoking. He turned and walked back to his car.

As he was about to open the door, his cell phone rang. It was Evan asking where Mike was; Charlie told him.

"What's he doing in a graveyard?"

"Search me; he's been acting strange ever since he went into that fabrication yard. He's been on about 'campanists' or words that sounded like that. I'm telling you Evan, he's just sitting on a grass verge smoking; it's been nearly forty minutes."

"It's a quarter to two Charlie, there's no way I suppose that you will be back before two."

"No way, Evan. I'm not sure we will be back before dark."

"Okay, Charlie, you stick with him and ring me if anything untoward happens."

"Like what Evan? Has this happened before?" asked Charlie.

"No, that's what's so worrying," said Evan.

"Look girls, I'm sorry. I don't know what's going on. Best leave the watch with Amber and we will present it to Mike when he returns, assuming he does," said Evan.

A disappointed Jasmine and Edna left dejectedly.

"I'm close Dad, I feel very close to solving your murder and getting revenge. I'm not sure what I should do when I get them. I don't know, it's been a long voyage and now suddenly I'm unsure."

For another half an hour he spoke; at last fully exhausted of what to ask, he said:

"How will I know Dad?" and then started crying.

Standing up, Mike started walking. It was five minutes before he realised he was going in the wrong direction. It was still drizzling, but that was of no consequence to Mike who was again wet through. He glanced at his wrist; he felt bad he'd broken his father's watch. Nearing the exit, he passed a blonde woman carrying a plant. She reminded him of his strawberry blonde, another failure. He tried to recall some good things. He was still trying when he reached the car.

"Where next Mike?" Charlie asked.

"The nearest garage, Charlie."

"What do we want there?"

"Petrol," said Mike. "I noticed you're on empty."

Charlie smiled; that's more like it, he thought to himself.

After paying for a full tank of petrol on his corporate card, Mike bought thirty pounds worth of flowers and the biggest box of chocolates the garage shop could provide; these too went on the card.

"These are for Maggie, Charlie."

"Is there something I should know, Mike?"

"Yes Charlie. You need to know that I'm just one hell of a great guy and you are one hell of a great friend. Drop me off at the office and go home and get some sleep: you look like you've been working all night."

Christ, Charlie thought. He's not far off.

When Amber saw Mike she immediately went and got her dressing gown. Without saying a word, Mike stripped back down to his boxers and put it on. Evan handed Mike a strong black coffee and waited for Mike to light up before handing him the box.

"What's this Evan?" Mike asked.

"Open and see, Mike."

Mike did; he just looked at it.

"It's from us, the Jones family – go try it on. It's inscribed on the back," Evan said.

Mike saw the inscription and was moved. He then tried it on; it was probably one link too big, even though Mike had large wrists.

"It's beautiful Evan. I am lost for words. You know you shouldn't have spent money to buy this for me."

"Don't be so humble Mike. This is the least we could do: after all you don't have a watch because of... you know."

Mike had turned away. He was about to cry for the second time that afternoon. After regaining his composure, Mike took the watch off, and then put it on, then off.

"Something wrong, Mike?"

"No Evan. Just trying to get the hang of this clasp. Look, first you push up and slide this along, otherwise I can't get it past my hand to my wrist."

"Yes, it is intricate Mike but it's nice and heavy like your old one and matches your lighter, see?" said Evan, picking up Mike's lighter and putting it next to the watch.

"Perfect," said Mike. "I'll always treasure it – as much as I did my father's."

Evan knew there was no greater compliment that Mike could give. He only wished the girls were here to see the pleasure on Mike's face.

"Edna and Jasmine were here Mike, during my daughter's lunch break. They wanted to present you with the watch but it was not to be. So Mike, give us your news."

Mike told them all that had passed since leaving the office, omitting just the part in the cemetery; that was personal.

"And we have found a retailer in Swansea," Amber said. "Peter's Electricals, who is willing to obtain forty of the latest CD players and recorders at eighty-five pounds apiece, inclusive of VAT. They retail at one nine nine. He will sell to us at one ten. So, he makes a grand on the goods and of course, he receives all the publicity we are putting in a small ad in the local paper and some posters outside. He's providing a room for us too!

"So it's costing us four thousand four hundred for the goods and about three, four hundred for the printing and advertising etc.," Amber concluded.

"Good old Tangent," said Mike.

"And of course we will have receipts for all that money which will please them no end. We will do the printing tomorrow. We have decided that we will go for Wednesday the fifth of December:

half between six and seven and the remainder from seven to eight. Any remaining items will be sold back to Peter's at one ten!" said Amber.

"That sounds good to me," said Mike.

"Oh, and I've arranged an audience for eleven a.m. tomorrow with Gareth Jones," said Amber.

"Can you find out if there were any bank jobs in the last three months of 1992, say within a radius of five miles of Cardiff, including Cardiff, Amber," said Mike.

"That won't be a problem Mike. What are you thinking?"

"I'm thinking that this Andrew Williams with the moniker 'Whistler' might not have upped sticks and gone to Scotland but that's what he wanted the others to believe. I think he used another group to do a bank as planned," said Mike.

"It makes sense," Evan said. "He had the money, bunged a bank official with some of it, then used the rest to tool up some professionals and that way his share of the proceeds would be much larger with a better chance of success."

Amber was already on the job; Mike and Evan just sat, Mike playing with his new watch, Evan with his old clay pipe.

"Here it is: Lloyds in Radyr. Hit for eight hundred thou, used bank notes, various denominations. Saturday night – no one arrested, no suspects. Very strange."

"When Amber?" asked Evan.

"First of the month. November the first or second. And there's more: that same night we have a massive fire in Whitchurch and a bomb scare in Cardiff city centre," said Amber.

"Let me guess," said Evan, "the fire was arson and the bomb scare was a false alarm."

"Diversions no doubt," said Mike. "Did they take anything else from the bank?"

"Just the money in notes. They left twelve thou in coins and didn't touch any of the safety deposit boxes."

"Well, it's a cold case and not ours anyway but I bet it was Williams behind all that," said Mike.

"What about the inside man? Surely, they must have had a lead to the person? How many staff would a small branch like that have?"

"Four, tops," said Evan.

"I think we should pass our findings to whoever is dealing with these old cases. It will help if we have someone else looking for Williams, because it's more than possible that he is still around in this area. And I could do with having a word or two with him," said Mike.

"I'll pass it on to the relevant people, if there are any, first thing tomorrow but I wouldn't hold your breath. We're talking about 1992/3; that's eighteen odd years ago," said Amber. "Oh, and I've got the copies of the photos Charlie took. What do we do with them?" asked Amber.

"Just hold on to them, Amber," said Mike.

"Okay Mike, and now what?" said Amber.

"And now I will get dressed again and if you're up to it Evan, I suggest we pay Mr Toby West a visit."

Mike drove the Beamer. Toby lived in a really rough part of the city. Even the rats kept their distance. Mike pulled up outside a six-storey block of flats. Toby lived on the fourth floor. The whole building looked as if it had been hit by a bomb. The smell was excruciatingly bad; it looked like people had mistaken the foyer for the toilets. Needless to say, both lifts had been vandalised and weren't working. Sixty steps. After two flights, Evan was visibly flagging and gasping for breath. Mike stopped.

"Are you okay, Partner?"

"Look Mike," Evan said in between his gasps for air, "I could climb forever."

"Yeah Evan, if forever comes within the next few steps,", said Mike.

Mike got to the flat before Evan had reached the third floor. The door was slightly ajar. He rapped on the door and shouted: "D.I. Karetzi here." He said it twice.

"And I'm busy, piss off." He said it twice, so Mike entered.

He was not surprise to find Mr West unshaven, half-dressed and as scruffy as his apartment. He had obviously been out sometime during the day. He had today's newspapers open on the racing page. The TV was also tuned into the racing. One ashtray and one saucer were overflowing with cigarette butt ends smoked down to the filters. No booze in sight. Mike was happy with that. At least West would be coherent.

"So what do you want?"

Mike gave him the spiel. West listened but kept one eye on the racing. The racing finished and Toby was ready to talk. He had a resigned look about him. He looked as if he was carrying more baggage than a jumbo jet. Mike guessed he'd just lost again. Evan came through the door. He was still breathing heavily.

"Is the pork pie with you?" said West.

Mike stared at him, noticing the tattoo on his left hand. West stared back. He was not intimidated. Mike spoke again. "Just some simple answers to a few simple questions, Mr West."

"Right," said Toby, standing up. A short very wiry type, aged about forty-eight, fifty. "Do you mind if I get myself a drink of water from the kitchen?"

"Go ahead," said Mike. "We've got all day." Looking at Evan, "So, you made it Partner. I was getting worried so I started without you but 'Pork Pie', what the hell is that meant to mean?"

"Pork equals pig, equals cop," answered Evan.

"He's taking his time," said Mike. "I'm going to look what the hell he's doing."

He walked into the kitchen. No sign of West but a large window was open. Mike looked out onto a small landing, a fire escape – a rusting iron mess. Mike carefully pulled himself onto it just in time to see Toby legging it down the street.

When Evan moved into the kitchen, he found Mike on all fours kneeling on the patterned platform. The whole thing was creaking and swaying slightly.

"What are you doing Mike? Where's West?" When Evan didn't receive any acknowledgement to his questions, he noticed that Mike, arms outstretched, was hanging onto the rail for dear life. It didn't need a doctor to know that his partner was petrified of heights. He didn't know what the proper medical term was but he knew he had to do something.

"Okay Mike, take it easy. Let go of the rail one hand at a time and place them on the platform." There was no movement from Mike. Evan was scared to go onto the platform. Their combined weight might be too much for the Victorian structure. Plus he couldn't get past Mike who was on his knees with his hands clutching the rail. Evan was determined to find a solution as much as his partner was determined to remain exactly where he was.

"Look Mike, you can trust me. Just talk to me. We can solve this without calling out the Fire Brigade."

"I can't move Evan, I'm scared."

"First thing Mike, don't look to either side, just look down at the solid platform. I'm going to get something to help."

Evan went back into the lounge. He poked around. Nothing he could use. The bedroom offered two dirty sheets, which Evan took into the kitchen and with the aid of a blunt kitchen knife, he cut the sheets lengthwise into halves. These he tied together with his best boy scout knots. He now had about a twenty-foot length of sheeting.

The platform was on the same level as the windowsill, so Evan with the aid of a broom handle, managed to push one end of his makeshift cotton rope through Mike's legs.

"You see that sheet Mike, it's as strong as, probably stronger than a rope made of sisal," he lied, "so let go of one hand, grab it and put it around your waist."

"I can't do it Evan, I can't."

"Of course you can. I tell you what: close your eyes and you will be able to do it."

Twice Mike let go for less than a half second and twice he clutched the rail again.

"Try your left hand, Mike. That's not your strong one. The right's enough to hold onto the rail."

Once, twice, and on the third attempt Mike grabbed the sheet and in one movement he was back onto the rail with both hands and the sheet around his waist. With the help of the broom handle, Evan slowly brought the sheet end back to him. Evan made a loop around the secure part of the sheet and pulled it taut around Mike's waist. That took ten minutes and Mike was still clinging on for dear life. It was weird: only the street lights, that is the one that was still working, cast a little light. The rest was coming from the kitchen's two remaining halogen lights. Not even one neighbour had appeared. Maybe West was the only inhabitant in the whole block.

"Look Mike, stay with me," Evan said as he noticed Mike beginning to tremble. "You're securely tied around your waist and I've secured this end around a big fridge. You can't go anywhere except back into the kitchen. I want you to put your hands one by one on the lower rail. You can do that, Mike."

"I'm having a panic attack, Evan."

"It's okay Mike, just put your hands one at a time on the lower rail."

Mike did but he was really starting to freak Evan out. Mike began to hyperventilate.

"Mike, if you are going to get your father's killers you need to be off the platform. Push your left foot back as far as possible, then you're right. Do it now, Mike. West and his mates are getting further and further away."

At last, Mike responded. He was now nearly horizontal. Evan grabbed an ankle in each hand. "Let go of the rail Mike and I'll pull you in." Nothing. "Can you hear me, Mike? There are papers and all sorts of stuff in here. We need to go through them together. Let go of the railing, Mike, now, please." Mike did. Evan pulled, Mike moved about six inches; his feet still nearly a foot from the sill.

Using his palms, Mike pushed backwards until he felt the sill. He then knelt and pushed both feet one by one through the opening. A minute later and he was in. He was soaked with sweat. It was pouring off his head. It was as if he'd just gone for a swim in the Taff. Both Mike and Evan sat on the dirty kitchen floor tiles, Mike still with the twisted sheet around his waist. Mike's breathing was slowly returning to normal. He was still sweating heavily and trembling from head to toe. Mike went to speak. Evan told him not to say anything. It was just one of those things. Everyone had phobias, it was nothing to be ashamed of and they would never mention the incident again.

Evan got up and then helped Mike up who was still unsteady on his feet. Evan searched the kitchen leaving Mike to himself. It was easier for both that way. Evan found a half bottle of Cointreau, smelt it and passed it to Mike who took a large swig, then another before passing it back to Evan who closed the bottle and replaced it back where he had found it. Mike visibly relaxed, enough to shake out a cigarette and light up. Evan leant back on the eye-level oven and for the first time during the last hour or so his heartbeat returned to normal.

Mike finished his cigarette, killing it in the filthy sink. He then closed the window and removed the sheet from around his waist. He then looked around, located the small fridge in the far corner and laughed. Evan knew why Mike was laughing and smiled but said nothing. They searched the flat, found nothing of interest. They switched the TV off, all the lights and slammed the door behind them on their way out. Four flights of stairs; much easier going down.

"So Mike, why do you think the guy did a runner?" said Evan.

"No idea, beats me," said Mike.

Evan dropped Mike at his apartment. "Pick you up at nine-thirty, Mike."

"Thanks again Evan, for tonight."

"Forget it Mike, it never happened."

"Unbelievable," said Edna when Evan told her and Jasmine about the Mike platform incident. "I mean, not scared of anything or anyone and yet heights put the fear of God into him. It just goes to show you can never tell."

"He loved the watch and thanks you all profusely. He said we shouldn't have and meant it," said Evan. Edna and Jasmine were happy.

Mike sat staring into space. He hadn't had an attack like that for probably twenty years. He was fine up to about ten, fifteen feet, but any higher and he'd start panicking. He would go when he had time and see a hypnotist, see if that would help or maybe he just wouldn't go out onto any more open-air structures on fourth floors. In truth, he was just scared of being put under by a hypnotist. That was another phobia.

At a quarter to ten on Saturday morning, the first day of December, Mike had joined the M4 motorway. Evan sat next to him in the BMW, deep in thought.

"About yesterday Evan, I'm sorry that I was a pain in the arse. I don't know what came over me; I panicked."

"As we said Mike, forget it. Nothing happened."

"Thanks Evan. I wish I knew why that Toby West guy ran, but I don't think it's something to do with my case."

"No Mike, I think he's probably been a naughty boy lately and thought we were on to him."

Four miles down the motorway Mike was now hitting ninety, ninety-five when suddenly and without warning he started slowing down, continuously looking in his rear view mirror.

"Something wrong Mike, are we being followed?" asked Evan who had turned his head attempting to see behind him.

"No Evan, I am checking the mirror to see what a dumb fuck looks like." By now, Mike had pulled over on to the hard shoulder. Work was in progress. It had been on that section of the M4 for years and cones were placed in neat rows for miles apart from the two dislodged by the BMW before it abruptly shuddered to a halt.

"Let's see your left hand and wrist, Evan."

Evan looked at Mike. He was now seeing the crazy Karetzi they all talked about when he asked people about his new partner. Evan humoured Mike and showed him his hand and wrist. Mike then put out his hand towards Evan. "What do you see, Evan?"

"I see a hand, wrist, the new watch and I guess that's it, Mike, and mine is exactly the same; different watch, wedding band, nothing else."

"Exactly, Evan, nothing else. How did my father see the numbers? The answer is he couldn't, unless the perp wasn't wearing a watch," said Mike.

"Or he was left-handed and wore his watch on his right hand as lefties do," said Evan.

"And that's what was wrong outside that fabrication place. One of the two suspects was sweeping the rain outside, his right hand below his left on the brush handle; he's a leftie.

"West is right-handed, I saw him writing something on the horse racing page and the other two at the fabrication place were right-handed, I'm sure of that.

"Cancel this meeting with Gareth Jones. Phone Amber to do it, Evan, and she is to get the authorities down there to tell us if he is left-handed or didn't wear a watch for any reason. Whilst I deal with the hard hat and his mate who are heading towards us."

Hardhat No 1 thumped the driver's window. Behind him stood Hardhat No 2. Hardhat No 1 indicated that he wanted the window wound down so he could converse with him. Mike pressed the open wallet with his warrant card against the window hoping that that would pacify him. Hardhat wanted his pound of meat and kept on thumping the window.

"For Christ's sake Mike, speak to him. I can't hear myself speak. I've got Amber on the line, she's wondering what's going on," said Evan.

Mike opened the door; both hard hats took a step back. "Now what's the problem my friends, I've shown you my warrant card, you know that I'm a Detective Inspector as is my partner."

"Dangerous driving, contravening motorway regulations, illegal parking in a work zone area. I've taken your number and will report you to my superiors, although for your information I'm in charge here," said Hardhat No 1.

"Problem Mike?" Evan said, having finished his call to Amber.

"I don't know Evan, this gentleman here says we've done a million things wrong and is going to report us to somebody."

"Have you spoken to the man nicely, Mike?"

"Of course I have Evan."

"Look Sir," said Evan, "we are on urgent police business and we needed to stop, simple as that, so let's keep it that way and we will be off and leave you to get on with whatever you've been doing on this motorway for the last decade."

"That's it," said Hardhat. "I want your names now," he said, pushing Mike against the car unintentionally. Before he could apologise, Mike had grabbed him by the throat and with his face up next to his, slowly spoke to the choking Hardhat.

"There are aspects of my job I find distasteful, but this isn't one of them amigo." After letting go, Hardhat No 1 dropped to his knees, his hand clutching at his throat. His workmate remained in situ like a frozen turkey on display at Iceland.

"Whoops," said Mike, "I think I've misplaced the rule book. Now my friend, get up off your knees and tell me your name and address. I'm not sure I've finished with you – you are pathetic."

Hardhat just looked down at the floor. Evan got back into the car; Mike was about to but turned and spoke to Hardhat No 1: "Just one more thing, would you like a complaint form?" Mike never got Hardhat's answer or name.

They drove off, Mike taking the first exit and turning back towards the office.

"Mike, we're going to be in deep shit after that little episode."

"Evan, he pushed me first," said Mike. "I wasn't sure what he was going to do next Evan, he provoked me, you were witness to that."

"I was Mike, but it won't cut it with Clarke."

"They need us Evan, remember why we were brought together."

"The Chief doesn't really see it that way, Mike, and now that they're putting pressure on the Chief from London, I don't see us getting a fair shake."

"I'm sorry Evan; I'm too involved with hunting down my father's killer instead of concentrating on the main thing, the Chessman. He's running rings around us and if our plan doesn't bear fruit then we have nothing."

"Mike, we've crossed the 't's and dotted all the 'i's. Do you realise how far we've come in just over a fortnight?"

"Maybe nowhere, Evan. Some days I think this Chessman is too clever for us and still no motive. That's where we are losing the game. We can't win. We have a handful of twos and threes and that bastard is holding bloody aces."

Evan sighed. His partner was right. Maybe they would never get anywhere near the Chessman. There would be more motiveless killings. The way things were going, he'd be retiring even quicker than he'd planned. If his partner didn't stop threatening people he might not even have that option; he'd be sacked.

Amber was happy to see them. She had news: "Gareth Jones is not left-handed and doesn't know anyone from the old gang who is or was and he won't or can't supply any names. He says he's erased that period of his life right out of his memory."

"I see," said Mike dejectedly.

"But I have other news on Williams."

"The gang leader," said Evan.

"The same," said Amber. "Early nineties moved to Malaga. Owns a restaurant/bar, car rental company and estate agency. Big house overlooking the sea, big cars, the works. Now calls himself Anton Walliams. Changed his name by deed poll," said Amber.

"How the hell did you track him down?"

"Through his name change; it's rather simple really," said Amber.

"Are you sure it's the same guy?" Mike asked.

"Without doubt. I've contacted the locals in Spain; they've been keeping an eye on him lately, because he's associating with some pretty unsavoury characters and they think he's involved in some high profile burglaries in the area. I have some pics on the computer – come over and have a look."

Mike and Evan did. The guy was wearing a watch on his left hand and in another photo had a pint of beer in his right.

"Can we print those off?" asked Mike.

"Will do Mike."

"Anything else, Amber?" asked Evan.

"Yes, I have sent off the forty-two prize winning letters and Charlie rang in to say he has another idea and will be in at around twelve," said Amber.

Charlie was true to his word. He found the three drinking coffee and eating doughnuts, which Amber had bought early that morning; they were from Cara's. Only one was left because Mike had had just the one.

"Is that for me?" said Charlie.

"It's got your name on it," replied Amber.

Charlie rested the two large envelopes he was carrying on Amber's desk, then grabbed the doughnut, and started chewing. Everyone waited for Charlie to speak which Charlie declined to do until he had polished off the doughnut.

"See those," he said, pointing at the envelopes. "They are going to help give time and save a lot of pussyfooting around."

"Time for what Charlie?" asked Evan.

"Time for whatever you need," said Charlie. "Take a Captain

Cook at them, they are addressed to the Chief Constable Clark, at his office and to you Evan and you Mike here, all block letters done with a common cheap biro. No fingerprints because I did them wearing these gloves and the envelopes are self-sealing – there will be no saliva on the stamp or anywhere so no DNA. Got it?"

Using a ruler Mike flipped them over. "Very clever Charlie, but you've spelt 'crescent' wrong, Clarke with the 'e' and bastardised my name. Were all those done on purpose?"

"Of course, and now I will fill them with photos of the Chief and what's her name and go into Cardiff and post them. Both you and the Chief will have them on Monday. When they arrive, you open the envelope, take out the photos, replace them in the envelope and keep them in a desk until they are needed. That way we accomplish a purpose, a lever to get something over the chief. Don't forget to wipe the chief's photos clean. The ones addressed to you will be handled again by your good selves but the Chief's must be clean."

"I like it Charlie; actually, I love it," said Amber. "I'll get the photos and wipe the Chief's copies down."

"That is great Charlie," said Mike.

"Brilliant," said Evan. "But blackmail. I don't like that at all for whatever reason."

"There's no blackmail Evan, we do not threaten the Chief with them or try to extort anything from him," said Charlie. "You just give him a call on Monday and hand him the envelope. He already has a set, now he will have two, but he will never be sure if you've got more or indeed if there are more."

"So he will feel obliged to us," said Evan.

"Dead on," replied Charlie.

"The same goes for Emma Andrews, I guess," Mike added.

The photos were cleaned and placed in the relevant envelopes, which Charlie sealed before affixing the stamps. He was of course still wearing the leather gloves.

"I'm off to see City play," said Mike.

"I'm off shopping," said Evan.

"And I'm off to do some posting," said Charlie.

Amber didn't bother telling them she was going to cook and eat; they all knew.

"She's got an eating obsession," said Mike.

"She sure has," said Evan.

"Reg Owen, 1960 sang 'Obsession'," said Charlie.

"Don't believe you," said Evan. "I'm going to check up this Reg Owen guy; bloody rock star calling himself Reg, that's ridiculous."

"Don't, late fifties, Elvis," said Charlie.

"Now that's a real rock name," said Mike.

"Now, Val Doonican 1968," said Charlie.

"Shut up," said Mike.

"Shut up," said Evan.

"Guy wore pullovers whilst singing," said Charlie.

"I remember him," said Evan.

"Pity you didn't say 'I remember you'," said Charlie.

"Why?" asked Evan.

"Because then I could have said Frank Ifield 1962," said Charlie.

"Please," said Mike.

"Just please, no other word? You could have had 'Please Mr Postman', 'Please don't go', 'Please please me', 'Please don't tease' and...."

"For Christ's sake shut up Charlie," said Mike. "Give it a break, I'm getting a headache."

"I already have," said Evan.

CHAPTER 19

The Chessman had been working non-stop for over twenty-four hours on the letter. He did the last bit of tweaking and then read it out aloud to all his associates. He stood up facing the mirror; in a way, he could see his audience.

DEAR MR...........................

Xmas is nigh and time to exchange gifts. Mine to you, the rest of your life.
Yours to me, ten per cent of your wealth
Be clever, have faith, just ten per cent
Is that worth a life?
Ninety per cent of zero is still zero
Just be ready, this is your Karma
Do not quibble about paying up
Direct any questions to D.I. Karetzi and D.I. Jones
Tel No .... The key word is Chess
Remember you have no obligations and
Remember you have family; they are the most important thing in your life.
Peruse the clippings enclosed carefully
Make provision for the exact amount to be readily available, that being £ ....
Wait for my next and final communication
Read the documentation again and again until you fully

understand that I am making no idle threat.

Never lose sight of the saying 'money doesn't equal happiness'.

Last but not least: good luck and thank you in anticipation.

Enjoy the rest of your family LIFE.

The Chessman took a bow in front of the mirror. He waited for the applause to die down in his head. This was a masterpiece of pure intimidation – something straight out of a Mickey Spillane novel. It was a pity so few people would read it.

Every letter of the alphabet was represented at least twice. Each individual letter was written a different way: some slanting to the left, others to the right. Some upright, some of the words connected, others half printed, half joined. The margin space and spaces between words irregular. Some of the words appeared squeezed together, some of them heavier print than others; some 'i's dotted, others not. A right mishmash of a letter. All in all no expert in the world could come to any sensible conclusion as to the character of the writer.

Instead of a signature, the Chessman had decided on two childlike faces with a question mark in between. One was a smiling happy face, the other a scowling unhappy one. The message was simplicity itself.

Each envelope was addressed carefully put in different styles; some ran from the top left to the bottom right, others straight down the middle. Some started high, others low. Some slanted to the right again, others did the opposite. Surgical gloves were worn throughout. Photocopies of the original were made on his own machine. Stamps were applied and he was finished. All he needed to do was go to Cardiff and post them. He didn't want them going from Swansea. A total of six letters, representing over 15 million pounds.

By the time Charlie had had his lunch, a cold beer and a pork pie with lashings of mustard, it was near on two. He walked around the centre looking for a post box. Having seen one, he stepped up his pace, his short little legs working overtime. In his hurry, he collided with another man who was also in a hurry. Both dropped their mail, both apologised and both bent down to retrieve their letters.

"After you sir," said Charlie politely to the distinguished well-attired grey haired man. The man thanked Charlie and posted his mail. Charlie did the same and walked off in a different direction to the Chessman who was now heading back towards his flat.

What a nice old man, thought Charlie. How wrong could he be? It was to be a day of close encounters or to be precise, near misses. Mike needed a black tie for Jane's funeral, which was to take place the following day, and Mel King's next Tuesday. It seemed strange they had kept the body so long, but he supposed it was because of the necessary arrangements that the authorities have to make. The whole capital would come to a standstill. This was the funeral of their most famous son.

Mike entered the store, cutting through the cosmetics department towards the men's accessories. Jasmine had bent down below the counter looking for an earring, which had become loose and fallen on the floor. Mike ogled the other girls, winking at one. She winked back still staring at him until he was out of her sight.

"Was that someone from the telly?" said Melanie to Davina, the one that Mike had winked at, "or maybe I've seen him in a film," Davina added.

"Who you on about?" asked Jasmine, who by now had retrieved her earring and was in the process of re-attaching it to her ear.

"Just some hunk who walked through and winked at lucky Davina," said Melanie, unable to hide her envy.

"I hope he comes back this way," said Davina. "He was so divine."

Tilly the fourth girl working at the cosmetics counter started giggling. "What's so funny Tilly?" asked Melanie.

"What a pair, Davina and the Divine one; good name for a film," said Tilly between giggles. No one else found it remotely funny, especially Melanie.

Mike picked a tie, bought it and was about to leave when his eye caught someone looking at him intensely from outside the store. Mike looked a little more closely but it was too late, the man had moved. Mike had this weird feeling. He rushed out but, too late, the stranger had melted into the heavy Saturday shopping crowd. Mike grabbed a passing cab and headed for Ninian Park.

It was a good day for the capital's sport followers. The Bluebirds won 4-1 and the Blues won 17-4. It was a bad day for Chief Constable Clarke. He'd received two calls and made one. The first call had come directly to him from the Director. They reckoned that they had a hundred thousand pounds worth of equipment in the safe house and needed it back. They also wanted rent of a thousand pounds a month or preferably they wanted it vacant by the end of the year. The Chief doubted if the equipment, now second-hand, was worth half their estimation and as for rent you could get a similar type of property in the area for 450 pounds.

The second call was from a daily tabloid, not directly to him but via his secretary. They were beginning to piece together a story about the chess murders and wanted confirmation of certain things. He had to keep a lid on it, so he agreed that they could talk face-to-face on Monday in Cardiff, if they didn't print anything. Meanwhile he would move heaven and earth to get a gagging order in place. That's why he made his call to the First Minister, via Emma.

The contrast for Mike between Saturday and Sunday was massive. With his ban cut to two games, a half fit Mike played for his team in the morning. As a team they played badly and deserved to get hammered. He changed and went to the cemetery. New black tie on, he missed the service at Jane's small country church. The Jones family were all present but Edna and Jasmine had all gone home and only Evan had gone on to the cemetery.

Mike paid his respects and left. He went directly to his mother's who surprisingly was not in. He later phoned and found that she had gone to a friend's for tea. She really needed a mobile phone, he thought.

CHAPTER 20

Another day, another rainy Monday. Everyone was there and it hadn't as yet turned nine. Charlie poured Evan and Mike a coffee before getting himself one. Evan lit his pipe, Amber crunched on another homemade cookie and Mike just sat reading the back page of the 'Cardiff Chronicle'.

The door buzzer sounded. Amber answered; it was the Chief. "Out the back, Charlie, quick. Make it snappy."

The Chief walked in. "Good morning, everybody."

"Good morning Chief," said Mike and Evan in unison.

"Glad to see that you're all on time for a change," he said looking at Mike.

The Chief told them of his conversation with the daily tabloid and that he had arranged a meeting with their top reporter that afternoon. All of them were to make themselves available here in the office at two p.m. However, before then the Chief needed to go through how much information they would give the reporter.

The mail had dropped through the letterbox. Amber picked it up. She recognised the big brown envelope. As she brought it in the phone rang. "It's a Mr Walter Atlas for either you or Mike," she said to Evan who was nearest.

"Yes Mr Atlas. How may I be of service and how did you get this number?"

"I received my mail about ten minutes ago. I opened one particular hand-written envelope, which contained various newspaper clippings and a letter, which will answer both your questions. I will read it out for you." Mr Atlas began to read out loud; Evan listened. In the meantime, the Chief had noticed four cups of coffee, one of which hadn't been touched. He dipped a finger in it; it was still lukewarm. Mike had seen the Chief dip his finger. Chief didn't make Chief because he was stupid, Mike thought.

"What's our fax number Amber?" asked Evan. Amber gave it to Evan who passed it on to Mr Atlas.

"Well Jones, are you going to tell us what all that was about?" asked the Chief. Evan sat down, wiped his brow and spoke.

"This Mr Atlas has just received a death threat by post from the Chessman. He's demanding two million odd pounds."

"Are you joking Evan?" asked Mike.

"See for yourself, the fax is printing first the envelope, then the letter."

Amber made three copies of each and handed one of each to the three men keeping the original copies for herself.

"These clippings..." the Chief asked.

"Local newspaper clippings reporting the various murders. We do have them all on file Chief," Amber said.

"An unusual sum of money," noted Mike. "Two million, one hundred and seventeen thousand, five hundred and eight pounds."

Amber was on one of the computers. "Mr Atlas is a very wealthy man. He could easily be worth twenty-odd million and ten per cent of twenty-odd million is what the Chessman is demanding."

"Family?" asked Evan.

"Wife, three kids, eight, six and one years old," Amber said.

"Cardiff postmark, posted Saturday. Any point in getting in a handwriting expert?" said the Chief, already knowing the answer.

"So now we have motive," said Mike.

"Two million plus motives," added Evan as that number was to rise by nearly one and a half million within five minutes when a second call from a Mr Alistair Winpenny came through.

"How many more?" thought Amber out loud. Another two that morning and one more later that same day. By eleven, it was obvious to all and sundry that the Chessman was attempting a big score. It was over eight million and rising. The mail remained unopened on the desk in front of Evan. The Chief excused himself and headed upstairs to the toilet.

"The Chief noticed Charlie's coffee," Mike said. "I bet you that right now he's going through every room looking for the missing coffee drinker." Mike would have won his bet. The Chief did go through every room before going to the toilet.

"What about the photos?" asked Amber, pointing at the large brown unopened envelope. Mike slit it open, checked the contents and left it on the desk. He then opened the other two bits of mail: both bills. The Chief, whilst passing water, had resigned himself to the obvious: the boys downstairs could not handle this case. It was way beyond their capabilities. He needed to bring in some proper people: Scotland Yard, MI5, the Tangent people, before there were more killings. That way, blame could be deflected and apportioned to others.

Even before entering, the Chief was giving his staff the bad news. By the time he had come to rest his message had been clearly received by the stunned trio.

"Even you lot must agree that we need more manpower; we need around the clock protection for these people and their families, more detectives on the case. I could go on but you must know the drill by now. We will create a new task force: six, seven, eight detectives from the various forces and add a couple of London boys and Scotland Yard and have a concerted effort on getting him. You can bring them up to speed and that's that."

"You are being too hasty Chief," said Amber. "The boys have been doing their utmost and...." The Chief raised his hand to stop Amber saying anything else.

"I am sure the boys have done their best," the Chief said sarcastically. "And now I'm doing what's best for all of us."

Evan's blood was boiling by now. He rarely lost it, if ever, but he had to say something and he did. "May I put my two pennyworth in Sir?"

"Yes, D.I. Jones, speak away," said the Chief.

"It's been less than three weeks. We are extremely close; we must be allowed to finish. It's only a matter of..."

"Enough," said the Chief. "What kind of operation do you think we're running? Act your age, man. Can't you see that you've failed. You had a good try but you failed and now it's someone else's turn."

"Someone else's turn to fail? Is that the way you see it Chief?" said Evan.

"Do I need to answer such a stupid remark, Detective Jones?" said the Chief. "You're very quiet Detective?" the Chief said, addressing Mike.

"Chief, we all do what we think is right but sometimes we get it wrong. Take this envelope for instance. We think passing it on might be the right thing to do but it could easily turn out to be the wrong thing to do."

"I'm not following you at all, Detective. It's frustrating for me not to understand you. Pray tell me who would you be passing it on to and what does it contain?" asked the Chief, completely baffled.

"I guess I'm not expressing myself clearly, Chief. Although this envelope is addressed personally to D.I. Jones and myself, it is of significant value to your good self, Sir. But before we hand it over, I would like you to consider the facts appertaining to the chessman case and other cases that we are involved in."

"Is this going to take long, Karetzi?

"No Sir, everything we are looking into is coming to a conclusion."

"A conclusion Detective? When, who, what, where?" said the Chief.

"Don't forget the 'why'," said Amber. The Chief looked at her, wondering what on earth she was talking about.

Mike glanced at his new watch. "This time next week we will have the name and hopefully the man we call the Chessman. We will also clear up and have arrested the mastermind behind the 1980 bank job in Radyr – about four mill in today's money. None of it recovered. He has assets which will help and we are homing in on a manslaughter, possibly a murder suspect or two from the same era."

"Proof, Detective; proof, that's what I want."

"It's in the pudding, Sir."

"What's in the pudding?" asked the Chief.

"Proof Sir, that's what they say. I've never fathomed out exactly what that means, but it sounds good."

"So you see Chief," said Evan "we need to carry on until Monday. Well, Mike told you what we would have. One week; it's not as if the Chessman is going to kill anyone else until he gets the money and to get the money he needs to send them at least one more communication."

"And the envelope, can I have it now?"

Evan handed it over to the Chief. The Chief turned his back on the group and flicked through the photos. Without turning, he said, "This is not what it seems."

"We do not judge Chief. We are just detectives trying to close a case or two, if we have the given time," said Mike.

"And giving me this is supposed to buy you time?" the Chief said, turning back to face them.

"No, Chief," said Evan. "My partner here and Amber all agreed to do the right thing."

"Even if you get the wrong result, isn't that so?" said the Chief. "Do we know who sent it?" asked the Chief.

"No idea, but we can exclude the Chessman: it's a Cardiff postmark, the address is not his style. It came this morning, just after you arrived. I doubt if we will get any prints," said Evan, "but we can try, if you leave them with us."

"No, I agree. I wonder if there are other copies? Even though it was totally innocent, people might construe it in another way. One thing odd about this whole business is why did they send them to you? It doesn't make sense," said the Chief.

"I agree. It's like someone is giving the ammunition to use on you, Chief, but why? First, it would mean that we are out to gain something and the sender must also profit in some way. What, I don't know," said Evan. "All I can say is that this somebody has got the wrong end of the stick."

"It was just a business meeting discussing a common cause," said the Chief.

"And with regards to our time problem?" said Mike.

"Under the circumstances, if you are that close, I will give you until Friday morning and then I want something more tangible, like a name or two," said the Chief.

"Okay Chief, now what about this Reginald Reed chap from the Press? He will be here in about forty minutes," said Mike.

"Tell him as much as he already knows. Promise him the whole shebang when we are nearer. Tell him that he will have a massive scoop, if he plays ball," said the Chief.

"What about the other potential victims?" asked Evan.

"Tell them to wait for further communication and that until then we are on the case. Make sure you tell them that others have received the same letter," the Chief said. "Oh, and one more thing that's puzzling me...," said the Chief who was getting ready to leave.

"Maybe we can help?" said Amber. The Chief pointed to the cup full to the brim with coffee. "I absent mindedly put milk in Mike's coffee, forgetting he doesn't use it."

"So it's remained not drunk," said Evan.

"I see," said the Chief, not entirely convinced.

With the Chief gone, Amber advised the others that they had barely half an hour to eat lunch and that she had made a hot curry with goat's meat. They all had a bowl with some warm French bread. It was different but delicious.

Reginald Reed was on time. Fortyish, upright, smart and very nosey. He accepted a cup of coffee. He knew a little but like a lot of reporters he made it sound as if he knew a lot.

"Look, I know there's more, much more and the country needs to be aware of this guy. If I print, people will ring in and who knows... My paper could be instrumental in helping you catch him. So give me some background. You're not in this. Why the office here, why not an established central police station? Has this serial killer left any clues, are there more than six victims, do you have any decent leads? I could go on. Either way, the story will go out on Wednesday. I understand from the Chief constable that you have orders to assist me for which in return I will hold off my story until the weekend."

"All we are willing to disclose at this point in time, said Evan, "is that what you have pieced together is the tip of the iceberg and you will have the lot, only you, when we are ready. We think it will be detrimental in the extreme if you were to start scare-mongering now, Mr Reed."

It took two hours, three coffees and half a pack of Park Drive cigarettes before Reginald Reed decided that half a story was better than none and as he rose, he made it clear where he stood. "You lot have wasted valuable time. My bloody time. You've told me nothing and I suggest you read my report on Thursday."

"And we suggest that you read the whole correct story in a rival paper on Friday, Mr Reed. You'll look pretty pathetic in front of your editor then, won't you?" said Karetzi.

Reed had stood up. He couldn't believe his ears. This was tantamount to blackmail.

"Sit down, man. Don't be an ass. This is the biggest story you will have in a dozen lifetimes. Don't piss it away because of your pride or whatever," Evan said.

"What guarantee do I have that I will get the scoop?" said Reed.

"Us," said Amber. "We will keep our side of the deal."

"Can't you give me anything at all?" asked Reed, his mind working overtime.

"We could give you a lot but it would all be a bunch of lies," said Mike.

"Okay then, fine. Then can we set some form of time limit?" said Reed.

Evan looked first at Mike, then at Amber before deciding to speak.

"Two weeks tomorrow you be down here at, say, noon."

"Two weeks: that's a lot of time to sit on a story of this magnitude," Reed countered.

"Fourteen days on and you will have the whole caboodle; a story that will make you rich and famous, Reginald," said Amber.

"Look, I just want the story for the good of the public. I'm not interested in becoming rich or famous," said Reed.

"Sure you don't. Have we got an agreement or what"? Evan said.

"I'm thinking about it. My editor won't like it if I come back empty-handed with just a promise," Reed replied.

"Well, take him a fucking bunch of flowers," Mike said sardonically.

Reed laughed. "It's a 'she'," he informed them.

"Well, add a box of chocolates then," added Amber feeling very peckish.

Reed stood up. "I'm going now and I'll come back a fortnight tomorrow if I've still got a job." He shook hands with everyone and left, a very sad man.

Chalky, as he was known to the underworld which he frequented, had fenced his ill-gotten jewellery to Fats Finnigan, eventually agreeing on sixteen thousand which was a very interesting amount. What was also interesting was that whilst negotiating with Fats, who loved small talk and gossip as much as he loved conning the crooks that provided him with a very comfortable living, the subject of the Demonic gang arose.

According to Finnigan, one of the Radyr banks' employees was a cousin or relative of some sort to one of the gang members. It was always Fats' contention that this gang had pulled off the robbery; although as he recalled, they were a pretty stupid bunch of individuals who at the time were no more than petty thieves.

Charlie headed off for the office as soon as he had deposited the cash, less four hundred, under the floorboards of his flat. He arrived at just gone five; everyone was still there. He then proceeded to tell them that he had won four hundred pounds on the horses (he'd already looked up the winners on the BBC's Ceefax) and that he wished to take all three of them out for dinner, as he wished to discuss various things with them.

"So, where do you all want to go?" asked Charlie.

"I'll tell you what," said Evan, "I really fancy going down to that Angelo's restaurant near Mike's again; the food was superb." Luckily Angelos is open this Monday it's the restaurant's tenth anniversary." Said Mike.

"So, half seven it is," said Charlie. "Oh, and by the way, I have some information; no cost" – and he told them what he had learnt from Fats.

"So, all we need to do is find this missing relative if your man is right, Charlie," said Evan.

"Amber, is it possible after nearly thirty years to get the staff list?" said Mike.

"Shouldn't be too much of a problem," Amber said.

"And a plan of the bank or, better still, we will pay them a visit tomorrow," said Mike.

"Let's leave it at that and meet at Angelo's at seven thirty," said Evan.

The five life-long friends sat together around one of the tables, drinking Champagne. They could easily have been mistaken for catwalk models. Four were beautiful but one whose birthday they were celebrating was more than beautiful. She was exquisite and knew it. When they laughed, and they were laughing a lot, one could see that they all had perfect white teeth to go with their perfect make-up and hair. Strangely, each wore a different coloured dress; no trouser suits here. All were slightly above the knees and all wore high heels. It was as if they had all agreed on some kind of dress code and stuck to it. Apart from the five, there were eight couples and a single man in his sixties and three tables of four. Even he must have fancied his chances. The odds were on his side. Amber and Evan arrived together in a taxi and Charlie appeared a few moments later, also by taxi. They ordered some white wine and settled down waiting for Mike to come. The restaurant started filling up.

"Evan, I don't think that I have ever seen a more beautiful woman in my life," said Charlie.

"You talking about the one in the red Charlie?"

"I am Evan, what a stunner," said Charlie.

"Absolutely gorgeous," said Evan "Don't you agree, Amber?"

"They're all fantastic looking women but I must admit the one in the red is by far the best looking," said Amber.

"Do you know, Amber, I'm invisible to beautiful women," Evan said wistfully.

"Not to Edna or me," said Amber.

"Thank you, Amber, that's very kind," said Evan, still staring at the woman in red, as was Charlie and the other male diners in the restaurant.

Doctor Crosby, the woman in red, giggled with happiness. She knew they were being talked about on the other tables and also knew that she was the centre of attraction. The bubbly had made her slightly tipsy; she wasn't used to it but it was her birthday and she had a good excuse for participating in a few glasses. She also had another reason to drink.

Mike had fallen asleep on the sofa. It was ten to eight when he realised the time. A very quick shower and quicker brushing of the teeth. He didn't bother shaving and he was ready to walk to the restaurant. He arrived just ten minutes late. Not bad really, the fresh air helped wake him. `

"My God," said Jackie. "Have you seen what's just walked in?" – and all the other four craned their necks to see what Jackie was on about. They were, in the most, impressed. Toni was gay and didn't give a rat's arse for men of any sort.

Mike stopped dead in his tracks. He could see and feel her watching him as he slowly crossed the floor towards her table.

"Hello Barbara, didn't expect to see you here."

Before Barbara could speak, Jackie piped up with it being Barbara's birthday and something else, which Mike didn't catch.

"Would you like to join us?" said Barbara who could see the 'want to' in his eyes but was afraid of what come out of his mouth.

"I'm afraid I can't. We are having an office dinner meeting," he said, pointing over to where the other three were sitting. "I see you are on the Champagne. Please allow me to get you one of Angelo's special reserves; he hides them away. He'd prefer it if no one ordered or even knew they existed," Mike said finding it difficult to know what to say. "It's good to see you again and I hope you have a good birthday meal." Mike turned and headed back towards his table, all eyes boring a hole in his back.

"Well, who the hell was that hunk, Babs? You didn't even introduce us! Wanted to keep him a secret from your best friends?" said Jackie playfully.

"I would do the same," said another of the women.

"Did you notice his eyes? I'd swear they were coal black and he's really fit. I love Dan, but if he asked me out it would be 'Tata Danny Boy'," said Jackie.

"He doesn't do anything for me," Toni said.

"Well, he wouldn't, would he?" said Pamela.

"His name's Mike, he's a cop. Russian blood somewhere and we had dinner at this very place," said Barbara.

"And then...? Come on, give us all the sordid details, Babs," said Jackie as they all moved their heads towards Barbara. Even Toni was interested in this part.

"Then nothing. I think I fucked up. He was a gentleman, walked me to the car and that was that," Barbara said.

"Is the man gay, or is he just stupid?" said Toni, acknowledging the fact that Barbara was the best looking. She actually fancied her enormously but knew it would never happen.

"No, he's not gay, I just fucked up. You know me girls; I was in my doctor mode. I even lectured him on drinking and smoking and I don't think he was too impressed when I picked at my food and told him I was a vegetarian," said Barbara taking another sip of her drink.

"I thought it strange you bringing us here and actually drinking, Babs. But now we know why, don't we? Don't tell me you're going to have a steak too?" said Jackie.

"No, I'm still vegetarian, although in the right circumstances that could change too," said Barbara.

"A friend of yours?" asked Amber, when Mike had seated himself.

"She's all woman, that one Mike," said Charlie.

"I guess so," said Mike, looking over and catching her and another three pairs of eyes, who he was sure were mentally stripping him naked. Mike felt uncomfortable. He wished that he could get up and disappear. He began squirming in his seat. He knew that this particular conversation had not concluded.

Evan was lost in thought. The woman really fancied Mike; it was obvious. She was very beautiful as was his lovely daughter Jasmine. Many people had commented on that during her life. Mike would hurt her as he had somehow hurt the woman in red who was pretending she was having a good time and didn't have a care in the world.

"So, Mike, are you going to enlighten us?" said Amber.

"What can I say? She turned out to be the wrong kind," said Mike. Mike caught Angelo's eye. Angelo came across. "Bottle of your best champers Angelo for the table with the ladies on. Wish them a 'happy birthday' and put the cost on my tab." Angelo winked, then saluted.

"Well Charlie, very kind of you to bring us for a meal. Let's order and then talk," said Evan. "Oh. and by the way, she turned out to be the wrong kind re words from the great George Jones record."

"Not a hit in this country, well not up to 1975," said Charlie.

"Some more bread and butter and some more cheese."

"Crostinis," added Amber after they had ordered. "Oh, and some mozzarella and some of what they are having on that table; and did we say calamari? Make it two."

"Yes Madam, no problem. I bring everyone," said a flustered Guilio.

"You mean you will bring everything very quickly, don't you?" said Amber, who wanted to make sure that the food would come and plenty of it.

Satisfied that the waiter had got it all correctly, Amber raised her glass: "To Mrs Edith Myson, aka Miss Edith Eastern, first cousin of a certain William Eastern, owner of Eastern's Fabrication," said Amber, her mouth full by now of calamari.

"The connection in the bank, the Easterns, Williams and I reckon the two stooges who work for Eastern," said Mike.

"Are you having a giraffe, Mike?" said Charlie.

All three looked at Charlie and Charlie looked back. Now what? He was thinking.

"Giraffes Charlie," said Evan. "'Giraffe, laugh' – are you having a 'laugh'? Look, the equivalent of four mill in today's money, right? Williams has got properties in Spain, businesses, etc. This Eastern chap too, he is well placed. A good business, probably freehold."

"Okay," Mike said. "We get the picture. Could two people do that job, Charlie?"

"With their inside man or, in this case, woman, easy; no problem getting in. One of them lugs in the cutting equipment, the type they use at Eastern's, cuts through the bars of the cage in the basement. No need for keys or codes or whatever they had. Helped themselves to all the used notes, piled up and ready. Three big bags and into their van, or large estate type car and off they go through the bloody front door, setting off the alarm purposely. It takes your boys ten minutes to get there by which time they are garaged up somewhere out of sight."

"Can we track down this Edith woman, Amber? Must be possible, she is married, or was at the time," said Evan.

"I've tried, Evan; she divorced end of 1994, moved to a council flat in Caerphilly, stayed about eighteen months and after that she just vanished," said Amber.

"No kids Amber?" asked Evan.

"No Evan, no kids," replied Amber.

"Did she work again for the bank?" asked Charlie.

"Yes, for about a year after the robbery and then went on the dole for a while before disappearing," said Amber.

"Is there any chance one of the other bank employees was also in on it?" said Evan.

"Possible, but I don't think so," said Amber.

"Are we set for Wednesday, Amber? I mean regarding the two-way mirror and a small room for the prize winners to fill in their forms."

"All will be ready in time," said Amber.

"But who will actually oversee the form filling? It can't be any of us," said Evan.

"No, Mr Peters himself; he's already agreed. Good for his ego, etc., etc.," said Amber.

Across the city, two people were also sharing a meal. They were being extremely careful not to touch hands, show any undue love, or care for each other, although both were yearning for much more than a polite conversation over a steak meal.

"So you see Emma, I've now got two sets of these photos which I will destroy tonight. There might be more but I have a feeling there's not; they've got what they wanted," said the Chief.

"Who are they, Clive, and what did they get?" asked Emma, her hope now rising that it was not over between them.

"They are our two detectives. I am sure about that and I gave them time," said the Chief.

"Time Clive? What time?" said Emma.

"Now that is the sixty-four thousand dollar question, Emma. Time to supposedly crack half the crime in Wales, including the Chessman business."

"And you don't think..."

The Chief interrupted her. "No, I don't think Emma, it's all Pie in the Sky stuff. They are living in another world, doing all sorts of madness and using their newly found positions as... my God, I'm not looking forward to checking their credit cards."

"Don't fret Clive. How long have you given them before you can close down their operations?"

"This week M, one more bleeding week and I can move them on," said the Chief.

"And then what?" said Emma.

"Well, I guess that Jones is ready to retire. Amber will go back to Bristol and I will try and arrange for the main pain in the arse to enjoy a few years in Anglesey. That will keep him occupied for a while and we can get on with what we got going for us, M. Just this week. We don't meet for these next few days. Agreed?"

"Agreed Clive. I'll miss you, you know."

"Same here but it's not too long. Fancy another bottle of Claret?" said the Chief.

The Chessman sat at home. He was eating a shop-made shepherd's pie and washing it down with ginger beer. He'd made his decisions and would stick to them steadfastly. He would not take up the offer of a free DVD recorder cum player. Having more stuff to leave behind was pointless. He would go to the karaoke night with Jim tomorrow. It would be the last time for Jim to be taken out of the equation, or at least out of the way for a while. A broken limb, preferably a leg, would do the trick.

Now he assumed that all the necessary money donors had received the letter and had contacted the Police. Big deal, maybe they had protection or backed up their own or both. Irrelevant. The one who had not been sent a letter was the next in line for a quick trip to the Promised Land. A crumpled letter would be found in his pocket, the same letter that had been sent to the others. It was the luck of the draw but in reality, the name swung it for him. McQueen – he wondered when the opportunity would arise for him to use the queen chess piece and travelling to Buckingham Palace was not really feasible with so much going on.

"This is a great meal," Amber said to no-one in particular. Everyone agreed but was too preoccupied with eating actually to verbally concur.

"You're not drinking, Mike?" Charlie asked.

"Course I am Charlie, I'm just pacing myself. No reason to rush, is there? You're still footing the bill, aren't you?"

Charlie laughed. "Actually, the meal's on my good friend William, William Hill."

"Bookies. Not often we can toast them," said Amber, raising her refilled glass.

The girls had drunk enough but didn't know it and ordered more. Clive and Emma hadn't had enough but called it a day. The Chessman hadn't had any but was ready for bed. Murder was hard work and he needed his sleep.

"You've got to do something, Barbara; you can't just let him go. At least give him your number. If you don't, I will," said Jackie.

"You fancy him that much?" said Barbara.

"I do, but I meant I will give him your number you silly moo, so that he can call you without losing face. I'm sure he will co-operate," said Jackie.

"And if he's recalcitrant, how does it help, Babs?" said Pamela who was a solicitor and at that very moment a very drunk one.

"Is that a legal word, Pam?" said giggling Tiffany, the quiet one.

"Recalcitrant, Tiffs. I'm not pissed you know. It means 'unwilling to co-operate'," Pamela said before throwing up into her embossed linen napkin.

Angelo moved quickly. He took the napkin and helped Pamela to her feet and to the door of the 'Ladies'. From then it was up to her. His obligation to the well-being of his female customers stopped at the entrance to the conveniences. A very suitable name for a loo, thought Angelo as he returned to the bar to dump the napkin and get some strong coffee made up for the hen party.

The girls wanted more wine; Angelo was reluctant to serve them but what could he do? He served them the alcohol and gave them the coffee free.

Pamela returned and sat down. Her faced was flushed and it wasn't the rouge that made it so. With Pamela seated, Jackie rose. In her hand, she had a paper napkin; none of her party took any notice of her, they had other things occupying their sozzled minds. Slowly but steadily Jackie weaved her way in and out of other diners' tables. No one complained but all held on to their glasses for dear life.

Evan noticed her just before Charlie did. Amber would have but was still busily finishing off the mountain of food. She didn't want it to go to waste and didn't have a dog. This was going to be very interesting, thought Evan but he wasn't looking forward to it and it was too late to go to the 'Men's'. The woman was nearly upon them.

Charlie nudged Mike who seemed deep in thought, head bowed. Mike looked up and realised why Charlie had been nudging him. Mike's reaction surprised everyone at the table. He rose, pulled out his chair and asked Pamela if she wanted to sit. He reckoned that she could hardly stand so she may as well sit. Pamela declined; she preferred using Charlie as a prop and Charlie welcomed her proximity. She handed Mike the napkin. "Give Babs a ring, doctor's orders."

"Thank you," said Mike pocketing the napkin without looking at it. She stood there swaying, looking intensely into Mike's eyes. "If for any reason you don't want to, I can give you my number," said Pamela, regretting her words as soon as she had said them. Even in her inebriated state, she knew that this man wasn't going to ring anyone, least of all her. She could tell from his four jet black eyes.

"Will do so, I promise, sometime soon. When the pressure of work dies down a little but again thank you," said Mike who was still standing. Pamela turned and headed for her own table. Everyone en route grabbed their glasses again.

Amber looked at Mike who had now sat back down in his chair. She was about to say something but changed her mind when she saw that a king prawn had escaped her attention and lying there begging to be eaten. She obliged.

It had gone deadly quiet around the table, so Charlie thought it was time to get everyone back into a happier frame of mind.

"Am I financing a wake here, or what? Here's to getting our man."

"Or woman," added Amber without meaning to have a poke at Mike who felt like a heel.

"You've done nothing wrong Mike," Evan said sensing his partner's discomfort.

"I know Evan, but this whole thing is just so seedy and in a way that I can't explain, degrading," said Mike.

"Like I said, you did nothing wrong. Come on, let's make a hole in Charlie's wallet; he might never win again," said Evan.

"Let's order some desserts," said Amber. They ordered two deserts: one for Evan and one for Amber. Coffee for three and four large brandies.

The girls had finished. They had paid and were awaiting taxis. Barbara was happy. Pam had told her that he would ring soon. That was great because she had taken quite a liking to the Champagne. It made her feel good. What she would feel like in the morning was another matter.

The taxis duly arrived. Barbara waved to Mike as she stumbled towards the door, making a phone sign with her hand. Mike waved back. There would be no more hassle that night, thank God. The coffee came with the desserts and brandies. All was well with the world for now.

"I'll go with Babs," Pam said. "Tiffany, you and Jackie take the other cab. Is that Okay with you Toni?"

"That's fine," said Toni. "Jackie's place is on my way." The three got into the cab. Two were white and one red. The cabbie had a good look. He was an expert in women's knickers. It was his lucky day. Three beautiful women all pissed out of their tiny little minds and showing flesh in abundance. He was in no hurry. He adjusted his mirror accordingly before slowly driving off.

Jackie managed to clamber into the second taxi. The Arab driver was uninterested. He liked his women big and fat, the opposite to the scrawny pair. When the aggressive one asked him to wait whilst she went back in to collect something, he was not amused. But it was a Tuesday and the meter was running.

Toni went back in and headed for Charlie's table. This time Mike didn't need to be nudged and Amber was well aware of the woman bearing down on them. On arriving at the table, she faced Mike, spread her legs and started to sing. Only Evan recognised the lyrics.

"He was a big man yesterday but boy you want to see him now." Three times the same verse before Angelo saved them from further earache.

"Madam, I'm a very sorry but we do not have an entertainment licence here at Angelo's. Please stop."

"No comediennes allowed, eh," said a wit on the next table.

Amber rose, all twenty-odd stone. "Lady, I don't know what your point is. I can guess you don't like men and I can assure you that the feeling is reciprocal. So zip your sweet little pussy mouth in a bag and piss off out of here before I slap you so hard, you'll end up in a rugby team's changing room next Saturday afternoon."

The first four words came out louder, the fifth not at all. The backhanded slap had seen to that. The men winced – that slap would have felled any of them. Never mind a little slip of a girl. Amber got a round of applause from the other customers.

A waiter, together with Angelo, helped Toni to her taxi. The evening's entertainment had come to an end. Angelo was glad; his customers on the whole were not. They were enjoying the show. Amber sat back down and proceeded to finish off her tiramisu. Evan, poor soul, had suddenly lost his appetite and couldn't finish his. Again, all was quiet until Amber had finished eating her dessert.

"Two things Evan," she said. Evan looked up, a worried furrow creasing his brow. "What song was she singing or trying to?"

"I think, Amber, it was a Kathy Kirby song from the sixties."

"Evan's right – 1962," said Charlie, "but it wasn't a hit."

"Ah, don't know her or it," said Amber.

"And your second query, Amber?"

"Have you finished with that dessert?"

"I have, thank you Amber," Evan said, passing over the half-eaten dessert.

Charlie called for the bill. For two hundred and fifty quid, he'd had one of the best nights he could remember. The most important aspect of it being that he felt that he was now one of them. He wasn't Chalky the clown, the petty thief, the appendix to the main story unfolding before his eyes. Who would have credited it, Charlie helping the Fuzz? He was so elated he left fifty pounds. Strangely enough in his old circle of acquaintances, the tip would have covered the whole cost of a meal for four.

A taxi was called. It would drop off Amber first; Charlie second and last would be Evan. Mike had decided to stay on and have a word with Angelo before he walked home. It was gone one when Mike got home. He took another shower before getting into bed and fell asleep as soon as his head hit the pillow. He had dreams: the usual ones about his strawberry blonde and a new one about him being a big man yesterday and a tiny little runt the next day. He woke up to find that he was still approximately six foot and a half inch. A good start to the day apart from a nagging headache.

He took two aspirin, smoked a cigarette and had two espresso coffees. He pulled back the curtain: it was raining. Par for the course. It actually made him feel good. He stood motionless for a good ten minutes, watching the rain. It was falling vertically; there was no wind. For some unknown reason, that also pleased him.

Evan also woke up at the same time and trudged into the kitchen to make himself a cup of tea. Even though it was raining he could hear birds singing and that made him smile. He crept along the corridor and slowly opened the door to his daughter's bedroom. She looked like an angel, her blonde hair cascading all over the place. It was good to have a nice family: a wife and daughter. He felt for Mike who had nothing but hassle. What an evening, he wouldn't forget it in a hurry. He wouldn't mention certain parts to his wife or daughter; some things were best left unsaid.

He could hear that the kettle had come to a boil. He also had a headache. He hoped a nice cup of tea would help. He didn't want to be incoherent when the girls woke up. He prepared his tea and his pipe and looked to see if his newspaper had been delivered. It had. He sat down; slippers, pyjamas, pipe, cup of tea and newspaper. What more could a Welshman wish for?

Charlie finished his tea. Maggie had just gone to bed after telling him that they would be spending Christmas in Wrexham with his mother-in-law. In general, Charlie was the boss in the house; he always had the last word apart from when Maggie's mother was involved. They were very close, her and Maggie. Most Christmases they spent in Wrexham; a week of pure purgatory but it was worth doing for the peace of the remaining fifty-one weeks.

After a decent breakfast, Amber had got on the phone and contacted the Spanish police in Malaga. She requested all photos, newspaper articles, etc., that they possessed on Walliams (aka Williams) and friends. The photos and articles duly arrived but had to wait their turn in the queue. Amber had much more important things to do: the Welsh cakes she had baked were ready. She sliced all four in half, buttered them and sat down to peruse the documentation from Spain. By the time she had finished the Welsh cakes, she had ringed in biro three faces on the photographs and three names in the articles, which unfortunately were in the main written in Spanish. By nine, all four were in feeling that all was going well with their various investigations.

Evan tapped one of the ringed photos. "So who's this then?"

"I think that is Erica Fairfield," said Amber.

"Are we supposed to know her?" said Evan.

"No, Evan," answered Amber.

"Is she a Miss, Ms, Mrs or a bloke who added on an 'a' to his name," quipped Evan.

"Looks a bit horsey to me. I think Evan might be right," said Charlie laughing.

"Why have you marked her then, Amber?"

"I'm not exactly sure. Call it gut feeling and let's be brutally honest here, I've got one hell of a gut," Amber said unsmilingly.

Mike had contented himself to whittling down another pencil to a stub. He found it therapeutic.

They passed the photos around. "Shall we get this lot translated, Amber?" said Evan.

"No need, I have a reasonable knowledge of the language and I don't think anything written there is of any use to us," Amber replied.

"Look here," said Mike.

"What are we looking at? It's just a marina full of boats," said Evan.

"This boat, the 'Anderi'," said Mike.

"Nice bit of boat," said Charlie.

"Nicer name," said Evan. "I now see the connection: the first three letters of Walliams and Fairfield's names: Andy, Erica: 'Anderi'. So we have a connection, they are partners," said Evan.

"Right," said Amber. "I have two addresses for the Bank's ex staff: John Arnold aged fifty-six and Amy Morris aged seventy-one and retired. Arnold still works for the Bank's branch in Cardiff. Manager passed away a few years back. Another is in an old people's home and gaga. Eastern and the other lady? No way of tracing them, unless...."

"Unless one of these two is her," said Evan.

"So, can we blow up the pictures? We have to zoom in on Erica's face and visit the two we have addresses for," said Charlie.

"Yes, I'll get right on to it," said Amber.

"Evan, you take the old woman and I'll take the other. That okay with you?"

"Fine Mike," said Evan.

"And what about me?" said Charlie.

"Take the photos down to the Cutty Sark. Anyone with any decent info gets fifty. Have you got fifty, Charlie?"

"I have Mike."

"Good, we'll reimburse you later then," said Mike.

John Arnold wasn't sure: it could be but he wasn't sure.

"So if the hair was darker, shorter, the nose shaped differently, it could be this Edith Eastern woman. Is that correct?" said Mike, exasperated with the man.

"Also, I think this woman looks much younger than what Edith would look like now. Is that a recent pic?"

"Yes it is, Mr Arnold."

"I'd say now that this woman is not Edith or Joss, but if it was one of them, I very much doubt it is more likely to be Edith, which I'm sure it isn't.

"Okay, Mr Arnold, thank you."

"No problem detective, glad to be of help," said Mr Arnold.

Of help, thought Mike, I wouldn't want to interview him when he didn't want to help. Mike walked back to the office; his mobile rang. "Mike here."

"It's me Mike, the old lady Amy gave me a positive ID; it's Edith, she recognised her unusual silver bracelet and according to Amy she's had a lot of plastic surgery, mainly to her nose and a lot of dental work. She used to have a big crooked tooth in the front. Now our Edith has got what looks like a new set of molars."

"Well done, Evan. Where are you now?"

"Still with Amy Morris, Mike, having a cup of tea and biscuits. Will see you anon."

So, Mike thought, they had found the insider! It was all coming together but which one of the bastards did in his father? He had to find out and soon. It was much more important than the bloody bank job.

"So, here we are again," said Mike.

"A little older and little wiser," said Evan.

Charlie was back a few minutes later, a huge smile on his face.

"Someone owes me twenty nicker," were his first words.

"No one recognised the woman but one nice chappie fingered Speedo, strong arm man and getaway driver par excellence. It's this big bugger here," Charlie said, pointing at a fifty-year-old baldie, "so I gave him a score."

"So we think we know who, why, where but we have no tangible evidence, do we?" said Evan.

"We need a confession," said Amber.

"DNA won't help us, the job was clean. No mistakes and as for the vehicle, we have no idea of the type and even if we did it's razor blades now," said Evan.

"If we follow the money?" asked Mike again.

"No go. Not marked, nor new. We know everything and can't do anything about it," said Amber.

"Tell you what," said Mike, "let's pack our bags, get down to Malaga and spend a few weeks interviewing our suspects."

"Not a bad idea Mike, but we've a big day tomorrow."

"All right boys, we can only wait on Bill Eastern. Where did he get the money to buy his business, house, whatever? When did he buy them, how did he source the money? Is there a tax angle on it? I could go on."

"I'm off, I've got to get a haircut," said Mike.

When Mike walked in, Andreas was just finishing off his last client before his break.

"Hi Mikhail, you come for a haircut?"

"No Andreas, I come on behalf of the Salvation Army, they're looking for someone to bang the big drum when they go marching," said Mike.

"Is that a joke?" said Andreas.

"Yes," said Mike.

The customer paid and left. Andreas turned the open sign to close. Andreas lit up, as did Mike.

"You like Greek coffee Mikhail?"

"No thanks," said Mike.

"It's very good, you know," said Andreas.

"It's okay," said Mike not wishing to offend Andreas but making sure that he didn't get stuck with the coffee.

"You know where the word 'okay' comes from Mikhail?"

"No I don't Andreas, but I'm sure you're about to tell me."

"From Greek who go to America to work, seamen who escape from ships and work on building bridges, very high. No problem because they work on ships high up masts and sails, you understand Mikhail?"

"Yes Andreas, your countrymen were the best workers on high structures."

"Yes Mikhail, they no speak proper English, my people."

"That's one thing I can believe," said Mike.

"Many times these peoples work very hard to make money to send home and when the Americans ask how they do, they only know to say 'Olla Kalla'. This mean everything is fine. 'Olla – O', 'Kalla – K': 'OK'."

"That sounds very feasible to me," said Mike.

"Yes, I hear lot of good things here. Every day I learn from my customers, you understand Mikhail?" Mike nodded. "And I tell you one thing, not many peoples know Mikhail, the English they talk all the time: 'fuck this', 'fuck that'. All the time and don't know what this mean."

"I think they do Andreas. Actually, I am positive they do. How do you think the population keeps expanding?"

"No, you don't understand Mikhail. They know how to make the fuck but not the word: why call it 'fuck'?"

"Andreas, am I going to get a haircut today? I'm very busy and this is my lunch break."

"Mine too Mikhail. I put this on you and wash your hair. Then when I wash your hair, I tell you about the fuck word."

"Anything you say Andreas."

"Water not too hot, eh?"

"It's fine, just fine."

"In old days, I think maybe three or four hundred years back, the English king not have any people to pay tax or to fight war with other country. He not have too many people, you understand, Mikhail." Mike grunted a reply. Andreas took it as a 'yes' and carried on.

"So the king he have idea to fix this problem, he made order to his people to make more babies. Good eh, Mikhail?" Another grunt from Mike. "So people made love and he call it fornications under the command of the king. Big words, I remember you see. This later spell 'fuck' because words too long for peoples to say. This is the truth. Mr Lampard he is top lawyer, he tell me."

"Christ, Andreas, don't tell me you believe that load of crap, surely not."

"This man lawyer, Mikhail, he read old English books. That is where he read this; he read many things. I will tell you what he tell me about King Arthur and his round table so everybody can see everybody and no one is more important than anyone else. Very good man, very clever," said Andreas.

"Who you talking about? The lawyer again?"

"No Mikhail, I talk about the Great King Arthur, he like Greek God, only English."

By now Mike had closed his ears to Andreas. He felt like telling Andreas that King Arthur was as real as the Greek gods but that would be too much for Andreas to take in.

"You learn very much today, Mikhail. Haircut worth it, you learn very much," said Andreas brimming with the joys of spring, even though it was near on Christmas. "You know me name, Mikhail, you know what it mean?"

"No Andreas, I have no idea."

"They no teach you old Greek in school?"

"Not in my school," said Mike. "No time for ancient Greek or modern," said Mike.

"Too bad for you my friend. Is very important to know, for mathematic, medicine, Olympic sports, everything if you know Greek. I will tell you 'Andreas', it mean 'man'. Strong man, big man, very brave man."

"That's very interesting," Mike said, wishing he'd had the coffee. It would have taken Andreas five minutes to make the bloody stuff, five minutes less of listening to the crap that poured out of his mouth.

"I'm sorry to call you on your mobile, Detective, but I was wondering about the letter opener, if you ever found it."

"Is that you Mr Arnold?"

"Yes, you came to the bank this morning and talked to me."

"What's all this about a letter opener then John?"

"Well, as you know Detective, when we had the burglary all those years ago, only used notes were taken. The deposit boxes were left untouched as was a large amount in coins, but the Manager's letter opener went missing and he was very upset."

"Missing a letter opener? Why the big deal?"

"Well, it was given to Patrick for twenty-five years' sterling work in the bank from Head Office in London," said John.

"Can you describe this letter opener to me John?"

"Yes, the blade was made of solid silver, the handle ivory with a ball depicting the world at the end, also made of ivory. On one side of the blade it was inscribed: 'Money makes the world go round' and on the other it read 'Patrick Bosman 1954 to 1979' or was it '1953 to 1978'?"

"And this thing went missing?" said Mike.

"Mr Bosman was very upset; he had the whole staff searching everywhere for it."

"How long was this opener John?"

"I would say about twenty centimetres," replied John.

"Well, thank you John, this could help us with our enquiries." Mike paid Andreas, good tip included and headed for the office.

"Nice haircut Mike," Charlie said cheekily. Mike didn't bother replying.

"Evan, does this Amy have a phone?" asked Mike.

"Yes, I've got her number here in my pocket, why?"

"Could you give her a call and ask her if she remembers anything about the Manager's letter opener which went missing at the same time as the burglary, and could she describe it," Mike asked.

Evan rang, posed the questions and listened, writing down some notes. When he'd finished he read from his notes: "Silver, solid, nine inches long, inscribed blade, both sides, ivory handle. Ball representing the world at the end also made of ivory. Inscription reads 'Patrick Bosman 1954 to 1979', and the other side..."

Mike put up his hand: "I know, Evan. I would say one of them pocketed it. We can discount Edith, she worked there and wasn't there on the night. We can also discount the getaway driver. He'd have been used as a lookout. Anyway, that's assuming he was part of the gang."

"That leaves Williams, the brain and Eastern, the man who cut through the bars and around the steel door," said Evan.

"It's got to be Eastern," Charlie said.

"Why Charlie?" asked Amber.

"By process of elimination. Williams was the gang leader and the brains. He made sure they didn't take the coins or open the deposit boxes. He knew that the time was limited and that it would be difficult to dispose of the coins and anything found in the boxes which would be easily traced if it wasn't in the form of hard cash."

"Makes sense to me," said Amber.

"And me," said Evan.

"But why take a stupid letter opener? It can't be flogged. Melted down for its silver content, yes. But the opener would not raise much, would it?" said Mike

"Does there have to be a reason Mike?" asked Amber.

"Maybe he just fancied it. Maybe he couldn't help himself. Some petty thieves can't, you know," said Charlie.

"Once a petty thief, always a petty thief," added Mike, knowing that he was talking rubbish. Maybe Andreas had rubbed off on him a little.

"Would he dump it, keep it, melt it down? If he kept it, would he still have it after all these years and what use is it to him?" said Evan.

"No use to him, unless he uses it as a letter opener and something tells me he's not the type," said Mike. "He's the type who rips things open with his finger."

"A lot of people in the trade keep something back as a souvenir," said Charlie. "It reminds them of the good days. It's about sentimentality I guess."

"It's a weakness," said Evan. "That's how half of these idiots get caught."

"Any chance of a search warrant, Amber?" said Evan. "His house, office, work place."

"No way. Case is too cold. No judge would entertain it," said Amber.

"We set an ex-thief to catch an ex-thief, if you get my drift Charlie," said Mike.

"Sorry Mike, can't do it. It's too specific and logically if he's still got it it's not going to be in open view, on his desk or filed under 'L' for letter opener."

"You're right Charlie. Sorry I mentioned it," said Mike.

"If only we knew for sure that Eastern has it, it's a big ask after all this time and that's assuming he was the one who took it to begin with."

"Have we checked Eastern out Amber?"

"We have Mike. Divorced, two kids aged about 15 and 16. Business stable, worth about two fifty thousand. Freehold premises, semi-detached property, another two fifty. No mortgage. Good credit, took a big hit – two hundred odd thou – very acrimonious divorce four years ago."

"Divorce, Tammy Wynette and Billy Connolly, both 1975," said Charlie.

"Is that the comedian, the Scots guy with long hair?" said Mike.

"Think so," said Charlie.

"Wife's name?" asked Evan, ignoring both Mike and Charlie.

"June Mattison. Reverted to her maiden name. I have an address for her. Lives in Llandaff. Runs some kind of B and B," said Amber.

"What's on your mind Evan?" asked Mike.

"I think we should pay her a visit. After all, if there is still bad blood between them, who knows what information she will impart to two nice gentlemen from the Law," said Evan.

"At least you look human now that you've cut your hair," said Amber.

"Yeah Amber, that will swing it for us," said Mike sneezing loudly.

"Wear a vest, take an umbrella with you always Mike and you won't catch a cold," said Evan.

Mike sneezed again. He reached into his pocket, extracted a paper napkin and blew his nose, throwing the paper napkin into the waste paper container next to his desk. And with that, Dr Barbara Crosby's telephone number was confined to the dustbin and she was out of his life.

June Mattison was at home and within seconds both detectives felt the hate that she still harboured for her ex. For ten minutes they sparred, asking insignificant questions and getting insignificant answers, most of which had no real bearing on their investigation. They heard about his meanness, his violence, their sex life or lack of it. On that point Mike was on Bill's side; the woman in front of him was ugly and that was being kind to her. Repulsive was a better way of describing the witch sitting cross-legged on her wooden chair. He couldn't help himself when his eyes scoured the old-fashioned dining room for a broomstick. He was actually surprised not to find one.

Evan carried on probing but getting nothing. "So why exactly are you here? What do you want?" said June Mattison.

"We want to know about the letter opener your ex stole."

"You're not talking about that bone-handled piece of steel are you, the one he said he bought in a flea market for a fiver? It had this guy's name on it and some dates. Is that the one? Did you say he stole it?"

"Correct, Ms Mattison."

"Call me June, Detective. Is this letter opener valuable?" asked June.

"Not particularly," said Mike.

"Well, why are you interested in it? He had it before we got married; when we started courting, actually," said June.

Mike looked at Evan who nodded. Mike leaned towards her as if he was about to impart a great secret but couldn't bring himself to make eye contact.

"Listen June, I'm not sure I should be telling you this and it must not go any further. It is difficult, you probably have some feelings for him but he could be in serious trouble."

"Like shit I do, I hope he rots in hell."

"Firstly, I want you to clear your mind and think back; it is most important that you give us a description of the item," said Mike.

"We are still talking about the letter opener aren't we?" said June.

"Yes," said Mike.

"I can do better than describe it. I can show you a picture of it. Hang on here a tick and I'll find it," said June.

True to her word, after sifting through about sixty odd photographs, she came up with a six by four colour photo. It showed her two sons aged about six. Both dressed up: one as a cowboy, the younger one as an Indian, headdress and all. The older boy, the one with the white cowboy hat, was holding the letter opener and pointing it at the other's throat.

"Is that good enough for you?" asked June.

"Fantastic," said Mike.

"So, will you now tell me why this thing is so important?" said June.

"Because it puts your ex at the scene of a crime which will put him away for a long time," said Evan.

"But we need to get hold of it; it's our only hope of tying him in with the robbery," said Mike. "Can you help on that score June?"

"I'd love to but I can't see how I can help," said June. "I haven't spoken to him for over four years, nor have the boys; he's just a slimy bastard from our past, I'm sorry."

"Where did he used to keep it?" asked Mike.

"Always in his desk. That one there," she pointed to a desk in the photo. "Middle drawer under lock and key. I still don't know how the kids got hold of it," said June.

"That picture, was it taken in this house?" asked Evan.

"Yes," said June, "happier days."

"So, he moved out after the divorce, is that so?"

"Yeah, he moved out, I kept the house; he the business. We split the furniture; the desk was one of the items he had. He rented at first then out of the blue he bought a house somewhere in Whitchurch. Where he got the money from, God only knows; he must have had a secret account someplace," said June.

"So it's more than possible that he still has the letter opener and that it's still kept in the middle drawer in that desk," said Evan.

"It's more than possible. Eastern is a mean man of habit. He never throws anything away, even if it's broken. He used to get up at exactly seven-thirty every morning. One boiled egg, one instant coffee, one piece of toast buttered with orange marmalade. He'd leave the house at precisely half eight and invariably be home at half six. Every day he would take a packed lunch: cheddar cheese and pickle sandwich, white bread and one apple.

"On the last Friday of every month, we would go to bed early to have sex. Twelve times a year unless Good Friday or Christmas Day fell on the last Friday. Shall I go on, or am I embarrassing you?"

"That's fine June," said Mike thinking once in twelve years would be once too much with this woman. He was beginning to feel sorry for Bill Eastern. "Can we keep the photo? We will of course return it within a few days."

"If it helps, put the fuck away. Keep it for as long as you want. I am sorry I haven't been a good host, have I?" said June. "I never offered you a cup of tea or coffee."

"That's okay June. You've been more than helpful. We will keep you informed," said Mike, getting up and heading for the door.

He needed out of there pronto. He needed fresh air. Evan, photo in hand, was right behind Mike.

They got back in the car, Evan driving. "I assume we're going back to the office, Mike?"

"Guess so Evan, you any other suggestions?"

"Nope. I'm glad we're out of there, she's spooky, that one and ugly as sin."

"You can say that again," said Mike.

"Ugly as sin," Evan said.

Both laughed. The sun came out, a good omen. It was the first time in four days.

"Right Amber, two things: a blow-up of that letter opener and half a dozen copies. Then get hold of someone; we need a search warrant for Eastern's house, business premises and if he's got a dog, then the dog kennel. Speak to your friend Mick's boss, we need six men and Mick Maloney. Four in uniform, Mick and two plain.

"Take Eastern down town. Don't let a lawyer near him; fob him off. You, Evan, take three people: one plain and two uniforms and search the house. Search the fabrication unit. Photos of the letter opener to all. That's all. We need to make sure no-one gets their grubby fingerprints on it."

"That's fine Mike. We must make sure Eastern doesn't take his mobile or keys with him," said Evan.

"Where's Charlie, Amber?" said Mike.

"No idea. Don't forget he doesn't officially work for us or with us, Mike."

"True, very true. Have a locksmith on standby in the event we come across a safe or two," said Mike.

"This is part of the Chessman investigation, isn't it boys?"

"What are you trying to say Amber?" said Mike.

"I'm not trying to say anything. I'm saying that Eastern business is part of our on-running investigation of the Chessman, otherwise no warrant."

"In that case Eastern is the focal point of our investigation into the Chessman murders," said Evan.

"I thought so," said Amber.

"Bring Big Mick up to speed on everything we know about the robbery. We owe him and realistically, tomorrow we're going to have to pass the case on to someone. Why not Big Mick? He deserves a good result. I'll get him on the blower now," said Evan.

"But remember, Evan, Mick, one plain and two uniforms. Don't move or say anything until we have found the opener," said Mike.

"And if we don't find it, we are in deep shit, all of us, including you Amber," Evan said. "Aren't you a bit apprehensive, Mike?"

"Of course I am, Evan. Tomorrow is D-Day. We might achieve a lot or a big fat zero. But I am not going to waste a good day today thinking about a possible bad tomorrow."

"Don't worry boys, tomorrow never comes," said Amber.

That night Jim met with a fatal accident. He got run over by a hit and run driver. There were no witnesses except for Peter but he was also the driver. Jim was pronounced dead on arrival in hospital. Poor old Pat suffered a scare. The pills provided by Peter the Chessman helped to exacerbate her condition. She ended up in hospital in intensive care. The only relative, a son who had not been in touch for years, made some noises, asked a lot of questions. Mainly about house prices in the area. He booked himself into a hotel. The house next door would remain empty for the foreseeable future and that suited the Chessman down to the ground. One more tomorrow evening, Idris McQueen. Shoe mogul with nearly one hundred outlets would be doing his last soft shoe shuffle.

Evan slept fitfully, as did Amber. Mike didn't sleep at all but the Chessman had no problem at all. He had lovely dreams: money, cars, servants, yachts and his new life was coming towards him at a rate of knots and even that wasn't fast enough.

CHAPTER 21

Amber was wrong, tomorrow did come just one second past midnight, like it did every day. Mike was the first to arrive in the office; nearly gave Amber a heart attack. Evan and Charlie arrived simultaneously and it was still only half eight.

"Warrants in order Amber?" said Evan.

"Mike's got them," Amber replied.

"So, we're ready to roll," said Evan.

"And me," said Charlie.

"Stay and keep Amber company. You might be needed somewhere along the line," said Mike.

"Irish Mick ready with the back-up Evan?"

"He is Mike."

"Tell him to get there, at the fabrication place just after nine, not before."

Evan did and they left, Mike driving the BMW. Two hundred yards from the workshop, they passed two unmarked police cars. One contained Mick, one plain clothes and two uniformed officers. The other, two uniformed and one plain. Mike stopped his car, "Morning Mick."

"Top of the morning to you squire," replied Mick.

Mike was hardly the country gentleman but then who was around here.

"You follow me, the other car to remain until we call them, preferably out of sight," said Mike.

"Count it as done," Mick said, giving the necessary instructions to the other car.

They pulled up outside. Thankfully it wasn't raining. Very cold and frosty but no rain. Mike was the first through followed by Evan and Mick. The other three remained outside.

"Mr Eastern, we have a warrant to search these premises. We are acting on information received about stolen goods. In this connection we need to have a talk with you down at the station. You are not under arrest and do not need a lawyer," Mike said watching Eastern carefully. He seemed completely unperturbed.

"This is nonsense, complete bullshit. Stolen goods? Are you people so fucking stupid? Go ahead; ask your lousy questions, I've nothing to hide."

"As I have already stated Mr Eastern, we will talk down town. Please try and remain calm and we will clear up this whole thing fast," said Mike.

"So who has sold you lot this pack of lies?" said Eastern now in control of himself.

"We are not at liberty to divulge our source," said Mike.

"Of course you're not. What a bloody waste of time, mainly yours," said Eastern,

Work had stopped; everyone was intent on finding out what was going on.

"I know my rights, Officer, why the hell are you hustling me? Stolen goods? We both know it's hogwash," said Eastern. "I am not moving, ask your questions, go ahead, let's just get on with it."

"You're right I suppose. We probably got off on the wrong foot Mr Eastern. Evan, could you get everyone out in the yard and start the search."

"Are you sure Mike?" asked Evan. "Would you mind staying with me Mick and take some notes?"

"Will do," said Mick, closing the door after Evan.

"What exactly do you make here? I can see you make boxes, but where do the pipes come into it? Like that one in the corner?"

"Why you interested Officer?" said Eastern.

"Curious, that's all Mr Eastern. I'm trying to make small talk, pass a bit of time."

"Well, these particular two-inch diameter pipes in old money were used for an old boiler contract. You see they are used horizontally, like this," Eastern said, picking up the two-foot length of steel.

"Don't threaten us Eastern," said Mike.

"Drop the pipe, arsehole," added Mick.

"I wasn't threatening anybody. I was just demonstrating how we fitted these pipes," said Eastern, dropping the pipe onto the desk.

"Threatening an officer with intent to harm, resisting arrest, blah blah blah," said Mick. "Empty your pockets onto the desk and then turn around please, Mr Eastern."

Eastern did as he was told. These two were crazy. He was getting scared. Mick handcuffed Eastern and then bagged the pipe in a bin bag that was lying around.

"Thank God he missed me with that swing; fortunately there were two of us to restrain him but he's very dangerous; I suggest before you interview the nutter, you let him cool off in the cells for an hour or two."

"And all we wanted was a nice quiet talk and we end up in a war zone," said Mick pushing over a chair and wiping the desk clean with one of his massive hands.

"I suggest you say nothing Mr Eastern; things could only get worse, much worse. Do you understand what I'm saying?" said Mike.

Eastern nodded; he would complain via his lawyer to the highest pig that was available. These two thugs shouldn't be walking the streets of Cardiff, they should be in Guantanamo Bay or the likes.

"What the hell happened in there?" asked Evan, when they led Eastern out.

"Bastard got nasty, took a swing at Mike with this here steel pipe; we managed to restrain him. Best take a picture or two in there before you search through," said Mick to his old friend and partner.

"He doesn't look the type," said Evan.

"No, he doesn't," said Mick.

And he probably isn't, thought Evan. Photos were taken and after Mick and Evan had left for their various destinations, Mike searched the offices and Eastern's car. As he expected, he found nothing and the other officers hadn't turned up anything remotely looking like the letter opener. Evan left with a couple of constables for Eastern's house.

It was just past eleven when Evan made his call. It was more bad news and Mike for the first time that day was worried.

"Shit Evan. Have you checked the desk with a microscope?"

" Mike, I tell you it's not here."

"Did you take out the draws, Evan?"

"Of course we did Mike, there are no hidden compartments. Nothing Mike, just a few bills, some stationery equipment, the usual stuff but no, I repeat, no bloody letter opener. We got problems Mike. I can't count the number of laws we've contravened."

"Are you finished then Evan?"

"Yes, Mike, I think we're finished in every which way."

"All right Evan, send the boys back. I'm coming over and I'll contact Charlie to come down too."

"Thanks Boys, you can get back to your station now," said Mike.

"Sorry, we couldn't find anything," said one of the plain clothes boys.

"Thanks anyway."

Mike told the workforce that they could resume, thanked them for co-operating and then phoned Charlie telling him to get down to Eastern's house. They stood around the desk like three stooges awaiting their cue from their puppet master but no help was forthcoming from any quarter.

"Have you told Mick our news?"

"I have Mike," said Evan, "he can't hold Eastern much longer without saying something to him. Do you think his wife contacted him Mike? He seemed pretty sure of himself."

"Possibly Evan, but I just don't see it. She came over as someone who wanted to do her ex no favours to say the least."

Mike and Charlie checked the drawers again and again. Evan didn't bother, he was resigned to the fact that they had lucked out and were now facing a lousy future.

"Let's turn it upside down Evan, look underneath."

"Already done it Mike, I tell you it's not here. I know you don't want to hear it but it's just not here, period."

"Nice desk," said Charlie, "lovely thick black leather; let me speak to Amber first then maybe I have the solution to all our problems."

Mike shrugged his shoulders and sat on the desk, lighting up a cigarette and blowing smoke bubbles at Charlie while he talked to Amber.

"Did I tell you Mike that we found over eighty porn videos? The dirty bugger. That's it!" shouted Charlie excitedly, "the leather baize on the desk was a greenish colour with a gold border when that photo of the desk that Amber has was shot."

"And now it's black with no border," said Evan.

Mike jumped off the desk. "Take a picture Evan, two, three, different angles."

"Fine," said Mike, "Go ahead Charlie, you've got a better touch than us. Here you are, use this," and Mike handed Charlie his knife.

Starting at one corner, Charlie started peeling back the leather from the two-inch thick mahogany desktop. A third of the way down and nothing untoward. Charlie started on the bottom half peeling the leather upwards towards the centre. Just six inches were exposed before he stopped and pointed. "Eureka!" he shouted. Mike and Evan strained their eyes and could just make out the faint lines of a nine by two inch oblong shape. Charlie pointed to the area. "More pictures please." Evan obliged.

"That's tight," said Evan.

"If he uses it he does not use a knife to prise it open," said Mike.

Charlie bent over the desk, his eyes just a few inches above the desktop. For a full two minutes, he remained in that position before rising and rubbing his hands together. Like a top surgeon, Charlie held out his hands and said, "Gloves please." Evan helped Charlie into them.

"There's some Blu Tack in one of those drawers Mike, I think the middle one. Can you get me two large pieces and roll them into balls."

When Mike had found the Blu Tack and rolled the two pieces as requested, he handed them to Charlie who placed the pieces at each end of the oblong; with a hand on each piece he lifted the wooden lid, and exposed the contents. Charlie stepped back and bowed. Without looking at each other, as if by telepathy, Mike and Evan started clapping. Evan's phone rang; it was Mick.

"My Super's telling me to let him go, I've no choice. Sorry Evan."

"Go back in Mick. We've just this second struck gold. We've hit the mother load. Book the bastard for the robbery. Let him call a lawyer if he wishes but advise him that it's in his own interests not to until he talks to us. We will be there in ten minutes."

More photos were taken, the letter opener bagged, room locked and cordoned off with tape and they left, dancing all the way to their cars.

"Can I sit in on the interview?" Mick asked

"It's your case Mick," said Mike.

"Has he called for a lawyer yet Mick?" asked Evan.

"Funnily enough he hasn't. He's just having a cheese and tomato sandwich with a coffee, which he requested, and I got for him. He knows we got something but I think he's still hoping it will all go away."

"All the equipment in place?"

"It is. He should be finished by now, eating I mean," added Mick.

"Any chance of a coffee?" asked Evan.

"On its way to the interview room," answered Mick.

The interview room had one table and five chairs on one side of the table. Bill Eastern sat; an empty chair next to him. The other three chairs were now occupied by the three detectives.

"Hi Bill, hope you enjoyed your sandwich," said Evan.

Eastern didn't answer.

"As you can see Bill, there's a chair for your brief, but may I suggest you listen and answer us truthfully – all off the record of course – before requesting your solicitor. That way we can come to some decent arrangement, which will suit us both. Is that clear Bill?" said Mike.

No answer.

"Don't make this difficult for yourself Bill. Give yourself a break and listen," said Evan.

Evan produced the letter opener and placed it in front of Eastern. It was still in its plastic police pouch.

"Do you recognise it Bill?" said Evan. "Your fingerprints are on it. They match the ones on the steel bar we bagged this morning," Mike lied.

"Look Bill," Evan said, "we know about Edith, Williams (Walliams) Speedo. We're picking them up tonight. No more super yachts, Bentleys, million-pound mansions for them. They've a lot to lose. Millions and I mean literally millions. But there is a problem: they are in Spain, they've no fingerprints anywhere, they can afford the best lawyers and there's three of them."

"Do you have anything to say Bill?" said Mick. Mike sipped his coffee. It was disgusting. He felt like a cigarette but that was out of the question. Still nothing from Bill Eastern.

"I'm going out for a sec to get the documents," said Mike standing up. Evan didn't have a clue about any documents.

Mike went outside and rang Amber. Gave her instructions and waited, enjoying a ciggie and watching all the pretty girls going about their business. Five minutes passed and Amber rang back.

Mike walked back in, walked over to the nearest desk and grabbed a bunch of papers from an in tray. He then took an empty folder from the adjacent desk and filled it with the documents he'd already grabbed.

Mike walked back in. "Sorry about that. It took me a while to get them off the Super. This is it Bill; scratch our back and we will scratch yours. Statements from your ex June, your sons Fred and Barry, Doctor Simpson, your bank managers. You will come out of clink ten years older. No business, no money. We're freezing all that. No home. We will get back one million pounds in today's money one way or the other and you will have at least three people waiting for you when you come out making sure you keep to the straight and narrow. No exes on the stand, no sons, no others and a stretch of say four, five. You could be out in two, with a business and have money.

"It's up to you Bill," Mike said opening the folder and extracting a document, which he passed on to Evan. Evan read it carefully. It was quite interesting; a toiletries requisition form. Evan handed it to Mick taking a second document offered by Mike. This had something to do with fire alarms and stations.

"Do you agree now Evan?" said Mike. "I think it's time we put everything on record. That way this bonzo could get a fifteen year holiday at her Maj's expense."

Evan wanted to laugh, but managed to look extremely thoughtful, as if in a great dilemma.

"I'm with you, let him have both barrels." And with that, he passed the Fire Precaution Notice to Mick who broke and started laughing as soon as he realised what it was.

"Christ, Man. Where did you get this information? It's dynamite," said Mick to Mike.

"I'm fed up with just fire fighting, Mick, that says it all."

"It sure does that," said Mick.

"Okay, let's see: the time is 1308 hours, Wednesday, the fifth of

December. Present are Detective Inspector Mick Maloney, Detective Inspector Evan Jones, Detective Inspector Mikhail...." but was interrupted by Eastern.

"Can you switch it off? I want to talk."

"Too late Billy Boy," said Mike, but switched off the tape recorder anyway.

"Two years, no more. No touching anything I own. I give you the works but I want guarantees and everything through my lawyer."

"There are no guarantees. We will recommend and they will listen, especially if we get the Chief Constable to put a word in but now, off the record, we need to know everything, so we can get the ball rolling in Malaga," said Evan.

Eastern spilled his guts. There were four people involved but Speedo wasn't one of them. The fourth was a good friend of Speedo's, a James Franklin, who two weeks after the robbery accidently drowned in the Taff.

"According to the coroner, Franklin was drunk, slipped and banged his head on a stone before tumbling down the embankment and drowning. He left no Will and no money was recovered from his house, which he rented from the council. All he left was a cheap watch, cheaper suits and an old Audi, which he kept in pristine condition. His only relative, a daughter, inherited. She lives somewhere up north, Sunderland, I think."

"How was the money divided, Bill?" Mick asked.

"Me, Edith and James got eighty grand each, ten per cent. We were informed that there was one point five million in the bank. Anyway, I got eighty k, the Whistler over half a million, a lot of money then, a lot now."

"Let's get back to Franklin a mo. Were you and he friends, Bill?" Mick asked.

"I knew him. Played snooker a few times, had a drink now and then together. Not best buddies but, yes, I would say he was a friend."

"So what did he do with his money Bill?" Mick asked.

"I know what he was planning to do," said Bill.

"What?" asked Mick, who wasn't letting this Franklin business lie down.

"Buy a garage in Sunderland. He was a great mechanic and driver and put down a deposit on a small house for him and his daughter."

"So you're not sure whether he achieved his dream?" said Mick.

"He didn't. I spoke to his daughter at the funeral. Had to lend her twenty quid to get back home. She said she'd send me the money. Anyway, she never has."

"Where we going with this Mick?" Evan asked.

"First Evan, I want to know what Bill thinks really happened to Franklin."

"I think Speedo helped him drown and stole the money," said Eastern.

"I'm inclined to agree with Bill on this Evan, you have a theory?"

"Nope, sounds about right. You Mike?"

"I'd take it further: Speedo finds out about the robbery, probably from Franklin, so he sets about blackmailing Williams. Williams promises Speedo money if he disposes of Franklin but gives him say twenty grand up front. Williams knows that if Speedo kills Franklin then he has something on Speedo. Speedo kills Franklin and takes the money but not before Speedo extracts some more from Williams and now takes Franklin's place in the gang. They now stick together because neither trusts the other for him to be out of sight for too long."

"I would say that is as near as we can get at this moment, but I think that our boys, what with DNA and modern technology can pin Speedo with a murder rap," said Evan.

"We can stop Speedo in his tracks," said Mick feeling that he was just about reaching the high point of his illustrious police career.

"Go on Bill, tell us the rest. How you got in, who drove, what type of vehicle was used. Where you went afterwards and just for me," said Evan, "please tell me why you pocketed the letter opener."

It took another two hours to get the lot. No one was unduly surprised when Bill told them that he took the opener as a souvenir. It was that simple.

"Are we done now?" Eastern asked.

"Unfortunately, Bill, we're not. You're going to have to say the same stuff, including the Franklin bit for the tape. Obviously, you can have your lawyer present, then we will get it typed for you to read and sign," said Evan.

"No Detective. I will sit down and write out my statement in long hand. You can then type it out after we correct any spelling mistakes and I sign, that is assuming that at the least a Chief Superintendent comes and tells me that he is going into bat for me, re the two years. I do not want a lawyer present." Eastern said.

"That's not the way it's done Bill," said Mick.

"Maybe, but that's the way it will be done. My Christ, what do you people want? I've handed you on a plate two bank robbers and a bloody murderer and something special just for you, Detective Karetzi."

Mike looked up at Eastern. Yes, he did have something. He's got an ace. It had to be something to do with his father's death, although it could be anything.

"Have it your way," said Mick, ushering Mike and Evan out.

"Hey, I want the toilet, a quarter pounder with cheese and fries, nuggets and a drink. Anything except shitty police coffee," shouted Eastern.

"This isn't the fucking Ritz," Mick shouted back.

"But he's spot on about the coffee," Mike said.

"I know," said Mick, "that's why I never drink the bloody stuff. I just give it to my enemies."

"And your friends Mick?" said Evan.

"I give them a refill," said Mick.

Mike took out a tenner. "Get the bugger something to eat."

Mick waved it away. "I'll deal with it Mike. Now we need to talk to Bateman, my Super, not the easiest of people but he's fair if bloody slow and indecisive. Do we agree, before we knock on the door, with our friend in there, two, three years? To me it's a good deal. I mean no-one got hurt, either in physical or monetary terms. Only a bank and look at the mess these people have created. The losses are in millions not thousands," said Mick.

Both Evan and Mike nodded. Mick knocked and entered. "Chief Super's on the phone. He wants five minutes," said Mick.

"All right, let's get our man CCC on it. I'll speak to Amber and explain she can speak to the Chief and hopefully he will agree and contact Bateman. The Chief can then talk to the CPS and whoever else needs to be party to our agreement with Eastern. The clock keeps ticking and we should be heading for Swansea soon," said Mike.

"How many hours in a day Mick?" Evan asked.

"Don't ask me. I'm just a thick Irishman but I can tell you that you don't seem to have enough."

Evan's phone rang. It was the Chief Constable explaining to Evan that they, the police, and he, the Chief Constable, do not make deals with known criminals under any circumstances, although all three detectives who could hear the Chief ranting, knew otherwise.

Evan was stuttering. He was holding the phone a foot from his ear and all Evan could say was "I understand Sir but, I agree but, but..." The 'buts' were winning hands down until Mike requisitioned the phone and listened for two seconds before calmly stating that Special Detective Inspective Mikhail Karetzi was now on the phone as Special Detective Inspector Evan Jones was suddenly indisposed. The chief had gone quiet; he was probably trying for a second wind.

"Chief, believe me, everybody in this station knows what's going on, and it's quite possible that our friend Eastern could squirm out of it and walk. Morale would plunge and the papers, especially Reed, would call us incompetent and worse. I mean, we solve a burglary, a national one involving big money in a financial institution, a murder and who knows what else. We'd be the laughing stock of all police regions up and down the country, the British Isles."

"Let him walk, Mick," Mike said. "There's no deal we can do and Evan, if you can get Amber and tell them to lay off Walliams and Edith or whatever she calls herself and that psycho Speedo."

"That's fucking ridiculous Mike," said Mick, not moving. This was a game if they didn't win he reckoned Evan would quit. He knew his ex-partner well enough to see what was going on in his mind.

"So," the Chief Constable said, "Did I make myself clear?"

"Yes Sir, you did. We are sorry to disturb you. We are dealing with the situation at this very moment."

The door opened to the Super's office and Mick went in. The Chief Constable carried on, "That's the way it goes sometimes, Detective, you can't win them all."

"He'll be out in about two minutes Sir. I'd better go and make sure he doesn't have any problems and Detective Jones is onto the police in Malaga, making sure they don't make any waves."

Just then, the door opened and Mick came out, thumbs up in triumph.

"Chief, before I go, may I say a few words off the record?" and before he could answer Mike carried on. "Chief, with all due respect, every officer here is on the phone to other departments to friends, to God knows who. Eastern walking will be big news. You have made a very big mistake. At least one murderer is getting away because of your high principles. It's a pity. Never mind, you will have my resignation in the morning. Now I'm going to try and finish off the Chessman. Let's hope he doesn't want a deal; say, only convict him on one murder instead of a dozen." And with that, Mike said goodbye and goodnight before closing the phone.

The Chief looked at Emma who was sitting opposite him on the other side of his desk. She smiled but the way she was smiling made the chief uncomfortable.

"We can't make deals, Emma."

"We do, every day of our lives, Clive – compromises from big things to little things. We do them automatically."

"It's not right Emma. We must uphold the Law, otherwise what do we have? We have murderers walking the streets and no maverick detectives interested or cunning enough to get them."

"Karetzi is probably one of the finest detectives in the UK and Jones complements him perfectly. For Christ's sake, Clive it's not even their case and they solve it thirty years later. And think about our relationship."

"What's wrong with our relationship Emma? They have seen the photos, probably as you rightly say, commissioned them."

"Get on the phone Clive. That guy resigns, others follow. The papers get hold of it through them in a roundabout way and you will be retired prematurely and our relationship will be history. For crying out loud Clive, can't you see what mayhem Karetzi will create and we, especially you, Clive, will be in the centre."

The Chief dialled Evan's number. Mike still had the phone. He was sitting on the toilet having a fag. Mick's boss Bateman was willing to have a word with Eastern and make a deal but needed the Chief Constable's authorisation. He would have gone ahead if the Chief constable wasn't involved and fought his corner later.

"Is that you Detective Jones?"

"No Sir, it's Karetzi."

"Have you released this Eastern chap?"

"No Sir."

"Why?"

"I don't know Sir; the boys here are making life difficult. They don't want him to walk and keep bringing obstacles in our way."

"Where's Jones?"

"I don't know Chief. He got a little upset and I haven't seen him since I last spoke to you."

"I've thought it over Karetzi. We can't let him walk, for whatever reason. Tell him we will do four."

"Four what Sir?"

"Years. That's the deal."

"Not for him Sir, he's been promised two."

"Who did the promising Detective?"

"I did Sir, but I'm resigning tonight and any promises I made will become null and void. I'll pass it on to Evan, I mean Detective Jones, Sir. He made no promises but I think he's also of the mind to resign. However, they have a good man here, a D.I. Maloney who was to take over the case when we had completed our part. He's good Chief. You can trust him."

"Three years. I'll try for three years and that is contrary to my principles and instincts. Three years. He'll serve one and a half and Karetzi, you and Jones are good detectives and good men. Don't resign. Get this fucking Chessman for me. For all of us."

"Thirty months, Sir. Maybe we can swing that with Eastern. It will be a feather in the cap for your force Sir."

"It's not my force; it's the people's force. I'm just a loyal servant. Two and a half is agreed but never mind, I'll give Chief Superintendent Bateman a call. Better still, ask him to ring me soonest and goodnight Detective, remember time is running out and tell Jones, 'good work'."

"Good work Sir?"

"Yes, I commend both of you on your good work."

"Thank you Sir, and goodnight."

Mike finished his cigarette and dumped it in the toilet before flushing. It was now gone four. Mike opened the toilet door and headed for the basins to wash his hands and splash some water over his head. He came face to face with a very pretty policewoman, who after eyeing Mike up and down, told him the obvious: he was in the 'Ladies'.

"Thank God for that. If all men started looking as good as you, I would be voting for Gay rights in the next election."

"I'm Jane," she said and quickly added, "Please don't tell me you're Tarzan."

"No Jane, I'm his twin brother Mikhail."

"A comedian eh? Can you tell me what you are doing in here?"

"Having a cigarette."

"Are you one of us, I mean the police?"

"I am. Special Detective Inspector Mikhail Karetzi at your service."

"I've heard of you, they call you 'crazy' don't they?" said Jane.

"Do I look crazy to you Jane?"

"Well, you are in the wrong toilets."

"So you say. Would you like to go out for a drink some time?"

"I don't think so, I'm engaged."

"So was that toilet over there, until I came out!" Mike said, brushing past her and out through the main toilet block door. Cute but crazy and a mite too old, thought Jane. She was only just twenty.

"Where have you been Mike, we've looked all over for you."

"In the 'Ladies' Evan, speaking to our Chief, who has now seen reason and will deal at thirty months. Mick, can you get your Super to give him a bell? I've got to see Eastern again," said Mike. "Won't be a tick, Evan."

"Okay, Bill. I see you got your quarter pounder meal. I think our boys are ready to deal at two and a half. Don't speak, just stick to your guns and don't say anything else. Got it? I'm paying you in advance for the information you're holding. That's for my ears only. Don't fuck me about Bill."

"My statement's ready. It's being typed at this very moment, so I'm told," said Eastern to Chief Superintendent Bateman.

"Three years, that's the best we can do," said Bateman.

"Please Sir, do not waste any of your precious time with unworkable deals. I said two years, that's twenty-four months. Seven hundred and thirty days. I can't work out the hours without a calculator; do you think you could provide one?"

"There's no need," said the Chief. "My last offer is two and a half years, that's thirty months or if my maths is correct nine hundred and twelve and a half days. Like you, Mr Eastern, I would need a calculator to work out the hours, but I can tell you that you would only serve fifteen months. Now that's not too long, is it, Mr Eastern?"

"Three months too long Chief. I will do a year, no more. Now that's plain enough isn't it Chief?"

"I'm going to turn and walk away, Mr Eastern. Please see sense and accept these terms, it's the best we can do, or will do."

"In that case goodnight Chief."

Mike, Evan and Mick stood behind the Chief. Mr Winfield sat alongside his client acting as his lawyer. He'd never seen such a circus in his life and was approaching sixty.

"Can you understand my client is not moving? Not one day past two years," said Winfield.

"It's two and half," said an animated Chief. "Can't you understand Mr Winfield, I can't go any further, it's a great deal."

Winfield whispered in Eastern's ear. He pleaded with him to accept. At exactly five, Eastern stood. "Eighteen months, that's the deal. I want no more than eighteen or you can charge me now and I'll live with the consequences and so will you Chief. Remember I gave you the opportunity. You have four witnesses to the fact."

"Give me a moment," the Chief said and walked out. Mike, Mick and Evan followed like puppies.

"A fat lot of good you lot were in there. Christ Mick, you of all people should have said something and now that lunatic wants to deal at eighteen, it will be twelve next. I'm not ringing the Chief

Constable again, what can I say?"

"May I speak Chief?"

"Yes D.I. um?"

"It's Karetzi, Sir.

"Well, what do you want to say?"

"It's two years Chief. Just agree. I'm sure the Chief Constable will agree. Just agree, make a decision either way but for Christ's sake let logic prevail and agree the two years."

"He's talking one and a half. He's not to be trusted Detective, that's the problem."

"Can I deal on your behalf?"

"And what do you expect to achieve?"

"The two-year deal Sir and an out of this place so that we can pursue other matters very close to our hearts."

"Do you have a date Detective?"

"Yes Sir, a date with destiny. We are in the middle of a serial killer maelstrom."

"A maelstrom, Detective?"

"Yes Sir."

"You're crazy Detective. Maelstrom?"

"I am Sir," said Mike.

"He is Sir," said Evan.

"Okay Mr Crazy, let's go back in and see how crazy you really are," said the Chief.

"Mr Winfield, would you kindly advise your client Mr Eastern, that we agree two years. Isn't that so Chief?"

"That is so D.I. Karetzi."

"We have a deal, D.I. Karetzi. I will now sign my statement. My witness to my signature and to the conversation we have just had is my lawyer Mr George Winfield." Bill Eastern then signed.

"It's your case now Mick. Get hold of the police in Malaga and good luck. We're off to Swansea," said Evan. They shook hands. Evan left the BMW at the station and travelled down to Swansea in Mike's.

They came: the tall, the short, fat, and thin. The only thing they had in common was greed. Everyone filled in the form before leaving with their free recorder/player. Everyone was on tape. Thirty-seven came; four didn't. Three of the thirty-seven were left-handed but only one fit the bill. The other two were only five foot two or three.

"So we're left with five," said Charlie.

"Yep, the four who didn't turn up and Mr Alan Ainsworthy," said Evan.

"It's only half eight," said Mike. "Why don't we ring Amber, get the addresses of the four remaining suspects and give them a visit."

"On what pretext?" asked Evan.

"Enquiries into something, Evan," said Mike. "I don't know. How about a missing person last seen nearby their house?" said Mike.

"Not possible. They will expect us to hit all the houses in their area, not just theirs," said Evan.

"Okay, how about noise pollution, a complaint from a neighbour or some busybody?" said Charlie.

"Let's go for it. Who cares as long as we get in and either eliminate or strike lucky."

The first house was only five minutes away. The ruse worked; a man, aged about fifty, opened the door. Evan explained why they were there and they were invited in. The pair of detectives went through the concocted rubbish about noise pollution. Obviously, the couple insisted that they had had no parties and the television was never loud and that they were usually in bed by ten. The husband was a milkman and was up at the crack of dawn. It was not surprising to note that the man was right-handed and could be eliminated from their list.

The second house they visited was only a couple of hundred yards from the first. Again, they had no problem entering and no problem eliminating the potential suspect even though he was left-handed, because his right leg was in plaster and had been for two weeks. Prior to that, he had been in hospital for nearly ten days.

"That leaves us with three: Ainsworthy, James and Swift. We've seen Ainsworthy and I think it's too late to go knocking on people's doors. The other two will have to wait until tomorrow night. It won't make much difference," said Evan.

"I guess you're right Evan. It's been a long day. The others can wait till tomorrow. I think we've got everything under control – the good people of Wales can sleep peacefully tonight," said Mike, who was very wrong.

Five minutes after setting off from Swansea the Chessman had garrotted the shoe magnate Idris McQueen with a pair of shoelaces. It had been easy. At half past nine, McQueen had left his office for home. The Chessman had done his homework. It took around half an hour for McQueen to reach his electronically gated mansion but the Chessman made it in twenty minutes. First, he hid the car down the avenue and then he disabled the automatic gate-opening device before he himself hid nearby awaiting his prey.

About his person, he carried a heavy wrench. Mr McQueen arrived and on finding that the automatic door would not open for him to drive through in his Bentley, he got out of the car to see what was wrong. The broken gate mechanism was the least of his problems. A blow to the head with the wrench brought him to his knees and the rest was simplicity itself.

The Chessman left a calling card, the severed head of a chess queen and a crumpled letter, which he put in McQueen's pocket. The chess piece he put into McQueen's right shoe. He then returned to Cardiff and posted the half dozen letters he had on him.

It was now time to go home. Five minutes out and he passed Mike's car going in the opposite direction. As they pulled up at the police station to drop off Evan so that he could pick up the BMW and go home, the call arrived. It was bad news. Another body, another chessman victim.

Evan gave Mike the address and told him he'd go in the Beamer. Mike sped off. After calling Edna to tell her he would be very late, Evan followed, lights flashing, siren on. It took Mike fourteen minutes, Evan twenty.

"Do we know who this is?" said Mike to Inspector Davies who was organising everything.

"Yes, an Idris McQueen. That is or was his house. Shoe factory owner with a hundred retail outlets."

"Any idea why he got out of his car? Surely those gates open electronically," said Mike.

"They should but my guess is that our killer tampered with them because they are not working and McQueen got out to see why they weren't working and bop, blunt instrument to the head and then strangled with this pair of laces tied in the middle." D.I. Davies added that they had found a chess piece or part of a chess piece in McQueen's shoe. Apart from a wallet full of credit cards and over two hundred pounds in cash, there was a letter addressed to Mr McQueen.

"How many men do you have here, D.I. Davies?"

"Five," replied D.I. Davies.

"This is a very expensive area. Only about eight, no nine houses in the avenue. I want three of your boys to do a house to house. Have they seen any strange cars, anyone walking around; you know what we're looking for. No one is going to walk here and no buses pass by. The nearest station is three odd miles away," said Mike.

"It's gone eleven," said Davies. These type of people don't take too kindly to being disturbed at this time of night."

"I guess not Detective Davies but they won't take too kindly to getting murdered by some madman. Think about it. They all have massive drives and garages. Not a car in sight in the whole of the road. Someone in these houses, a servant, kids, someone must have noticed a new car to the area parked somewhere in this street," said Mike.

"You're in charge. I'll get right on to it," said D.I. Davies.

"Thank you," said Mike.

"What have we got Mike?" said Evan on arrival. Mike told him everything he knew and showed the letter. The same one the others had received; different amount.

"How long Mike?"

"According to him," Mike said pointing to a guy in a white coat, "one and a half hours max."

"About half nine then, Mike," said Evan.

"Why was the guy carrying around the letter Evan?"

"But was he, Mike? Or was it planted by the Chessman, a message of some kind?"

"Possibly misdirection Evan."

"Can't agree there Mike. It means something to him, to us, to someone," said Evan.

"Oh shit," said Mike.

"What now?" said Evan.

"The Chief Constable has just arrived," said Mike.

"Good evening Chief," said Evan and Mike.

"Good evening to you all. Thought I'd find you two down here. I understand we have another Chessman victim," said the Chief.

"Yes Sir. A Mr Idris McQueen. A very rich and prominent citizen by all accounts," said Evan who then proceeded to tell the Chief everything they knew about the murder.

"Who's with the family?" asked the Chief, looking towards the mansion.

"Doctor, brother and friends," said Mike.

"This letter is significant, isn't it?" said the Chief.

"We think so Sir, but we can't work out why," said Evan.

"It's a warning to the others," said the Chief.

"You mean pay up when I tell you because I can get you anytime, anywhere I feel like. Just like I got Mr McQueen at home," added Evan.

"Something along those lines. He knows they will read about it tomorrow and will ask questions which we the guardians of the law must answer. I've had a couple of complaints from this street. I understand you're doing a door-to-door looking for witnesses, etc.," said the Chief.

"Yes Sir. I thought it might come to nothing but keeping up the good folks an extra half an hour or so is hardly criminal," said Mike.

"I agree," said the Chief.

"You agree?" said Mike.

"Yes, you heard me the first time, I agree."

By midnight, all except for D.I. Davies had returned. Nobody saw anything. Fifteen minutes later an exasperated detective turned up with an old tramp in tow.

"I found this poor beggar going through some bins. I think he knows something but he's a little drunk or mad or both."

All three, the Chief, Mike and Evan stepped back. The poor old guy stank to high heaven.

"I've done nothing wrong guv," he said, looking at the Chief. "What's happening here? I didn't do anything. I was just walking and minding my own business."

"What's your name and where do you live?" asked Evan.

"It's Everard."

"And your first name?"

"That's it, Everard, Everard Entwistle."

"Where do you live?" asked Evan.

"Here, there, everywhere."

"So you're homeless?" said Evan.

Everard just looked at them.

"My Christ. It's the one-eyed leading the blind in this bloody street. I'll leave him to you," and with that the Chief was gone.

"Right Everard, do you smoke?" asked Mike.

"When I have some," said Everard. Mike handed him a cigarette, which he lit for him.

"Now Everard, this is very important, what were you doing in this street?"

"It's Wednesday," said Everard.

"Yes, it is," said Mike, "so why were you here?"

"I told you it's Wednesday, I come every Wednesday night."

"Why Everard?"

"Because tomorrow is Thursday."

"Okay, tonight's Wednesday, tomorrow is Thursday. So what?"

"The rich people put out their bins on Wednesday for collection in the morning."

"I see. You look through the bins for drink, food and whatever else catches your fancy," said D.I. Davies.

"Good. That's logical for a man in your position, Everard. We have no gripe with that, do we Detectives?" said Mike.

"Nothing wrong with that," said Evan.

"Nothing at all," said D.I. Davies.

"About two, two and a half hours ago, were you here?" asked Mike.

"Yes, I guess so. I don't have a watch but I'm usually here about seven. I start at the end when the bins start coming out and I work up the street and cross coming back down," said Everard.

"How do you carry the stuff you find?" said D.I. Davies.

"In my case," said Everard. "It has wheels. It's easy to pull along. I'm over seventy you know," said Everard.

"You had no case when I found you," said D.I. Davies.

"I hid it when I saw the coppers coming down the road. I wasn't stealing just taking things people don't want any more."

"There's no problem there, we're not interested in that," said Evan. "Did you see anybody during your walk, Everard, any person or vehicle?"

"Yes, I saw the lady from No 2. She came in her car and I saw a man in black clothes, he was running up the street. I think maybe he was jogging; he was quite fast and he had a hat on, a woollen type, black too. Maybe for the cold."

"Where did he go Everard?" asked Mike.

"Don't know, he just disappeared," said Everard.

"Which way was he running: up this way or going down the other way?" asked Mike.

"Coming up this way. I saw him but he didn't see me 'cause I hid behind a tree until he passed me, then I carried on. I knows that the guy with the brown car, that one always comes home at a certain time, so I move faster down the street, not looking into some bins in case I get caught," said Everard.

"And no cars or motorbikes except for the lady in No 2. Is that correct Everard?"

"There was a car down there, about a hundred or so yards under some bushes, very hard to see it but nothing gets past me you know. I might be seventy but I'm not blind you know," said Everard.

"Show us exactly where," said Mike. Keeping downwind of Everard, they walked to the spot where the old man had spied the car. Unfortunately, it was hard standing, completely sheltered by two trees and a bush.

"It was a medium sized car, dark blue or possibly black. Didn't notice the make, sorry."

"You've been helpful enough my friend," said Mike. Mike took D.I. Davies aside.

"Can you do me a big favour detective?"

"If I can, I will," said D.I. Davies.

"Get the old boy back to the nick. Get him to have a shower and a shave. Get him some breakfast and find him some kind of place where he can stay for a couple of days. You know the type of place I'm talking about," and Mike went into his trouser pocket and counted his money. Evan walked over, wondering what was going on.

"Here's one twenty. Buy the guy some clothes," said Mike. Evan took out his wallet. "Add that," he said, giving D.I. Davies another fifty.

"I'll round it up to two hundred," said D.I. Davies.

Mike walked back to Everard and gave him the remaining cigarettes in his pack less one, which he lit up and smoked. D.I. Davies had gone for a car. They loaded Everard in the back. The car was just about to go when Mike tapped the driver's window. D.I. Davies wound it down. "Don't forget Mr Entwistle's suitcase, and thanks."

"No, I thank you D.I. Karetzi. That's a decent thing you were doing for our friend back there. We could all end up like him, he deserves a break."

As they walked back towards the crime scene Evan wondered. He wondered what went on in his partner's head; he was human after all, but he still wasn't meeting Jasmine. That was for sure.

"Anything else for us here Evan?"

"I doubt it Mike. We know who did it. Let's get back to the office. Amber will probably be up working on something or other and having a meal or two in between working," said Evan.

"That's reminds me, Evan. Have we had anything to eat today?" said Mike, his stomach rumbling.

"At least I had some breakfast, but it's nearly bloody breakfast time again," said Evan looking at his watch. It was actually twenty past one.

"So," Amber said, "in about six hours the Swansea boys will hit the last three and ascertain where they were last night between the hours of eight and eleven. They will remain with the occupants until they had thoroughly checked any alibis they might have. They will also check their cars, etc. They will report here soonest. Now do you boys want an early breakfast? The Amber special, or do I have to eat the lot myself?"

"Why are we waiting until eight?" said Mike, "Why not do them tonight? We're wasting time!"

"There's a good chance it's none of them, you both know that."

"Do we have anyone else? No, we don't and that's something

else you both know," said Amber. "Now I am going to make breakfast and you two can talk some sense to each other. You're no use as you are, all gung ho and crazy."

"She's got a fair point Mike. It's all guesswork, coincidental, gut feelings, eliminations, Mike. I'm beginning to think that it's not one of the three."

"Come on Evan, even if we're wrong, what the hell do we lose? We eliminate another three."

"But not before we can check their alibis and we can't do that until the earliest nine o'clock, can we Mike?"

"No we can't Evan," said Mike, his eyes closing.

The aroma of food brought Mike round. They all ate heartily. It was going on for three when they finished; even the coffee had failed to stop both of them dozing on and off for the next half an hour, when neither felt like moving.

There was no more talk of four a.m. raids, no more talk of the Chessman or McQueen. There was literally no more talk because both were fast asleep. One on the couch, the other sitting with his head on the table. Amber woke them at eight with some hot piping coffee. When both were in the same world as her, she explained to them that Charlie was on his way with toothbrushes, toothpaste and a pack of cigarettes for Mike, who was by now gasping for one.

08.13 hrs. Charlie arrived. Mike nearly kissed him he was so happy to see him and the pack of cigarettes.

08.34 hrs. A worried Edna rang. Evan tried to explain; his not calling didn't help in calming down his wife who had been up all night.

08.55. Evan checked his mobile; he'd switched it off last night after calling Edna. He switched it back on.

09.01. Swansea rang. Information at hand so far. Ainsworthy: dinner with wife, daughter and son in law to be at local Italian restaurant. Arrived half seven ate about eight, left about ten fifteen/ten twenty. Checking with staff – it might take a while. Definitely left-handed.

Roger Swift: playing snooker, Swansea town centre. Some kind of league match. Partnered by a Bob Chisholm. Checking staff. And, Chisholm, according to Swift, played six frames from six-thirty onwards to nine-thirty then had a few drinks at the bar before his wife picked him up about ten to ten. Anyway, not left-handed, this gathered from pictures on his wall playing tennis and snooker.

Peter James: away in North Wales, Lancashire buying coins for his business. His uncle, one Paul James, tried to contact him on mobile. "We have the number but were getting no answer. Both ourselves and uncle have tried but phone switched off. Uncle says that he usually calls him at six. Uncle is about sixty-four/five and right-handed, as is his nephew."

Amber switched off the party line. All just sat and waited for more news.

"I don't need to be Einstein to fathom out that if any of them is the Chessman it has to be this Peter James guy. The other two have given alibis involving public places. They are plausible and will prove so," said Charlie.

"We can all agree there, Charlie," said Amber.

"But how could he be in South Wales at say nine and Lancashire or North Wales at six, just three hours earlier?" said Evan. "And he's right-handed."

"Firstly, we don't know that he is in Lancashire. Maybe his uncle doesn't know either. He's away from home, so he had to stay somewhere. B & B, hotel, friend somewhere? How come his uncle doesn't seem to be able to contact him? Secondly at a push he could easily make it in say three hours from there if he drives straight through," said Mike.

"Especially if he drives like Mike," Evan added.

"Then he could do it in two and a half max," said Mike laughing but not meaning it.

"But he's still right-handed," said Evan.

"Only according to his uncle," said Charlie.

"Amber, could you do me a favour and check with D.I. Davies, here's his number, about Everard Entwistle. Ask if he had a meal last night, breakfast, a shower, shave, warm cell, new clothes and find out where they are trying to place him."

"Is this Everard Entwistle important Mike?"

"Extremely, Amber. He's a man that has to be looked after. D.I. Davies understands." Amber looked at Evan, who nodded. She left it at that.

"Right, no point in us sitting around. I'll go and brush up first, then you can, Evan. Then we'll get off down to Swansea. I think we better pay a visit to Uncle James, I'm sure he has a lot more to say," Mike said.

How the hell did they come around to suspecting him, thought the Chessman, what did they know, how long before they would realise that Uncle Pauli was in fact Peter who was all the others. But they didn't know Carl and they couldn't know about his flat in Cardiff or the other two passports. It was time to walk away, regroup and get himself ready for handling the money that would come soon enough. He needed a little time.

He'd already packed the things he needed. Two cases, one full of documentation, the other full of Carl's clothes, or to be more precise, clothes that he thought Carl should wear. One last look around. One large ginger in front of the mirror and one last goodbye to all his associates.

This done, he slipped out of the back and headed to his secret lock-up garage where he kept the two litre BMW. The Rover and Mini he left; one in his garage, the other outside the house. Again, their paths crossed. Evan driving West, Peter or now Carl, driving East.

"So you know what you've got to do, Charlie," Mike said, his head turned to face Charlie who was on the back seat.

"I do Mike. After you enter, I give you five minutes before I get around the back or wherever and get a gander at his car, extracting anything that I might think worthwhile. If I find anything suspicious, I call you on your mobile. But wouldn't it be easier just to get a search warrant Mike?"

"Not if our suspect is supposedly in North Wales or wherever. Too much fannying around. No Charlie, we do this by the book," said Mike.

"Except for the breaking into the car and garage part," said Charlie.

"Well, yes Charlie, but you're not a policeman and we are," said Mike.

"I see," said Charlie, not seeing anything that made sense.

They found the address after stopping to ask a newsagent for directions. It was now a quarter past eleven. Evan parked behind the Mini and they walked up to the front door. Charlie remained next to the car.

They rang, they knocked, they banged. No one came to the front door so they, including Charlie, went round to the back, which they opened and walked into a paved garden with a locked garage and plastic double glazed French doors leading into the house. These too were locked. Mike, Evan and Charlie all took a turn at peeping in through the doors into the kitchen. There was no sign of life.

"Uncle James must be out, shopping or maybe down the pub," said Evan.

"Is there a car in the garage Charlie?" asked Mike.

"Can't tell, can I?" said Charlie.

"Well, open it and see," said Mike. Charlie did.

"Christ," said Evan, "it's a Rover exactly like mine, same colour, age, the works. I think we passed it on the motorway once. In fact I'm bloody sure. Do you remember that Mike? I pointed it out to you."

"So you did. That was a while ago. That's very strange," said Mike.

"I suppose there must be lots of similar cars, Evan."

"Just a coincidence," said Charlie.

"There's a Mini outside, too. He must have gone for a stroll or gone shopping. It's a reasonable day. No rain, not too cold," said Evan.

"Shall we wait or go and get a coffee and come back?" said Evan.

"Let's go round the front and try again," said Mike. "But this time we will take Charlie."

"Why would anyone leave their front door open Charlie?" said Mike.

"I thought we were doing things by the book," said Evan.

"We are Evan, but an open front door and the smell of gas needs investigating and quick, don't you think so Charlie?"

"After you," said Charlie, a satisfied look on his face. Mike went straight for the kitchen and turned on all four hobs, without igniting any of them.

"I suggest you turn off the gas Evan, that way you don't have to lie." Evan did.

"Don't touch anything. Just look around," said Evan. "Five minutes and we'll call in a SOCO team, then you'd better go Charlie."

"Where to?" said Charlie. "This is the middle of nowhere; maybe I should borrow the Mini out there." Evan panicked. Mike laughed.

"Only joking, don't worry. I'll go for a walk, have a nosey around the area."

Mike's cell rang. It was Amber. He listened. It was a good few minutes before he said, "Thanks, Amber."

"Our friendly murderer is Uncle Paul James and nephew Peter James and God knows who else. Amber has checked out Paul James or rather tried to. There is no record or file on him anywhere. He does not exist. Peter James does of course. He owns this house, the two cars, both financed to the hilt, as is the house.

He deals in antique coins, works from home, hours flexible. He's our man."

"And?" said Evan.

"And he has sent all the potential future victims another letter asking them to read today's article on McQueen in the Cardiff Chronicle who he anonymously rang from a Cardiff call box yesterday at half ten, night time of course. Amber is trying to obtain a photo of our Chessman but that's not going to help, is it?" said Mike.

"Are you saying that we know everything about our murderer and yet don't know what he's going to look like?" said Charlie.

"That about sums it up. We can get fingerprints, DNA. Maybe some photos but we can't recognise him," said Mike. "Let's look around."

Ten minutes later and they were finished. Not one piece of paper, not one clue to help them identify the Chessman in the future.

"Well, he won't miss the newspaper; it's today's edition," said Mike.

"And the rest," said Evan pointing to a stack of Cardiff Chronicles in the corner under the T.V.

"There must be at least fifty of them," said Charlie, picking them up.

"Are they in chronological order?" asked Mike.

"Yes, Mike," said Charlie.

"Let's take them then," said Evan.

"Why?" asked Mike.

"I don't know. Let's just take them," said Evan.

"Okay, let's just get out of here," said Mike.

"He's gone, new car," said Charlie.

"New car, neighbours will know about that. It could be our only lead," said Evan.

"You take across the road Evan; I'll take next door."

Ten minutes and both were back to the car.

"Hardly knew them and I mean them: Peter and his uncle, never together and only on rare occasions. Really on nodding terms as such," Evan said.

"No one in next door, husband just died, wife in hospital, nervous breakdown plus other problems. And next door but one: old couple knew both of them. Again, just to say 'hello', no more. Never seen any cars. Hardly ever get out and you, car-wise Evan?" said Mike.

"No cars apart from the Mini which Peter drove and the Rover which Uncle Paul drove," said Evan.

"He must have another car," said Charlie, "I saw no suitcases anywhere but on the other hand all the clothes and shoes seem to be there," said Charlie.

"Assume he's flown the coop. He's either gone light in a hurry or took what he needed and ordered a taxi or got himself another car, which surely someone around here would have noticed this morning."

"I'm crossing over. Someone over there is giving us a good looking over. They haven't left that window since we arrived," said Mike. "I'll get Amber to contact all the local taxi firms, see if they picked up anyone from the Chessman's address or nearby."

"That leaves just me," said Charlie, "I'm going to break into one of those houses over there and rob them of their jewellery."

Even Evan realised that Charlie was joking. When Mike returned he had news. "She was wheelchair bound and spent the daylight hours, when her husband was at work, looking out of her front window. She knew both Uncle Paul and Peter by sight but had never seen them together. They only had the two cars. She had never seen another one outside. No one had left the house that morning, no taxis. She finished by saying that she might have a problem with her legs but she had 20:20 vision."

"So he left through the back, hence the back door leading on to the street wasn't bolted," said Evan.

"Let's get back there," said Mike. "He obviously didn't come back this way or the lady in the wheelchair would have spotted him."

"So he came out and he had a choice: go left, go straight ahead, or go straight ahead and after twenty yards turn right," said Evan.

"We take a route each," said Mike, "walk for ten minutes, see where it takes us, then turn and come back. We will all meet in say twenty minutes; same place, right here."

"I'll go straight ahead," said Charlie, "if you go left Mike and Evan to the right as such."

Mike lit up and started walking but within two hundred yards, he came to a dead end, so he turned and walked back. Charlie walked on and on looking down the streets that criss-crossed the road, he was following. Rows and rows of terraced housing, a shop or two dotted here and there. He had walked for over thirty-five minutes when he realised the time, so he phoned Mike.

"Keep walking Charlie and when Evan comes back we will pick you up. Keep to the same road. Don't veer off anywhere."

"Okay Mike, will do, but all I see is houses. Normal, run of the mill houses. What exactly are we looking for?"

"I've no idea Charlie, but you'll know if you come across it," said Mike.

"Course I will Mike," said Charlie, cursing his luck for picking the worst route.

Evan could hardly walk. He was all over the place, probably covering twice the distance that was necessary. If he'd walked in a straight line, he would have been back ten minutes ago. "Whose bloody idea was this?" said Evan huffing and puffing, "we've got a car and I've just done about ten miles."

"Christ Evan, you did a mile at the most. Anyway, anything to report?"

"Nothing, Mike. Interestingly about two/three miles down the road, there's about ten lock-ups in a row, all seem well maintained. All locked, mostly with padlocks."

"What's that mean to us Evan?"

"Probably nothing, but if you want to hide another vehicle, it's handy enough," said Evan.

"Not if it's two miles away Evan," said Mike. "Let's go and pick up Charlie, he got carried away and walked too far."

They picked up Charlie and Evan turned the car around and headed for the lock-ups. "Half a mile Evan," said Mike.

"Seemed much further to me," said Evan.

"Now Charlie, have a look at the locks and find the easiest one to open," said Mike.

"Are you sure?" said Evan, "I'm not too happy about another break-in; that's all we seem to be doing."

"It's Charlie who's doing it all, Evan. We will nick him if anyone turns up. Handcuff him, put him in the back of the car and drive off, back to Cardiff."

"You're crazy Mike," Evan said.

"We've had this conversation before Evan and you couldn't prove it beyond a reasonable doubt," Mike said in all seriousness but inside he was laughing at Evan's discomfort.

"All right, keep a look-out then," said Charlie. In four minutes, he'd opened five of the ten. They were all 'up and overs'. Plants in one; paint and ladders in one, a motorbike, an empty one and one with furniture.

"Do the rest Charlie," and Charlie did. They were all full of various bits of furniture, apart from two, which were full of whisky.

"What do we have here then?" Charlie asked Mike.

"I'd say three hundred cases of Red Label whisky in each," said Charlie.

"Close them all up, apart from the empty one Charlie. Let's get a good look inside that one."

Mike and Evan entered the empty one. Evan bent down and

dipped his finger in a small oil patch. "Car's been here recently Mike."

"Yeah, but whose car? Could we have struck oil, the odds are stacked against us?" said Mike.

"Okay, let's hang around. There's some houses up the top there. Maybe they know who owns them. I don't think the whisky's been here too long, it's not very secure is it?" said Evan.

"Listen up Evan. Can we say that the Chessman will have a different identity, new clothes, new appearance, new home? What are we looking for, who are we looking for? For some reason I don't think he's in this area."

"Okay," said Evan, "this is what we should do. Call SOCO into the house; fingerprints etc. Maybe he's got a record. Not that that will help us in any way. Call the Swansea boys and tell them about the lock-ups. Call Amber, tell her what we know and get her to speak to Reed. Get him down here from London. At the same, get someone in from the 'Cardiff Chronicle'. We must have a local paper on our side. That about it, Mike?"

"No Evan. Before we do anything, we lift twenty cases of whisky and fill up the car. Then we take it to my flat and drink ourselves into oblivion," said Mike.

They did what Evan suggested and whilst waiting for someone to turn up at the lock-ups, did the round of houses at the end of the street. Charlie though got the breakthrough. A small newsagents run by an Asian family had posted an advert for the lock-up being for rent in their shop window. They didn't know who rented it because he went directly to the owner who requested that he remove the card as he had found someone to take it for a year. The service cost five pounds and as he didn't want any hassle from the tax boys, he kept a record of all the payments received, together with their addresses and phone numbers.

The owner lived nearby so Evan paid him a visit. Mike and Charlie remained. Charlie was busying himself wiping off all his fingerprints from the lock-up handles, whilst Mike paced up and down the street, wondering why nobody had ever seen a car going into that particular lock-up.

It was Amber. This time she rang Evan. All was in hand; no taxis picked up at the address or nearby that day. Bus route on main road, probably half a mile away. Mr Reed contacted; on his way down. Mr Alex Symonds also contacted and ready for meeting. Chief Constable up to date with everything. She herself was standing by for any new developments. Evan passed them on to Mike, with the other information he had gathered from the lock-up owner. A Mr Endover had rented the lock-up for a year about eight months ago. The owner had no idea what he kept in the lock-up and didn't care. Endover paid a year in advance and he had no idea who owned the others.

After nearly fifty minutes, a car arrived. A sergeant and a Detective Inspector Rains. "So what do we have here then?" said Rains to Evan, assuming as the older of the two that he was of higher rank, and in charge.

Evan pointed at the lock-ups with the whisky. "Gear's in those two."

"And how do you know? They're locked," said D.I. Rains.

"Because we're fucking magicians," said Mike. Charlie, who was leaning on the BMW laughed.

"And who's that:" asked the D.I.

"Oh, him," said Mike, "he's our assistant."

"So, how can I verify that those two contain whisky?" said D.I. Rains.

"We've just told you, that's enough. Now do you want us big city boys to tell you how to go about this?" said Evan.

"I can't break in; no, I won't break in," said D.I. Rains. "Not without a search warrant."

Mike phoned Amber. "I have a D.I. Rains from Swansea, spelt RAINS, Edward, with a sergeant, in a car reg... and two lock-ups full of whisky, Red Label – that's Johnnie Walker. Largest selling whisky in the world. Ninety-five per cent is exported. I think the parent company is Guiness plc, or it used to be anyway. Find out if any stuff has gone missing in the past week or so. Thank you Amber. Oh, and before I go, keep the Chief Constable informed about this." As he was closing the phone, he started shouting to Charlie, "Stop that bike; stop that bike Charlie!"

Charlie saw the boy riding a bicycle and just managed to get him to stop. "Hold him there Charlie, I'm coming over," said Mike.

"You seem to know a hell of a lot about whisky, D.I. I assume it's D.I."

"It is, D.I. Karetzi and my partner D.I. Jones, and yes, I do know a lot about whisky. I told you we're magicians when we're not policemen.

"Now do me a favour. Stake out the lock-ups, follow whoever picks them up and you might grab yourself a juicy bust. This could be the tip of the iceberg; and please call this number and keep our colleague Amber up to date. Nice meeting you." And with that, Mike and Evan moved towards where Charlie was holding the boy.

"Hello son, hope we didn't frighten you," said Evan showing his warrant card. "What's your name?" asked Evan to the thirteen/fourteen year old boy who was dropping off some freebie newspaper to all the houses in the vicinity.

"What's it to you?" said the boy.

"Just your name please," asked Evan.

"I'm a minor. You can't stop me for nothin'," said the boy.

"Look son, you're not in any trouble, we just want to ask you a few questions, that's all."

"I'm not your fucking son, Mister," said the boy. Mike lit up. Why was everything so difficult when one was deadbeat from tiredness, he thought.

"Can I go now?" said the boy, "time is money."

"Look, forget your name," said Evan, "did you notice any car entering or leaving that garage over there?"

"I don't notice nought, I just do what I'm paid for," said the boy.

"My my," said Mike, "we have a toughie here. Get off your bike sonny and into the back of the car. We will go down to the station and sort this out. We have all the time in the world."

"And if I don't want to go with you?"

"Then, sonny, I'll cuff you and carry you into the car and you will also lose twenty quid," Mike said. "The twenty quid I have for information rendered," said Mike.

"Rendered, what's that?"

"Means... never mind. Do you want a ride to the station in the car, or twenty quid and you go on your way?"

The kid put his hand out. Mike felt in his pocket. Everard had got all his money and Evan's too. Turning to Charlie, he asked if he had any. Charlie did and passed Mike two twenties.

"Before you get the twenty, what's your name?" asked Mike, "first name will do."

"It's Billy," said the boy.

"Age?" asked Mike.

"Thirteen," said Billy.

"Simple so far, Bill. Now one last question, you know what it's about. Here take the twenty as a sign of good faith," said Mike.

"Yeah, I do this route two times a day and once on Saturday and Sunday."

"Go on Billy," said Evan. By this time they had been joined by D.I. Rains and the sergeant.

"Dark Blue BMW. Very clean. I think quite new. Four doors, teddy bear in the back, about this size," Billy said indicating with his hands. "Colour white, fluffy type."

"Well done, Billy. Now the registration number, any ideas?" asked Evan.

"It had a 'B' and an 'L' in it and I think a one," said Billy.

"'B' and 'L' as in 'Billy' eh?" said Mike. "That's why you remembered the one. Why the one?"

"Because I'm thirteen. I play a game, it helps pass the time. I look to see how many 'Billy thirteens' I can see. Last year I looked for 'Bill twelve', you understand?" said Billy. "I got a six about two weeks ago, but never a seven."

"You've been a great help Billy. Here's another twenty," Mike said, passing over Charlie's other note. Now between the three of them they could only muster a few pounds in loose change. The kid gratefully accepted it and rode off.

"Was he telling us the truth Mike?" asked Evan.

"I think so, but one can't be certain."

D.I. Davies was just about to speak when Mike put his hand up to stop him. He needed Amber urgently.

"Amber I want you to try and run down a reg for me. Four door BMW, one to three years old, a 'B' and an 'L' and a 'one' in the number. No 'Y's or '3's; oh, just one 'L', probably bought in the Swansea area about a year ago. I know it's impossible Amber but start with car salesrooms, garages. Colour? Yes, sorry, navy blue." Then Mike listened. "Thanks, Amber. We will be leaving in half an hour. It's now half three, be there at six. Call it half six, we haven't slept, eaten, washed for Christ knows how long. We need to change, have a shower. The bloody Chessman will smell us before we get within half a mile of him. See you later. Get the Chief down, get the Welsh Assembly woman down. We don't want to say anything that might be misconstrued or used out of context and two tape recorders. Thanks Amber."

"I'm sorry for back there," said D.I. Rains, holding out his hand. "I've just phoned in and been told who you guys are and to make myself and my sergeant available if you need us."

Mike shook his hand, and then Evan did. Charlie wandered off. "By the way D.I. Rains, six hundred cases went missing, a truck just disappeared between Aberystwyth and Fishguard. Three hundred cases each of Red and Black Labels. Retail value over one hundred and twenty grand and the truck of course," said Mike.

"Time to go," said Evan, who had now lit up his pipe. "I'm dead beat. I think we've got another long sleepless night ahead of us."

"You okay here, D.I. Rains?" asked Mike.

"I am, just waiting for our surveillance van then I can organise the rest from the station and good luck with the Chessman saga."

"Thanks," said Evan and Mike simultaneously, "and goodnight to you."

"It's only just gone half three," said Charlie "and you two look like you've seen better days, maybe I should drive."

"Don't be ridiculous Charlie, you can't be seen driving a police car," said Mike, getting behind the steering wheel and getting ready to drive off. Mike stopped at a bank in Port Talbot and drew two hundred pounds on both his and Evan's credit cards. He extracted twenty pounds from each and handed the money to Charlie. Evan said nothing.

Evan managed to get there by six-thirty. He had his grey suit and white shirt with a red tie and brown polished shoes. The Chief Constable, Emma Andrews, Reginald Reed and Alex Symonds had been there since five-thirty and were acting a little tetchy to say the least. They'd already had tea and biscuits and a homemade lemonade each.

"Where's the other guy?" Reed asked Evan.

"You mean Special Detective Mikhail Karetzi, do you?" said Evan.

"Yes, you know I mean him," said Reed.

"Haven't a clue," said Evan hoping that Mike would appear soon. He wasn't cut out for this type of thing and he was very tired.

At ten to seven, Mike arrived, casually dressed. Armani jeans, open blue shirt, moccasins and carrying a long black leather jacket. Having apologised, he sat down. Amber had brought two chairs up from downstairs. They took it in turns to talk: Mike first, then Evan. They told it from the beginning but never mentioned Tangent or anything remotely connected to them. They had reached that very morning when the phone rang. It was D.I. Rains. Five arrests, six hundred cases of whisky, two hundred vodka, gin, cigarettes, a whole Aladdin's cave. The reporters heard every word. They were amazed that just two detectives and an assistant could bring about so many closures in such a short time span. Symonds was moved enough to shake both their hands and give Amber a kiss.

"So where do we stand with this Chessman case right at this very moment?" asked Reed.

"Difficult to say. We have no description of what he looks like now and he really is a master of disguises. You have a picture of him as Peter James. He's threatened half a dozen people demanding money, large amounts. I understand from the Chief here that they now have round the clock security. Here, at this moment, we're working on a small lead but it may come to nothing and that's about it.

"Do you think these newspaper articles will goad him into doing something rash? What if we print your names, print your pictures looking smug. Do you think he will have a go at you? Will you become targets?" said Symonds.

"He already has-remember Jane," said Mike.

"Am I speaking for you, Mike, when I say that you can print anything you like but no pictures?" said Evan.

"It's nearly ten you know," said Evan, just after everyone had left. "I'll bring in the papers for Amber to look through. Maybe something will crop up."

"What about the car sales Amber?" said Mike. "I'm working on it, but it's going to be a long haul," Amber replied.

They sat around the desks, coffees all round. Each had about sixteen papers. They started on the first page and read through to the back page. There was not one pencil, biro or ink mark in any of them.

"Why keep them?" said Evan.

Neither Mike nor Amber had an answer.

"There are no dog-eared corners. The folds are consistent. Why the hell did he keep them?" said Mike.

"No logical explanation," said Evan.

"Logic," Mike said. "Logic. The bastard has taken the logic, thrown it on the ground and stamped it out of existence."

"You've lost me there," said Amber.

Evan wanted to agree but was too dog-tired to offer any words. Evan went home to Edna and his daughter. He told them about the newspapers and after an hour's discussion, they gave up trying to find any reason for the Chessman to have kept them.

Mike went to Angelo's, had a few snifters with the proprietor and his wife Donna. He ran the newspaper mystery by them and came up with nothing. He got back to his apartment at one in the morning, listened to his answering service – five calls, all women. One from his mother and four from Tanya. Fully clothed, he slumped on to his bed and within seconds was fast asleep.

CHAPTER 22

The Chessman counted out his money, twelve thousand pounds, seven thousand Euros and seven thousand five hundred U.S. dollars. Plus of course his coins, worth in the right market probably another twenty thousand pounds. Things had drastically changed. He'd needed another fortnight, at best ten days.

Now, all his plans had to change. He slept well that night and woke in very good spirits. He'd done the hard work but how had they got on to him, where had he made a mistake?

As was his usual practice, the Chessman bought the 'Chronicle'. His face, that is his old face, stared at him from the front page. He rushed and read the article twice before he could admit to himself that somebody had blown his future into smithereens.

Could he manufacture something from the small fragments of his broken dreams? Of course he could. He had money, new identities and was now on a mission. He would destroy this bloke with the foreign name and at the same time rekindle his future.

Mike awoke with a headache. He really shouldn't have had the last large brandy or the four before that. Two were enough. He showered and shaved. Had his black coffee, which he needed to wash down the two Anadin tablets and then he switched on the T.V. Nearly every news channel was leading with the Chessman story.

"Well Prof, I guess we can now put all this Nakamaru horse crap to bed, can't we?" bellowed the Director. Brian sat next to the Director, a frown on his face, a smile in his heart. The boyos had done well, extremely well. He was pleased with his part, although if truth be known, they could have helped a lot more.

"You've got to admire them," said the Doc, "but this Chessman is still at large," he added.

"Jimmy."

"Yes Sir."

"Take your best men and get down to Cardiff. I want them protected 24/7."

"What if they don't want us Mr Director?"

"Take two of your best, assign one each to the men and stay yourself in the house with the woman. She's the most likely target and go now, please. And Jimmy..."

"Yes Sir?"

"Be armed."

Jimmy nodded and left. Life was strange. Only a while ago he'd been sent down to teach them a lesson and now... he hurried along, there was no point in thinking too deeply about things.

The Chessman folded his paper and threw it into the corner. He would get around reading the rest when he had a spare minute. Funny that, he thought, all the papers he had saved to read when he had time were left unread and now would never be. He got up, he needed to go to the library. He needed out of his flat, at least they had no idea that he was mobile. There was no mention of his car, thank God, unless of course they were being disingenuous.

On exiting his block of flats, the Chessman started humming. It was one of the tunes that poor old departed Jim used to sing on the karaoke at the pub. Now what were the words? Ah, yes.

"As I walk along, I wonder what went wrong.

I'm a walking in the rain and I feel the pain..."

He didn't know who sang the song but anyway the words were right. That's exactly how he felt. There was no getting away from it. He upped his pace; a stroll had now become a brisk walk. Charlie would have named the song, artist and year.

Mike went onto his balcony, cigarette in one hand, second coffee in another. Someone was hanging about near the front entrance; he had a camera around his neck. A fucking reporter, Mike thought. He had no problem finding an address. Mike finished his fag and drank the coffee. Getting to his car would be impossible without passing by the guy, but he had to get to work, things were moving.

As he opened the foyer door to go out into the courtyard, the man approached. Mike turned his back to him and walked quickly towards the undercroft where he garaged his car.

"Hey you, can I have a word please!" the man shouted to Mike.

Mike turned. By now, the guy was in his face, camera at the ready.

"You can have two: fuck off!" – and Mike turned and went to his car.

Mike couldn't park anywhere near the office. It was heaving with reporters and television paraphernalia. Three uniformed police held them at bay. Mike eventually parked a half a mile away and before getting out of his car, he called Amber.

"Hi Amber, good morning, I see we're very popular today," said Mike.

"Hello Mike, it's bad. Evans says he's being hounded by the press and has gone to ground. Charlie's meeting him there and I can't get out to go shopping. I'm running out of food. It's a complete disaster. I think they are trying to starve me out."

"Where Amber?"

"Where what, Mike?"

"Where is Evan?"

"At Morrison's," said Amber.

"Is he shopping, Amber?"

"He's having breakfast in the cafeteria, then I've given him a shopping list. It will be hours before these buggers disperse."

"Okay Amber, thanks. By the way, anything on the car?" said Mike.

"No," said Amber.

"Anything likely on the car?" said Mike.

"I don't think so, but a reward of one hundred thousand pounds has been posted on the internet, television stations and press," said Amber.

"Who by, who's paying this?" asked Mike.

"A consortium of business people," said Amber.

"I think I can guess who," said Mike.

"And you would be right; it's the people who received the Chessman fan mail."

"Christ Amber, this is going to end up like a circus with us acting the part of clowns." said Mike.

"And the Chessman, the ringmaster," said Amber.

"Okay Amber, I'm off to Morrison's," said Mike.

"Don't forget the shopping Mike, otherwise we will have a lot of problems. I'm already feeling a little faint," said Amber polishing off another buttered teacake.

Mike grabbed himself a diet coke, paid and sat down opposite Evan who was sitting next to Charlie. Both were drinking tea and eating iced buns of some sort. They said their good mornings and immediately Charlie stood up and said 'goodbye'. They couldn't be caught cavorting with him, it was bad for the detectives and just as bad for him.

"Did you hear about the reward, Evan?" He hadn't so Mike told him.

"Nothing on the car, no ideas on the newspaper angle. If there is one, no idea where the bastard is, or what he looks like or what he's going to do next. So what are we going to do?" said Evan.

"Do you think he'll give up and fade away into the twilight zone?" said Mike.

"No way," said Evan. "I think he might go for one of us and if he succeeds then I think our rich friends will be falling over themselves to pay up."

"I think you're right Evan. He could strike out at any of us, including Amber, Edna, your daughter, my mother. It will look bad if we can't protect our own. How will we be able to protect anyone else?"

"He's not averse to hitting easy targets, or women Mike. Look at poor old Jane."

"He's probably seething with rage over all the coverage. He'll know that security will be beefed up, so what will he do?" said Mike.

After returning from the library, the Chessman sat and made himself a coffee. It was too early to start on the ginger beer. His girlfriend and her son Alex were away again visiting her mother. Maybe she was hoping for a windfall when the old dear popped her clogs and was keeping in with her. If only she knew, he would have hastened the old bag's departure.

So, three paintings worth near on ten million. Not one larger than six square feet. Okay, so he didn't know how to dispose of them or at this very moment of how to acquire them. So what exactly did he know? He knew they were originals and not fakes. He knew that they were all in one specially air-controlled room. He knew that Sir Quentin Reardon-Smythe was seventy, a widower and lived together with his butler, cook and maid in his large Victorian mansion on the outskirts of Llandudno, overlooking Conwy Bay.

Does he drive himself; does he have a chauffeur, gardener? There were a lot of imponderables. Maybe he had a live-in lady friend, maybe he was gay. It needed more research. Compared to this, killing was a piece of cake and he would get his piece to eat soon enough. The foreigner would be next or maybe the other one, Jones; he would be easier; he wasn't really in the correct frame of mind to have a close encounter with the foreigner. He looked much fitter than Jones and of course, he was much younger.

Evan's phone rang. He listened quietly for half a minute. "What's that Evan?"

"People phoning to various stations around the country, of which at least a quarter know who the Chessman is. No normal calls are getting through. A hundred grand is a lot of money in this recession," said Evan.

"It's a lot of money at any time, that's the problem. Police resources are now being used up chasing nonsense," said Mike.

"But it's the one that might be, you know Mike, the one," said Evan.

"I don't see it Ev. This guy has led us a merry dance. He's been extremely careful and cunning as a fox and we've been lucky to get this far and where we have got to. Still no nearer than we were on day one," Mike said, taking another sip of his diet coke.

"We can't sit here all day twiddling our thumbs," said Evan.

"So what shall we do?" said Mike.

"Go outside into the car park and have a smoke," said Evan.

"Right, let's go. People are beginning to look and point at us," said Mike.

The Chessman was back on the street, heading for W.H. Smith's. He needed some magazines; he bought three. Decisions, decisions. From his pocket, he took out his lucky ninety-nine year old penny. Heads he would take out Jones, tails and his wife would buy it. He spun the coin into the air and watched it as it rotated going up and rotated coming down. It took less than three seconds and incredulously it landed upright.

The Chessman stared and stared at the coin. The impossible had happened. It was still upright. Slowly and carefully the Chessman knelt down, his knees now on the old pine floor. He moved his head downwards towards the coin, his eyes never leaving it for a microsecond.

He examined the coin for a full five seconds before it dawned on him that the damn thing had landed in a crack. What did this mean? It must mean something but what? He picked up the coin and then he picked up himself, clutching the coin in his left hand. Strangely, it felt very warm, yet he himself felt cold. What did all this mean, what was the significance of this?

He couldn't unclench his fist. Panic was setting in. His heart was beating faster and he began to sweat. He was having difficulty breathing. Two steps and he reached the sash window, which he managed with difficulty to open with his right hand. He poked his head out and took large gulps of fresh air. Both his hands were also outside. Slowly, he began to regulate his breathing until finally after what seemed an eternity he felt better. His left unclenched, the penny dropping onto the pavement below. He had no wish to retrieve it.

Now that he felt more his normal self, he decided he needed a drink. A strong drink. The only thing he could find was a quarter bottle of gin, something his girlfriend was partial to. Without bothering to pour it into a glass, he drank straight from the bottle. It tasted like shit but it did the trick and steadied his jangling nerves. He felt more like his old self, confident and in control.

He took a piece of paper and a pen from the sideboard and started drafting a letter. He wrote in block capital letters with his good hand, his left. To each he assigned a place of worship: a Baptist church, a Methodist, Church of England, Roman Catholic, United Reform, a synagogue and a Greek one. All local to Cardiff. He wasn't sure what the difference was with some of them, but he felt good about giving them a million pounds each. That should save a few souls although he didn't count himself as one of them. He would send them to the same people. Luckily for him, Sir Quentin Reardon-Smythe would save a million; he was insured for the art.

He'd also decided that he would spare the detectives. The coin had decreed that. That left the car. He was worried about that. These people were smart. Either way he needed to do something just in case. He had to remain mobile. He had to have wheels.

He picked up one of the magazines. He flicked through the pages until his eyes reached something that suited his purpose. He rang the number and told Mr Harker that he would be around in ten minutes. Haling a taxi on the street, he was standing alongside Mr Harker fifteen minutes after his telephone call.

"She's a good runner, no rust, only eighty thousand miles. Had her since new. Do you want to drive her around the block Mr Sandlewood?"

"No. I see you've still got five month's MOT. That's good. Could you turn the engine over for me? That will be enough. Five thousand pounds cash sound agreeable to you Mr Harker?"

"I was hoping for a little more as I told you over the phone. She's got to be worth another two hundred, Mr Sandlewood."

"This is cash Mr Harker. I tell you what, let's split the difference. I'll add another hundred. Do we have a deal?"

"I guess so," said Mr Harker.

The Chessman drove direct to the nearest car insurance brokerage firm. It took over an hour before Mr John Wallis left three hundred and seventy pounds lighter in the pocket. Another seventy disappeared when he purchased petrol for his new car, a Jag.

The black handlebar moustache, bushy black eyebrows and wart on the side of his nose made Mr Wallis as unforgettable as a walking walrus. It was time to dump the disguise and resemble at least a little the photo on the driving licence, plus the fact that he might have a problem with his neighbours when he entered his apartment block. He drove his BMW three miles, found a quiet spot, doused the inside of the car with petrol from the car he had purchased when he filled up the jaguar and set it alight. The time was 12.45. Less than five minutes later, he was on a bus heading for his apartment.

The second magazine helped to locate a twenty-eight foot motor boat with its own berth in Deganwy Marina. It was connected for electricity, had a small galley, fridge, W.C., shower, a decent size cabin, and a lounge with a small table. It also of course had an engine of some sort. However, that was of no interest, as he wasn't going to sea with the boat. He just wanted to avoid B&Bs and hotels.

This the Chessman would rent after inspection, which was to take place on Tuesday. He would have normally paid in advance on his credit cards, but he had now trashed them, as they were now useless to him.

By now, the reporters had given up on the office and after purchasing Amber's food, the detectives headed back. Mike arrived first and parked in the next street. Evan parked behind him. Each took two bags of shopping and walked the rest of the way. They were surprised to find Charlie there waiting with Amber, who was all excited.

Both Mike and Evan assumed wrongly that her excitement stemmed from her sighting of the four food bags. However, when she told them that she had found the registration number of the Chessman's BMW only a few minutes ago and had just that second alerted the various traffic and highway police throughout the principality and beyond into Chester, Liverpool, Manchester, the border towns and Bristol area to be on the look-out. It would only be a matter of time before it was physically located. It was time for high fives all round. Even the Chief had rung to congratulate them. Mike looked up at the large wall clock. It was three minutes to one.

Amber grabbed the four carrier bags and marched off upstairs to the kitchen. Things were getting better by the minute.

Mike took out his knife. He didn't expose the blade but just held it in his hand and played with it. He felt elated. The saga of the Chessman was coming to an end and for that, he was extremely grateful. It wasn't long before he opened up the knife, grabbed one of the pencils and started whittling it down. It felt good. The blade was razor sharp as was his mind.

"Did you know, Detective Jones and Detective Karetzi, that there is no 'J' or 'K' in the Welsh alphabet? Strange eh?" said Charlie.

"Interesting," said Evan, "no 'J or 'K' ."

"Is there an 'F' Charlie?"

"Yes, Mike," said Charlie.

"Is there an 'O' Charlie?"

"There is Mike, both an 'F' and an 'O'."

"Well, that's reassuring to know, don't you agree Evan?"

"I do Mike," replied Evan, wondering again if sometimes Mike was on the same planet as the rest of them.

Amber called down on the intercom. She had made a lovely Spanish omelette and there was enough for anyone who was interested. They all were; even Charlie who had no idea what a Spanish omelette was but was hungry enough not to care.

They sat and ate, their mood was jovial. The banter between them light. All was well until the call, which Amber answered.

At first, it seemed good news when they heard Amber proclaim loudly, "That's great news. You've actually found the car." But then when she said, "Oh shit, are you sure it's our car?" the three men sitting around the table prepared themselves for bad news. After replacing the receiver, Amber just plonked herself down on the remaining vacant chair, nearly breaking it in the process.

"They have found the Chessman's car or what remains of it. It's been torched early today. Nothing but a shell," said Amber.

"I just can't believe it," said Evan.

"How is he always just one step ahead of us?" said Charlie, the disappointment heavy in his voice.

Mike bowed his head; he was suddenly very tired.

"We're looking for a ghost with brains," said Amber.

"He's beaten us again," murmured Mike, his head still bowed.

"What can we do now?" said Evan. "I'm this bloody close to chucking it all in," he said, thumb and index finger nearly touching, an indication of how close, 'close' was.

"We're going to see it through together," said Amber, emphasising the last word.

"I think what Amber's says makes sense. Look, this is hard but so much work has gone into getting him. Nobody expected you guys to get anywhere near a result. Just read the papers, switch on the news, the radio. You've done wonders. He's in our sights," said Charlie, wondering where all that came from.

Mike looked up and said, "Thanks Charlie. You've been a great help, considering you don't even get paid."

"Let's have no more defeatist-type talk," said Amber. "Let's see what we got and try to fathom something out, shall we? You start the ball rolling Evan, and I will take notes," said Amber.

"Can we go back downstairs?" Mike said. "I think better downstairs, there aren't so many distractions."

"Like eating, like a human being Mike, you're too thin," said Amber.

"Too thin, Amber? I'm probably three, four pounds overweight," said Mike, "and why do you keep looking at the window, Amber? Are they delivering food by pigeons these days?"

"Don't be smart, Mike. I'm old enough to be your mother and big enough to box your ears," said Amber.

"Sorry Ma'am," quipped Mike.

"Anyway, enough sparring, I'm looking out of the window because someone is acting suspiciously outside. I've noticed him twice already today," Amber said.

"Where?" asked Evan.

"Once in the back and once in the park. He's wearing a dark overcoat and black cap," said Amber.

"Shoes," said Charlie.

"What about them?" asked Amber.

"Very important are shoes," said Charlie.

"I'm sure they are," said Amber, "but I didn't see his shoes Charlie."

"This bloke worrying you, Amber? Do you think it's our Chessman?" said Evan.

"No, I don't, he's not that stupid. It's okay now that there are three men in the house and it's daytime, but I do feel a little uneasy."

"Right then. Let's deal with our peeper. Evan, you and Charlie take the back, I'm going into the park. Keep your mobiles on."

It was Charlie who spotted him first. He was walking away from them at a fast pace. He was heading for the park. Evan told Mike, who closed in from the opposite direction. He was now trapped in the narrow lane a few houses away. The man stopped and nonchalantly, lit up a cigarette. Mike slipped his knife into his right hand and with his left opened the blade. He let it dangle from his hand.

"No need for the knife, Mike," said the man, still not looking up.

"Who are you?" said Mike.

"It's your friendly footballer, Jimmy," said the man.

"Why all the creeping around, why the subterfuge Jimmy? What you doing here down in little old Cardiff?"

Jimmy told them. "I've got a good guy watching your house Mike and your Detective Jones. The only reason I let you see me was because I needed to speak to you," said Jimmy.

"Come in Jimmy and see Amber. Oh, and this is Charlie, he's uh, helping us with our enquiries."

"I'm sure he is," said Jimmy.

"So the car's gone and with it your only real lead. Is that about it?" said Jimmy.

No one answered.

"He could be anywhere," said Evan.

"And anyone," said Charlie.

"We will watch your backs but I now have a feeling that he's not going after you or anything in this area. There's round the clock protection for all those who received the letters and I can't see how he would get the money. I mean it's near on impossible to pick up any huge cash amount and then the money would be marked," said Jimmy. "Electronically transmitted, going through a dozen offshore accounts, nigh on impossible," added Jimmy.

"Now Charlie, if it was you, what would you do?" said Jimmy.

"How would I know," said Charlie.

"It's just hypothetical," said Jimmy. "If it was you in his position what would you do? Rob a bank, a post office, what?"

"Like I said, I've no idea. What do you think I am?"

"He knows," said Mike.

"How?" said Charlie.

"He just knows Charlie. So, hypothetically, what would you do?"

"Well, to start with I wouldn't go around killing anyone else. He doesn't need to. The threat is enough. He's proved that he has no qualms about doing so."

"Carry on," said Amber. "I think what you are saying is correct. He can't get close to those he has sent the letters to and like Jimmy said, he's realised by now that even if he did and somehow extracted the money, he couldn't spend it."

"So now I would pick my second string that have not received letters and hit one of them who is unprepared and unaware. A Plan B as such!" said Charlie.

"Two problems there," said Mike. "People don't have hundreds of thousands of pounds hanging around and if for some reason they do, it will be secured in a safe or something, and I don't think our friend belongs to the safe crackers' union."

"No need," said Charlie. "The owner will open the safe, no problem getting someone to do that when they realise that he is the Chessman. But I don't think..., I mean if I was him I would be after jewellery, works of art probably. Yes, that's it! I'd go for someone with a coin collection; he knows their value and how to get rid of them for top dollar."

"Some of these coins are worth thousands," said Jimmy. "Not too heavy or bulky to carry a million or two, is it?"

"He's invested too much time and money in the others to change his M.O. now. I personally think he's still going to go for one of them. He's obviously working on something," said Mike.

"I like Charlie's theory," said Jimmy.

"And you Amber, Evan, what do you think?" said Mike.

"Charlie's got a point," said Amber.

"No way he's going to change this far down the road," said Evan.

"I'm with Mike on this."

"You asked the question, I gave you an answer," said Charlie. "Who am I to know what the madman will do next?"

"Okay," Mike said. "Let Amber check out any coin dealers or whatever who hold large amounts of valuable stuff, especially rich old buggers living within the normal operating parameters of the Chessman."

"Right, come on Jimmy, we're going to see a friend," said Mike. "You'll like him; he's got some info for me. His name's Eastern and they're still holding on to him downtown. You got documents on you Jimmy?"

"I have Mike, impeccable ones, get me in to see the Queen if need be," said Jimmy.

"Evan, try and get Mick. Tell him I'm on the way down with an old friend. We need to have a word with Eastern, privately," said Mike.

"Oh Christ Mike, don't do anything stupid," said Evan.

"Don't fret Ev, this is personal, I've to see the finishing line before I completely run out of steam. Things are getting to me too, you know. I'm not Superman, I'm not even Robin," said Mike.

"Robin was with Batman, not Superman Mike," said Amber.

"Whatever," said Mike and walked out. Jimmy followed him full of anticipation of a little bit of rough stuff.

"Look Mike," Mick said, "this is highly irregular, he's moving to remand tomorrow – I'm taking a big risk."

"It's about our Chessman case Mick, that as you know takes precedence over everything."

"Sure it does Mike, that's why I see that you've got Jimmy with you. Is he part of the case Mike?" said Mick.

"Come on Mick, you know the situation; give me a form, I will sign it. We're wasting time; it will be fine, just a few minutes Mick," said Mike.

"Follow me, he's in cell number three," said Mick.

"Well, I can't speak to him through bars, Mick! Open the fucker, he won't attack us I promise you," said Mike. Jimmy laughed.

Mick got the cell opened, turned to Mike and said, "Three minutes, no more. I'm timing you and I will be standing just outside."

"Thanks Mick, I owe you," said Mike.

"Hello Bill, you remember me don't you?" said Mike. "When we last talked you said you had information which was personal to me, only and I would like that information now Bill, if you don't mind."

"I said I might have information and that was conditional to my getting the correct sentence," said Bill, dropping the book he was reading and sitting upright on his bunk.

"Are you packing Jimmy?" said Mike. Jimmy nodded and opened first his coat then his jacket. Eastern could see the gun.

"Have you a licence for that Jimmy?" asked Mike.

"I have more than a licence Mike."

"And what sort of gun is it, it seems very big to me," said Mike.

"Walther P38, 30 rounds per minute. It would take Bill's head off in less than one hundredth of a second. German, has never let me down," said Jimmy, smirking.

"Come on you guys, you've got to be kidding," said Bill, beginning to feel very nervous.

Mike reached into his pocket, extracted the knife, opened the blade and threw it down onto the bunk next to Eastern.

"Christ Jimmy, how did he get hold of my knife?" said Mike. "Maybe we should defend ourselves."

"How much time we got left Mike?" said Jimmy, unholstering the Walther.

"A minute Jimmy, and then its boom, boom time. Pity really, all I want to know is what Mr Eastern wants to tell me.

"Rider and Reece," said Eastern.

"What about them?"

They were involved with your father's accident," said Eastern.

"How do you know?" said Mike.

"They used to have newspaper cuttings and I put two and two together. Can you please go now? I've told you everything."

Mike picked up the knife and pocketed it. Jimmy put the gun back in its holster and quickly buttoned up his jacket and coat.

"Listen Bill, this conversation never happened, do you understand?" said Mike.

Bill nodded; he was still shaking with fear.

"Say Yes, you understand," said Jimmy, "I don't want to come looking for you. I've got too much work on right now."

"Yes, I understand. No meeting, nothing, I never saw you or anything," said Eastern.

"Time's up Mike," Mick said, opening the cell door and letting them out.

"Get anything useful Mike?" said Mick.

"No, the guy's a waste of space Mick, but thanks anyway."

"Yeah, pity that," said Mick glancing over at a white-faced Bill Eastern.

"Is this what that Demonic business is about Mike?" said Jimmy as they got out.

"Sorry Jimmy, it is," said Mike.

"You lied to me and the others," said Jimmy.

"I did out of necessity Jimmy. It's for my father. Twenty-two bloody years, twenty-three years of mental torture," Mike said, the tears streaming down his face.

Jimmy turned away. He hated seeing big men cry. He recalled his own nightmare; how they stopped when he caught up with his mother's lover, the man who drove his father to suicide when Jimmy was just fourteen. It took him seven years but he caught up with the bastard and for sixteen hours tortured him before hanging him from the Forth Bridge, in exactly the same place that his father had hung himself seven years earlier. Jimmy had never been the same since, how could he be.

"Twenty-two years, Mike?"

453

"Yes Jimmy, that's the main reason I joined the Force. I thought it would help me find the truth. It's very difficult for me to make you understand. I needed you in there, I didn't know how I was going to get the information. I couldn't take Charlie. You probably know why and Evan is too decent a man to be involved with a lunatic like me in this instance."

"Yes, I know you Mike. You're not a lunatic, believe me; we both took a big risk in there, as did the big Irishman. And you're right about D.I. Jones, he's a good family man. That goes a long way in my book. As for Charlie, I checked. I know he's got a record, so that left me. I conveniently turned up and you used me, just like I would have you in the same situation. I've had my share of… let's call them the uncertainties of life.

"I've been there Mike and because of that I'm going to come with you and help you get through it in one piece. Jimmy never forgets. I owe you and now here I am. Let's go and do whatever."

"Thanks Jimmy, but I can handle my own problems from here on. I'll drop you off at the office. Keep your eye on Amber, I think she's vulnerable," said Mike.

"That woman, no way Mike, she's as tough as teak. Could take us both on with one hand tied behind her back and still beat the crap out of us. No, Mike, I'm going with you – at least I can stop you doing something really stupid."

"It's personal Jimmy. You don't owe me a thing, you're best out of it. I can handle it myself."

"That's what you think at this very moment. Reality is different. I'm coming, things might not be what they seem, Mike."

"Remember Jimmy, I am in charge. These guys are innocent until I prove otherwise, if that is the case."

They arrived at a quarter to five; five people were welding. The man left in charge, the foreman, was sitting at Eastern's desk drinking tea.

"You again," said the man drinking tea.

"Me again," said Mike. "What time do you pack up today?"

"Five sharp, it's Friday. Why?" said the foreman.

"I need to interview two of the men," said Mike.

"Which ones?" asked the foreman.

"Rider and Reece," said Mike, lighting up.

"It's against the Law to smoke in public places such as this," said the foreman.

"Is that a fact Mr... Um?"

"Roberts, Mr Roberts, and you can put that cigarette out now or go outside and finish it."

Mike took a large drag and then stubbed it out on the dirty desk.

Roberts smiled. "You can wait outside, you have no business in here," he said.

"Too cold out there boyo. I'll wait here, you go call the two. I will use Mr Eastern's office to interview them," said Mike.

"At five and outside," said Roberts.

"Jimmy, what do you say?" said Mike.

"I say according to my watch it's five and you're right about the weather, it's cold, too cold for interviews."

"It's ten to," said Roberts.

"It's five, said Jimmy, taking out the gun.

Roberts went for the phone; it was one of those old-fashioned finger-dialling types with a twisted cord cable. Mike reached out and put his hand on the receiver. "Don't be an ass Roberts, my friend would love a reason to send you to hell, he has a licence for that thing," said Mike.

"Piss off, you don't scare me," said Roberts.

Mike hit him with his other hand so hard Roberts crashed into the wall behind him and crumpled onto the floor, bleeding from his mouth and nose. There was too much noise going on inside the workshop for anyone to hear.

Mike went around the desk and was about to kick Roberts in a delicate area when the phone rang. Mike picked it up and said, "Eastern's."

"Hello, is George there?"

"Who's speaking please," said Mike.

"It's his wife Anthea."

"Is that my wife Anthea?" mumbled Roberts.

"Mr Roberts has gone out for a meeting and said he would be late home tonight if you rang."

"Why didn't he ring me? Anyway, I'm out, his tea's in the oven. He can get me on my mobile – and who are you by the way?"

"I'm the new man, just started. Nice speaking to you Mrs Roberts, I'll pass on the message." Mike replaced the receiver.

"Get up, clean up your face and get out there and tell them all to go home except for Rider and Reece; and your wife said she's going out."

It took five minutes to clear the men. Reece tried to sneak out but Mike caught hold of him and shoved him back in. With all the movement and commotion, Mike didn't notice that Roberts had got hold of a mobile phone and had started dialling. Unfortunately for him, Jimmy noticed and that cost Roberts four front teeth and a crushed phone. But Roberts was a tough nut. He started mouthing obscenities at Jimmy who was particularly affronted by the word 'motherfucker'. A broken nose was the price paid for that.

"Look laddie, you've still got two ears and two eyes, don't push my patience any further, try to hold on to what's left of your face," Jimmy told him nicely. Roberts had got the message; he zipped it and just lay on the concrete floor whimpering. Jimmy found some cable flex and tied Roberts' hands and feet.

The right-handed one of the two picked up a steel bar and came for Mike, who fortunately had the desk in between him and the one with the pipe. The other just egged him on, that is until Jimmy walked through the door, gun in hand and said, "Drop it sucker or I'll drop you where you stand."

"Okay," said Mike. "You sit here and you there. We're going to have a talk: first me, then you," he said pointing to Rider, "and then you," he said looking at Reece. "If I don't like what I hear, if I don't believe what I hear then you will both crawl out of here on your hands and knees. Believe me, I've waited a long time for this." Rider and Reece sat. What else could they do? One was pointing a gun at them.

"Are you both sitting comfortably, because if you are, you're in the wrong place," said Mike. "Regard me as your doctor, I'll decide on the medicine and I'll dish it out. Are we clear?" Mike said. He continued: "I want to talk about something that has haunted me for the whole of my adult life. I want you both to cast your minds back twenty-two years to July 1987 at approximately seven p.m. Can you do that for me?

"I'm going to have a smoke and then you, Reece, will tell me your story," he said looking at Rider. Mike smoked and played with his knife. He felt bitter anger and he was afraid. Deep down he wasn't sure he wanted to know the truth. All these years it had suited him to have this goal in life and now he wasn't sure he had been right in pursuing it.

Jimmy walked over to him and put his arm around Mike's shoulder. "It's not too hard Mike, they will talk. I promise you."

Big Mick Maloney knocked hard on the window. Charlie and Evan peeped out from behind the heavy curtains. What's he doing here, Evan asked himself before letting him in.

"I think Mike and that Jimmy fellow are going to do something real stupid. Mike knows who killed his father and the Scotsman – he's got a gun. I think they are at Eastern's factory and I don't think we have much time."

"Let's go then Mick," said Evan.

"I'm coming too," said Charlie.

"And so am I," said Amber.

They all piled in to Mick's waiting car, the engine was still running.

Mike placed the knife on Rider's ear whilst keeping the man in a headlock with his other hand. "This ear first, then the other."

"And I will kneecap this one at the same time," said Jimmy, placing the gun on Reece's left knee.

Rider and Reece both started talking.

"One at a time arseholes, one at a time. You first," said Mike pressing the knife down a little harder and causing blood to flow down Rider's face and mix with his tears before dripping onto his filthy boiler suit.

When the gang arrived, they were surprised to see five people enjoying a cup of coffee, well, four were. Roberts was finding it a little difficult.

"Have we missed all the fun?" Mick said.

"I'm afraid you have," said Jimmy.

"Everything okay here Mike?" asked Amber.

"Of course it is," answered Mike.

"Are we ready to go then?" said Mick.

"We are," said Mike, writing something down on a piece of paper and handing it to Rider.

"Remember boyos, every Sunday, you know the words and make sure they're decent, no poxy pansies, proper gear, I will be checking. And, don't send anyone, you go yourselves and don't forget the words, I will be checking every Sunday. If you miss out any one time, I'll find you. No questions and you can guess the rest," Mike said.

"Let's get the fuck out of here," said Jimmy "before I get bored and take it out on one of you three; and get this bloke to hospital."

They left in two cars: Mike and Evan in one and the rest in the other.

"Twenty-two years, Evan, and all it was really was an accident as such," said Mike.

"An accident Mike?" said Evan.

"Yep. They confronted my father, threatened him with a knife; wanted money. My father wouldn't play ball and grabbed one of them. There was a scuffle. My father slipped and hit his head on the hard ground. They ran off. They caused it but hard to put all the blame on them," said Mike.

"So that's it, finished?" said Evan.

"In a way, yes Evan."

"What do you mean 'in a way yes'? That doesn't make sense Mike. Is the matter closed to your satisfaction or not?"

"I guess so Evan, in time."

"Christ Mike, can't you give me a straight answer?"

"It's like this, Evan. Our friends Rider and Reece have kindly agreed to put flowers on my father's grave every Sunday with a nice card stating how sorry they are," Mike said.

Evan nodded. He'd never heard of anything like that in his life. He sat next to Mike and realised that maybe, just maybe, he didn't know his partner that well. Nothing was making sense to him. He wondered if Mike was now at peace with himself. He felt old; well, in this game he probably was old. He'd give it until the sixth of January and he would resign; a birthday present to his daughter who would be thirty. He looked at Mike. He seemed happy. He looked at the speedometer. Mike was cruising at twenty-five miles an hour dead.

CHAPTER 23

Mick dropped off Amber, Charlie and Jimmy for whom Amber had made up the bed in the spare room.

Charlie had gone home. He was taking Maggie out for a night in town, a nice Chinese meal. She was back on days at the hospital.

Mike dropped off Evan and carried on to his mother's. He desperately needed to have a talk and he needed to tell her about the flower arrangement, so that it would not come as a surprise to her.

Evan was also in a rush to get home. His brother was coming around for dinner and then they would all play Monopoly or Scrabble or both, a perfect evening as far as he was concerned.

Amber was preparing a meal, a three-course meal. She had a guest, Jimmy and he looked like the type of person who liked his food. She made more than enough anyway and that wouldn't go to waste.

The happiest of them all was the Chessman. Mario Fratelli works of art were few; only twenty-seven known paintings, of which fourteen were in museums. The rest in private hands of which only three were held outside the United States – the three owned by Sir Quentin Reardon-Smythe. He didn't care how this knight of the realm acquired them, he cared only how he would dispose of them once they were in his hands. Somewhere he had read that all ten in the USA were owned by Italian Americans. If they were, he would have no problem selling. Mafia Dons had the money and didn't ask the wrong questions; well, not in this case anyway.

The second piece of good news that the Chessman had concerned Sir Quentin's Christmas and New Year travel plans. Every year he spent the festive period in his villa in Naples and he was due to leave on the fifteenth for a period of three weeks. But with the good news came unwelcome ones; the other occupants, namely the butler, cook and maid, together with a nine-to-five secretary, a Mrs Adele Histon, would still be around. There was no chauffeur, as the butler doubled up if required. It seemed Sir Quentin drove himself around in a mixture of grand cars. The gardening was done by a local company; three acres was a lot of ground, the Chessman guessed.

The third magazine had repaid in full plus the three pound sixty cost and it was still producing. Mrs Adele Histon was fifty-eight, drove a red Fiat Uno and always arrived ten minutes early for work. What more information could one want for less than four pounds outlay?

He needed another hour in the library. It would wait until Monday. Everything had to be finished by Monday because the following day he would be travelling in his new car to North West Wales.

Saturday came and went like the weather; fine and sunny in the morning, dull and cloudy from then until about six, when it started pouring with rain before eventually giving way to high winds just before midnight.

The Chessman did his research, assembled a letter, which he would type on Monday after a last visit to the library and made his decisions concerning his two new identities. He knew he was the master of disguises. He looked at himself in the mirror and that's all he could see. He felt sad. He missed his old friends and colleagues. No more Uncle Pauli or Abergele or Bala or Dinas Powys. Maybe he needed another friend: yes, Larry Llandudno. He still had a knight, some pawns, and a bishop. The knight was perfect but he wouldn't be there. It would have to be the butler. It's usually them that did it. It was time for the roles to be reversed. The butler didn't do it; he was the victim.

That night Jimmy ate more at Amber's table than he had eaten the whole of the previous week. He slept until midnight and then sat downstairs until eight when Amber advised him that she was

461

preparing breakfast. Jimmy made his excuses and did a runner straight into the park where he sat on a bench feeling and acting like a beached whale.

His two colleagues fared little better, Edna insisting that her minder Tim should eat with them and then join in the game of Monopoly with them, which lasted until half one in the morning, when Bryn fell asleep on the sofa and Tim rested on the stiff armchair, awake all night.

Sean, Mike's minder, fared better; not food-wise – all they had to eat was a shared three-egg omelette and a bottle of Macallan whisky. They also finished off a pack of cigarettes between them, even though Sean had quit six months previously.

It was late morning, Saturday, when Amber received the first email. By noon, she had two faxes and two emails. The Chessman had made his move, or a move of some sort, demanding that the various recipients of his first letter and now a second each donated a million pounds to a different charity. A few calls to the charities named ascertained that they had no idea of what was going on – neither did the Chief Constable or anyone else she called.

She called Evan. He was on his way immediately, Charlie too but Mike seemed a little hazy about what he was going to do. He sounded as if he had just woken up from a drunken sleep. Amber put on the coffee and opened a pack of six thick sausages. She had only four eggs and five rashers of bacon, a small tomato and a measly-looking mushroom. That had to suffice. Fortunately, she'd had breakfast and half a large Victoria sponge.

Mike got Sean to ring Jimmy to come and pick them up. Both Sean and he were way over the limit and would be for quite a while yet. He hoped Jimmy wasn't.

"Do you know Amber, you woke me up," said Mike on entering.

"It's midday Mike," retorted Amber.

"There's a bloody reason one leaves sleeping dogs to lie," said Mike holding a desk for support.

"Are you going to bite me?" said Amber.

"What are you on about, Amber? I'm not in the mood for small talk yet, I need a black coffee or two."

"I'm talking about sleeping dogs left to lie. You wake them and they are liable to bite you," said Amber.

"On the bum," said Jimmy.

"Have some breakfast Mike, you too Jimmy," said Amber.

"Thanks Amber, you know a way to a man's heart," said Mike.

Jimmy cried off, he didn't even want to look at food for a good few days.

Mike had his coffees, a bacon and egg sandwich and a stale cigarette, which he fished out from one of his desk drawers, before Evan or Charlie had even arrived.

"I thought you had given up, Sean," Jimmy said.

"I have after this one," said Sean dragging on his cigarette until it was redder than his nose, which was a lovely scarlet red.

"So as I see it," said Jimmy, "Tim's given up playing board games, I've given up eating and you've started smoking again, Sean."

"So what's going on in there Jimmy?" asked Tim.

"Fuck knows," replied Jimmy, "but I'm going back in to find out. They are as weird a group of people as I have ever come across and I've come across some bloody weird fuckers in my time."

"Detective Jones seems a regular kind of guy Jimmy."

"Sure, he's regular; uses the toilet at the same time every day. Man, he's something out of those Agatha Christie programmes, the ones who play the Sunday school teacher, the vicar, the bumbling colonel. Then we have a bloody burglar. Do you hear me Tim, a fucking cat burglar, a woman who eats for fucking England and Jamaica or wherever she originates from, she's got a massive arse and an even bigger brain."

"And my guy, the one with the strange name?" said Sean.

"Fucking Jekyll and Hyde. You never know which guy is going to turn up but to be fair a good man to have on your side," said Jimmy. "What a fucking quartet," he added.

"I didn't know that," said Sean.

"Know what?" said Jimmy.

"That they sing," said Jimmy.

"For Jesus Christ sake, Sean, are you a fucking moron?" said Jimmy. "Who said anything about singing, idiot?"

"You did, just now Jimmy, you said they were a quartet. You heard him, didn't you Tim?" said Sean.

"When we get back Sean, I'm going to recommend you go and visit one of the company's doctors," said Jimmy walking off towards the office, shaking his head in amazement. He didn't regard himself as an Einstein but compared to Sean he was. Well, that's why he was a leader and Sean and his ilk, sheep.

"Anything I should know about?" said Jimmy.

Amber handed him one of the faxes. Jimmy took a while reading it before speaking. "This is crap; excuse my French, unadulterated crap. He doesn't honestly expect these types to give money to charity. Surely to goodness, if anything these rich types do the opposite; they steal from charity."

"What he expects or doesn't is irrelevant," said Evan.

"I agree," said Jimmy, "he's just tying your hands. There's no personal gain. His target is someone else."

"And it's not us," said Amber.

"Again, I agree Amber, so what's next, what's on his mind?" said Jimmy.

Amber handed him a list of names. There were twenty-three, of which two were ringed.

"Why this David Dalton and Henry Winterburn?"

"They are the largest coin collectors, both of whom have collections worth over one and half a million. Our Chessman knows the business; it's the most logical thing for him to do next. He can pick up the best, the rarest and fit everything in one holdall," said Mike, his head still thudding.

"And the others?" said Jimmy.

"Works of art, sculptures, jewellery, not his scene and I think he might have a go at one of our six who have received the letters, probably a relative, someone easy to take out and make us think that he's still after them. Otherwise, why give them until the twenty-first of the month, why is that date important?" said Evan.

"Is it important? We're reading too much into this date. It's arbitrary, making us think that nothing will happen until after said date," said Amber.

"Which probably means that the next move is before the twenty-first," said Charlie.

"Let's take a reality check here. We have no description, no car, no idea of where he is and can only guess at his next move," said Mike.

"Where is he living? He has no relatives. We could check hotels, B&Bs, but we could end up with thousands of names. Who the hell could check them out? Impossible," said Evan.

"Have you contacted this Dalton and Winterburn?" asked Jimmy.

"That's my next job," said Amber.

"Well, me and my two boys are finished here. I'm happy to stay on but it's not going to help is it?" said Jimmy.

"I'm okay," said Mike.

"Ditto," said Evan.

"And you Amber?" asked Jimmy.

"I have no problem; I can look after myself, but thank you anyway Jimmy." Jimmy breathed a sigh of relief.

They shook hands and Jimmy left.

"Going to the football Mike?" asked Evan.

"No Evan, I'm going to get myself some sleep, unless of course we can do something constructive here, in which case I'll stay."

"You Charlie?" said Evan.

"Taking the missus for a spot of shopping, then a drink and a bite to eat," said Charlie.

"Not the Cutty Sark surely, Charlie?" said Mike.

"No way Mike. I don't like to mix business and pleasure," answered Charlie. "And their culinary expertise only stretches to sandwiches," he added.

"Makes sense Charlie, and you Amber?" asked Mike.

"Need to replenish my larders, what with Jimmy eating like a horse. I ran out of basics. Mind you, he was good company. You wouldn't think he was a government hit man," said Amber.

"Now that's slanderous Amber," said Evan, unable to resist laughing.

"I'm not sure Evan. I don't think you can say slanderous when you don't have proof," said Charlie.

"You're quite the lawyer Charlie," said Amber. "Now can we all get on with what we need to do, I'm starving."

"You got a car Charlie?" asked Mike.

"No, Maggie's using it at the moment."

"Well, let's walk up to town together. I need some fresh air Charlie. Okay with you or are you in a rush?" said Mike. Together they walked through the park to the city centre. Mike's head was still a little sore and he walked slowly.

The centre was heaving. The weather was reasonable. Pre-Christmas sales on and a Saturday. One could hardly walk for people and then Mike saw her. She was about to cross the road. He shouted and started to run in the strawberry blonde's general direction. If only he had a name! Charlie followed. Mike bumped into one, two people. Knocked the shopping out of a young lady's hand and then ran straight into a wall, a wall of tough black flesh. A huge black arm grabbed Mike by his arm and pinned him against a telephone box. A gruff voice made it clear that he was very angry. If he'd been white he would have been purple with rage.

"What's your problem running like a mad bull in the street?" His wife or girlfriend was shouting. "Let it be Lance, don't get involved," she kept saying. A crowd had formed. The black man had an audience and wanted to perform. "I'm asking you what your problem is."

"I'm a police officer, just let me go otherwise you will have a problem," said Mike.

"It's you who have the problem," said the black man tightening his hold. "Don't diss me cause I'm black and don't give me any untruths about yous being the police, I'm not stupid."

Mike tried to crane his neck to see if he could catch the movement of the strawberry blonde, who by now was long gone and all because of this arsehole.

"You scared to look at me, arsehole?" said the black man.

"Look Mister, I don't need any hassle. Just let me go and I will say no more about it," said Mike. By now, the man's head and body were inches away from Mike, who couldn't move anything but his head.

"This is your last chance. Walk away." He said to the black man.

"Or what, you'll arrest me, arsehole?" said the black man.

"No," said Mike, head butting the black man with such velocity that the man just dropped in a heap, blood running down his face. Mike produced his warrant card and showed the crowd.

"Disperse now, the show's over," Mike said. The crowd started moving, only he, Charlie, the black man and his girlfriend remained.

"Is this your boyfriend?" he said addressing the woman who was now crying. She nodded.

"Do you think he's learnt a lesson here today or shall I call in reinforcements and haul him down to the station, where we can find out what makes him tick?" said Mike.

The black man was now on his feet. "What's it to be then my friend?" said Mike stepping back and watching the black man's hands.

"Let's give him a break," said Charlie.

"Get lost," said Mike to the black man who was still contemplating giving the cop a good hiding. Mike took out his phone and started dialling; the black man started walking away fast, his girlfriend trying to keep pace with him. Blood was everywhere. Mike watched him until he too was lost in the crowds. Mike lit up, his hand shaking.

"One good thing Charlie."

"What's that Mike?"

"I think my headache's cured," said Mike.

"Why were you running Mike, who were you chasing?" said Charlie.

"I thought I saw the Chessman," Mike said, noticing the street cameras and wondering if the black man would make a report. All he needed was a charge of police brutality. The Chessman was the perfect excuse and one which would override any potential inquiry of what just happened.

"How did you know it was him?" said Charlie.

"I just know Charlie, and one more thing, we just met a few minutes ago and were passing the time of day, exchanging info, you understand?"

"I do," said Charlie.

"I'm going now Charlie. Wait a minute and then go in the opposite direction. We've got to be careful and if you can give Amber a call and tell her what happened."

"Right Mike, see you Monday. Have a nice weekend."

"You too Charlie. Give my regards to Maggie."

Mike walked off following what he thought would have been the strawberry's route. One never knew, he could strike lucky. Mind you, pigs might fly. After half an hour of walking up and down, Mike gave up. He looked up into the sky. He didn't see any pigs. He grabbed a passing cab and gave his mother's address. The cabbie had City on his radio; they were four nil up. It was five nil by the time he reached his mother's. She was out.

Mike decided to walk down to the shops and have a look around. He needed to start buying a few Christmas presents. Two hours later the only thing he had bought was another packet of non-filtered cigarettes. By the time he'd walked back to his mother's she had returned.

"Mam, you must get yourself a mobile phone. They're easy to use you know."

"I know they're easy Mikhail but why would I want one? I've got a phone here and that's all I need. Why make life complicated?" she replied.

"Well, get a car of some sort, you can drive," said Mike.

"I was driving before you were born Mikhail but what need would I have for one? The shops are only a short distance and all my friends live around here."

Mike was about to speak when his mother went on. "If they're so useful, why didn't you ring me to tell you were on your way? That way I wouldn't have gone out. And how come you didn't drive your car down?"

"Mam, my phone's playing up and I've got a problem with the car. I've got a flat tyre or something," Mike said.

"So the two things you insist on me getting are no good for you. Is that so Mikhail? More trouble than they're worth."

"Okay Mam, it was just a suggestion," said Mike.

"Cup of tea and cake then, Mikhail?"

"That would be nice," said Mike not, particularly wanting either.

"Tell me Mikhail, why aren't you playing or watching football? It's a Saturday."

"Too busy Mam," said Mike.

"And how come you have no girlfriend, Mikhail? You are getting older. I want grandchildren while I can still enjoy them," his mother added.

Before Mike could answer, his mother was asking him about any special girlfriends and why she never met any. Was he ashamed of his dear old mother?

"I have girlfriends Mam but nothing special yet. That's why I don't bring them round. Don't worry, I'm not gay."

"I know you're not Mikhail. Mrs Alibi is always tidying up after you've had visitors for the night."

"Mrs Alibi, my cleaner?" Mike said.

"Yes, the same cleaner who I found for you and lives just around the corner," Alice said.

"Is there anything you don't know?" said Mike, promising himself to be more careful on Tuesdays, the day before the cleaner came.

"I know enough," said Alice.

"Enough of what?" said Mike.

"That you are still searching for the perfect partner Mikhail, and having a good time searching."

"That about sums it up, Mam. I will just keep plugging away and one day – boom! I'll be at your door with your future daughter-in-law," said Mike.

Alice poured her son some tea and cut him a piece of Dundee cake. "Don't leave it too long, Mikhail. Life's too short to be alone without a good woman," Alice said.

"I'll do my best," said Mike, putting a piece of cake into his mouth. It was good. It was homemade. He was sure that made all the difference.

Mike left after calling a taxi and after arriving home, he felt dejected. Nothing was going right. He didn't want a drink, he didn't want company. He didn't know what he wanted. He switched on the TV and within minutes, he switched it off again. His concentration levels were at zero. He made himself an espresso, took a sip and left it. He wasn't in the mood for Angelo's and couldn't be arsed to make himself something to eat; he wasn't hungry.

He opened the balcony doors and looked out. He could hear a dog howling; he felt like joining it. He thought of his late father. The phone rang; he let it ring. His mobile rang; he didn't answer it. Mike mooched around. Even Cardiff's big win didn't make him feel any better.

He lay on the bed fully clothed, closed his eyes and tried to sleep. Again, he got up within minutes and paced around the house. He wished he had a brother or sister; someone who could act as a release valve for whatever malady he had. In a way, he was jealous of Evan who had a loving wife and loving daughter. Maybe his mother was right. He needed a wife. He had friends but it wasn't the same. Even Charlie had someone who was always there for him, good times and bad. He made a decision. He would take the car and go for a drive; see where it took him, kill an hour or so.

He opened the door. Amber was eating pork chops. She was surprised to see Mike, who himself was surprised to be there. He had made no conscious decision to go to the office.

Amber immediately recognised that Mike was under the weather. He was, or seemed extremely stressed about something.

"Are you okay Mike, have you eaten?" she asked.

"Um, yes, I've eaten, I think. No, I can't remember Amber," said Mike.

"Would you like something to eat or maybe I can get you a drink, whisky if you like," Amber said.

"No thanks Amber. I'm sorry if I caught you just when you were having a bite to eat," said Mike, still standing and staring at nothing in particular.

"I'm always eating Mike," Amber said, putting down her knife and fork. "Are you sure that you're okay Mike? Is there any specific reason you're here and not out enjoying yourself?"

"I'd best be going," Mike said.

"No, please don't go, Mike, sit down. I'd welcome a little company," said Amber clearing the half-eaten food from the table.

Mike didn't want to sit or stand, he couldn't make up his mind.

"Something is troubling you, isn't it?" said Amber, plonking a large glass of rum in front of Mike, who by now had decided to sit. "I have whisky but this always perks me up when I'm down," said Amber.

For five minutes, not another word was exchanged. Mike was far away. Amber got herself a drink and an ashtray, which she placed on the table. Mike stared at the ashtray and then into space. Amber waited. She'd never seen Mike like this; he was usually in control of everything going on. This was a first and it worried her.

Leaning over, she pushed the rum nearer to Mike and said, "Drink Mike. Nothing is ever as bad as it first seems."

Without thinking, Mike automatically picked the glass up and drank. The rum hit his insides and sent shock waves straight up to his brain and that at least registered with him.

"Fuck, Amber. What the hell is this?" Mike said, his stomach doing somersaults.

"Just a little West Indian medicine," Amber said, glad that Mike had joined her in the present world.

"What am I doing here?" said Mike.

"You've come to talk, get things off your chest. Come to someone you trust and who isn't judgmental," Amber said.

Mike looked as if for the first time into Amber's big round beautiful black face and a smile crossed his worried face. He liked this woman; she was in some ways homely, decent, and upstanding. He wasn't about to burden her with his problems.

"You know Mike, I know what you're thinking. You're thinking that you can't unload your problems on a delicate little woman like me and you would be wrong Mike. I can feel your problems. I don't know what they are but little Amber here has a sixth sense and knows that something is troubling you."

"I'm fine Amber. I should be going. I've got things to do," said Mike.

"Just sit, Mike. You've nothing urgent that can't wait, otherwise you wouldn't have come to me. You can trust me. Just tell me what's eating you up, Mike."

"Where do I start Amber? I've so many things on my mind, it's jammed up and I'm not sure I care where it takes me."

"That's stupid talk, Mike. You're one of the bravest and most decent types of people I've come across. Look what you did for Evan, how you treated Charlie, how you stood up to Fowler and Jimmy and more. They're all good things Mike."

"That's my good self, Amber, but I have a nasty self too. I'm not very proud of it and I keep it quiet from everyone."

"Well I've only seen the good, so let me help you. Tell me your problems. You can share them with me," said Amber.

"Twenty-two years Amber, I've waited for my revenge and what do I find out? It was an accident as such."

"Are you talking about your father Mike?" Mike nodded. "If you can call getting mugged an accident." Mike nodded again. Amber wasn't sure what he meant by that.

"The Chessman, where are we with him? Nowhere Amber. He'll kill again and we are partly responsible."

"Why?" said Amber.

"Because it's taken us too long to get him, Amber. Far too long."

"I disagree, Mike. We have done well. The police forces of England and Wales got nowhere. We did. Just the three or four of us and in the process solved another murder, a bank job and the whisky racket."

"True Amber, we did some good," said Mike.

"Some good? Our success rate is ten times better than anyone's in the country, no not ten, a hundred times, if you take into account our resources."

"You might have a point. Did you know that Evan is contemplating retirement? Clarke's going to move us on; you back to Bristol, me to that place with the long name, you know the place Amber, Llan goff goff goff..."

"I know Mike. It's got about fifty-five letters in its name. I can't say it either. Even if it was written here in front of me."

"And then I've got my mother. She wants grandchildren. She's been alone for a long time and unfortunately, I can't do much about that. I mean, how am I ever going to meet somebody in this job?"

"Sport Mike. I know you like to play football and you play tennis to a reasonable standard or so I'm led to believe, that must help," said Amber.

"I'm getting slower and aching more and more after every game and I don't have time for training. I'm beginning to let the team down," Mike said sadly. "Not that I was much good to begin with," he added.

Amber looked at Mike, who was now staring, head bowed, at his drink. She felt uncomfortable. She wished Evan or Charlie were there, preferably both. She could see the scar very clearly under his eye. The one shaped like a teardrop. Somehow, she felt that tears would be flowing soon, her tears.

"Take our address here," Mike carried on. "111 Nelson Street. According to Evan, it's unlucky. He's convinced of it and to be truthful, I think he's right Amber."

"Just superstition Mike, take no notice of Evan, it's just a stupid cricketers' thing Mike, nothing that means anything to others outside the game."

Mike reached into his pocket and took out his pack of cigarettes, extracted one and placed it in his mouth. "Explain Amber, I'm curious. Evan's always on about it."

"Simple Mike, the superstition is that if the score is on 111, 222 etc., a wicket will fall unless all the team waiting to bat have their feet off the ground."

Mike started laughing, "I like it, but why is it called a Nelson, Amber?"

"Nelson, the famous seafarer had only one eye, so eye, eye, eye, means 111 and called a Nelson, a Double Nelson 222 and so on."

"Must admit it doesn't make much sense Amber, so we have a double Nelson, correct?"

"I think it's just a Nelson," said Amber.

"Look Amber, I don't know anything about a game that's played for five days and still ends up as a draw but I do know that in our address we have a Nelson and 111 which is another Nelson, two Nelsons or maybe we just have four 1's. Nelson's one and the other three in 111."

"That's very good Mike. I've no idea if you can interpret it like that but I think you've grasped the general idea."

"Four 1s are better than two, Amber, that's for sure. I'll have to tell Evan to stop worrying. It's a lucky address."

"Yes Mike, you're right," Amber said, trying to make light of everything. Mike was still fumbling for his lighter so Amber rooted through her handbag and came up with a box of matches, which she passed over to Mike. Mike took another swig of rum and inhaled the cigarette smoke deeply into his lungs. He was beginning to feel better; he was feeling a little mischievous.

"Can you now explain what a googly is? Does it have anything to do with a man's private parts?"

"Do you really want to know Mike?"

"Of course I don't. I was just kidding. I've had my lesson for today Amber, for which I thank you not. Tell me Amber, are you ever scared?"

"Sometimes, it's only human to be."

"That's a good answer Amber."

"Why is it a good answer Mike – are you scared of something?"

"I get scared about a lot of things, Amber, but at this very moment I'm not. Thanks for the drink and the talk," Mike said rising from his chair. "I guess I will see you on Monday," Mike said. "One last thing Amber, did Charlie ring you about a little problem I had with some fella in the town centre?"

"He did Mike, and he also told me that you were chasing the Chessman," replied Amber.

"Well, goodnight Amber. You can finish your meal now."

"I will and I don't Mike."

"Sorry Amber, what's that?"

"I said I would finish eating and I don't believe you were chasing the Chessman, Mike."

"You're a clever lady Amber. Remind me never to play poker with you for money."

After five minutes, Mike found himself driving down Bute Street towards Cardiff Bay station. Suddenly he braked hard and stopped. He got out of his car and walked the hundred or so yards to the Greek Orthodox Church of Saint Nicholaos, the Patron Saint of Seafarers. It was open, a service of some kind had just finished and people were coming out.

Mike went in, put a five-pound note on a tray and took a candle, which he lit and placed in the place that held many other, still burning candles. He made the sign of the cross and silently prayed for a good two minutes. He thanked God for helping him make it thus far and when he had finished he left. The priest stood at the door and looked at him. Mike said goodnight and the priest answered in Greek – well, Mike thought it was.

He then drove the short distance to his apartment, had a shower and retired to bed. It was only nine p.m. He slept for a full twelve hours. He felt safe and secure and that good feeling remained with him for the whole of the next day.

Sunday started well for everyone except poor Miss Zoe Pritchard who slipped and fell whilst walking to the local shop for a magazine. She died instantly; she was only thirteen.

The grand house, complete with stables, tennis court and indoor swimming pool, was owned by Henry J Pritchard, founder of the Pritchard Banking Group. His granddaughters Zoe and Chloe were spending the week with him whilst their parents, his son and daughter-in-law were away on business. The twins loved riding, tennis and swimming and looked forward to leaving London and travelling to Monmouth to see their grandfather.

There was a short piece on the local news about the accident and this only because old man Pritchard was one of the richest men in the United Kingdom. The Chessman caught the news. Strangely enough, this Pritchard was one of the six to whom he had sent a letter. Amber and Evan also saw the piece but thought nothing more of it. Within six hours, they would have a lot more to say about it.

Mike picked up his mother and took her to the cemetery.

"Someone's put flowers on Dimitri's grave and there's a card too," said Alice, Mike's Mum. "Let me get my glasses out so I can read it."

"No need Mam, the note reads 'Lest we forget.' By this time Alice had found her glasses and was reading the card. "How did you know Mikhail? Did you come earlier? These look fresh and very expensive."

"Look Mam, there's a bench just over there. Let's go and sit down. I need to tell you something," said Mike. "Nothing is wrong Mam. I'm not ill; I just want to explain about the flowers." And he did, everything, leaving out the violence from his story. His mother was in floods of tears. Mike put his arm around her and then remained like that for ten minutes.

"Maybe Mikhail, you can now get on with your life in a proper and dignified way. The way your father would have liked from his only child."

"Mam, I don't know what a proper and dignified life is. I joined the Force to help me get my father's killers, who turned out to be muggers who caused Dad to die. It was an accident. Twenty-two years. Anyway Mam, before I go rambling on, my objective is complete and now I think it is time to resign from the Force, as is my partner, very soon."

"But you're good at your job Mikhail, and as I understand it, your partner's much older than you."

"Yes, Mam, my partner's much older and as for being a good detective, I've reason to believe that I'm not that hot. Actually, I'm not that good."

"You shouldn't talk like that Mikhail. You're a very good police officer."

"And you are my mother," said Mike. "Only a mother sees no wrong in her child," said Mike.

"That's true Mikhail, but I can't see wrong where wrong doesn't exist. You're a good, kind hearted man, just like your father."

"Mam, why don't we go to Archangel and spend a week or two?" said Mike.

"One day we shall Mikhail, all of us will go."

"All of us?" said Mike.

"Yes, me, you, your wife, my grandchildren," said Alice.

"Okay Mother, but it might take a while to get everything into place," Mike said, killing the conversation.

After revisiting the grave, Mike took his mother home where she changed ready to be taken out for Sunday lunch at Angelo's. By three-thirty, Mike was back in his apartment; Alice was with him. Mike made two coffees but his mother was more interested in cleaning his apartment.

"What can you find to clean Mam? Mrs Alibi does all that on Wednesday." He might as well have been talking to the wall – his mother just carried on cleaning. "It's Sunday Mam and it doesn't need cleaning," said Mike unable to concentrate on his newspapers. He always bought half a dozen when City won, especially Wales on Sunday as they carried bigger stories on the local sporting teams.

"When was the last time you made up the bed, Mikhail, or cleaned the fridge? What you need is a good woman. You can't eat at Angelo's every day."

Mike thought about it. Yes, he did need a good woman but fate had decreed that the strawberry blonde was unobtainable. Where the hell was she, would he ever find her?

"I hear no answer from you Mikhail," said Alice.

"Yes Mam, you're right. I need a good woman; even a bad one will do right this minute."

"Don't be funny with me Mikhail and did you hear what I said about the bed and fridge?"

"I don't do the bed on Sundays, it's my lying in day, and as for the fridge, well, I do it now and then."

"And what about the oven, Mikhail?" Alice asked. "This will take me a good half hour to clean."

"I hardly ever use it Mam, so how can it be dirty?"

"And how many clothes do you need? You have too many and they all look the same to me."

Mike didn't bother replying – it was a lose, lose, lose situation when his mother started on about cleaning and clothes.

"What you need is a good wife, Mikhail, who can cook and clean, sew and..." There Alice stopped. Mike guessed she was going to say 'and have babies' but was happy that for the time being his mother was occupied doing whatever she was doing in the kitchen and he could read his papers.

As the Chessman drove past, windows open, he briefly stopped at the point where the girl's accident had occurred and threw out the beheaded chess pawn. It bounced once on the pavement and then settled on the small grass verge next to a few large stones.

He returned to his flat and wrote a letter, which he copied four times. Envelopes and stamps he had. All he needed to do now was post his letters and make one phone call – a free one.

After receiving the call and ascertaining to whom to pass it on, the sergeant on duty called Amber. It was now twenty past four.

"Oh no," said Evan, when he got the message. He'd had three large glasses of white wine with his roast chicken dinner and thought it prudent to a call a taxi.

Mike, who had avoided drinking too much in front of his mother, was fine to drive. He explained to his mother that he had to go and that she should call a taxi to get her home.

Amber had given instructions to the sergeant that two men were to be immediately dispatched to the scene but not to do anything or touch anything until Special Detective Inspectors Karetzi and Jones arrived.

Mike got to the office just before Evan and they set off in Mike's car to the scene. On arrival, one of the constables pointed out the chess piece. Mike thanked them and told them they could go.

"Three questions, Evan."

"Only three Mike?"

"Well, let's start with three, Evan: one, where was the security and why did she go out alone? Two, the Chessman has never touched children before. Why now? Three, is this what it purports to be or are we missing something? And four, why? He's nothing to gain."

"That's about six, Mike. The girl obviously got out without anyone knowing and this is not the Chessman's work. This I think was a pure accident. The girl slipped here," Evan pointed to a bit of moss on the pavement, "fell and cracked her head on these rocks here, hence the blood just here and there," Evan said, pointing out the dry stained blood.

"I agree with all you say, except for one thing Evan."

"I know you're talking about his calling card, Mike."

"Yes, the chess piece which we can check for fingerprints and match them with those we have, but what does that mean?" said Evan.

"Nothing," said Mike, "because the piece is a recent placement."

It had started to drizzle but both men stood like marble statues looking at the ground. The rain became heavier and still neither man sought shelter.

"You are obviously very preoccupied Evan. You okay?"

"I'm fine Mike, why do you ask?"

"You've forgotten our umbrella, Evan, this must be a first," said Mike and that was the first time that Evan noticed it was raining and that he was wet through.

"Let's get back to Four Eyes, Evan."

"Four Eyes, Mike?"

Mike explained the Nelson business to his partner. Evan approved, he liked it and it would do until the 6th of next month. Roll on retirement, he thought to himself. Mike drove slowly back; neither was talkative.

Amber was drinking coffee when they reached the office, not the usual stuff they drank daily but something with a great aroma, which both men appreciated before actually tasting.

Bedraggled Mike and Evan might be but they weren't as yet beat, although they were pretty close to losing it; the Chessman was still running rings around them. Two cups of coffee were served up by Amber; they hadn't bothered to get out of their wet clothes.

"This is great coffee Amber," said Mike. "I'll have to get some of this myself."

"It's a blend of Blue Mountain from Jamaica and Kopi Luwak in London. It will set you back forty pounds a cup if you can find a retailer," said Amber.

"My God," said Evan, "how the Dickens can you afford it Amber?"

"Corporate credit card," said Amber.

"Oh shit," was Evan's reply.

"Well, are we going to talk about the cost of coffee beans or about Zoe Pritchard? I assume that's where you have just been," Amber said.

"We don't think it's a Chessman victim," said Mike.

"And the chess piece?" said Amber.

"That we can't fathom out," said Evan.

"The Chief expects his weekly report first thing every Monday," said Amber.

"I say Plan A is to interview both the coin collector people and then get some form of trap," said Mike.

"And do we have a Plan B, boys, if that comes to nothing and we're on the wrong track?" Amber asked. "What will I tell the chief in the report?"

"Tell him we've got a whole alphabet of plans," said Mike, lighting up.

"And we do?" asked Evan.

"Do you expect a reply, Ev?" said Mike.

"No, 'cause there isn't one, is there, Mike?" said Evan, who was loading his pipe. "We can't flush him out, tempt him in some way?"

"Is that a question, answer or just a plain 'we're fucked' statement, Evan?" said Mike.

"I think all three," said Amber. "Our days are numbered as a force operating out of Nelson Street," said Amber.

"We know," said Mike.

"Wish we could close this bloody case," said Evan. "I'm beginning to have nightmares about it."

"I don't want to say it, but I have to," said Amber.

"Say what?" said Mike.

"What's crossed all our minds from nearly day one of this investigation."

"That he has someone in the organisation helping him. That's how he's always one step ahead," said Evan.

"It's possible Evan, but how, not who, how?" said Mike.

"Surely it's 'who' Mike, a somebody, not a 'how'," said Evan.

"It's a 'how'. Look, the way I see it, forget who. It could be the Chief, those arseholes at Tangent, Charlie, someone who works closely with the Chief. His wife, his girlfriend Emma, someone in the local force; my mother, Edna, your daughter Evan."

Mike was cut up at that stage by Amber who said, "Don't be so ridiculous Mike, you're implying that it could even be one of us three."

"No, that's my point. It's how. Think about it. Most of our findings have been from gut feelings, luck, bits of information, off the cuff movements. So how could the 'who' tip off the Chessman, when we ourselves have no idea of what we're going to do from one minute to the next?" said Mike.

"Mike's correct Evan. Sometimes I'm in the dark, never mind the Chief, but it wouldn't be a bad idea to run another bug scan in this building," Amber said. "That's the only way someone would know," she added.

"The Chief isn't going to like it when we tell him that Zoe Pritchard had an accident and is not, nor was not, a Chessman victim, even though evidence suggests otherwise," said Evan.

"And any day now the credit card invoices are going to hit his desk and he will have a fit," said Amber, looking at her coffee cup.

"Well, let's get our Christmas shopping while we still have

time," said Mike. Everyone laughed including Amber, who was still looking at her coffee cup.

"I'll get the two interviews arranged for tomorrow afternoon. I'll leave the morning open in case the Chief needs to see us. Is that okay with you both?" Mike and Evan told Amber it would be fine.

"See if you can obtain some cyanide pills, Amber, just as a precaution."

"I'll run down to Boots in the morning Mike." Again, everyone laughed.

"One more thing Amber: could you get hold of the photos taken at the scene of Zoe's accident and the street camera videos from the town centre between the hours of say, two p.m. and four p.m., or at least copies," said Mike. "Oh, and get Charlie in first thing," Mike added.

"What about the sweep?" asked Amber.

"First thing," said Evan, "best use Jane's husband again, tell him we'll pay him."

"I forgot to tell you boys: the reward money has been cancelled. They've had nearly five thousand Elvises and decided it was time to put a halt to it," said Amber.

"Elvises, what are they then?" asked Evan.

"Sightings which they know are rubbish," said Amber.

"Did they follow up any?" asked Mike.

"Of course they did, hundreds, all a complete waste of money and manpower," said Amber.

"Has Zoe's accident been on telly today?" said Evan.

"Yes, a few times," replied Amber.

"From the site where she met her death or from the newsroom?" asked Mike.

"Both," said Amber.

"Well, I guess we've solved that particular mystery," said Evan.

"We have Evan. He saw the report and decided to make some use out of it, so he just went down and deposited the chess piece. I bet we won't see it on any of the photographs," said Mike.

"One up to us," said Amber beaming.

"Only nine more to catch up," said Evan.

Before they left, Mike had one more piece of wisdom to leave with Amber. "Don't drink all the coffee, Amber, the Chief might want to try it and see where his money is being spent."

"I'll drop you off home then Evan," said Mike as they walked out to his car.

"No thanks Mike, I'll get a taxi, no point in you going out of your way," said Evan, ever fearful of a meeting between his partner and his daughter.

"I insist Evan. For God's sake, it's not a problem."

"It's just that I could do with a little walk and a little fresh air Mike, that's all."

"Get in the car Evan. I'll keep both windows open. You'll get your fresh air, I guarantee you. Come on Evan, you hiding something from your partner? Have you got a party on at home and you don't want poor old Mike to show you up."

"Of course not Mike, it's that I know you're a busy man with things to do and I don't want you to go out of your way when it's easy for me to grab a taxi."

By this time, they had reached the car and Mike had practically manoeuvred Evan into the passenger seat.

"There are no tyre marks on the grass verge, Evan. He must have just driven by and lobbed the piece onto the verge straight out of the window."

Evan was deep in thought. He was thinking of a reason to be dropped off without Mike coming into the flat. He was still working on his plan when Mike pulled up and parked outside his block. Both men got out and Evan, being the type of person he was, found himself asking Mike up for a drink. Mike noticed that Evan didn't knock or ring the bell, but tried to open the door with trembling fingers. It was the wrong key; the second attempt was more successful and they entered.

"Hello Edna. I've got a surprise. Mike my partner is with me," he shouted as they entered.

Edna appeared from nowhere and after kissing Evan on the lips, kissed Mike on his cheek. "My, my, your clothes are damp and yours, Evan. Where have you both been? Give me your jackets, I'll put them both in the airing cupboard, then I'll fix us a drink. Is whisky fine for you Mike?" Edna said without waiting for a reply but taking both jackets with her.

"You've just missed Evan; she's gone to the pictures with a friend, left about fifteen minutes ago."

"That's a pity," said Mike "I still haven't had the time to thank you both for this fantastic watch. As I told Evan, it's greatly appreciated but unnecessary. Being able to help was reward enough."

"Rubbish," said Edna who had returned with the drinks. "That was the least we could do, Mike. It's something we will never forget."

Evan fully agreed, head bowed with shame for his stupid high morality. The man who avenged his daughter was too much a man to meet her. He now wished his daughter had not gone to the cinema but was here to thank Mike herself. He deserved that and more.

"It seems a little big Mike – the wrist strap," said Edna.

"It is," said Mike, "I need to take one or two links out. They always make the straps much bigger because everybody's wrist size is different."

"And you have large wrists," said Evan. "God knows what it would be like on Charlie. He could probably wear it around his neck."

Mike laughed. He noticed the change in Evan. It was as if somebody had thrown a switch. Evan was now completely relaxed – and they called him crazy!

A mobile rang, then stopped, then rang again and stopped. Everyone looked around the room. It wasn't Edna's. "Where did you put the jackets, Edna?" Evan asked.

"In the airing cupboard love," replied Edna.

"Thanks," said Evan leaving the room. Edna looked at Mike, puzzlement written all over her face.

"He's gone to get our mobiles, Edna, and I hope my cigarettes." Mike was half right. Evan returned with both mobiles but no cigarettes, so Edna got up and collected Mike's cigarettes from his jacket pocket.

"It's Amber," said Evan. Mike looked at his, scrolled back and said, "Me too." Using the landline Evan contacted the office.

"Half an hour, we've only been gone half an hour," said Evan when he put the phone down. "Not more bad news?" said Mike.

"Not exactly Mike; the photos are not conclusive, that is to say they don't show where we found the chess piece. The coin buffs refuse to see us; one is out of the country and the other says he has enough security. Anyway, both are too busy doing whatever they do."

"That's okay Evan, we can still set something up without their knowledge," said Mike.

"That's a no-no Mike, they have spoken to the Chief and we will not be allowed to use any men," said Evan.

"Pathetic, that's bloody pathetic," said Mike.

"That's not all Mike; we have a meeting with Henry Pritchard, nine o'clock sharp tomorrow morning at his residence."

"What for? It's not our case. It was an accident," said Mike, knocking back the whisky in one go and then lighting up. Edna poured Mike another. Evan hadn't touched his sherry yet.

"There will be other parties at this meeting Mike; the Chief Constable, a chappie from Scotland Yard and our old mate Brian," said Evan.

"You're joking me; all these people for what amounts to a tragic accident," said Mike who by now had lit another cigarette and had two on the go.

"It turns out that this Pritchard is an ex-foreign secretary and one of the richest people in Europe, if not the world. His daughter-in-law owns a newspaper and various magazines and the son runs the banking group and various brokerage houses. We're talking massive money, heavy political clout," said Evan.

"Best I wear a suit then Evan."

"Best you do Mike," said Evan in all seriousness.

"Did I tell you it's Lord Pritchard, Mike?"

"No, you didn't mention it," said Mike.

Mike didn't drink the second whisky, he needed to get home and then have a drink.

"So I'll pick you up at eight then, Mike. No point in us going in separate cars."

Five to and Evan rang the bell. Mike answered and let him in. Evan was all dressed up as if he was going to meet the Queen. Edna must have dressed him. He looked relatively well attired apart from the ultra-shined brown brogue shoes, which didn't match his blue suit and tie.

"They your best shoes Evan?"

"They are, Mike. I've had them nearly eleven years. They were bloody expensive but have worn well," said Evan.

Pity, thought Mike. Mike had a pair of black slacks and a black jacket, all of which perfectly matched his black moccasins.

"You look like Johnny Cash, Mike."

"All I need to do is practise my singing and get myself a guitar," said Mike. As they approached the mansion, Evan lit his pipe; Mike put both the windows down. "Better smoke before we get in," said Evan. Mike acknowledged Evan's thoughtfulness and lit up.

A guard at the gatehouse looked them over. Checked their warrant cards, then his list, before opening the gates. Mike counted the gardeners and a security guard before they had reached the visitors' parking spaces. Security cameras were in abundance and the door opened before they had actually reached it. A flunky disguised as a penguin opened the door and took Evan's umbrella before motioning them to a small room where another flunky dressed in a business suit, but obviously some form of security man, again asked for their warrant cards before leading them to a large heavy wooden door. The hall itself was bigger than both the detectives' combined flats. The floor was chequered marble and if you looked at it for too long you got cross-eyed. Antiques were everywhere, suits of armour, desks, occasional tables and more. A maid crossed the hall whilst they waited outside the big wooden door.

The flunky knocked and was told to enter. He did not, he just held the door open for the detectives. The room they entered was very large and decorated in art deco style. Another maid took charge and bade them follow her, which they did into another slightly smaller room. Obviously, they had arrived at their destination because the Chief, Brian, an older man, who by his demeanour was Lord Pritchard, and a fifty-year-old balding, badly dressed man who was, by process of elimination, the Scotland Yard detective chappie.

The introductions were made; the man from Scotland Yard was called Commander Spallow. Mike wasn't sure if it was Swallow or Scallow so he would stick with Commander. Evan was sure it was Swallow but also decided to stick with Commander. Two seats were unoccupied and the Lord stretched out his hand indicating where they should sit. Everyone remained standing like soldiers on parade until Lord Pritchard sat. The maid remained, waiting to be dismissed.

"Would you like a coffee, tea, soft drink, anything?" the Lord asked in a quiet and kindly sounding voice. Both detectives declined but Mike noticed there were ashtrays everywhere and could smell cigar smoke.

"I understand that my granddaughter Zoe was murdered by some madman you call the Chessman. Is that so?"

Mike noticed the tears in the old man's eyes. He'd been crying. God knows how Evan was going to answer this. Evan saw the same thing and was glad that his partner was going to answer. Neither spoke and no one from the three helped by saying something.

"I see," said the Lord. "Am I correct in saying that this Chessman's calling card is a severed white chess piece, and that one was found next to my little Zoe's body?"

"That is correct your Lordship," said Evan.

"And you, I presume, are D.I. Jones?" said the Lord.

"Yes Sir, I mean your Lordship, that is correct," said Evan.

"May I call you Evan and Mikhail, will that be in order? And I'm Lord Henry if that's okay with you." Both nodded. "That's good. So Evan, we have this calling card but for some reason there is doubt, that's what I seem to be reading."

"I don't think, your Lordship, that the detectives are saying that," said the Chief Constable.

"And I don't think I asked you to answer for them Clive, so shut up." The Chief shut up. Lord Pritchard was not a man to cross swords with.

"So, Evan, please try to explain to me why you have doubts. I need to get to the bottom of this before my son arrives here in about two hours' time. He'll want answers. Zoe was in my care."

Evan tried to speak but just couldn't. He wanted out. Maybe it was the Chessman. That's what his Lordship wanted to hear, but nothing would come out of his mouth.

"I hope I'm not being too intimidating, I don't mean to be. I just need the truth as you see it," said the Lord.

"May I say something, Lord Henry?" said Commander Spallow.

"Go ahead David."

"It's that our two detectives here, good fellows that they are, have been after this Chessman for a while and regrettably have failed. Not of course through any fault of their own and are probably too close to everything concerning the murderer to let's say make the right diagnosis."

"How many victims David?" asked Lord Henry.

"Quite a few: twelve or so," said Spallow.

"And what resources, or let's put it another way: this serial killer is still at large to kill my little girl. How many men do you have on the case, David?" No answer. "I guess that means none and your people Brian, another 'nothing' is it? So it was left to the local

South Wales police to deal with and I suppose resources are tight. How many Clive? Six, seven, eight, how many? Come on man, it's an easy question. How many?"

"It's just us two and a civilian cum police person," said Mike.

"How many victims, Mikhail?"

"Twelve positives, Lord Henry, Sir."

"Including Zoe."

"No Lord Henry."

"Tell me why, Mikhail" – and Mike told him. Evan's phone went off. Lord Henry told him to answer it. Evan did. It was Amber. Two large amounts had been paid out to charities.

"Anything of concern to us here in this room?" said Lord Henry. Evan told him.

"My God," exclaimed Brian. "What on earth made them do that?"

Lord Henry produced two letters from his pocket and said, "I too as you know have received these letters and I have no intention of parting with any money, not now, not ever. It's a drop in the ocean to me but if money could buy back my Zoe's life, I would walk out here with just the clothes on my back." Lord Henry stopped there because he was crying so much he couldn't speak and he seemed to have difficulty breathing. Everyone looked away until he had composed himself again.

"So detectives, speak to me. What went wrong? Was it just Karma with my poor little Zoe?"

"We must ask the following questions, Lord Henry," said Evan. "Who knew that Zoe was going out to buy a magazine, apart from her sister Chloe? Why didn't she send one of the staff? There seem a lot of them around. Why wasn't she accompanied? How did she get out undetected? There's a lot of security cameras about. It will help a lot if we have answers to that lot," said Evan.

"There's one more Evan," said Mike.

"What's that Mikhail?" asked Lord Henry.

"Who does she know in the village and I mean a boy, and who

was she going to meet, and I mean a boy again. She's at that age and she didn't take her twin sister with her."

"What are you suggesting Detective?" said the Chief Constable.

"The obvious," retorted Brian. "Mike's right, it makes sense to me."

"I have to disagree," said Spallow. "She's only been down here two days and don't forget the chess piece."

"Why do you come to this conclusion, Mikhail?" asked Lord Henry.

"Easy Lord Henry, we can't answer any of the questions my partner posed which means that Zoe didn't want to be driven, seen, accompanied, etc., because she wanted to meet somebody and that has to be a boy. Let us speak to her sister Chloe and within half an hour I promise you we will have your answer."

Lord Henry stood and crossed the room to a phone, which he picked up and spoke into. He requested that his granddaughter Chloe should come down immediately and wait in the adjoining room.

"Please feel free to smoke. This is the smoking room," said Lord Henry. He also offered various Havana cigars. Mike lit up. Evan was too nervous to so he just played with the pipe. It took Evan and Mike five minutes to extract the information from Chloe. The boy's name was Jack. He was fifteen and they met last year when the twins spent a week in Wales. He was the local paperboy. Two phone calls later and the boy admitted all, not that he had done anything wrong.

Commander Spallow was astonished. This was police detection at its very best. Brian wasn't, he'd come to expect miracles from the boyos in Wales and he was never let down. The Chief basked in their glory; after all they were his men.

"My son has been delayed for an hour. Tell me everything about yourselves and the Chessman, I want to help."

They told Lord Henry everything. They tried not to put down the Chief or Brian too much but Lord Henry was no fool, he could read between the lines better than people could actually read what was on the lines.

"Will you please excuse me for a minute or two?" said Lord Henry, walking out of the room.

"Well done boys, you've done our force proud here today," said the Chief, meaning every word.

The Commander shook their hands and said the usual; anytime they wanted a job in London, no problem. He of course didn't mean a word of what he said. Brian was happy for them; he knew they were good detectives. He'd known that a long time. Lord Henry returned after approximately ten minutes. He addressed Brian first.

"I've just spoken to your Director and he's agreed to sell the property and contents at 111 Nelson Street to me for a cut-down price. This same property I'm renting out to the South Wales Police Force for ten years at a peppercorn rent of fifty pounds per annum on the condition that it is used for the purposes it is now used for and that an additional member of staff is taken on by the unit now occupying said building. This additional member of staff shall be chosen by S.D.I.s Karetzi, Jones and Mrs Gilberts. Is this okay Clive with you? All the additional documentation is being written up as we speak. I want it finished by Friday."

"Of course Lord Henry, it's fine. It is very magnanimous of you to help in this way. I can't thank you enough; our budget is very tight and..."

"Oh stop waffling on Clive. I want this Chessman caught and I think these are the lads that can do it. Thank you all for coming at such short notice. I wish I had better news for my son but at least it was an accident and nothing more sinister. I can only blame myself and I always will."

Lord Henry shook hands with everyone and walked them to the outside door. Five minutes later and everyone was heading back to their bases.

"Well, that was a result," said Evan.

"Henry's a wise old bird; it's inconceivable that he wasn't fully aware of everything we have achieved and that his granddaughter's accident was just that."

"You mean Lord Henry, Mike."

"For Christ's sake Evan, yes, I mean Lord Henry. There's only us two in the car, I'm sure he won't mind us calling him Henry when he's not around," said Mike.

"Anyway Mike, Lord Henry promises everything that is decent in a human being but why help us out? I mean, why help out the police?"

"Lord Henry, that is Henry as I know him when I'm not addressing him, is very rich. There's a little part of his mind that says, it could be the Chessman, so he throws money at it, just on that one per cent chance that it is," said Mike. "Evan, we need to talk about the future. There is no point in say hiring Charlie if the Chief breaks up our unit or if you or I retire, or Amber wants out for whatever reason. Even I have been having negative thoughts lately," said Mike.

"Chief can't do anything now after today. Do you know of the Peter Principle Mike? Well, I guess you don't, not many people do know it."

"To use one of your silly cricketing terms Evan, you've stumped me with that one."

"Well, Laurence Peter, a Canadian sociologist, after conducting research into large organisations such as the police, big business, etc., etc., came up with his principle which states that in any organisation, people are promoted to the level of their incompetence and remain there. Don't you see Mike, he's right? I've reached my level of incompetence."

They had arrived at the office at the same time Brian pulled up and before they could exchange words, the Chief Constable came around the corner, his driver having been instructed to come direct to the door.

"I see we have a full house," the Chief said.

"Where's Mr Swallow?" asked Evan, fully expecting another arrival.

"It's Commander Spallow Detective," said the Chief.

"Yes Sir," said Evan.

"There is no reason for the Commander to be present," said the Chief.

Everyone walked in. Thankfully, Charlie was not already there and a quick call from Mike stopped him on his way. Amber had the coffee ready, not the good stuff but the office's normal fare.

"So, that was a turn up for the books," said the Chief. "Tell me Mike, have you met Lord Henry before?"

"No Chief," said Mike.

"Strange then, that he should call you by your given name. He really must have done his homework."

Mike nodded, yes, it was unusual to be called by your given name and yes, Henry seemed to know a lot about what was going on.

"The documentation was in hand Chief, as if Lord Pritchard had already made his mind up," said Brian.

"He knew everything yesterday, or to be more precise last night after he asked me to send him a fax with all our details from the day we started working out of Nelson Street," said Amber.

"You told him everything, police confidential stuff, Mrs Gilberts?" asked the Chief incredulously.

"I did Chief. I appealed for help. You have been talking about disbanding the unit, days only remaining and so much unfinished business," said Amber.

"Have you spoken to your Director today Brian?" asked the Chief.

"No Chief, but if Lord Pritchard says the Director agrees to whatever, then that's how it is. I think Lord Pritchard can bring a lot to bear on any one situation, when he has a mind to and my prognosis of the situation is simply that he's still unsure whether or not the Chessman killed his beloved granddaughter or if it was, as he would like to believe, just an accident."

"So?" said the Chief.

"So, as his money is unlimited, he decided, after talking to Mike and Evan, that they had the best chance of getting a result and so he would throw some small change into their pot to expedite the Chessman's capture."

"That's it, Brian, and what happens if our boys don't apprehend the Chessman? What will he do then?" said the Chief.

"Nothing," said Mike, "he knows if we don't get him no one will."

"You have a very high opinion of yourself, Karetzi."

"No Sir, I don't as a matter of fact. At this very moment in time I have a very low opinion of myself but I also have two great colleagues who make up for any deficiencies I might possess."

"I disagree with my partner, Chief; he's a top-class detective. The best I've worked with and as a team, together with Amber, we will get a result, of that I'm sure," said Evan.

"This new person, anybody in mind?" the Chief asked.

"We will find someone that fits in," said Evan.

"One more thing: the Chessman's always a step ahead of us."

"How?" asked the Chief.

No one answered.

"Do we have a leak on the inside?" said the Chief.

"I don't think so, Chief. We did a bug sweep this morning and found nothing," Amber said.

"The ten thousand pounds, any accounts Amber?"

"Yes Sir, here are the receipts for four thousand, one hundred and eighty pounds. You can safely assume that the remainder will go to our informants." Amber handed a sealed envelope to Brian, who didn't open it but put it straight into his briefcase.

"Now Chief, can we have half a dozen men for some surveillance on our two coin collectors?" asked Evan.

"Sorry, it's just not possible. We don't have the resources and can't take a chance on your gut feelings. We need something concrete," said the Chief, "and furthermore I understand that the two in question do not want our help and say that they have adequate security.

"One more thing before I let you get on with your work: the two charities in question did not receive a million pounds each, but much smaller sums. A deal was made as will others," said the Chief.

"How much then Chief?" asked Evan.

"Substantially less, Evan," the Chief replied.

"It's important that we know Sir," said Mike.

"Why? Suffice it to say that everyone is happy," said the Chief.

"Except those of us trying to work on the case," said Mike.

"I don't see the importance," the Chief countered, trying to close the subject.

"It is," said Mike. "We can't keep on operating unless we are in receipt of the full facts."

"And we can't keep on working with one hand tied behind our backs," said Evan.

"Give me your reasons why it's so important and I can then decide whether or not to tell you," said the Chief.

"All this is a diversionary tactic, Chief. If the Chessman realises that we are making deals with the charities, he then knows that we know he's planning something else and will start looking elsewhere, where now he wants us concentrating on these people, using up our time and the little resources we have," said Evan.

"Not good enough," said the Chief.

"Fine," said Mike. "Can we at least make sure that no one else makes a deal in the near future? It would seem strange that suddenly everyone pays up Chief," said Mike.

"That I can do, but apart from Lord Pritchard, everyone is pretty scared after this business with the little girl," said the Chief.

"To conclude," said Amber, "we will not be closed down or moved sideways somewhere else. We can hire a civilian of our choice but we cannot have any manpower for surveillance."

"That sums it up," said the Chief. "I wish I could do more but like everyone I am beholden to others."

"Anything you can do Brian?" asked Amber.

"Times are tough, Amber. We're in a bloody recession and I've heard rumours of us downsizing," said Brian.

"I guess we will just sit here and twiddle our thumbs, until we are called out to the next Chessman victim," said Mike.

"Don't be sarcastic D.I. Karetzi. You know how it goes. Go through everything you have again and again. Be detectives, something will break," said the Chief, standing up and ready to go.

The Chief and Brian left together. Amber opened a new packet of biscuits. Evan loaded his pipe and lit up. Mike kicked the paper bin from one end of the room to the other and still felt like shit.

Thor Ingerson sat waiting patiently in the reception area. He was ten minutes early. The only other person in the room was the receptionist, who as far as he could ascertain doubled up as a typist. He gave it a couple of minutes then took out a small bottle containing tablets, two of which he tapped out loudly into the palm of his left hand. His briefcase lay unlocked beside him.

"Excuse me Madam, would it be possible to have a glass of water? I need to take these pills," Thor said.

"Of course Mr Ingerson, I'll go fetch you some."

"Thank you, you are very kind," he said.

As soon as she had moved out of sight, Thor jumped up, extracted two sheets of headed paper from a tray, and placed them in his briefcase. He again thanked the receptionist on her return and used the water to wash down two aspirins. A few moments later, he was shown into Mr Paul Hart's office where he explained his need for insurance cover for various antiquities. He also managed to extract two of Mr Hart's calling cards, before arranging to meet him again the following week. From Hart's office, he went directly to the library where he spent half an hour. He was now ready, as ready as he could be.

On returning to his flat, he started typing and when finished he added Hart's signature or what he thought Hart's signature should be. He then took a copy and burnt the original in his small sink.

After eating a cheese and tomato sandwich and drinking the last two ginger beers from the fridge, he started packing, taking as much as he could in the two suitcases he had. He knew he would never sleep in the flat and he was not sorry. He would rise early so as to avoid the return of his girlfriend from next door and head for his last assignment. Mr Ingerson had completed his job; now it was Mr Hart's turn.

06.30 hours, Tuesday, 11th of December and Peter had left. The car was tanked up, washer fluid vessel full, oil okay and Peter aka the Chessman in good spirits. He drove steadily, not too fast or too slowly. He joined the M4 and headed for Carmarthen where he would come off on the A48 and join the A484 to the West coast near Newquay, and then take a turn onto the A487. The intention was to breakfast at the Port Abraham Services but he wouldn't refill with petrol until he reached Carmarthen. By eight he was sitting eating breakfast and reading his newspaper. All was going to plan.

CHAPTER 24

On arrival, Peter's first job was to contact the boat's owner, which he did. They met shortly afterwards and Peter looked over the 'Maggie May'. Hadfield was obviously a fan of Rod Stewart.

It was more than adequate for Peter. It was large enough for him to be comfortable whilst he completed the writing of his novel. As he explained to Hadfield, he needed three things: peace and quiet, somewhere to lay his head, a table for his small typewriter and of course electricity. That was four things but Hadfield didn't seem to notice, especially after receiving three months' rent in advance.

The car was parked about fifty yards away and after sorting out his belongings Peter went into town and did some food shopping. Fortunately, the boat had a small fridge, not that he needed one – it was minus ten outside, too cold for snow.

After shopping, Peter found a fish restaurant and ate. He'd also purchased a powerful torch and a dozen batteries. He'd also bought a new bolt, a hammer and a screwdriver. He fixed the new bolt on the wooden door and checked out the surrounding area with his torch. He needed to know every inch of the area between his boat and his car. By now, he was tired; the boat's movement made him sleepy and after drinking a couple of ginger beers, he fell asleep; a deep sleep.

He rose early the next morning and fixed himself a coffee, which he made with bottled water. Again, he went into town and purchased a local map. That afternoon he took a drive up to the Reardon-Smythe residence, a big ugly sprawling Georgian mansion. No electric gates, no CCTVs, no security. Things were looking better and better.

He drove past it four or five times. It was slightly off the main roads and not one other car passed him either way. He then drove around the immediate area and found himself a Spar shop which was about half a mile from the mansion.

He returned to town, parked up and searched for a restaurant. He found himself a Chinese that was open. Very unusual for that type of restaurant to open in the daytime, same with Indian restaurants. The food was surprisingly good and Peter was more than satisfied.

On the Thursday, he followed the secretary Adele Histon to her home, which happened to be in Conwy. He'd seen her arrive promptly at ten to nine and leave at ten past six. This woman was regular; that however would soon change – Peter was planning everything for the 17th, a Monday.

It was decided that Charlie would be employed on a forty-hour weekly basis, split thirty hours officially and ten hours unofficially. It was simply that if anything needed doing using Charlie's unique talents, then that would be done during the unofficial hours. For two whole days, the team at Four 1s turned up at the office. Mike taught Evan and Charlie how to play poker properly, Amber already could. They watched television; it was like a little grown up family.

Amber cooked; Mike went to the gym and fitted in some jogging. Amber cooked and ate as they all did. Amber kept on winning all the matches they were using as chips for Texas Hold'em. Charlie kept on buying more to redistribute until Amber had a drawer full. In a way it was a pity they weren't edible.

Boredom set in. Mike lost 3lbs, which Evan gained. Charlie seemed the same weight and no one dared ask Amber. By Wednesday, the men had had enough. They'd lost their matches and were beginning to lose their marbles. Amber was in her element, cooking, eating, cooking and so on. It was decided by Amber that it was time for the house to be thoroughly cleaned and after some gentle persuasion, the men began cleaning. Amber was a hard taskmaster and the men just weren't used to it. They were pleased when the Chief called and told them he was on his way down.

The Chief was not a happy bunny. In his hand, he carried their credit card bills. Meeting Charlie didn't make him any happier. He had grave misgivings about the new recruit. The Chief laid into them all, including Amber and Charlie. Petrol, repairs, food, restaurants, bar bills, everything.

"Who the hell do you think you are, MPs?" said the Chief, throwing the bills onto the desk. Evan tried to hide behind Amber. Mike picked up the bills and read through them.

"Nothing about overtime then, Chief?" said Mike.

"They're credit card invoices Karetzi," said the Chief.

"I know," said Mike, "but I don't see anything about our overtime."

"There is no overtime, you're detectives. You work all hours that God sends," said the Chief.

"If there is such a thing as overtime, then when we are doing this non-overtime, we've got to eat and drink Sir, and we..."

"Enough bullshit Karetzi! There is no overtime and there will be no credit cards if these bills carry on. And as for you, Amber, the amount of food passing through here is enough to feed an army."

The Chief's parting words were "You've been warned" as he walked out.

Poor old Evan had gone the colour of Charlie's surname. Amber was flustered and Charlie bemused.

"Let's order a pizza," Mike said.

"Are you serious?" said Evan.

"You're right Evan, one won't go far, best we order four and some drinks. We can't sit here all day eating Amber's cooking."

"You heard what the Chief said, didn't you Mike?" said Evan.

"Oh, he's okay, let's order some pizzas, it's another month before we have to go through this again."

"You really are crazy Mike," said Amber.

"How come I haven't got a card?" said Charlie.

"Because you're not a full employee. You only work thirty hours," said Mike.

"It's forty hours on the books," said Charlie.

"Give the Chief a ring and tell him, Charlie," said Mike. Charlie didn't answer.

"On whose card are these pizzas going on to?" said Evan.

"Mine," said Mike.

"In that case, let's order," said Amber. Evan still wasn't sure; Charlie didn't care.

The pizzas duly arrived and everyone enjoyed them immensely. "Well, that was well worth it," said Amber, finishing off whatever the others had left.

"Let's raise our glasses to the Chief for providing our lovely meal," said Mike. Charlie and Amber did. Evan thought it was a little tasteless to do so.

"Did I tell you that another one of our guys has paid into a charity? That makes half of them," said Amber.

"And now what shall we do?" said Evan.

"Well, we can't just sit here doing nothing, why don't we go through the inventory of the Chessman's belongings from his house and cars?" said Amber.

"What, again?" said Mike. So they did and as per usual found nothing of interest.

The Chessman spent all Friday checking train timetables and then went back to the boat and rested until it was time to have dinner. This time he found a Thai restaurant and ate leaving at half nine for the 'Maggie May'.

Amber spent her weekend at the International Food Fair; she bought a lot of different foods. The rest of the time, she spent cooking and eating. She also managed to get in some Christmas shopping.

Charlie took Maggie to the local pub, the cinema, the pub, a day out in the Brecon Beacons, Christmas shopping and the local pub where Charlie played darts and pool.

Evan went shopping, watched rugby on telly and rugby live down at the Arms Park. Together with Edna, he went to chapel and then visited his brother Bryn where they had a meal and played Scrabble. Edna arranged collection of their Christmas turkey and various other things needed at that time of year.

Mike managed to get Vicky the barmaid to go out with him for a meal on Saturday night. They went for an Indian as most other places, including Angelo's, were closed by then. After the meal, Mike took her home and that was as far as he got. He returned home alone, a little drunk but a lot wiser. His cheek was still stinging. Sunday he took his mother Alice to the cemetery. New flowers were on the grave but he noticed that his mother was a little agitated about something.

He didn't have the time to find out why, as he was playing that afternoon and he was in a rush. He scored but they still lost. Toby his friend and defensive partner invited him round for a meal that night and Mike accepted. He liked Fiona and loved the kiddies.

The Chessman spent the time planning and re-planning. One quick call and he had confirmed that Sir Quentin had left; it was all on for Monday. Once again, he checked his briefcase: sheet, surgical gloves, Stanley knife, magnifying glass, insurance folder, letter, tape and nylon rope.

Sunday night and he dyed his hair silver grey, the same colour as his false moustache. His spectacles had clear glass and his suit was a non-descript navy blue, the shirt cream, the tie a plain red, the colour of one of those old-fashioned telephone boxes. He wanted people to remember the tie and the glasses with a white unforgettable paint spot on the frame which he himself had daubed on with a cotton bud. He wore black leather shoes and red socks. On his left hand pinkie finger he wore a cheap Masonic ring and on the same wrist a five-pound chrome plated watch which had a large red face. Again, something people would remember.

There was to be no connection with his past. No chess pieces, that was why his disguise had to be perfection itself. He practised his new voice over and over again until he thought it suited his new self. An eccentric seventy-year-old art and antiques insurance expert with the plumy voice.

He wrapped up the book with brown paper, wrote Adele Histon's name and address on the parcel, then tied a piece of string around the parcel and put three first-class stamps on the top right-hand side. These he had to glue down as they had already been used.

The Chessman parked a good five hundred yards from the house and walked, parcel in one hand, tape and card in his pocket. It was a bright start to the morning; the Chessman was sure that the sun would remain all day. He rang the bell at exactly half past eight. Mrs Histon answered. She was alone in the house, divorced with no children. It just made things easier for the Chessman.

"Adele Histon?" asked the Chessman.

"Yes," she replied.

"I have this parcel for you, I need a signature."

"Who's it from?" asked Adele

"I've no idea," said the Chessman, turning it over and pretending to look to see if there was a sender's address.

"Okay, I'll sign," said Adele.

"Do you have a pen? I seem to have mislaid mine," said the Chessman, looking through his suit pockets.

"I'll go and get one," said Adele, turning to go back in. Two quick steps and one karate-style chop to the back of the head and Adele was out of it. The Chessman closed the door and dragged her into what seemed to be a living room. He noticed that she was an avid reader. The shelves were full of books. It was thoughtful of him to bring her another. She probably wasn't really interested in the 'Maintenance of Marine Diesel Generators' but that was all he could lay his hands on.

He got her onto one of the aluminium style chairs and with the cord tied her legs and left hand securely to it. Smelling salts brought her around and as she slowly focused, she could see the old man who by now had located the kitchen and was holding one of her knives in his gloved right hand.

"Are you okay Adele, would you like some water?" he asked. Adele shook her head. "I would like you to do me a favour, Adele, and if you do it properly in exactly two hours from now you will be freed by the police to carry on your life. If, on the other hand, you don't, you will not have a life."

Adele was crying softly, actually she was whimpering. The Chessman handed her a small lace doily, which was on a small table underneath her phone. With her free hand, she dabbed her tearful eyes with the doily. The Chessman sat patiently, time he had. There were to be no mistakes. After a few moments, the Chessman asked her if she was feeling better and understood the prevailing situation. She nodded, keeping her eyes fixed on the knife.

"I do not intend hurting you, Adele, but before I tell you what you must do, I need to ask a few questions. Remember, any lies and I will have no option but to hurt you badly." Adele nodded. "Right then Adele, some simple questions. Firstly, are you expected in today for work?" Adele nodded. "From now on, Adele, you must answer me verbally in case I misinterpret your body language. What time Adele are you expected?"

"Nine but I'm invariably early," she answered.

"What is the butler called?" asked the Chessman.

"Baccus, or to be precise everyone addresses him as Mr Baccus on account of his standing and age," she said.

"When did you last visit a dentist?" he asked.

"What? The dentist? I don't understand," she replied.

"When did you last visit your dentist or any dentist?" asked the Chessman in a very soft voice.

"I would say about three, maybe four months ago," Adele said.

"Did you have any problems, was it just for a check-up or clean? Tell me, Adele, it's important," said the Chessman.

"I went for my six monthly check-up and had a clean at the same time," replied Adele.

"That's fine Adele. End of questions. I told you it's simple. Now you have to make a phone call to Mr Baccus." It was ten to nine.

By nine, there was a full house at Four Is. They sat around one of the desks on the ground floor offices, drinking regular coffee and eating biscuits.

"What's occurring then?" asked Charlie. Evan and Amber laughed but Mike was wondering what the hell was so funny. He had never seen or heard about the Gavin and Stacey programme on T.V. Evan explained as best he could.

"So where to now?" said Evan.

"Why don't we rob a bank or something?" said Charlie.

"Best we do something," said Amber.

"Not poker again," said Evan.

"Any interesting crimes over the weekend, Amber?"

"The big fire out in Caerphilly; two days to get it under control, probably arson; a hit and run case, fatal, ten-year-old girl; a smash and grab – some jewellers in Bridgend; six arrests outside the City ground, I could go on," said Amber.

"Talking of Caerphilly, did you know that the local castle has a tower which since 1648 leans 11 degrees whereas Pisa only leans 4?" said Evan.

"It's depressing, all this crime," said Charlie without thinking.

"It sure is," said Mike, whittling down another pencil.

"How about some elevenses?" said Amber, warming to the thought of eating some more.

"It's only half nine," said Mike.

"Elevenses doesn't mean that it's got to be eleven before we have a snack," said Amber.

"I suppose not," said Mike, "but it's still a little early. Maybe I should go for a brisk walk up to the centre."

"Well, if you are going into town, buy five dozen pencils please, Mike," said Amber.

"What for?" said Mike.

"Because we've run out Mike. You're going through ten a day," replied Amber.

"Sorry," said Mike, folding his knife and placing it in his inside jacket pocket.

"I tell you what we should be doing right now," said Evan. Everyone waited for Evan to tell them. "Buy a Christmas tree, decorations, lights, crackers, the works."

"Sounds good to me," said Charlie. "It's only another eight days to Christmas and we have nothing."

"Artificial or real?" said Amber.

"Real," said all the men together.

"Let's do it then. First stop that greengrocer's near Charlie's," said Mike.

"Then B&Q," said Evan.

"Come on then, let's go," said Mike.

"Don't forget the fairy," said Amber.

No one answered. Fairies were not on their mental lists.

The two-metre tree with stand was delivered. Forty gold-looking baubles were bought, 144 lights, a dozen of the most expensive crackers, some large golden balls and lanterns, a Father Christmas and sledge, a musical roundabout that played carols, various boxes of chocolates, shortbread, After Eights. The three unwise men bought everything that they could think of except of course a fairy for the top of the tree.

On their return, they found the tree already up. It took half an hour of going through the packages before Amber realised there was no fairy and having drawn the shortest straw, Charlie was dispatched to go and get one. With everyone helping, it still took another hour to decorate the room and tree. It was twelve when Amber flipped the switch and the tree lit up. It was magnificent;

it now felt like Christmas at Four I's. Amber opened up a special bottle of rum, took out four mugs and poured each of them a drink. It tasted good. Everyone's mood was sky high, nearly as high as the fairy with the big white wings standing on the top of the tree.

"Now Adele, it's time for us to see how badly you want to live. Pick up the phone and ask for Mr Baccus – you will tell him as follows: one, that you will be in late today, as you need to see your dentist. Two, at about half past nine you are expecting a Mr Hart from the insurance company who has come to revalue the three Fratellis. Three, that he has to take them off the wall, as they need to be horizontal when inspected. Four, he is to advise the police that he is doing so. We don't want any alarms going off in the local nick now do we? Now can you do that for me Adele, it's not too much to ask, is it?" said the Chessman, picking up the knife again and running a finger over the sharp end of the blade.

"You're a very good actress, Adele. I think you have missed your vocation. I'll keep my promise. You will be freed in less than two hours but now I must tie your other hand to the chair and to the radiator.

"Now I'm going to have to cut off your phone and take your mobile, just in case, before I gag you with this tape. Don't panic, breathe through your nose and you will be fine," said the Chessman.

Half an hour he had spent dealing with Adele and everything had gone according to plan. He replaced the knife in its rightful place in the kitchen and left, still wearing gloves and carrying the brown-papered parcel with him, together with Adele's phone, which he would dump into the nearest river.

He drove as fast as he possibly could to the Spar shop, situated a half mile from Sir Quentin's mansion and parked his car out of sight in a field, firstly making sure that the ground was dry. He then unwrapped the book and burnt the paper. He had already disposed of the mobile on route. He called a cab from a nearby telephone box, the number that he had already on his person and stood outside the Spar until it came. He gave them the address of the mansion and arrived outside at a quarter past nine. He rang the bell and after what seemed like a lifetime, the big door opened.

"Good morning," the Chessman said in his much-practised posh voice. "I am Mr Hart and I have an appointment with Adele Histon. Here is my card and this letter confirms our arrangement." The letter was a copy of a letter written by himself and signed by a Mr A Donahue, Managing Director of the insurance company on the headed paper he had stolen. The card was of course one of the two given to him by Mr Hart himself.

The butler, God bless him, took a quick glance at the letter and the card before letting the Chessman through. The Chessman went back to the cab and paid him off. It was important that the staff noticed that he had come by cab; after all, he had come by train from Cardiff.

"We were expecting you Sir. Unfortunately, Mrs Histon has been delayed and has requested me to look after you. Please follow me – this way Sir. I am Baccus the butler. As requested, I have switched off the alarms and notified the police. The paintings are of course off the wall and lying on the full size snooker table in the next room. I hope that meets with your approval, Sir.

"May I offer you some tea or other beverage Sir?" the butler said after leading the Chessman into the room where the paintings lay flat on a full size snooker table.

"That is very considerate of you Mr Baccus but I've just had breakfast on the train coming up," the Chessman said, simultaneously opening his briefcase and extracting the surgical gloves, which he put on, and the sheet and magnifying glass.

"Will you be long Sir? I have a few small duties that I must be getting on with."

"Half an hour or so," said the Chessman, "then if it is possible to call a cab to take me back to the station – I've got another job in Chester this afternoon."

"That won't be a problem Sir," said the butler, turning and shuffling back out the way they had come in.

The Chessman was amazed by the beauty of the paintings. All three were set in orchards. One in an olive orchard where a family of four were sitting on a blanket having a picnic; one with lemon trees – in this one three beautiful young Italian women were picking lemons and putting them in baskets; and his favourite with the two old Italian men sitting under a huge fig tree smoking pipes, drinking red wine and playing Chess.

He gazed at the three for a minute before eventually deciding that time was running out and, from his briefcase, he produced the Stanley knife and set to work. He was careful not to cut into the thick green baize covering the table; it would be a pity if the old man couldn't have a game of snooker on his return from his holidays with his mates. As for the paintings, the cunning old bastard would be insured at way over their actual value, so all in all he was doing Sir Quentin a big favour.

After cutting out the paintings, he rolled them up and placed them in the sheet that he had. They were too large for the briefcase. He checked his watch: fifteen minutes had elapsed; he needed to make a move, so he did by calmly walking to the front door, opening it and strolling down the drive. As soon as he had passed through the gates, he started jogging. He reached the car in six minutes.

Opening the boot, the Chessman changed into jeans and an old cotton shirt. He changed socks and piled the suit, shirt, shoes, glasses, moustache and everything else that would be of no use to him into the briefcase. He looked round, found two heavy stones and threw them in too. With the cream, he rubbed his hair. Slowly it darkened and then he plonked a blue baseball cap on top. He was once again John Davids, author and tenant of the good boat 'Maggie May'.

A small detour and he dumped the briefcase. With the heaviness of the case, together with the stones, it sank like a lead balloon. Stopping at a phone box, he called 999 and left a message about Adele. He used his posh voice. It was now a quarter past eleven.

Within twenty minutes, he was back on the boat. His first job was to wrap up the paintings in Clingfilm and then into a large plastic bag which he made watertight. These he taped onto the sides of the vessel just below the waterline. He then washed his hair and put on the darker dye; he had no intention of leaving the boat for a few days. He had enough food and a radio. He needed to know what was going on.

First, the butler phoned the police and they arrived twenty minutes later. He then tried to contact his boss but was unable to do so. Adele was freed five minutes after the Chessman's phone call.

"How much did all this cost?" said Amber.

"I suppose about three-fifty," said Mike.

"Three hundred and fifty pounds?" exclaimed Amber.

"About that," said Mike, "but remember, you can use most of it next year and the year after."

"If we get that far," said Evan.

"I suppose you purchased these things on the credit cards," said Amber. "Evan's right," said Amber, "if we get to next year. The Chief will crucify us," she said, opening up one of the many boxes of chocolates.

"I paid for the tree," said Mike, "Evan the rest."

Wanting to change the subject, Amber asked if anyone had heard about that art robbery in Llandudno. An old man of seventy plus walked into some guy's mansion and walked out again half an hour later with paintings worth millions, she told them.

"Good for him," said Charlie, "I guess his old age pension wasn't enough." Everyone laughed and forgot about the whole thing.

"Let's open some crackers," said Mike.

"No, wait until Christmas," said Evan.

"We've got twelve, Evan, let's open up just one each," said Mike.

"No way," said Evan, "it's unlucky."

"What's bloody unlucky about opening a few crackers?" said Charlie.

"I don't rightly know but I know it's unlucky," said Evan.

"Can we at least put on that musical roundabout thing, Evan, or is that unlucky too?" said Charlie.

"Don't be ridiculous Charlie, of course that's not unlucky."

"I'm going upstairs to watch 'Loose Women' on TV and make myself a bite to eat. Anyone interested?" said Amber. Nobody was.

The men sat and talked soccer, rugby and fishing. Charlie was keen on fishing. Time passed slowly. Amber came rushing down the stairs and headed straight for the fax where she waited until whatever she was expecting came through; all in all, four sheets.

"Take a gander at this. I know it's in black and white but take a close look." All three men looked.

Evan spoke first: "It's two guys drinking wine under a tree."

"Look closer Evan," said Amber.

"They're smoking pipes," said Evan.

"And?" said Amber.

"And they are playing Chess," said Amber. "Can't you see that?"

"I can," said Mike. "So what?"

"It's one of the three Fratelli paintings stolen. A bit of a coincidence, don't you think?" said Amber.

"Any chess piece at the scene?" said Charlie

"No," said Amber, "and no one was hurt either."

"It's not our man," said Mike.

"No way," said Evan.

"Speak to Chief Inspector Stevens," said Amber, "and then tell me I'm wrong."

"Okay. Evan, will you do the honours?" said Mike.

Evan rang leaving the phone on loudspeaker. "Do you know Mike, I think Amber's right," Evan said, after concluding the call to Stevens.

"I think she is too," said Mike.

"So now how do we work it?" said Evan.

"Let's both go home, pack our suitcases and head up to Llandudno," said Mike. "Amber, could you book a decent hotel for us and try to get as much information about these paintings as possible? Can you pick me up at my apartment, Evan, and Amber, could you inform the locals that we're coming?"

"You can stay here, Charlie, and help where you can. Who knows what's going to happen next."

It was Evan who drove until they got to within thirty miles of Llandudno where Mike took over and drove at nearly twice the speed that Evan had been doing. Evan was glad to have reached Llandudno in one piece. Mike was taking sharp corners at seventy plus and there were times when Evan was saying his prayers. Mike never noticed a thing – driving was driving.

"You drive far too fast, Mike. Not only is it dangerous but we missed the sights," said Evan.

"What sights?" asked Mike.

"The slate piles and railway in Blenau Ffestiniog, Betws-y-Coed and other things," said Evan.

"Don't worry Evan, we can see them at our leisure on the way back down to Cardiff," said Mike.

"Right then, let's find the name of our hotel, dump our bags and get out to the mansion. I will give Amber a tinkle and see what she has arranged," said Evan.

"Everyone's at the mansion. It's near a village called Bryn-y-Maen, about three or four miles away. And Mike, I'll drive," said Evan.

"Fine with me," said Mike, opening up a local map which he had borrowed from the hotel reception desk. They didn't know that Mike had borrowed their map.

Ten miles and half an hour later they decided to stop and ask directions from the next person they saw, who happened to be in the small village they came across next. Evan came to a halt right alongside the man who was about thirty years old and wore his trousers exactly like Simon Cowell – half way up his chest.

Evan opened the window and politely asked the man for directions to Bryn-y-Maen. The man shook his head. Bryn was dead, he died last year in an accident. After five minutes of fruitless questions, all they had managed to find out was that Bryn had been cremated.

Evan drove off in a huff. Bryn's friend carried on walking, hitching his trousers up even further. "Trust me to find the village idiot," said Evan, whose head was spinning.

"He hasn't been promoted yet," said Mike.

It took a further mile of driving before Evan understood what Mike was getting at. He smiled and said, "Good one, Mike, I like it." Another mile and they found a pub. Mike went in and after five minutes returned with a hand-drawn map, which they followed, reaching their destination in five minutes flat, even with Evan driving.

Everyone was there: Chief Inspector Stevens, a D.I. named Harrison, the butler Baccus and the secretary Adele Histon. Introductions were made; the Detectives looked around the crime scene and spoke to both Adele and Baccus.

Stevens handed them a sheet of paper with both Baccus's and Histon's descriptions of the robber. They were near on identical, only in height did they vary; Baccus said about 5ft 8in, Histon 6ft, probably because she was sitting throughout her ordeal and the assailant looked taller.

"Let's see what he's not," said Mike. "Silver hair and moustache, 70 years old, navy blue suit, black shoes, cream shirt, red socks, glasses with white speck on frame, telephone box red tie, Masonic ring noticed by both before he wore the black leather gloves at Histon's house and before he wore the surgical gloves in the Mansion. Brown leather briefcase."

Evan complimented both on their observational qualities and Adele Histon on her bravery under the circumstances.

"So, he was softly spoken, plummy accentless voice, is that correct?" said Evan. Both Histon and Baccus agreed. Evan dismissed them both for the time being.

Chief Inspector Stevens now spoke. "This isn't your man Detectives, it's just an art theft. Well organised. I'll bet you my house that the paintings are in London, Manchester or Birmingham by now and that's the last we will hear of them. Go back home boys, enjoy Christmas, forget this."

Mike and Evan said their goodbyes and headed back to the hotel. "I'm still not convinced it's not our Chessman," said Mike.

"Nor am I," said Evan, "I don't know why but call it a sixth sense. It's him."

When Evan came into Mike's room for them to go down for dinner, he was all kitted up as if he was on his way to evening chapel, if there was such a thing. As usual, Mike had dressed casually.

"You're taking this police thing a bit far Evan," said Mike.

"What police thing?" said Evan.

"Wearing a tie with blue pigs," Mike said, enjoying his joke. He was the only one enjoying his joke.

"Amber did us proud, Evan, this is five star luxury. Let's open the mini bar and see what a can of coke will cost in ten years' time."

"Let's get down and have a drink. I really could do with a pint of Brains."

They didn't serve Brains, so Evan joined Mike in a whisky and soda. They found themselves a seat next to the piano; no one was playing. Maybe it was too early or maybe it was just for show.

Evan's phone rang. It was the Chief – he'd just found out that they were in Llandudno and he was pretty angry. The conversation was mainly one-sided.

"So Mike, the Chief thinks we're on holiday. The hotel is too expensive; we shouldn't have come. He has it on good authority that it was nothing to do with our case and the locals do not want us stepping on their toes. Oh, and by the way, Scotland Yard have sent someone up from the Art and Antiques Squad but according to the Chief, he will be staying in a cheap B&B, like we should have. Oh, and we're to leave immediately after breakfast and he won't, repeat won't accept our expenses for this jaunt," said Evan.

"Is that all, Evan? I must admit I've built quite an appetite and some decent wine won't go amiss."

Half way through their steak, Chief Inspector Ray Stevens walked in and headed for their table. "I'm sorry to interrupt your meal, Detectives. May I sit down and join you?" he said. Mike indicated a chair and asked a passing waiter to bring another wine glass. When the glass came, Mike poured one for Stevens, who he guessed was off duty. Stevens didn't refuse, why should he? It was a forty-pound bottle of wine, the detectives' second bottle of the night. Stevens looked around the room enviously. These South Wales boyos had it easy; life was good for them. No one spoke whilst they finished their meal. Mike ordered espressos for him and Stevens and a cup of tea for Evan. The coffees came, Mike took out his cigarettes then realised he couldn't smoke and replaced them in his pocket.

"So Chief Inspector, I assume this is unofficial," said Evan.

"Yes and no," said Stevens, "and the name is Ray."

"I'm Mike and this is Evan."

"My Super has just had a call from Sir Quentin and another from some Lord Pritchard. I think the bottom line is that we should explore all avenues for a day or two together," said Ray.

"We would like to assist but we've been ordered back."

"I understand that your Chief Constable will be advised of the new arrangements by Scotland Yard and some other people in London. I'm not sure who they are, my super doesn't tell me everything. Anyway, I took the liberty of booking Detective Utis from the Arts and Antiques people into this very hotel and we're having a get-together in about twenty minutes' time, in the lounge area. She will find us, as I haven't met her," said Ray.

"Right, let's go outside and have a smoke," said Mike.

"What about my tea?" said Evan.

"Don't worry Evan, it will still be here," said Mike.

"And it will be cold," said Evan.

"Order another, Evan, for God's sake, let's go and have a ciggie," said Mike. They had their smoke and returned.

"What a looker," said Ray, ogling a petite blonde in a tweed suit who had just wandered in from the next room.

"Reminds me of that song," said Evan.

"Song?" said Ray.

"Yes, you know, 'Five foot two, eyes of blue, couchy, couchy, couchy coo'," sang Evan.

"She's heading our way," said Ray excitedly.

"Excuse me, is there a Chief Inspector Stevens amongst you?" said the blonde.

"That's me," said Ray, standing up and towering over her; he was six foot five without shoes.

"I'm Detective Inspector Utis and I assume you two are Detective Inspector Jones and Karetzi. Have I got that right?" By now, both Mike and Evan were on their feet.

"Please sit down. Would you like a beverage of some kind?" said Evan.

"No thank you," Utis said, sitting down on the last available chair.

She was absolutely gorgeous, thought Mike, looking her over from top to waist; he'd already seen her legs and they were top drawer.

"I'm here at the request of Sir Quentin and others. I will add insight into the case and as such will be in charge. Is that clear?"

"Well, I'm Mike, this is Evan and this Ray."

"We will keep this formal," said Utis. From her bag, she produced four photos, which were passed around.

"I understand you have a good description of the man who stole the paintings; these four account for most art thefts of this magnitude. Do any fit?"

Ray shook his head, as did Evan.

"D.I. Utis, we do not have the thief's description, we only have what he wanted us to have, which is no use to man or beast." Mike fished in his pocket and produced a photo of Peter James aka the Chessman. "This is how he really looks when not in one of many disguises."

"Ah yes, you boys have some ridiculous theory that it is someone you call the Chessman, but from what I understand, he always kills and leaves a certain calling card, so I've been asked to let you waste everyone's time for a day or two before you go back to Cardiff," said Utis. "And you, Chief Inspector Stevens, where do you stand?" said Utis. About two foot taller than you, thought Mike.

"I do not think it's this Chessman guy but the two detectives here have a very impressive record, so I'm not ruling anything out."

"Let me fill you all in: art and antique thefts of note average one a month. This size of theft, moneywise, maybe two or three times a year. Experts like the PMSA believe there is an illegal art and antique black market out there, a massive one. Their problem is, as is ours to a certain extent, that they do not have a proper record of what exists in the public domain, never mind the private, yet the bad guys do."

"Who is this 'PMSA'?" asked Evan.

"Public Monuments and Sculpture Association," answered Utis.

"And you think one of these usual suspects is behind this?" Evan said, tapping the photos.

Ray was mesmerised by Utis's eyes. They were big and blue. He would like working with her; she seemed unapproachable for anything else but Ray lived in hope; everything was possible.

"Tell me D.I. Utis, if it's one of these, why are you here? Surely these people would be back wherever by now; they might have even disposed of the paintings, if they were stolen to order."

I'm here Detective because I was ordered to be. I will have a look around and go back. The chances of getting a result are slightly below zero," said Utis.

"And you, what are you going to do?" she said, looking directly at Mike.

"We, that is, Evan and myself, will of course keep a sharp eye out for your suspects here."

"Don't play silly games with me Detective, I've come across your type before – think they're smart, clever, witty and they always turn out to be stupid, dull and pedantic morons. I asked you a civilised question, so please answer me in the same manner," said Utis.

"Never mind Mike," said Evan jovially, "he's always cracking his little jokes. He doesn't mean any harm."

Ray turned to Mike, "Go ahead, what are you going to do?"

"Last week the perp was in Cardiff. We know that he went and stole some headed paper from the insurance company; slightly different description but, like I said, it means nothing. He was organised, he knew Mrs Histon's address, her times of work, everything, yet we know he's not local. Question: how did he get to Mrs Histon's house and from there to Sir Quentin's? We know he arrived by taxi at the mansion yet left on foot. Question: did anyone see him walking along with a briefcase and rolled up paintings which are too large to fit in the case? Another question: how did he get from Cardiff to here and where is he staying, or was staying? Now our man would have done at least two, three days looking over the lay of the land. Question: did he buy a map locally? Sir Quentin's place is a hard place to find, even with a map. Question: Why these Fratellis? Our sources in Cardiff tell us they are the only three in Britain that were in private hands. Question: who under those circumstances can, a) afford them and b) want them?"

"Lots of questions," said Ray, "we're already looking into the taxi that brought him to the mansion."

"Our man's long gone," said Utis, "I know how they work. Those paintings will never be seen again, I can guarantee you," Utis added.

"What about the butler, Baccus?" said Ray.

"I don't think he's involved. He's been working with Sir Quentin over thirty years, he has a good life," said Evan.

Ray's phone rang; he listened for a moment and then closed the line. "The taxi picked up our man outside the Spar shop about half a mile or so from Sir Quentin's. No taxi made a pick up from around Mrs Histon's. The call was made from a telephone box outside the Spar shop. We're checking for fingerprints. Unfortunately, the taxi's already been cleaned down ready for tomorrow's shift."

"Good work Ray," said Evan.

"I see it this way: the guy drives up from Cardiff, does a recce or two, then the next day drives to Mrs Histon's, leaving the car out of her sight," said Ray. "He does his thing in her house, then drives to near the Spar shop where he hides his car somewhere nearby. He then calls a taxi and after leaving the mansion runs back to the car."

"I see it the same way. Somewhere he must have dumped Mrs Histon's mobile phone and his gear, changing into another person again. We need to find where he parked his car twice. We need door-to-door around Histon's and go ourselves to the Spar shop and look around," said Mike.

"No Detectives, we'll meet here at eight o'clock and then we will go to Sir Quentin's. We need to interview all the staff again. I am positive there's an inside man or woman. It was just too easy. The clues are in the mansion, not outside looking for car tracks. This is my area of expertise, not I guess yours," Utis said, standing up, and without even a 'goodnight' she marched off.

"So," said Ray, "a tough little cookie that one. See you boys at eight."

"Well, what do you think Mike?"

"She's well fit Ev."

"That she is Mike, but I was talking about the case," said Evan.

"It's him, Evan; it's been a hell of a day, so why don't we get a good night's kip and worry about it tomorrow. See you for breakfast Evan. Goodnight."

"Goodnight Mike." I suppose I should ring Edna; yes, I will, he said to himself, pulling out his phone to make the call to his wife.

Hannah Utis climbed into bed. This case would go the same way as most of the others – a dead end. She didn't know why they'd sent her up and she didn't seem to be getting much sense from the other three. She re-read her notes on all three. Pretty impressive, especially the South Wales boys, but this crazy idea about the Chessman was laughable. It was one of the four; she knew it but couldn't prove it.

When Evan came down at twenty past seven for breakfast, he was surprised to see that his partner had nearly finished his. "Morning Mike, hungry were you?" he said.

"Not particularly, Evan. I wanted to get an early start. No point in us both going to re-interview the butler and secretary. I'm taking the car and I'm going to have a look around the Spar shop."

"But didn't Madam Utis say that..."

"I didn't hear that bit, Evan. My mobile will be switched off until I contact you. That way I can get some work done. You haven't seen me this morning, Evan."

"I don't like it, Mike," Evan said. "This woman can cause us a lot of trouble."

"Maybe, Evan, but she's on the wrong track. We also might be but nevertheless I intend to follow my instincts. See you later," Mike said.

Detective Utis was down five minutes after Mike left. She nodded acknowledgement to Evan who had moved to a clean table and ordered. Utis sat alone and all she had was a piece of toast and coffee. Evan took a full English and some more. When Stevens arrived just before eight and sat with Evan, Utis wandered over and made enquiries as to the whereabouts of Evan's partner. Evan said he had no idea but that Mike had taken the car. Utis insisted that they phone Mike. Evan went through the motions.

"I am not happy with this. We agreed that we would all go to the mansion together, didn't we?" Utis said, not waiting for an answer.

Mike found the shop. It was open as they also sold newspapers. He asked some questions; nobody had seen anything. His next visit was to the telephone box. He wanted to see if the Chessman, or whoever, had found the taxi telephone number from inside the box or whether he already had the number. It could prove important as to which area he was staying in. The telephone box was empty of directories, phone numbers, graffiti; it was the cleanest telephone box he had ever seen.

He stepped out into the morning sunshine. A paperboy nearly ran him over on his bicycle. Mike followed him into the shop. With his third question, he struck lucky; the boy had passed a car at about nine, when he was on his way to school. He could show Mike where it was. He didn't get a good look at it as he was already late for school and was travelling at speed. It was a four door, dark blue, big car. No, he didn't know the make or notice the registration number. Together Mike and the paperboy went to where the mystery car had been parked. Mike thanked the boy who left to tell his friends that he was helping the police with their enquiries. It would be the same excuse for being late for school.

There were no tyre marks or anything to indicate that a car had been parked there. Mike was about to turn away and go to his car when his eyes noticed a brown, frayed piece of paper. He carefully picked it up. The edges bore the marks of a fire. On his hands and knees, Mike scoured the immediate area. Someone had burned paper there recently. Luckily, it hadn't rained.

He returned to the shop and asked if they sold brown parcel paper. They did and he bought a sheet. Mike rang Evan.

"Can you talk Evan?"

"Yes Mike, our new boss is interviewing the cook, together with Stevens."

"Anything of interest Evan?"

"No Mike, only that the telephone box revealed no fingerprints as such, someone wiped it clean."

"Not surprising Evan, he's not bloody stupid but can you get the secretary by herself and ask her about this parcel that the perp was holding with her name and address on it? How was it wrapped? It's important and ring me back Evan, soonest."

"Okay, Mike, but you're in big trouble with Utis. I'd watch my step if I were you," said Evan.

"Sure Evan. Remember: how was the parcel wrapped?"

The answer came as no surprise to Mike. Now all he had to do was find a navy blue four-door saloon car. Mike opened the door of the BMW and was about to step in when a gruff, yokel-type voice told him that he was parked on private land and was fed up with people using his land as a parking lot. Mike's was the second car in the space of a day to park on his land.

Mike showed Farmer Giles his warrant card and asked about the other car. It was an old navy blue Jaguar and no, he hadn't noticed the number. Mike thanked him and drove off towards the mansion; he needed to speak to Stevens urgently.

The Chessman was in a very good mood. It was a bright sunny day. A little cold but not freezing. The papers had said the value of the paintings was over ten million pounds. He could expect to get at least half if sold to the right people and through his antique coin American connections he would get to the right people. All he needed now was to make the necessary travel arrangements. First stop after breakfast would be a travel agent.

The Chessman parked just off the promenade near the North Wales Theatre and walked up past the regal-looking four-storey terraced hotels, towards the Great Orme. On reaching the pier, he doubled back but this time down through Upper Mostyn Street where he located a travel agent. He booked a ticket on the Irish ferry from Holyhead to Dublin. For this, he used his Dutch passport. From there he would book a flight to Toronto with his Canadian passport. After a day or two, which he needed to identify potential buyers, he would rent a car and drive down south to wherever he needed to go.

"So what we're looking for is an old-style Jaguar, navy blue in colour," said Ray, amazed at how far Detective Karetzi had progressed.

"Yes, we need to concentrate on this area. Llandudno, Conwy, Rhos on Sea and Colwyn Bay," said Mike.

"Two of our four suspects have no alibis; one is supposedly in a place called Denbigh visiting friends," said Utis.

"That's only about twenty miles from here," said Stevens.

"Too much of a coincidence for me to ignore," said Utis. "I suggest we find Robertson soonest. Let's notify the police there and have him brought in, and this time we will all go – that is, everyone except Chief Inspector Stevens who has no jurisdiction there."

"I'm afraid that's not going to happen, Detective Inspector Utis. We have the highest authority to pursue anything connected to the Chessman case and we think he's around here, so we will remain in this area until such time as it is proven otherwise."

"Detective, I don't like your tone. I don't like your attitude and I don't like you, but I'm in charge and we will follow up the lead we have in Denbigh. Isn't that so, Chief Inspector Stevens?"

"I have no idea. I just take my instructions from my immediate boss, the Super. I have no real authority on your case or theirs. I have been instructed to help and that's what I am doing," said Stevens.

"And you call yourselves men," said Utis.

"I can prove it, just give me the chance," said Mike.

"That is a sexist remark and I will report you on my return to London," said Utis. "Now, are we going to Denbigh or not?"

"Not," said Mike. "It's not our remit and if you want some advice from a raving, crazy sexist detective, I suggest you forget Denbigh until this Robertson is in the police station and concentrate your mind on our immediate problem – finding the car."

"Have we finished here?" said Stevens, who'd already been on the phone to his station about the Jaguar. They would relay the particulars onwards to the other stations.

By now, everyone was on their phones – Evan to Amber, Mike to his mother, Stevens again to his Super and Utis to someone at Scotland Yard.

Evan finished his call. "Amber and Charlie are checking out all second-hand car dealers in the South Wales area with the help of another two staff and Mick from his station. It's a long shot. I've also asked her to ring Lord Henry, the Chief Constable and Brian to sort out the mess with Utis."

Utis, phone in hand, marched over to Mike and pushed the phone over to him. "My superiors wish to have a word with you, Detective Karetzi."

Mike took it and immediately pushed the cut-off button. "Oops, I think we've been cut off, D.I. Utis. Who wanted me? I can ring them back." Mike looked straight into Utis's deep blue eyes.

"You disgust me. You're worse than the scum we're chasing," she said, frantically redialling the number.

Mike walked away to the front door where he lit up. The butler Baccus moved him on to around the corner. Mike felt like a little schoolboy. He knew he was in deep shit and would go down the pan if his car hunch didn't come up trumps. Evan joined him. He'd witnessed the phone palaver and wasn't happy.

"Christ Mike, you are crazy. You know what this means if the car isn't found or if it's found and has nothing to do with the robbery or the Chessman. You're dead meat, finished, no pension, nothing."

By this time, Ray had joined the group. He looked at Mike and shook his head before saying, "You're going about this the wrong way, Mike. I'll probably be called as a witness if this goes the way our D.I. Utis wants."

"I know Ray. I would expect you to tell the truth and Evan here, but I just got carried away."

"Again," said Evan.

"Yeah, again Evan. I'm sorry if you're dragged into this."

"Don't worry about me," said Evan, "but it would not be a bad idea if you were to apologise to our pocket battleship in there."

"I guess you're right. I should, it's hard, but I should," said Mike.

"Well, here's your chance Mike, our pocket battleship is steaming towards us."

The Chessman meanwhile was having a ball. He liked this old genteel town. The queen of seaside resorts, he'd read somewhere. He'd taken in the pier, the Alice in Wonderland Centre, the Llandudno Museum and the World War II experience. He'd lunched and was now contemplating whether or not to take a ride up on the Great Orme San Francisco-style railway. After all, time he had plenty of. Eventually, he decided upon a walk around the shops. He needed a few bits and pieces and he could do the railway another day.

D.I. Utis came right to the group. She noticed that all three were smoking. It was difficult for her, she'd just found out that the Chessman case held precedence over all other cases, as did any serial killer, with at least a dozen kills in such a short space of time. She would hold off until this bloody car was located.

"Look Detective Inspector Utis, I would like to say that I'm sorry that..." Midsentence and Utis raised her hand. Mike stopped speaking.

"We all make mistakes," Utis said. "There is no need to compound them. You and your partner chase down the car. I will find Robertson and deal with him. This is my mobile number if you get a break on anything to do with the art theft."

"Can I arrange transport?" said Ray Stevens.

"Yes please," said Utis, turning on her three-inch heels and walking back into the mansion. All three men noticed her nice firm arse but no one commented.

"Spot of lunch Chief?" said Evan, "It's nearly one o'clock."

"May as well," said Ray "we can only wait and pray."

Lunch was fish and chips. The Chief's treat, washed down with Tizer and in the Chief's case Iron Bru. He was of Scottish descent. After lunch, the Chief returned to his station, Mike and Evan to the hotel where they had a beer each before settling in the lounge and reading the papers. By three, they were bored. Evan had an idea and rang Amber. Amber was already trawling through the private car sales of the last month. She was way ahead of Evan. Fifteen minutes later the call came through. Amber had found what seemed to fit the bill. All the hard work put in had paid dividends and now they had a registration number. Evan phoned through to Stevens and passed on the information.

At five minutes past four, P.C. Evans had found the car on his rounds. Ray, a D.I. and two uniforms descended on the car from one direction, Mike and Evan from another direction.

The Chessman had completed his shopping and after taking tea and cakes in a small cafe, strolled down Mostyn Street towards his car. On turning left off Mostyn Broadway, he immediately sensed something was amiss. There were people milling around his car. Police people. He turned and walked back into the busier Mostyn Street, where he made some enquiries and caught a bus.

He spent an hour walking around the marina until he was a hundred per cent sure that the 'Maggie May' was not being watched. It was those damn fucking detectives from Cardiff again. He recognised the shorter, squatter one and possibly the other with the strange name. He was now carless. Did he try to move on or keep to his plan? What would they expect him to do? He thought long and hard and decided they would expect him to run, so he would sit tight. They didn't know about the 'Maggie May'.

Stevens called a locksmith and a SOCO team who took fingerprint impressions from the mirrors, door handle, steering wheel and anywhere else they could. Apart from a cheap road map and some tyre changing tools in the boot, the car was bare.

"We shouldn't have rushed in," said the Chief Inspector. "We should have staked it out and caught whoever red handed."

"Not easy Ray," said Evan. "If it's our Chessman, he's way ahead of us. How, I don't know, but he's always one step ahead."

"It's as if he wanted us to find it," said Mike. "I think he might have dumped it here on purpose, but why? Is he trying to put us off the scent, buy time, or is he just lucky?"

"Get the car into the police garage," Ray said to the plain-clothes detective alongside him. "In an hour or so we will know if the prints match."

At precisely five o'clock Mike received a call from Utis. Robertson was in custody, had no alibi for the whole of Monday morning and they were awaiting his brief before charging him. Mike told her to hold fire; they had found the car and were waiting for news on the fingerprints. At half past five, it was confirmed that they were indeed the Chessman's fingerprints and Robertson was released. Tail between her pretty legs, Detective Inspector Hannah Utis of Scotland Yard's Art and Antiques Squad made arrangements to return to Llandudno.

"Are you okay to meet tonight, Ray, at the hotel?" said Mike.

"No problem, I'm divorced, no kids," the Chief Inspector replied.

"Well, in that case, come and have a meal with us in the hotel. It's on expenses, so don't worry," Mike said.

"Thanks, I will," said Ray. "I'll just pop home and change into something more comfortable and meet at the hotel, say half seven?"

"Half seven it is then," said Mike.

Mike and Evan drove back to the hotel. "Do you know Mike,

this is a wonderful town, I feel really comfortable here," said Evan.

"We're staying at a five-star hotel, unlimited expenses, the weather's good, as is the food and wine, who wouldn't feel comfortable?" said Mike.

"It's best I choose the wine tonight," said Evan.

"Why?" asked Mike.

"Because there are good wines at half the price, Mike, and we might end up paying if the Chief Constable has his way," said Evan.

"Old Clarkey's okay Evan, he will understand that we are acting on behalf of our whole force. We can't be seen to be penny pinching in front of the local boys and Scotland Yard."

"I don't see it that way," said Evan, "and to be perfectly honest I can't tell the difference between a twenty-pound bottle of wine and a forty-pound one," said Evan.

"But our guests can, Evan."

"Guests plural?" said Evan.

"Yes, Evan, Ray and Hannah," said Mike.

"Hannah?" repeated Evan.

"Hannah Utis, our friendly person from Scotland Yard, Hannah Utis."

"Have we invited her, and if we do, will she come? I don't think she likes us much Mike, especially you."

"I know Evan," said Mike.

"Yes, you do know," said Evan.

'The three amigos (friends) request the pleasure of your company tonight at eight p.m. for dinner and discussion.' He signed it Ray, Evan and Mike and gave it to one of the staff to slip the note under Hannah Utis's door. Mike then reserved a table near the window and overlooking the bay for half past eight.

The three men sat together and talked about various matters, namely sporting ones. Evan asked Ray if they served Brains in any establishment; the answer was affirmative, there were a couple.

"Is Detective Utis joining us for dinner?" asked Ray.

"No," said Evan.

"Yes," said Mike; he was expecting her at a quarter past eight and as it turned out she arrived at ten past, dressed to the nines. Out had gone the tweed two-piece suit and the horrible trouser suits, in had come a lovely red dress, cut just above the knee and strapless. She reminded Evan of another song but this time he didn't sing it out loud. It was, he thought, a David Bowie one. He sang it inside to himself: 'With your long blonde hair and your eyes of blue...' She was stunning. Both the other two men thought the same as did the rest of the people seated around them. Mike remembered the name of the song; appropriately it was 'Sorrow'.

"I'm sorry I'm late," she said.

"But you're not," said Ray, looking at his watch. Mike told us eight-fifteen." It was at that very moment that the penny dropped and Ray went as red as the Republic of China's flag.

"I've booked for eight-thirty, Detective Inspector Utis. Would you like a drink before we sit?" said Mike.

"No, I'll wait for the wine, and it's Hannah."

"Well, you know who we are," said Mike, taking a call on his mobile. It was Amber. He listened, thanked her and closed the line.

"Sorry about that. It was just the office, Four Is."

"Did you say Four Is?" said Ray, "eyes like in sight or the letter iota?"

"It's a long story," said Evan. "It will be boring if you're not a cricket fanatic." Obviously, they weren't so they changed the subject to the weather. There was always mileage in the weather. They had a fantastic meal, three bottles of wine, followed by brandies and coffee. Mike and Ray excused themselves and went out for a smoke. Evan, forever the gent, remained with Hannah, even though he was dying for a smoke.

"I would like to thank you for ringing with news on the car. Another twenty minutes or so and we would have charged Robertson and I would have looked a real idiot," said Hannah.

"Look Hannah, we are good people trying to do the best job we can. Mike may be a little, let's say crazy and rough sometimes, but he really is the best detective I will ever meet or have ever met. He calls a spade a spade, isn't cowed by any authority and never backs down if he thinks he's right; and let me tell you, he's rarely wrong."

"You like him, don't you Evan? Even though he seems the opposite to you," Hannah said.

"I will miss his wisecracks, the way he stands up for the underdog, his tenacity, his calmness under any circumstances thrown at him, his big-heartedness and most of all his crazy ideas, which always come up trumps. Anyway, enough of Mike, they're coming back in."

"Before we talk shop, can I thank you all for today? You saved my bacon," Hannah said to an embarrassing silence.

"Right," said Ray, "firstly, thank you for a beautiful meal. I haven't eaten that well since, well, for a very long time."

"You can thank Chief Constable Clarke for that," said Mike.

"And whilst I'm on the subject, the wine was superb. It must have cost an arm and a leg," said Ray.

"That is called 'Chief Constable's Choice', wine of the week. He's a connoisseur you know, but he doesn't know it yet," said Mike. Everyone laughed, Evan half-heartedly.

"To business then," said Ray. "What do you want us to do next? Personally, I can't see a way forward, because I think that this Chessman guy is long gone from this area and possibly this island."

"That's the logical answer," said Hannah.

"Question: where has he been staying? It's not here in Llandudno, I don't think," said Mike.

"Because he would have left his car in the hotel car park or outside, not where we found it," said Evan.

"Unless Evan, he is staying with a friend or someone he trusts, because he has to change, shave, make up somewhere decent, which cuts out an empty barn or derelict house," said Mike.

"Are you saying that you think this guy is still in the area Mike?" asked Ray.

"Ninety-nine per cent, according to Amber, and Hannah will have better information than Amber. He will find it impossible to fence the paintings in Europe and the only other buyers are American, where all the other Fratellis not in museums or such are," said Mike.

"What you say is correct," said Hannah, "but nobody is sure who in America owns them."

"Amber's sources don't have names but confirm that they are owned by Italian Americans of dubious backgrounds," said Mike.

"You mean the Mafia bosses or whatever they're called now?" said Ray.

"These people have the money and ask no questions," said Mike.

"To sell, he would have to go to them, they won't come to him," said Hannah.

"So, he's got a lot of arranging to do. He can't just hop on a plane and go to America, hoping for the best," said Mike.

"He might have an American passport but they are extremely difficult to come by," said Hannah.

"When we checked the accounts: he sent over three hundred thousand pounds half way around the world, ending up in the Cayman's, so that doesn't help and the money was legit by the way," said Evan.

"So, why come into Llandudno today?" said Ray.

"To make travel arrangements," said Mike.

"He's got to get to America somehow," said Evan.

"True," said Mike, "he deals a lot in American coins, or he used to. He will have contacts out there."

"So why not move immediately?" said Ray.

"Because the paintings are too hot; he's got to lie low until everyone forgets the robbery or something more important crops up," said Mike.

"I think he left the car purposely for us to find. We now think he's fled the area and has no further use for the car," said Evan.

"I agree," said Hannah.

Ray shook his head. "No, I don't think he left the car on purpose. There was no reason. He couldn't know or assume that we would track down the vehicle. It was a one in a million chance. No, he needed that car and now he's got a problem."

"How many travel agents in this town?" asked Hannah.

"Two or three," said Ray.

"Well, let's hit them first thing tomorrow and see what falls out of the bushes," said Mike.

"That's a strange saying. I haven't heard that one before," said Ray.

"Nor had I until it came out of my mouth," said Mike.

Again, everyone laughed – the mood was getting better by the double brandies.

Time had flown. Ray was tipsy and ordered a taxi to go home. Evan was tipsy and decided to go up to his room and call Edna. He might as well get his telling off over and done with. That left Mike and Hannah and a bald-headed coot playing the piano badly.

"Looks like you're stuck with me for a while," said Mike, his black eyes sparkling like diamonds. The teardrop scar under his eye looked more pronounced but he wasn't drunk in any way or form.

Hannah appreciated his rugged but handsome face, loved his jet-black curly hair and could see that he looked after himself physically.

"We have a choice," said Mike. "Either we dance, and I've got to warn you I have two left feet, or you can accompany me to the pier so that I can have a smoke. That will save me hanging my head outside the bedroom window."

"Maybe the third option," said Hannah.

"Which is?" said Mike.

"I say goodnight and see you in the morning."

"If it is to be the third option, I will escort you to the lift Hannah, where I will thank you for joining us for dinner."

"Do you have your cigarettes on you?" said Hannah.

"I do, and my gold and silver lighter."

"Well, let's go and see what this place looks like at night."

They leant on the rails looking out to sea. It was peaceful and beautiful. Both noticed the full moon – one couldn't miss it. Mike was not sure where he was going with this, nor was Hannah. Evan, who could see them from his bedroom window, knew exactly where he was going with this. Mike never failed to amaze him. This morning he was public enemy number one in Hannah's eyes and now this. Ooh, to be young and good looking, he thought, but then did Mike have an Edna, or his Jazzy? All in all, he was better off but he did wish he was a little younger.

Mike's hand strayed around her back. She welcomed the strength and warmth it brought but she was afraid of herself. She had to remain professional; things were getting a little too intimate and she didn't want to hurt Mike, like she had many others. Mike removed his hand. "That was nice, Hannah." He needed the fresh air and now he needed to get away from her strong scent and his sexual desires.

"Time we went back," Mike said. "It's getting a little breezy out here." Hannah didn't know what she wanted but like every other person, she had desires. There was no one special in London. Compared to this man they were nothing, just playthings for when she got bored. Use them and dump them, easy. As promised, Mike escorted her to the lift, thanked her as promised and bade her goodnight, as promised.

He returned to his drink and asked the piano player to play something sad. He played something; Mike didn't have a clue what, but dropped him a ten-pound note. That did the trick; he stopped playing. A waiter kept hovering. Mike turned to him and asked him what his problem was. The waiter explained that the bar had closed five minutes ago and that he wanted to clear up and go home.

"Fair enough," said Mike and left for his bedroom. Another ten pounds on expenses and with the wine coming out at over one hundred pounds for the three bottles, it had been a good night. On entering the room, he opened the window and put his head out for a smoke. Someone in the adjoining room was doing the same thing. Mike said hello and they both griped on about the new smoking laws until both had finished and said goodnight.

By 11.15 they had procured 73 different travel arrangements, which had been processed in the last forty-eight hours. There were families, groups, singletons, the works. One of them might be the Chessman. It was a long shot. There were lots of agents in the area and it was quite possible that their man had not visited a travel agent at all.

It took another two hours to find that a Mr Van Deal had given a false address and phone number. He had booked a trip on the ferry from Holyhead to Dublin on the 27th. They had him; it was just a matter of time.

The Chessman sat on his boat and thought it all through. They had made the connection to him through the car. How, he didn't know or care. By a process of elimination, they would run a check with the airports, ferries and travel agents. It wouldn't take them long to find that Van Deal wasn't what he seemed to be. He burnt the ticket and passport. These arseholes were causing him a lot of grief and a lot of money. He needed a new plan. It didn't take him long to make one.

Information was passed to everyone: throughout Wales, in London, Manchester, Liverpool, Birmingham and Bristol. They were to remain on the case. Both the South Wales boys and Hannah. They would liaise through Ray Stevens. This was to be their last night in five-star luxury; the rooms were needed for the pre-booked Christmas parties. A B&B which usually closed at that time of year had been persuaded to open up for the group. It had four bedrooms and had been booked and paid for until the 2nd of January. The best room was taken by Hannah, the biggest by Evan; there was a possibility that Edna would come up and stay. The smallest and the worst by Mike, which was fine by him; he had other ideas which was sharing another room with someone small and blonde.

The landlady lived next door. They were to supply their own food and do their own cleaning. The landlady would change their sheets every three days. The fourth bedroom, which was similar to Mike's, was also made up. The only good point was the bathroom. There were two and both had baths and showers. It was decided that the bathroom next to Hannah's bedroom would be solely for her use and the two detectives would share the other one, which happened to be between their two respective bedrooms. After agreeing all this, and taking two sets of keys, the group headed back to their hotel.

Transport was the main problem. The only problem. Any plan can work if you have the correct equipment and the Chessman didn't, he needed transport. The problem with small towns is that they're small. A stolen car is reported immediately and just as quickly found. He had the money to buy one but again he needed to travel to somewhere like Liverpool to make his purchase and he didn't have the transport to get there. The train was risky, especially at small stations with little traffic. There were no ferries and taxis were a no go.

The solution did eventually come. A bus ride to Llandudno Junction, then a freight train out to wherever. The wherever turned out to be Manchester. Another train ride; this time a passenger train got him to the airport where he rented a black Fiat and drove back to the marina. He used his Cardiff name and address and the documentation that went with them. He was now mobile.

Mike and Evan sat alone that night. Hannah had food served

in her room and Ray was otherwise engaged on some other problems at the station.

"How did it go then Mike?" said Evan over coffee.

"How did what go?" asked Mike.

"I saw you on the pier," said Evan.

"Ah, that. How did it go, Evan?" said Mike, smiling at Evan's inability to ask the direct question.

"You're making it hard for yourself Mike."

"Evan, it was calm on the water; no wind, a full moon, a cigarette, a little conversation and then a walk back to the hotel where I said goodnight."

"I see," said Evan, embarrassed again.

"And you, Evan, did you have a convivial conversation with Edna?" said Mike.

"I shouldn't have pried. It's nothing to do with me," said Evan.

"It's okay Ev, stop worrying about everything. Nothing happened, okay? And did I mention that the drink came to over two hundred pounds last night?" said Mike.

"No, you didn't Mike, and let me tell you a fact: that wine tasted even worse than the first lot we had," Evan retorted.

"There I think you have a point, Evan. Next time we'll go for the really expensive stuff. You can't go wrong with wine that costs nearly a hundred quid a throw," Mike said, slapping his partner on the back before saying goodnight and heading off into the night. He walked around the town for over an hour. It looked like he'd have to get used to his new dingy bedroom alone as from tomorrow night. Hannah was giving him the cold shoulder. For different reasons, Mike, Evan, Hannah and the Chessman didn't sleep well.

Mike felt uneasy. He'd felt the Chessman's presence on his walk. He could feel him, he seemed everywhere. He was still in control and Mike felt helpless. He tossed and turned. The Chessman was winning. For all their good work, they had nothing. Mike wanted to go home. Was it time for Russia or not? It was very near, that was another thing he could feel.

Evan worried about the expenses they were running up. Two hundred pounds would have been sufficient for him and Edna to drink for a month and still have change.

Hannah wanted the detective. She knew it was reciprocal but and there was a big 'but' – she wanted more than just a work's fling and she knew that was impossible with this man. That she knew, but then on the other hand she wanted him desperately. There was no easy answer to her confusion. She was after all a professional and a good one at that. She would resist her desires but then she wasn't sure. It kept her awake most of the night.

The Chessman had used his brains. The only way out was by sea, not through the conventional routes the ferries took, that was too dangerous even with the best of disguises and papers. The problem was finding someone he could trust. Those types could only be found if you knew where to look and he did. He was so excited he couldn't sleep.

Half past seven and both Hannah and Evan were eating hearty breakfasts. Mike turned up at eight, ordered some scrambled eggs and coffee and sat down next to Hannah, opposite Evan. He hadn't shaved or combed his hair. He looked ten years older and felt twenty years older. The nightmares persisted all through the night – he couldn't shake them out of his mind. The Chessman was playing with him; he was bouncing metal marbles around the inside of his head. Conversation between the three was strained and Mike only ate a forkful of his meal. He just kept staring out of the window. He could see the Chessman clearly and he was laughing at him.

Mike automatically pulled out his cigarettes, shook one out and lit it, oblivious to the stares. After a few puffs, Evan took it out of his hand and dumped it into Mike's coffee. An officious head waiter had reached the table by now and was about to say something when Hannah turned all five foot two of her and looked at the man in such a manner as to make him regret coming over. He turned on his heels for the kitchen.

Mike sat there impassively, still staring out of the window. He couldn't see the laughing Chessman anymore. All he could see was the sea and ships and more sea. He reached out for his coffee. Evan restrained him with one hand and moved the cup to a safe position with the other.

"What's happening here, Evan," asked Hannah.

"I'm not sure. Mike seems in another world, a world I don't have any knowledge of. A bad world, one I am glad I don't have to share with my partner. One which he wouldn't want to share with anyone."

"Poor man. I wonder what demons are torturing him," said Hannah, looking at Mike with tears in her eyes.

Evan lifted Mike up and walked him to the lounge where they sat together on a leather sofa. Within minutes, they were joined by Hannah who had a large espresso and a large brandy.

"I saw him Evan. He was laughing at me but I saw other things too. I saw the sea; it was rough, dark green. I saw boats. Do you understand what I'm saying, Evan?" Evan didn't but let his partner ramble on.

"He needs a doctor," Hannah said.

"No, he needs to get whatever is on his mind out in the open," said Evan.

"A doctor could help, prescribe something," said Hannah.

"He was laughing at us. You, me, Amber, Charlie and we can't do anything. But now we have the key," Mike rambled on.

"Look Mike, drink the brandy please. Please, you must drink up, it's good for you" – and with that Evan held the glass to Mike's lips. Mike drank, drank it as if it was water, and then started on the coffee.

"Who was laughing Mike?" asked Hannah.

"The Chessman. Surely you could see him? He was just outside the window, laughing at us," said Mike.

"Oh my God," said Evan, "Mike needs help."

"I'll call Ray, he'll get a doctor fast," said Hannah.

It was just after nine when Ray appeared, doctor in tow. By now, Mike had drunk another brandy and another coffee.

"What happened exactly?" asked the doctor of Evan.

"Who are you?" Mike suddenly asked the doctor.

"I'm Doctor Roberts, son."

"And what do you want?" said Mike.

"I want to see if I can be of help to you," said Doctor Roberts kindly.

"Why would I need your help, Doctor? I'm not ill. I'm probably fitter than anyone in this room," said Mike.

"I can see that you are a fine specimen of a man, Michael, but sometimes even a man blessed with physical powers can be ill in other ways not so apparent," said the doctor.

"It's Mikhail, not Michael, Doctor, and you're trying to tell me that I'm really crazy, that you can help me with pills or something. Am I right?"

"It's best I examine you, up in your room. I understand you are staying here. We can also have a chat in private of course."

"Doctor, I have a question for you," said Mike.

"I'm listening Mikhail," said the doctor.

"Do you have nightmares?" asked Mike.

"Sometimes," replied the doctor.

"Well, I think I've just had the equivalent but in daytime. Is that so unusual?" said Mike.

"Did you sleep well last night Mikhail, or did you have problems?" asked the doctor.

"I had nightmares, Doctor."

"Can you remember them at all?"

"Yes," said Mike. "I know or think I know what they were about," said Mike.

"Could you tell me?" asked the doctor.

"They were about my failure to comprehend a serial killer," said Mike.

"And you think that you're the only person responsible for this failure?"

"Yes, I am to blame more than anyone else. I've been too slow not been thorough enough, lots of other reasons."

"And this laughing man you saw today, is he the serial killer, Mikhail?"

"Yes, and he knows I can't touch him."

"Have you accepted that Mikhail?" Mike didn't answer, he badly needed a smoke. "All you need is rest. I will give you some tablets. Take them three times a day and talk with your colleagues. It's good to talk to people you know and can trust. See your own doctor when you return home." The doctor shook hands with Mike.

Evan and Ray walked the doctor to his car. "Your friend is exhausted. His mind is at breaking point and he's depressed. He's on the brink of a breakdown. It could go either way. Keep an eye out for him and if he remains as he is or seems to be getting worse, get him back home and to a doctor."

"Thanks Freddy," said Ray.

"Yes, thanks Doctor Roberts," said Evan.

As they walked back to the hotel, they met up with Mike and Hannah who had just come out. Mike wanted a smoke. All four crossed over to the pier and those who smoked lit up. It had been a long day and it still wasn't ten o'clock. The fresh air and pills were working wonders on Mike. He wasn't exactly dancing in the street, but he wasn't lying in it either.

"Do you need any help packing?" Hannah asked Mike. "You know we must vacate the hotel by eleven."

"Thanks, but I'll be fine," said Mike.

Any other time Mike would have let someone like Hannah help him. It would have been a good excuse to get her alone in his room but today he didn't have the strength or inclination for any of that stuff. Although Mike was finding it difficult to concentrate, he did manage to hold things together for enough time to pack.

Once at the boarding house, Hannah and Evan unpacked. Mike couldn't be bothered. He just plonked himself on the one decent chair, which was situated next to the large bay window. He could see what he wanted, water.

Above the door, there was a 'No Smoking' sign, the same as in the kitchen. The heating was on yet Mike felt a little cold. By the time the pair had finished unpacking and returned downstairs, Mike was fast asleep. Hannah found a blanket and covered him before leaving with Evan for the local station where they were going to meet Ray and talk strategy.

Charlie had packed and driven like a bat out of hell. He was armed with the B&B address, a local map and a bottle of Macallan. He left as soon as Amber had received the call from Evan. She remembered the night that Mike had come round for a chat. He was a little unstable then. Her last word to Charlie was to tell Mike to eat often and well, that was the secret.

Charlie's car was old but it could really move. By noon he was there, knocking on the door. There was no answer. He walked around the house and could see Mike fast asleep on a chair. It was obvious to Charlie that Evan wasn't there, so Charlie let himself in; another cheap lock. He found the room where Mike was sleeping and then the kitchen from where he extracted two glasses, which he set on the dining table together with the bottle of whisky.

Mike began to come out of his slumber. His eyes focused slowly and rested on Charlie's beaming face.

"Call an ambulance Charlie. I think I nearly killed him. The man fought like an animal, but I got him Charlie, I got him good and proper. He won't be causing any more trouble. Get an ambulance. You know the..." Mike stopped for a moment, as he gathered together his senses. "Where the fuck am I?" Sweat ran down his brow and he threw off the blanket.

He stood up unsteadily. Realisation had at last set in. He was in a disgusting little boarding house somewhere in Llandudno on the trail of the Chessman who'd stolen some paintings.

"What are you doing here Charlie, is there something wrong?"

"Nothing Mike, everything's fine. I couldn't find anyone to share my twenty-year old malt with. Then I thought of you and remembered that it's your favourite. So I got in the old jalopy and hey presto, here I am."

"I don't believe a word of that crap but I can see the unopened bottle and the two glasses so what are we waiting for? It's good to see you, Charlie."

Charlie poured two good shots. Mike took out his cigarettes and was about to light up when he noticed the sign. "Take that down, will you Charlie?" he said, pointing at the 'No Smoking' sign. Charlie did and then went into the kitchen and found a small cereal bowl. It would do as an ashtray.

They drank in silence, each with his own thoughts. Mike looked rough but didn't seem too bad. Charlie was glad. He just hoped that Evan would come back before he got completely pissed.

Ray, Evan and Hannah talked, had lunch, talked and by four had still not come to any logical conclusions. All three headed back to the B&B. They were hoping that Mike was still asleep. Mike was asleep – after a half bottle he felt drowsy and drunk. Charlie was also very drunk and also sleeping on the tatty sofa in the corner of the room. He'd had a quarter of the bottle and after his long drive, he felt like he'd been hit with a sledgehammer. Having had nothing to eat hadn't helped.

Evan opened the door. He turned and whispered to the others, "I think he's still asleep."

"I think that will do him the world of good," said Hannah as they entered the so-called living cum dining room.

"Charlie's here," said Evan.

"And he's who?" said Ray. Evan explained.

"It looks like they had a drinking party," said Hannah, picking up the bottle of Macallan.

"No food," said Ray.

Charlie woke. The first thing he saw was Hannah. "Am I dreaming?" he said out loud.

"No Charlie, you're just pissed," said Evan. "This is Chief Inspector Ray Stevens and this is D.I. Hannah Utis from Scotland Yard."

Charlie tried to stand up, try being the operative word. It took two large coffees and half a gallon of water to get Charlie up and into the last bedroom. Mike slept through everything and eventually surfaced from his sleep at six. He had had no nightmares.

"Glad to see that you're still alive and kicking," said Ray.

"Have you taken your pills?" said Hannah.

"Had anything to eat?" said Evan.

"Hey, good afternoon to you all," said Mike. "Where's my drinking partner?"

"Bombed out of his mind and asleep upstairs, Mike. How are you feeling?" said Evan.

"I'm a little tipsy and could do with a long cold drink of any sort, preferably diet type."

Hannah brought him a can of diet coke and a glass. Mike didn't bother with the glass, he drank it dry without taking it away from his mouth. He still felt thirsty. Hannah brought him another. This time Mike could only manage half. He took out a cigarette and lit up. Evan reminded him that it was a non-smoking establishment.

"All except this room," said Mike, "there's no sign in here because I took it down." Both Ray and Evan smoked their respective poison.

"So, how are you feeling Mike, have you taken your pills?" asked Hannah.

"I've felt better and will again as soon as I have a shave and shower and get a bite to eat. As for the pills, I don't need them.

I've got my medicine over there," Mike said pointing to the whisky.

"In the long run Mike, that won't help and you know it," Ray said.

"What's the harm in taking a few pills Mike?" said Evan.

"No harm at all Evan."

"So you're going to take them then?" said a relieved Hannah.

"No," said Mike. "Now, can somebody give me a half hour and we can talk about something other than pills?" Mike got up and went upstairs where he woke Charlie and told him to have a cold shower and get ready for a meeting.

"Christ, he's stubborn," Hannah said to Evan.

"And that's one of his good points," retorted Evan.

Ray couldn't fathom out what Mike's bad points could be. Hannah found the 'No Smoking' sign in the kitchen and was about to put it back up but thought better of it.

Two hours, that's how long the Chessman needed in the library. He'd been through every local paper for the last three years before he struck gold.

James Mason, not the old film star guy, but a fishing boat owner and operator. In court, seventeen months ago for alleged smuggling of weapons. Not guilty due to lack of evidence. It seemed that Mason caught wind of his impending arrest in the UK and dumped all the merchandise at sea except for a pistol, which he fancied himself. To cut a long story short, he said he had bought it in a pub in exchange for some fish. Luckily, he had also dumped the ammunition so it was hard to prosecute. The gun was confiscated, a fine was levied and Mason was free to go about his own business.

Times were strange. In the old days of the IRA, traffic was one-way, Britain to Ireland. Now whatever was left of the weaponry was slowly being sold off to the people across the water. No wonder crime involving guns had rocketed.

The Sea Sparrow, Mason's boat, worked out of Malpas Harbour, a small port on the Welsh side of the Dee, between Prestatyn and Holywell. Fortunately, there was a picture of

Mason in that same article. He looked cunning and crooked, just the man for the Chessman.

They all gathered round, all five of them eating pizzas and drinking various cold drinks.

"Right then," said Mike. "We have a wanted man who does not have transport but he has many identities, passports, money and three paintings. He's trapped in a small area and he needs to get to the USA. He can't take a plane, can't take a train or a ship. How does he do it? That my friends is the question."

"He waits us out until our guard is down and either takes a chance on the train to say Manchester or London and then arranges from there," said Evan.

"He steals a car or hitchhikes. No, forget the hitchhiking part," said Hannah, "and he can't use a taxi, far too risky," she added.

"So he waits us out," said Mike. "Where is he doing this waiting?"

"Not anywhere like a barn or disused house. Maybe one of the hotels or B&Bs. There's thousands up in the area. We can't check them all, it's an impossibility, especially without a name or current description," said Ray.

"Could he have wangled himself into a hospital, an old people's home or the like?" said Evan.

"Easier to check," said Ray. "I'll get the boys onto it first thing tomorrow."

"You only have men working at the police station Ray?" said Hannah.

"Let me rephrase my statement: I will put the police persons onto it first thing."

"What if he got himself an army uniform and police uniform?!" Evan asked. "It would be easy for him to move around without too many questions."

"Don't think so," said Mike, "he's still got luggage for his coins and paintings; no, I can't see him doing that."

"You've not said much, Charlie," Evan said. "Feeling a little under the weather after the party, are you?"

"I'm just thinking Evan, what would I do if I was in his position?" said Charlie.

"And have you come to a conclusion, Charlie?" asked Ray, wondering why the boys in Wales would want to employ someone like Charlie. The same thing had crossed Hannah's mind.

"Yes, I have," said Charlie.

"Well, can you tell us?" said an irritated Ray.

"The way I look at it is this way: join a ship as crew or paying passenger, there's a lot of greedy captains out there. Now before you tell me that the nearest foreign-going port is Liverpool and our friend can't get there due to lack of transport, etc., etc., I say to you, it doesn't need to be a freighter or a big ship, a small fishing boat will suffice. All he needs is to find the right one. That's the hardest part, someone he can trust, even if that means parting with big money. Tomorrow's the twentieth, five days to Christmas. He'll make a break for it on either the Monday before Christmas Day or the 26th, Wednesday, Boxing Day, two of the quietest days of the year. Everyone's either getting ready for the big day or getting over it, do you follow? Can I now go back to sleep? I'm dead beat," said Charlie.

"Goodnight Charlie, nice to see you and thanks for the Macallan. For a while there I wasn't my normal self but the whisky did the trick, it always does."

After Charlie had gone upstairs, Ray was the first to speak. "The little fellow makes complete sense. It's obvious and in all truth I thought he was a waste of space."

"So did I," said Hannah. "As Ray said, it's the obvious – we never went for the obvious."

"Charlie could be completely wrong," Mike said, "but, and this may sound ridiculous, when I saw him laughing outside the window in the hotel, I could also see the sea, which you can't from that point unless you're standing up. For a while I thought it had some connection to my father but now I think it's something to do with the Chessman."

"Have you seen or think you've seen anything since this morning Mike?" asked Hannah.

"The only thing I think I've seen is a quarter bottle of undrunk Macallan," said Mike.

Evan got up, found some glasses and between them, Hannah included, polished it off.

"Right," said Mike. "I'm going for a walk. I need the fresh air."

"I'll join you, if it's okay with you," said Hannah. "It's cold outside, I'll grab a coat," she added.

After they had left, Ray looked at Evan, awaiting an explanation.

"They're just good friends," said Evan, tongue in cheek

"I bet they are," said Ray, a little jealousy creeping into his voice. "I wish I had good friends like her," he added, putting emphasis on the word 'good'. "Fancy a pint Evan? One of the pubs serving Brains is only a short walk from here."

"Aye, that would be good. Just the ticket after a day like today," said Evan.

Evan had his pint and a half and walked back to the house. Mike and Hannah were in bed, separate rooms. Hannah had bolted hers, thus avoiding any temptations that might come her way. She was the only woman in the house with three men.

Charlie was first up at the crack of dawn. It was still pitch black outside. He made himself a cup of tea and had a round of toast with marmalade. Evan was next followed quickly by Mike and ten minutes later Hannah joined them.

The Chessman was up and about early too. He drove carefully to the port. There was no gate at the entrance, so he drove in. There were two fishing boats and a barge. One of the fishing vessels was the Sea Sparrow, a rusting hulk that hadn't seen paint for at least ten years. Taking the rented car back out of the small dock, he parked outside the main entrance, his car mainly hidden by a huge derelict building. He got out and walked. Even inside the dock, the boat bobbed like a cork but that didn't bother him unduly.

Outside the boat he stopped next to the old wooden gangway, which itself had seen much better days. He shouted out, "Anyone aboard?" He felt like an idiot but kept on shouting until a scruffy young boy appeared.

"What do you want Mister?" the boy said.

"I want to see James Mason," answered the Chessman.

"Skipper's asleep. Come back this afternoon, Mister," said the boy.

"I have a lot of money for him and if I don't see him now, he will lose out and blame you Sonny." The boy thought it over, then without a word disappeared.

It was a full five minutes before he resurfaced and beckoned the Chessman with his finger to follow him. Skipper James Mason was a huge man with a dirty greyish black beard. He sat alone in what could be termed a mess room. It was suitably named; it was a room and it was a mess and it stank. Mason hadn't bothered to put on a shirt, that is, assuming they made them big enough to fit him and just wore a dirty vest under an even dirtier pair of dungarees. On his feet, he wore sandals. He was smoking some kind of aromatic pipe tobacco; it smelt as bad as rotten fish. His chipped mug had some liquid in it; the Chessman didn't know what.

"My son said something about money," said Mason.

"Yes, that's correct Mr Mason, two thousand pounds worth of money."

"And how do I get this money?"

They talked for over half an hour before they had an agreement.

"So let me get this straight," said Mason. "You come back here tonight and stay in the deckhand's cabin until Sunday when we cast off for Wicklow. You give me five hundred when we cast off and five hundred when I drop you off at Wicklow. My brother-in-law Shamus then takes you to Dublin, no immigration control, police or anything. You give him two hundred. You do your business and then the following Sunday you find your own way back to where we drop you off in Wicklow, between the hours of 18.00 and 20.00, that is six to eight at night. On boarding, you give me five hundred and the same on arrival back here at Malpas? Have I got everything correct so far?" asked James Mason.

"You have, but I don't understand the 'so far' part," said the Chessman.

"Board and lodgings for three days at say thirty pounds daily comes out at a round ton, which of course I need up front."

"I'll tell you what I'll do," said the Chessman. "Let's meet half way and I'll give you fifty quid," said the Chessman. Mason rubbed his beard as if giving the problem great thought.

The Chessman turned and headed for the door leading onto the deck. He could hear Mason shouting. He was reminding him not to forget the fifty pounds. The Chessman was smiling all the way back to his car. After parking in Colwyn Bay, he visited an art shop where he purchased five cheap oil paintings and a cylindrical three-foot long box of four-inch diameter. The total cost was just under 300 pounds. In the car, he cut out the paintings from the frames, rolled up the paintings and placed them in the box. Then he drove for a few minutes and parked at the edge of a steep cliff. He threw the frames over and walked back to the car.

At precisely five o'clock, he retrieved the three Fratellis and mixed them with the new ones that he had purchased before replacing them in the box, making sure that the top one was one of the new ones. The box fitted perfectly into his large black holdall which took the box, his clothes, coins and toiletries easily, with a little room to spare for the Luger which still had four rounds left. He secured the holdall with a small padlock and put the key in his pocket.

The biggest potential problem the Chessman could foresee was Mason. He wasn't in the least bothered by his son Aled or the so-called engineer who was seventy if he was a day. The other deckhand he'd not yet met but dismissed him anyway. It was Mason. He was big, uncouth and greedy, hence the Luger. Of course, he had no intention of coming back, but the promise of more money might help keep Mason honest. The Chessman was also slightly concerned as to the seaworthiness of the Sea Sparrow. From the small amount of nautical knowledge he had, he reckoned that at 12 knots it should take the Sea Sparrow about ten hours to complete the journey, weather permitting. If they left at about seven in the morning, he would be in Dublin by nine, ten p.m. at most. Finding a cheap hotel should be easy enough or come to that an expensive hotel. It would only be for one night or two at the most.

Transport was still a problem. He had to dump it somewhere where it wouldn't be found for at least a week. He took the A55 heading south and after a few miles cut right onto the small lanes and roads in the area. He drove around and around for over forty minutes before finding the perfect spot to hide the rental. He laid the keys down under a smaller tree underneath a rock at the base of the tree. Satisfied, he walked towards the village of Trefnant bag in hand. The mile and a half took him another thirty minutes. A bus got him to Rhyl, another to Ffynnongroyw and from there another mile of walking took him to the Malpas docks.

There were three cabins: one double with bunks and two singles. They were for the skipper and engineer. The double was for the two deckhands, one of which was in hospital with some problem or other. It was this bunk that was to be the Chessman's new sleeping quarters. They hadn't even bothered to change the grey sheets, which once were white. Fortunately, it was the bottom bunk in the eight by eight steel prison. The whole room stank of a mixture of sick, cheap booze, cigarettes and damp. The Chessman tried to open the one porthole so that some fresh air could be let in. It wouldn't budge.

There was one toilet for all and they weren't allowed to flush whilst in port. The bowl was full and there was no toilet paper anyway. The galley was indescribable, had grease on the stove on the four bulkheads and on the floor – a fire hazard, and there wasn't an extinguisher in sight. He had to spend three days in this shithole.

"He is not to the best of our knowledge a resident in either a rest home or a patient in one of the hospitals, so that leaves us where?" said Ray.

"A trawl of the marinas," said Charlie.

"Good," said Ray. "I suggest that I go with Hannah, do half; you three, who are used to working together, do the remainder. We will keep in touch hourly."

"Good with me," said Mike.

"I'll do the driving Mike, you can do the navigating," said Evan. "Charlie can sit in the back, he's the smallest."

"Okay, we're coming up to the first," said Mike. "You try to find the head honcho Evan; me and Charlie will spread out and mooch around."

"Don't do too much mooching around Mike," said Evan. "I want to be home by Christmas Eve."

The three split up. For an hour they looked, then they met up again and had a coffee in the marina bar and coffee house. "According to the man in charge, he can't tell you zilch. As long as they pay their fees, they don't have a track of who is here and who isn't. Generally, though at this time of year, there is only a five per cent occupancy ratio. I do have a list of those paying the berthing fees," Evan said passing the list to Mike.

Mike looked at the list and was about to ask a question when Evan butted in again. "Over ninety per cent of these on the list are local and known to the people here. The others, well, none have a telephone or post code in or around the Cardiff area. A few in Chester, one or two Manchurians, half a dozen Scousers etc., etc."

"Fine," said Charlie. "Let's see where they park, those who are still here."

"Why?" asked Mike.

"I'm not sure," said Charlie. "But I do know 'Why' was a hit for Anthony Newley in 1960 and for Roger Whittaker in 1972."

"You can add Frankie Avalon to that – early 60s," said Mike.

"And don't forget Donny Osmond a decade later than Avalon," said Evan.

"He's got no transport, Charlie," said Evan.

"That's what you think Evan. He could have stolen or borrowed one," Charlie replied.

"No cars reported stolen," said Mike. "We're continuously monitoring the situation. As for borrowing one, who does he know up here?"

"Motorbike, bicycle?" said Charlie.

"Bicycle too cumbersome. Slow, and you can't carry much load safely. Motorbike a possibility. We will get Ray to check out all the shops selling the gear: leathers, helmets, and boots. There can't be many such shops in the area," said Evan.

"Okay, I'm on to it, Evan. Any luck your end, 'cause we've lucked out so far," Ray said.

Mike looked at Evan who shook his head. It was the same with the next two. One to go, plus a few odd private berths dotted here and there.

"This is pointless Evan," Mike said.

"There's still one to go," said Charlie.

"Ray got any news on the bikers' gear?" asked Mike.

"Guess not, he would have called us if he had," said Evan.

"It's dark, do you know it's nearly six?" said Mike.

"Let's give Ray a ring and see if they've finished. We can then call it a day and do the last one in the morning," said Mike, who was now beginning to feel the effects of yesterday's drinking session.

"He's on the last one of his list. Another half hour and he's finished."

"Where is he?" said Mike.

"Portmadog," replied Evan.

"That's quite a way from Llandudno isn't it?" said Mike.

Before answering, Evan consulted his road atlas. "About thirty-five, maybe forty. An hour on these roads, Mike."

"Well, we may as well do the one in Conwy," said Charlie. "It won't take that long."

"Let's go, get it over with," said Mike.

"Same as before, Mike?" asked Evan.

"Same, why change a losing formula?" said Mike.

Half an hour or so proved fruitless. Evan trudged up to the other two slowly, list in hand.

"Anything Mike, Charlie?" Both shook their heads.

"You Evan?" asked Charlie.

"Same old crap but one writer chappie, famous author, has rented one of the boats."

"Back to our luxurious abode then," said Mike.

"I'm bloody hungry; we haven't eaten all day," said Evan, quickening his step.

"How you feeling now Mike?" asked Evan.

"Tired, frustrated and hungry Ev."

"Won't take us long, we're just up the road," said Evan, driving faster than he normally did.

"What's his name then, Evan?" Charlie asked.

"Whose name, Charlie?"

"The famous author. What books he written?"

"No idea Charlie, didn't get a name," he said, pulling up outside their residence. He was about to get out when Mike put a restraining hand on him.

"What famous author would live on one of those crummy little boats over Christmas, Evan?" said Mike. "I wouldn't if I had money, being a famous author."

"Maybe he wants the peace and tranquillity that type of place brings, especially if he's writing," said Charlie.

"Rubbish," said Mike. "Do we have the boat's name, berth number, something?"

"I have the harbour master's mobile on his card," said Evan.

"Give it to me," said Mike, "and drive back to the bloody marina."

"You say 'Maggie May', Berth B, No. 13? Thank you, there's no need for you to be present."

"Did you get that Charlie?" said Mike.

"I did, 'Maggie May', Berth B, No. 13," replied Charlie. "Rod Stewart – '71," he added.

"Vipers 1957," said Mike.

"Do you think it's the same song?" asked Evan.

"Not sure, never heard them sing it," said Mike.

They parked in the same place and hunted down the 'Maggie May'. Mike jumped on board and shone a light through the plastic window. It was dead inside, no sign of life, so he tried the door; it was locked. Charlie unlocked it and they entered.

"Is it connected to electricity?" said Evan.

"I think so," said Mike, locating a switch and pushing it down. Now they had light. Evan opened the cupboards and drawers. Mike went direct to the small fridge. "It's our man and he's flown, not so long ago," said Mike.

"How do you know Mike?" asked Charlie.

"Because he's got three ginger beers in the fridge and three in that rubbish bag there, together with today's newspaper, which has obviously been read."

"And why do you think he's gone?" asked Charlie.

"Because there are no clothes," said Evan.

"Bag up the fridge's contents, Charlie, and let's take the bag of rubbish. We can get fingerprints off something."

"Shall we call Ray?" asked Charlie.

"No," said Mike. "He can't do much for us here."

"Shall we get someone to stake this place out?" said Evan.

"He's gone Evan; one step ahead of us as usual," said Mike.

"The bastard," said Evan.

Charlie looked on. If only he'd come up a day earlier, if only. Now he felt useless.

"Well, shall we at least have a word with the boat's owner?" said Evan.

"We could, but to learn what?" said Mike.

"Maybe he knows if our man has acquired transport. Maybe the Chessman let slip something that could be of use to us," said Evan.

"Evan's right you know Mike," said Charlie.

"Of course Evan's right; I'm just down at this moment and can't think straight."

"Here we are," said Evan, "here's the list – he's left a mobile number; I'll give it a ring and see if I can get him down. He lives locally, according to this list. Shit," said Evan, "shit, shit, shit!"

"Bad news I presume?" said Charlie

"The guy's in Tenerife, he's been there three days now," said Evan.

"Everything but everything is working in his favour," said Mike spitefully.

"Let's go," said Charlie, "we can't just sit here looking like life's perpetual losers."

"We don't have to look like it, we are," said Mike.

On their way back to the house, everyone kept their thoughts to themselves. Mike felt into his pocket, found the pills and took them out. He looked at them and returned them to his pocket. From the corner of his eye, Evan had seen Mike's battle with his pills and felt that he needed to say something. "Mike, those pills will help you feel better."

"Even if the pills will make me feel better, then first they'd better work out a way to catch the Chessman, then I'll feel great. Till then they remain in my pocket," Mike said in a near whisper.

On their return, they found Hannah alone, cooking. Ray had returned to wherever he went after seven.

"Hello Boys, I'm doing a spot of cooking but I'm warning you in advance, I'm not Delia Smith."

You're bloody right there, thought Charlie, noticing her slim yet voluptuous figure.

"I've got cold beers, fresh French bread and a warm Irish-type stew. It should go down nicely on a cold night, assuming I don't poison you."

"Hannah, don't worry about me, I'm starving and it does look good to me," said Evan.

"It smells good too," said Mike.

The meal turned out to be surprisingly good. They had a couple of beers each and shared a supermarket-made trifle. With the meal finished and coffee on the table, the group discussed the day's events.

"So where is he now?" asked Hannah.

"Your guess is as good as ours," said Evan.

"Well, what's your guess Evan?" said Hannah.

"I reckon he's back in Swansea. If I'm not mistaken a ferry runs from there to Cork and another runs from Milford Haven or Pembroke to Rosslare in Ireland."

"You Charlie?" said Hannah.

"I've been thinking about this for a while. Again, in his shoes I would find a way out of Wales, head for Newscastle or Hull, which have international ferry terminals and vast amounts of traffic with little or no security. If I had to choose, it would be Hull. It's bigger and nearer than say Newcastle or Harwich and gets you to Amsterdam or Rotterdam which have of course international airports. Also, we must not forget that he has or had a Dutch passport, that's what swings it for me; and remember one more thing; he has money, that's a big plus for him. You can buy a lot of silence with that."

"Lastly Mike, what's your theory?" asked Hannah.

"He's gone Hannah, where only God and he know. My gut feeling says London. Massive population, big criminal elements of all kinds. A place where money talks and one can get lost for as long as one wants to," said Mike.

"Come on Mike, you don't for one minute believe that, do you?" said Hannah.

"Why do you say that? My theory is as good as Evan's or Charlie's surely?"

"Your theory's fine Mike and actually I'm thinking on the same lines, but my woman's intuition tells me that you do not really believe that the Chessman is in London," said Hannah.

"So, what do you think I believe?" said Mike.

"That he's still in the area," said Evan.

"Why would I think that?" said Mike.

"I don't know why you think that but I know you, Mike. We wouldn't be sitting around this table, smoking and drinking coffee if you thought he was in London. We would be travelling at a hundred and twenty plus miles per hour on our way to London by now."

"With Mike driving like a lunatic, we would be in London already," added Charlie.

"Okay, okay, hands up, I surrender. I do think he's around here. He left in a hurry. The unopened ginger beer, the uneaten fresh food, today's newspaper, the water on the deck. It's the little things; they don't add up. Nothing adds up. Maybe I should take the fucking pills," said Mike.

"Water on the deck Mike?" asked Evan.

"Don't ask me Evan, it bothered me. Did you notice anyone else's deck Charlie?"

"And you Evan?"

"I don't think so Mike," replied Evan.

"I can't see the importance of such a small detail, Mike, but forgive me if I'm missing some clue, but I can't see the relevance of some water on a boat's deck," said Hannah.

"Nor can I, Hannah, but relevance it has," said Mike. "We just don't know what."

"Shouldn't we call Ray and get some prints sorted out?" suggested Charlie. "After all, Mike, we are not a hundred per cent sure it's the Chessman."

"It's him," said Mike.

"But what about Ray?" said Evan.

"Right, this is how it will work," said Mike. "Charlie, you bring in the rubbish from the boat and empty it on that rug over there."

"On the rug?" said Charlie.

"On the fucking rug, Charlie, we're wasting precious time. Evan, ring Ray; tell him everything and tell him to get someone down here first thing for fingerprints. Hannah, go through that newspaper. We're looking for anything to do with the cost of transportation of any kind. I don't know what. The paper is important. Why go out and buy one and bring it back?" said Mike, finally finishing.

"Tell him Mike?" said Evan. "You mean ask Ray don't you?"

"Yes Evan, Ray is of superior rank, so we ask him politely," said Mike.

"Maybe he wanted to know last night's soccer scores," said Charlie.

"The rug Mike, anything could be in that rubbish bag," Hannah said. "It could get ruined."

"You can't ruin rubbish with a rug," said Mike.

"You're living up to your nickname Mike," said Hannah.

"What nickname's that Hannah?" said Mike.

"Crazy," she replied.

"That's not my nickname, that's my middle name," said Mike, pushing around the emptied rubbish with a carrot.

Charlie looked on spellbound. They'd laugh their heads off down at the Cutty if he dare tell them about the scene unfolding before his very eyes.

"What's that Charlie?" Mike said, prodding a half-eaten apple with the carrot.

"Half an apple, Mike."

"And that?"

"Wrapping from some kind of pie or coke."

"This here?"

"A piece of paper."

"And these?"

"More pieces of paper, the same paper, ripped into tiny pieces, Mike."

"Everything back in the black bin bag, Charlie, except the pieces of paper. Don't miss one."

"Okay Mike, will do," said Charlie. "Shouldn't we be wearing gloves? Who knows what diseases are lurking in this rubbish."

"Just make sure you don't come in contact with the rug, that's where the bloody germs are hiding," said Mike laughing.

"That's funny Mike. How come I got to do all the dirty work?" said Charlie.

" 'Cause you're the smallest and therefore nearer the floor," said Mike, turning and going over to where Hannah was reading the paper.

"Anything of interest Hannah?" asked Mike.

"Yeah, there's a section on Liverpool shipping movements that is arriving and departing Liverpool and associated docks."

"Good, that's it. Where's that page, Hannah?"

"Um, not much, is there?"

"Three ships expected today and tomorrow. Two ships E.T.D. today, one tonight. Four still discharging or loading, no E.T.D. E.T.D., 'estimated time of departure', is that correct Hannah?"

"That's correct!" shouted Evan from across the room. "Does it give destinations?"

"It does. Bilbao, Piraeus, Buenos Aires, Miami, Jacksonville, that's the lot," said Hannah.

"That's only six," said Mike.

"Well, the other one hasn't found a charter yet," said Hannah.

"How we doing, Charlie Boy?" Mike asked.

"One ruined rug and about two dozen pieces of paper of various sizes," said Charlie.

"Bring them up to the table, Charlie," Mike said. "Let's put our jigsaw together and fast."

Charlie did as he was told. When Mike was on a run, there was no stopping him and he wasn't about to be the first.

"Well, I'll be fucked," said Charlie. It's a receipt from Hertz at Manchester Airport, dated yesterday. Black Fiat, reg no, rented for two weeks, pre-paid. It's all here. Name, Carl... address in Cardiff and mobile phone contact number."

"Firstly, is Ray coming? Second, when? Third, call the mobile," Mike said. "Fourth, get Amber to contact Mick and get around to that Cardiff address. Make sure they get in, whichever way. Tell them not to wait for a warrant. We want anything that they can get before they get it. Fifth, get in touch with Hertz. Sixth, dump the rug, it stinks to high heaven. Seventh, I need a glass of water," which Mike went and got and in front of the astonished group took out two tablets and washed them down with the water.

It looked like Mike had taken charge and he wasn't finished yet. "Hannah, if you could do the mobile and Hertz, Evan, Amber and Big Mick. Charlie can dump the rug and I will get Ray moving in the right direction and at speed when he eventually arrives," which was only seconds away.

Ray's first words were "What's going on here?" to nobody and everybody.

"Ask Mike," said Hannah. "He seems to have taken control of the situation."

"Is he all right, I mean you know what I mean," Ray said to Hannah out of the side of his mouth, thereby assuming that it was a private conversation.

Mike could hear every word that Ray spoke. "Thanks for your concern Ray, I'm fine and I've taken my tablets, so let's get on with it. We need search warrants for eight vessels in Liverpool. If need be we can go hand in hand with Immigration, Customs and Excise, the local darts team, anyone, but we need those warrants now, tonight."

"What are we looking for Mike?"

"A stowaway, a passenger, a crew member or whatever the bastard is masquerading as, right? He might even be the fucking ship's pilot. I've no idea but he's on one of those ships."

"Forget it Mike, no hope, whatever pull you think you've got, whoever you think you know, trust me you won't get a warrant for these ships without some kind of proof," said Ray. "Have you got that? No, of course, you haven't. Do you have anything of substance? No, you don't. You haven't even checked any fingerprints. You're not sure it's even him who was on the 'Maggie May'. Think about it, Mike. I know you've spent so much time on the ruthless killer, but that's police work. We work on evidence and you don't have any. I'm sorry Mike."

A deflated Mike sat down on one of the dining table's hard-back chairs. He knew that Ray was right. They wouldn't get a warrant; not today, not tomorrow, not ever without any supporting documents.

"How did he get to Liverpool?" Mike asked Ray.

"He's hired a Fiat from Hertz in Manchester," said Evan.

"The airport," added Charlie.

"And how the fuck did he get there?" said Ray.

"God knows," said Evan.

"God and the Chessman," added Charlie.

"Right, let's start with the car. Let's keep an extra eye out for the car in the Liverpool area," said Ray, using his mobile.

Evan took a call. It was Mick; he was in the Chessman's flat, illegally.

"Mike, Mick's in, he and a mate. Just a few clothes, books, CD player, television, kitchen equipment. Some toiletries, a few unopened bills. Nothing of interest to the case. Will speak to the neighbours in the morning but he's left it clean," said Evan.

"Ask him if there's any hidden compartments. Have they looked under any loose floorboards? Mick knows."

"I'll pass it on Mike," said Evan. "What are we looking for anyway?"

"A Luger pistol," said Mike. "The one he used on the pawnbrokers. If it isn't there and it wasn't in the Swansea house or the 'Maggie May', then we have an additional problem. He's armed and very dangerous."

"Oh no," said Hannah. "What can we do?"

"As it stands, not much. If the car doesn't turn up, then he really could have got anywhere by now. Three hundred, four hundred miles. My geography ain't great but he could have got to John O'Groats or Land's End in that time," said Charlie.

"So we just accept failure, sit on our arses and then go back home," said Mike. "Forget any pride we still have, forget we're the Police, forget that we represent justice, the Law of the country. Forget all our lives. Is that all it's come down to?"

Evan, his head down, felt Mike's emotion, understood it. He wished he could say the words that would make his younger partner happier but he didn't know the words. It was at times like this when he wished he'd had a better education. It was at times like this that he was glad his days in the Force were numbered. He wondered what would happen to his partner and good friend. He felt sad for himself, for Mike, for Charlie and for some reason even for Hannah. This was a backward career step. She was young but he doubted if she could recover from this debacle. Then she had the other problem. She didn't know it but Mike was a problem looming. Evan could see how she looked at Mike. It would all end in tears. The problem was that neither Mike nor Hannah knew that the problem was heading their way. He had tried to warn Mike, but Mike was Mike, the crazy one.

Ray left at midnight. He didn't want to leave but stay to keep Mike company. They didn't drink any hard liquor, just coffee upon coffee, matched in number by cigarettes. They talked and talked. It was chucking it down outside. The heavens had opened. Ray normally hated the rain; tonight though he walked slowly to his car letting the rain encompass him like a blanket. He felt ashamed by saying the truth; he'd let the others down, especially Mike. What he'd done was take any slight lingering hope they had of apprehending the Chessman away. Deep down they must have known they were up against impossible odds, but the system wouldn't change. However strong your instincts were, no evidence, no search warrants, no arrest. Not that he personally thought this guy was stupid enough to try and leave by boat. If the guy had any sense, and he seemed to possess a sack full of it, he would have got down to the Big Smoke. With money, everything was possible in London.

Mike stood at the door watching Ray walk slowly back to his car, some sixty yards away. Poor old Ray, Mike thought, trapped up here in the sticks. Nothing ever happening, and when it did, not being allowed to deal with it. Poor bastard, nice bloke though, good cop too.

The rain eased off a little and Mike crossed the road. He could see the town. It looked good. Nice people, nice place. His thoughts ran to Russia. He wondered what his father's hometown Archangel looked like at night. He thought of the strawberry blonde; it was so unlike him not to even get her name. Would he ever see her again? He thought of his mother Alice. Was she happy or was she just lonely? It didn't help her, him being away.

He lit up and inhaled. It felt good. His mind wandered to the Chessman. Was the bastard really laughing at him? And finally, he thought about Hannah. She really was beautiful, clever and on her way up in life, unless the Chessman business pegged her back. Would she reject any advances, did he really want to make any advances? He didn't have an answer. He didn't have answers for much lately. The way things were panning out he would retire before Evan and retirement for Evan would mean good things, like travel with his wife and his daughter. For him, another job, starting once again at the bottom.

Hannah had seen Ray leave and watched as Mike crossed the road and leant across the brown, brick wall. The man was an enigma. He had a big heart and a sharp mind. He looked good, very good, film star good but there was vulnerability about his person. She wanted to be close to him, to protect him from his demons but wasn't sure if she could last the pace. She welcomed a move from him. Last night she'd bolted the door; tonight she left it slightly ajar.

Mike shut the door behind him, took off his shoes and crept silently up the stairs to his bedroom. Opening his bedroom door, he slipped off his clothes and got into bed. He'd noticed that Hannah's door was ajar. Was this a message for him? He couldn't really tell and he was in no mood for games, of the mind or of any other type. The old Hank Locklin song 'Please help me I'm falling' came to mind, especially the lines 'Close the door to temptation. Don't let me walk in' or something along those lines.

Hannah had heard Mike. She waited a few minutes and then got up and closed the door, bolting it securely. In a way she was pleased, in another way not so.

The Chessman spent all evening on deck, sitting, holdall by his side. Mason and the engineer were getting paralytic on cheap whisky. The boy, Mason's son, had gone ashore. Just before midnight, he went to the cabin and stripped down the bunk. He turned over the mattress and laid down his coat on top. After taking out the Luger, he used the holdall as a pillow. The Luger he kept by his side but out of sight. He knew he wouldn't sleep. He couldn't anyway.

The lad came in at one o'clock. He hadn't been drinking, not excessively, that was for sure. He clambered up to the top bunk and within minutes was fast asleep. The Chessman rose and placed the one chair in front of the door. He didn't wedge it under the handle, just placed it in front of the door so that anyone opening the door would make a racket and that would be warning enough.

At seven the Chessman rose. His roommate was still fast asleep. He needed a pee badly, so he went on deck, looked around, ascertained that no one could see him and urinated into the dock. That done, he returned to the room, opened his holdall, replaced the gun and took out his toothpaste. Putting some on his finger, he then rubbed his teeth. He was also hungry but didn't intend eating anything cooked on the boat. He went on deck again, this time taking his holdall. During the night, he had made a decision. They would leave tomorrow, Saturday. He knew it would cost him more but he also knew that he couldn't do more than one more night in the prison they called a cabin.

Two hours later and the crew were awake. For the skipper and the engineer the drinking had resumed. The Chessman needed to have a word before they became incoherent. As he walked towards the mess room, another young lad of about twenty was crossing the gangway to board.

"Hi," he said. "Who are you?"

"Friend of the skipper's, and you?" asked the Chessman.

"Louis, deckhand, been in hospital but am okay now."

"Tell me Louis, if I give you thirty quid, could you go and get a few things?"

"Like what?" said Louis.

"A loaf of bread, not sliced; a pack of Cheddar, some ham and four big bottles of still water."

"Is that it?" said Louis.

"That's it, about ten quid's worth. The rest, twenty pounds, you keep. What do you say?"

"I say give me the money and I'll be back in about thirty minutes," said Louis. The Chessman gave him the money. From somewhere Louis produced a bicycle, old and rusty but still better than walking.

"What about butter?" said Louis as he left.

"Thanks, I forgot that," said the Chessman.

It looked like he would be sleeping in the mess room tonight, probably better than the cabin down below.

"So you want to leave tomorrow, do you Mr Smith?"

"That's what I said, Mr Mason."

"Could be done but a lot of rearranging to be done so what's the rush eh?" said Mason.

"That will cost you," said the engineer.

"Of course it will, doesn't everything in life?" said the Chessman.

"What's in the bag, Mr Smith?" asked Mason.

"Nothing of interest to you," the Chessman retorted.

"Everything is of interest to me. We don't do anything illegal on board my ship, Mr Smith, do we Angus?" said Mason.

"Not unless of course we profit accordingly," said Angus the engineer.

"You are profiting. Another two hundred and we leave tomorrow," said the Chessman.

Mason now stood. "Open the bag," he said menacingly. Angus smirked. The skip could take this little runt apart blindfolded and with one hand tied behind his back. The Chessman hesitated; he wasn't afraid, he knew that this moment would come and he was prepared but something in his head was telling him to be careful and not rush.

"Look, all I've got are my clothes for a week and a few presents for my friends in Dublin; nothing more than that," the Chessman said.

Mason had now moved around the table and was facing the Chessman, only the width of the table between them. The Chessman unzipped the holdall and took out his toiletries bag, then the tube containing the pictures. He pushed the bag nearer to Mason and said, "As you can see the rest is clothes."

"What's in the tube? Open it up," said Mason.

The Chessman obliged and then he extracted the middle

painting, which showed sheep grazing in a field. Mason looked at it from every conceivable angle. Even Angus got off his arse and had a look; neither seemed too impressed.

"These are the presents I told you about. Nice, don't you think?" said the Chessman.

Mason grunted and Angus murmured something inaudible.

"Can I repack my gear now?" said the Chessman, already packing.

Mason grunted again. The Chessman took it as a 'yes' and carried on.

"Why you going to Dublin?" asked Mason, sitting back down again and pouring himself another shot of cheap whisky.

"Personal business matters," said the Chessman.

"That's your business then?" said Mason.

"That's right," said the Chessman, taking another two hundred from his pocket and laying it on the filthy table.

"I'll make the arrangements," said Mason. "We leave on the high tide, about eight in the morning."

As he left the mess room, he again found Louis sitting on a bollard, shopping at his side.

"Get everything?" he asked Louis. Louis pointed to the bag and nodded.

"Thanks mate," the Chessman said, picking up the bags and moving to the other side of the boat.

Firstly, he opened one of the bottles of water, splashed it over his face and then had a drink. With his small penknife, he cut some slices of cheese off the block and after buttering a chunk of bread, which he broke off with his hands, he made an open sandwich and ate.

Everyone in the house had eaten something for breakfast and was now awaiting the arrival of Ray. Hannah had been told to report to her London office for Monday. Charlie had decided he could bring nothing more to the table other than ignorance and would leave that afternoon. He could at least have the weekend with his partner.

Mike and Evan agreed that they had lost the scent and would leave Sunday morning, taking Hannah down as far as Cardiff, thus saving her from the worst part of the train journey.

When Ray arrived at half ten, he had already done nearly five hours in his office. He was trying to catch up with his own paperwork, which he had neglected over the last three days.

"Nothing on the car, I'm afraid," said Ray.

"Didn't expect anything," said Evan.

"Have spoken to the port authorities in Liverpool; they are keeping an eye out but they cover a large area."

"And the fingerprints?" asked Charlie

"They match, on the boat, the rubbish. This Chessman must have a sixth sense," said Ray.

"He's just plain lucky," said Mike.

"Or are we just plain unlucky?" said Evan.

"I'd say both," Hannah chipped in.

"What's on your agenda now then?" asked Ray.

"We must remain belligerent, he's bound to make a mistake," said Charlie.

"Do you know what our problem is right now?" said Evan. Not waiting for an answer he went on, "It's Parkinson's Law, that's the problem."

"Michael Parkinson, the TV chat show host?" said Hannah.

"No, Cyril Parkinson, English historian and author," said Evan.

"And what did Cyril Parkinson come up with, Evan?" asked Charlie.

"He said something like this: that work expands to fill the time available for its completion."

"So how does that have anything to do with our current predicament?" asked Ray.

"Well, the way I see it, whenever we run out of ideas, clues or things to do, something else comes our way like, say we find his car, a receipt, the travel agent and so on. This gives us more things to follow up – more work and therefore more time is needed," said Evan.

"Yes Evan, that may be so but it's a crap theory," said Mike. "It's not valid in our case because we might fill our time up but we're not going to get any more time available to us to complete our mission and apprehend the Chessman."

"You've lost me," said Charlie.

"And me," said Hannah.

"Maybe he said something more than I can remember but I'm sure that's the gist of his theory," said Evan.

"Could be," said Ray.

Evan's phone rang, it was Amber. "Are you boys eating properly up there?" she asked.

"We're getting by," said Evan.

"Look, I'm ringing to warn Mike, I don't want him hurt unnecessarily."

"I'm not following you, Amber."

"I understand that D.I. Hannah Utis is sharing the B&B with you all?"

"That is correct, Amber."

"She's got a bad reputation down in London, a man-eater. Is she really as gorgeous as they say?"

"Correct again, Amber."

"Has Mike gone for her?"

"Err, um," said Evan.

"That means yes, I suppose. Warn Mike off her. She's bad news; she'll hurt Mike."

"Look, Amber," Evan said walking into the kitchen so that he wouldn't be overheard, "I think it's too late and even if it wasn't, what do you think I could do about it? He's an adult and I'm not my partner's keeper."

"Do something Evan," Amber said before closing the line.

"Anything interesting?" asked Mike.

"No, just Amber. Wants to know if we are eating properly, you know what she's like," said Evan.

Mike laughed, as did Charlie. The others, namely Ray and Hannah, didn't know Amber and therefore couldn't join in the merriment. Ray had brought a large map of the Merseyside area and was showing it to Mike who was engrossed with the detail marked by Ray. The position of every ship in and the berthing arrangements of those expected. Hannah had gone upstairs for something, so Evan called Charlie into the kitchen and had a word. He told Charlie what Amber had told him.

"For God's sake Evan, I think it's already too late and do you think Mike would listen? It's his business and we must not get involved. Mike won't be hurt, that's absolute."

"That's absolute? What kind of English is that Charlie?" said Evan wishing he hadn't taken the call from Amber and now wishing he hadn't confided in Charlie.

"Leave it be, Evan, Mike can look after himself," Charlie said. "You remember what happened at the restaurant? She was beautiful too and begging. No, don't worry about Mike, he'll be fine."

"So we've checked out five ships so far Boss and nothing. What about the ferries?" Hannah asked.

"Every case, every lorry, everything. You remain close to the two Welsh boys, just in case something comes up and if they leave on Sunday, go down with them to Cardiff. Be in the office first thing."

"Yes Boss, will do. I'll speak to you tonight and keep you up to speed with any breaking news."

"That's it then Mike," said Ray. "You can keep the map, a fat lot of good it will do you. I'll be around if you want me but in all honesty I don't think I can be of any use, unless you boys get a speeding ticket or parking fine in Llandudno. Even then, the way things are these days, I'm not sure I could help too much there. Go shopping, have a look around our town. There's nothing anyone can do now."

Ray said goodbye to everyone including Hannah who had returned downstairs. Fifteen minutes later and it was Charlie's turn to say his goodbyes.

"So there's just the three of us left," said Hannah.

"Anyone fancy a spot of lunch?" asked Evan.

"I've got some work to catch up on," said Hannah. "I'll see you both later."

She waited five minutes and once sure that they had gone, went through their belongings, carefully putting everything back in its original position. She found nothing to interest her.

Mike and Evan wandered around town, had lunch, one drink and then wandered around some more. They walked to the end of the pier and sat down. The seats were wet but Mike had bought a newspaper and instead of reading it, they used half of the paper each as seat cushions. Evan loaded his pipe and then with difficulty lit it. The wind was getting up and it was quite cold.

Mike pulled out his phone, dialled and spoke; he was talking to Charlie. He turned to Evan and told him that Charlie was only half an hour from home. Evan could feel Mike's relief; there was a strange bond between Mike and Charlie. Actually, there was a bond between all of them; they'd come together as a unit under great adversity and made it.

"Do you realise Mike, we've come a long way together you, me, Amber and even Charlie? We've gone through lean times and fat times. We always punch way above our weight and I for one am proud of what we have done."

"I'm also very proud of what we have done, Evan, but leaving a job half done because we don't have the manpower or pull to get things done really gets my goat. I get depressed thinking that we can't act. Look at us, like two old farts sitting on a pier, staring at the sea, hoping we might catch a glimpse of the Chessman as he sails past us on a boat to foreign parts."

"Mike, I'm going to tell you a secret, something my wife and daughter do not know. I was going to retire on the sixth of next month, my daughter's birthday. It was to be a surprise for them. You notice I use the past tense, Mike. I can't retire, it's not just this Chessman business, it's you and Amber and Charlie, we're a unit; we're like a family. As I see it, Amber's got nobody, Charlie's got just... and you, your mother." Evan finished. He hadn't intended to come out with that, but it made him feel a whole lot better.

Mike stood. "Thank you, Evan. Strangely enough, I've been thinking the same thing."

"What do you mean by the same thing, Mike?" asked Evan.

"I had a feeling you were contemplating retirement. I knew or rather I guessed it was imminent. I was myself thinking the same. I just wanted to wrap up, you know, and then give it all up. I think he's given us the slip, Evan. He's well away. I'll give him one thing, he doesn't make many mistakes, does he Evan?"

"No he doesn't, Mike, and some of the mistakes I think he's made on purpose. We had a good go Mike. Very near on a few occasions but no cigar for us."

"In that case Evan I'll stick to these and you to that little clay pipe."

"And Amber to her cooking," said Mike.

"And Charlie?" said Evan.

"Best we don't find out," said Mike.

Evan laughed. He loved this man. Was this a good time to bring up the Hannah subject? He decided that it wasn't. Thank God they had decided to leave first thing the next morning. Now they had to tell Hannah of the new travel arrangements.

"Let's get back, Mike, have a meal with Hannah somewhere and then an early night so we're ready to leave early tomorrow. At least we can still make the most of tomorrow; Christmas shopping, odds and ends," said Evan.

Mike's phone rang. Charlie was home. Mike told him he'd see him on Monday. When Mike and Evan returned they were surprised to see that Hannah had gone out. They both went to their respective rooms. Evan stopped mid-step – his room had been searched. Everything was in place where he had left it but his suitcase was a quarter of an inch out. He could see the clean strip where the suitcase had previously been. He turned and went immediately to Mike's room. Mike was shaving.

"Okay if come through?" said Evan.

"Course it is Ev, what's the problem?"

"What makes you think I've got a problem, Mike?"

"You rush in, slightly out of breath, 'upset' written all over your face, so what's wrong?"

"Someone has been through my room, Mike. They were careful but made a slight mistake."

Mike came out, lather covering his face, razor in hand. He looked around. Evan just behind him waited. Mike looked at his bag, turned to Evan and nodded. He pointed at the zip. "Habit, Evan, I always leave the zip two inches open from the end. Always have, always will I suppose. Don't know why I do it but as you can see this has been zipped up tight."

Mike opened the case, and then went through all the draws. There was nothing missing. "Nothing missing Evan, not that anything I have is worth stealing anyway. You Evan?"

"Like you, nothing missing."

"Do you know its mid-winter Mike?" Mike just looked at Evan. "You're not wearing a vest. For Christ's sake Mike, you can't just wander around without a vest, you'll catch pneumonia."

"Let me shave Evan and we'll talk."

Evan sat on Mike's bed. God, it was a small room, depressing; a bed, a sink, a wardrobe that housed two drawers.

"Why?" said Mike on finishing shaving.

"Why indeed," said Evan.

"What the hell did she expect to find Evan?"

"Beats me Mike. She must be hiding something and assumes we're doing the same," said Evan.

"What could we be assumed to be hiding, Evan? If we can work that out then we have a good idea of what she's hiding."

"Pity Charlie isn't still here," Mike said. "When you need his expertise the little bugger is somewhere else."

"We wouldn't stoop that low," said Evan.

"I wouldn't bet your house on that Evan, if only Charlie was here."

"So, what can we do, if anything?" said Evan.

"Nothing Evan. I wonder if she did this off her own bat or is someone else pulling her strings? The big question is, why?" Mike splashed some Grey Flannel on his face.

Mike had put on a clean shirt and indicated to Evan that he was ready to leave. Evan was glad. There was hardly room for one, never mind two. Downstairs they sat and read some newspapers which Evan had bought in Llandudno. Hannah turned up at six, various bags in hand, she'd been Christmas shopping.

Evan told her that they would be leaving in the morning and she was welcome to join them for the trip to Cardiff. She thanked them but declined. She would be staying on until Sunday but she did accept an invitation to dine with them at a local bistro. They took a taxi and ate. Conversation was somewhat muted. Brandies and coffee went down better until Hannah asked Evan if there was a problem. Evan told her it was a personal problem and that was the reason they were leaving a day early. Fortunately, Hannah didn't pry.

Mike got the call when he was actually visiting the toilet. It was Ray; he needed to meet alone. Mike told him half an hour. He closed the phone, re-opened it, and dialled Evan. "Don't say a word Evan, refer to me as Charlie and listen." Evan played his part, "Hi Charlie, you got back all right, what can I do for you?"

"Ray's just phoned, he wants to meet me alone, something

important. I'm going to stay in the restaurant. You must get Hannah out of the way; take her back to the house."

"I'll have a look Charlie and if it's there I'll bring it with me tomorrow. I'll leave it with Amber. Is that fine?"

"That's great Evan; we have a new Olivier in the making."

"Yeah, goodnight Charlie."

"Charlie okay?" said Hannah.

"He's fine, says he has misplaced his driving licence. Thinks it's in the house. I doubt it but I'll have a look," said Evan, finding it easy to lie to someone who'd just rifled through his belongings. "Anyway, I'm tired. Long journey tomorrow, shit roads. I'll organise a taxi if that's okay with you Hannah."

"That will be fine, I'm a little tired. Here comes Mike," Hannah said.

"Right then, let's have another large brandy or two" said Mike.

"I was just about to order a taxi," said Evan. "I'm dead beat and so is Hannah. It's a long ride tomorrow," said Evan.

"Only when you drive Evan. You Hannah, you fancy a few drinks?"

"No thanks Mike, I'll go with Evan, but thanks anyway."

"Looks like I'm not Mr Popular round here," said Mike laughingly.

Within ten minutes, the taxi had come, picked them up and gone. Mike called Ray and gave the name of the restaurant.

"Brandy Ray?" asked Mike.

"Thanks," said Ray, sitting down.

Mike waited for the brandies, as did Ray. Ray took a sip before speaking.

"I have a cousin, a D.I. in Southport. I gave him a call to see if he wanted to go and see Everton tomorrow. We talked a little and he told me that they had a big thing going on in Liverpool and that he'd be on duty together with the Customs and Excise boys. They were searching every ship for drugs and illegal immigrants. They were also checking every car and lorry going in and out.

"Up until the time I spoke to him, they had found nothing. I then called an ex-colleague working in Felixstowe. The same's happening there and they are being escorted by three armed policeman on every ship," said Ray.

"Do you think Hannah knows?" said Mike.

"Without a doubt. I've checked up on her too. Extremely ambitious, will stop at nothing to advance her career and by the way, she's a ball breaker."

"She went through our rooms when we were out and she's staying on after we leave. She is expecting a result, here in Liverpool. Have they found the rented car, Ray?"

"Not to my knowledge," said Ray.

"That's our problem Ray, you didn't know about the search warrants being issued. Somebody very high up is suppressing information, which rightfully we should be the first to have. It's our case. We've been on it for six fucking weeks solid."

"Sorry Mike, I know how you feel. What are you going to do now?"

"Ring Amber, Ray. Amber, hi, it's Mike."

"Hi Mike, are you okay?"

"I will be when you get me some information, Amber, and I need it fast."

"Shoot."

"First, check up on a D.I. Hannah Utis, Arts Squad, Scotland Yard. Then, do you remember the rented Fiat? Check with Brian if it's been located. Lord Pritchard might help there. We've got Brian's home number on file, or we did and who the fuck issued a glut of search warrants for all the major ports; that is the ships in the ports?"

"Is that it Mike? I can answer the first about Utis." She then told Mike what she had told Evan, which tallied with what Ray had said. "As for the second, it would have come from the Home

Secretary via MI5. If I can find anything about the car, I'll come back but I can't see why you need me to find out. You're on the spot," said Amber.

"It's not that easy. There's a lot of weird things going on up here and we're being by-passed," said Mike.

Mike ordered another brandy for Ray and a large espresso for himself. Amber called.

"Brian says he knows nothing. He's no idea of anything to do with the art robbery. I believe him, Mike. If anything is going on it's on a higher level than Brian. It could only be the Director."

"Thanks Amber," Mike said, closing down the line.

"No luck?" said Ray.

"Nothing Ray. We're not getting anywhere. Ray, where do you house cars which have been in accidents, used for robberies, being taken apart for examination, etc.?"

"As you know Mike, each force uses certain garages local to them and special police pounds. You must have them down in Cardiff."

"Yeah, we do Ray. I need the numbers of all the pounds in North Wales and Merseyside."

"How do you expect me to get that?" said Ray.

"Ring up the one you use. I know they're closed but you will have an emergency number and he will know the rest in the area. As for Merseyside, contact your cousin. He can do the same thing. He starts with the Southport one and gets us the rest," said Mike.

"Christ Mike, it's nearly ten," Ray said, already dialling a number.

It was Amber who came back before they even had one telephone number. "Mike, the car has been found. It's in a police pound in Denbigh. That's all I could find out. It was found this morning sometime. I pretended to be the Manager at Hertz, Manchester Airport. They are working on the car right this minute, so someone's there. Here is the address."

"Thanks Amber, a big kiss from me and from my new friend, Chief Inspector Ray Stevens," Mike said, closing the phone.

"Let's go Ray, tell your cousin not to proceed and to forget our conversation, same with your man here."

"Where are we going Mike, Denbigh?"

"No Ray, we don't want anyone to know that we know. I just need to get out of here and have a smoke." Mike paid and left a good tip – he was in a good mood. They walked out into the fresh air where both lit up as they aimlessly strolled down the main street.

"It's question and answer time again," said Mike. "I ask, you answer."

"Go ahead, fire," said Ray.

"Question: why was the car taken to Denbigh?"

"Answer: it was found near Denbigh."

"Question: why was it dumped in Denbigh?"

"Answer: to make us think he's in that vicinity and not say in Liverpool or Hull."

"Question: if he went to say Liverpool or Hull, how did he get there?"

"Answer: trains, buses, those are the only options."

"Question: did he want us to find the car?"

"Answer: can't tell unless we know where it was left and if it was hidden well."

"Question: is it a double bluff, I mean, does he want us to think that he's moved on, yet he hasn't, or does he want us to think that he's still in the area but isn't?"

"Answer: I have none."

"Question: when did he dump the car?"

"Is that important Mike?" asked Ray.

"I think so. Denbigh and the surroundings are quite rural. People would remember someone walking around, suitcase in hand, probably asking questions about bus routes or stops."

"I'd better get back and have a word with Evan – he's a man of habit, you know Ray, and goes to bed roughly the same time every day," said Mike.

"I'll drop you off Mike," said Ray.

"Could you stop around the corner from the house?" Mike asked. "I don't want Hannah to know that we've been in touch."

"Speaking of our spy, what do you intend to do about her?" said Ray.

"I'll think of something," said Mike, smiling.

"I bet you will, Mike. I could think of a few things too!" said Ray, also smiling.

Evan heard Mike come in, as did Hannah. They couldn't have not heard him after he slammed the door shut. Mike had noticed Hannah's light on. Evan was down first, he was expectant of news and the first thing Mike told him was that they would speak later. He was expecting Hannah down any second and he was right, she had only taken time to comb her hair and put on her dressing gown.

"Had a nice time?" she asked Mike in rather a shy manner.

"Bit lonely but I made the most of it. Got talking to a fellow, he was quite interesting," said Mike.

"Anyone fancy a cup of tea?" said Evan. Hannah declined, so Mike said he'd love one.

"Early start tomorrow," said Hannah.

"No, I think we should take it easy, leave around eleven, twelve. There's something I want to buy in Llandudno," said Mike. "What about you, Hannah?"

"Oh, I think I'll go and have another word with Ray and then take a bus and have a look around the area," Hannah said. "I guess I'll never have another opportunity of coming to these parts again. I'll go up now," she said, "goodnight."

Mike and Evan said goodnight. Evan poured the tea and Mike told him everything.

"Now what are we going to do, Mike?"

"Nothing Evan, nothing we can do. If they find him and of

course the paintings, Hannah will somehow be there in the forefront. All the kudos, promotion, picture in the dailies wearing her finest and we, we will be forgotten. Your Peter's principle thing for us Evan."

"And we are going to sit here and do nothing?" said Evan incredulously.

"We can't go around searching every ship in the UK, Evan; we can't even get a search warrant to search a public convenience."

Evan looked at Mike, before deciding not to say anything. He couldn't tell and he didn't want to ask Mike what were his intentions. Some things it was best not to know.

"See you in the morning Mike."

"Cheers Evan," said Mike.

Mike sat alone, smoking and drinking cold tea. He would give her half an hour. Mike rang Charlie, who was just about to go to bed. "How's your Welsh accent Dai?" asked Mike. "Ring me in exactly one hour Dai, that's your new name, best heavy Welsh accent. The Chessman has been sighted in Swansea, someone will be listening in to my conversation, my answers or questions will seem strange, bear with me. Ten minutes after we finish our conversation, I will phone you back. You, being Charlie, and give you instructions to go immediately to Swansea with Big Mick and wait for us. Completely ignore them and I'll ring you in the morning. Do you understand all that Charlie?" said Mike.

"I do Mike," said Charlie.

Mike poured himself a whisky and waited. It took Hannah forty minutes to doll herself up and come back down. "I couldn't sleep, too much on my mind. Where's Evan?"

"Gone up," said Mike, noticing Hannah's fresh mascara and lipstick.

"Mind if I join you?" asked Hannah.

"Please do, I'd be glad of the company," said Mike.

"So, where do you think this Chessman has got to?" said Hannah.

"Probably got a ship out," said Mike.

"Could have," said Hannah.

Like hell he could, thought Mike. His phone rang. Mike looked at Hannah as if to say who is ringing at this time of night. It was nearly one in the morning.

"Karetzi," Mike said into his phone.

"It's Dai, Dai Roberts," said Charlie.

"Long time no talk, Dai. What can I do for you?" said Mike, getting up and walking towards the kitchen. "Yes, I'm still on the case with old Evan Jones, you remember Evan don't you Dai? Are you fucking sure Dai? You say Pembroke, near Milford Haven, that place? Of course, Dai, of course, thanks Dai. Yes, usual place, like the old days." By now, Mike was nearly shouting. He was a hundred per cent sure that Hannah had heard the parts he wanted her to hear.

"Everything okay Mike?" asked Hannah.

"Just an old friend from long ago, met up with another old friend. Neither of us has seen each other for yonkers. Why he couldn't wait till morning beats me but Dai was always excitable," said Mike, feigning a yawn. "I'm suddenly so tired," said Mike, "sorry but I think I'll go up."

"I'll tidy up and follow," said Hannah.

Mike got into his room. He heard Hannah following ten minutes later. He dialled, Charlie answered. Mike whispered, then said, "Look Charlie, just get Big Mick and get down to Pembroke now, no not in the fucking morning, now. Keep me advised Charlie, I'll get there when I can."

Again, Hannah heard most of it. A call to the emergency number and another to her boss and she then started packing. When she had finished dressing and had packed, she wrote a short note to Evan and Mike:

'Something urgent has arisen, had to dash. Thought it best not to wake you as it's been such a tiring day for you both. Good luck, Hannah.'

Scotland Yard were quick. A chauffeur-driven car picked up D.I. Utis at precisely three o'clock. They were headed for Pembroke, for the docks to be precise. A ferry was scheduled to leave from there to Rosslare harbour in Eire later that day.

Mike saw her leave; from behind the curtains in Evan's darkened room. Evan was still in bed but awake. "Can you tell me what's going on?" said Evan.

"Yes, Hannah has just left by car."

"Why and to where?"

"Goose hunting in Pembroke."

"Crazy Mike, you're crazy. Tell me something that makes sense please."

"Wild goose chase, Evan. She thinks the Chessman's going to board a ferry in Pembroke."

"And what made her think that Mike?"

"I did," said Mike, telling Evan the whole story.

"Oh no, Mike."

"Oh yes, Evan, I never told her to go, did I?"

"May I ask what our plan is?" asked Evan.

Mike shrugged. "All we can do is wait, see if anything happens."

"Do you think he's going or gone by ship Mike?"

"I don't know Evan. Anyway, I promised I would call Charlie again when Hannah left.

"It's gone three Mike," said Evan.

"I know but he won't be asleep Evan, he'll wait for my call."

Mike called. Charlie was awake. Mike spoke then listened and on finishing with Charlie dialled the office number. Amber answered. "Christ Amber, you should be asleep, what's the problem?"

"No problem Mike; on the contrary we haven't checked out fishing boats because they go out to sea, fish and return with their catch, isn't that so Mike?"

"It is Amber, that's what they do," said Mike.

"But what's stopping them going to another country and dropping off someone? Money talks. What's a few lost hours when they sometimes spend days out in the middle of nowhere fishing?" said Amber.

"What do you have for us then Amber?"

"By eight, maybe half eight, I'll have a list of all fishing boats operating out of your area within a radius of about sixty miles. Fleetwood in the north to Aberystwyth in the south."

They stopped at six-thirty at the only open place in Haverfordwest that was open. If they hadn't needed petrol and a visit to the toilets, Hannah would have preferred to carry on. Her big moment was just around the corner. She'd kept a lookout for Mike and Evan's BMW; it hadn't passed them. Plus the fact that Mike had been drinking excessively and wouldn't risk it. Also, from what she'd heard, Evan drove like a tortoise. What a pair of plonkers, although she would have slept with Mike. She'd been looking forward to putting another chauvinist pig in his rightful place but first she'd wanted to have her way with him, show him what a real woman was like. What an idiot. Did he think she was stupid? She'd love to see his face when she retrieved the paintings and caught this Chessman bloke, obviously another dumb idiot. Were all the Welsh males stupid? That's what it looked like to her; she couldn't wait.

"Cast off Danny and you Louis," said Mason, as he stood over the vessel's steering wheel.

The Chessman watched with interest from the porthole in the mess room. He would not come out onto the deck until they were a mile or so out. By eight, the Sea Sparrow had set a course at 295 degrees. The wind coming from the West had freshened considerably, headway was laboured and the vessel was down to seven, eight knots through the water.

It was half past eight when Evan received the list from Amber, who immediately contacted Ray and arranged a meeting. Mike spoke to Amber and they agreed that Charlie was not to answer any calls from the office landlines. He was after all supposed to be in Pembroke and that was the way it would remain.

Ray was late. It was ten before he arrived at the house. "Sorry about the time," he said.

"That's okay," said Evan, not actually meaning it. Mike didn't say anything. Ray sat down and fiddled with his cigarettes and matches. He didn't seem to be in any hurry, but Evan was. He started pacing up and down. They should be out checking the fishing boats, warrants or no warrants. Mike sat down. He could tell from Ray's demeanour that there was no rush.

"Something happened Ray?" asked Mike casually.

"Something's happening Mike. Look out of the window." Mike did.

"I don't see anything Ray, what am I looking for?" said Mike.

Ray rose and crossed to the bay window. "Where's Hannah by the way?" he asked.

"Gone" said Mike.

"The weather," said Ray, pointing a long bony finger at the sky.

"Yeah, it's a shitty day, Ray. So what? Most days are around this time of the year," said Mike.

"A storm is brewing up out there in the Irish Sea, a big bugger, could reach force 8 or 9. The fishing fleets around here will not go out until the storm passes. Those already out will be making their way back into port. No one's going anywhere today."

"What time will it be at its worst? Any idea Ray?" said Evan.

"Two, three onwards," said Ray.

"That's good news for us," said Mike.

"There's more," said Ray.

"More bad weather?" said Mike.

"No, Mike, more news which I find very interesting. A rust bucket, the Sea Sparrow left Malpas this morning at six-thirty. They must have had the weather forecast. The old tub's top speed is ten knots.

She can't outrun the storm. She'll have to heave to somewhere and ride out the storm. Only a lunatic would head out to sea, knowing that a storm was coming his way. It's suicidal," said Ray.

"That's it," said Evan. "I reckon our man's aboard that boat unless of course the crew have something else to hide or move desperately."

"Anything's possible; he might be doing an insurance job. We know fishing's in the doldrums, what with all these quotas and red tape. We also know it's a floating museum piece and worth peanuts as such, but insurance wise, who knows?" said Mike.

D.I. Utis was in her element. Every ferry leaving West Wales was covered. Swansea, Pembroke and Fishguard, every available cop, customs' personnel, fraud squad, Scotland Yard were on hand. She was calling the shots. No one could get on a ferry without her knowing it. Security was tighter than a duck's arse. Yet, she hadn't located Charlie White. He was not in his office, he was around nearby, she was sure of that.

Feet up on the desk, coffee in one hand, a slab of Christmas cake in the other, life was good for Charlie. He didn't even have to answer the phone. Amber was doing all that.

The weather had veered to a northwesterly direction; it was force six and rising. Mason changed course another twenty degrees to starboard. He didn't want the weather on the side. It was easier to navigate head on. By one, Mason had realised he was in trouble. The small fishing boat was being battered by huge waves. The engine was racing. Ten-foot swells were lifting the boat out of the water and the single propeller was rotating in mid-air. The vibration coming from the engine compartment was deafening.

The Sea Sparrow was rolling like a pig in mud. Mason was afraid every time a wave supported the vessel amidships, she was vulnerable to hogging; the bow and stern were applying a downward stress and there was a possibility of the vessel breaking her back. He gave orders for half speed. This reduced the punishment from the weather but rendered the vessel nearly unnavigable. Slowly, he was being pushed towards the dangerous rocks around Little Orme's Head. If only he could get into Conwy Bay, he could then make a run to Beaumaris in Anglesey where he would be protected from the weather. Anywhere else and he was in trouble.

The Chessman sat in the corner of the small bridge. He was sitting on the deck, one arm around a stanchion, the other around his case. He had never felt so scared. Surely, it wouldn't end here. Not after all his hard work. The two deckhands were on the opposite side of the bridge – both had been sick. Water swirled around them. From one side of the bridge to the other, then from aft to forward. All three, the Chessman and deckhands, were wet from the waist down. None cared.

Down below, the engineer was singing; he was half-cut but still had enough booze to help him get through. He wasn't afraid; he'd been through storms like this before. The skipper was a good seaman; he knew what he was doing. Together they would get the boat to safety.

"Will we be all right Dad?" asked Tony, the deckhand and skipper's son.

"Sure we will Tony, when we get a window of opportunity, that is a lull in the weather, we'll get around Great Orme's Head and shelter off Anglesey," said Mason, not really believing his own words.

"And if the weather doesn't break?" said the Chessman.

"It will, it will," said Mason.

It didn't. Half an hour later and only half a mile off the coast, Mason resumed at full speed. An hour later and the Sea Sparrow had made just one mile and a half. Things were looking ominous. The storm had reached force eight. Waves were fifteen and more feet high. Decisions had to be made and fast.

"Louis, take the wheel, come on boy, you too Tony. Keep her on this heading. I'm going to use the ship-to-shore radio and get help. We're in big trouble. The Sparrow can't take much more."

"I wouldn't do that if I were you Mason," said the Chessman, pointing a gun at the skipper.

"Are you fucking mad, Smith? We're all going down unless we call for help," said Mason.

"This is accurate to a hundred feet but at five feet, even with the boat pitching and rolling, I don't think I'd miss, do you Mason?"

"What do you propose then Smith? She's taking in water, the engine's nearly knackered and I'm the only fucking sailor on board."

"You beach the rotting hulk, but first you break the ship-to-shore communication system, then you just run the ship aground."

"It will break her up," said Mason.

"Think insurance Mason, use your bloody brains. If you can't call for help and your engine gives in, what could you do?"

"I've got flares," said Mason.

"What use would they be if they were soaked? Do you understand?" the Chessman countered and Mason did the necessary.

Without any warning, the lull that Mason had promised his son had come. The wind had died a little, not completely; it was back around a force five or six, no more.

"We've got a chance Smith, just half an hour and we can get around the Great Orme's head. Another hour and we can ride out the storm, north of Beaumaris," said Mason.

"Let's go for it then Captain," said the Chessman, who'd now found his sea legs.

"Is that her?" asked Evan.

"Must be," said Ray, taking the binoculars off Evan.

"Can't understand why they haven't made any distress calls. She must have taken a hammering these past hours," said Mike.

"There's a man on the bridge," said Ray.

"Can you make out any faces?" said Evan.

"No, not with these binoculars and these weather conditions," said Ray.

On the Sea Sparrow, the Chessman was using the Captain's binoculars. He could see three men at the side of the pier. He didn't need to see their faces to know who they were. Two of them anyway. It was unbelievable; these arseholes had been dogging him for all of seven weeks. He just couldn't shake them off. He felt for the Luger. It felt good. He had maybe four or five rounds left; he wasn't sure. More than enough, he only needed two.

"Turn round and head for the pier Mason. I need to get off now – I've got unfinished business," said the Chessman.

"Don't be daft Smith, Ireland's your best bet if you're on the run. No one knows where we're going to land and at what time," said Mason.

"I'm not on the run Mason. Like I said, I need to make closure on a certain matter," said the Chessman.

"It looks like he's turning," said Ray, "what's going on? Shall I call in the troops, armed response, how we going to play it?" said Ray.

Mike looked at Evan. "Get three, four men Ray, no guns," said Mike.

"Are you sure Mike?" said Ray.

"We're sure," said Evan, "he's ours. We don't want an OK Corral shoot-out down on the promenade."

"Newspapers," said Ray.

"Absolutely not," said Mike.

"So, four unarmed men," said Ray.

"That's it, and they just cover the beach, no heroics," said Mike.

Amber picked up the phone; it was the Chief Constable.

"So, where are they?" asked the Chief.

"Who?" asked Amber.

"D.I.s Karetzi and Jones. Where are they?"

"I cannot tell you Sir. I last heard from them this morning – they were still in Llandudno."

"The other one, White, do you know where he is?" said the Chief.

"Yes, Sir, he's right here," said Amber.

"Does he know where the others are?" said the Chief.

"No Sir, he's no idea. He came down yesterday," said Amber.

"Have you tried to contact them, Gilberts?" asked the Chief, by now exasperated.

"Yes Sir, but I've had no luck. I have left messages on their phones. I'm sure they're on their way back; probably not getting a signal up there in the mountains of Wales."

"Don't be ridiculous Amber, you know as well as I that they are probably up to no good. I've got Customs, Scotland Yard, Port Authorities, the Post Office and the Dylan Thomas Appreciation Society and they all seem to be looking for our intrepid detectives."

"Did you say the Dylan Thomas Appreciation Society Chief?" said Amber.

"Well, they haven't called yet; it's only a matter of time, as is a call from the Tom Jones Fan Club. Everyone, especially me, wants to know where the Dickens Karetzi and Jones are. Find them, Gilberts and fast, something's wrong. I can feel it in my bones," said the Chief, slamming down the phone.

You get me alongside the pier and you get the other five," said the Chessman.

"Now we got fog," said Mason.

"You've got radar, echo sounder. Come on Mason, don't fuck me about, it's not worth dying for nothing."

"Louis, Tony, get the big tractor tyre up over the bow. Standby for collision, then use the grappling iron to keep us alongside whatever we collide with. Move; we don't have much time. I'm cutting out the engine Chief, stand by to go into reverse as soon as we make contact. Do not, repeat, do not wait for my orders."

"Very efficient Skipper. I take my hat off to you," said the Chessman, applauding Mason's skills and mastery of the situation.

"Collision is imminent," said Mason, wrenching the wheel hard to starboard. "You ready Smith?" said Mason.

"I'm always ready," answered the Chessman, placing the ten fifty pound notes under the binoculars.

"Hold on up front Boys; hold on for dear life until contact is made."

Contact was expected but still came as a surprise. Mason and the Chessman were thrown backwards, hitting the bulkhead with force. Both were stunned but both were tough men, not easily beaten. Tony had the presence of mind to get the grappling hook around a metal stanchion. Together with Louis, they had managed to wrap one of the boats mooring ropes around the stanchion before retrieving the grappling hook and throwing it onto the pier's upper rails. It was now up to the Chessman.

The Chessman was up for it. The fog was so thick he couldn't see the end of his outstretched hand. With the end of the grappling hook, he tied his holdall. Luger tucked into his belt, he waited for the next high swell before stepping onto the boat's rail and clambering up the remaining ten feet or so. Once he had a decent footing but without turning around, he warned Mason that if he went anywhere near the holdall, it would be his last act on earth.

Mason believed him. Knife in hand, he was about to cut the grappling line and release the holdall when he got the call. He couldn't see Smith and was ninety-nine per cent sure Smith couldn't see him. He decided that one per cent wasn't worth finding out.

The engine was at full astern and straining. Mason gave the boys orders to release the mooring rope. The engine grunted and the boat moved slowly astern. New orders for full ahead to the engineer, followed by taking the boat hard to port until the compass spun around to 20. The weather was on the side, he would give it an hour, get two or three miles out to sea. Allowing for drift from the wind and prevailing currents, he should be in a position where he could plot a course of about a hundred, one two five and head directly for the River Dee with a following wind. He needed a drink. He'd send Louis down for a bottle as soon as he changed course.

The Chessman was now up on the pier, holdall intact, Luger still in his belt. This wasn't the time for sitting happily; he needed to use the fog before it lifted. From what he remembered, the pier was about a quarter of a mile long, four hundred plus yards. They'd be waiting but in this dense fog, he had a fighting chance. He opened his holdall; everything was still dry. He wiped himself dry with one of his shirts and then changed both his trousers and shirt for other clean ones. He changed his shoes, leaving a pile of wet clothes where he stood.

For a moment, he stood there. It was still. He decided to move down the middle of the pier, not the sides. They would be waiting for him somewhere, probably with reinforcements.

"This is how our luck's been going. We get close, something happens and he slips away like the Invisible Man. Now we get the heaviest fog I have seen in my life. I'm not even sure you two are still here next to me," said Evan.

"Look Ray, where are the men?" said Mike.

"I'm not a hundred per cent sure Mike; they should be here by now. Christ, this fog's bad."

"Okay Ray, this is how we will do it: Evan will stand on the right, you on the left. Don't move. Remember: keep your eyes peeled. He's either on the pier or underneath it. Either way, his only way out is through us. Remember he might be working his way underneath us," Mike said. "I'm going to zigzag up all the way to the end and do the same coming back."

"And if you bump into him Mike, what then?" said Ray.

"I arrest the bastard," said Mike.

"That's not a plan Mike; he could still be on that fishing boat," said Evan. "He could swim ashore somewhere up the other end of the beach. He could be hiding somewhere amongst those rocks on the other side of the pier. He could shock you Mike, remember he could be armed."

"He won't see me coming," said Mike.

"You won't see him coming," said Ray.

"Evan, switch your phone on, I'm to dial you and keep the line open until it's finished. I've got fifty quid credit on it. It should last. You of course are only five yards from Ray, you might not be able to see each other but you sure as hell can hear each other."

The Chessman stopped half way down. He just stood there, right in the middle of the pier, equidistant from the top and bottom and from the left rails and the right rails. He couldn't see him, he could feel him; instinct had always served him well, just as it was doing now. He wondered, was it the short, older one or the tall, younger one? He didn't particularly care, he wanted them both.

It was moonless and dark. The fog thick and heavy. Mike moved slowly, his eyes not accustomed to the prevailing conditions. The Chessman waited; someone was very near. He didn't want to fire a shot; that would only bring more hassle. He needed to take out whomever quietly, so that the others wouldn't be aware that they were a man down.

Mike was beginning to feel uncomfortable. This wasn't one of his better plans. He moved to his left, took a small step and felt the blow behind his left ear sending him sprawling into one of the kiosks. He was out cold. The Chessman replaced the pistol in his belt; he'd hit Mike with the butt and was sure he had killed him. He was sure it was the taller, younger, copper, Karetzi.

One down, one to go, the others would be at the bottom, separate, probably on either side. He was still lugging his holdall around, although now it was much lighter. Just as Mike was coming round, the Chessman had reached what he thought to be the end of the pier. He stopped and crouched, opening his holdall as quietly as possible. He took out the pouch with the antique coins and placed them in his pocket. He then took out the tube containing the various works of art and zipped up the bag again. He now moved sideways to the rails, he placed the tube and pistol on the floor. Then he picked up the holdall above his head and with all his strength, threw it into the water.

"Over there!" shouted Evan to Ray.

"Where is he, in the water?" asked Ray, who had now managed to join Evan. "He's nearby, I think he's in the water."

Both men leant over the rails but couldn't see anything. The Chessman moved in the direction of the voices; one was on the phone trying to raise the one he'd just killed.

"Come on Mike, answer me, we've got him down here, I'm sure. Just get down here."

Mike was still dazed. He could hear Evan but couldn't fathom out where he was or what he was saying. Blood was streaming down the back of his head past his ear and onto his leather jacket. Mike felt the cut with his left hand; it was a nasty gash. He tried to stand up but couldn't. He had nothing to hold on to. He crawled to the side until he reached the railings.

It took three goes but he did it. He was now bent over the railings. He could feel and smell the sea as it sprayed him. He was physically sick, not once but twice. He still wasn't a hundred per cent sure where or why he was there. Mike tried to light a damp cigarette with his damp lighter in a gale force wind. He failed.

One more step and he knew he was only a matter of six or seven feet away. The Chessman raised the Luger in the general direction of where he thought the two men were standing. He waited, left hand outstretched.

"We can't just stand here," said Evan, "doesn't make any sense; if he's in the water we'd hear something. All I hear is the water crashing."

The Chessman adjusted his stance and loosed off three rounds. One missed completely. One hit Evan in the upper part of the arm and the third hit Ray in the thigh. Neither of the hits was life threatening; both flesh wounds.

The Chessman heard them both hit the deck. He lowered the

594

pistol and went to fire again but the gun had jammed. In disgust, he threw it at the fallen men. This time he hit Ray on the bridge of his nose, shattering it.

"Fuck," said Ray, "Fuck, fuck, fuck, I've been hit."

"Me too," said Evan. "We need help down here, we need a fucking ambulance! Where the hell are the reinforcements, where's Mike?"

Mike heard the shots and came to his senses. He felt light-headed and his legs felt like jelly. With difficulty, he took out his phone and spoke. "Evan, Evan, Mike here, what's going on. I heard gunfire, are you okay?"

"Thank God Mike, where have you been, are you okay?" asked Evan.

"Just a sore head, you?"

"Flesh wound in the arm and Ray I think the same in the thigh and a broken nose," said Evan.

"A bust nose, did you say Evan?"

"Yes, the bastard first shot at us and then threw the bloody gun at us, hitting Ray.

"Ray's calling the station. There are four men down here. Christ knows where, they're going to send an ambulance if they can, but like I said, we've only got flesh wounds," said Evan.

"I'm coming down, Evan."

"Okay Mike, you know where we are?" said Evan.

Mike took a few deep breaths; left hand on the rail, he started walking towards where Evan was. After Ray had used his belt as a tourniquet for his thigh wound, he then helped Evan with a tourniquet for his arm. He used Evan's handkerchief.

The Chessman had worked it out. Soon, all three would be down at the bottom of the pier. He would now go the opposite direction; no one would expect him to double back. He would find a way out of his predicament later. All he had to do now was avoid meeting up with the cop coming down. He guessed he was

595

probably hugging the rails, so the Chessman started walking slowly towards the end of the pier, tube extended in front of him just in case he strayed off course and walked into something.

He stopped when he heard the detective. He was obviously labouring. He had hit the bastard with all his might. It was a miracle the guy was still alive. The Chessman contemplated finishing the detective off. It would be easy in the state he was in, but thought better of it; he didn't want to give his position away.

Mike didn't have any idea that the Chessman was close by. A whole battalion could have walked past and Mike wouldn't have had a clue.

Ray took the call. The four police were on their way across the beach. Progress was painfully slow and more good news was forthcoming – a doctor was staying at one of the hotels opposite them and for some reason had taken his medical bag with him on holiday. He, together with the hotel manager, was making his way across.

Mike arrived just after Doctor Marsden. Having already finished with Evan and after giving Ray a jab, insisted that the Manager and two policemen, who'd found their chief at last, get Ray across the road to the hotel where the facilities were obviously better.

Mike was relieved to see Evan and Ray and was glad to see the Doctor who, from his accent, was obviously a Manchurian. He cleaned Mike's wound and dressed it. He indicated that both men needed more treatment and that they would also be better off in the hotel. By now, another five policemen had arrived, two detectives, a sergeant and two uniforms.

One, a small, mousey, thin man asked Evan what they should do. They'd locked up the town tight. Train and bus stations, hospitals, roads everywhere they had men. Everyone had been called in. The Super was running the police station with one sergeant and two civilians.

"He'll go into hiding," said Evan. "Go where you don't really expect him to be because that's where he'll be," said Evan.

"Where's the gun Evan," Mike asked.

"Ray's got it," said Evan.

"So he's unarmed but still approach with care. He's a lunatic," said Mike.

The doctor moved off with Detective Mousey who had somehow driven there. He was going to patch Ray up and together with the detective, they would get him to the hospital which was about two miles away. The news had spread like wildfire. The Chessman had shot two police officers, maimed another and was now at large somewhere in Llandudno.

"Time to phone Amber and Charlie and the Super," said Evan.

"And Edna, Evan, her first. I'm ringing my mother; I don't want her hearing something on the News."

Evan spoke to Amber, who told Charlie. She then contacted the Super. Evan phoned Edna, told her he was just grazed, not hurt. Edna passed on the news to Jasmine. Mike had bummed a few cigarettes off one of the police and had lit up. He spoke to his mother, told her he should be back by Monday. There was a lot of paperwork to clear up and of course the small matter of the Chessman, which of course he didn't pass on to his mother.

"Are you okay Mike, should we get to the hotel across the road? Not much for us here," Evan said, noticing his partner's reluctance to move. Mike didn't answer; he could do with a brandy or two. Help was at hand.

"Hello D.I. Karetzi, D.I. Evans, you guys still here?" a voice said. It wasn't the Chessman's; it was the other D.I., not the mousy one but the other one.

"We're still here," said Evan.

"Compliments of our Chief Inspector Stevens," said the D.I., holding out a half bottle of brandy. "He said you would probably need this."

"God bless him," said Mike. "How is he?"

"He's fine, on his way to the hospital with that doctor and D.I. Edwards."

Evan took the proffered bottle, unscrewed the top and handed it to Mike.

"You first, Evan, there might not be any left if I go first," he said jokingly.

Evan took a gulp, paused then took another gulp. It was cheap and nasty stuff but it did the trick. Mike took a sip and was immediately sick.

"Thank God that cop left," said Mike. "He must think we're a pair of winos," he said, getting up and moving unsteadily down a couple of yards. He still had the bottle in his hands. This time he took a sip and kept it down, so he took a large gulp and it stayed down, as did the next one. Evan took the bottle off Mike, replaced the cap and set it down on the floor. Mike lit up, took a couple of puffs and passed it on to Evan. Evan took it automatically and took a few puffs, inhaling deeply before passing it back to Mike. That was his first puff of a cigarette in nearly twenty years. He didn't know why he did it; it just felt right. He knew it was Mike's last cigarette and yet he was willing to share it with his partner. How could he not accept in those circumstances?

"Sorry Evan, I'm not thinking straight. I know you don't smoke cigarettes."

"Not a problem Mike, a couple of puffs every twenty years won't harm me."

"So the little rat threw his holdall into the sea, misdirected you and Ray, then started shooting wildly!" said Mike.

"That about sums it up Mike, how did he get behind you?" said Evan.

"Beats me, he really cracked me hard. I think I was out for a while," said Mike.

"I think the fog's beginning to lift. What do you want to do?" asked Evan.

"Sit here for a little while Evan. Try to get our heads around this," said Mike.

Down in Pembroke and West Wales everyone had been told to stand down. A complete waste of time and money. D.I. Utis had been recalled, she was to get the next train out of Swansea. She'd been duped, made to look like a first-class idiot. The Welsh dumb asses had done for her. Promotion, no way. Demotion, very possible. She was not looking forward to seeing her colleagues on Monday. Most hated her but until now respected her as a good professional. Now they would be laughing behind her back. Another thing that riled was that curly-haired detective, though known to all and sundry as a womaniser, didn't really go for her. It didn't make sense. The world had turned upside down and it felt like it had landed on her pretty blonde head.

She travelled back from Pembroke dock heading for Swansea Station in a police van, sitting in the font. Two dogs, Alsatians, were in the caged area at the back. Her driver, a sergeant, smelt worse than the dogs. Her mobile rang; it was Mike Karetzi.

"Hello Hannah, I suppose you're at home now, you should have woken us. Anyway, I just rang to say thank you."

"Thank you for what exactly?" said Hannah icily.

"Thank you for having the good grace to let us, your bumbling Welsh idiots, I mean police, get on with a job that was a little out of your league."

"Fuck off, all three of you," said Hannah and closed the line.

CHAPTER 25

"Was that called for Mike? Making enemies won't help our cause," said Evan.

"Will sleeping with them do any good Evan?" said Mike, now getting to his feet. "By the way Evan, I forgot to give you her parting half dozen words."

"Go on then Mike, tell me," said Evan. Mike told him.

"The little bitch," said Evan.

"Now Ev old chap, what do we know?" said Mike.

"We know he's somewhere within a mile or two of this very point. We know he's not armed; he may have a knife but no gun. We know he's travelling light, just the paintings, I would assume. We know he's a clever chap and won't baulk at killing. Where is he Mike?"

"Same place as your umbrella Evan," said Mike.

"Bloody good point Mike. Where is my umbrella?"

"The last place you think it is, Evan. Where did you lose it?" said Mike.

"I didn't lose it," said Evan, "I've misplaced it. Thinking about it, it's either in the hotel or the B&B or Ray's car. I honestly don't know Mike and, to be truthful, right now I don't care. Why is it important Mike?"

"It isn't Evan. It just proves that if you think logically, you can get results."

"That's crazy Mike. The umbrella is somewhere safe. I will pick it up tomorrow."

"Where is the safest place for the Chessman, Evan? Somewhere we won't think about."

"Nowhere in Llandudno Mike. Our boys are everywhere. This isn't a big place, he won't just walk into a hotel or B&B. Firstly, they're full and secondly they will be on the look-out for him."

"Agreed Evan, the shops are shutting up about now. The streets empty because of the weather. Nowhere for him to go."

"So he stays put," Evan said.

"Why does he stay put, Evan?"

"Because it's the safest place where no one is going to look. Tomorrow the town will be full. The pier crowded. He mingles in with the people and just disappears into thin air."

"So what we are saying is that crazy as it sounds, he doubled back after taking the pot shots at you and Ray, knowing that the whole area would be swarming with police."

"You got that D.I.'s number Evan?" asked Mike. "I've got a D.I. Edwards. We'll need four men here at the pier. Make it six a.s.a.p. Don't tell him anything else."

"And you worked all this out from my misplaced umbrella Mike? Incredible."

"Of course I didn't. I just was just curious. You're a man of habit and your umbrella was part of your habit. I couldn't understand it, Evan and no umbrella, that's what's incredible.

"When they come Evan: two down on the beach that side, two on the beach that side, two on the pier and you come up and join me. I'm on my way up; the fog's lifting. If he's there he won't catch me unawares a second time."

"Mike, why don't you wait till help comes, then we will go up together?"

"I'll be okay Evan. He won't sucker punch me again," Mike said as he slowly headed up the pier, knife open and ready in his hand.

He tried every window and door of every kiosk on the way up but nothing. Visibility was getting better and the throbbing in his head was subsiding. The Chessman could just about see him. Not that fucker. Surely to goodness not, he thought. He had to act quickly;

he had no weapon, no element of surprise and was up against a bigger, fitter opponent. The odds were stacked against him.

When Mike had reached the end, where the biggest kiosk lay, the chessman waited for Mike to start circling it as he had done with the others. He moved in the same clockwise direction until he was near to the railings. He knew he could make it over the rails and under the pier where there was a ledge. The paintings he had taken out of the box and had hidden them under one of the loose planks. They were dry and safe for the time being.

Mike detected movement. He turned and saw the Chessman, one leg already over the rail. The Chessman froze. Mike didn't hesitate; with all the venom he could muster, he threw the knife. It imbedded itself three inches into the flesh. Despite horrendous pain in his thigh, the Chessman still managed to get his leg over the rail and then, catastrophe: he slipped on the wet two-inch thick ledge and only by luck grabbed the wrought iron metalwork barrier as he fell.

As he rushed to the barrier, Mike stubbed his foot on a loose timber and nearly fell. He made it to the barrier. He could see the Chessman's hands; he was afraid to peep over the rail, which was over 30ft above the water, but he forced himself to and at last, he came face to face with the Chessman. A face that lacked any remorse, a face which he wanted to beat to a pulp but first he had to rescue him.

By the time Evan had come panting up, Mike, with no thought for his phobia of heights, had climbed over the barrier and bending his legs, offered his left hand to the Chessman. His right was firmly clenched around one of the metal links that made up the barrier.

"Take my hand arsehole; you fall and you're dead meat. I'll pull you clear." Evan watched on, he couldn't believe what he was seeing: his partner, so afraid of heights, standing over a 30ft drop.

"Come on Peter, you can't hang on much longer. You want to go down like this, a nobody, a piece of history shit, which everyone will forget in a few weeks. Is that what it's all come down to, is that what you want as an epitaph? 'Here lies the Chessman, a man whose pride got in the way and he was checkmated'."

The Chessman made his decision and with his weaker hand, grabbed Mike's dangling left, covering his watch. Mike pulled; there was no way he had the strength to heave up what was practically a dead weight. The Chessman could no longer hold on to the metal barrier with his left. The metal was cutting into his hand. Water was crashing all around them. The Chessman's fingers slipped and were now wedged in between Mike's watch and wrist.

"Not the watch, Peter, not the watch; it won't hold you!" Mike shouted but still hardly audible above the sound of the crashing sea. The bracelet fastener popped open making the already oversized watchstrap three inches longer. Now only the flimsy metal lengthening slide kept the Chessman from falling to near certain death. Evan turned and ran for a life buoy but by the time he returned, the Chessman was in mid-air. Evan threw the lifebuoy after him.

"Call the lifeboat station or someone!" shouted Mike as he climbed back onto the pier.

"He can't survive that; he's got no hope," said Evan.

"I know he can't but the bastard's got my knife and watch; he's not getting away with that. I hope the watch is waterproof Evan or I'll kill the bastard again."

"They're sending down some divers Mike."

"Good. We will wait," Mike said. "The way I see it, the weather will smash him across those stanchions holding up the pier and then push him under where he will probably get snagged."

"Christ Mike, it's freezing, let's at least go across the road to the hotel," said Evan.

"I need to see him dead and I need my gear back before some arsehole out here decides to confiscate my knife and watch as evidence," said Mike.

"There's no way he will hold on to the watch Mike; don't fret, we're insured, we can get another one, exactly the same," said Evan.

"I want that watch Evan and I want that knife. It's all I have left of my father apart from an icon, an icon of Saint Demetri. You can understand that can't you Evan?"

"Of course I do Mike. There is also the problem of the paintings."

"What problem?" said Mike.

"Where are they, Mike?"

"Dumped in the water, I suppose," said Mike.

"I don't think so; he's put them somewhere safe. He reckoned on outfoxing us and coming back for them," said Evan.

"Left them on the fishing boat maybe, because I saw him going over the side and he wasn't holding any paintings," said Mike.

"No, he wouldn't have trusted them but as soon as she gets into port, we will get a search crew on board and take the thing apart. However, like I said, I don't think he would have trusted that lot, he hardly knew them," countered Evan.

"Let's go talk to the men down on the end. Nobody apart from us really knows what's going on," said Mike "and I'm desperate for a few fags," he added.

The fog had now completely dispersed, the wind was abating and Mike had found someone with cigarettes. Things were looking up, even more so when the divers arrived. It took them less than an hour to bring the battered body ashore, during which time the detective with the mousy look drove Chief Inspector Ray Stevens from the hospital to the pier.

The first person to the body was Mike. He pulled out his knife, folded it without cleaning it first and put it into his pocket. His watch was still in the Chessman's clenched fist. It was a struggle but eventually Mike prized it out and noted the time. It was ten to seven and the second hand was still merrily ticking away.

"What time you got, Ray?" Mike asked him.

"Nearly five to seven," said Ray.

"It's a few minutes fast," said Mike.

"Probably," said Ray.

"Can we interest you in a drink?" said Mike.

"Sounds good to me," said Ray.

Mike turned, spat at the battered body and then kicked it viciously, before turning on his heels and marching up the stony beach. Evan and Ray followed. It was over. SOCO had already arrived. Evan phoned Amber who contacted the Chief. Evan helped Ray, who had crutches, cross the road to the hotel. Mike had ordered two whiskies for him, Ray, and a pint of bitter for Evan and a small cup of olive oil to clean his knife. He used two nice clean white starched linen napkins; nobody at the hotel complained.

They had their drinks, ate their steaks, shook hands and parted. "I'll drive us back home," said Mike, "you're in no fit state with that arm of yours."

"Oh shit," said Evan "and I thought my troubles were over."

Mike laughed. "I'll be back in a moment," he said to Evan who was already sitting in the car. Mike actually took two but with a present for Evan: his umbrella.

It was now half eight, pitch black, moonless and drizzling. Remnants of the fog and narrow A roads made Mike keep the speed down to seventy. Within an hour, Evan was fast asleep but woke up with a start ten minutes later as Mike braked hard to avoid running into a parked lorry in the middle of the road, showing no hazard lights or warning of any sort that he was stationary.

"It's okay Evan, just some nutter parked in the middle of the road without hazard lights," said Mike.

"Where are we?" said Evan.

"Just outside Caersws," said Mike, getting out of the car, as did Evan who was now on the phone.

Two steps in and Evan stumbled. He'd stepped on a protruding piece of rock on the narrow footpath. Mike helped him up and together they walked to the lorry's cabin, which was empty. Mike shone the torch around. Evan pointed to a coffee cup, half-full. It was warm.

"It's warm Evan." Evan dipped his finger in and agreed.

"Let's get around to the rear," said Evan, his upper arm now aching after his fall onto his flesh wound.

They got around. Mike climbed up and opened one of the big steel doors; that too was completely empty. Mike felt the back of his neck; it was sticky with blood, his wound had re-opened. He took off his leather jacket and Evan could see the blood on his white shirtsleeve.

"Let's get back to the cabin Mike." They did and still no one was there.

"It's not the Marie Celeste, it's the Lorry Celeste," said Mike.

Mike got down on the ground and shone his torch under the truck – just air. Evan checked the tyres; they all seemed fine.

"Where's the flask?" asked Evan.

"What flask?"

"The flask containing the coffee, Mike."

"Not here Evan; gone, with the keys."

"Bloody strange," said Evan looking all around him. Just fields either side, nothing else. No buildings, farms, no sign of another human being or animal; just nothing as far as the naked eye could see.

"I'm baffled," said Evan.

"Where the hell are the locals?" said Mike.

Two minutes later a police car came screeching to a halt, stopping just six inches behind the detectives' BMW. Two uniforms got out; one was chewing gum and making what sounded like cow noises; the other, his cap lopsided with his uniform half unbuttoned. Both were about thirty.

"You call in this?" said the gum chewer, in a slight Scottish accent.

"We did," said Evan.

"How long you been here?"

"About fifteen minutes," said Evan.

"You guys in some kind of trouble?" said the other.

"No, we are..."

Before he could finish, the one with the lopsided cap pointed at Mike's neck and then Evan's arm and said, "Is that blood?"

"It is," said Evan.

Mike had acquired a packet of filter cigarettes from the hotel. He broke off the filter and lit up, leaning against the lorry. Tiredness had finally caught up with him and he was feeling very uncomfortable about the blood flowing even more freely from his head wound.

"Tell me about it," said the gum chewer.

"About what?" said Evan.

"About the blood," said the one with the lopsided cap.

"It's a very long story and as I was about to say, we are..." Again, Evan was interrupted mid-sentence by the gum chewer.

"Can't your friend speak?"

Mike took one last drag and killed the stub with his feet. "What my partner was trying to tell you..."

Gum chewer was getting quite excited, "Partner eh, lovers' quarrel, was it?"

Mike surprised even himself with the speed with which he'd grabbed the chewer by the arm. He spun him hard around before smacking him with a gut punch that made the chewer swallow his gum before falling to his knees. Evan by now was holding up his warrant card and Mike shone his torch on it.

"Now sonny, it's been a long day, an even longer week and we are only running at ten per cent, which is more than enough to see the likes of you two idiots off. So, be a good chap, do up your uniform, straighten your cap and then help Mr MacGum up," said Mike. "You," Mike said pointing at the cop who used to chew gum, "move your fucking car back five yards and get out a traffic cone, triangle, hazard lights on blah, blah, blah. You know what to do and make it quick. I've a date tonight in Cardiff."

Evan smiled. Mike was back on form. He just loved the guy. There was no one better when the chips were stacked against you or even when some arsehole overstepped the line.

"Now that we have introduced ourselves, this is the situation: the truck is empty, there is or was some warm coffee in a cup in the cabin and there is no sign of the driver and or passenger," said Evan.

"That's not possible," said one of the uniforms.

"Look, it's not our case. Run the licence plate, get the coffee to a lab and test it. As you will see, the flask is missing. Strange eh? One thing for sure…" said Mike.

"What would that be Sir?" said the other uniform.

"They weren't abducted by aliens and if they were, it's still not our case," said Mike laughing.

"Excuse me Sir," said the ex-chewer, "what exactly do you really think happened here?"

"One, the coffee was drugged, hence them taking the flask but not being bright enough to take the cup," began Evan. "They follow the lorry and when the driver is too weary to carry on and stops for a sleep or some fresh air, they nab him, make him open the doors and then steal whatever he's carrying. Two, same scenario but they are really after the driver only for whatever reason. Remember, the keys are missing. What else was on those keys? Three, the driver's in with them; why I've no idea until you find out who owns the lorry, his cargo, his destination, etc."

"Do you need a medic?" asked the cop who hadn't been chewing gum.

"No, we're fine," said Mike, "here's our names, telephone numbers and place of contact if you need any more from us."

"Thank you Sir, sorry about the problems a little earlier," said one of them. They were both beginning to look the same to Mike who was so tired.

"What problems Boys?" said Mike, walking back to the car.

"Here Mike, use this handkerchief," said Evan.

"Thanks Evan, I suggest we get out of this area, head another ten, twenty miles and find ourselves a hotel or somewhere to sleep and a doctor if possible," said Mike.

"I'll give Amber a ring," said Evan. "She can arrange something, she's good at that."

Amber found a hotel and had a doctor standby in Llandrindod Wells; it was on their way.

"Ever been to Llandrindod Wells, Mike?"

"Can't say I have, Evan. What's it like?"

"Nice Mike, Victorian, opulent, grand public buildings, a spa pump room, recently restored to a very high standard. For 10p, you can buy a small glass of water from the spa taps in one of the cafes. Lots of little individual type shops selling all sorts of things. There's a grand pavilion, where they have tea dances and the like. Edna likes that and believe it or not, they have a museum for old cycles. I say cycles because they have penny-farthings, trikes, tandems, boneshakers. There's hundreds of them dating back nearly two hundred years."

"Interesting Evan, but you haven't mentioned pubs, drinking and eating establishments; they must have them."

"I'm afraid that when it comes to pubs, I don't think there are many, if any; it's very much a place living in the past Mike, a very straight-laced past."

"And where are we staying?" asked Mike.

"The Metropole; elegant, large, old spa town hotel. It's got a good restaurant, very refined and a fantastic indoor swimming pool. Stayed there with Edna, must have been about five years ago."

"I hope they serve decent brandy, Evan."

"I'm sure they do Mike."

"Great. It sounds like a decent enough place then," Mike said, his eyes half closed.

"Not much further, Mike. About a mile or so," said Evan, looking at his road atlas, which indicated they had nearly four to go.

After about two miles, Mike saw a sign: another two to go. He smiled. Evan saw the same sign; he also smiled.

They checked in. The doctor checked them out, redressed their wounds, gave them some tablets and went back to wherever. Both had baths, both shaved and both were down in the bar by eleven. They ordered large brandies, the finest the hotel could provide and they sat in huge soft leather chairs happily, each with their own thoughts.

"We should ring Ray," said Mike.

"Why?" asked Evan.

"Tell him about the paintings," said Mike.

"Do you know where they are Mike?"

"No Evan, but I know where they might be."

"Look Mike, it's late, I'm tired. Please don't talk in riddles."

"Evan, you know when you stumbled and fell when we got out to look at the lorry, do you remember?"

"I remember, Mike."

"Well, the same thing happened to me when I saw the Chessman climbing over the rail, barrier thingy."

"So?" said Evan.

"We stumbled because we stepped or trod on something uneven, do you agree?"

"Obviously Mike, otherwise we wouldn't have stumbled."

"On a pathway in the middle of nowhere it's more than possible, but on a wooden pier used by thousands of people weekly, you would expect a very even walk, would you Evan? You know, health and safety, people suing you at the drop of a hat; you would have to make sure that there were no imperfections to avoid any unnecessary hassle. The Council, or whoever owns the thing, would keep on top of it. Do you agree?"

"I do Mike."

"So Evan, one night all's fine and dandy, the next day we have a protruding plank of timber; why?"

"Because someone has tampered with it in between," said Evan.

"So who, why and when did someone tamper with the planking, Evan? The Chessman, to hide something. When he was hiding out there and wanted to lighten his load, he could hardly walk around with three paintings in his hand, could he?"

"Hi Ray, how you feeling?" asked Mike, when he had raised him on the phone.

"Good, 'cause I'm taking a week off, good because we got that little bastard and not so good because although we found about fifteen grand's worth of antique coins on his person, we have no idea where the paintings are. We searched the Sea Sparrow from top to bottom when she came into Malpas a few hours ago. The captain's a slimy big bastard but I believe him when he said the Chessman had paintings of sheep or something in a three-foot tube which he took with him."

"Evan and I have a theory, Ray. I would advise you to get down to the pier at first light. About fifteen yards or so from the end of the pier, in about the middle, a plank of wood has been lifted and not placed back properly. It's sticking out. Our guess is that the Fratellis are there."

"How the hell did you come to that conclusion Mike?" said Ray.

"It's a long story Ray. Good hunting and please give us a call after eight in the morning. We're in Llandrindod Wells at the Metropole Hotel and before you ask Ray, it's another long story, we're too tired to tell you it, and you're too ill to hear it. Goodnight and again, thanks for all your help."

"It's been a pleasure Mike, give my best to Evan. Have a good night's sleep and I hope that I can bring you some good news in the morning."

Mike and Evan slept like logs. Both men were down to breakfast at seven-thirty. Eight on the dot, Ray called with the good news.

The Fratellis had been found.

"Please contact the Special Fraud Squad, Ray, and tell them our good news," said Mike.

"It's time to start Christmas," said Mike, getting into their car and turning on the radio which was aptly playing 'I'll be home for Christmas' by Bing Crosby.

"Perfect," said Evan. "Just perfect," as he strapped himself in for the journey home.

BV - #0007 - 220426 - C0 - 229/152/33 - PB - 9781909020696 - Matt Lamination